REIMAGINING REALISM

REIMAGINING REALISM

*A New Anthology of
Late Nineteenth- and
Early Twentieth-Century
American Short Fiction*

EDITED BY

CHARLES A. JOHANNINGSMEIER
AND JESSICA E. McCARTHY

SWALLOW PRESS
ATHENS, OHIO

Swallow Press
An imprint of Ohio University Press, Athens, Ohio 45701
ohioswallow.com

The following is reprinted here with permission by the University of California Press: "The Second Advent," in *Mark Twain's Fables of Man,* by Mark Twain, Edited with an Introduction by John S. Tuckey, © 1972 The Mark Twain Company. Published by the University of California Press.

The author has made a good-faith effort to reach all rights holders for figures and tables. If the current rights holder is unknown or has not responded to multiple inquiries, the original source is noted.

Printed in the United States of America
Swallow Press / Ohio University Press books are printed on acid-free paper ∞ ™

30 29 28 27 26 25 24 23 22   5 4 3 2 1

Library of Congress Cataloging-in-Publication Data available upon request.
Names: Johanningsmeier, Charles, editor. | McCarthy, Jessica E., 1976– editor.
Title: Reimagining realism : a new anthology of late nineteenth- and early twentieth-century American short fiction / editors, Charles A. Johanningsmeier and Jessica E. McCarthy.
Description: Athens, Ohio : Swallow Press, [2022] | Includes bibliographical references and index.
Identifiers: LCCN 2022027998 (print) | LCCN 2022027999 (ebook) | ISBN 9780804012379 (paperback ; acid-free paper) | ISBN 9780804041218 (pdf)
Subjects: LCSH: Short stories, American. | American fiction—19th century. | American fiction—20th century. | LCGFT: Short stories.
Classification: LCC PS648.S5 R45 2022 (print) | LCC PS648.S5 (ebook) | DDC 813/.0108—dc23/eng/20220816
LC record available at https://lccn.loc.gov/2022027998
LC ebook record available at https://lccn.loc.gov/2022027999

To my wonderful wife, Gina, who throughout this project's long genesis not only always supported it in so many different ways but also gave valuable advice whenever I needed it. As with all my academic endeavors, I know I couldn't have done it without her.

—Chuck

To my partner in all things, Andrew, for his unflagging support and wise counsel and for always making time to read the "fascinating!" things I share. I would be lost without him. And to my children, Alex, John, Blake, and Jane, for cheering me on and making sure I never ran out of snacks. Thank you, this is yours too.

—Jess

Contents

Acknowledgments

First and foremost, we would like to thank Lawrence I. Berkove ("Larry"), long-time professor of English at the University of Michigan–Dearborn. An esteemed colleague, accomplished scholar, and wonderful human being, Larry was the one who had the initial idea for an anthology such as this, and he put in a great deal of work on it during its early stages of development. We very much wish he could have been here to see the final product, but, unfortunately, he passed away in 2018 without seeing his final academic project come to fruition. Nevertheless, readers should know that there is a lot of him in this book.

Because this anthology has been in the making for quite some time, there are many people who deserve our thanks for contributing to its completion.

Many different librarians have assisted us immeasurably by procuring various short fictions that originally appeared in quite obscure periodicals. At the University of Nebraska at Omaha's Criss Library, three different interlibrary loan coordinators, over a large span of years, carried out this work for Charles: Mark Walters, Jonathan Nitcher, and Laura Mirras. A special thanks goes to Catie Huggins, public services coordinator of the Charles Deering McCormick Library of Special Collections and Archives at Northwestern Libraries, for providing us with a scan of a rare publication of Jack London's entitled "The League of the Old Men," which was originally published in the very short-lived *Brandur Magazine* in 1902. Also helping us procure a Realist text that has all but disappeared from view—the original newspaper version of Stephen Crane's "An Experiment in Misery"—was Paul Sorrentino, professor emeritus of English at Virginia Tech, one of the foremost Crane scholars and, fortunately for us, someone who kept great files even in retirement.

Once we had obtained copies of all the texts we wished to include in our anthology, we were faced with the difficult task of turning them into Word documents that we could edit and annotate. For their key role in doing this work, we owe a particular debt of gratitude to Andrew, Emma, and Randall Johanningsmeier, all of whom devoted many hours to accurately transcribing and reformatting original periodical printings of various texts (and even offering valuable feedback about which pieces they found most interesting!).

After we had created usable versions of our fiction selections and written headnotes and endnotes for them, we wanted to make sure that in all these materials, issues of great racial and ethnic sensitivity were presented in an appropriate manner. We turned to a number of expert colleagues who, at our request, read over some of the anthology's selections as well as many headnotes and endnotes to them and provided valuable suggestions, which we then drew on when making needed editorial revisions. Many thanks to Dr. Sterling Bland (Rutgers University–New Brunswick), Prof. Peggy Jones (University of Nebraska at Omaha), Dr. Joan Latchaw (University of Nebraska at Omaha), and Dr. Barbara Robins (University of Nebraska at Omaha) not only for agreeing to do this invaluable work but also for educating us on these important matters.

For financial support, we would like to thank the University Committee on Research and Creative Activity at the University of Nebraska at Omaha for awarding Charles a Summer Research Fellowship in 2013. This fellowship allowed him to search through, and read, an incredibly great number of short fictions as he and Larry began the selection process as well as to travel to Michigan to work with Larry in person for an entire weekend. The Department of English at the University of Tennessee at Chattanooga also invested in this project, notably by providing honoraria for our outside sensitivity readers.

We would also like to acknowledge the team at Ohio University Press. The efforts of Rick Huard, Beth Pratt, Adonis Durado, Anna Garnai, Laura André, Jeff Kallet, and Sally Welch contributed greatly to this project. Special thanks to Tyler Balli, whose careful eye and thoughtful queries polished this book into its best possible form.

Finally, we both would like to thank our families, who patiently listened to us talk about this project, graciously understood when we had to miss certain activities to work on it, and always offered their encouragement.

GENERAL INTRODUCTION

Jessica E. McCarthy

The earliest story in this anthology, Louisa May Alcott's "Hospital Sketches: A Day" (1863), and the latest, Theodore Dreiser's "Free" (1918), were published fifty-five years apart. In fact, Dreiser was not even born until eight years after the publication of Alcott's story. To say that much changed in the United States during the nearly six decades covered by this collection is a tremendous understatement. In 1863, Abraham Lincoln issued the Emancipation Proclamation, West Virginia became the thirty-fifth state in the Union, ground was broken in San Francisco for the first transcontinental railroad, and the United States was at the midpoint of the Civil War. By the end of 1918, there were forty-eight states, the United States Post Office Department (later the United States Postal Service) employed airplanes to deliver mail, World War I had come to an end, and an influenza pandemic had begun. Of course, these changes are only a small sample, and much, much more took place in the United States during the years covered by this anthology. The texts included here are intended to be illustrative of these immense changes and the upheaval that characterized the latter half of the nineteenth century and the first decade of the twentieth. Readers will find that many of the stories take on familiar themes and topics, while others defy expectations and stand apart as unusual exceptions.

When the first story in this collection was published, the Civil War was underway. Tension had risen in the 1850s between the Northern states and the Southern ones as the latter sought to preserve slavery as a means of economic production and to expand it into newly added territories. Abraham Lincoln campaigned against expanding slavery and, in 1860, was elected president of the United States. The Southern states subsequently formed the Confederate States of America (also called "the Confederacy"); however, they were never formally recognized as an independent government by the United States or any foreign country. The Northern states (often called "the Union") wanted to keep the country together and stop the South from seceding. With no apparent possibility of reconciling these divisions, the Confederacy attacked the federal Fort Sumter in South Carolina in April 1861, thus beginning the American Civil War. Each side subsequently formed a large army of volunteers and conscripted men.

1

The ensuing war would last four years and result in the deaths of approximately 620,000 to 750,000 men; it remains the bloodiest armed conflict in American history. On April 9, 1865, Confederate general Robert E. Lee surrendered to Union general Ulysses S. Grant, effectively ending the war.

The Civil War marks an important turning point in American history and is notable as one of the first industrialized wars. Both the Union and Confederacy made use of factories, steamships, railroads, telegraphs, and mass-produced weapons to support their efforts. The Union initially fought to keep the states united, but it quickly became clear that slavery was at the heart of the conflict. On January 1, 1863, Abraham Lincoln issued the Emancipation Proclamation and declared all enslaved persons free. But because this proclamation was made while the country was still at war and Southern states were controlled by the Confederacy, many remained enslaved even after its issuance.

The decade following the Civil War, roughly 1865 to 1876, is referred to as the Reconstruction era. During this time, the Southern states worked to recover and rebuild, while those newly freed from slavery struggled to build lives for themselves. Congress passed two important amendments to the United States Constitution, the Fourteenth Amendment (1868) and the Fifteenth Amendment (1870). The Fourteenth Amendment granted automatic citizenship to all persons born in the United States and ruled that no state could deprive citizens of their rights. The Fifteenth Amendment gave all men the right to vote, regardless of "race, color, or previous condition of servitude." Although its ratification was a watershed moment for civil rights, the Fifteenth Amendment was not perfect. Many Southern states responded by implementing barriers to voting, such as poll taxes and literacy tests. It also must be noted that women of all races were pointedly left out of this amendment, despite having campaigned for over two decades for their rights.

Women's ongoing struggle to be included as full members of society continued to be a major social issue during the years covered in this anthology. The women's suffrage movement began in earnest in 1848, but it lost momentum during the Civil War. In 1869, however, Elizabeth Cady Stanton and Susan B. Anthony formed the National Woman Suffrage Association to lobby for a constitutional amendment granting women the right to vote. After an 1886 proposal for women's suffrage was defeated by the US Senate, women turned their efforts to lobbying individual states for voting rights. They made some gains in states and territories, but women would not be granted the right to vote by the federal government until the passage of the Nineteenth Amendment in 1920. At times, there was tension within the women's suffrage movement when White women activists' goals did not align with those of their African American colleagues. One can see this misalignment in numerous historical moments. For instance, despite having worked closely with Frederick Douglass, Stanton and Anthony opposed the Fifteenth Amendment for its exclusion of women, even though it granted voting rights to African American men. The 1913 Women's Suffrage Procession in Washington, DC, asked African American women to march in the back, a request defied by journalist and suffragist Ida B. Wells. Furthermore, some women's rights activists, including Native Americans and Asian Americans, did not even have access to citizenship. Unfortunately, after the passage of the Nineteenth Amendment and despite supporting the suffrage movement from its inception, women of color, like their African American male counterparts, were blocked from voting by racist poll taxes, local voting restrictions, and intimidation.

As the world around them changed, women saw potential opportunities to improve their daily lives and expand their reach beyond the domestic sphere. Middle- and upper-class women typically stayed at home to care for their families—usually with the help of servants—while lower-class women labored in factories or service jobs. Women's role in the home was often seen as nurturing and providing a positive moral influence. Some women used this characterization as a way to argue for a voice in more public forums, claiming that their civilizing influence was needed to create more humane and just laws. Many women authors, including some in this anthology, supported the women's rights movement by writing stories that showed women making significant contributions outside of the home and challenging conventional gender roles.

Even as women and members of various racial minority groups struggled to be recognized as full US citizens, the nation as a whole grappled with understanding how it would come together and what the future would look like in the aftermath of the Civil War. Virtually every aspect of the country was undergoing dramatic changes, including its expanding borders as well as the size and constitution of its population. During the 1830s and 1840s, a great number of settlers headed to newly acquired western territories in search of land and opportunity; some followed the Oregon Trail all the way to the Pacific Northwest. Later, with the passage of the Homestead Act in 1862 and the completion of the transcontinental railway across the western United States in 1869, settlement of the Great Plains became even more widespread. In addition to seeking land, many people ventured west in hopes of finding wealth in other ways. The California gold rush began in 1848 and drew approximately three hundred thousand people toward the Pacific coast. Even after the initial boom ended around 1855, the lasting impacts of the rapid influx of people would continue to be felt. Similarly, the Klondike gold rush inspired large numbers of people to travel to Alaska and Canada's Yukon Territory after the discovery of gold there in 1896. It should be remembered that as settlers and fortune seekers moved west after the Civil War, and even to Alaska, they caused great damage to the natural environment as well as to the Indigenous peoples who were violently displaced. Many were forcibly relocated to reservations on land deemed undesirable to non-Native settlers, and a great number of their children were taken away and sent to boarding schools where students learned to "be American" and thereby lose their Native languages and cultures.

While many Americans headed west in the nineteenth century, even more people were immigrating to the United States. Nearly twelve million immigrants entered the US from 1870 to 1900, hoping to build a new life. Most immigrants to the eastern states came from European countries such as England, Germany, Italy, and Ireland. On the West Coast, a large number of immigrants came from China. Intense competition over jobs fueled racism and ethnocentrism and consequently high levels of hostility toward almost all these newcomers throughout the country. Just one terrible result of this prejudice was the passage of the Chinese Exclusion Act (1882), which explicitly prohibited the immigration of Chinese workers. In 1892 the Geary Act extended the ban for another decade and added a new requirement that Chinese residents carry and present proof of residency or face deportation or hard labor. This act was not repealed until 1943, and even after that date approximately only one hundred visas were granted annually to Chinese immigrants until the Immigration and Nationality Act of 1965.

Expansion into the West, as well as the increasing population of the United States, coincided with a number of industrial developments that helped secure the country's position as a global economic force. New industries emerged, such as steel, electricity, and petroleum. Expanding industries created economic prosperity for some, especially those at the top; they also helped create a growing and flourishing middle class. Simultaneously, however, the increasing mechanization and production capacity of these industries meant that a great many skilled craftspeople were replaced by factory workers, most of whom toiled for low wages at repetitive tasks for more than ten hours a day, six days a week. The poor working conditions of so many laborers led to the creation of workers' unions. Differences between socioeconomic classes widened, both in terms of financial wealth and overall quality of life.

One of the other major developments of this period was the increasing urbanization of the American population. The industrial boom created new jobs in urban centers and drew people from rural areas to the cities, especially as technological developments increased means of production and made family farms less profitable. It was also more efficient to operate factories near a readily available urban workforce. The tremendous influx in people meant new demands for transportation, sanitation, and adequate living spaces, all of which were met quite unevenly. Resources were divided along class lines. Wealthier residents enjoyed the amenities of urban living, such as restaurants, museums, and theaters. At the other end of the spectrum, impoverished people and immigrants often lived in overcrowded slums and tenements. These terrible conditions were brought to the public's attention when journalist and photographer Jacob Riis published *How the Other Half Lives: Studies among the Tenements of New York* (1890). The photographs in Riis's book exposed the grim reality of poverty and helped prompt social reforms to improve housing and working conditions. As the public became increasingly aware of social inequities and political corruption, it demanded change. The period that spans from approximately 1895 to 1915 is known as the Progressive Era. During this time, reformers sought to remove corruption from government and industry while improving living conditions for average citizens. For instance, they advocated for anti-trust laws and the creation of government agencies that would improve public health, such as the Food and Drug Administration, founded in 1906.

Another significant development of the nineteenth century was the implementation of free standardized public education. Rather than being restricted to private or religious educational institutions, many children were now able to attend public schools that taught a curriculum approved and regulated by a board of education, usually by state. This development helped establish a common knowledge base because children were learning the same materials, even if they did not reside in close proximity to each other. Increased access to education also resulted in an increasingly literate population with a desire for reading materials.

As the population became more literate, so did the broad distribution of printed materials increase. In many ways, the local or regional newspaper was a perfect embodiment of modern society: heterogeneous, confusing, yet trying very hard to "order" current events. It also helped satisfy people's interest in "the others" who lived far away from them, and it seemed to have the potential to connect the disparate parts of America—divided by region, class, gender, ethnicity—together in a united nation after the Civil War. But until the end of the century, objectivity was not a stated goal of newspaper journalism and readers likely questioned the truthfulness of these publications and photographs.

The standardization of manufacturing also enabled the development of an expanded print network that helped play a large role in crafting a national identity for a country recently divided by war. Magazines became extremely popular due to their greater affordability, the result of numerous technological innovations that drove down the costs of production. Editors and publishers catered to audiences' interests, which ranged from news to literary features. Many of the stories included in this anthology were first published in some of the most influential of these periodicals, such as *Harper's Weekly*, *Atlantic Monthly*, and *Scribner's Magazine*. Because of the exponential increase in the availability of media, Americans during this era were exposed to more ideas, places, and people than ever before. Modern scholar Benedict Anderson has astutely described this expansion of "print capitalism" as having helped forge a national identity by creating "imagined communities" that fostered understanding between people despite geographical distances.

American literary authors were acutely aware that the expanded print network afforded them the opportunity to play a significant part in the country's search for identity. One important way they responded to this challenge was by transitioning from literary Romanticism to Realism. Prior to the Civil War, Romanticism dominated American literature. Born out of national optimism that followed the War of 1812, Romanticism sought to depict the ideal country America *could* be. Romantic American authors were both male and female, but they were also predominantly White, Christian, and financially secure members of the middle class who could afford to be writers. Many of these authors believed America had the potential to be a perfect society for the world to emulate.

There was also an emphasis on breaking from the traditions of the past and a high regard for individualism and trusting one's own instincts. With this optimism came an idealistic view that writers should portray life as it *should* be, not as it was. This belief resulted in many stories in which moral behavior and general "goodness" are rewarded, malice and immoral behavior are punished, endings are happy, and a useful moral "lesson" is given. Nature figures prominently in Romantic writing because it was identified as a place to reclaim innocence and draw closer to God. Of course, there was not a single strain of Romanticism. There were Sentimental Romantics, whom Nathaniel Hawthorne famously called "that damned mob of scribbling women," whose works did generally end with wedding bells; people like Hawthorne, Herman Melville, and Edgar Allan Poe, who used the term "Romance" to define a middle space between reality and fantasy; Historical Romance writers, such as James Fenimore Cooper; and Transcendentalists, such as Ralph Waldo Emerson and Henry David Thoreau, who focused especially on nature. However, one must question whether Romanticism has ever died in America. One need not look far to find examples of media celebrating a sense of national destiny and pride in achieving an ideal through constant improvement and refinement. If one accepts the usual definition of Romanticism as involving the human relation to nature, and its byproduct Sentimentalism as dealing with domestic reality in unrealistic ways, examples of persistent American Romanticism can easily be found today on television, online, and in any number of popular novels.

Literary genres do not have absolute lines of demarcation, but most scholars conveniently date the end of Romanticism in American literature to 1861, when the Civil War severely challenged the country's idealism and optimism. In the aftermath of the Civil War, literary focus on the *ideal* gave way to a desire for the *real*. Americans found themselves living in a more complex, diverse, and often confusing nation. Romanticism, many felt, was incapable of reflecting and capturing the emerging society, and its happy endings felt hopelessly naive to many Americans reeling from the trauma of a war that had killed roughly 2.5 percent of the population in the short span of four years. The shift from Romanticism to Realism is especially evident in Louisa May Alcott's "Hospital Sketches: A Day," presented in this anthology. In the fictionalized account of her time as a Civil War nurse, Alcott illustrates the tension between belief in a noble, patriotic duty and the exhausting reality of injury and death in a military hospital. Other stories in this volume similarly combine Romantic elements with more Realistic ones.

American Realist authors' desire for verisimilitude resulted in numerous works that aimed to depict average people—particularly from the growing middle class—engaged in often unremarkable tasks, and without interjection from the author or the obvious use of manipulative plot devices. As William Dean Howells challenged his peers in an Editor's Study column published in the April 1887 issue of *Harper's Monthly* magazine: "We must ask ourselves before we ask anything else, Is it true—true to the motives, the impulses, the principles that shape the life of actual men and women?" Of course, one must remember that no matter how objective authors might claim to be, their own identity greatly influenced what they presented as "truth."

One way Realist authors sought to differentiate themselves from Romantic authors was by avoiding explicit moralizing or didacticism in their fictions. Rather than presenting the world as it could be and leading the reader to a specific conclusion, Realism let readers reach their own conclusions. Literary critic Thomas Sergeant Perry explained this new approach in an 1885 review of *Adventures of Huckleberry Finn:* "That is the way that a story is best told, by telling it, and letting it go to the reader unaccompanied by sign-posts or directions how he shall understand it and profit by it. Life teaches its lessons by implication, not by didactic preaching; and literature is at its best when it is an imitation of life and not an excuse for instruction." In short, Realism challenged writers to "show, don't tell." In his influential essay "The Art of Fiction" (1884), Henry James denigrated Romantic novels because they "hand out rewards at the end and tie up all ends neatly." In contrast, Realists sought to depict probable everyday events. Romantic plot contrivances were removed, and as would be expected, endings were not always happy or ideal, a characteristic often heightened by the author's use of irony. Realism lacked the optimism of Romanticism, but success was still possible. Howells and his colleagues subscribed to the idea that humans had God-given individual wills and thus they could make choices—both good and bad. The lessons of these fictions resulted from readers discovering which choices were "better" and which were "worse." More-perceptive characters were more likely to make good choices that resulted in achievement or enlightenment. Ultimately, the ability to succeed was based on one's choices, a characteristic that reinforced the long-held American ideal of individualism.

As was the case with Romanticism, not all authors interpreted Realism in the same way. There were roughly three primary strains: Genteel/Psychological, Regional, and Urban. Genteel Realists were generally middle-class authors who tended to view the world from a distance, such as through the windows of houses, apartments, or trains. These authors include Howells and James. Genteel Realism attempted to faithfully depict life, although some critics derided it as "parlor realism" because to them it lacked action and relevance to everyday life, particularly if the authors were writing from within the bubble of their own privilege and comfort. Regionalists and Local Color writers, such as Sarah Orne Jewett, chiefly sought to render an accurate and sympathetic representation of very specific American locales and the people who inhabited them. In some Regionalist stories, especially those that took place in rural areas, the author's intense connection to a specific location often resulted in engagement with themes of conservation. In Genteel/Psychological and Regionalist Realist works, humans did possess an innate spiritualty that could result in edification. Urban Realists, on the other hand, wrote about the bleak realities of life in the growing cities, particularly the struggles facing members of the lower class, including poverty, unemployment, food insecurity, child labor, and homelessness. While these authors sought to present a faithful representation of their subject, they, too, were undeniably limited by their own perception and experience. Stephen Crane's "An Experiment in Misery," for example, offers a fascinating illustration of the potential and limitations of Urban Realism. As is made clear by the original narrative frame included in this version of the story—it was removed in subsequent publications—the main character assumes the appearance of a homeless person to experience his daily life, but he is never really in peril because he is always free to return to his more comfortable and secure "real" life.

Because Realism placed so much stock in the veracity of an author's depiction of a place, it is no coincidence that many Realist fiction writers were also journalists, with their fictional stories set in current society and real places; plots were often based on actual current events. However, just as newspaper writers and photographers during this time period could not always be trusted to present an accurate or objective account, the world as depicted by Realist fiction writers was not free of bias either. Even if objectivity or truth were the goals of many Realist authors, today we recognize that ultimately the "truth" they presented heavily depended on their own backgrounds. For instance, as is evident in many of the stories gathered here, authors often went to great lengths to faithfully represent the speech of characters as it would have been heard rather than how "proper" grammar would dictate; this accounts for the widespread use of colloquial language and attempts at writing dialect. Despite their efforts, the accuracy of that depiction often fell short or relied too heavily on stereotypes. For all Realists, there was the risk that their work would reinforce the legitimacy of negative stereotypes and social or cultural hierarchies. Because modern scholars have increasingly questioned the biased "reality" presented by the mostly White, male, and middle-class authors of this period (as well as by a number of White women), there have been efforts—such as the construction of this anthology—to broaden our understanding of American Realism by turning attention to works by a more diverse group of authors, including African Americans, Native Americans, and Asian Americans.

Just as the Realists criticized Romanticism, so did the Naturalists—the Realists' successors, beginning in the 1890s—point out the shortcomings of Realism. In "A Plea for Romantic Fiction" (1901), a response to Realism, Frank Norris wrote: "Realism is minute; it is the drama of a broken teacup, the tragedy of a walk down the block, the excitement of an afternoon call, the adventure of an invitation to dinner." For him, the type of Realism previously offered had not actually been *real* because it had a myopic focus. Taking their inspiration from grittier Urban Realists, Norris and his peers (including Stephen Crane, Theodore Dreiser, Hamlin Garland, and Jack London) introduced literary Naturalism. Many—but not all—Naturalists took their readers even further into the margins of society than did the Realists, depicting lower- or lower-middle-class characters struggling against obstacles that included poverty, addiction, and violence.

When many readers first see the term "Naturalism," it suggests a literary philosophy that would celebrate nature and stories set in the natural world.

However, it refers to the idea that human beings are a part of nature and subject to its indifference, randomness, and chance. The emphasis on evolution stems from Naturalists' interest in the ideas of Charles Darwin's *On the Origin of Species* (1859) and *The Descent of Man* (1871) and Herbert Spencer's theories of social Darwinism and the "survival of the fittest." Authors such as Norris were also influenced by French author Émile Zola, whose groundbreaking essay "The Experimental Novel" (1880) suggested authors should assume a position of detachment from characters by placing them into an environment and watching them without interference, as one might observe a lab specimen. As he said of his own work: "I chose characters completely dominated by their nerves and their blood, deprived of free will, pushed to each action of their lives by the fatality of their flesh." In works of Naturalism, heredity and environmental factors—natural, social, or economic—are everything, and the goodness or moral fortitude that could guarantee a Realist happy ending count for nothing. Some critics argue that Naturalism is, despite being descended from Realism, a distinct genre of its own; in truth, though, the two are difficult to separate on a time line, and principles of both often coexist in a single text.

In "Late Nineteenth-Century American Literary Naturalism: A Re-introduction" (2006), noted scholar Donald Pizer writes, "The nature of this [genre] is not easy to describe, given the dynamic flexibility and amorphousness of naturalism as a whole in America, but it appears to rest on the relationship between a restrictive social and intellectual environment and the consequent impoverishment of both social opportunity and of the inner life." While Romanticism generally depicted an ideal, and Realism depicted the ordinary, Naturalism typically grappled with the consequences for people who struggled within the ordinary but who lacked the resources to improve their situation. In Romanticism nature brings humans closer to God, but in the strongly atheistic Naturalism, nature frankly could not care less about humans, who are often brought to a tragic end by their own flaws or succumb to natural disasters that take no notice of their presence. In general, Naturalist authors tended to have little faith that an individual's success depended primarily on will or effort, and they drew attention to the havoc wreaked by external forces beyond an individual's control. Because many of the authors most frequently associated with Naturalism came from backgrounds less privileged than those of the Realists, they likely had much less confidence in average people's ability to overcome the forces—both natural and human made—that formed their environment. Significantly, like the Realists, many Naturalists took their material from real life; unlike them, though, they were often drawn to stories that highlighted the worst examples of human behavior. For example, Norris's novel *McTeague* (1899) was inspired by a brutal murder in a San Francisco kindergarten, and Dreiser's *An American Tragedy* (1925) was based on the callous murder of a pregnant young woman in the Adirondack Mountains of upstate New York.

Historically, critics have aligned Naturalism with predominantly White male writers, but others are now reconsidering how the genre might be expanded to include works by White women and minority writers, including some of the writers in this collection: Kate Chopin, Willa Cather, Paul Laurence Dunbar, and Edith Wharton. For example, Canute in Cather's "On the Divide" is an excellent example of a naturalistic brute whose actions seem predetermined by "barbarian ancestors."

During the period this anthology covers, from 1863 in a Civil War hospital to 1918 among the glittering skyscrapers of New York City, the United States was utterly transformed. Realist and Naturalist authors, coming from diverse backgrounds, employing a wide range of techniques, and speaking with a multiplicity of voices and viewpoints, sought to deal with the many significant changes in American society and contribute to the creation of a new national identity. As the stories included here demonstrate, American Realism was not at all a straightforward, univocal genre but instead offered an extremely complex response to an increasingly complicated nation.

INTRODUCTION FOR INSTRUCTORS

Charles A. Johanningsmeier

Literary anthologies, it is now widely acknowledged, are not simply compilations of what everyone agrees are the "best" works of literature from a particular period, genre, or group of authors, as they were once believed to be, but are instead reflections of the interests and biases of both their creators and their anticipated readers. As Jane Tompkins wrote in *Sensational Designs: The Cultural Work of American Fiction, 1790–1860* (1985), "Works that have attained the status of classic, and are therefore believed to embody universal values, are in fact embodying only the interests of whatever parties or factions are responsible for maintaining them in their preeminent position." Quite naturally, then, as the characteristics of the people creating anthologies—as well as those of their readers—change, the elements of the literary past that are deemed most important for students, instructors, readers, and researchers to remember and learn about are also revised. The present anthology is no exception to this truism, for it, like many an anthology before it, seeks to address what its editors see as the many shortcomings evident in the general and targeted anthologies of American literature, and specifically American Realism, published during the last forty years. It is our fervent hope that the short fictions found in this anthology will not only inspire interesting, lively classroom discussions but also, in many ways, encourage instructors and their students to "reimagine Realism" by questioning its boundaries and assumptions.

We believe this collection, by exposing readers to the extraordinary vitality, variety, and complexity of this period of American history and literature's role in it, will prove valuable to students, instructors, and readers alike. To represent the complexity of that period's history and literary record, it was necessary to present texts that would force students to grapple with the difficult issues that this era's fiction authors raised, instead of excluding or downplaying certain views. It is tempting to selectively choose and present only those literary texts from the period that imply a smooth, steady, easily comprehensible narrative of Americans' nascent liberalism and seemingly "natural" march toward ever-increasing progressivism, for few students in modern American classrooms would likely object to such texts. Whether intentionally or not, by presenting only a certain group of works, this is what many recent targeted and general anthologies have suggested "Realism" was all about. But American history of the late nineteenth and early twentieth centuries, as well as the Realist genre, were anything but simple or smooth, and there was little unanimity on any of the most significant issues, certainly not among fiction authors. Here we present a diverse group of texts intended to complicate many of the usual narratives about Realism and help shed light on the nation's true, rough-around-the-edges history, which is less easily understood or explained. This volume's contents will prompt a reassessment that will go a long way toward helping students more fully and accurately understand both this period's history and what exactly constitutes the genre of Realism. In our work we are inspired by the words of James Baldwin, who wrote in *The Fire Next Time* (1963): "To accept one's past—one's history—is not the same thing as drowning in it; it is learning how to use it. An invented past can never be used; it cracks and crumbles under the pressure of life like clay in a season of drought."

Granted, most literary anthologies currently in use offer, at least compared to the anthologies that preceded them, a relatively broad range of viewpoints as to what constituted "reality" during the period from 1860 to 1920. This is because, beginning in the 1980s and then even more so in the 1990s, most American literature anthologists began to include texts by authors who challenged readers' notions of "reality" as defined chiefly by the White male authors whose works had previously predominated in them. These volumes brought to the forefront previously under-studied works by women authors, African American authors, and Native American authors and at least a few by authors from the Asian American and Latinx communities. All these anthologies are to be applauded for helping democratize the literary canon.

However, while the selection of works and authors contained in these anthologies has changed only slightly since the 1990s, our understanding of the period from 1860 to 1920 has changed a great deal. We wanted to reflect these developments in our anthology.

One significant development is that scholars have recovered, from many previously lesser-examined sources, even more excellent fictions and authors that deserve to be seriously considered as part of the period's literary history. Exposing students to more of these works and writers is especially crucial because many of the "fresh new voices" once introduced by anthologies have, during the past few decades, become frequently read and written about and are no longer especially "fresh." Today, for example, Sarah Orne Jewett, Kate Chopin, Charles W. Chesnutt, Mary Wilkins Freeman, Sui Sin Far, Charlotte Perkins Gilman, and Zitkala-Ša, as well as a small number of their works, are now somewhat familiar to most students of this period's literature. This wider recognition and readership is a very good thing. At the same time, though, most anthologies have not given these authors their proper due, chiefly in the way they continue to be represented by only a limited selection of their works. For instance, readers of current anthologies could be forgiven for not knowing that Sarah Orne Jewett wrote anything more than "A White Heron"; that Mary Wilkins Freeman wrote

other fictions besides "A New England Nun" and "The Revolt of 'Mother'";
that Charlotte Perkins Gilman authored short stories other than "The Yellow
Wall-Paper"; that Charles W. Chesnutt did not include the character of Uncle
Julius in all his fictions; that Kate Chopin had a larger oeuvre than "The Story
of an Hour" and "Désirée's Baby"; or that Sui Sin Far penned many excellent
works besides "Its Wavering Image" and "Leaves from the Mental Portfolio of
an Eurasian." Such treatment is not limited solely to "recently discovered" authors either, as seen in the way particular stories, such as Stephen Crane's "The
Open Boat," Willa Cather's "Paul's Case," and Jack London's "To Build a Fire,"
are almost invariably chosen to represent these authors.

This persistent repetition of the same small group of short fictions in anthologies has, quite unintentionally, come to represent a problem for students and
their instructors in numerous ways. First, students quite understandably become
tired of the usual cast of authors and texts they encounter in the wide-scope
anthologies used in their introductory classes, because later they are assigned to
read the same ones in more narrowly focused anthologies for an upper-division
course. The interest level in some discussions, not surprisingly, is not always as
high as the instructor might wish it to be. Second, because students have been
misled into believing that all the represented authors—especially those more
recently added to the canon—wrote only a handful of truly exceptional fictions,
the likelihood has diminished that students regard these authors as "major";
after all, one key criterion for such a designation has always been an extensive
oeuvre of high-quality work. Third, a plethora of online study guides, sophisticated critical articles, and even books on commonly reprinted stories—as well as
ready-for-purchase essays to hand in for class assignments—have made it seem
that there is nothing new to say about any of these authors. This, we feel, has
discouraged students from investigating further and offering their own interpretations on essays and exams. For all these reasons, we wanted to create an anthology that included a broader collection of short fictions from this era than had
previously been available, one that would both generate excitement and prompt
a reconsideration of Realism that is long overdue.

We have purposely included many texts that, although written by familiar
authors, are not themselves well-known at all. These stories will allow students,
instructors, and readers to see dimensions of such authors rarely acknowledged
but richly deserving of recognition and further study. Mark Twain's "The Facts
concerning the Recent Carnival of Crime in Connecticut," for example, exemplifies the way he sometimes put his considerable satirical powers to use in
examining individuals' psychological and moral struggles. Louisa May Alcott's
"Hospital Sketches: A Day" is nothing at all like *Little Women,* just as Rebecca
Harding Davis's "A Day with Doctor Sarah" has almost nothing in common with
Life in the Iron Mills. Charlotte Perkins Gilman's "Mrs. Beazley's Deeds" demonstrates her keen use of irony to communicate her ideas about women's rights
in ways quite different from how "The Yellow Wall-Paper" does. Mary Wilkins
Freeman's "Old Woman Magoun" chronicles a much darker and insidious side

of male control than is found in, for example, "The Revolt of 'Mother.'" And her story "One Good Time" (as well as Sarah Orne Jewett's "Tom's Husband" and "Stolen Pleasures") shows that women authors of this period did sometimes pen endings that portrayed heterosexual marriages as mutually beneficial and desirable. In addition, although Jack London's "The League of the Old Men," included here, does indeed take place in the Yukon, as many of his more famous stories do, it focuses neither on dogs, wolves, nor desperate prospectors. Furthermore, while Owen Wister is widely celebrated for his 1902 novel, *The Virginian: A Horseman of the Plains,* almost no one has read his first published story, "Hank's Woman," a much less Romantic treatment of gender relations in backcountry Wyoming in the 1890s that defies many common expectations of the Western genre. Finally, the textual version of Stephen Crane's "An Experiment in Misery" presented here is significantly different from the one occasionally reprinted; to our knowledge, it has never been included in an anthology.

To further expand the range of readings available to students and probe the boundaries of Realism, we have also included a handful of stories by authors who were quite popular during their day but who, for various reasons, have not been highly regarded by later critics. As a result, these works have never appeared in a major literary anthology—yet they offer valuable new viewpoints to consider. In this category are Octave Thanet's "The Face of Failure," Kate Cleary's "Feet of Clay," Lafcadio Hearn's "In the Twilight of the Gods," Elia Peattie's "After the Storm: A Story of the Prairie," and Ruth McEnery Stuart's "The Unlived Life of Little Mary Ellen." The reasons why such texts have not been republished are extremely varied. Some of their authors lacked advocates powerful enough to promote their work among publishers, especially after their deaths, while others were the victims of critical bias against particular regions or simply expressed ideas that ran counter to those that many anthologists from the 1970s forward wished to emphasize.

Also contributing to the breadth of this collection and adding to the range of choices available to instructors are a number of pieces that possess strong Romantic and Sentimental elements. This is not something typically found in most anthologies that seek to represent the genre of Realism. As scholar Nancy Glazener has well documented in *Reading for Realism: The History of a U.S. Literary Institution, 1850–1910* (1997), genteel cultural commentators and literary reviewers, as early as the 1860s, began to more highly value fictions that exhibited more "realistic" attributes. They also negatively judged those that, because of their coincidental events, strong doses of pathos, happy endings, and so forth, were regarded as overly Romantic or Sentimental. She writes, "The construction of realism at midcentury as a uniquely democratic and modern form was simultaneously the construction of the romance as aristocratic and outmoded; the construction of realist authorship as professional authorship around the 1880s was simultaneously the construction of sentimental and sensational authorship as unprofessional." This bias in favor of Realism was continued by most academic critics in the twentieth century, and for almost a century thereafter, texts "tainted" with Romantic and Sentimental elements have, for the most part, been tacitly yet powerfully excluded from general and more focused literary anthologies. Yet Realist authors frequently incorporated Romantic and Sentimental devices in their work, in part because they knew that the most popular—and thus remunerative—fictions in the late nineteenth and early twentieth centuries involved romance and sentiment. Most students, though, due to the absence of such texts from modern anthologies, are unaware that the boundaries between these genres were much less rigid than they have been led to believe. We believe students should know that calling the period from 1860 to 1920 the "Age of Realism" is quite misleading.

To rectify this situation, the present anthology does not discriminate against Romanticism or Sentimentalism. Instead, we have chosen to include a number of texts that most modern literary critics would dismiss, for various reasons, as "unrealistic"; these include Octave Thanet's "The Face of Failure," Frank Norris's "The House with the Blinds," Rebecca Harding Davis's "A Day with Doctor Sarah," and Ruth McEnery Stuart's "The Unlived Life of Little Mary Ellen." This anthology's lack of anti-Romantic bias is especially evident in certain western Regionalist fictions included herein. In the 1970s, modern anthologies began to excise almost all western writers besides Mark Twain, including Bret Harte and many of his contemporaries, because they were judged to be simplistic, predictable, and unrealistic. To counter the stereotype of western, Romantic fiction as less artistically advanced than Realist works, we have included Harte's "The Luck of Roaring Camp" and "Wan Lee, the Pagan," as well as "Sister Celeste," by C. C. Goodwin, and Samuel Post Davis's "A Christmas Carol," all of which take place in or near "exotic" western mining towns and involve numerous "unlikely" events.

Many Realist authors, too, incorporated Sentimental elements to produce some excellent, gripping tales that profoundly moved their readers. Indeed, instructors will likely learn that such works can prove quite popular among their students. This popularity should not be distrusted; after all, as a number of excellent studies of women's writing of this period have documented, if one judges the excellence of literary works at least in part by the influence they exerted over readers, then one must make room for texts that elicit strong emotional responses. Some works of this type included here are Sarah Orne Jewett's "Stolen Pleasures," Harriet Prescott Spofford's "Her Story," Constance Fenimore Woolson's "Miss Grief," Rebecca Harding Davis's "A Day with Doctor Sarah," Grace King's "Making Progress," and Louisa May Alcott's "Hospital Sketches: A Day." All are outstanding works that make their readers feel great empathy for certain characters, and discussions with students about the roots of their emotional resonance and great success among readers of the late nineteenth and early twentieth centuries will, we believe, not only lead them to question how "un-Sentimental" the Realist genre actually was but also afford them a better understanding of the period's literary marketplace and how Realist authors navigated it.

This anthology further expands the boundaries of Realism by including a small number of works written by authors who are almost completely unknown to modern readers, having been discovered only recently. These authors typically published only a handful of works in their lifetimes, did not have their stories appear in major magazines, or never had their fictions collected and republished in book form. Although Hannah Lloyd Neall and Lucy Bates Macomber, for instance, each wrote and published fewer than ten stories in their lifetimes and dropped completely out of sight afterward, one cannot help but admire how Neall's powerful story "Placer" grapples seriously with the moral implications of White Americans' displacement of Native Americans in California, and how Macomber's "The Gossip of Gold Hill" highlights the great toll the California gold rush took on the wives that male fortune hunters left behind.

To further interrogate the current understanding of late nineteenth- and early twentieth-century "reality" as defined in literature, we have consciously not applied any type of political litmus test to the fictions we chose to include. Some of the works in the volume consequently depict themes and characters in ways contrary to those typically found in most modern literary anthologies. Student readers who have never been exposed to fictions of this period that include the type of nonprogressive ideas and language found in them will likely feel unsettled and possibly even disturbed. For instance, in the works in this anthology a number of female characters find happiness in traditional heterosexual relationships, not all rich people are evil, and some characters and authors manifest views on race, class, and gender that are now considered extremely problematic. We feel that such texts should be included for a number of reasons. For one, students will get from them a more accurate sense of Americans' varied views on these topics during this time period; for another, they give students the opportunity to actually use the critical literary theories they have learned about race, ethnicity, class, gender, and sexual orientation and thereby learn to recognize the sometimes subtle, and sometimes more overt, ways that texts of this era reflected the ideologies surrounding race, ethnicity, class, gender, and sexual orientation.

Unfortunately, modern literary anthologies have also far too often avoided texts that include certain aspects of American history, as well as American literary history, that raise a number of uncomfortable questions. We have consciously chosen not to do so, because we believe that well-conducted discussions about such texts can help students better understand the pervasive racism, ethnocentrism, and sexism of this era. We hope the disequilibrium these texts are thus likely to produce in today's readers will be justified by the way they inspire spirited, thoughtful, critical discussions, not only about how these literary works reflected and contested prevailing ideologies during the period in which they were written but also about why certain texts have been privileged or marginalized in the twentieth and early twenty-first centuries. We contend that students today have a right to know the truth about the American past, even when it includes certain elements that are contrary to what they have been taught to believe and which most Americans today find unconscionable. Students today need to be exposed to texts such as these because if they are not, these aspects of American history will be forgotten and students will not have an opportunity to understand what so many people have been fighting against—and for—in hopes of a better future.

Instructors should take special note that we have not avoided stories that employ racial, ethnic, class, and gender epithets that are today deemed offensive by most people. This is not a decision we have taken lightly. We understand that some readers might be quite disturbed by these terms, so to caution these readers, we have placed warning notes directly preceding any stories that include them. We of course do not wish to condone or endorse the use of such language; however, its casual and frequent use in fictions of this era was an unfortunate reality.

Those who teach these works should thus expect to engage in some difficult—yet necessary—conversations about these terms and the power dynamics involved in their use, both in the past and in the present. Instead of regarding these discussions with trepidation, instructors should approach them as educational opportunities, ones that can take place only if students are exposed to these terms and the attitudes and assumptions behind them.

Because of the potentially contentious ideas and offensive language present in some of these stories, instructors must carefully prepare for, and sensitively moderate, the discussions that result from them; only in this way can these conversations be educational rather than hurtful and divisive. Based on her many years of experience leading educational discussions, Professor Peggy Jones of the University of Nebraska at Omaha suggests that instructors spend a good deal of time beforehand engaging students in a dialogue about the choice of course materials and how the class will be conducted. For instance, instructors should candidly explain their rationale for choosing particular texts, despite the fact that they might make some students feel uncomfortable or insulted. They should also make clear to students their expectation that they all be open to learning about very challenging, provocative material without negatively judging other students for their expressed views. In addition, she suggests students should be informed from the start that their grades will not depend on the personal views they express but rather on assessments such as quizzes, exams, and papers that will be judged by the objective criteria established beforehand. Prof. Jones adds—and we fully agree—that one good way to work these issues out is to have students discuss them in small groups, in which they could possibly also create a type of class charter that spells out mutually agreed-upon ground rules for discussions.

Once students are properly prepared, the class will be ready to engage in substantive, meaningful dialogues that might address questions like the following: Why did particular characters in these works use demeaning and dehumanizing terms to refer to people different from themselves? Why did authors during this time period depict people from different identity groups the way they did? Did readers of this era actually think these fictions presented "reality"? Why did readers back then not object to these portrayals and to the use of such hurtful language? Should we read such works today if they include offensive language as well as distasteful themes? These are the types of meaningful questions students might ask; with your guidance, they can explore them in a productive, educational way.

Other elements of this anthology are intended to help instructors generate student discussions that will prompt them to think about certain subjects in new ways. For instance, we have intentionally not grouped these selections by particular subgenres of Realism or by the racial, gender, or regional identities with which their authors identified. Such categorization by other anthologists has, in our view, often predisposed readers to restrictively interpret works and to miss evidence of the complexities and cross-pollination between categories that greatly enriched these stories. The best literary works are those which cannot be easily pigeonholed. The very fact that so many of the texts in this anthology cross conventional boundaries and thus fit in many different categories is itself strong evidence of their excellence. To avoid such pigeonholing, we have instead simply provided a chronological listing of when the texts were published and then presented the fictions in alphabetical order according to their authors. We hope this organization will allow instructors and students maximum flexibility to make their own connections among the texts. We trust all will appreciate this freedom and respond positively to the challenge.

Another way this anthology affords readers as much interpretive latitude as possible is by providing only brief headnotes and a limited number of endnotes. Our headnotes are not miniature biographies/bibliographies of the authors, for we assume that anyone wishing to know more about a particular author or text can easily find such information online. Instead, the headnotes limit themselves to providing thumbnail sketches of the author's life, situating each text in its original biographical and literary context, and briefly recounting the circumstances of its production and publication. In the headnotes we also consciously avoid telling readers the standard critical opinions about what each text "means," for these too often overly circumscribe readers' approaches to the text by giving them preconceptions about the "correct" interpretation of each story. Our endnotes, too, are designed to inform rather than prescribe. Thus, we have included only annotations we thought were especially helpful or absolutely necessary to understand the fictions, and we have striven to present this information as objectively as possible; we hope that, in at least some cases, they will inspire students to further inquiry.

There are numerous parallels between what took place in the United States from 1860 to 1920 and what is occurring today, and these similarities will likely continue to be of great importance to many people in the decades to come. Today the United States is experiencing an epic, transformative period in which questions of national identity and how to respond to various manifestations of modernization are once again being fiercely debated throughout its culture. The questions of what is "real" and what is "fake," and of how the agendas of those making such judgments are influenced by their own personal biases, pervade the news. In addition, the project of learning more about, and respecting, the viewpoints of Americans different from ourselves is still ongoing—and remains vital to our nation's cohesiveness.

Because of these parallels, we contend that now is a highly propitious time to rededicate ourselves to the project of discussing and studying as diverse a set of Realist literary texts, representing as many different views on the American experience as possible. The tasks of determining how we wish to remember the origins of our modern nation and of gathering together the literary evidence that can help explain ourselves to ourselves are truly never-ending. It is our sincere hope that this collection will not only reenergize interest in the period's literature among students, instructors, and readers but also do its small part in improving the national conversation about the issues its texts raise, thereby helping lead us into a less fractious future.

CHRONOLOGY OF SHORT FICTIONS' ORIGINAL PUBLICATION DATES

1860s

Louisa May Alcott, "Hospital Sketches: A Day" (1863)
Bret Harte, "The Luck of Roaring Camp" (1868)

1870s

William Dean Howells, "A Romance of Real Life" (1870)
Hannah Lloyd Neall, "Placer" (1871)
Harriet Prescott Spofford, "Her Story" (1872)
Lucy Bates Macomber, "The Gossip of Gold Hill" (1873)
George Washington Cable, "Belles Demoiselles Plantation" (1874)
Bret Harte, "Wan Lee, the Pagan" (1874)
Mark Twain (Samuel Langhorne Clemens), "The Facts concerning the Recent Carnival of Crime in Connecticut" (1876)
Rebecca Harding Davis, "A Day with Doctor Sarah" (1878)
Samuel Post Davis, "A Christmas Carol" (late 1870s)

1880s

Constance Fenimore Woolson, "Miss Grief" (1880)
Mark Twain (Samuel Langhorne Clemens), "The Second Advent" (written 1881; first published 1972)
Sarah Orne Jewett, "Tom's Husband" (1882)
C. C. (Charles Carroll) Goodwin, "Sister Celeste" (1885)
Sarah Orne Jewett, "Stolen Pleasures" (1885)
Ambrose Bierce, "The Affair at Coulter's Notch" (1889)

1890s

Hamlin Garland, "Up the Coulé. A Story of Wisconsin" (1891)
Octave Thanet (Alice French), "The Face of Failure" (1892)
Owen Wister, "Hank's Woman" (1892)
Kate Cleary, "Feet of Clay" (1893)
Kate Chopin, "A Gentleman of Bayou Têche" (1894)
Stephen Crane, "An Experiment in Misery" (1894)

Alice Dunbar Nelson, "Titee" (1895)
Lafcadio Hearn, "In the Twilight of the Gods" (1895)
Willa Cather, "On the Divide" (1896)
Ruth McEnery Stuart, "The Unlived Life of Little Mary Ellen" (1896)
Mary E. Wilkins Freeman, "One Good Time" (1897)
Frank Norris, "The House with the Blinds" (1897)
Elia Wilkinson Peattie, "After the Storm: A Story of the Prairie" (1897)
Sui Sin Far (Edith Maude Eaton), "Sweet Sin. A Chinese-
    American Story" (1898)
Alice Dunbar Nelson, "When the Bayou Overflows" (1899)

1900s

Abraham Cahan, "The Daughter of Reb Avrom Leib" (1900)
Paul Laurence Dunbar, "One Man's Fortunes" (1900)
Zitkala-Ša (Gertrude Simmons Bonnin) "The Soft-Hearted Sioux"
    (1901)
Charles W. Chesnutt, "The March of Progress" (1901)
Grace King, "Making Progress" (1901)
Jack London, "The League of the Old Men" (1902)
Paul Laurence Dunbar, "The Lynching of Jube Benson" (1904)
Mary E. Wilkins Freeman, "Old Woman Magoun" (1905)
Jack London, "The Apostate: A Child Labor Parable" (1906)
John Oskison, "The Problem of Old Harjo" (1907)
Sui Sin Far (Edith Maude Eaton), "The Success of a Mistake"
    (1908)
Henry James, "The Jolly Corner" (1908)

1910s

O. Henry (William Sydney Porter), "A Municipal Report" (1910)
Charlotte Perkins Gilman, "Mrs. Beazley's Deeds" (1911)
Edith Wharton, "Xingu" (1911)
María Cristina Mena, "The Education of Popo" (1914)
Theodore Dreiser, "Free" (1918)

LOUISA MAY ALCOTT

(1832–88)

Louisa May Alcott was born in Germantown, Pennsylvania, on November 29, 1832. Her father, Amos Bronson Alcott, was a philosopher and educator, and her mother, Abigail May, was the daughter of a prominent liberal Boston family, an energetic philanthropist who advocated for women's suffrage, the temperance movement, and the abolition of slavery. In 1847, the Alcotts had even served as station masters on the Underground Railroad and sheltered a runaway slave. The humanitarian values and political activism of the Alcotts colored all aspects of the family's life as well as, eventually, Louisa's writing.

Alcott's childhood was spent in Concord and Boston, Massachusetts, at that time lively hubs of intellectual activity. She found herself frequently in the company of her parents' friends, a circle that included Transcendentalist philosophers, intellectuals, and authors such as Ralph Waldo Emerson, Margaret Fuller, Nathaniel Hawthorne, and Henry David Thoreau. However, Bronson Alcott's intellectual pursuits did not always create an easy time for his wife and daughters. The Alcotts struggled financially. Louisa herself worked a wide array of jobs to contribute to the meager family finances, finding employment as a governess, teacher, seamstress, domestic helper, and writer.

When the Civil War began in 1861, Alcott longed to contribute to the Union effort and so enlisted as a nurse at a military hospital in Washington, DC. Unfortunately, she contracted typhoid fever there and served for only about three weeks. Her health would never completely recover, in large part because doctors treated her typhoid with doses of toxic mercury. The experience nonetheless proved valuable for Alcott, for during her short time as a nurse, she sent many letters home telling of her impressions and adventures caring for the wounded men. She later used these letters as the basis for a series of sketches about the energetic and empathetic nurse Tribulation Periwinkle, which were published in the *Commonwealth*, a Boston-based abolitionist newspaper, in the spring of 1863. Alcott's keen observations and witty remarks made the serialized sketches very successful, and they helped establish her literary reputation. Alcott then revised these for a book entitled *Hospital Sketches*, published later that year. In an 1863 advertisement for the collection, its publisher, James Redpath, appealed to readers' sympathies and promised "at least five cents for every copy sold to the support of orphans made fatherless or homeless by the war," and that "should the sale of the little book be large, the orphans' percentage will be doubled."

Although *Hospital Sketches* was commercially successful, a much greater portion of Alcott's income came from her pseudonymously published thriller novels that appeared serially in a wide range of "nongenteel" periodicals, such as *Flag of Our Union* and *Frank Leslie's Illustrated Newspaper.* One of her best known, *Behind a Mask; or, A Woman's Power* (1866), is a suspenseful gothic novella about a shrewdly manipulative governess who deceives her wealthy employers until she commands their love and controls their fortune.

Despite these prior successes, Alcott became best known for her juvenile fiction, especially the perennial favorite *Little Women* (1868–69), which fictionalizes Alcott's childhood experiences from the early to mid nineteenth century. Written chiefly to earn money for her struggling family, this novel conforms to many of the formulas then prevalent for domestic Sentimental fiction. Focused primarily on the four March sisters, this novel continues to resonate with readers even to this day. It should be mentioned, too, that Alcott also published novels for an adult audience, including *Work: A Story of Experience* (1873) and *A Modern Mephistopheles* (1877).

As noted earlier, after serving as a nurse to wounded Civil War soldiers, Alcott suffered from chronic health problems the rest of her life. She died in Boston from a stroke at the relatively young age of fifty-five and is buried in Concord in the family plot in Sleepy Hollow Cemetery, near the graves of Emerson, Hawthorne, and Thoreau. Alcott's popularity continues today: in 1996 she was inducted into the National Women's Hall of Fame, and in 2016 her image was even used as a Google Doodle on the search engine's homepage. More recently, in 2019 *Little Women* was adapted and made into a highly popular, Academy Award–winning film.

*Readers should be aware that this story includes some language which, while commonly used during this time period, is no longer considered acceptable because of its offensive nature.

HOSPITAL SKETCHES: A DAY (1863)

"They've come! they've come! hurry up, ladies—you're wanted."

"Who have come? the rebels?"

This sudden summons in the gray dawn was somewhat startling to a three days' nurse like myself, and, as the thundering knock came at our door, I sprang up in my bed, prepared

> *"To gird my woman's form,*
> *And on the ramparts die,"*[1]

if necessary; but my room-mate took it more coolly, and, as she began a rapid toilet,[2] answered my bewildered question,—

"Bless you, no child; it's the wounded from Fredericksburg; forty ambulances are at the door, and we shall have our hands full in fifteen minutes."

"What shall we have to do?"

"Wash, dress, feed, warm and nurse them for the next three months, I dare say. Eighty beds are ready, and we were getting impatient for the men to come. Now you will begin to see hospital life in earnest, for you won't probably find time to sit down all day, and may think yourself fortunate if you get to bed by midnight. Come to me in the ball-room when you are ready; the worst cases are always carried there, and I shall need your help."

So saying, the energetic little woman twirled her hair into a button at the back of her head, in a "cleared for action" sort of style, and vanished, wrestling her way into a feminine kind of pea-jacket as she went.

I am free to confess that I had a realizing sense of the fact that my hospital bed was not a bed of roses just then, or the prospect before me one of unmingled rapture. My three days' experiences had begun with a death, and, owing to the defalcation of another nurse, a somewhat abrupt plunge into the superintendence of a ward containing forty beds, where I spent my shining hours washing faces, serving rations, giving medicine, and sitting in a very hard chair, with pneumonia on one side, diptheria on the other, five typhoids on the opposite, and a dozen dilapidated patriots, hopping, lying, and lounging about, all staring more or less at the new "nuss,"[3] who suffered untold agonies, but concealed them under as matronly an aspect as a spinster could assume, and blundered through her trying labors with a Spartan firmness,[4] which I hope they appreciated, but am afraid they didn't. Having a taste for "ghastliness," I had rather longed for the wounded to arrive, for rheumatism wasn't heroic, neither was liver complaint, or measles; even fever had lost its charms since "bathing burning brows" had been used up in romances, real and ideal; but when I peeped into the dusky street lined with what I at first had innocently called market carts, now unloading their sad freight at our door, I recalled sundry reminiscences I had heard from nurses of longer standing, my ardor experienced a sudden chill, and I indulged in a most unpatriotic wish that I was safe at home again, with a quiet day before me, and no necessity for being hustled up, as if I were a hen and had only to hop off my roost, give my plumage a peck, and be ready for action. A second bang at the door sent this recreant desire to the right about, as a little woolly head popped in, and Joey,—a six years' old contraband,[5]—announced—

"Miss Blank is jes' wild fer ye, and says fly round right away. They's comin' in, I tell yer, heaps on 'em—one was took out dead, and I see him,—hi! warn't he a goner!"

With which cheerful intelligence the imp scuttled away, singing like a black-bird, and I followed, feeling that Richard was *not* himself again,[6] and wouldn't be for a long time to come.

The first thing I met was a regiment of the vilest odors that ever assaulted the human nose, and took it by storm. Cologne, with its seven and seventy evil savors,[7] was a posy-bed to it; and the worst of this affliction was, every one had assured me that it was a chronic weakness of all hospitals, and I must bear it. I did, armed with lavender water, with which I so besprinkled myself and premises, that, like my friend Sairy,[8] I was soon known among my patients as "the nurse with the bottle." Having been run over by three excited surgeons, bumped against by migratory coal-hods,[9] water-pails, and small boys, nearly scalded by an avalanche of newly-filled tea-pots, and hopelessly entangled in a knot of colored sisters[10] coming to wash, I progressed by slow stages up stairs and down, till the main hall was reached, and I paused to take breath and a survey. There they were! "our brave boys," as the papers justly call them, for cowards could hardly have been so riddled with shot and shell, so torn and shattered, nor have borne suffering for which we have no name, with an uncomplaining fortitude, which made one glad to cherish each as a brother. In they came, some on stretchers, some in men's arms, some feebly staggering along propped on rude crutches, and one lay stark and still with covered face, as a comrade gave his name to be recorded before they carried him away to the dead house. All was hurry and confusion; the hall was full of these wrecks of humanity, for the most exhausted could not reach a bed till duly ticketed and registered; the walls were lined with rows of such as could sit, the floor covered with the more disabled, the steps and doorways filled with helpers and lookers on; the sound of many feet and voices made that usually quiet hour as noisy as noon; and, in the midst of it all, the matron's motherly face brought more comfort to many a poor soul, than the cordial draughts she administered,[11] or the cheery words that welcomed all, making of the hospital a home.

The sight of several stretchers, each with its legless, armless, or desperately wounded occupant, entering my ward, admonished me that I was there to work, not to wonder or weep; so I corked up my feelings, and returned to the path of duty, which was rather "a hard road to travel"[12] just then. The house had been a hotel before hospitals were needed, and many of the doors still bore their old names; some not so inappropriate as might be imagined, for my ward was in truth a *ball-room*, if gun-shot wounds could christen it.[13] Forty beds were prepared, many already tenanted by tired men who fell down anywhere, and drowsed till the smell of food roused them. Round the great stove was gathered the dreariest group I ever saw—ragged, gaunt and pale, mud to the knees, with bloody bandages untouched since put on days before; many bundled up in blankets, coats being lost or useless; and all wearing that disheartened look which proclaimed defeat, more plainly than any telegram of the Burnside blunder.[14] I pitied them so much, I dared not speak to them, though, remembering all they had been through since the rout at Fredericksburg, I yearned to serve the dreariest of them all. Presently, Miss Blank tore me from my refuge behind piles of one-sleeved shirts, odd socks, bandages and lint; put basin, sponge, towels, and a block of brown soap into my hands, with these appalling directions:

"Come, my dear, begin to wash as fast as you can. Tell them to take off socks, coats and shirts, scrub them well, put on clean shirts, and the attendants will finish them off, and lay them in bed."

If she had requested me to shave them all, or dance a hornpipe[15] on the stove funnel, I should have been less staggered; but to scrub some dozen lords of creation at a moment's notice, was really—really—. However, there was no time for nonsense, and, having resolved when I came to do everything I was bid, I drowned my scruples in my wash-bowl, clutched my soap manfully, and, assuming a business-like air, made a dab at the first dirty specimen I saw, bent on performing my task *vi et armis*[16] if necessary. I chanced to light on a withered old Irishman, wounded in the head, which caused that portion of his frame to be tastefully laid out like a garden, the bandages being the walks, his hair the shrubbery. He was so overpowered by the honor of having a lady wash him, as he expressed it, that he did nothing but roll up his eyes, and bless me, in an irresistible style which was too much for my sense of the ludicrous; so we laughed together, and when I knelt down to take off his shoes, he "flopped" also, and wouldn't hear of my touching "them dirty craters. May your bed above be aisy darlin', for the day's work ye ar doon!—Whoosh! there ye are, and bedad, it's hard tellin' which is the dirtiest, the fut or the shoe." It was; and if he hadn't been to the fore, I should have gone on pulling, under the impression that the "fut" was a boot, for trousers, socks, shoes and legs were a mass of mud. This comical tableau produced a general grin, at which propitious beginning I took heart and scrubbed away like any tidy parent on a Saturday night. Some of them took the performance like sleepy children, leaning their tired heads against me as I worked, others looked grimly scandalized, and several of the roughest colored like bashful girls. One wore a soiled little bag about his neck, and, as I moved it, to bathe his wounded breast, I said,

"Your talisman didn't save you, did it?"

"Well, I reckon it did, marm, for that shot would a gone a couple a inches deeper but for my old mammy's camphor bag," answered the cheerful philosopher.

Another, with a gun-shot wound through the cheek, asked for a looking-glass, and when I brought one, regarded his swollen face with a dolorous expression, as he muttered—

"I vow to gosh, that's too bad! I warn't a bad looking chap before, and now I'm done for; won't there be a thunderin' scar? and what on earth will Josephine Skinner say?"

He looked up at me with his one eye so appealingly, that I controlled my risibles,[17] and assured him that if Josephine was a girl of sense, she would admire the honorable scar, as a lasting proof that he had faced the enemy, for all women thought a wound the best decoration a brave soldier could wear. I hope Miss Skinner verified the good opinion I so rashly expressed of her, but I shall never know.

The next scrubbee was a nice-looking lad, with a curly brown mane, and a budding trace of gingerbread over the lip, which he called his beard, and defended stoutly, when the barber jocosely suggested its immolation. He lay on a bed, with one leg gone, and the right arm so shattered that it must evidently follow: yet the little Sergeant was as merry as if his afflictions were not worth lamenting over; and when a drop or two of salt water mingled with my suds at the sight of this strong young body, so marred and maimed, the boy looked up, with a brave smile, though there was a little quiver of the lips, as he said,

"Now don't you fret yourself about me, miss; I'm first rate here, for it's nuts to lie still on this bed, after knocking about in those confounded ambulances, that shake what there is left of a fellow to jelly. I never was in one of these places before, and think this cleaning up a jolly thing for us, though I'm afraid it isn't for you ladies."

"Is this your first battle, Sergeant?"

"No, miss; I've been in six scrimmages, and never got a scratch till this last one; but it's done the business pretty thoroughly for me, I should say. Lord! what a scramble there'll be for arms and legs, when we old boys come out of our graves, on the Judgment Day: wonder if we shall get our own again? If we do, my leg will have to tramp from Fredericksburg, my arm from here, I suppose, and meet my body, wherever it may be."

The fancy seemed to tickle him mightily, for he laughed blithely, and so did I; which, no doubt, caused the new nurse to be regarded as a light-minded sinner by the Chaplain, who roamed vaguely about, informing the men that they were all worms, corrupt of heart, with perishable bodies, and souls only to be saved by a diligent perusal of certain tracts, and other equally cheering bits of spiritual consolation, when spirituous ditto[18] would have been preferred.

"I say, Mrs.!" called a voice behind me; and, turning, I saw a rough Michigander, with an arm blown off at the shoulder, and two or three bullets still in him—as he afterwards mentioned, as carelessly as if gentlemen were in the habit of carrying such trifles about with them. I went to him, and, while administering a dose of soap and water, he whispered, irefully:

"That red-headed devil, over yonder, is a reb,[19] damn him! You'll agree to that, I'll bet? He's got shet of a foot, or he'd a cut like the rest of the lot.[20] Don't you wash him, nor feed him, but jest let him holler till he's tired. It's a blasted shame to fetch them fellers in here, along side of us; and so I'll tell the chap that bosses this concern; cuss me if I don't."

I regret to say that I did not deliver a moral sermon upon the duty of forgiving our enemies, and the sin of profanity, then and there; but, being a red-hot Abolitionist, stared fixedly at the tall rebel, who was a copperhead,[21] in every sense of the word, and privately resolved to put soap in his eyes, rub his nose the wrong way, and excoriate his cuticle generally, if I had the washing of him.

My amiable intentions, however, were frustrated; for, when I approached, with as Christian an expression as my principles would allow, and asked the question—"Shall I try to make you more comfortable, sir?" all I got for my pains was a gruff—

"No; I'll do it myself."

"Here's your Southern chivalry, with a witness," thought I, dumping the basin down before him, thereby quenching a strong desire to give him a summary baptism, in return for his ungraciousness; for my angry passions rose, at this rebuff, in a way that would have scandalized good Dr. Watts.[22] He was a disappointment in all respects, (the rebel, not the blessed Doctor,) for he was neither fiendish, romantic, pathetic, or anything interesting; but a long, fat man, with a head like a burning bush, and a perfectly expressionless face: so I could dislike him without the slightest drawback, and ignored his existence from that day forth. One redeeming trait he certainly did possess, as the floor speedily testified; for his ablutions were so vigorously performed, that his bed soon stood like an isolated island, in a sea of soap-suds, and he resembled a dripping merman, suffering from the loss of a fin. If cleanliness is a near neighbor to godliness, then was the big rebel the godliest man in my ward that day.

Having done up our human wash, and laid it out to dry, the second syllable of our version of the word war-fare was enacted with much success. Great trays of bread, meat, soup and coffee appeared; and both nurses and attendants turned waiters, serving bountiful rations to all who could eat. I can call my pinafore to testify to my good will in the work, for in ten minutes it was reduced to a perambulating bill of fare, presenting samples of all the refreshments going or gone.[23] It was a lively scene; the long room lined with rows of beds, each filled by an occupant, whom water, shears, and clean raiment, had transformed from a dismal ragamuffin into a recumbent hero, with a cropped head. To and fro rushed matrons, maids, and convalescent "boys," skirmishing with knives and forks; retreating with empty plates; marching and counter-marching, with un-varied success, while the clash of busy spoons made most inspiring music for the charge of our Light Brigade:

> *"Beds to the front of them,*
> *Beds to the right of them,*
> *Beds to the left of them,*
>
> *Nobody blundered.*
> *Beamed at by hungry souls,*
> *Screamed at with brimming bowls,*
> *Steamed at by army rolls,*
>
> *Buttered and sundered.*
> *With coffee not cannon plied,*
> *Each must be satisfied,*
> *Whether they lived or died;*
>
> *All the men wondered."*[24]

Very welcome seemed the generous meal, after a week of suffering, exposure, and short commons; soon the brown faces began to smile, as food, warmth, and rest, did their pleasant work; and the grateful "Thankee's" were followed by more graphic accounts of the battle and retreat, than any paid reporter could have given us. Curious contrasts of the tragic and comic met one everywhere; and some touching as well as ludicrous episodes, might have been recorded that day. A six foot New Hampshire man, with a leg broken and perforated by a piece of shell, so large that, had I not seen the wound, I should have regarded the story as a Munchausenism,[25] beckoned me to come and help him, as he could not sit up, and both his bed and beard were getting plentifully anointed with soup. As I fed my big nestling with corresponding mouthfuls, I asked him how he felt during the battle.

"Well, 'twas my fust, you see, so I aint ashamed to say I was a trifle flustered in the beginnin', there was such an allfired racket; for ef there's anything I do spleen agin, it's noise. But when my mate, Eph Sylvester, caved, with a bullet through his head, I got mad, and pitched in, licketty cut. Our part of the fight didn't last long; so a lot of us larked round Fredericksburg, and give some of them houses a pretty consid'able of a rummage, till we was ordered out of the mess. Some of our fellows cut like time; but I warn't a-goin' to run for nobody; and, fust thing I knew, a shell bust, right in front of us, and I keeled over, feelin' as if I was blowed higher'n a kite. I sung out, and the boys come back for me, double quick; but the way they chucked me over them fences was a caution, I tell you. Next day I was most as black as that darkey yonder, lickin' plates on the sly.[26] This is bully coffee, ain't it? Give us another pull at it, and I'll be obleeged to you."

I did; and, as the last gulp subsided, he said, with a rub of his old handkerchief over eyes as well as mouth:

"Look a here; I've got a pair a earbobs[27] and a handkercher pin I'm a goin' to give you, if you'll have them; for you're the very moral o' Lizy Sylvester, poor Eph's wife: that's why I signalled you to come over here. They aint much, I guess, but they'll do to memorize the rebs by."

Burrowing under his pillow, he produced a little bundle of what he called "truck," and gallantly presented me with a pair of earrings, each representing a cluster of corpulent grapes, and the pin a basket of astonishing fruit, the whole large and coppery enough for a small warming-pan.[28] Feeling delicate about depriving him of such valuable relics, I accepted the earrings alone, and was obliged to depart, somewhat abruptly, when my friend stuck the warming-pan in the bosom of his night-gown, viewing it with much complacency, and, perhaps, some tender memory, in that rough heart of his, for the comrade he had lost.

Observing that the man next him had left his meal untouched, I offered the same service I had performed for his neighbor, but he shook his head.

"Thank you, ma'am; I don't think I'll ever eat again, for I'm shot in the stomach. But I'd like a drink of water, if you aint too busy."

I rushed away, but the water-pails were gone to be refilled, and it was some time before they reappeared. I did not forget my patient patient, meanwhile, and, with the first mugful, hurried back to him. He seemed asleep; but something in the tired white face caused me to listen at his lips for a breath. None came. I touched his forehead; it was cold: and then I knew that, while he waited, a better nurse than I had given him a cooler draught, and healed him with a touch. I laid the sheet over the quiet sleeper, whom no noise could now disturb; and, half an hour later, the bed was empty. It seemed a poor requital for all he had sacrificed and suffered,—that hospital bed, lonely even in a crowd; for there was no familiar face for him to look his last upon; no friendly voice to say, Good bye; no hand to lead him gently down into the Valley of the Shadow;[29] and he vanished, like a drop in that red sea upon whose shores so many women stand lamenting. For a moment I felt bitterly indignant at this seeming carelessness of the value of life, the sanctity of death; then consoled myself with the thought that, when the great muster roll was called, these nameless men might be promoted above many whose tall monuments record the barren honors they have won.

All having eaten, drank, and rested, the surgeons began their rounds; and I took my first lesson in the art of dressing wounds. It wasn't a festive scene, by any means; for Dr P., whose Aid I constituted myself, fell to work with a vigor which soon convinced me that I was a weaker vessel, though nothing would have induced me to confess it then. He had served in the Crimea, and seemed to regard a dilapidated body very much as I should have regarded a damaged garment; and, turning up his cuffs, whipped out a very unpleasant looking housewife,[30] cutting, sawing, patching and piecing, with the enthusiasm of an accomplished surgical seamstress; explaining the process, in scientific terms, to the patient, meantime; which, of course, was immensely cheering and comfortable. There was an uncanny sort of fascination in watching him, as he peered and probed into the mechanism of those wonderful bodies, whose mysteries he understood so well. The more intricate the wound, the better he liked it. A poor private, with both legs off, and shot through the lungs, possessed more attractions for him than a dozen generals, slightly scratched in some "masterly retreat;" and had any one appeared in small pieces, requesting to be put together again, he would have considered it a special dispensation.

The amputations were reserved till the morrow, and the merciful magic of ether[31] was not thought necessary that day, so the poor souls had to bear their pains as best they might. It is all very well to talk of the patience of woman; and far be it from me to pluck that feather from her cap, for, heaven knows, she isn't allowed to wear many; but the patient endurance of these men, under trials of the flesh, was truly wonderful. Their fortitude seemed contagious, and scarcely a cry escaped them, though I often longed to groan for them, when pride kept their white lips shut, while great drops stood upon their foreheads, and the bed shook with the irrepressible tremor of their tortured bodies. One or two Irishmen anathematized[32] the doctors with the frankness of their nation, and ordered the Virgin to stand by them, as if she had been the wedded Biddy to whom they could administer the poker, if she didn't;[33] but, as a general thing, the work went on in silence, broken only by some quiet request for roller, instruments, or plaster, a sigh from the patient, or a sympathizing murmur from the nurse.

It was long past noon before these repairs were even partially made; and, having got the bodies of my boys into something like order, the next task was to minister to their minds, by writing letters to the anxious souls at home; answering questions, reading papers, taking possession of money and valuables; for the eighth commandment[34] was reduced to a very fragmentary condition, both by the blacks and whites, who ornamented our hospital with their presence. Pocket books, purses, miniatures, and watches, were sealed up, labelled, and handed over to the matron, till such times as the owners thereof were ready to depart homeward or campward again. The letters dictated to me, and revised by me, that afternoon, would have made an excellent chapter for some future history of the war; for, like that which Thackeray's "Ensign Spooney" wrote his mother just before Waterloo,[35] they were "full of affection, pluck, and bad spelling;" nearly all giving lively accounts of the battle, and ending with a somewhat sudden plunge from patriotism to provender, desiring "Marm," "Mary Ann," or "Aunt Peters," to send along some pies, pickles, sweet stuff, and apples, "to yourn in haste," Joe, Sam, or Ned, as the case might be.

My little Sergeant insisted on trying to scribble something with his left hand, and patiently accomplished some half dozen lines of hieroglyphics, which he gave me to fold and direct, with a boyish blush, that rendered a glimpse of "My Dearest Jane," unnecessary, to assure me that the heroic lad had been more successful in the service of Commander-in-Chief Cupid than that of Gen. Mars;[36] and a charming little romance blossomed instanter in Nurse Periwinkle's romantic fancy, though no further confidences were made that day, for Sergeant fell asleep, and, judging from his tranquil face, visited his absent sweetheart in the pleasant land of dreams.

At five o'clock a great bell rang, and the attendants flew, not to arms, but to their trays, to bring up supper, when a second uproar announced that it was ready. The new comers woke at the sound; and I presently discovered that it took a very bad wound to incapacitate the defenders of the faith for the consumption of their rations; the amount that some of them sequestered was amazing; but when I suggested the probability of a famine hereafter, to the matron, that motherly lady cried out: "Bless their hearts, why shouldn't they eat? It's their only amusement; so fill every one, and, if there's not enough ready to-night, I'll lend my share to the Lord by giving it to the boys." And, whipping up her coffee-pot and plate of toast, she gladdened the eyes and stomachs of two or three dissatisfied heroes, by serving them with a liberal hand; and I haven't the slightest doubt that, having cast her bread upon the waters,[37] it came back buttered, as another large-hearted old lady was wont to say.

Then came the doctor's evening visit; the administration of medicines; washing feverish faces; smoothing tumbled beds; wetting wounds; singing lullabies; and preparations for the night. By twelve, the last labor of love was done; the last "good night" spoken; and, if any needed a reward for that day's work, they surely received it, in the silent eloquence of those long lines of faces, showing pale and peaceful in the shaded rooms, as we quitted them, followed by grateful glances that lighted us to bed, where rest, the sweetest, made our pillows soft, while Night and Nature took our places, filling that great house of pain with the healing miracles of Sleep, and his diviner brother, Death.

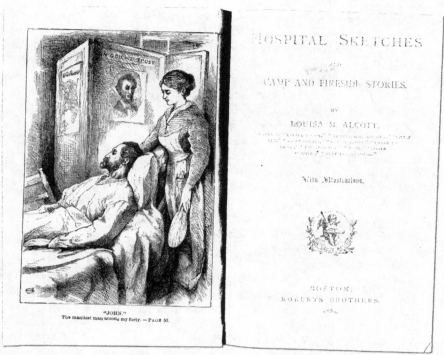

"JOHN."
The manliest man among my forty. — PAGE 53.

Nurse Periwinkle, about "John": "The manliest man among my forty." Illustration from Louisa May Alcott, *Hospital Sketches and Camp and Fireside Stories* (Boston: Roberts Brothers, 1889).

NOTES

1. The narrator, who was introduced to readers in an earlier sketch as "Nurse Periwinkle" (Alcott herself), here quotes a piece by English poet Felicia Hemans (1793–1835), "Egypt, Nubia, and Abyssinia: Damietta. Marguerite of France." These lines are spoken by Marguerite, queen of St. Louis, to rally her knights against their enemy, the Turks.
2. "To make one's toilet" in this era meant simply to prepare for going out, typically by washing one's face, brushing one's hair, etc.
3. Nurse.
4. Spartans were inhabitants of Sparta, in ancient Greece; they were well known as excellent warriors who were very physically fit.
5. In this context, "contraband" refers to an African American who has escaped slavery.
6. "Richard" has no antecedent here; possibly Alcott intended to refer to another wounded soldier.
7. Unknown reference. It is possible that the city of Cologne, Germany, was known for its foul stench.
8. Nickname for Sarah.
9. Steel buckets for carrying coal, which at this time was used to fuel small heater stoves.

10. African American nurses; the term "colored" was commonly used at this time to refer to African Americans but is now considered offensive and is no longer used.

11. A drink of sweet liqueur. Alcoholic drinks were often given to patients at this time to relieve pain.

12. On the surface, this appears to simply mean "a difficult course of work ahead." However, it is also possibly a reference to the folksong "Jordan Is a Hard Road to Travel" (1853), originally composed by Daniel Emmett for a blackface minstrel show (an extremely offensive type of once-popular performance in which White people blackened their faces with stage makeup and grotesquely caricatured Black people). Or it could be referring to the Confederate adaptation entitled "Richmond Is a Hard Road to Travel," which was intended to rally the Confederate troops and warn Union soldiers that capturing the Confederate capital of Richmond, Virginia, would be much more difficult than they believed.

13. Nurse Periwinkle here makes a joke with a pun; during this era bullets were in the shape of balls, and people danced in ballrooms.

14. In 1862, Union general Ambrose Burnside planned to cross the Rappahannock River at Fredericksburg, Virginia, and to subsequently attack the Confederate capital of Richmond. However, the essential pontoon bridges arrived two weeks after Burnside and his troops had arrived at the river, giving the Confederate Army ample time to prepare defenses before Burnside's force could cross. Due in large part to this delay, Burnside lost over twelve thousand men in the battle.

15. A Scottish Highland dance, similar to a jig.

16. By force and arms (Latin).

17. Facial muscles used when smiling and laughing.

18. A cup of tea containing alcoholic spirits.

19. A rebel, or Confederate soldier.

20. This soldier had been shot in the foot, and as a result he was unable to run ("cut") in retreat.

21. In the 1860s, many Republicans in the North who supported the Civil War called the small faction of antiwar Democrats "copperheads," believing that, like the venomous snakes known by this name, they were dangerous to the war effort; it also likely refers to the soldier's red hair.

22. Dr. Thomas H. Watts, a prominent Alabama politician who advocated secession from the Union; he served as governor of Alabama from December 1, 1863, to May 1, 1865.

23. A pinafore is a loose, sleeveless garment worn over young women's dresses at this time to keep them clean; here Nurse Periwinkle is noting that it had accumulated numerous food stains.

24. Nurse Periwinkle here adapts stanza three of "The Charge of the Light Brigade" (1854), by British poet Alfred, Lord Tennyson (1809–92), which is about the Battle of Balaclava during the Crimean War, fought from 1853 to 1856 between Russia and a combined force of British, French, and Ottoman Turkish troops. Stanza three reads:

> *Cannon to right of them,*
> *Cannon to left of them,*
> *Cannon in front of them*

Volleyed and thundered;
Stormed at with shot and shell,
Boldly they rode and well,
Into the jaws of Death,
Into the mouth of hell

Rode the six hundred.

25. Munchausen syndrome is a mental disorder in which a patient acts ill or claims symptoms that do not exist.
26. The term "darkey" to refer to African Americans is extremely offensive, but at this time some White people—both Northerners and Southerners—used it to derogatorily refer to African Americans. Here the Union soldier offers further evidence of his racism by implying that obtaining food by secretly licking plates is something a Black person would do.
27. Earrings.
28. "Truck" was a term synonymous with "loot"; it is clear that these earrings were stolen from the previously mentioned house in Fredericksburg. Alcott took the risk of offending her Northern readers by portraying a Union soldier as not being above looting.
29. In Psalm 23:4 (King James Version), David says to the Lord, "Yea, though I walk through the valley of the shadow of death, I will fear no evil: for thou art with me; thy rod and thy staff they comfort me."
30. Slang for a type of knife, usually used to prepare food.
31. An early anesthetic that would make a patient unconscious and unable to feel pain.
32. To curse someone that one dislikes.
33. The Virgin Mary, the mother of Jesus. These Irishmen, almost certainly Catholics, would have looked to her for solace in their moment of need. Alcott here critiques the men for being so coarse as to liken the Virgin Mary to a "biddy" (hired girl) on whom they could use a "poker" stick from a fire to help them in their time of suffering.
34. "Thou shalt not steal" is one of the Ten Commandments spoken by God to Moses, to serve as rules of conduct for all believers (Exodus 20:15, KJV).
35. A character from *Vanity Fair* (1848), a novel by British author William Makepeace Thackeray (1811–63). This character fights at the Battle of Waterloo (June 18, 1815), where French emperor Napoleon Bonaparte was defeated.
36. According to Roman mythology, Cupid—son of Venus, the goddess of love, and Mars, the god of war—serves as a god of love and erotic desire; here Alcott is insinuating that this soldier was more successful in love than in war.
37. In Ecclesiastes 11:1 (KJV), the Preacher, son of David, the king of Jerusalem, states that a true believer in God's goodness will "cast thy bread upon the waters: for thou shalt find it after many days." In other words, if one practices charity by giving one's own food or belongings to others, be assured that God will return your gift to you.

AMBROSE BIERCE

(1842–ca. 1914)

American short-story writer, journalist, poet, and Civil War veteran Ambrose Bierce was born in Meigs County, Ohio, on June 24, 1842. The Bierce family was quite large, and Ambrose was the tenth of thirteen children, all of whom had names beginning with "A." Although the large family struggled financially, Bierce's parents encouraged a love of reading and writing. Thanks to his acquired literacy, in 1857, at the age of fifteen, Bierce was able to get a job as a printer's assistant at the *Northern Indiana,* a small abolitionist paper.

Bierce joined the Ninth Indiana Infantry of the Union Army in 1861 and fought in a number of notably bloody Civil War battles, including the Battle of Shiloh (1862) and the Battle of Chickamauga (1863). Bierce sustained a significant head wound in 1864 at the Battle of Kennesaw Mountain but returned to the army after his recovery; he was not discharged until 1865. Bierce headed west in 1866 as a surveyor of military outposts, eventually arriving in San Francisco in 1867. His first job there, as night watchman at the United States Mint, gave him ample time to write, thus allowing him to begin to pursue a literary career. He soon became well-known for his short stories and articles that appeared in periodicals published in the Bay Area, including the *Californian,* the *Wasp,* the *Argonaut,* and the *San Francisco News Letter and California Advertiser.* During the course of his career, Bierce would serve as editor of the latter two publications.

In December 1871, Bierce married Mollie Day, and shortly thereafter the couple moved to London, where they stayed for three years before returning to San Francisco. The Bierces' marriage produced three children, but the couple separated in 1888 when Bierce found incriminating letters his wife had received from a male admirer. Their divorce was finalized in 1904.

Although his personal life was in upheaval, Bierce continued to solidify his place in the literary culture of California. Beginning in 1887, he was one of the first regular columnists to be featured in the *San Francisco Examiner;* in his "Prattle" columns especially, Bierce built a reputation for himself as a writer known for his dry wit and keen sarcasm. In addition, the economy of language and unadorned description often associated with journalism significantly influenced Bierce's short stories and poetry. Many of these characteristics are evident in the short stories and essays Bierce wrote about the Civil War, which broke new ground with their graphic and moving depictions of wartime horrors. Many of the best of these—including "The Affair at Coulter's Notch" as well as the frequently anthologized "Chickamauga" and "An Occurrence at Owl Creek Bridge"—were first published in the *San Francisco Examiner* and subsequently revised for his collection *Tales of Soldiers and Civilians* (1891), for which Bierce had difficulty finding a publisher due to its graphic presentation of war. This book achieved a moderate success and was republished in 1892 under the title *In the Midst of Life*, by which it has been known ever since.

By 1912, Bierce, after a decade-long journalism career in New York, was nearing the end of his life. Having been predeceased by many of his children and even his ex-wife, Bierce decided to travel to Mexico with the intention of supporting the Mexican Revolution by joining Pancho Villa's army. He began his journey by visiting many of the Civil War battlefields of his youth, but then continued to southern Texas, where he crossed the border into Mexico in December 1913. The last letter anyone ever received from him was dated December 26, 1913, from Chihuahua, Mexico; he was never heard from again. He likely died in battle in January 1914, but details remain unknown to this day. For many years the mysterious circumstances of Bierce's death overshadowed his work; in fact, the Mexican author Carlos Fuentes was so moved by the story of an American author who served in the American Civil War and then likely died in the Mexican Revolution that he based the main character of his 1985 novel, *The Old Gringo*, on Bierce.

During the past few decades, literary critics have increasingly appreciated Bierce's not-easy-to-classify works and the sharp satire of much of his writing. Bierce's growing reputation might also be ascribed to Bierce's strong commitment to challenging traditional power structures, hypocrisy, various ideologies, and corruption. "The Affair at Coulter's Notch" is one such story. As noted earlier, it first appeared in the *San Francisco Examiner* (October 20, 1889); Bierce then revised it in a number of ways for inclusion in *Tales of Soldiers and Civilians* two years later. Although the latter version is the one that has been most commonly read and discussed by scholars, the version reprinted here follows the original *San Francisco Examiner* text, which would have been read by tens of thousands of readers at the time.

*Readers should be aware that this story includes some language which, while commonly used during this time period, is no longer considered acceptable because of its offensive nature.

THE AFFAIR AT COULTER'S NOTCH (1889)

"Do you think, Colonel, that your brave Coulter would like to put one of his guns in here?" the General asked.

He was apparently not altogether serious; it certainly did not seem a place where any artillerist, however brave, would "like" to put a gun. The Colonel thought that possibly his division commander meant good humoredly to intimate that Captain Coulter's courage had been too highly extolled in a recent conversation between them.

"General," he replied warmly, "Coulter would like to put a gun anywhere within reach of those people,"—with a motion of his hand in the direction of the enemy.

"It is the only place," said the General. He was serious, then!

The "place" was a depression, a notch, in the sharp crest of a hill. It was a pass, and through it ran a turnpike which, reaching this highest point in its course by a sinuous ascent through a thin forest, ran straight away toward the enemy. For a mile to the left and a mile to the right the ridge, though occupied by a line of [Union] infantry lying close behind the sharp crest and appearing as if held in place by atmospheric pressure, was inaccessible to artillery. There was no place but the bottom of the notch, and that was barely wide enough for the roadbed. From the Confederate side this point was commanded by an entire battery posted on a slightly lower elevation beyond a creek and a mile away.[1] All the guns but one were masked by the trees of an orchard; that one—it seemed a bit of impudence—was directly in front of a rather grandiose building, the planter's dwelling. The gun was safe enough in its exposure: the rifles of that day would not carry a mile without such an elevation as made the fire, in a military sense, harmless; it might kill here and there but could not dislodge. Coulter's Notch—it came to be called so—was not, that pleasant summer afternoon, a place where one would "like to put a gun."

Three or four dead horses lay there, sprawling in the road, three or four dead men in a trim row at one side of it and a little back, down the hill. All but one were cavalrymen belonging to the Federal advance. One was a quartermaster:[2] the General commanding the division and the Colonel commanding the brigade, with their staffs and escorts, had ridden into the Notch to have a look at the enemy's guns—which had straightway obscured themselves in towering clouds of smoke. It was hardly profitable to be curious about guns which had the trick of the cuttlefish,[3] and the season of observation was brief. At its conclusion—a short remove backward from where it began—occurred the conversation already partly reported. "It is the only place," the General repeated thoughtfully, "to get at them."

The Colonel looked at him gravely. "There is room for but one gun, General—one against six."

"That is true—for only one at a time," said the Commander with something like, yet not altogether like, a smile. "But then, your brave Coulter!—a whole battery in himself."

The tone of irony was now unmistakable. It angered the Colonel, but he did not know what to say. The spirit of military subordination is not favorable to retort, nor even deprecation. At this moment a young officer of artillery came riding slowly up the road attended by his bugler. It was Captain Coulter. He could not have been more than twenty-three years of age. He was of medium height, but very slender and lithe, sitting his horse with something of the air of a civilian. In face he was of a type singularly unlike the men about him: thin, high-nosed, gray-eyed, with a slight blonde moustache, and long, rather straggling hair of the same color. There was an apparent negligence in his attire. His cap was worn with the visor a trifle askew; his coat was buttoned only at the sword belt, showing a considerable expanse of white shirt, tolerably clean for that stage of the campaign. But the negligence was all in his dress and bearing; in his face was a look of intense interest in his surroundings. His gray eyes, which seemed occasionally to strike right and left across the landscape, like search-lights, were for the most part fixed upon the sky beyond the Notch; until he should arrive at the summit of the road there was nothing else in that direction to see. As he came opposite his division and brigade commanders at the roadside he saluted mechanically and was about to pass on. Moved by a sudden impulse, the Colonel signed to him to halt.

"Captain Coulter," he said, "the enemy has a battery of six pieces over there on the next ridge. If I rightly understand the General he directs that you bring up a gun and engage them."

There was a blank silence; the General looked stolidly at a distant regiment swarming slowly up the hill through rough undergrowth, like a torn and draggled cloud of blue smoke; the Captain appeared not to have observed him. Presently the captain spoke, slowly and with apparent effort:

"On the next ridge, did you say, sir? Are the guns near the house?"

"Ah, you have been over this road before! Directly at the house."

"And it is—necessary—to engage them? The order is imperative?"

His voice was husky and broken. He was visibly paler. The Colonel was astonished and mortified. He stole a glance at the Commander. In that set, immobile face was no sign; it was as hard as bronze. A moment later the General rode away, followed by his staff and escort. The Colonel, humiliated and indignant, was about to order Captain Coulter in arrest, when the latter spoke a few words in a low tone to his bugler, saluted, and rode straight forward into the Notch, where, shortly, at the summit of the road, his field glass at his eyes, he showed against the sky, he and his horse, sharply defined and motionless as an equestrian statue. The bugler had dashed down the road in the opposite direction at headlong speed and disappeared around a corner. Presently his bugle was heard singing in the cedars, and in an incredibly short time a single gun with its caisson,[4] each drawn by six horses and manned by its full complement of gunners, came bounding and banging up the grade in a storm of dust, unlimbered under cover and was run forward by hand to the fatal crest among the dead horses. A gesture of the Captain's arm, some strangely agile movements of the men in loading, and almost before the troops along the way had ceased to hear the rattle of the wheels, a great white cloud sprang forward down the declivity, and with a sharp shock which turned up the white of the forest leaves like a storm the affair at Coulter's Notch had begun.

It is not intended to relate in detail the progress and incidents of that ghastly contest—a contest without vicissitudes, its alternations only different degrees of despair. Almost at the instant when Captain Coulter's gun blew its challenging cloud six answering clouds rolled upward from among the trees about the plantation house, a deep multiple report roared back like a broken echo, and thenceforth to the end the Federal cannoneers fought their hopeless battle in an atmosphere of living iron whose thoughts were lightnings and whose deeds were death.

Unwilling to see the efforts which he could not aid and the slaughter which he could not stay, the Colonel had ascended the ridge at a point a quarter of a mile to the left, whence the Notch, itself invisible but pushing up successive masses of smoke, seemed the crater of a volcano in thundering eruption. With his glass he watched the enemy's guns, noting as he could the effects of Coulter's fire—if Coulter still lived to direct it. He saw that the Federal gunners, ignoring those of the enemy's pieces, whose position could be determined by their smoke only, gave their whole attention to the one that maintained its place in the open—the lawn in front of the house, with which it was accurately in line. Over and about that hardy piece the shells exploded at intervals of a few seconds. Some exploded in the house, as could be seen by thin ascensions of smoke from the breached roof. Figures of prostrate men and horses were plainly visible.

"If our fellows are doing such good work with a single gun," said the Colonel to an aide who happened to be nearest, "they must be suffering like the devil from six. Go down and present the commander of that piece with my congratulations on the accuracy of his fire."

Turning to his Adjutant General[5] he said: "Did you observe Coulter's damned reluctance to obey orders?"

"Yes, sir, I did."

"Well, say nothing about it, please. I don't think the General will care to make any accusations. He will probably have enough to do in explaining his own connection with this uncommon way of amusing the rear guard of a retreating enemy."

"Colonel," said the Adjutant General, "I don't know that I ought to say anything, but there is something wrong in all this. Do you happen to know that Captain Coulter is from the South?"

"No; *was* he, indeed?"

"I heard that last summer the division which the General then commanded was in the vicinity of Coulter's home—camped there for weeks and—"

"Listen!" said the Colonel, interrupting with an upward gesture. "Do you hear *that?*"

"That" was the silence of the Federal gun. The staff, the orderlies, the lines of infantry behind the crest—all had "heard," and were looking curiously in the direction of the crater, whence no smoke now ascended except desultory cloudlets from the enemy's shells. Then came the blare of a bugle, a faint rattle of wheels; a minute later the sharp reports recommenced with double activity. The demolished gun had been replaced with a sound one.

"Yes," said the Adjutant General, resuming his narrative, "the General made the acquaintance of Coulter's family. There was trouble—I don't know the exact nature of it—something about Coulter's wife. She is a red hot Secessionist,[6] as they all are, except Coulter himself, but she is a good wife and high-bred lady. There was a complaint to army headquarters. The General was transferred to this division. It is odd that Coulter's battery should afterward have been assigned to it."

The Colonel had risen from the rock upon which they had been sitting. His eyes were blazing with a generous indignation.

"See here, Morrison," said he, looking his gossiping staff officer straight in the face, "did you get that story from a gentleman or a liar?"

"I don't want to say how I got it, Colonel, unless it is necessary"—he was blushing a trifle—"but I'll stake my life upon its truth in the main."

The Colonel turned toward a small knot of officers some distance away. "Lieutenant Williams!" he shouted.

One of the officers detached himself from the group, and, coming forward, saluted, saying: "Pardon me, Colonel, I thought you had been informed. Williams is dead down there by the gun. What can I do, sir?"

Lieutenant Williams was the aide who had had the pleasure of conveying to the officer in charge of the gun his brigade commander's congratulations.

"Go," said the Colonel, "and direct the withdrawal of that gun instantly. Hold! I'll go myself."

He strode down the declivity toward the rear of the Notch at a break-neck pace, over rocks and through brambles, followed by his little retinue in tumultuous disorder. At the foot of the declivity they mounted their waiting animals and took to the road at a lively trot round a bend and into the Notch. The spectacle which they encountered there was appalling.

Within that defile, barely broad enough for a single gun, were piled the wrecks of no fewer than four—they had noted the silencing of only the last one disabled. The *débris* lay on both sides of the road; the men had managed to keep an open way between, through which the fifth piece was now firing. The men?— they looked like demons of the Pit! All were hatless, all stripped to the waist, their reeking skins black with blotches of powder and spattered with gouts[7] of blood. They worked like madmen, with rammer and cartridge, lever and lanyard.[8] They set their swollen shoulders and bleeding hands against the wheels at each recoil and heaved the heavy gun back to its place. There were no commands; in that awful environment of whooping shot, exploding shells, and shrieking fragments of iron and flying splinters of wood, none could have been heard. Officers, if officers there were, were indistinguishable; all worked together—each while he lasted—governed by the eye. When the gun was sponged,[9] it was loaded; when loaded aimed and fired. There was no clashing; the duty of the instant was obvious. When one fell another, looking a trifle cleaner, seemed to rise from the earth in the dead man's tracks to fall in his turn.

With the ruined guns lay the ruined men—alongside the wreckage, under it and atop of it; and back down the road—a ghastly procession!—crept on hands and knees such of the wounded as were able to move. The Colonel—he had compassionately sent his cavalcade to the right about—had to ride over those who were entirely dead in order not to crush those who were partly alive. Into that Hell he tranquilly held his way, rode up alongside the gun, and, in the obscurity of the last discharge tapped upon the cheek the man holding the rammer—who straightway fell, thinking himself killed. A fiend seven times damned sprang out of the smoke to take his place, but paused and gazed up at the mounted officer with an unearthly regard, his teeth flashing between his black lips, his eyes, fierce and expanded, burning like coals beneath his bloody brow. The Colonel made an authoritative gesture and pointed to the rear. The fiend bowed in token of obedience. It was Captain Coulter.

Simultaneously with the Colonel's arresting sign silence fell upon the whole field of action. The procession of missiles no longer streamed into that defile of death; the enemy also had ceased firing. His army had been gone for hours, and the commander of his rear guard who had held his position perilously long in hope to silence the Federal fire, at that strange moment had silenced his own. "I was not aware of the breadth of my authority," thought the Colonel, facetiously, riding forward to the crest to see what had really happened.

An hour later his brigade was in bivouac[10] on the enemy's ground and its idlers were examining, with something of awe, as the faithful inspect a saint's relics, a score of straddling dead horses and three disabled guns, all spiked. The fallen men had been carried away; their crushed and broken bodies would have given too great satisfaction.

Naturally, the Colonel established himself and his military family in the plantation house. It was somewhat shattered, but it was better than the open air. The furniture was greatly deranged and broken. Walls and ceilings were knocked away here and there, and there was a lingering odor of powder smoke was everywhere. The beds, the closets of women's clothing, the cupboards were not greatly damaged. The new tenants for a night made themselves comfortable, and the practical effacement of Coulter's battery supplied them with an interesting topic.

During supper that evening an orderly of the escort showed himself into the dining-room and asked permission to speak to the Colonel.

"What is it, Barbour?" said that officer, pleasantly, having overheard the request.

"Colonel, there is something wrong in the cellar; I don't know what—somebody there. I was down there rummaging about."

"I will go down and see," said a staff officer, rising.

"So will I," the Colonel said; "let the others remain. Lead on, orderly."

They took a candle from the table and descended the cellar stairs, the orderly in visible trepidation. The candle made but a feeble light, but presently, as they advanced, its narrow circle of illumination revealed a human figure seated on the ground against the black stone wall which they were skirting, its knees elevated, its head bowed sharply forward. The face, which should have been seen in profile, was invisible, for the man was bent so far forward that his long hair concealed it; and, strange to relate, the beard, of a much darker hue, fell in a great tangled mass and lay along the ground at his feet. They involuntarily paused; then the Colonel, taking the candle from the orderly's shaking hand, approached the man and attentively considered him. The long dark beard was the hair of a woman—dead. The dead woman clasped in her arms a dead babe. Both were clasped in the arms of the man, pressed against his breast, against his lips. There was blood in the hair of the woman; there was blood in the hair of the man. A yard away lay an infant's foot. It was near an irregular depression in the beaten earth which formed the cellar's floor—a fresh excavation with a convex bit of iron, having jagged edges, visible in one of the sides. The Colonel held the light as high as he could. The floor of the room above was broken through, the splinters pointing at all angles downward. "This casemate[11] is not bomb-proof," said the Colonel gravely; it did not occur to him that his summing up of the matter had any levity in it.

They stood about the group awhile in silence; the staff officer was thinking of his unfinished supper, the orderly of what might possibly be in one of the casks on the other side of the cellar. Suddenly the man, whom they had thought dead raised his head and gazed tranquilly into their faces. His complexion was coal black; the cheeks were apparently tattooed in irregular sinuous lines from the eyes downward. The lips, too, were white, like those of a stage Negro.[12] There was blood upon his forehead.

The staff officer drew back a pace, the orderly two paces.

"What are you doing here, my man?" said the Colonel, unmoved.

"This house belongs to me, sir," was the reply, civilly delivered.

"To you? Who then are—were these?"

"My wife and child. Colonel, I am Captain Coulter."

NOTES

1. Here the colonel, the general, and the captain referred to are Union soldiers in the American Civil War; opposite them is a Confederate position of six cannons (an artillery battery consists of six pieces) that has a clear line of fire on the notch where the Union general is proposing placing a cannon to fire at the enemy.
2. An officer in charge of providing clothing and food for troops.
3. When threatened, a cuttlefish can eject a type of ink from its body that serves as a smoke screen in order to evade attack.
4. A wagon carrying ammunition.
5. An officer whose duties include communicating orders and performing various administrative tasks.
6. Someone who believed in the right of states to secede from the Union and thus a supporter of the Confederacy. During the Civil War many families had such divided loyalties.
7. Gushes.
8. Various parts of a cannon involved in its firing.
9. After a cannon was fired, the "sponger" would dip a pole with rags on its end into water and then put it down the barrel of the cannon to both scour it and make sure no sparks were still there that might prematurely ignite the next powder charge loaded into the barrel. When Bierce revised the text for its appearance in *Tales of Soldiers and Civilians*, he added this passage to make the scene even more horrific: "The Colonel observed something new to his military experience—something horrible and unnatural: the gun was bleeding at the mouth! In temporary default of water, the man sponging had dipped his sponge into a pool of his comrades' blood."

10. A temporary encampment.
11. A fortified chamber within a defensive position, usually to hold ammunition. Clearly, the house's basement was not intended as such.
12. For what were known as "minstrel shows," White performers would put on theatrical makeup to make their faces black and their lips white; these caricatures of African Americans, and the mocking, inaccurate portrayals involved in the shows, were very racist. Minstrel shows mostly disappeared after approximately 1910, except in the South.

GEORGE WASHINGTON CABLE

(1844–1925)

As a young man, George Washington Cable appeared to be a relatively typical son of prosperous parents living in New Orleans before the Civil War, even duly enlisting in the Confederate army in 1863, at the age of nineteen. Yet after the war, Cable began to show signs of discontent with the South. While holding down an accountant's position at the Cotton Exchange, he began to write a regular column of observations, often rather satirical, for the New Orleans–based *Times-Picayune* newspaper. Then in 1873 he was "discovered" by Edward King, a literary scout sent by *Scribner's Monthly* magazine (based in New York City) to find talented writers who could tell the inside story of the New South to a national readership. At the time, *Scribner's Monthly,* like many other genteel northern magazines, wished to expand its circulation in the South, and thus actively sought out stories about this seemingly "exotic" region that would simultaneously satisfy northern readers and not offend southern readers.

Cable's early fictions appeared to meet these requirements quite well. His story "'Sieur George" was published in the October 1873 issue of *Scribner's Monthly,* and "Belles Demoiselles Plantation" followed not long thereafter, appearing in the April 1874 issue. These, along with five other stories set in Louisiana, were collected and published by Scribner's as *Old Creole Days* in 1879. It is important to note that Cable himself, just two years later, told readers in the preface to his novel *Madame Delphine* that this "happy title" had been given to the collection by his publisher, not by him; it is clear he felt there was more to these stories than simply pleasing depictions of quaint ways in a southern locale. Nonetheless, in these fictions, Cable's critique of the complex and often hypocritical attitudes and actions of the region's inhabitants, especially concerning race, is rather muted.

During the following years, however, Cable's criticism of the South would become much more explicit, not only in his first novel, *The Grandissimes* (1880), but also in a number of nonfiction essays published in various periodicals and collected in *The Silent South: Together with "The Freedman's Case in Equity" and "The Convict Lease System"* (1885). Many of his fellow southerners were not pleased by one of their own revealing unpleasant facts about their attitudes and activities, and their severely negative response to Cable's work prompted him to relocate with his family to Northampton, Massachusetts, in 1885. Throughout the rest of his career, Cable published a great many short stories and novels but struggled to break out of the expectation (both from editors and readers) that he write romances of the South rather than expose the region's problematic aspects with more realistic treatments.

"Belles Demoiselles Plantation" is one of Cable's most critically renowned stories, and with good reason, for it offers excellent passages of dialogue in regional dialect (a hallmark of Regional Realism) and an incisive look into how historical racial intermingling affected land ownership and wealth in the South during this period. As noted earlier, it was originally published in *Scribner's Monthly* in April 1874; however, because a number of typographical errors from the serialized version were quietly corrected for the *Old Creole Days* collection of 1879, that is the version reproduced here.

*Readers should be aware that this story includes some language which, while commonly used during this time period, is no longer considered acceptable because of its offensive nature.

BELLES DEMOISELLES PLANTATION (1874)

The original grantee was Count—, assume the name to be De Charleu; the old Creoles[1] never forgive a public mention. He was the French king's commissary. One day, called to France to explain the lucky accident of the commissariat having burned down with his account-books inside,[2] he left his wife, a Choctaw Comptesse,[3] behind.

Arrived at court, his excuses were accepted, and that tract granted him where afterwards stood Belles Demoiselles Plantation. A man cannot remember every thing! In a fit of forgetfulness he married a French gentlewoman, rich and beautiful, and "brought her out." However, "All's well that ends well;" a famine had been in the colony, and the Choctaw Comptesse had starved, leaving nought but a half-caste orphan family lurking on the edge of the settlement, bearing our French gentlewoman's own new name, and being mentioned in Monsieur's will.

And the new Comptesse—she tarried but a twelvemonth, left Monsieur a lovely son, and departed, led out of this vain world by the swamp-fever.

From this son sprang the proud Creole family of De Charleu. It rose straight up, up, up, generation after generation, tall, branchless, slender, palm-like; and finally, in the time of which I am to tell, flowered with all the rare beauty of a century-plant, in Artemise, Innocente, Félicité, the twins Marie and Martha, Leontine and little Septima: the seven beautiful daughters for whom their home had been fitly named Belles Demoiselles.[4]

The Count's grant had once been a long Pointe, round which the Mississippi[5] used to whirl, and seethe, and foam, that it was horrid to behold. Big whirlpools would open and wheel about in the savage eddies under the low bank, and close

up again, and others open, and spin, and disappear. Great circles of muddy surface would boil up from hundreds of feet below, and gloss over, and seem to float
away,—sink, come back again under water, and with only a soft hiss surge up
again, and again drift off, and vanish. Every few minutes the loamy bank would
tip down a great load of earth upon its besieger, and fall back a foot,—sometimes
a yard,—and the writhing river would press after, until at last the Pointe was
quite swallowed up, and the great river glided by in a majestic curve, and asked
no more; the bank stood fast, the "caving" became a forgotten misfortune, and
the diminished grant was a long, sweeping, willowy bend, rustling with miles of
sugar-cane.

Coming up the Mississippi in the sailing craft of those early days, about the
time one first could descry the white spires of the old St. Louis Cathedral,[6] you
would be pretty sure to spy, just over to your right under the levee, Belles Demoiselles Mansion, with its broad veranda and red painted cypress roof, peering over
the embankment, like a bird in the nest, half hid by the avenue of willows which
one of the departed De Charleus,—he that married a Marot,—had planted on
the levee's crown.

The house stood unusually near the river, facing eastward, and standing four-
square, with an immense veranda about its sides, and a flight of steps in front
spreading broadly downward, as we open arms to a child. From the veranda nine
miles of river were seen; and in their compass, near at hand, the shady garden
full of rare and beautiful flowers; farther away broad fields of cane and rice, and
the distant quarters of the slaves, and on the horizon everywhere a dark belt of
cypress forest.

The master was old Colonel De Charleu,—Jean Albert Henri Joseph
De Charleu-Marot, and "Colonel" by the grace of the first American governor.[7]
Monsieur,—he would not speak to any one who called him "Colonel,"—was a
hoary-headed patriarch. His step was firm, his form erect, his intellect strong
and clear, his countenance classic, serene, dignified, commanding, his manners
courtly, his voice musical,—fascinating. He had had his vices,—all his life; but
had borne them, as his race do, with a serenity of conscience and a cleanness
of mouth that left no outward blemish on the surface of the gentleman. He
had gambled in Royal Street, drunk hard in Orleans Street, run his adversary
through in the duelling-ground at Slaughter-house Point, and danced and quarreled at the St. Philippe-street-theatre quadroon balls.[8] Even now, with all his
courtesy and bounty, and a hospitality which seemed to be entertaining angels,
he was bitter-proud and penurious, and deep down in his hard-finished heart
loved nothing but himself, his name, and his motherless children. But these!—
their ravishing beauty was all but excuse enough for the unbounded idolatry
of their father. Against these seven goddesses he never rebelled. Had they even
required him to defraud old De Carlos—

I can hardly say.

Old De Carlos was his extremely distant relative on the Choctaw side. With
this single exception, the narrow thread-like line of descent from the Indian wife,

diminished to a mere strand by injudicious alliances, and deaths in the gutters of old New Orleans, was extinct. The name, by Spanish contact, had become De Carlos; but this one surviving bearer of it was known to all, and known only, as Injin[9] Charlie.

One thing I never knew a Creole to do. He will not utterly go back on the ties of blood, no matter what sort of knots those ties may be. For one reason, he is never ashamed of his or his father's sins; and for another,—he will tell you—he is "all heart!"

So the different heirs of the De Charleu estate had always strictly regarded the rights and interests of the De Carloses, especially their ownership of a block of dilapidated buildings in a part of the city, which had once been very poor property, but was beginning to be valuable. This block had much more than maintained the last De Carlos through a long and lazy lifetime, and, as his household consisted only of himself, and an aged and crippled negress, the inference was irresistible that he "had money." Old Charlie, though by *alias* an "Injin," was plainly a dark white man, about as old as Colonel De Charleu, sunk in the bliss of deep ignorance, shrewd, deaf, and, by repute at least, unmerciful.

The Colonel and he always conversed in English. This rare accomplishment, which the former had learned from his Scotch wife,—the latter from up-river traders,—they found an admirable medium of communication, answering, better than French could, a similar purpose to that of the stick which we fasten to the bit of one horse and breast-gear of another, whereby each keeps his distance. Once in a while, too, by way of jest, English found its way among the ladies of Belles Demoiselles, always signifying that their sire was about to have business with old Charlie.

Now a long-standing wish to buy out Charlie troubled the Colonel. He had no desire to oust him unfairly; he was proud of being always fair; yet he did long to engross the whole estate under one title. Out of his luxurious idleness he had conceived this desire, and thought little of so slight an obstacle as being already somewhat in debt to old Charlie for money borrowed, and for which Belles Demoiselles was, of course, good, ten times over. Lots, buildings, rents, all, might as well be his, he thought, to give, keep, or destroy. "Had he but the old man's heritage. Ah! he might bring that into existence which his *belles demoiselles* had been begging for, 'since many years;' a home,—and such a home,—in the gay city. Here he should tear down this row of cottages, and make his garden wall; there that long rope-walk should give place to vine-covered ardors; the bakery yonder should make way for a costly conservatory; that wine warehouse should come down, and the mansion go up. It should be the finest in the State. Men should never pass it, but they should say—'the palace of the De Charleus; a family of grand descent, a people of elegance and bounty, a line as old as France, a fine old man, and seven daughters as beautiful as happy; whoever dare attempt to marry there must leave his own name behind him!'

"The house should be of stones fitly set, brought down in ships from the land of 'les Yankees,' and it should have an airy belvedere,[10] with a gilded image tiptoeing and shining on its peak, and from it you should see, far across the gleaming folds of the river, the red roof of Belles Demoiselles, the country-seat. At the big stone gate there should be a porter's lodge, and it should be a privilege even to see the ground."

Truly they were a family fine enough, and fancy-free enough to have fine wishes, yet happy enough where they were, to have had no wish but to live there always.

To those, who, by whatever fortune, wandered into the garden of Belles Demoiselles some summer afternoon as the sky was reddening towards evening, it was lovely to see the family gathered out upon the tiled pavement at the foot of the broad front steps, gayly chatting and jesting, with that ripple of laughter that comes so pleasingly from a bevy of girls. The father would be found seated in their midst, the center of attention and compliment, witness, arbiter, umpire, critic, by his beautiful children's unanimous appointment, but the single vassal, too, of seven absolute sovereigns.

Now they would draw their chairs near together in eager discussion of some new step in the dance, or the adjustment of some rich adornment. Now they would start about him with excited comments to see the eldest fix a bunch of violets in his button-hole. Now the twins would move down a walk after some unusual flower, and be greeted on their return with the high pitched notes of delighted feminine surprise.

As evening came on they would draw more quietly about their paternal center. Often their chairs were forsaken, and they grouped themselves on the lower steps, one above another, and surrendered themselves to the tender influences of the approaching night. At such an hour the passer on the river, already attracted by the dark figures of the broad-roofed mansion, and its woody garden standing against the glowing sunset, would hear the voices of the hidden group rise from the spot in the soft harmonies of an evening song; swelling clearer and clearer as the thrill of music warmed them into feeling, and presently joined by the deeper tones of the father's voice; then, as the daylight passed quite away, all would be still, and he would know that the beautiful home had gathered its nestlings under its wings.

And yet, for mere vagary, it pleased them not to be pleased.

"Arti!" called one sister to another in the broad hall, one morning,—mock amazement in her distended eyes,—"something is goin' to took place!"

"*Comm-e-n-t?*"[11]—long-drawn perplexity.

"Papa is goin' to town!"

The news passed up stairs.

"Inno!"—one to another meeting in a doorway,—"something is goin' to took place!"

"*Qu'est-ce-que c'est!*"[12]—vain attempt at gruffness.

"Papa is goin' to town!"

The unusual tidings were true. It was afternoon of the same day that the Colonel tossed his horse's bridle to his groom, and stepped up to old Charlie, who was sitting on his bench under a China-tree, his head, as was his fashion, bound in a Madras handkerchief. The "old man" was plainly under the effect of spirits and smiled a deferential salutation without trusting himself to his feet.

"Eh, well Charlie!"—the Colonel raised his voice to suit his kinsman's deafness,—"how is those times with my friend Charlie?"

"Eh?" said Charlie, distractedly.

"Is that goin' well with my friend Charlie?"

"In de house,—call her,"—making a pretense of rising.

"*Non, non!* I don't want,"—the speaker paused to breathe—"ow is collection?"

"Oh!" said Charlie, "every day he make me more poorer!"

"What do you hask for it?" asked the planter indifferently, designating the house by a wave of his whip.

"Ask for w'at?" said Injin Charlie.

"De *house!* What you ask for it?"

"I don't believe," said Charlie.

"What you would take for it!" cried the planter.

"Wait for w'at?"

"What you would *take* for the whole block?"

"I don't want to sell him!"

"I'll give you *ten thousand dollah* for it."

"Ten t'ousand dollah for dis house? Oh, no, dat is no price. He is blame good old house,—dat old house." (Old Charlie and the Colonel never swore in presence of each other.) "Forty years dat old house didn't had to be paint! I easy can get fifty t'ousand dollah for dat old house."

"Fifty thousand picayune;[13] yes," said the Colonel.

"She's a good house. Can make plenty money," pursued the deaf man.

"That's what make you so rich, eh, Charlie?"

"*Non,* I don't make nothing. Too blame clever, me, dat's de troub'. She's a good house,—make money fast like a steamboat,—make a barrel full in a week! Me, I lose money all de days. Too blame clever."

"Charlie!"

"Eh?"

"Tell me what you'll *take.*"

"Make? I don't make nothing. Too blame clever."

"What will you take?"

"Oh! I got enough already,—half drunk now."

"What will you take for the 'ouse?"

"You want to buy her?"

"I don't know,"—(shrug),—"maybe,—if you sell it cheap."

"She's a bully old house."

There was a long silence. By and by old Charlie commenced—

"Old Injin Charlie is a low-down dog."

"*C'est vrai, oui!*[14] retorted the Colonel in an undertone.

"He's got Injin blood in him."

"But he's got some blame good blood, too, ain't it?"

The Colonel nodded impatiently.

"*Bien!* Old Charlie's Injin blood says, 'sell de house, Charlie, you blame old fool!' *Mais,* old Charlie's good blood says, 'Charlie! if you sell dat old house, Charlie, you low-down old dog, Charlie, what de Compte De Charleu make for you grace-gran'muzzer, de dev' can eat you, Charlie, I don't care.'"

"But you'll sell it anyhow, won't you, old man?"

"No!" And the no rumbled off in muttered oaths like thunder out on the Gulf. The incensed old Colonel wheeled and started off.

"Curl!" (Colonel) said Charlie, standing up unsteadily.

The planter turned with an inquiring frown.

"I'll trade with you!" said Charlie.

The Colonel was tempted. "'Ow'l you trade?" he asked.

"My house for yours!"

The old Colonel turned pale with anger. He walked very quickly back, and came close up to his kinsman.

"Charlie!" he said.

"Injin Charlie,"—with a tipsy nod.

But by this time self-control was returning. "Sell Belles Demoiselles to you?" he said in a high key, and then laughed "Ho, ho, ho!" and rode away.

A cloud, but not a dark one, overshadowed the spirits of Belles Demoiselles' plantation. The old master, whose beaming presence had always made him a shining Saturn, spinning and sparkling within the bright circle of his daughters, fell into musing fits, started out of frowning reveries, walked often by himself, and heard business from his overseer fretfully.

No wonder. The daughters knew his closeness in trade, and attributed to it his failure to negotiate for the Old Charlie buildings,—so to call them. They began to depreciate Belles Demoiselles. If a north wind blew, it was too cold to ride. If a shower had fallen, it was too muddy to drive. In the morning the garden was wet. In the evening the grasshopper was a burden. *Ennui*[15] was turned into capital; every headache was interpreted a premonition of ague;[16] and when the native exuberance of a flock of ladies without a want or a care burst out in laughter in the father's face, they spread their French eyes, rolled up their little hands, and with rigid wrists and mock vehmence vowed and vowed again that they only laughed at their misery, and should pine to death unless they could move to the sweet city. "Oh! the theatre! Oh! Orleans Street! Oh! the masquerade! the Place d'Armes! the ball!" and they would call upon Heaven with French irreverence, and fall into each other's arms, and whirl down the hall singing a waltz, end with a grand collision and fall, and, their eyes streaming merriment, lay the blame on the slippery floor, that would some day be the death of the whole seven.

Three times more the fond father, thus goaded, managed, by accident,— business accident,—to see old Charlie and increase his offer; but in vain. He finally went to him formally.

"Eh?" said the deaf and distant relative. "For what you want him, eh? Why you don't stay where you halways be 'appy? Dis is a blame old rat-hole,—good for old Injin Charlie,—da's all. Why you don't stay where you be halways 'appy? Why you don't buy somewheres else?"

"That's none of your business," snapped the planter. Truth was, his reasons were unsatisfactory even to himself.

A sullen silence followed. Then Charlie spoke:

"Well, now, look here; I sell you old Charlie's house."

"*Bien!* and the whole block," said the Colonel.

"Hold on," said Charlie. "I sell you de 'ouse and de block. Den I go and git drunk, and go to sleep de dev' comes along and says, 'Charlie! old Charlie, you blame low-down old dog, wake up! What you doin' here? Where's de 'ouse what Monsieur le Compte give your grace-gran-muzzer? Don't you see dat fine gentyman, De Charleu, done gone and tore him down and make him over new, you blame old fool, Charlie, you low-down old Injin dog!'"

"I'll give you forty thousand dollars," said the Colonel.

"For de 'ouse?"

"For all."

The deaf man shook his head.

"Forty-five!" said the Colonel.

"What a lie? For what you tell me 'What a lie?' I don't tell you no lie."

"*Non, non!* I give you *forty-five!*" shouted the Colonel.

Charlie shook his head again.

"Fifty!"

He shook it again.

The figures rose and rose to—

"Seventy-five!"

The answer was an invitation to go away and let the owner alone, as he was, in certain specified respects, the vilest of living creatures, and no company for a fine gentyman.

The "fine gentyman" longed to blaspheme,—but before old Charlie!—in the name of pride, how could he? He mounted and started away.

"Tell you what I'll make wid you," said Charlie.

The other, guessing aright, turned back without dismounting, smiling.

"How much Belles Demoiselles hoes me now?" asked the deaf one.

"One hundred and eighty thousand dollars," said the Colonel, firmly.

"Yass," said Charlie. "I don't want Belle Demoiselles."

The old Colonel's quiet laugh intimated it made no difference either way.

"But me," continued Charlie, "me,—I'm got le Compte De Charleu's blood in me, any'ow,—a litt' bit, any'ow, ain't it?"

The Colonel nodded that it was.

"*Bien!* If I go out of dis place and don't go to Belles Demoiselles, de peoples will say,—dey will say, 'Old Charlie he been all doze time tell a blame *lie!* He ain't no kin to his old grace-gran-muzzer, not a blame bit! He don't got nary drop of

De Charleu blood to save his blame low-down old Injin soul!' No, sare! What I want wid money, den? No, sare! My place for yours!"

He turned to go into the house, just too soon to see the Colonel make an ugly whisk at him with his riding-whip. Then the Colonel, too, moved off.

Two or three times over, as he ambled homeward, laughter broke through his annoyance, as he recalled old Charlie's family pride and the presumption of his offer. Yet each time he could but think better of—not the offer to swap, but the preposterous ancestral loyalty. It was so much better than he could have expected from his "low-down" relative, and not unlike his own whim withal—the proposition which went with it was forgiven.

This last defeat bore so harshly on the master of Belles Demoiselles, that the daughters, reading chagrin in his face, began to repent. They loved their father as daughters can, and when they saw their pretended dejection harassing him seriously they restrained their complaints, displayed more than ordinary tenderness, and heroically and ostentatiously concluded there was no place like Belles Demoiselles. But the new mood touched him more than the old, and only refined his discontent. Here was a man, rich without the care of riches, free from any real trouble, happiness as native to his house as perfume to his garden, deliberately, as it were with premeditated malice, taking joy by the shoulder and bidding her be gone to town, whither he might easily have followed, only that the very same ancestral nonsense that kept Injin Charlie from selling the old place for twice its value prevented him from choosing any other spot for a city home.

But by and by the charm of nature and the merry hearts around him prevailed; the fit of exalted sulks passed off, and after a while the year flared up at Christmas, flickered, and went out.

New Year came and passed; the beautiful garden of Belles Demoiselles put on its spring attire; the seven fair sisters moved from rose to rose; the cloud of discontent had warmed into invisible vapor in the rich sunlight of family affection, and on the common memory the only scar of last year's wound was old Charlie's sheer impertinence in crossing the caprice of the De Charleus. The cup of gladness seemed to fill with the filling of the river.

How high that river was! Its tremendous current rolled and tumbled and spun along, hustling the long funeral flotillas of drift,—and how near shore it came! Men were out day and night, watching the levee.[17] On windy nights even the old Colonel took part, and grew light-hearted with occupation and excitement, as every minute the river threw a white arm over the levee's top, as though it would vault over. But all held fast, and, as the summer drifted in, the water sunk down into its banks and looked quite incapable of harm.

On a summer afternoon of uncommon mildness, old Colonel Jean Albert Henri Joseph De Charleu-Marot, being in a mood for revery, slipped the custody of his feminine rulers and sought the crown of the levee, where it was his wont to promenade. Presently he sat upon a stone bench,—a favorite seat. Before him lay his broad-spread fields; near by, his lordly mansion; and being still,—perhaps by female contact,—somewhat sentimental, he fell to musing on his past. It was hardly worthy to be proud of. All its morning was reddened with mad frolic, and far toward the meridian it was marred with elegant rioting. Pride had kept him well-nigh useless, and despised the honors won by valor; gaming had dimmed prosperity; death had taken his heavenly wife; voluptuous ease had mortgaged his lands; and yet his house still stood, his sweet-smelling fields were still fruitful, his name was fame enough; and yonder and yonder, among the trees and flowers, like angels walking in Eden, were the seven goddesses of his only worship.

Just then a slight sound behind him brought him to his feet. He cast his eyes anxiously to the outer edge of the little strip of bank between the levee's base and the river. There was nothing visible. He paused, with his ear toward the water, his face full of frightened expectation. Ha! There came a single plashing sound, like some great beast slipping into the river, and little waves in a wide semi-circle came out from under the bank and spread over the water!

"My God!"

He plunged down the levee and bounded through the low weeds to the edge of the bank. It was sheer, and the water about four feet below. He did not stand quite on the edge, but fell upon his knees a couple of yards away, wringing his hands, moaning and weeping, and staring through his watery eyes at a fine, long crevice just discernible under the matted grass, and curving outward on either hand toward the river.

"My God!" he sobbed aloud; "my God!" and even while he called, his God answered: the tough Bermuda grass stretched and snapped, the crevice slowly became a gape, and softly, gradually, with no sound but the closing of the water at last, a ton or more of earth settled into the boiling eddy and disappeared.

At the same instant a pulse of the breeze brought from the garden behind, the joyous, thoughtless laughter of the fair mistresses of Belles Demoiselles.

The old Colonel sprang up and clambered over the levee. Then forcing himself to a more composed movement he hastened into the house and ordered his horse.

"Tell my children to make merry while I am gone," he left word. "I shall be back to-night," and the horse's hoofs clattered down a by-road leading to the city.

"Charlie," said the planter, riding up to a window, from which the old man's nightcap was thrust out, "what you say, Charlie,—my house for yours, eh, Charlie—what you say?"

"Ello!" said Charlie; "from where you come from dis time of to-night?"

"I come from the Exchange in St. Louis Street." (A small fraction of the truth.)

"What you want?" said matter-of-fact Charlie.

"I come to trade."

The low-down relative drew the worsted off his ears. "Oh! yass," he said with an uncertain air.

"Well, old man Charlie, what you say: my house for yours,—like you said,—eh, Charlie?"

"I dunno," said Charlie; "it's nearly mine now. Why you don't stay dare youse'f?"

"*Because I don't want!*" said the Colonel savagely. "Is dat reason enough for you? You better take me in de notion, old man, I tell you,—yes!"

Charlie never winced; but how his answer delighted the Colonel! Quoth Charlie:

"I don't care—I take him!—mais, possession give right off."

"Not the whole plantation, Charlie; only"—

"I don't care," said Charlie; "we easy can fix dat. *Mais*, what for you don't want to keep him? I don't want him. You better keep him."

"Don't you try to make no fool of me, old man," cried the planter.

"Oh, no!" said the other. "Oh, no! but you make a fool of yourself, ain't it?"

The dumbfounded Colonel stared; Charlie went on:

"Yass! Belles Demoiselles is more wort' dan tree block like dis one. I pass by dare since two weeks. Oh, pritty Belles Demoiselles! De cane was wave in de wind, de garden smell like a bouquet, de white-cap was jump up and down on de river; seven *belles demoiselles* was ridin' on horses. 'Pritty, pritty, pritty!' says old Charlie. Ah! *Monsieur le père*, 'ow 'appy, 'appy, 'appy!"

"Yass!" he continued—the Colonel still staring—"le Compte De Charleu have two familie. One was low-down Choctaw, one was high up *noblesse*. He gave the low-down Choctaw dis old rat-hole; he give Belles Demoiselles to you gran-fozzer; and now you don't be *satisfait*. What I'll do wid Belles Demoiselles? She'll break me in two years, yass. And what you'll do wid old Charlie's house, eh? You'll tear her down and make you'se'f a blame old fool. I rather wouldn't trade!"

The planter caught a big breathful of anger, but Charlie went straight on:

"I rather wouldn't, *mais* I will do it for you;—just de same, like Monsieur le Compte would say, 'Charlie, you old fool, I want to shange houses wid you.'"

So long as the Colonel suspected irony he was angry, but as Charlie seemed, after all, to be certainly in earnest, he began to feel conscience-stricken. He was by no means a tender man, but his lately-discovered misfortune had unhinged him, and this strange, undeserved, disinterested family fealty on the part of Charlie touched his heart. And should he still try to lead him into the pitfall he had dug? He hesitated;—no, he would show him the place by broad daylight, and if he chose to overlook the "caving bank," it would be his own fault;—a trade's a trade.

"Come," said the planter, "come at my house to-night; to-morrow we look at the place before breakfast, and finish the trade."

"For what?" said Charlie.

"Oh, because I got to come in town in the morning."

"I don't want," said Charlie. "How I'm goin' to come dere?"

"I git you a horse at the liberty stable."

"Well—anyhow—I don't care—I'll go." And they went.

When they had ridden a long time, and were on the road darkened by hedges of Cherokee rose, the Colonel called behind him to the "low-down" scion:

"Keep the road, old man."

"Eh?"

"Keep the road."

"Oh, yes; all right; I keep my word; we don't goin' to play no tricks, eh?"

But the Colonel seemed not to hear. His ungenerous design was beginning to be hateful to him. Not only old Charlie's unprovoked goodness was prevailing; the eulogy on Belles Demoiselles had stirred the depths of an intense love for his beautiful home. True, if he held to it, the caving of the bank, at its present fearful speed, would let the house into the river within three months; but were it not better to lose it so, than sell his birthright? Again,—coming back to the first thought,—to betray his own blood! It was only Injin Charlie; but had not the De Charleu blood just spoken out in him? Unconsciously he groaned.

After a time they struck a path approaching the plantation in the rear, and a little after, passing from behind a clump of live-oaks, they came in sight of the villa. It looked so like a gem, shining through its dark grove, so like a great glow-worm in the dense foliage, so significant of luxury and gayety, that the poor master, from an overflowing heart, groaned again.

"What?" asked Charlie.

The Colonel only drew his rein, and, dismounting mechanically, contemplated the sight before him. The high, arched doors and windows were thrown wide to the summer air; from every opening the bright light of numerous candelabra darted out upon the sparkling foliage of magnolia and bay, and here and there in the spacious verandas a colored lantern swayed in the gentle breeze. A sound of revel fell on the ear, the music of harps; and across one window, brighter than the rest, flitted, once or twice, the shadows of dancers. But oh! the shadows flitting across the heart of the fair mansion's master!

"Old Charlie," said he, gazing fondly at his house, "You and me is both old, eh?"

"Yass," said the stolid Charlie.

"And we has both been bad enough in our times eh, Charlie?"

Charlie, surprised at the tender tone, repeated "Yass."

"And you and me is mighty close?"

"Blame close, yass."

"But you never know me to cheat, old man!"

"No,"—impassively.

"And do you think I would cheat you now?"

"I dunno," said Charlie. "I don't believe."

"Well, old man, old man,"—his voice began to quiver,—"I sha'n't cheat you now. My God!—old man, I tell you—you better not make the trade!"

"Because for what?" asked Charlie in plain anger; but both looked quickly toward the house! The Colonel tossed his hands wildly in the air, rushed forward a step or two, and giving one fearful scream of agony and fright, fell forward on his face in the path. Old Charlie stood transfixed with horror. Belles Demoiselles, the realm of maiden beauty, the home of merriment, the house of dancing, all in the tremor and glow of pleasure, suddenly sunk, with one short, wild wail of terror—sunk, sunk, down, down, down, into the merciless, unfathomable flood of the Mississippi.

Twelve long months were midnight to the mind of the childless father; when they were only half gone, he took his bed; and every day, and every night, old Charlie, the "low-down," the "fool," watched him tenderly, tended him lovingly, for the sake of his name, his misfortunes, and his broken heart. No woman's step crossed the floor of the sick-chamber, whose western dormer-windows overpeered the dingy architecture of old Charlie's block; Charlie and a skilled physician, the one all interest, the other all gentleness, hope, and patience—these only entered by the door; but by the window came in a sweet-scented evergreen vine, transplanted from the caving bank of Belles Demoiselles. It caught the rays of sunset in its flowery net and let then softly in upon the sick man's bed; gathered the glancing beams of the moon at midnight, and often wakened the sleeper to look, with his mindless eyes, upon their pretty silver fragments strewn upon the floor.

By and by there seemed—there was—a twinkling dawn of returning reason. Slowly, peacefully, with an increase unseen from day to day, the light of reason came into the eyes, and speech became coherent; but withal there came a failing of the wrecked body, and the doctor said that monsieur was both better and worse.

One evening, as Charlie sat by the vine-clad window with his fireless pipe in his hand, the old Colonel's eyes fell full upon his own, and rested there.

"Charl—," he said with an effort, and his delighted nurse hastened to the bedside and bowed his best ear. There was an unsuccessful effort or two, and then he whispered, smiling with sweet sadness,—

"We didn't trade."

The truth, in this case, was a secondary matter to Charlie; the main point was to give a pleasing answer. So he nodded his head decidedly, as who should say— "Oh yes, we did, it was a bona-fide swap!" but when he saw the smile vanish, he tried the other expedient and shook his head with still more vigor, to signify that they had not so much as approached a bargain; and the smile returned.

Charlie wanted to see the vine recognized. He stepped backward to the window with a broad smile, shook the foliage, nodded and looked smart.

"I know," said the Colonel, with beaming eyes, "—many weeks."

The next day—

"Charl—"

The best ear went down.

"Send for a priest."

The priest came, and was alone with him a whole afternoon. When he left, the patient was very haggard and exhausted, but smiled and would not suffer the crucifix to be removed from his breast.

One more morning came. Just before dawn Charlie, lying on a pallet in the room, thought he was called, and came to the bedside.

"Old man," whispered the failing invalid, "is it caving yet?"

Charlie nodded.

"It won't pay you out."

"Oh, dat makes not'ing," said Charlie. Two big tears rolled down his brown face. "Dat makes not'in."

The Colonel whispered once more:

"*Mes belles demoiselles!* in paradise;—in the garden—I shall be with them at sunrise;" and so it was.

NOTES

1. At this time in Louisiana history, "Creole" referred to a White person descended from one of the early French settlers of the area; almost all still spoke French and practiced Catholicism.
2. A "commissary" here refers to the person overseeing the store, called a "commissariat," which provided supplies. It is implied here that the Count De Charleu had been engaging in illegal activities with the accounts and that the burning of both the building and the account books fortuitously saved him from having his crimes discovered.
3. "Choctaw" is the name of a Native American tribe from the region; *comptesse* means "countess" in French, and thus this reference implies a marriage between her and the count, people of different races.
4. Beautiful, unmarried ladies (French).
5. The Mississippi River, which was—and still is—a main thoroughfare through the state of Louisiana.
6. Despite its name, this cathedral, which held its first mass in 1794, is located in New Orleans.
7. The area surrounding New Orleans was under French control until the United States purchased the Louisiana Territory from France in 1803; William C. C. Claiborne governed the Territory of Orleans from 1804 to 1812, when Louisiana became a state, and he then served as its first governor from 1812 to 1816.
8. A "quadroon" at this time referred to someone who was one-quarter African American (i.e., one grandparent was African American); this term is now considered offensive and is no longer acceptable. Legend had it that "quadroon balls" were dances at which White men could meet nonenslaved quadroons and engage them as their mistresses, but historians today regard this as no more than a myth.
9. "Injin" was a derogatory slang term for "Indian" used by some non-Native people at this time to refer to a person who would now be known as Native American.
10. A roofed area recessed into the top floor of a building and open to the elements on one side.
11. "What?" or "How's that?" (French).
12. "What's that!" (French).
13. A Spanish silver coin of little worth, approximately six cents, and still in circulation during the time of this story.
14. "Yes, it's true!" (French).
15. Boredom (French).
16. A fever that involves chills and sweating.
17. Many parts of New Orleans, including the area occupied by the fictional Belle Demoiselles Plantation, are below the level of the Mississippi River; the only protection for these areas are large earthen levees, which, like dams, act as barriers to hold back the water.

ABRAHAM CAHAN

(1860–1951)

Born to Russian Jewish parents in what is now Lithuania, Abraham Cahan fled to the United States in 1882 to avoid arrest by the czar's forces for his socialist activities. He arrived knowing almost no English, but he worked hard to quickly learn the language; his proficiency as both a reader and writer of English subsequently allowed him to go beyond the limits of the Yiddish-speaking Jewish world and become a part of mainstream American culture. His early years in the United States were spent as a successful labor organizer in New York City, but he soon became enamored of the idea of becoming a writer. He succeeded admirably at this endeavor; in just a few short years he not only began publishing stories for English-language newspapers and became the leading figure in Yiddish journalism as the editor of the newspaper *Jewish Daily Forward* (1897, then 1903–51), but also became the first truly great Jewish American fiction author.

Cahan's first published work of fiction was in Yiddish and entitled "Mottke Arbel un zayn shiddokh" (Arbel gets his match); it appeared in the *Arbeiter Zeitung* (Daily worker), a New York–based socialist newspaper. When this story was translated into English and published in 1895 as "A Providential Match," the influential magazine editor William Dean Howells was greatly impressed and encouraged Cahan to write more fiction in English. Cahan complied with Howells's suggestion and, between that point and 1917, produced a relatively small yet very significant body of work that served to inform the larger American public both about Jewish culture and what the millions of Jewish immigrants arriving during these years were experiencing. Cahan's novels *Yekl: A Tale of the New York Ghetto* (1896) and *The Rise of David Levinsky* (1917), along with most of the stories in *The Imported Bridegroom and Other Stories of the New York Ghetto* (1898), examine in one way or another the conflicted feelings many Jewish immigrants had about assimilating into their new homeland, which often involved leaving their ethnic ghettos and living among non-Jews.

"The Daughter of Reb Avrom Leib," one of six stories Cahan published in leading American magazines from 1899 to 1901, was undoubtedly influenced by his experiences as a reporter for the *New York Commercial Advertiser* from 1897 to 1901. During this period he had the opportunity to absorb many tales of life on the Lower East Side of Manhattan, where many Jewish immigrants initially settled. In the way it immerses the reader in Jewish life, employing many Hebrew and Yiddish terms that would have been unfamiliar to almost all non-Jewish readers, this story realistically depicts the dilemmas many Jewish immigrants faced. In this story, as well as in his other fictions and the great many nonfiction pieces he published in the *Jewish Daily Forward* over the course of his career, Cahan served as the foremost voice for a group that hitherto had not been heard from or taken seriously in American culture, thereby earning greater respect for its members.

THE DAUGHTER OF REB AVROM LEIB (1900)

I.

Welcoming Sabbath, the Bride.[1]

As Aaron Zalkin emerged from the Broadway[2] hotel where he usually dined, and it dawned upon him that there was not a single house where he might pass an hour or two in intimate, hearty conversation, a great feeling of loneliness took hold of him. The dazzling affluence of the stores and cafés amid which he always felt at home, seemed like a practical joke on him. The married poor devils who worked under his "sweaters"[3] were at this moment enjoying their homes. He was homeless. His heart began to yearn for the Jewish quarter,[4] his old home, and crossing over to Second Avenue he boarded a downtown elevated train.[5]

The markets were deserted. Old people in their Saturday clothes were shuffling along on their way to the synagogues. It was Friday evening. Sabbath[6] was settling over the great Ghetto.

Zalkin had not entered a synagogue since he left his native town. Now the house of worship across the street drew him into its fold.

As always on Sabbath eve, the synagogue was peopled very sparsely, but the empty pews only added a sense of roominess and comfort to the repose and festive self-complacency which shone out of every face. The women's gallery was deserted, save for an elderly matron in a discolored wig.[7] Zalkin surveyed the holy ark, the golden "shield of David" on its velvet curtain, the illuminated omud, the reading-platform in the center, the faces of the worshipers as they hummed the Song of Songs or chatted in subdued tones.[8] Usually he made these things the subject of banter. Now his heart warmed to them and he was glad that it did.

The cantor[9] came in—a plump, narrow-shouldered, florid-faced, bustling little man with a massive grizzly beard which disturbed one's sense of equilibrium. At the same time a tall, good-looking girl of twenty-five or six, with a care-worn smile and sparkling black eyes, appeared on the gallery above.

The cantor took a seat by the side of the rabbi[10] near the holy ark, and at once fell to talking with ringing merriment, often bursting into a hearty laugh which caused him to throw back his head and slap his knees.

An old man by Zalkin's side was at this moment preparing to dip his fingers into his snuff-box, but noticing that the well-dressed stranger was looking at the new-comer in the women's synagogue,[11] he said, in Yiddish:[12]

"The cantor's girl."

"She comes ev'ry time he' fathe' sings," a boy added, in English.

Zalkin was interested. Another worshiper craned his neck to volunteer information. Reb Avrom Leib, the cantor, was a well-to-do member of the congregation, and in addition to saving it the expense of a professional "master of prayers," he contributed to the maintenance of a large choir during the autumn festivals.[13]

The cantor mounted the platform. The sexton slapped the reading-desk for order.[14] Some of the old men cleared their throats. Then there was silence.

"O come, let us sing unto the Lord: let us make a joyful noise to the rock of our salvation!"

Reb Avrom Leib jerked the words out, as though calling his congregation to arms. The "joyful noise" came with a cordial outburst. Zalkin was thrilled. It was as if the corners of the house of God, the holy ark, the glistening chandeliers and the shimmering letters on the omud, broke forth singing of his childhood to him.

Reb Avrom Leib warmed up to his song of welcome. At first it was all an extemporaneous recitative, and he gave himself free rein. He bellowed, he moaned, he trilled, he sighed. Once or twice he puckered up his lips into the fond smile of a mother cooing to her baby, and dropping into a falsetto he sang with quiet ecstasy. Then, suddenly, his voice would blaze out again, bidding defiance, threatening, crying for help.

Zalkin received a nudge from his neighbor.

The ancient hymn was sung in a tune of the cantor's own composing:[15]

"Come, my beloved, let us meet the Bride; the face of Sabbath let us welcome!

"Arise, arise, for thy light is come! Awake, awake and utter song, for behold! the glory of God is revealed upon thee.

"Come, my beloved, let us meet the Bride," et cetera.[16]

As the whole congregation burst out chanting the refrain in the traditional melody, Zalkin found it more impressive than the cantor's own tune. He reflected that Reb Avrom Leib's song had little or no bearing upon the text. Some of his gesticulations inclined him to laughter, while his abrupt transitions jarred his nerves. As to the cantor's composition, Zalkin thought he could point out in it Hebraized snatches of popular opera and recent street music.[17]

His first flush of exultation had died down. He had not seen the inside of a Jewish house of worship for fifteen years, yet he now felt as if he had never left off going to synagogue. Nevertheless each time he looked from father to daughter, the service acquired a fresh charm for him. Sophie was leaning forward, closely following her father. Now there would come a pained look into her face, now she would nod beaming approval.

During Maariv, when Reb Avrom Leib and the whole congregation were whispering the Eighteen Blessings,[18] Zalkin met her eye. She forthwith looked away.

The service over, the congregation struck out for the door.

"Good Sabbath! Good Sabbath!" said the patriarchs, festively.

Zalkin could almost smell the fresh-baked Sabbath loaves and the steaming lokshen-soup[19] awaiting them at home where things had been made tidy and the dining-table shone beneath the light of blessed candles. He paused at the head of the front steps to see the cantor and his daughter meet.

"Good Sabbath, father!"

"A good Sabbath and a good year to you, my child."

They were surrounded by several worshipers. Everybody chaffed the girl.

"When will we dance at your wedding?" asked Zalkin's pew-fellow. "I am tired of waiting."

"Are you? Then get me a suitor—only a nice one," she returned, with a laugh. "Foolish girl that you are," interposed her father. "A nice fellow he would keep for himself. He has his own marriageable girls to get rid of."

Zalkin tried to get a good look at her, but he could not and was vexed inordinately. He watched them turn the corner and then he slunk off in the direction of the elevated train.[20]

II.

Sabbath of "Comfort Ye."

Zalkin's impressions of the cantor and his daughter soon faded out of his mind. Nevertheless, next Friday evening he at once remembered that it was Sabbath eve and started off to Reb Avrom Leib's synagogue, as a matter of course. The melody of his "Come, my beloved," he recognized with a quiver of pleasure, and mentally proceeded to sing it with the cantor. He looked up at Sophie again and again, and several times he caught her eying him.

The next few days Zalkin went about with the echo of a disquieting little adventure in his heart. Reb Avrom Leib's hymn rang in his brain. The melody had sparkling eyes, a healthy girlish face and a preoccupied, "housewifely" smile. He seemed to hear every note of it, yet, try as he would, he could not recall it. His heart craved to hear it once more. Even when his attention was absorbed in business, the synagogue song seemed to dwell in him, filling his every limb and whispering in his heart as the soul of something living, femininely lovable, luring, unrelenting.

He had a feeling that unless he was introduced into the cantor's house his peace of mind would be sorely disturbed; and to make the proceeding the more old-fashioned and old-country-like, he sent a marriage agent to Avrom Leib.[21]

When Zalkin called to "view the bride," he was struck by the slight resemblance she bore to the image which he had formed of her at a distance. She was pretty, sure enough, "domestically" pretty—just what he was looking for—but she seemed quite another girl.

Sophie was disappointed.

"Not good-looking at all, and oh, what a figure!" she said to herself.

Her two little brothers, stubborn Joe and laughing Davy, who were ridiculously alike and ridiculously black,[22] were saying their evening prayers under protest.

"These are my two little black saints," said Reb Avrom Leib, with mock reverence. He was as ill at ease as the visitor, and he was at pains to talk himself out of his embarrassment. "They would be blacker still if they had not faded a bit, rioting around the streets, rain or shine, don't you know."

Joe frowned; Davy grinned.

"What's the use of it all?" resumed the cantor, seriously, with a wave of despair at the open prayer-book. "When their father is gone, they won't turn their tongue to a Hebrew word. They are American boys, don't you know, and I am a hen breeding duck's eggs. Only Sophie and I are all right." He aimed a caress at her which she dodged with a shamefaced smile. Zalkin felt a little flutter at his heart. "Besides," the cantor proceeded, "a girl need not be over-religious. 'A maiden who prays too much and a widow who is a busybody bring ruin upon the world,'" he quoted.

"Ah," Zalkin objected, "but 'We may learn of a maiden to dread sin, and of a widow to pursue divine reward.'"

Reb Avrom gave a start.

"Why, you are quite a scholar!" he exclaimed, raising his hands.

The quotation of the rest of the passage was a hot race, each beamingly trying to outrun, outshout and outgesticulate the other, in true Talmudist[23] fashion:

"Rabbi Yohanan heard of a maiden who fell on her face and said: 'Master of the Universe! Thou hast created the garden of Eden; Thou hast created hell; Thou hast created the righteous; Thou hast created the wicked: may it please Thee to save sons of men from stumbling in their righteousness over me.'"[24]

Reb Avrom Leib fell in love with his daughter's suitor on the spot.

Sophie played her father's compositions, the old man sweeping the air with his great beard and snapping his fingers with might and main, by way of beating time, as he sang along.

Zalkin reveled in it all. Sophie played by ear. She had a knack at memorizing a light tune and picking it out on her piano, but her musical education was barely sufficient to enable her to represent the keys she touched by notes and "accidentals," without indicating either the time or the phrasing. Zalkin could see that her playing was a sorry performance, but he had never heard a Yiddish melody from a piano before;[25] much less from one played by an old-fashioned maiden like his sisters and cousins at home; and the room was so redolent of "heaven-fearing" peace and affection, so full of the ancient Judaism and the family warmth to which he had been a stranger since a boy.

"O thou crown of my life!" his heart cried out to Sophie and his childhood at once. "It was God who brought me hither!"

The swing of Sophie's form and the droop of her head as she fingered the keyboard, and her old father, all gesticulation and radiance, by her side, parched his lips with a desire to kiss them both; and failing that he said:

"A golden tune! One's heart melts away!" Whereupon the cantor felt like kissing him.

"It is a sin to make fun of an old man," he said, shaking his plump finger at the visitor. "I am only an old-fashioned botcher. I pray to God as my father did. None of your written music! None except what she will scribble down to start her father on a forgotten tune once in a while. And, for that matter, what is the good in written music?" he appealed to Zalkin half in jest and half in earnest. "It's like those bills of fare they give you in the restaurants, while a tune which comes straight from one's own head and heart without scrawling is like the dinner that comes from your own kitchen." Zalkin burst out laughing, and the cantor, in the seventh heaven, joined him. "Restaurant dinners are no good. Sophie's are much better. I can tell you that," he concluded with a merry wink; and pleading some work at his desk, he left the Uppermost to his business of "pairing pairs."[26]

Sophie was a good girl, but she knew it and talked too much. She complained to Zalkin how helpless her father was and how she had to take care of him and the whole house.

"If I didn't play for him he could not remember a bit," she said, with a resigned air. "He is good at thinking up tunes all right, but he is so quick to forget them."

She said it with a confidential heartiness of manner and voice, as though the visitor were an old friend of the family and she herself were much older than she was. Zalkin sat, vainly trying to study her face and to weigh her every word, but little by little his embarrassment wore off and he fell into the familiar, friendly tone which she took with him.

"Do you go to the opera? I do, quite often. I am very fond of music," he rattled on, without letting her answer his questions. "Last winter I—" But she interrupted him:

"Last winter papa was to the opera sixteen times, and I twelve."

"And yet he is such a pious Jew!" he laughed.

"He says it isn't much of a sin, after all; is it?"

"No, I don't think it is."

He was burning to say, "Will you marry me?" and got around to the question again and again; but each time he came face to face with it, he turned coward. Finally, when he least intended it, he said in a bashful undertone:

"Your father will be waiting for an answer."

"Oh, there is plenty of time to discuss that," she replied, in quite a business-like way.

"You see, you shine so brightly, that I have no patience to wait," he said, coloring once more. It was the first compliment he had ever made a young woman.

"Thank you for the compliment," she returned, with the frankest coquetry.

"She is a crown and glory. She is a daisy," he said to himself, clinching the verdict in English.

"What a funny mouth he has," thought Sophie. "When he speaks he works his lips like a duck." As though to accentuate the suggestion, his legs were too short for his loosely build frame; but his pale, intellectual face had something meek and peculiarly attractive in it, and its appeal was not lost upon her. "He looks good-natured, though," she added. "I'll get used to him. We'll live like a couple of doves."

He wanted to have the betrothal and even the wedding as soon as possible, but the Nine Days were near at hand and who would make merry while one was mourning the fall of the Temple?[27] So the formal engagement was fixed for the night of the Sabbath of "Comfort Ye"—the great Sabbath of engagement parties and weddings in Israel.[28]

Meanwhile Zalkin called every evening and took her out to amusements. She was forever bubbling over with the solemn consciousness of being on the eve of the greatest event in her life, but she was haunted by a dim impression that there was an annoying tang to her otherwise complete happiness. What that was, she never paused to ask herself.

* * * * * * *

"Comfort ye, comfort ye, my people, saith your God," intoned Zalkin at the reading-desk of Reb Avrom Leib's synagogue. "Speak ye comfortably to Jerusalem and cry unto her that her warfare is accomplished, that her iniquity is pardoned."

He had not chanted the Prophets for years, and as the old intonation came back to him his voice rang out with confidence and relish.[29] Eyes wandered from him to the bride on the gallery. Some of the women around her were nodding admiringly. Reb Avrom Leib was struggling against an overflow of emotion by uttering loud sighs and slapping his snuff-box with two fingers. Sophie, over-dressed and with Zalkin's huge diamond brooch flaming at her throat, made a feint of reading the English translation in her prayer-book. Her heart swelled with the warmth and joy with which Zalkin's recitation filled the synagogue, but she never thought of him. "So I am a bride and everybody is looking at me and my brooch," she said in her heart, as if all this had nothing to do with the man at the reading-desk.

In the evening Reb Avrom Leib's house was crowded. The articles of betroth-ment having been read, in a mixture of Chaldaic and Hebrew,[30] bang went a plate against the door,[31] and by an uproar of felicitations Zalkin and Sophie were declared bridegroom and bride, to become man and wife a few weeks later, and their severance to be as unlikely as the reunion of the broken plate.

Sophie shone. She hovered about the guests, smiling and jesting like a happy mother at the engagement party of her daughter rather than as the bride. Reb Avrom Leib's huge beard was all over the house. He bustled about everybody in general and Zalkin in particular. He made jokes at his expense, winked at him, dug in his ribs, and once even pinched his arm. Then, suddenly, he beckoned him into a small side-room, and locking the door, said, tremulously:

"I love you as if you were my own child; Aaron, for you have a Jewish heart and a Jewish head. But do you know what you are taking from me? Merely a daughter? No. It's a treasure. Pray hold her dear, Aaron. 'If ye take this also from me and mischief befall her, ye shall bring down my gray hairs with sorrow to the grave. . . . for behold! my soul is bound up in her soul.'"[32] He fell upon Zalkin's shoulder and broke out weeping.

When the cantor and his daughter were left alone amid the debris of the feast, it was some time before they could speak. As Sophie looked at her father, a feeling of homesickness came over her. "Now he will be all alone," she said to herself in dismay. She seated herself by his side, and as she stroked his hand, so familiar to her touch, her eyes filled.

"What are you crying for, foolish girl that you are? You ought to thank God for such a bridegroom," he said, struggling with his own tears.

III.

Yom Kippur Eve.[33]

As long as Zalkin, like the "bashful Talmud student" that he was, held himself at a respectful distance, Sophie took his presence and his love-lorn eyes as part and parcel of the great change which was coming over her. When, with throbbing heart, he finally ventured to take her by the hand, however, her whole being revolted. She was angry with herself. The feeling seemed like something unholy breaking in upon the sanctity of her present state of mind, and she told herself that it was all imagination, but she knew that it was not.

* * * * * * * *

It was the eve of the Day of Atonement. The Bird of Redemption had been swung three times around one's head and slain as a ransom for one's life; the graveyard had been visited.[34] Sundown was drawing near. The family, including Zalkin, who had been invited by his future father-in-law for the autumn festivals, were at the supper-table. It was the supper which makes one ready for Kol Nidre, the song of awe, and for the twenty-four hours of praying and fasting which it initiates.[35]

The redemption birds were eaten in grave silence. Everybody's heart throbbed with the anticipation of the tears to come. At last grace was begun. Reb Avrom Leib needed his voice for the great service at the synagogue, but it would not be kept down, and coming from the bottom of his heart, it filled the room with the accumulated grief of the past year. Joe eyed the table-cloth. Davy watched his father with a piteous look.

As Reb Avrom Leib rose, Sophie approached him with bent head. He laid his hands on her, and after the traditional Hebrew benediction, he said sadly, in Yiddish:

"A happy new year to you, my child—to you and your predestined one. May you be inscribed in the Book of Life.[36] Maybe I have sinned against you, by deed or in thought—forgive me, my daughter. 'The Day of Atonement will atone for sins against God, but not those between man and his fellow,'" he quoted.[37]

When they had exchanged pardons, Zalkin stepped up to the old man and bowing his head, said, with emotion:

"Bless me, too, Reb Avrom Leib."

"Of course, my son," answered the cantor, as he rested his hands on him. "What is the difference between you and Sophie? Both of you are my children. God grant that you live out your days in happiness together. Maybe I have sinned against you by deed or in thought—forgive me."

When the two boys came up to be blessed, he wished them to be God-fearing Jews.

"My poor little doves! It was not ordained that your mother should bring you up," he added, brokenly.

Sophie buried her face in her arm and burst out sobbing. Zalkin felt a tremor run through his heart. "My flesh will I cut to make her happy," he said to himself.[38] There were tears in his eyes, and even Joe began to cry. Reb Avrom Leib was stroking his beard nervously.

Suddenly Sophie leaped to her feet, her face red and wet with weeping, and beckoned her lover into the parlor.

"Forgive me, Aaron dear," she said, vehemently. "I love you as I do the eyes in my head, as true as I wish to be inscribed for a happy year. Only a day or two I had thoughts against you. It has all passed off. I love you with all my heart now."

His heart turned to ice.

"What was it?" he asked.

"Oh, nothing to tell about, nothing at all." But she blurted it all out:

"I thought I didn't care for you. Once I was so cranky that I cursed you in my mind—so hateful I thought you were to me: but I was mistaken. I'm sure I was. Forgive me."

"There is nothing to forgive," he answered, sullenly.

They went to the synagogue in grave silence.

At sundown the house of worship was white with shrouds and aglitter with silver-laced praying-shawls and skull-caps.[39] The doors of the holy ark were open. The silk vestments of the scrolls within loomed many-colored. The worshipers stood in their stocking-feet. The wax candles in front of them burned mournfully. The women above were nodding over their Books of Tears.[40]

The laments of the evening came from the caves and forests of Spain where the sons of Israel sang them under breath, at the peril of the stake. Some gave up their lives rather than their faith. Others escaped death by making promises and vows of which they prayed God to be absolved.[41]

The sexton slapped for order. The women raised their heads from their books and looked down upon the omud where the cantor, robed in a white shroud, striped praying-shawl and white skull-cap, stood in the center of the choir. There was a stir. The sexton slapped again. Silence fell, and then—softly, cautiously, as though looking around to see if some spy of the Inquisition was not hidden in bushes near by, Reb Avrom Leib began in Chaldaic: "All vows and self-prohibitions, vows of abstinence and promise—"

The text of the prayer is out of touch with modern conditions, but its strains retain the frightened whisper of hiding worshipers. Reb Avrom Leib's congregation scarcely thought of Spain and the Inquisition, but each worshiper was conscious of his own "pack of sorrow" and that he stood before God on the fast-day of Atonement when it is "sealed and determined who shall live and who shall die, who shall reap enjoyment and who shall be afflicted." "All vows and self-prohibitions, vows of abstinence and promise!"

Zalkin was oblivious of his surroundings, but the terrible song passed through his soul like an accompaniment to his misery. "I'm so hateful to her that she cursed me. She cannot stand me." The unuttered words were crawling over his brain.

Sophie, prayer-book in hand, was trying to catch his eye. Her father's song, the multitude of death-shrouds and gigantic candles, spoke of her cruelty. She pitied Zalkin and she pitied herself. She was aiming an affectionate gaze at him, but he never looked up. His heart lay heavy within him and he could not lift his eyes to the gallery.

The next day Zalkin wrote Sophie a long letter, full of open resentment and ill-disguised misery, declaring their engagement off.

IV.

The Rejoicing of the Law.

Gloom settled in Reb Avrom's house. Sophie felt relieved on her own account, but her father's speechless anguish gave her no rest. Now that it was all over and she had returned to Zalkin his engagement gift, she was sincerely congratulating herself upon her deliverance from the match: but the old cantor had become attached to the manufacturer, and the disappearance of his blazing brooch from under Sophie's chin brought darkness into his soul.

Zalkin went about with a lump in his throat. He kept away from the synagogue during the Feast of Tabernacles,[42] but his burden grew on him till he often caught himself crying like a baby. "I cannot, I cannot live without her," he lamented in his heart. For hours together he paced his room like a prisoner in his cell. The little box containing the brooch he never parted with, and once even touched the sparkling stones with his lips. At last he gave up the struggle. It was the evening of the Rejoicing of the Law, when the rule prohibiting the mingling of the sexes in a house of worship is winked at by the rabbis, and Zalkin went to Reb Avrom Leib's synagogue.[43]

He found it overcrowded. The curtain of red and gold was drawn aside; the holy ark was deserted; the scrolls of the Law were out on their yearly pageant.[44]

"O thou God of spirits!" sang Reb Avrom Leib, as attired in his praying-shawl and velvet cap and bearing a sefer Torah (scroll of the Law) in his arms, he led the procession round and round the reading-platform.

"Save us!" responded the choir from the platform.

The refrain was an adagio of joyous solemnity. Following the Master of Prayers were some thirty venerable men, each with a gaily robed Torah in his arms: red Torahs, blue Torahs, white Torahs; Torahs with crowns and Torahs without crowns; some in humble silence, with their vestments unadorned; others with jingling, glittering shields of silver suspended from their "trees of life."[45]

"O Thou, who knowest all of our thoughts—"

"Save us!"

After the scroll-bearers came a number of boys, some striding along by themselves, others carried in their fathers' arms. Each boy held a paper flag with texts and pictures and with a red apple holding a lighted candle impaled upon its staff. Young daughters of Israel standing on the benches bent over and kissed the scrolls as they filed by, or merely touched them and then kissed their own sanctified fingers. Sophie was among them, and Zalkin pushed his way to a point within earshot from which he could see without being seen.

"Oh, father, stop! I haven't kissed your Purity,"[46] she said in mock despair, as she leaned forward and reached out for his scrolls.

"O thou eternal King!" he sang, giving her a deprecating smile over his shoulder, and passed on. His grief was drowned in the all-pervading glee of the feast. Besides, a score or two of the worshipers were humming his refrain with the choir.

Sophie forced the next man to stop till she and the girls near her had kissed his Torah.

"That's right, my daughter!" shouted an old woman from the gallery. "Don't miss a single Purity, or the Uppermost won't send you your predestined one during the coming year."

Zalkin colored. Sophie exchanged a glance with two of the girls by her side and then the three burst into a laugh in which some of the bystanders joined. She was the queen of the crowd around her. Young fellows were trying to attract her attention; some of the older people were eying her fondly. She wore a dress of blue silk dotted with red fleurs-de-lis which well became the radiance of her flushed face. She exhaled health and joy, and each time the cantor marched by, a look of delight in one another passed between father and daughter.

Zalkin could not take his eyes off her. His heart writhed with agony. "It will kill me, it will kill me!" he whispered to himself.

"Oh Thou who art holy!" sounded Reb Avrom Leib's voice in the distance.

When the scrolls had been restored to the ark, the congregation burst into a deafening welcome to the Law; for the two Torahs which had been left without were now on their way to the platform to be read.

"And this," began the master reader, bending over the unrolled parchment, "is the blessing wherewith Moses, the Man of God, blessed the children of Israel before his death." He could scarcely be heard for the merry tumult around the platform, but the rabbi, the cantor and a few other pious men followed the reading in their Pentateuchs.[47]

Most of the girls had gone home. Sophie lingered. She had caught sight of her former suitor. She convinced herself once more that he did not interest her, and yet she felt held to the spot.

The reading over, Reb Avrom Leib, who was known as "the biggest Rejoicing of the Law romp" in the congregation, intertwined his arm with the arms of several other men and the group launched out into a hop.[48]

"Make merry and rejoice on the Rejoicing of the Law!" they shouted.

"Out with our new hop!" the cantor commanded his choir. "Hi-da-da! Hi-da-da!"

"What makes you so jolly, Reb Avrom Leib? Brandy has not come within four ells of you," somebody jested.

"No matter," the cantor answered, gasping for breath, as he stopped spinning. "I like strong wine and old, but the Law is the strongest and the oldest wine there is. Even Vanderbilt could not afford it, could he?[49] Here is health!" he said, tossing off an imaginary goblet, and was off again. To be drunk on the Rejoicing of the Law is a good deed. The next best deed is to imagine oneself befuddled, and Reb Avrom Leib's was quite a lively imagination. "Hi-da-da! Hi-da-da! Why, Zalkin, Aaron!" he shouted, suddenly tearing himself loose from the others. "My heart has told me all along you'd turn up. Come, let us hop!" With which he took him in his arms and carried him to the dancers.

Then he took him to his daughter.

"This is the Rejoicing of the Law, children," he said, puffing for breath. "Come, make peace and let us have a merry holiday."

Sophie was about to shake her head, but her father was so exuberantly happy that she had not the heart to do it, and smiled instead.

"Let her take it back," said Zalkin, handing Reb Avrom Leib the brooch.

"Here, stick it right into your dress, I say!" the old man shouted.

She obeyed, gravely.

The cantor went back to the hoppers.

"My rabbis! I have got my daughter's suitor back!" he yelled. "When does a beggar rejoice? When he is restored to his loss! Make merry and rejoice on the Rejoicing of the Law. To-morrow after the service you must all come to my house. Sophie, do you hear? The whole lot of them!"

About half an hour later, the raw October air outside was filled with merry voices. Reb Avrom Leib and several other members of his synagogue went home singing.

"A merry holiday to you!" he greeted every elderly passer-by boisterously. "Hi-da-da! Hi-da-da!"

"You'll catch cold, papa!" Sophie called to him. "You have been perspiring and it is so chilly."

She offered to turn up his collar, but he pushed her from him.

"What does a girl know about the Law! You only know of suitors. A merry holiday-ay-ay!"

V.

Blessing the Dedication Lights.

Reb Avrom Leib did catch cold. He went to bed shivering with fever and the next morning he woke with a severe headache and a burning pain in his side. Toward evening he felt better, however, and the following day he was able to attend to business.

A few weeks later he caught another slight cold, after which he frequently complained of headaches, fatigue, and pains in his side. Still, he had a big sign hung up on the outside wall of his synagogue announcing that he would bless the Dedication Lights with a large choir and a band.[50]

Zalkin's suit did not thrive. He was forever nagging Sophie for her indifference to him and bewailing his fate as a lover.

"You need not let me kiss you if it is repulsive to you," he often said, with
some venom. She would drop her arms in despair at such moments, and once,
losing all patience, she flamed out:

"Then why do you do it?"

The engagement was broken off once more.

On the "first candle" of the feast commemorating the miracle which attended
the recovery and reconsecration of the Temple by the Maccabees,[51] Zalkin went to
Reb Avrom Leib's synagogue, in the hope of being reconciled to Sophie. "She will
yield again," he thought, "and then we must be married at once. I'll cherish her like
the apple of my eye. It's all a foolish fancy in her, and once she is my wife it will wear
off and she will get to love me. They are all like that." He felt a joyous tug at his heart.

The cantor was at first embarrassed, and when his diffidence had passed off
he conducted the band and the choir in a spasm of excitement. He stamped
his feet, smote his beard, pinched the air, bored it with his index-finger and
dispersed imaginary clouds of smoke before him.

His tune met with decided success. Some of the worshipers attested their
admiration by saying, "May your strength be upheld," in formal Hebrew; others
merely wagged their heads and smacked their lips; still others kept groaning: "Ai!
ai! ai!" One man declared that the cantor had "blessed the lights so well that the
end of the world had come." Reb Avrom Leib was so overcome that he had not
the strength to simulate modesty, and sitting down, ghastly pale with exertion, he
simpered grateful assent.

Zalkin had been hiding from Sophie under the gallery. When the crowd
around the cantor had thinned out, he went up to him and said, tremulously:

"I have heard the best operas, but such a tune I have never heard."

It was the warmest and heartiest compliment of all.

Tears came to the old man's eyes.

"My heart has been aching after you, Aaron," he said.

At this moment Sophie, in a ferment of enthusiasm, bent over the rail as far
as she could and cried out:

"It was so good, papa, that you don't know yourself how good it was. Don't
you dare leave before you have rested, and don't forget your muffler." As she recognized Zalkin, she checked herself, and resumed her seat with a clouded face.

When they met in front of the synagogue, she said, with agitation:

"Take pity on me. You know nothing will come of it all. You had better look
for your predestined one."

When she was left alone with her father, the old man gave her a look full of
reproach and yearning, but said nothing.

For some minutes they walked in silence.

Then Sophie said, testily:

"What makes you so low-spirited? I know, I know—you won't rest until I have
married him. You are my murderer, papa."

"Who says I have been thinking of Zalkin?"

"But you have. He is never out of your mind."

"And what if he isn't?" Reb Avrom Leib confessed, helplessly. "Is it my fault that he has grown into my heart and that I want to see you happily married? Do I want him for myself?"

"You are my murderer, papa!" she gasped.

VI.

Reb Avrom Leib's Last Composition.

Reb Avrom Leib sat up in his folding bed, in the parlor, leaning against his two big pillows as he gazed at the locust-tree rustling in front of the open window. It was a mild afternoon in July. Rose-colored sunlight threw his yellow, emaciated face into ghastly relief. His enormous beard seemed a mass of discolored cotton. He had taken to his bed shortly after Passover, and he had been slowly wasting ever since. The doctors had diagnosed the case as a species of kidney disease. Sophie knew that her father was doomed, and every time the situation dawned upon her she would grow faint with terror.

Presently Reb Avrom Leib's lips began to move and his head to nod, as if keeping time to a song. A smile spread over his deathly face. He reached out for his medicine spoon and rapped several times at the chair by his bedside.

"What is it, father dear, what is it?" asked Sophie, running in and bending over him.

"I have hit upon an excellent 'be-Rosh Hoshanah,'"[52] he said, in a feeble voice, pointing at the piano hard by.

"Sing it; only very softly," she replied, with a deprecating, tender look.

It was a plaintive melody for the most solemn part of the service on the three Days of Awe.[53] His voice was pitifully weak, but his notes were clear, and in the stillness of the sickroom, when Sophie paused to listen, they sounded with tragic distinctness. Only once or twice the note in his mind was beyond his strength, whereupon he would shut his eyes and, screwing up his face, raise his finger, as though to indicate the height to which his voice would have ascended if it could. Sophie read the note in the expression of his countenance.

"Is that right?" she asked over her shoulder, striking a key.

"Yes, yes, my daughter," he answered, with a grateful gleam in his eye.

When she had mastered the tune and he sang it to her accompaniment, his peaked face was now contorted to express the tearful supplication of a penitent spirit praying for mercy, now all but melting in an ecstasy of anguish.

"Who shall pass by and who shall be born, who shall live and who shall die," he sang, in Hebrew.

He thrust out his lips like a child about to cry and let his head fall on his breast. "Why should I die?" he seemed to say. "What have I done to be excluded from the Book of Life?" After a pause he said, dismally:

"If I could see you married happily, it would be easier for me to die."

"Have mercy, papa!" she implored him, with a gesture of despair. "Your words saw my heart. You know you'll get well. Do you want me to beg Zalkin to come and marry me? If he wanted me, he would not have kept away so long. Why should you torment yourself, papa darling? You are so weak."

Reb Avrom Leib sighed. At the bottom of his heart he never believed he was going to die, but his daughter's indifference to Zalkin grieved him.

A few days later, he was so weak that he could not even hum his "be-Rosh Hoshanah." He had Sophie play it for him again and again. As he listened, his bloodless face beamed.

"The best thing I have ever composed," he said, faintly. "When I sing it with the choir, please God, it will make a hit."

The next morning he lay on his side breathing heavily, as he eyed the floor with a look of weary indifference.

To please him, Sophie struck up his new "be-Rosh Hoshanah." There were suppressed tears in her soul and these she seemed to put into her every tone. She had never played the tune with so much feeling. When she had finished and faced about, she found her father gazing at the floor, more indifferent than ever.

"Did you like it, father?"

"Oh, I don't care," he said, with a feeble groan, as he let his head slide to the other side.

VII.

Days of Awe.

The frowzy, crowded street through which Sophie dragged herself, a roll of music-paper in her hand, was mournfully lighted by a flickering jumble of ped-dlers' torches and gas lamps. The light which showed her pale, sorrow-worn face, seemed part of the squalor of the place. Suddenly voices of a synagogue choir burst upon her ear. Her heart stood still. "Rehearsing for the Days of Awe," she said to herself, pausing in front of a tenement-house.

The fire-escapes of the towering block were heaped and overhung with odds and ends of household effects which in the gloom of the upper stories loomed like a medley of moss, lichen and cobweb on a deserted castle. It was from be-hind a pile of this kind of junk that the voices rang out into the tumult of the market-place. The choristers shrieked and moaned and whispered with gusto. Now accompanying them and now checking their rapturous vociferation was the guiding old tenor of the cantor. It was Reb Avrom Leib's successor.

When Sophie reached his apartments and knocked at the door, the choir stopped short. The cantor, a gaunt man with a dirty white necktie, received her politely.

"Father—peace upon him—has left some tunes. He composed them on his death-bed," she said, flushing.

A gleam of irony came into the cantor's eyes. After a glance at some of her music, he said, with an amused laugh:

"No, my daughter, that's not the way music should be written. Besides, I have my own tunes."

"But I can play it all, and they are the best tunes my father ever got up," she said, with a tone which implied Reb Avrom Leib's superiority over his successor. The cantor, who had his full share of the vanity for which his profession is noted, reddened to his skull-cap.

"I have heard his tunes," he retorted, with a sneer.

Sophie came out of the big tenement-house with her heart in her mouth. "Poor dear papa!" she thought. "Now that you are in your grave every nobody will raise his head."

She had not gone many paces when another choir gave her a pang, and then there was a third, and a fourth and a fifth. The Ghetto was priming itself for the great season of song and prayer. Sophie felt like the daughter of a forgotten general while the forces of her country are mustered and paraded on the eve of war.

She offered her father's compositions to several other cantors, but they would not even unroll her music. Her anguish seemed to be growing on her heart like a physical load. So cruel, so terrible, was its weight that she wondered how she could suffer it all and live. "Nobody will even so much as speak of him, nobody, nobody!" she would moan. "He is gone—gone and forgotten, as if there had never been a Reb Avrom Leib. And you?" she would turn upon herself. "Are you better? Didn't you make his last months dark enough for him? Now that you have lost him, your father, you miss him. Why didn't you hold him dear when you had him?" She felt like moving heaven and earth to bring her father to life again that she might show him her readiness to marry Zalkin and to do anything, anything to please him. But he was gone, gone forever. She thought of Zalkin. He was the only man that admired her father and his songs sincerely. She would see him, speak to him of her father, of his songs, of his good heart. But what was the use? Her father was dead, never to be her father again, never, never, never.

The tears of New Year did her good. To please her father in his grave she would sit for hours and hours over her Hebrew or Yiddish prayer-books. She was in a transport of sorrow and piety. Her religion bade her stand forth before God with a resigned spirit, and she did. Even the new cantor she accepted without criticism.

On Yom Kippur Eve she took supper with her two little brothers, as usual. Her father's chair, where a year ago he had chanted grace in disconsolate accents, was empty. Sophie served the meal on tiptoe, and ate it in silence. It was getting late. As she looked out of the window she saw people with shrouds and prayer-books under their arms stop, on their way to the great Kol Nidre service, to ask one another's forgiveness. Joe was morose. Davy threw a look at his father's empty seat and burst out crying. Sophie gnashed her teeth.

"What are you crying for?" she said, in a rage. "Hush, I say, hush!" But the next minute her own pent-up sobs broke loose. "There is nobody to bless us this year, children!" she moaned. "We have no father. He is over there, under a mound, is our father!" And in her frenzy of grief she flung herself down on the lounge, tore at her hair and shrieked.

VIII.

Rejoicing of the Law Once More.

"O Thou who art pure and just!" sang the new cantor.

"Save us!" responded his choir.

"O Thou who compassionest the poor!"

"Send us happiness!"

The synagogue was again crowded; again the Torahs were out on their procession around the platform; again girls stood on the benches jesting, giggling and throwing glances at each other and at the young men, as they kissed the passing scrolls. Only one of these touched the "Purities" with unsmiling devotion. The others were making jokes to her, but she never unbent.

"Rejoice and make merry on the Rejoicing of the Law!" shouted the worshipers.

Tears started to Sophie's eyes.

"What, crying on the Rejoicing of the Law! It's a sin, Sophie!" said an old man, kindly.

Then she heard somebody else call her by her first name. It was Zalkin. He of all men appreciated her father and his tunes, and how dear he had been to Reb Avrom Leib! Her lover seemed to her like an angel sent from heaven to share her grief and her ecstasy over her father's memory.

"Sophie, I have heard of your misfortune. I cannot live without you," he whispered.

"Do you remember last year's Rejoicing of the Law?" she said, brightening up. "How he did romp! Over there, near the platform—do you remember?"

"Do I! He was like a father to me. When I heard of his death, I cried like a boy."

"I'll marry him, I'll marry him," she thought to herself, with a rush of tearful happiness at her heart. Then she said audibly: "Did you? You alone knew what a gold he was. Do you remember how he sang the hop? Now people would not even admit that he could get up a fine tune."

"I hum his tunes often, Sophie. I sigh over them, Sophie. They are the sweetest I ever heard," he said, with a shaking voice.

Sophie was sure she loved him. "Oh, how happy father would be if he could see us together now," she thought.

When they were out in the street he asked her, beseechingly:

"Will you marry me?"

"Yes, yes," she answered, impetuously. The street was dark. From the Synagogue came the hum of muffled merriment. It sounded like a wail. "Yes, yes," she repeated in a whisper. And as if afraid lest morning might bring better counsel, she hastened to bind herself by adding, with a tremor in her voice: "I swear by my father that I will."

NOTES

1. Jewish ritual pictures the Sabbath as a "bride" to Israel.
2. Broadway is a main thoroughfare of New York City.

3. Many Jewish immigrants worked in clothing factories that were known as "sweat-shops," due to their arduous working conditions; a "sweater" was a foreman in one of these establishments who was responsible for making workers sweat.

4. In many cities of Europe, where Zalkin had come from, Jewish people were restricted to living only in a certain neighborhood, often called a "quarter" or "ghetto"; Zalkin's desire to return to Judaism identifies him as a *ba'al tshuvah,* Hebrew for "a repentant Jew."

5. Zalkin is depicted in this story as a wealthy Jew who has become distant both literally and figuratively from others of his faith. Further evidence of this distance is seen in the way he has to take an "elevated train" to his home (many sections of the New York subway were at that time aboveground), which implies that he lives and eats in an area of New York City distant from the bulk of the city's Jewish population, at this time located in the southeast section of Manhattan.

6. In Judaism, the holy day of worship lasts from sundown on Friday to sundown on Saturday. (Judaism defines a single day as the interval from one sundown to the next.) Because the Sabbath begins on Friday evening, traditional Jews wear their best clothes not only then but also on Saturday, for attending synagogue services.

7. In traditional Jewish synagogues, women often occupy the balcony ("gallery") seats. When married women leave their homes, they customarily wear wigs out of modesty to make themselves less attractive to other men.

8. All the things mentioned in this sentence are important elements usually found in a Jewish synagogue. The ark is an ornate cabinet located at the front and contains the congregation's most holy documents, its Torahs; the ark often is enclosed by a curtain known as a "parocheth." During the nineteenth century in Europe, the Star of David, made up of two overlapping equilateral triangles, became a symbol of Judaism. Softly chanting the Song of Songs is a preliminary part of the regular Friday-night services.

9. A person who leads the congregation in song and sometimes in prayer.

10. Leader of a Jewish congregation. This person must be well versed in Jewish law.

11. The women's part of the synagogue (the balcony), not one completely separate from the men.

12. A language once widely used by German and Eastern European Jews, consisting mostly of a mixture of German and Hebrew.

13. Many synagogues hire professional cantors to lead the congregations in chanting the prayers of a service; in others, knowledgeable members of the congregation volunteer to perform the cantorial functions. It is customary in Judaism to use both first and middle names in addressing someone, and in this story Reb Avrom Leib's last name is not given. "Reb" is an honorific form of address acknowledging the piety, learning, or social standing of a man; "Avrom" is the Hebrew and Yiddish pronunciation of the name of the prophet Abraham; and "Leib" (pronounced "Labe," meaning either "heart" or "lion") is his middle name.

14. Here Cahan uses the term "sexton," more familiar to Christian readers, to refer to the "gabbai," who in Jewish services assists the rabbi in performing Jewish religious services; here he is pounding a desk in order to quiet the congregation.

15. Although most prayers have traditional tunes, new tunes are often introduced to keep their recitals fresh and inspiring; a congregation may or may not adopt the new creations.

16. The Sabbath hymn of "L'chah dodi" (Come, my beloved) combines elements of Isaiah 60:1 and Judges 5:12.

17. Many traditional Jewish hymns are adaptations of familiar and secular melodies, both classical and popular; here the cantor is clearly trying to incorporate modern elements into his compositions.

18. Maariv, the evening prayer, is the third of three daily times of prayer; the "Eighteen Blessings" (*Shemonah esrei*) are a unit of this prayer that a congregation customarily chants, while standing, in an undertone.

19. Noodles (Yiddish).

20. Jewish law forbids riding in any conveyance on the Sabbath, so Zalkin's riding on an elevated train after Friday-evening services indicates his Americanization.

21. A marriage agent (Yiddish: "shadchan") was traditionally used by families to make formal contacts between potential grooms and brides.

22. Observers of ultra-Orthodox Judaism dress wholly in black.

23. The Talmud is the compilation of writings by thousands of rabbis that make up Jewish civil and ceremonial law, as well as the religion's theology.

24. This dialogue occurs in the Babylonian Talmud, Sotah 22a. The fact that Zalkin is familiar with it is evidence of the thoroughness of his Talmud training before he emigrated to America and stopped being religiously observant, as well as of how much he remembers of traditional Judaism.

25. Musical instruments are banned from use in traditional Jewish services to show perpetual mourning for the destruction of the Temple in Jerusalem. Instruments may be used, however, outside a synagogue to play secular music and even in a synagogue when nonbiblical celebrations take place (e.g., marriages and Hanukkah).

26. Many people believe that one of the duties of God ("the Uppermost") is to match pairs of people for marriages "made in heaven."

27. Jewish weddings are traditionally not performed during the first nine days of the summer month of Av. The ninth day of Av, called Tisha b'Av, is a rabbinically ordained solemn day of mourning that commemorates the destruction in 586 BCE of Solomon's Temple of Jerusalem—Judaism's holiest site—with a twenty-five-hour-long fast, as well as the reading of the book of Lamentations and many dirges.

28. The first Sabbath after Tisha b'Av is named after a passage in Isaiah 40:1, which begins with "Comfort ye."

29. After the period of restrictions, Jews return to the comforts and joys of life on the Sabbath of "Comfort Ye"; given the way that Zalkin is able to handle the honor of chanting the passage beginning with Isaiah 40:1 in front of the entire congregation, it is clear his boyhood training in traditional Judaism is coming back to him.

30. Judaism treats a wedding engagement very seriously, almost as much as the wedding vow itself. The announcement of an engagement is made in the Aramaic (here referred to as "Chaldaic") language, as well as the Jews' holy language, Hebrew, because Aramaic was for some centuries the popular language of the Jews.

31. It is a Jewish custom at engagements to throw a plate and break it.

32. See Jacob's charge to his sons in Genesis 44:29.

33. Yom Kippur is Judaism's holiest day, during which worshipers fast for twenty-five hours, attend synagogue services, and restore their relationship with God and others through atonement.

34. Traditional customs among some Jews at Yom Kippur time.

35. Kol Nidre, the solemn opening prayer of Yom Kippur Eve, asks God to nullify all vows made to him during the year so that the penalties for breaking them will not be carried out.

36. According to Judaism, God records the names of all the righteous in the Book of Life.

37. Judaism teaches that if a sinner is sincere in repenting and atoning for breaking a vow to God, God will be forgiving. But this applies only to vows made by human beings to God; broken vows between human beings can be forgiven only by the offended party. Hence the obligation of Jews to sincerely ask forgiveness from those they might have sinned against and to offer amends.

38. An exaggerated statement of his love. To perform such an act, though, would be heresy, as Jewish scripture forbids inflicting cuts upon one's own body (Leviticus 19:28 and 21:5).

39. Many traditional Jews wear shrouds at the Yom Kippur service, as well as prayer shawls; rimless caps (in Hebrew "kippah" and in Yiddish "yarmulke") are worn by men to honor God. Here Cahan once again uses more anglicized terms ("praying-shawls" and "skull-caps") in order to reach non-Jewish readers.

40. Figuratively, the Book of Tears is God's recording of human sorrows.

41. The power of the Kol Nidre prayer derives in large part from particular historical situations. Here the allusion is to Spain during the Inquisition, begun in 1478 by the monarchs to impose religious (Catholic) homogeneity and orthodoxy. According to a royal decree of 1492, Jews and Muslims were given a choice of converting to Christianity, being expelled from Spain, or being executed; for many Jews who allowed themselves to be converted but who remained secretly Jewish, saying the Kol Nidre prayer was a great comfort.

42. The biblical festival of Sukkot, which begins shortly after Yom Kippur.

43. The holiday of Simchat Torah—the Rejoicing of the Law—occurs nine days after the beginning of Sukkot and marks the end of the High Holy Days season.

44. To celebrate God's gift to the Jews of having been chosen to receive the Torah, during this holiday every Torah scroll is taken out of a synagogue's ark and paraded throughout the synagogue with joyous dancing and singing. The prohibition against the mingling of the sexes is relaxed, and an almost madcap atmosphere prevails until everyone who wishes to hold a scroll has the wish gratified, at which point the scrolls are returned to the ark.

45. Silver ornaments are hung from the two wooden posts on which the Torah parchments are rolled and unrolled. Crowns are fitted on those posts, symbolizing that God, represented by his law, is the king of Israel.

46. It is customary to kiss the covering of a Torah scroll as it is paraded through the congregation; calling a Torah scroll a "Purity" appears to have been a local custom in Cahan's time.

47. The annual cycle of the reading of the Torah concludes on Simchat Torah with the chanting of Deuteronomy books 33 and 34; the Pentateuch is a Greek name for the first five books of the Hebrew Bible: Bereshit, Shemot, Vayikra, Bamidbar,

and Devarim, which taken together are called the Torah. Christians include these five books in their Old Testament and call them Genesis, Exodus, Leviticus, Numbers, and Deuteronomy.

48. A type of circle dance used in worship that involves hopping.

49. Railroad magnate Cornelius Vanderbilt (1794–1877) was one of the richest Americans ever, and his son William and his descendants were also very wealthy.

50. The Jewish holiday of Hanukkah is known as the Festival of Lights and marks the time when Jews regained control of Jerusalem and rededicated the Holy Temple; although it often occurs around the same time as Christmas, the eight-day festival of Hanukkah is not considered a major Jewish holiday.

51. As blessings are said and hymns sung on the first night of Hanukkah, candles or oil cups on an eight-branched menorah are lit in succession—that is, one on the first night, two on the next, and so on.

52. The "B'Rosh Hashanah" (here anglicized as "be-Rosh Hoshanah") is a solemn hymn sung as part of the Rosh Hashanah (new year) liturgy. Its most important part translates as, "On Rosh Hashanah it is written, and on Yom Kippur it is sealed . . . who shall live and who shall die [in the coming year]."

53. The Days of Awe are the ten days between Rosh Hashanah and Yom Kippur, when Jews are asked to repent and seek atonement for sins in order to avert severe decrees of punishment.

WILLA CATHER

(1873–1947)

Born in Virginia in late 1873, Willa Cather moved to rural Webster County, Nebraska, with her family in April 1883, when she was nine years old. She lived in the state only until June 1896, when she departed for an editing job in Pittsburgh. But during those thirteen years she gained (or, as she once said in a 1921 interview, "absorbed") an incredibly deep understanding of life on the plains and in her small hometown of Red Cloud, knowledge that she would later put to effective use not only in a great number of excellent short stories but also in such classic novels as *O Pioneers!* (1913), *My Ántonia* (1918), and *A Lost Lady* (1923). In comparison, Cather incorporated into her fiction relatively little of her experience living in Pittsburgh from 1896 to 1906 or in New York City, where she lived from 1906 until her death in 1947.

During her lifetime most of Cather's works were highly regarded by critics but only modestly popular among readers. After writing chiefly about the plains and Midwest until the mid-1920s, she branched out to write about many other locales and cultures; indeed, one of her most famous novels, *Death Comes for the Archbishop* (1927), focuses on the work of two French priests in early nineteenth-century New Mexico. Unfortunately, during the last decade of Cather's life, health problems greatly diminished her literary output. For a long time after her death, in 1947, Cather's fiction was not deemed as complex as that of her male contemporaries, such as F. Scott Fitzgerald and Ernest Hemingway. Rediscovered in the 1970s by feminist critics—many of whom identified Cather as a lesbian whose texts were deeply influenced by her sexual orientation—Cather is now recognized as one of the best American authors of the early twentieth century.

According to a letter Cather wrote on the last day of 1938 to a university English professor named Edward Wagenknecht, who had asked her about republishing her early fiction, "On the Divide" was merely "a college theme written for a weekly theme class" during her time at the University of Nebraska (1891–95), and that not only had the instructor embellished the story himself but he had submitted it to the *Overland Monthly* magazine in her name but without her permission; it was published in the January 1896 issue. In this same letter, Cather disparaged "On the Divide" as among a group of her early stories she regarded as "immature work," which she wished would be forgotten and never republished. In all likelihood, however, Cather's protestations were, as the editors of *The Selected Letters of Willa Cather* (2013) concluded, "fabrications constructed to convince Wagenknecht to leave her alone."

The editors of this anthology believe the story is well worth republishing, not only because of the way it deals forcefully and skillfully with a number of important themes that had hitherto been unaddressed in fictions about pioneer life on the plains, such as Scandinavian immigrants, alcoholism, and town-country frictions, but also because of how Cather depicts the main character's assertion of brute masculinity. In addition, the story reflects many of Cather's own personal concerns at this time: uncertainty about her sexuality, as well as her fear that she might have to spend the rest of her life trapped on the plains and never get to experience the wider world. Often an author's early, less polished works are just as powerful as their later ones, and "On the Divide" is a very good example of this.

ON THE DIVIDE (1896)

Near Rattlesnake Creek, on the side of a little draw stood Canute's shanty.[1] North, east, south, stretched the level Nebraska plain of long rust-red grass that undulated constantly in the wind. To the west the ground was broken and rough, and a narrow strip of timber wound along the turbid, muddy little stream that had scarcely ambition enough to crawl over its black bottom. If it had not been for the few stunted cottonwoods and elms that grew along its banks, Canute would have shot himself years ago. The Norwegians are a timber-loving people, and if there is even a turtle pond with a few plum bushes around it they seem irresistibly drawn toward it.

As to the shanty itself, Canute had built it without aid of any kind, for when he first squatted along the banks of Rattlesnake Creek there was not a human

being within twenty miles. It was built of logs split in halves, the chinks stopped
with mud and plaster. The roof was covered with earth and was supported by
one gigantic beam curved in the shape of a round arch. It was almost impossible
that any tree had ever grown in that shape. The Norwegians used to say that
Canute had taken the log across his knee and bent it into the shape he wished.
There were two rooms, or rather there was one room with a partition made of
ash saplings interwoven and bound together like big straw basket work. In one
corner there was a cook stove, rusted and broken. In the other a bed made of
unplaned planks and poles. It was fully eight feet long, and upon it was a heap
of dark bed clothing. There was a chair and a bench of colossal proportions.
There was an ordinary kitchen cupboard with a few cracked dirty dishes in it,
and beside it on a tall box a tin wash-basin. Under the bed was a pile of pint
flasks, some broken, some whole, all empty. On the wood box lay a pair of shoes
of almost incredible dimensions. On the wall hung a saddle, a gun, and some
ragged clothing, conspicuous among which was a suit of dark cloth, apparently
new, with a paper collar carefully wrapped in a red silk handkerchief and pinned
to the sleeve. Over the door hung a wolf and a badger skin, and on the door itself
a brace of thirty or forty snake skins whose noisy tails rattled ominously every
time it opened. The strangest things in the shanty were the wide window-sills. At
first glance they looked as though they had been ruthlessly hacked and mutilated
with a hatchet, but on closer inspection all the notches and holes in the wood
took form and shape. There seemed to be a series of pictures. They were, in a
rough way, artistic, but the figures were heavy and labored, as though they had
been cut very slowly and with very awkward instruments. There were men plowing with little horned imps sitting on their shoulders and on their horses' heads.
There were men praying with a skull hanging over their heads and little demons
behind them mocking their attitudes. There were men fighting with big serpents,
and skeletons dancing together. All about these pictures were blooming vines and
foliage such as never grew in this world, and coiled among the branches of the
vines there was always the scaly body of a serpent, and behind every flower there
was a serpent's head. It was a veritable Dance of Death[2] by one who had felt its
sting. In the wood box lay some boards, and every inch of them was cut up in
the same manner. Sometimes the work was very rude and careless, and looked
as though the hand of the workman had trembled. It would sometimes have
been hard to distinguish the men from their evil geniuses but for one fact, the
men were always grave and were either toiling or praying, while the devils were
always smiling and dancing. Several of these boards had been split for kindling
and it was evident that the artist did not value his work highly.

It was the first day of winter on the Divide.[3] Canute stumbled into his shanty
carrying a basket of cobs,[4] and after filling the stove, sat down on a stool and
crouched his seven foot frame over the fire, staring drearily out of the window
at the wide gray sky. He knew by heart every individual clump of bunch grass
in the miles of red shaggy prairie that stretched before his cabin. He knew it
in all the deceitful loveliness of its early summer, in all the bitter barrenness of

its autumn. He had seen it smitten by all the plagues of Egypt.[5] He had seen it parched by drought, and sogged by rain, beaten by hail, and swept by fire, and in the grasshopper years he had seen it eaten as bare and clean as bones that the vultures have left. After the great fires he had seen it stretch for miles and miles, black and smoking as the floor of hell.

He rose slowly and crossed the room, dragging his big feet heavily as though they were burdens to him. He looked out of the window into the hog corral and saw the pigs burying themselves in the straw before the shed. The leaden gray clouds were beginning to spill themselves, and the snow-flakes were settling down over the white leprous patches of frozen earth where the hogs had gnawed even the sod away. He shuddered and began to walk, trampling heavily with his ungainly feet. He was the wreck of ten winters on the Divide and he knew what they meant. Men fear the winters of the Divide as a child fears night or as men in the North Seas fear the still dark cold of the polar twilight.

His eyes fell upon his gun, and he took it down from the wall and looked it over. He sat down on the edge of his bed and held the barrel towards his face, letting his forehead rest upon it, and laid his finger on the trigger. He was perfectly calm, there was neither passion nor despair in his face, but the thoughtful look of a man who is considering. Presently he laid down the gun, and reaching into the cupboard, drew out a pint bottle of raw white alcohol. Lifting it to his lips, he drank greedily. He washed his face in the tin basin and combed his rough hair and shaggy blond beard. Then he stood in uncertainty before the suit of dark clothes that hung on the wall. For the fiftieth time he took them in his hands and tried to summon courage to put them on. He took the paper collar that was pinned to the sleeve of the coat and cautiously slipped it under his rough beard, looking with timid expectancy into the cracked, splashed glass[6] that hung over the bench. With a short laugh he threw it down on the bed, and pulling on his old black hat, he went out, striking off across the level.

It was a physical necessity for him to get away from his cabin once in a while. He had been there for ten years, digging and plowing and sowing, and reaping what little the hail and the hot winds and the frosts left him to reap. Insanity and suicide are very common things on the Divide. They come on like an epidemic in the hot wind season. Those scorching dusty winds that blow up over the bluffs from Kansas seem to dry up the blood in men's veins as they do the sap in the corn leaves. Whenever the yellow scorch creeps down over the tender inside leaves about the ear, then the coroners prepare for active duty; for the oil of the country is burned out and it does not take long for the flame to eat up the wick. It causes no great sensation there when a Dane is found swinging to his own windmill tower, and most of the Poles after they have become too careless and discouraged to shave themselves keep their razors to cut their throats with.[7]

It may be that the next generation on the Divide will be very happy, but the present one came too late in life. It is useless for men that have cut hemlocks among the mountains of Sweden for forty years to try to be happy in a country as flat and gray and as naked as the sea. It is not easy for men that have spent their youths fishing in the Northern seas to be content with following a plow, and men that have served in the Austrian army hate hard work and coarse clothing and the loneliness of the plains, and long for marches and excitement and tavern company and pretty barmaids. After a man has passed his fortieth birthday it is not easy for him to change the habits and conditions of his life. Most men bring with them to the Divide only the dregs of the lives that they have squandered in other lands and among other peoples.

Canute Canuteson was as mad as any of them, but his madness did not take the form of suicide or religion but of alcohol. He had always taken liquor when he wanted it, as all Norwegians do, but after his first year of solitary life he settled down to it steadily. He exhausted whisky after a while, and went to alcohol, because its effects were speedier and surer. He was a big man with a terrible amount of resistant force, and it took a great deal of alcohol even to move him. After nine years of drinking, the quantities he could take would seem fabulous to an ordinary drinking man. He never let it interfere with his work, he generally drank at night and on Sundays. Every night, as soon as his chores were done, he began to drink. While he was able to sit up he would play on his mouth harp or hack away at his window sills with his jack knife. When the liquor went to his head he would lie down on his bed and stare out of the window until he went to sleep. He drank alone and in solitude not for pleasure or good cheer, but to forget the awful loneliness and level of the Divide. Milton made a sad blunder when he put mountains in hell.[8] Mountains postulate faith and aspiration. All mountain peoples are religious. It was the cities of the plains that, because of their utter lack of spirituality and the mad caprice of their vice, were cursed of God.

Alcohol is perfectly consistent in its effects upon man. Drunkenness is merely an exaggeration. A foolish man drunk becomes maudlin; a bloody man, vicious; a coarse man, vulgar. Canute was none of these, but he was morose and gloomy, and liquor took him through all the hells of Dante.[9] As he lay on his giant's bed all the horrors of this world and every other were laid bare to his chilled senses. He was a man who knew no joy, a man who toiled in silence and bitterness. The skull and the serpent were always before him, the symbols of eternal futileness and of eternal hate.

When the first Norwegians near enough to be called neighbors came, Canute rejoiced, and planned to escape from his bosom vice. But he was not a social man by nature and had not the power of drawing out the social side of other people. His new neighbors rather feared him because of his great strength and size, his silence and his lowering brows. Perhaps, too, they knew that he was mad, mad from the eternal treachery of the plains, which every spring stretch green and rustle with the promises of Eden, showing long grassy lagoons full of clear water and cattle whose hoofs are stained with wild roses. Before autumn the lagoons are dried up, and the ground is burnt dry and hard until it blisters and cracks open.

So instead of becoming a friend and neighbor to the men that settled about him, Canute became a mystery and a terror. They told awful stories of his size and strength and of the alcohol he drank. They said that one night, when he went out to see to his horses just before he went to bed, his steps were unsteady and the rotten planks of the floor gave way and threw him behind the feet of a fiery young stallion. His foot was caught fast in the floor, and the nervous horse began kicking frantically. When Canute felt the blood trickling down into his eyes from a scalp wound in his head, he roused himself from his kingly indifference, and with the quiet stoical courage of a drunken man leaned forward and wound his arms about the horse's hind legs and held them against his breast with crushing embrace. All through the darkness and cold of the night he lay there, matching strength against strength. When little Jim Peterson went over the next morning at four o'clock to go with him to the Blue to cut wood, he found him so, and the horse was on its fore knees, trembling and whinnying with fear. This is the story the Norwegians tell of him, and if it is true it is no wonder that they feared and hated this Holder of the Heels of Horses.

One spring there moved to the next "eighty"[10] a family that made a great change in Canute's life. Ole Yensen was too drunk most of the time to be afraid of any one, and his wife Mary was too garrulous to be afraid of any one who listened to her talk, and Lena, their pretty daughter, was not afraid of man nor devil. So it came about that Canute went over to take his alcohol with Ole oftener than he took it alone. After a while the report spread that he was going to marry Yensen's daughter, and the Norwegian girls began to tease Lena about the great bear she was going to keep house for. No one could quite see how the affair had come about, for Canute's tactics of courtship were somewhat peculiar. He apparently never spoke to her at all: he would sit for hours with Mary chattering on one side of him and Ole drinking on the other and watch Lena at her work. She teased him, and threw flour in his face and put vinegar in his coffee, but he took her rough jokes with silent wonder, never even smiling. He took her to church occasionally, but the most watchful and curious people never saw him speak to her. He would sit staring at her while she giggled and flirted with the other men.

Next spring Mary Lee went to town to work in a steam laundry. She came home every Sunday, and always ran across to Yensens to startle Lena with stories of ten cent theatres, firemen's dances, and all the other esthetic delights of metropolitan life. In a few weeks Lena's head was completely turned, and she gave her father no rest until he let her go to town to seek her fortune at the ironing board. From the time she came home on her first visit she began to treat Canute with contempt. She had bought a plush cloak and kid gloves, had her clothes made by the dress-maker, and assumed airs and graces that made the other women of the neighborhood cordially detest her. She generally brought with her a young man from town who waxed his mustache and wore a red necktie, and she did not even introduce him to Canute.

The neighbors teased Canute a good deal until he knocked one of them down. He gave no sign of suffering from her neglect except that he drank more and avoided the other Norwegians more carefully than ever. He lay around in his den and no one knew what he felt or thought, but little Jim Peterson, who had seen him glowering at Lena in church one Sunday when she was there with the town man, said that he would not give an acre of his wheat for Lena's life or the town chap's either; and Jim's wheat was so wondrously worthless that the statement was an exceedingly strong one.

Canute had bought a new suit of clothes that looked as nearly like the town man's as possible. They had cost him half a millet crop; for tailors are not accustomed to fitting giants and they charge for it. He had hung those clothes in his shanty two months ago and had never put them on, partly from fear of ridicule, partly from discouragement, and partly because there was something in his own soul that revolted at the littleness of the device.

Lena was at home just at this time. Work was slack in the laundry and Mary had not been well, so Lena stayed at home, glad enough to get an opportunity to torment Canute once more.

She was washing in the side kitchen, singing loudly as she worked. Mary was on her knees, blacking the stove and scolding violently about the young man who was coming out from town that night. The young man had committed the fatal error of laughing at Mary's ceaseless babble and had never been forgiven.

"He is no good, and you will come to a bad end by running with him! I do not see why a daughter of mine should act so. I do not see why the Lord should visit such a punishment upon me as to give me such a daughter. There are plenty of good men you can marry."

Lena tossed her head and answered curtly, "I don't happen to want to marry any man right away, and so long as Dick dresses nice and has plenty of money to spend, there is no harm in my going with him."

"Money to spend? Yes, and that is all he does with it I'll be bound. You think it very fine now, but you will change your tune when you have been married five years and see your children running naked and your cupboard empty. Did Anne Hermanson come to any good end by marrying a town man?"

"I don't know anything about Anne Hermanson, but I know any of the laundry girls would have Dick quick enough if they could get him."

"Yes, and a nice lot of store clothes huzzies you are too. Now there is Canuteson who has an 'eighty' proved up and fifty head of cattle and—"

"And hair that ain't been cut since he was a baby, and a big dirty beard, and he wears overalls on Sundays, and drinks like a pig. Besides he will keep. I can have all the fun I want, and when I am old and ugly like you he can have me and take care of me. The Lord knows there ain't nobody else going to marry him."

Canute drew his hand back from the latch as though it were red hot. He was not the kind of man to make a good eavesdropper, and he wished he had knocked sooner. He pulled himself together and struck the door like a battering ram. Mary jumped and opened it with a screech.

"God! Canute, how you scared us! I thought it was crazy Lou,—he has been tearing around the neighborhood trying to convert folks. I am afraid as death of him. He ought to be sent off, I think. He is just as liable as not to kill us all, or burn the barn, or poison the dogs. He has been worrying even the poor minister to death, and he laid up with the rheumatism, too! Did you notice that he was too sick to preach last Sunday? But don't stand there in the cold,—come in. Yensen isn't here, but he just went over to Sorenson's for the mail; he won't be gone long. Walk right in the other room and sit down."

Canute followed her, looking steadily in front of him and not noticing Lena as he passed her. But Lena's vanity would not allow him to pass unmolested. She took the wet sheet she was wringing out and cracked him across the face with it, and ran giggling to the other side of the room. The blow stung his cheeks and the soapy water flew in his eyes, and he involuntarily began rubbing them with his hands. Lena giggled with delight at his discomfiture, and the wrath in Canute's face grew blacker than ever. A big man humiliated is vastly more undignified than a little one. He forgot the sting of his face in the bitter consciousness that he had made a fool of himself. He stumbled blindly into the living room, knocking his head against the door jamb because he forgot to stoop. He dropped into a chair behind the stove, thrusting his big feet back helplessly on either side of him.

Ole was a long time in coming, and Canute sat there, still and silent, with his hands clenched on his knees, and the skin of his face seemed to have shriveled up into little wrinkles that trembled when he lowered his brows. His life had been one long lethargy of solitude and alcohol, but now he was awakening, and it was as when the dumb stagnant heat of summer breaks out into thunder.

When Ole came staggering in, heavy with liquor, Canute rose at once.

"Yensen," he said quietly, "I have come to see if you will let me marry your daughter today."

"Today!" gasped Ole.

"Yes, I will not wait until tomorrow. I am tired of living alone."

Ole braced his staggering knees against the bedstead, and stammered eloquently: "Do you think I will marry my daughter to a drunkard? a man who drinks raw alcohol? a man who sleeps with rattle snakes? Get out of my house or I will kick you out for your impudence." And Ole began looking anxiously for his feet.

Canute answered not a word, but he put on his hat and went out into the kitchen. He went up to Lena and said without looking at her, "Get your things on and come with me!"

The tone of his voice startled her, and she said angrily, dropping the soap, "Are you drunk?"

"If you do not come with me, I will take you,—you had better come," said Canute quietly.

She lifted a sheet to strike him, but he caught her arm roughly and wrenched the sheet from her. He turned to the wall and took down a hood and shawl that hung there, and began wrapping her up. Lena scratched and fought like a wild thing. Ole stood in the door, cursing, and Mary howled and screeched at the top of her voice. As for Canute, he lifted the girl in his arms and went out of the house. She kicked and struggled, but the helpless wailing of Mary and Ole soon died away in the distance, and her face was held down tightly on Canute's shoulder so that she could not see whither he was taking her. She was conscious only of the north wind whistling in her ears, and of rapid steady motion and of a great breast that heaved beneath her in quick, irregular breaths. The harder she struggled the tighter those iron arms that had held the heels of horses crushed about her, until she felt as if they would crush the breath from her, and lay still with fear. Canute was striding across the level fields at a pace at which man never went before, drawing the stinging north wind into his lungs in great gulps. He walked with his eyes half closed and looking straight in front of him, only lowering them when he bent his head to blow away the snowflakes that settled on her hair. So it was that Canute took her to his home, even as his bearded barbarian ancestors took the fair frivolous women of the South in their hairy arms and bore them down to their war ships. For ever and anon the soul becomes weary of the conventions that are not of it, and with a single stroke shatters the civilized lies with which it is unable to cope, and the strong arm reaches out and takes by force what it cannot win by cunning.

When Canute reached his shanty he placed the girl upon a chair, where she sat sobbing. He stayed only a few minutes. He filled the stove with wood and lit the lamp, drank a huge swallow of alcohol and put the bottle in his pocket. He paused a moment, staring heavily at the weeping girl, then he went off and locked the door and disappeared in the gathering gloom of the night.

Wrapped in flannels and soaked with turpentine,[11] the little Norwegian preacher sat reading his Bible, when he heard a thundering knock at his door, and Canute entered, covered with snow and with his beard frozen fast to his coat.

"Come in, Canute, you must be frozen," said the little man, shoving a chair towards his visitor.

Canute remained standing with his hat on and said quietly, "I want you to come over to my house tonight to marry me to Lena Yensen."

"Have you got a license, Canute?"

"No, I don't want a license. I want to be married."

"But I can't marry you without a license, man. It would not be legal."

A dangerous light came in the big Norwegian's eye. "I want you to come over to my house to marry me to Lena Yensen."

"No, I can't, it would kill an ox to go out in a storm like this, and my rheumatism is bad tonight."

"Then if you will not go I must take you," said Canute with a sigh.

He took down the preacher's bearskin coat and bade him put it on while he hitched up his buggy. He went out and closed the door softly after him. Presently he returned and found the frightened minister crouching before the fire with his coat lying beside him. Canute helped him put it on and gently wrapped his head in his big muffler. Then he picked him up and carried him out and placed him in his buggy. As he tucked the buffalo robes around him he said: "Your horse is old, he might flounder or lose his way in this storm. I will lead him."

The minister took the reins feebly in his hands and sat shivering with the cold. Sometimes when there was a lull in the wind, he could see the horse struggling through the snow with the man plodding steadily beside him. Again the blowing snow would hide them from him altogether. He had no idea where they were or what direction they were going. He felt as though he were being whirled away in the heart of the storm, and he said all the prayers he knew. But at last the long four miles were over, and Canute set him down in the snow while he unlocked the door. He saw the bride sitting by the fire with her eyes red and swollen as though she had been weeping. Canute placed a huge chair for him, and said roughly,—

"Warm yourself."

Lena began to cry and moan afresh, begging the minister to take her home. He looked helplessly at Canute. Canute said simply,—

"If you are warm now, you can marry us."

"My daughter, do you take this step of your own free will?" asked the minister in a trembling voice.

"No sir, I don't, and it is disgraceful he should force me into it! I won't marry him."

"Then, Canute, I cannot marry you," said the minister, standing as straight as his rheumatic limbs would let him.

"Are you ready to marry us now, sir?" said Canute, laying one iron hand on his stooped shoulder. The little preacher was a good man, but like most men of weak body he was a coward and had a horror of physical suffering, although he had known so much of it. So with many qualms of conscience he began to repeat the marriage service. Lena sat sullenly in her chair, staring at the fire. Canute stood beside her, listening with his head bent reverently and his hands folded on his breast. When the little man had prayed and said amen, Canute began bundling him up again.

"I will take you home, now," he said as he carried him out and placed him in his buggy, and started off with him through the fury of the storm, floundering among the snow drifts that brought even the giant himself to his knees.

After she was left alone, Lena soon ceased weeping. She was not of a particularly sensitive temperament, and had little pride beyond that of vanity. After the first bitter anger wore itself out, she felt nothing more than a healthy sense of humiliation and defeat. She had no inclination to run away, for she was married now, and in her eyes that was final and all rebellion was useless. She knew nothing about a license, but she knew that a preacher married folks. She consoled herself by thinking that she had always intended to marry Canute some day, any way.

She grew tired of crying and looking into the fire, so she got up and began to look about her. She had heard queer tales about the inside of Canute's shanty, and her curiosity soon got the better of her rage. One of the first things she noticed was the new black suit of clothes hanging on the wall. She was dull, but it did not take a vain woman long to interpret anything so decidedly flattering, and she was pleased in spite of herself. As she looked through the cupboard, the general air of neglect and discomfort made her pity the man who lived there.

"Poor fellow, no wonder he wants to get married to get somebody to wash up his dishes. Batchin's[12] pretty hard on a man."

It is easy to pity when once one's vanity has been tickled. She looked at the window sill and gave a little shudder and wondered if the man were crazy. Then she sat down again and sat a long time wondering what her Dick and Ole would do.

"It is queer Dick didn't come right over after me. He surely came, for he would have left town before the storm began and he might just as well come right on as go back. If he'd hurried he would have gotten here before the preacher came. I suppose he was afraid to come, for he knew Canuteson could pound him to jelly, the coward!" Her eyes flashed angrily.

The weary hours wore on and Lena began to grow horribly lonesome. It was an uncanny night and this was an uncanny place to be in. She could hear the coyotes howling hungrily a little way from the cabin, and more terrible still were all the unknown noises of the storm. She remembered the tales they told of the big log overhead and she was afraid of those snaky things on the window sills. She remembered the man who had been killed in the draw, and she wondered what she would do if she saw crazy Lou's white face glaring into the window. The rattling of the door became unbearable, she thought the latch must be loose and took the lamp to look at it. Then for the first time she saw the ugly brown snake skins whose death rattle sounded every time the wind jarred the door.

"Canute, Canute!" she screamed in terror.

Outside the door she heard a heavy sound as of a big dog getting up and shaking himself. The door opened and Canute stood before her, white as a snow drift.

"What is it?" he asked kindly.

"I am cold," she faltered.

He went out and got an armful of wood and a basket of cobs and filled the stove. Then he went out and lay in the snow before the door. Presently he heard her calling again.

"What is it?" he said, sitting up.

"I'm so lonesome, I'm afraid to stay in here all alone."

"I will go over and get your mother." And he got up.

"She won't come."

"I'll bring her," said Canute grimly.

"No, no. I don't want her, she will scold all the time."

"Well, I will bring your father."

She spoke again and it seemed as though her mouth was close up to the key-hole. She spoke lower than he had ever heard her speak before, so low that he had to put his ear up to the lock to hear her.

"I don't want him either, Canute,—I'd rather have you."

For a moment she heard no noise at all, then something like a groan. With a cry of fear she opened the door, and saw Canute stretched in the snow at her feet, his face in his hands, sobbing on the door step.

"SAW CANUTE STRETCHED IN THE SNOW, AT HER FEET, SOBBING."

When Lena opened the door, she "saw Canute stretched in the snow, at her feet, sobbing." Illustration from Willa Cather, "On the Divide," *Overland Monthly* 27 (January 1896).

NOTES

1. A small flimsily constructed cabin or hut.
2. In 1538, German artist Hans Holbein the Younger published the book *Dance of Death*, which included numerous woodcarving prints he had begun creating over a decade earlier; these often gruesome prints depict death interacting with humans from all walks of life, demonstrating that no matter one's worldly status, everyone will face inescapable death.
3. An area of land in central Nebraska that represents the dividing line between the watersheds of the Republican River to the south and the Little Blue River to the north.
4. Dried corncobs were often used as fuel on the prairie due to the unavailability of wood.
5. In the Bible's book of Exodus, God inflicts ten terrible plagues on Egypt during the period of the Israelites' enslavement there.
6. A mirror.
7. The term "Dane" refers to someone from Denmark, and "Pole" to someone originally from Poland.
8. English poet John Milton (1608–74) first published his epic *Paradise Lost* in 1667 and revised it extensively for a second edition in 1674; in the second edition he describes Heaven, Hell, and Chaos, the last of which lies between the other two.
9. In the *Inferno*, the first book of *The Divine Comedy*, by Italian poet Dante Alighieri (ca. 1265–1321), the character of Dante travels with his guide Virgil through various circles and subcircles of hell, corresponding to different sins; in each area they observe sinners undergoing various kinds of torture.
10. Under the provisions of the Homestead Act of 1862, each individual was entitled to a "claim" of 160 acres; "eighty" here refers to a half claim.
11. At this time, soaking a cloth in turpentine—a liquid solvent created by distilling resin from trees, usually pine trees, and commonly mixed with paint or tar to make them easier to use—and applying it to one's body was a common home remedy for a cold.
12. Living as a bachelor.

CHARLES W. CHESNUTT

(1858–1932)

Charles W. Chesnutt has the honor of being the first African American to achieve significant distinction as a fiction author during his lifetime. Decades before the Harlem Renaissance of the 1920s, Chesnutt wrote dozens of excellent short stories and three important novels that sympathetically represented the experiences of African Americans; many of them also contested the injustice of Whites' racial discrimination at both a personal and a systemic level.

Born in Cleveland, Ohio, to parents of mixed-race backgrounds, Chesnutt moved with his family to Fayetteville, North Carolina, in 1866. Chesnutt himself had extensive experience with the type of school described in the story presented here, "The March of Progress," and in general with efforts to educate formerly enslaved Black people in the South. Soon after his family moved to Fayetteville, Chesnutt, at the age of nine, began attending the Howard School, which had been built with funds from the Freedmen's Bureau, a federal government initiative that assisted Black people in the South from 1865 to 1872. Proving himself an adept and intelligent student, he officially earned his teaching certificate in 1874, and from 1873 to 1876 he served during the school year as the assistant principal of the Peabody School in Charlotte (likely supported by the Peabody Fund, established in 1867 and also mentioned in the story); over the summers he taught in rural schools in both North Carolina and South Carolina to earn money for his family. In 1877 he became the assistant principal of the State Colored Normal School in Fayetteville, which trained African American teachers; he became principal in 1880.

Despite his success as an educator, Chesnutt became increasingly frustrated with the racial prejudice he faced in the South and began to formulate plans to become a writer. In 1880 he wrote in his journal (now published): "If I do write, I shall write for a purpose, a high, holy purpose, and this will inspire me to greater effort. The object of my writings would be not so much the elevation of the colored people as the elevation of the whites." As early as 1881 he determined to leave for the North, where he believed conditions would be more amenable for him not only as a Black man but also as a writer. Finally, in May 1883 he resigned his secure position as principal of the State Colored Normal School to move to New York City and pursue his dream of becoming a full-time author.

After a short time living in New York, where he learned that it was very difficult to make enough as a writer to support a family, Chesnutt returned to Cleveland, his childhood home. There he worked first as an accountant and simultaneously studied law, passing the Ohio bar exam with high grades in 1887. Confined by racial prejudice to working solely as a court stenographer instead of being able to practice law, Chesnutt eventually established his own stenography business. In his spare time, though, he continued to try his hand at writing fiction. At first Chesnutt sold short fictions for little remuneration to S. S. McClure's Associated Literary Press syndicate, which distributed them to multiple newspapers across the United States. But it was the publication of his story "The Goophered Grapevine" in the August 1887 issue of *Atlantic Monthly* magazine, the era's premier literary monthly, that first brought him to the attention of literary critics. For the next decade he was able to place many of his stories, typically set in the South and drawing on his personal experiences in the region, in the *Atlantic* as well as in other prestigious magazines. Many of these stories featured a formerly enslaved Black man named Uncle Julius and "conjure," a system of Black folk beliefs; these works often directly challenged the Plantation school of fiction popularized by the White Georgian author Joel Chandler Harris, with his Uncle Remus tales. Chesnutt's works, in sharp contrast to Harris's, often highlighted how unhappy African Americans had been when enslaved, as well as their intelligence and humanity; his works also frequently, but very subtly, critiqued the actions and attitudes of their White characters and, by extension, their White readers. Many of these stories were collected in *The Conjure Woman*, published by the prestigious Boston firm of Houghton, Mifflin, in 1899; it was received quite well by both the public and by critics.

In that same year, Houghton, Mifflin, published another collection of Chesnutt's stories under the title *The Wife of His Youth and Other Stories of the Color Line*. Chesnutt, for many years, had wanted to move away from providing what were known as "dialect stories" about rural, uneducated African Americans for the entertainment of White readers, and the stories in *The Wife of His Youth*, many of which had been previously published in various periodicals, reflect that desire, especially those that dealt with a topic hitherto unaddressed in American fiction: life among free Black people in the postbellum North. Chesnutt was disappointed, however, by the relatively low sales and tepid critical reception, both likely due to Whites wishing to continue reading stories that comported more with their stereotypes of African Americans.

Chesnutt wrote "The March of Progress" in the mid-1890s, and it was one of two stories (the other being "The Wife of His Youth") that the *Atlantic Monthly* accepted for publication in February 1897. To Chesnutt, having two stories accepted by the most prestigious literary magazine of its day represented a major career milestone. However, while "The Wife of His Youth" appeared in the magazine's pages in July 1898, the *Atlantic* never published "The March of Progress." Instead, its editor, Walter Hines Page, kept delaying its publication, eventually asking Chesnutt if they could instead publish another one of his "conjure" tales featuring Uncle Julius and set in the rural South. Chesnutt, wishing to please Page and the book publisher Houghton, Mifflin, with whom Page was affiliated, agreed to this plan. Chesnutt then submitted "The March of Progress" to *Century Magazine*, another one of the most important American publications of that era; it was accepted there in May 1899 and published in its pages in January 1901.

*Readers should be aware that this story includes some language which, while commonly used during this time period, is no longer considered acceptable because of its offensive nature.

THE MARCH OF PROGRESS (1901)

The colored[1] people of Patesville had at length gained the object they had for a long time been seeking—the appointment of a committee of themselves to manage the colored schools of the town. They had argued, with some show of reason, that they were most interested in the education of their own children, and in a position to know, better than any committee of white men could, what was best for their children's needs. The appointments had been made by the county commissioners during the latter part of the summer, and a week later a

VOL. XLIII. DECEMBER, 1891. No. 2.

T̤ḤE̤ CENTURY
ILLUSTRATED
MONTHLY
MAGAZINE

CHRISTMAS NUMBER

18 91

THE CENTURY·CO·UNION·SQUARE·NEW·YORK
T. FISHER·UNWIN. PATERNOSTER·S♀ LONDON

Cover of the *Century Illustrated Monthly Magazine* (December 1891).

meeting was called for the purpose of electing a teacher to take charge of the grammar school at the beginning of the fall term.

The committee consisted of Frank Gillespie, or "Glaspy," a barber, who took an active part in local politics; Bob Cotten, a blacksmith, who owned several houses and was looked upon as a substantial citizen; and Abe Johnson, commonly called "Ole Abe" or "Uncle Abe," who had a large family, and drove a dray, and did odd jobs of hauling; he was also a class-leader in the Methodist church. The committee had been chosen from among a number of candidates—Gillespie on account of his political standing, Cotten as representing the solid element of the colored population, and Old Abe, with democratic impartiality, as likely to satisfy the humbler class of a humble people. While the choice had not pleased everybody,—for instance, some of the other applicants,—it was acquiesced in with general satisfaction. The first meeting of the new committee was of great public interest, partly by reason of its novelty, but chiefly because there were two candidates for the position of teacher of the grammar school.

The former teacher, Miss Henrietta Noble, had applied for the school. She had taught the colored children of Patesville for fifteen years. When the Freedmen's Bureau, after the military occupation of North Carolina, had called for volunteers to teach the children of the freedmen,[2] Henrietta Noble had offered her services. Brought up in a New England household by parents who taught her to fear God and love her fellow-men, she had seen her father's body brought home from a Southern battle-field and laid to rest in the village cemetery; and a short six months later she had buried her mother by his side. Henrietta had no brothers or sisters, and her nearest relatives were cousins living in the far West. The only human being in whom she felt any special personal interest was a certain captain in her father's regiment, who had paid her some attention. She had loved this man deeply, in a maidenly, modest way; but he had gone away without speaking, and had not since written. He had escaped the fate of many others, and at the close of the war was alive and well, stationed in some Southern garrison.

When her mother died, Henrietta had found herself possessed only of the house where she lived and the furniture it contained, neither being of much value, and she was thrown upon her own resources for a livelihood. She had a fair education and had read many good books. It was not easy to find employment such as she desired. She wrote to her Western cousins, and they advised her to come to them, as they thought they could do something for her if she were there. She had almost decided to accept their offer, when the demand arose for teachers in the South. Whether impelled by some strain of adventurous blood from a Pilgrim ancestry, or by a sensitive pride that shrank from dependence, or by some dim and unacknowledged hope that she might sometime, somewhere, somehow meet Captain Carey—whether from one of these motives or a combination of them all, joined to something of the missionary spirit, she decided to go South, and wrote to her cousins declining their friendly offer.

She had come to Patesville when the children were mostly a mob of dirty little beggars. She had distributed among them the cast-off clothing that came from their friends in the North; she had taught them to wash their faces and to comb their hair; and patiently, year after year, she had labored to instruct them in the rudiments of learning and the first principles of religion and morality. And she had not wrought in vain. Other agencies, it is true, had in time cooperated with her efforts, but any one who had watched the current of events must have been compelled to admit that the very fair progress of the colored people of Patesville in the fifteen years following emancipation had been due chiefly to the unselfish labors of Henrietta Noble, and that her nature did not belie her name.

Fifteen years is a long time. Miss Noble had never met Captain Carey; and when she learned later that he had married a Southern girl in the neighborhood of his post, she had shed her tears in secret and banished his image from her heart. She had lived a lonely life. The white people of the town, though they learned in time to respect her and to value her work, had never recognized her existence by more than the mere external courtesy shown by any community to one who lives in the midst of it. The situation was at first, of course, so strained that she did not expect sympathy from the white people; and later, when time had smoothed over some of the asperities of war, her work had so engaged her that she had not had time to pine over her social exclusion. Once or twice nature had asserted itself, and she had longed for her own kind, and had visited her New England home. But her circle of friends was broken up, and she did not find much pleasure in boarding-house life; and on her last visit to the North but one, she had felt so lonely that she had longed for the dark faces of her pupils, and had welcomed with pleasure the hour when her task should be resumed.

But for several reasons the school at Patesville was of more importance to Miss Noble at this particular time than it ever had been before. During the last few years her health had not been good. An affection of the heart similar to that from which her mother had died, while not interfering perceptibly with her work, had grown from bad to worse, aggravated by close application to her duties, until it had caused her grave alarm. She did not have perfect confidence in the skill of the Patesville physicians, and to obtain the best medical advice had gone to New York during the summer, remaining there a month under the treatment of an eminent specialist. This, of course, had been expensive and had absorbed the savings of years from a small salary; and when the time came for her to return to Patesville, she was reduced, after paying her traveling expenses, to her last ten-dollar note.

"It is very fortunate," the great man had said at her last visit, "that circumstances permit you to live in the South, for I am afraid you could not endure a Northern winter. You are getting along very well now, and if you will take care of yourself and avoid excitement, you will be better." He said to himself as she went away: "It's only a matter of time, but that is true about us all; and a wise physician does as much good by what he withholds as by what he tells."

Miss Noble had not anticipated any trouble about the school. When she went away the same committee of white men was in charge that had controlled the school since it had become part of the public-school system of the State on the withdrawal of support from the Freedmen's Bureau.[3] While there had been no formal engagement made for the next year, when she had last seen the chairman before she went away, he had remarked that she was looking rather fagged out, had bidden her good-by, and had hoped to see her much improved when she returned. She had left her house in the care of the colored woman who lived with her and did her housework, assuming, of course, that she would take up her work again in the autumn.

She was much surprised at first, and later alarmed, to find a rival for her position as teacher of the grammar school. Many of her friends and pupils had called on her since her return, and she had met a number of the people at the colored Methodist church, where she taught in the Sunday-school. She had many friends and supporters, but she soon found out that her opponent had considerable strength. There had been a time when she would have withdrawn and left him a clear field, but at the present moment it was almost a matter of life and death to her—certainly the matter of earning a living—to secure the appointment.

The other candidate was a young man who in former years had been one of Miss Noble's brightest pupils. When he had finished his course in the grammar school, his parents, with considerable sacrifice, had sent him to a college for colored youth. He had studied diligently, had worked industriously during his vacations, sometimes at manual labor, sometimes teaching a country school, and in due time had been graduated from his college with honors. He had come home at the end of his school life, and was very naturally seeking the employment for which he had fitted himself. He was a "bright" mulatto,[4] with straight hair, an intelligent face, and a well-set figure. He had acquired some of the marks of culture, wore a frock-coat and a high collar, parted his hair in the middle, and showed by his manner that he thought a good deal of himself. He was the popular candidate among the progressive element of his people, and rather confidently expected the appointment.

The meeting of the committee was held in the Methodist church, where, in fact, the grammar school was taught, for want of a separate school-house. After the preliminary steps to effect an organization, Mr. Gillespie, who had been elected chairman, took the floor.

"The principal business to be brought befo' the meet'n' this evenin'," he said, "is the selection of a teacher for our grammar school for the ensuin' year. Two candidates have filed applications, which, if there is no objection, I will read to the committee. The first is from Miss Noble, who has been the teacher ever since the grammar school was started."

He then read Miss Noble's letter, in which she called attention to her long years of service, to her need of the position, and to her affection for the pupils, and made formal application for the school for the next year. She did not, from motives of self-respect, make known the extremity of her need; nor did she mention the condition of her health, as it might have been used as an argument against her retention.

Mr. Gillespie then read the application of the other candidate, Andrew J. Williams. Mr. Williams set out in detail his qualifications for the position: his degree from Riddle University; his familiarity with the dead and living languages and the higher mathematics; his views of discipline; and a peroration[5] in which he expressed the desire to devote himself to the elevation of his race and assist the march of progress through the medium of the Patesville grammar school. The letter was well written in a bold, round hand, with many flourishes, and looked very aggressive and overbearing as it lay on the table by the side of the sheet of small note-paper in Miss Noble's faint and somewhat cramped handwriting.

"You have heard the readin' of the applications," said the chairman. "Gentlemen, what is yo' pleasure?"

There being no immediate response, the chairman continued:

"As this is a matter of consid'able importance, involvin' not only the welfare of our schools, but the progress of our race, an' as our action is liable to be criticized, whatever we decide, perhaps we had better discuss the subjec' befo' we act. If nobody else has anything to obse've, I will make a few remarks."

Mr. Gillespie cleared his throat, and, assuming an oratorical attitude, proceeded:

"The time has come in the history of our people when we should stand together. In this age of organization the march of progress requires that we help ourselves, or be forever left behind. Ever since the war we have been sendin' our child'n to school an' educatin' 'em; an' now the time has come when they are leavin' the schools an' colleges, an' are ready to go to work. An' what are they goin' to do? The white people won't hire 'em as clerks in their sto's an' factories an' mills, an' we have no sto's or factories or mills of our own. They can't be lawyers or doctors yet, because we haven't got the money to send 'em to medical colleges an' law schools. We can't elect many of 'em to office, for various reasons. There's just two things they can find to do—to preach in our own pulpits, an' teach in our own schools. If it wasn't for that, they'd have to go on forever waitin' on white folks, like their fo'fathers have done, because they couldn't help it. If we expect our race to progress, we must educate our young men an' women. If we want to encourage 'em to get education, we must find 'em employment when they are educated. We have now an opportunity to do this in the case of our young friend an' fellow-citizen, Mr. Williams, whose eloquent an' fine-lookin' letter ought to make us feel proud of him an' of our race.

"Of co'se there are two sides to the question. We have got to consider the claims of Miss Noble. She has been with us a long time an' has done much good work for our people, an' we'll never forget her work an' frien'ship. But, after all, she has been paid for it; she has got her salary regularly an' for a long time, an' she has probably saved somethin', for we all know she hasn't lived high; an', for all we know, she may have had somethin' left her by her parents. An' then again, she's white, an' has got her own people to look after her; they've got all the money an' all the offices an' all the everythin',—all that they've made an' all that we've made for fo' hundred years,—an' they sho'ly would look out for her. If she don't get this school, there's probably a dozen others she can get at the North. An' another thing: she is gettin' rather feeble, an' it 'pears to me she's hardly able to stand teachin' so many child'n, an' a long rest might be the best thing in the world for her.

"Now, gentlemen, that's the situation. Shall we keep Miss Noble, or shall we stand by our own people? It seems to me there can hardly be but one answer. Self-preservation is the first law of nature. Are there any other remarks?"

Old Abe was moving restlessly in his seat. He did not say anything, however, and the chairman turned to the other member.

"Brother Cotten, what is yo' opinion of the question befo' the board?"

Mr. Cotten rose with the slowness and dignity becoming a substantial citizen, and observed:

"I think the remarks of the chairman have great weight. We all have nothin' but kind feelin's fer Miss Noble, an' I came here to-night somewhat undecided how to vote on this question. But after listenin' to the just an' forcible arguments of Brother Glaspy, it 'pears to me that, after all, the question befo' us is not a matter of feelin', but of business. As a business man, I am inclined to think Brother Glaspy is right. If we don't help ourselves when we get a chance, who is goin' to help us?"

"That bein' the case," said the chairman, "shall we proceed to a vote? All who favor the election of Brother Williams—"

At this point Old Abe, with much preliminary shuffling, stood up in his place and interrupted the speaker.

"Mr. Chuhman," he said, "I s'pose I has a right ter speak in dis meet'n? I *s'pose* I is a member er dis committee?"

"Certainly, Brother Johnson, certainly; we shall be glad to hear from you."

"I s'pose I's got a right ter speak my min', ef I is po' an' black, an' don' weah as good clo's as some other members er de committee?"

"Most assuredly, Brother Johnson," answered the chairman, with a barber's suavity, "you have as much right to be heard as any one else. There was no intention of cuttin' you off."

"I s'pose," continued Abe, "dat a man wid fo'teen child'n kin be 'lowed ter hab somethin' ter say 'bout de schools er dis town?"

"I am sorry, Brother Johnson, that you should feel slighted, but there was no intention to igno' yo' rights. The committee will be please' to have you ventilate yo' views."

"Ef it's all be'n an' done reco'nized an' 'cided dat I's got de right ter be heared in dis meet'n', I'll say w'at I has ter say, an' it won't take me long ter say it. Ef I should try ter tell all de things dat Miss Noble has done fer de niggers[6] er dis town, it'd take me till ter-morrer mawnin'. Fer fifteen long yeahs I has watched her incomin's an' her outgoin's. Her daddy was a Yankee kunnel, who died fighting fer ou' freedom. She come heah when we—yas, Mr. Chuhman, when you an' Br'er Cotten—was jes sot free, an' when none er us didn' have a rag ter ou' backs. She come heah, an' she tuk yo' child'n an' my child'n, an' she teached 'em sense an' manners an' religion an' book-l'arnin'. When she come heah we didn' hab no chu'ch. Who writ up No'th an' got a preacher sent to us, an' de fun's ter buil' dis same chu'ch-house we're settin' in ter-night? Who got de money f'm de Bureau to s'port de school? An' when dat was stop', who got de money f'm de Peabody Fun'?[7] Talk about Miss Noble gittin' a sal'ry! Who paid dat sal'ry up ter five years ago? Not one dollah of it come outer ou' pockets!

"An' den, w'at did she git fer de yuther things she done? Who paid her fer de gals she kep' f'm throwin' deyse'ves away? Who paid fer de boys she kep' outer jail? I had a son dat seemed to hab made up his min' ter go straight ter hell. I made him go ter Sunday-school, an' somethin' dat woman said teched his heart, an' he behaved hisse'f, an' I ain' got no reason fer ter be 'shame' er 'im. An' I can 'member, Br'er Cotten, when you didn' own fo' houses an' a fahm. An' when yo' fus wife was sick, who sot by her bedside an' read de Good Book ter 'er, w'en dey wuzn' nobody else knowed how ter read it, an' comforted her on her way across de col', dahk ribber?[8] An' dat ain' all I kin 'member, Mr. Chuhman! When yo' gal Fanny was a baby, an' sick, an' nobody knowed what was de matter wid 'er, who sent fer a doctor, an' paid 'im fer comin', an' who he'ped nuss dat chile, an' tol' yo' wife w'at ter do, an' save' dat chile's life, jes as sho' as de Lawd has save' my soul?

"An' now, aftuh fifteen yeahs o' slavin' fer us, who ain't got no claim on her, aftuh fifteen yeahs dat she has libbed 'mongs' us an' made herse'f one of us, an' endyoed havin' her own people look down on her, aftuh she has growed ole an' gray wukkin' fer us an' our child'n, we talk erbout turnin' 'er out like a' ole hoss ter die! It 'pears ter me some folks has po' mem'ries! Whar would we 'a' be'n ef her folks at de No'th hadn' 'membered us no bettuh? An' we hadn' done nothin', neither, fer dem to 'member us fer. De man dat kin fergit w'at Miss Noble has done fer dis town is unworthy de name er nigger! He oughter die an' make room fer some 'spectable dog!

"Br'er Glaspy says we got a' educated young man, an' we mus' gib him sump'n' ter do. Let him wait; ef I reads de signs right he won't hab ter wait long fer dis job. Let him teach in de primary schools, er in de country; an' ef he can't do dat, let 'im work awhile. It don't hahm a' educated man ter work a little; his fo'fathers has worked fer hund'eds of years, an' we's worked, an' we're heah yet, an' we're free, an' we's gettin' ou' own houses an' lots an' hosses an' cows—an' ou' educated young men. But don't let de fus thing we do as a committee be somethin' we ought ter be 'shamed of as long as we lib. I votes fer Miss Noble, fus, las', an' all de time!"

When Old Abe sat down the chairman's face bore a troubled look. He re-membered how his baby girl, the first of his children that he could really call his own, that no master could hold a prior claim upon, lay dying in the arms of his distracted young wife, and how the thin, homely, and short-sighted white teacher had come like an angel into his cabin, and had brought back the little one from the verge of the grave. The child was a young woman now, and Gillespie had well-founded hopes of securing the superior young Williams for a son-in-law;

and he realized with something of shame that this later ambition had so dazzled his eyes for a moment as to obscure the memory of earlier days.

Mr. Cotten, too, had not been unmoved, and there were tears in his eyes as he recalled how his first wife, Nancy, who had borne with him the privations of slavery, had passed away, with the teacher's hand in hers, before she had been able to enjoy the fruits of liberty. For they had loved one another much, and her death had been to them both a hard and bitter thing. And, as Old Abe spoke, he could remember, as distinctly as though they had been spoken but an hour before, the words of comfort that the teacher had whispered to Nancy in her dying hour and to him in his bereavement.

"On consideration, Mr. Chairman," he said, with an effort to hide a suspicious tremor in his voice and to speak with the dignity consistent with his character as a substantial citizen, "I wish to record my vote fer Miss Noble."

"The chair," said Gillespie, yielding gracefully to the majority, and greatly relieved that the responsibility of his candidate's defeat lay elsewhere, "will make the vote unanimous, and will appoint Brother Cotten and Brother Johnson a committee to step round the corner to Miss Noble's and notify her of her election."

The two committeemen put on their hats, and, accompanied by several people who had been waiting at the door to hear the result of the meeting, went around the corner to Miss Noble's house, a distance of a block or two away. The house was lighted, so they knew she had not gone to bed. They went in at the gate, and Cotten knocked at the door.

The colored maid opened it.

"Is Miss Noble home?" said Cotten.

"Yes; come in. She's waitin' ter hear from the committee."

The woman showed them into the parlor. Miss Noble rose from her seat by the table, where she had been reading, and came forward to meet them. They did not for a moment observe, as she took a step toward them, that her footsteps wavered. In her agitation she was scarcely aware of it herself.

"Miss Noble," announced Cotten, "we have come to let you know that you have be'n 'lected teacher of the grammar school fer the next year."

"Thank you; oh, thank you so much!" she said. "I am very glad. Mary"—she put her hand to her side suddenly and tottered—"Mary, will you—"

A spasm of pain contracted her face and cut short her speech. She would have fallen had Old Abe not caught her and, with Mary's help, laid her on a couch.

The remedies applied by Mary, and by the physician who was hastily summoned, proved unavailing. The teacher did not regain consciousness.

If it be given to those whose eyes have closed in death to linger regretfully for a while about their earthly tenement, or from some higher vantage-ground to look down upon it, then Henrietta Noble's tolerant spirit must have felt, mingling with its regret, a compensating thrill of pleasure; for not only those for whom she had labored sorrowed for her, but the people of her own race, many of whom, in the blindness of their pride, would not admit during her life that she served them also, saw so much clearer now that they took charge of her poor clay,[9] and did it gentle reverence, and laid it tenderly away amid the dust of their own loved and honored dead.

Two weeks after Miss Noble's funeral the other candidate took charge of the grammar school, which went on without any further obstacles to the march of progress.

NOTES

1. A term used by many White people at the time to refer to African Americans. It is now considered offensive and is no longer acceptable.

2. After the Civil War officially ended on May 9, 1865, the federal government—dominated by Northern representatives and senators—sought to ensure the safety, rights, and fair treatment of newly freed people ("freedmen") throughout the South. Key to accomplishing these ends was the continued Northern military occupation of formerly Confederate states; North Carolina was under military rule until July 1868. Another measure intended to assist formerly enslaved people was the creation of the Bureau of Refugees, Freedmen, and Abandoned Lands, usually referred to as simply the Freedmen's Bureau, which operated from 1865 to 1872. Among its many accomplishments was the creation of over one thousand free public schools for formerly enslaved people in the South; this necessitated the recruitment of many teachers, including a good number from the North.

3. The Freedmen's Bureau was widely challenged throughout its history by most Southerners and by many northern Democrats; as a result, by 1869 most of its funding had been cut off by Congress, and in 1872 the bureau was abruptly terminated.

4. A person of mixed racial heritage. At this time it most commonly referred to a person with one White and one Black parent. It is now considered offensive and thus unacceptable.

5. A formal speech.

6. An extremely offensive term sometimes used by non-Black people to refer to Black people. While it is sometimes used among Black people to refer to other Black people, in both the past and the present this term was and is usually intended to be derogatory and hurtful when used by non-Black people; it is thus deeply offensive and should not be used.

7. George Peabody established the Peabody Education Fund in 1867 to provide financial support to already-existing schools in poor areas throughout the South; because schools for African Americans founded by the Freedmen's Bureau did not count as "already existing," they did not usually qualify for Peabody Fund assistance, and thus if Miss Noble had actually obtained such funding, it would have been an especially great achievement.

8. Among many Christians, "crossing the river" has a great deal of biblical resonance and metaphorically represents the transition from life to death—and "freedom" from this world's burdens.

9. In the Bible there are many instances where people are referred to as being made out of "clay"; this symbolizes their having come from the earth and been molded by God.

KATE CHOPIN

(1850–1904)

The work of Kate Chopin, born Katherine O'Flaherty, was rediscovered in the 1960s by a Norwegian scholar named Per Seyersted, and ever since the rise of feminist literary studies in the 1970s, Chopin has been widely recognized as one of the most accomplished American authors of the late nineteenth century. The daughter of an Irish immigrant father and a Creole (descended from early French settlers) mother, Chopin grew up in a well-to-do, devotedly Catholic family in St. Louis, Missouri. She married Oscar Chopin in 1870 and moved with him first to New Orleans, where he was a cotton broker, and then to rural northwest Louisiana, where his family plantation was located. Soon after her husband died of malaria in 1882, leaving her with six children to raise, Chopin returned to St. Louis in 1884 to be near her family. She began to write seriously and for publication in 1888; she never remarried.

The details of Chopin's complex life have supplied ample material for those scholars who have wished to link her biography with her work. Given her extensive experience of life in both rural Louisiana and New Orleans, for instance, it is not surprising that Chopin's fictions are almost all set in those locations and include "exotic" Acadian and Creole characters who speak various dialects. These elements undoubtedly played a key role in inducing editors at many of the most prominent magazines of her day—including the *Atlantic Monthly, Century, Harper's Monthly,* and *Vogue*—to accept Chopin's submissions for publication, for they satisfied their mostly urban and genteel readers' desire for a kind of "print tourism." In addition, though, Chopin was a strong advocate for women's rights, and this is reflected in the way she often depicts her female characters as fighting for their physical and spiritual freedom in a male-dominated world. Over forty of her stories and sketches—some of which had been previously published in various periodicals—appeared in two relatively popular collections, *Bayou Folk* (1894) and *A Night in Acadie* (1897). Chopin's masterpiece, a novel entitled *The Awakening* (1899), combined the regional elements evident in so much of her previous work with the story of a married woman, Edna Pontellier, living in Louisiana and staking a claim for her own selfhood and control of her body. Such a work, however, was too progressive for its time, and while there were some positive reviews, most reviewers condemned its main character as well as Chopin, her creator, for having transgressed a variety of commonly accepted boundaries about women and sex in fiction.

"A Gentleman of Bayou Têche," which addresses the issue of how northern magazines wished to depict southern subjects, was among three Chopin stories that editor Horace E. Scudder of the prestigious *Atlantic Monthly* magazine of Boston rejected in 1893; it was first published in Chopin's well-received collection entitled *Bayou Folk* (1894).

*Readers should be aware that this story includes some language that, while commonly used during this time period, is no longer considered acceptable because of its offensive nature.

A GENTLEMAN OF BAYOU TÊCHE (1894)

It was no wonder Mr. Sublet, who was staying at the Hallet plantation, wanted to make a picture of Evariste. The 'Cadian[1] was rather a picturesque subject in his way, and a tempting one to an artist looking for bits of "local color" along the Têche.[2]

Mr. Sublet had seen the man on the back gallery just as he came out of the swamp, trying to sell a wild turkey to the housekeeper. He spoke to him at once, and in the course of conversation engaged him to return to the house the following morning and have his picture drawn. He handed Evariste a couple of silver dollars to show that his intentions were fair, and that he expected the 'Cadian to keep faith with him.

"He tell' me he want' put my picture in one fine '*Mag*'zine,'" said Evariste to his daughter, Martinette, when the two were talking the matter over in the afternoon. "W'at fo' you reckon he want' do dat?" They sat within the low, homely cabin of two rooms, that was not quite so comfortable as Mr. Hallet's negro[3] quarters.

Martinette pursed her red lips that had little sensitive curves to them, and her black eyes took on a reflective expression.

"Mebbe he yeard 'bout that big fish w'at you ketch las' winta in Carancro lake. You know it was all wrote about in the 'Suga Bowl.'"[4] Her father set aside the suggestion with a deprecatory wave of the hand.

"Well, anyway, you got to fix yo'se'f up," declared Martinette, dismissing further speculation; "put on yo' otha pant'loon' an' yo' good coat; an' you betta ax Mr. Léonce to cut yo' hair, an' yo' w'sker' a li'le bit."

"It's w'at I say," chimed in Evariste. "I tell dat gent'man I'm goin' make myse'f fine. He say', 'No, no,' like he ent please'. He want' me like I come out de swamp. So much betta if my pant'loon' an' coat is tore, he say, an' color' like de mud." They could not understand these eccentric wishes on the part of the strange gentleman, and made no effort to do so.

An hour later Martinette, who was quite puffed up over the affair, trotted across to Aunt Dicey's cabin to communicate the news to her. The negress was ironing; her irons stood in a long row before the fire of logs that burned on the hearth. Martinette seated herself in the chimney corner and held her feet up to the blaze; it was damp and a little chilly out of doors. The girl's shoes were considerably worn and her garments were a little too thin and scant for the winter season. Her father had given her the two dollars he had received from the artist, and Martinette was on her way to the store to invest them as judiciously as she knew how.

"You know, Aunt Dicey," she began a little complacently after listening awhile to Aunt Dicey's unqualified abuse of her own son, Wilkins, who was dining-room boy at Mr. Hallet's, "you know that stranger gentleman up to Mr. Hallet's? he want' to make my popa's picture; an' he say' he goin' put it in one fine *Mag'*zine yonda."

Aunt Dicey spat upon her iron to test its heat. Then she began to snicker. She kept on laughing inwardly, making her whole fat body shake, and saying nothing.

"W'at you laughin' 'bout, Aunt Dice?" inquired Martinette mistrustfully.

"I is n' laughin', chile!"

"Yas, you' laughin'."

"Oh, don't pay no 'tention to me. I jis studyin' how simple you an' yo' pa is. You is bof de simplest somebody I eva come 'crost."

"You got to say plumb out w'at you mean, Aunt Dice," insisted the girl doggedly, suspicious and alert now.

"Well, dat w'y I say you is simple," proclaimed the woman, slamming down her iron on an inverted, battered pie pan, "jis like you says, dey gwine put yo' pa's picture yonda in de picture paper. An' you know w'at readin' dey gwine sot down on'neaf[5] dat picture?" Martinette was intensely attentive. "Dey gwine sot down on'neaf: 'Dis heah is one dem low-down 'Cajuns o' Bayeh Têche!'"

The blood flowed from Martinette's face, leaving it deathly pale; in another instant it came beating back in a quick flood, and her eyes smarted with pain as if the tears that filled them had been fiery hot.

"I knows dem kine o' folks," continued Aunt Dicey, resuming her interrupted ironing. "Dat stranger he got a li'le boy w'at ain't none too big to spank. Dat li'le imp he come a hoppin' in heah yistiddy wid a kine o' box on'neaf his arm. He say' 'Good mo'nin', madam. Will you be so kine an' stan' jis like you is dah at yo' i'onin', an' lef me take yo' picture?' I 'lowed I gwine make a picture outen him wid dis heah flati'on, ef he don' cl'ar hisse'f quick. An' he say he baig my pardon fo' his intrudement. All dat kine o' talk to a ole nigga[6] 'oman! Dat plainly sho' he don' know his place."

"W'at you want 'im to say, Aunt Dice?" asked Martinette, with an effort to conceal her distress.

"I wants 'im to come in heah an' say: 'Howdy, Aunt Dicey! will you be so kine and go put on yo' noo calker dress an' yo' bonnit w'at you w'ars to meetin', an' stan' 'side f'om dat i'onin'-boa'd w'ilse I gwine take yo' photygraph.' Dat de way fo' a boy to talk w'at had good raisin'."

Martinette had arisen, and began to take slow leave of the woman. She turned at the cabin door to observe tentatively: "I reckon it's Wilkins tells you how the folks they talk, yonda up to Mr. Hallet's."

She did not go to the store as she had intended, but walked with a dragging step back to her home. The silver dollars clicked in her pocket as she walked. She felt like flinging them across the field; they seemed to her somehow the price of shame.

The sun had sunk, and twilight was settling like a silver beam upon the bayou and enveloping the fields in a gray mist. Evariste, slim and slouchy, was waiting for his daughter in the cabin door. He had lighted a fire of sticks and branches, and placed the kettle before it to boil. He met the girl with his slow, serious, questioning eyes, astonished to see her empty-handed.

"How come you didn' bring nuttin' f'om de sto', Martinette?"

She entered and flung her gingham sunbonnet upon a chair. "No, I did n' go yonda;" and with sudden exasperation: "You got to go take back that money; you mus' n' git no picture took."

"But, Martinette," her father mildly interposed, "I promise' 'im; an' he's goin' give me some mo' money w'en he finish."

"If he give you a ba'el o' money, you mus'n' git no picture took. You know w'at he want to put un'neath that picture, fo' ev'body to read?" She could not tell him the whole hideous truth as she had heard it distorted from Aunt Dicey's lips; she would not hurt him that much. "He's goin' to write: 'This is one '*Cajun* o' the Bayou Têche.'" Evariste winced.

"How you know?" he asked.

"I yeard so. I know it's true."

The water in the kettle was boiling. He went and poured a small quantity upon the coffee which he had set there to drip. Then he said to her: "I reckon you jus' as well go care dat two dolla' back, tomo' mo'nin'; me, I'll go yonda ketch a mess o' fish in Carancro lake."

Mr. Hallet and a few masculine companions were assembled at a rather late breakfast the following morning. The dining-room was a big, bare one, enlivened by a cheerful fire of logs that blazed in the wide chimney on massive andirons. There were guns, fishing tackle, and other implements of sport lying about. A couple of fine dogs strayed unceremoniously in and out behind Wilkins, the negro boy who waited upon the table. The chair beside Mr. Sublet, usually occupied by his little son, was vacant, as the child had gone for an early morning outing and had not yet returned.

When breakfast was about half over, Mr. Hallet noticed Martinette standing outside upon the gallery. The dining-room door had stood open more than half the time.

"Is n't that Martinette out there, Wilkins?" inquired the jovial-faced young planter.

"Dat's who, suh," returned Wilkins. "She ben standin' dah sence mos' sun-up; look like she studyin' to take root to de gall'ry."

"What in the name of goodness does she want? Ask her what she wants. Tell her to come in to the fire."

Martinette walked into the room with much hesitancy. Her small, brown face could hardly be seen in the depths of the gingham sun-bonnet. Her blue cotton-ade skirt scarcely reached the thin ankles that it should have covered.

"Bonjou'"[7] she murmured, with a little comprehensive nod that took in the entire company. Her eyes searched the table for the "stranger gentleman," and she knew him at once, because his hair was parted in the middle and he wore a pointed beard. She went and laid the two silver dollars beside his plate and motioned to retire without a word of explanation.

"Hold on, Martinette!" called out the planter, "what's all this pantomime business? Speak out, little one."

"My popa don't want any picture took," she offered, a little timorously. On her way to the door she had looked back to say this. In that fleeting glance she detected a smile of intelligence pass from one to the other of the group. She turned quickly, facing them all, and spoke out, excitement making her voice bold and shrill: "My popa ent one low-down 'Cajun. He ent goin' to stan' to have that kine o' writin' put down un'neath his picture!"

She almost ran from the room, half blinded by the emotion that had helped her to make so daring a speech.

Descending the gallery steps she ran full against her father who was ascending, bearing in his arms the little boy, Archie Sublet. The child was most grotesquely attired in garments far too large for his diminutive person—the rough jeans clothing of some negro boy. Evariste himself had evidently been taking a bath without the preliminary ceremony of removing his clothes, that were now half dried upon his person by the wind and sun.

"Yere you' li'le boy," he announced, stumbling into the room. "You ought not lef dat li'le chile go by hisse'f *comme ça*[8] in de pirogue."[9] Mr. Sublet darted from his chair; the others following suit almost as hastily. In an instant, quivering with apprehension, he had his little son in his arms. The child was quite unharmed, only somewhat pale and nervous, as the consequence of a recent very serious ducking.[10]

Evariste related in his uncertain, broken English how he had been fishing for an hour or more in Carancro lake, when he noticed the boy paddling over the deep, black water in a shell-like pirogue. Nearing a clump of cypress-trees that rose from the lake, the pirogue became entangled in the heavy moss that hung from the tree limbs and trailed upon the water. The next thing he knew, the boat had overturned, he heard the child scream, and saw him disappear beneath the still, black surface of the lake.

"W'en I done swim to de sho' wid 'im," continued Evariste, "I hurry yonda to Jake Baptiste's cabin, an' we rub 'im an' warm 'im up, an' dress 'im up dry like you see. He all right now, M'sieur; but you mus'n lef 'im go no mo' by hisse'f in one pirogue."

Martinette had followed into the room behind her father. She was feeling and tapping his wet garments solicitously, and begging him in French to come home. Mr. Hallet at once ordered hot coffee and a warm breakfast for the two; and they sat down at the corner of the table, making no manner of objection in their perfect simplicity. It was with visible reluctance and ill-disguised contempt that Wilkins served them.[11]

When Mr. Sublet had arranged his son comfortably, with tender care, upon the sofa, and had satisfied himself that the child was quite uninjured, he attempted to find words with which to thank Evariste for this service which no treasure of words or gold could pay for. These warm and heartfelt expressions seemed to Evariste to exaggerate the importance of his action, and they intimidated him. He attempted shyly to hide his face as well as he could in the depths of his bowl of coffee.

"You will let me make your picture now, I hope, Evariste," begged Mr. Sublet, laying his hand upon the 'Cadian's shoulder. "I want to place it among things I hold most dear, and shall call it 'A hero of Bayou Têche.'" This assurance seemed to distress Evariste greatly.

"No, no," he protested, "it's nuttin' hero' to take a li'le boy out de water. I jus' as easy do dat like I stoop down an' pick up a li'le chile w'at fall down in de road. I ent goin' to 'low dat, me. I don't git no picture took, *va!*"

Mr. Hallet, who now discerned his friend's eagerness in the matter, came to his aid.

"I tell you, Evariste, let Mr. Sublet draw your picture, and you yourself may call it whatever you want. I'm sure he'll let you."

"Most willingly," agreed the artist.

Evariste glanced up at him with shy and child-like pleasure. "It's a bargain?" he asked.

"A bargain," affirmed Mr. Sublet.

"Popa," whispered Martinette, "you betta come home an' put on yo' otha pant'loon' an' yo' good coat."

"And now, what shall we call the much talked-of picture?" cheerily inquired the planter, standing with his back to the blaze.

Evariste in a business-like manner began carefully to trace on the tablecloth imaginary characters with an imaginary pen; he could not have written the real characters with a real pen—he did not know how.

"You will put on'neat' de picture," he said, deliberately, "'Dis is one picture of Mista Evariste Anatole Bonamour, a gent'man of de Bayou Têche.'"

NOTES

1. A "'Cadian" refers to someone who is of "Acadian" heritage; colloquially, such a person is known as a "Cajun." The Acadians in Louisiana were descended from chiefly French-speaking settlers expelled from Nova Scotia by the British between 1755 and 1764 and who, after being treated harshly by people in the British colonies along the East Coast, moved west in the late eighteenth century; they were generally regarded in Louisiana as White yet lower in class status than the Creoles, who at this time period in Louisiana history were regarded as White people descended from early French settlers of the area and who almost all still spoke French.

2. The Bayou Têche is a 125-mile-long waterway in south-central Louisiana. A bayou can be either a slow-moving stream or river in a flat landscape or a marshy area.

3. A term commonly used at the time to refer to African Americans. It is now considered offensive and is no longer acceptable; the term "negress," used later in the story to refer to Aunt Dicey, was frequently used to refer to a female African American. Slavery was officially abolished in 1865, but many African Americans continued out of necessity to work as servants for the White people who had formerly enslaved them.

4. Likely the title of a local newspaper.
5. Underneath.
6. While sometimes used among African Americans to refer to other Black people, in both the past and the present this term was and is usually intended to be derogatory and hurtful when used by non-Black people; it is thus deeply offensive and should not be used.
7. "Bonjour," or, in English, "Hello" (French).
8. Like that (French).
9. A narrow canoe created from a hollowed-out tree.
10. Immersion underwater.
11. Even though Evariste and Martinette are Acadians and thus, by the standards of that time and place, "White," their sitting at the same table with upper-class White people would have been a severe violation of the region's social norms; Wilkins is, as previously indicated in Martinette's conversation with Aunt Dicey, the African American "dining-room boy" for the Hallets, and he resents having to serve two Acadians who would not usually be regarded as much higher in the social order than African Americans—who themselves would never be invited to sit at a table with Creoles.

KATE M. CLEARY

(1863–1905)

Kate McPhelim was born to Irish parents in Canada in 1863 and came with them to the United States in 1879, eventually settling in Chicago. There, she met Irish immigrant Michael Cleary and married him in 1884. Just one month later they left the burgeoning metropolis of Chicago for the tiny frontier town of Hubbell, Nebraska, where Michael had established a lumber and coal business. That same year Kate, having already successfully placed a number of her short pieces in various publications, published her first novel, *Lady of Lynhurst*. For many years after, she ceased writing and instead focused on fulfilling the traditional duties of a nineteenth-century wife and mother. Her bucolic, happy life in Hubbell took a turn for the worse in 1892, however, when both her husband and small baby experienced severe health problems. Cleary returned to writing as a way to support her family, and she experienced substantial success, selling numerous stories to national magazines, newspaper syndicates, and the *Chicago Tribune*, where her brother Edward was an editor. Many of these were formulaic, humorous pieces about life in Nebraska and Chicago, but she was also able to publish some excellent, more realistic pieces that reflected Cleary's own difficult life experiences from 1892 onward. These challenges included severe financial difficulties, multiple family health crises, the deaths of two of her six children, and her own addiction to the painkiller morphine. A number of these fictions also offered critiques of the prevailing Victorian gender standards and roles by portraying women standing up to men and, similar to Hamlin Garland, by highlighting how difficult farm life could be for women.

Due to her husband's failed business ventures in Hubbell, Cleary returned to Chicago with her family in 1898. There, she continued to write and publish a great number of short stories, yet she was frequently worn down from overwork and relied heavily on morphine and alcohol to cope with her difficult life. In 1903 she was admitted to a hospital for the insane in Elgin, Illinois, where she stayed for almost four months; when the opportunity came for her to be released on probation, her husband refused to sign the papers taking responsibility for her welfare. Fortunately for Cleary, however, her writer friend Elia Peattie, whom she had befriended in Nebraska, signed the release papers and welcomed her into her family's home for three months. Two years later Michael Cleary tried to have Kate declared insane, but a panel of judges ruled she was not, and she was released to live on her own. Weakened by all her struggles, though, Cleary died not long afterwards while her husband and some of her children were visiting her.

It is clear from the extremely high quality of Cleary's best short stories, among them "Feet of Clay" (1893), "Told on a Prairie Schooner" (1893), "The Rebellion of Mrs. McLelland" (1899), and "The Stepmother" (1901), that had she not been burdened with family demands and consequently died at such a young age (forty-one), she likely would have developed into one of the Midwest's premier authors of this period, possibly rivaling her fellow Nebraskan and contemporary Willa Cather. However, because Cleary was forced to produce fictions of a certain type, and at a high rate of speed, in order to support her family, she was unable to write a greater number of the types of works that would have brought her more critical acclaim. In addition, because no collection of her short stories appeared in print until 1958 (*The Nebraska of Kate McPhelim Cleary*, a vanity press edition edited by her eldest son), for a long time critics and academics had no access to her work. Tragically, her only opportunity to publish such a collection came in 1905, when the prestigious Boston firm of Houghton, Mifflin, entered into negotiations with her to produce a short story collection; such negotiations, though, came to a halt with her death, and no book was ever published.

In the 1990s, scholar Susanne K. George carried out extensive research on Cleary and brought a number of her best works to light in *Kate M. Cleary: A Literary Biography with Selected Works* (1997). Among these is "Feet of Clay," which originally appeared in *Belford's Monthly Magazine* in April 1893; it is a gripping narrative of what hard work, strict gender expectations, and extreme isolation on the prairie could do to a farmer's wife.

FEET OF CLAY (1893)

Sometimes it seemed to her that she could endure everything save the silence. That was terrible. Days when Barret was too far in the corn for the rattle of the machine he drove to reach her, she could feel the silence settling down upon her like a heavy cloud. Then, if she were washing the dishes, she used to clatter them needlessly to make some sound. But all that was before she began to hear the voices of the corn. Perhaps she would not have dreaded the silence and isolation so much if she were a happy woman. There is little woman cannot bear if she has the kind of thoughts in her heart which make her smile unconsciously. But one who has lost interest in the present, hope in the future, and dares not look into the past lest the old delights mock and sting, does not smile when alone.

The worst of it was that she had brought it on herself. Young, delicate, cultured, the only child of wealthy parents who adored her, was Margaret Dare when she married Barret Landroth. She had been brought up in such a hothouse atmosphere of luxury, had been such a gay girl[1] always, and so fond of balls and theaters and parties that her friends heard with incredulity the announcement that she was to marry a Western farmer, and live her life with him on a Kansas prairie. She had met him at the house of a mutual acquaintance. That he was impressed from the first was evident. He was thirty-five then, tall and largely built, with a heavy, regular-featured face, pale blue eyes, and reddish hair and mustache. He did not possess the manners of the men she was accustomed to meeting. He lacked their repose, their subtle deference, their habitual courtesy. Recognizing this, the infatuation which controlled her found in it cause for admiration. For the superficial defects she accredited him with unrevealed perfections. "Unpolished," she admitted, "but profoundly truthful; awkward, but honest to the heart's core!"

It was with a gentle contempt she listened to the protests of those privileged to advise her. How petty must be their ideals, how restricted and conventional the confines of their affections! The attractions of which they spoke, the material comforts, the social pleasures, even the intellectual and artistic stimulus which one finds only in cities, became minimized when weighed in the balance with the devotion of a true heart. Here was the sacrificial spirit of youth which is glad to make surrender of things dear. To the man she loved she gave the devotion of a perfect wife, which embodies triply the tenderness of a mother, the passion of a mistress, and the reverence of a child. It was a chill, gray November afternoon when the train which had borne her westward on her bridal journey slacked speed in the little Kansan town, south of which Landroth's farm was situated. It was a raw, new, straggling settlement, lacking all that was picturesque, even in suggestion. North of the trim, red-roofed station-house the brown prairies melted into a sullen sky. South of the track lay the town, about twenty houses huddled on the sunburned, withered grass. Some of the buildings had been moved from a decaying Bohemian village, others were in process of erection. There was a livery-barn, and a lumber-yard also—at least lumber was piled on an unfenced bit of ground, and a rough box of a shed did duty for an office. "Better wait inside till I get a team, Margaret," Landroth advised, and strode away. But she did not go into the hot, stuffy waiting-room. She stood on the platform, where he had left her, and looked up the one deserted street, where the mud was axle-deep. Involuntarily she shuddered at the desolate stagnation of the place. Far in the west were bluffs, curving with refreshing boldness against the amethystine sky, but south—and there her home lay—were level plains, blank, boundless and unbroken. A skurrying wind, that peculiar wind with a wail in it, which springs up in the west at sundown, came rioting along, tore an auction poster from the boarded wall of the depot, and blew backward the skirt of her soft cloth gown. Two men, plodding by, looked at her with the stolid curiosity of cattle in their eyes—no more, no less. They were not impressed by her gentle beauty, by the elegance which was the appropriateness of her attire, nor by the distinction of her air; still they were duly conscious of her aloofness from the women they knew intimately.

"From Back East, I reckon," grunted one.

"Reckon so," indifferently assented the other.

Landroth drove up, and, getting down, assisted his wife into the buggy. When they were well out on the darkening road, with the wind that was like the wind of the sea, blowing from off interminable stretches in their faces, a kind of wild content came to her. She would be so happy here with Barret. Having him she had all. The weird glamour of the hour, the strangeness of the scene, the dear, protecting presence beside her, all thrilled her with delicious enthusiasm. She could have cried out with him who felt the fierce rapture of the "Last Ride": "Who knows but the world may end to-night?"[2] Long hedges, like black, wavy ribbons, went running by; ragged bushes that skirted the creek; silent and un-lighted farmhouses; little, dull, purplish pools, dimly discernible; "bunches" of cattle, motionless, as if cut from granite; and now and then a light in the window, more brilliant than the distant stars; fields, where the stacked cornstalks looked like huddled dwarfs; and, over all, that brooding sky closing down on the plains, until only that cold, strong, surging wind seemed to keep earth and sky asunder.

They had been driving for more than an hour when she became aware that they had left the road, and that the wheels of the buggy were crunching over the rough prairie. A square house, uncompromisingly bare of porches or bay-windows, loomed up before them. Landroth lifted her out.

"Welcome home, my Margaret!" he said softly.

Tired and dazed as she was, the loverly words thrilled her with an exquisite sense of satisfaction. She could feel her cheeks grow hot in the dark. She slipped her hand under his arm, and they went to the house together. To her surprise he led her by an uneven path, around to the rear of the building.

"Mother doesn't use the parlor often," he explained.

He pushed open the back door. Margaret found herself in a large, low-ceilinged kitchen. The stove glistened like a black mirror. The table, covered with a red-checked table-cloth, was already set for the morning meal. Near the door hung a cracked looking-glass, and under it, on a backless chair, was a tin basin and a piece of soap. A woman came from an inner room at the sound of the opening door. She was gowned in an ill-fitting black-and-white print, which re-vealed all the angles of her spare and slightly-stooped form. Her face reminded

Margaret of those grotesque images the Chinese cut from ivory. It was thin, of a pale yellow, and covered from brow to chin with a spider web of minute wrinkles. Her eyes were black and piercing.

"Oh," she ejaculated, addressing Barret, "you've got back!"

"This is my wife, mother," Landroth said.

She extended a bony hand and gave a quick shake to the slim, gloved fingers, but vouchsafed no word of greeting to the stranger. Instead she turned to her son:

"T'was a bad time of the year for you to be away so long. The men that's been huskin' have needed some one to drive them. They're a shiftless set. Most hard work they do is at meal times."

Landroth had never seen "The Lady of Lyons." On his rare visits to the city he used to take in the cycloramas and the burlesque shows. He had never heard of Pauline Deschapelles.[3] But the similarity of their positions struck Margaret. But Pauline had been deceived; she had not. When she married Barret Landroth, she knew she was not marrying a man of wealth, of position, not even of common culture. Still she had loved him for himself, and had been quite willing his life should be her life—only, she had not exactly comprehended what his life was.

"It is right," she told herself silently over and over. "This indifference of manner is like the snow that covers mountains in which fire smolders; there is a volcano of affection under it. I have been accustomed to color, to intensity. I am selfish and hypercritical."

So she strove; so she dissimulated. Solecisms[4] which startled her she affected to regard as eminently natural and proper. She permitted no brusquerie of speech or action to astonish her. When her mother-in-law declared she must get print dresses "to save washin'," she obediently consented. The first day she sat down to the dinner of coarsely-cooked food, at which the huskers gathered. Her husband watched her furtively. With an indrawn breath of relief he noticed that she did not court attention by the manner of one unaccustomed to such fare or surroundings. She would make a good farmer's wife when broken in. He had not made a mistake. Singularly enough, it was not borne in upon his consciousness that she might have made one.

The scant knowledge of life which was hers had come to her through books. She had read how the affections of men were alienated by fault-finding on the part of their wives. She had also read pathetic stories of old people who were thrust out of the homes and hearts of their children by those whom marriage had brought into propinquity with them. In her heart she vowed she would endure any annoyance in silence rather than be the aggressor in domestic disturbance. There was a good deal to endure. Much of it, while existing, was not tangible. There were slights she could not openly resent, did she desire to do so.

The winter set in bleak and bitter. Margaret had imagined she would be glad when the husking was over, and the men for whom such incessant frying of pork and baking of pies was in progress had departed. But the sweet sanctity of isolation she had seen from afar proved to be but a mere taunting mirage, for Barret's mother seemed to be omnipresent. The young wife likened her sometimes to a malevolent old fairy who never slept. Always alert were those sharp black eyes of hers; always curved in a sneering smile her thin white lips. She was not to be won over or conciliated. In Barret's presence she was suavity itself to Margaret; only when he had gone back to the endless labor stock and granaries entailed did she vent her spleen and jealousy in smooth, purring words of insult. With a heroism there was no one to appreciate, Margaret kept dumb under the fire; she had given up venturing protest or denial. The few times she had dared to offer either, she had been confronted with the lachrymose reproach: "That is right! Make me the victim of your temper. I am only a helpless old woman. If Barret knew! He would never permit me to be abused."

One day a package of magazines came for Margaret. A neighbor who had called for her mail at the office handed them in as he passed. The dishes were washed, the cream skimmed, the rooms set in order, so she felt free to enjoy her treasure. A sibilant voice sounded in her ear.

"Wasting your time, of course. I thought perhaps you'd help me a little."

Margaret dropped her books guiltily and sprang to her feet.

"I shall, gladly," she assented with eagerness. "What can I do?"

"Put them away first," commanded Mrs. Landroth, pointing to the magazines and speaking much as she might have spoken to a disorderly child. Margaret obeyed. Then she followed the old woman into the kitchen. The back door stood ajar. Pointing to it, Mrs. Landroth handed her a tin pan.

"Go to the shed. They're stickin' hogs[5] for winter picklin'. Hold this pan after they hang 'em up, and get it full of blood to make black sausage."[6]

Margaret was not obtuse, but for a couple of minutes she actually failed to comprehend the command. Suddenly she dropped the pan with a clatter. She grew taller, whiter. All the lightnings of an angry heaven blazed in the stormy eyes she turned on her tormenter.

"I!" she panted hoarsely. "I!" In a lower voice she declared: "I would—will die first!"

And she went back to her magazines.

That evening, while the three were seated at supper, the elder woman made her antagonism openly manifest.

"You must look out for a housekeeper, my son," she began. "The work is too heavy for me."

"Too much?" glancing up stupidly. "Now? When you have Margaret to help you?"

"Margaret? Oh, she is a lady! She refused to help me to-day."

"Impossible!" And he looked angrily toward his wife. She did not speak; the meal was finished in silence. After that Margaret knew she need no longer look to her husband for faith or sympathy. Like the gourd of the prophet,[7] the seed of disunion grew. There was no outbreak, no open warfare, but there was the awful, creeping paralysis of estrangement, the grinning ghastliness of disillusion.

Then the baby came. That was a day of horror never to be blotted out. Barret was in the pasture, not a quarter of a mile off, and his mother refused to send for him.

"He's gettin' in the last of that late hay," she grimly responded to every agonized appeal. "He can't be put about for whimsies."

So the supreme crisis of a woman's life found Margaret exiled and practically alone.

She got around after awhile—not nearly so soon as Mrs. Landroth urged. Barret took a deal of interest in his daughter. Margaret found a wan kind of pleasure in that. Only once did a single soldering ember of spirit flare up in a fierce flame. That was when Barret suggested calling the child Rebecca, after his mother.

"No," she answered, in a tense voice. "After any one else. Never after her!"

He stood aghast. He had always feared his mother too much to condemn her even in thought. From that moment on he took less notice of the child. He had gradually omitted toward Margaret all tenderness. He now failed in common civility. He even began to echo his mother's carping remarks. Once he said a farmer had no right to marry a woman who considered herself above him.

Margaret had lived on the Kansas farm, proudly deaf to all voices from her old home, for two long years. Occasionally women came in "to set awhile." Some of them had young babies; but they all looked so sallow, so haggard, so old. They had a hunted look in their eyes, the look that is begotten of crushing, monotonous work, and the possible failure of crops. Their hair was almost always dry and scanty; their teeth out, or dark with decay. The knobby, nail-worn hands, the petty tyranny shown to the children, the fretful complaints as to their unaccomplished labor, the paltriness of their ambitions, the treadmill whirl of their mildly-malicious gossip all hurt her with a queer, prescient pang of pain.

"My God!" she used to murmur passionately to herself, "shall I grow to be like those women? Oh, my God!" For she felt the hideous conviction crawling up on her that she would be as one of these. The knowledge forced itself in upon her one day when she found herself laughing aloud at a tale of vicious slander. She was fairly startled. She formed a desperate resolve; she would not have all the energy, vitality, individuality, all love for the lofty and the beautiful, filched from her, stamped out of her! She must keep them for her child. She went straight to Barret. She was quite calm, but very pale.

"Let me go home awhile," she pleaded. "I—I am not well."

He turned and looked at her. Her slender figure, gowned in gingham, was outlined against the young greenness of the osage-orange hedge. Her sun-bonnet had fallen back on her neck; her hands were clasped. He had just learned his latest shipment of steers had brought a poor price. He was not in the mood to be besought.

"You look well enough," he declared. "Wait awhile. My mother hasn't been off this farm for twenty years." And he walked away.

That night she found herself talking aloud, repeating his words over and over. A heavy fall interrupted her. She left the cradle, and ran up the steep stairway to

the room of her mother-in-law. Prone on the floor lay a stark form. With a great
effort Margaret lifted it, bore it to the bed.

"No—no!" came the querulous protest. "The chair. I'm—all right. Don't
try—to put me to—bed. Don't make me—out sick—when—I ain't!"

Margaret fled downstairs.

"Barret!" she screamed. "Barret!"

He came running in. They hastened upstairs. The old woman sat straight up
in her chair; her stiff fingers were clenched convulsively; her thin gray hair straggled over her ashy countenance; the glazed eyes were wide open. She was dead.

When Margaret had the house to herself she began to think she could live,
to a certain extent, her own life after all. She did her best—but vainly. From
downright indifference Barret passed to a less endurable mood, that of facetious
brutality. He expected the service of a slave, not the dutiful homage of a wife. He
spoke continually of how other men prospered—men whose wives worked and
saved. He became controlled by a penury so extreme, he denied, as unattainable,
many mere necessaries of life. And yet people on market days said to Margaret:
"A fine man, yours—smart, my! He'll make his mark. There ain't many as doubts
he kin get to the Legislatur' ef he wants to."

Mrs. Landroth had been dead more than a year, and life had rolled on and on
in the same unbroken routine. Season succeeded season, and, working or tossing, too tired to sleep, Margaret kept her finger upon the pulse of nature. This
cold meant hail, this cloud foreboded rain, the droop of this flower presaged
lightning, the shrill cry of that bird was a prelude to winter. The maddening
monotony of it all! Then it was that she first began to dread the silence, began to
think she could bear anything rather than that.

It was not so bad when the child was around, although she was a quiet little girl
at all times. It was in the hours of early morning, in the afternoon while the baby
slept, chiefly in the night. Many a day Margaret stood at the door and stared straight
ahead. Corn, corn, corn! Corn, short and green in spring, higher and greener in
summer, still higher and yellow in fall. Springing, growing, and attacked. Nothing
but corn and that low-lying sky. A fear of it came upon her. She felt that she was
hemmed in by corn, prisoned by it. Sometimes it seemed an impenetrable forest
that shut her in, again a tawny, turbulent ocean, through which she could not battle.

When little Lillian was three years old a letter came to Margaret. Enclosed
was a check for five hundred dollars. She made it payable to Barret. She had
never valued money till now. Now she prized it as a possible means of escape.
Not of escape in the actual, outer world. She could not bear that those who had
known her therein should look with pity upon her, but as a final hope of losing
sight and sound of corn. For, since its terrible voices had begun to haunt her, she
wondered why she had ever hated the silence. A few days after the receipt of her
letter she spoke to Barret concerning it. He had just come from town, and was
pulling off his wet boots by the kitchen stove.

"Barret, I wish to get a piano out of that money, and some books. I fancy I
would not feel as—as I do, if I had those."

"A piano—books!" he repeated with a harsh laugh. "If you keep the calves fed and the soap made, you won't have time to fool away on such things. When my mother got an hour to herself she used to sew rags again the spring house-cleaning.[8] Besides, I paid off the mortgage on the new pasture with half that money, and made a payment on a thrasher with the other half. Don't," he said irritably, "look as if you'd seen a ghost!" And he flung his boots behind the store.

The following week the thrashers[9] were at the house. She had a woman to help her cook for them, but still the work was savagely hard. More frequently now she found herself talking aloud, always repeating some senseless words. She got in the habit of putting up her hand to cover her mouth, there was such a spasmodic twitching at one corner.

"I wish you'd brush my clothes, Margaret," Barret said one night. "I'm going to the county-seat to-morrow to pay my taxes." She did as bidden. The clothes were the ones he had worn on his wedding-day, and which he had only since donned when he went from home. As she brushed the coat she felt something hard in the inner pocket. She drew out a photograph. A young, radiant face, with soft curls clustering around the forehead, and lovely, eager eyes, smiled up at her. She was still looking at it when Barret came in. He glanced over her shoulder.

"Lord!" he exclaimed. "Have I been carrying that around all this time? You were a good-looking girl, Margaret!"

Later the child found the picture where she had laid it down, and brought it to her.

"Who's ze pitty lady?" she cooed.

"That is mamma," Margaret answered.

"Oh, zis lady is pitty!" she averred, with charming cruelty.

Margaret took the picture from the child, looked at it again for several minutes, and then, still with it in her hand, walked to the glass. The face that glared back at her was of a chalky hue. The features were sharpened. The hair, brushed straight back, was dull and rough. There were heavy, dark veins around the throat and temples. The mouth every few moments twitched nervously.

That night the voice of the corn roared louder than ever. It was like the surge of a hungry sea. There was something menacing in it. Ever nearer it sounded, and louder. Those frightful, relentless yellow waves! Were they closing in on her?

Shrieking, she sprang from her bed.

"What is the matter?" Barret cried.

"The corn!" she screamed, frantically. "Don't let it close in on me! Can't you hear what it is saying? 'Forever, ever, ever!'"

He leaped out of bed, caught her by the arm. The moonlight was streaming into the room.

"Margaret!" he gasped in fear.

Her eyes were quite vacant, but her mouth was smiling. "I—I must go down-stairs," she muttered. "There's the washing—and the soap-grease to be boiled, and the—the carpet rags, and"—

There were those who said when Margaret's people took her and the child home that it was too bad such trouble should have come upon so fine a man as Barret Landroth—a man who was almost certain to go to the Legislature. There had been nothing in her life to cause insanity. It must have been hereditary.

NOTES

1. Carefree and happy.
2. In the poem "The Last Ride Together" (1855), by English poet Robert Browning (1812–89), the male narrator begs his beloved to accompany him for one last ride and hopes that their futures will be together.
3. In "The Lady of Lyons; or, Love and Pride" (1838) by the English author and playwright Sir Edward Bulwer-Lytton (1803–73), the rejected male lovers of Pauline Deschapelles conspire to disguise a gardener's son as Prince of Como, whom Pauline subsequently falls in love with and marries; cycloramas and burlesque shows were popular forms of entertainment at this time.
4. An error in grammar or syntax.
5. To slaughter hogs.
6. Sausages consisting chiefly of animal blood but combined with some type of filler, such as meat, bread, cornmeal, oatmeal, barley, or onion.
7. In the Bible, God provides the prophet Jonah a vine that grows extremely quickly; the name of this plant has been mistranslated for centuries as a "gourd" (Jonah 4:6–11, King James Version).
8. To sew seemingly worthless scraps of fabric into larger cloths in anticipation of spring cleaning.
9. A person who beats harvested plants in order to separate the seeds from the stalks, or who operates a machine that performs this operation.

STEPHEN CRANE

(1871–1900)

Despite its brevity, the life of American author Stephen Crane was filled with adventure and accomplishment. Many biographies of Crane highlight the degree to which he embodied a "live fast, die young" ethos, and while he may have lived and written for only a short time, he left an important mark on American literature.

Born on November 1, 1871, in Newark, New Jersey, Crane was the youngest of fourteen children, only nine of whom survived infancy. His father, Jonathan Townley Crane, was a prominent Methodist minister and abolitionist who published writings arguing that popular leisure pursuits, such as drinking and dancing, corrupted young people. Crane's mother, Mary Helen Peck Crane, was also a church writer and temperance activist. Despite—or possibly because of—the strict religious environment of his youth, Crane possessed a rebellious streak and indulged in many of the activities his parents deemed inappropriate, including reading novels, playing baseball, drinking, and smoking.

Crane began composing fictional stories at a young age, and at sixteen he began to publish articles in the *New York Tribune*. In 1890, Crane briefly enrolled in Pennsylvania's Lafayette College before transferring to Syracuse University for the spring semester of 1891, during which time he demonstrated more passion for baseball than academics. During his one semester as a student at Syracuse, Crane served as a regular "stringer" for the *New York Tribune*, reporting on events both at the college and in the community. Crane was particularly drawn to the drama of court cases and crime. Crane likely began to write his first novella, *Maggie: A Girl of the Streets* (1893), while at Syracuse, but much of its content is based on material he gathered after he left Syracuse and moved to New York City in the summer of 1891.

In New York, Crane worked as a newspaper reporter and lived in the slums of New York's Lower East Side, in an area known as the Bowery, where he immersed himself in the local culture. There he met the types of poor people who would populate not only *Maggie*—which tells the story of a young girl's tragic descent into prostitution and the circumstances that ultimately lead to her death—but also many of his later writings, including "An Experiment in Misery." Now commonly identified as one of the most representative texts of literary Naturalism, *Maggie* had to be self-published in 1893 because of its controversial subject matter and language.

Crane's first popular and critical success as a fiction writer, however, came only with the serial publication of an adumbrated version of his Civil War novel *The Red Badge of Courage* in multiple newspapers across the country in December 1894 through the auspices of the Bacheller Syndicate. Soon thereafter the publishing firm of D. Appleton offered to publish Crane's complete text as a book, which proved extremely popular.

Following the publication and success of *The Red Badge of Courage* (1895), Crane secured his reputation as an author with a unique talent for writing about war. In late 1896 he accepted an assignment from the Bacheller Syndicate, this time to travel to Cuba and cover the anti-Spanish insurgency there. Unfortunately, his journey had barely begun when the ship sank and Crane was stranded at sea for a day and a half in a small dinghy before reaching Florida. Crane dutifully filed a news story about his harrowing experience, but the most important and long-lasting result was his short story "The Open Boat" (1897), which is often anthologized as a prime example of Naturalist fiction. Blocked from returning to Cuba in early 1897, Crane made arrangements with S. S. McClure's Associated Literary Press newspaper syndicate and William Randolph Hearst's *New York Journal* newspaper to cover the Greco-Turkish War. By April 1897 Crane and his common-law wife, Cora Stewart (still married to another man), had arrived in Greece. Within a month, however, the conflict ended and the two moved to England, where Crane would publish not only numerous serialized works but also his last two novels, *The Third Violet* (1897) and *Active Service* (1899), as well as a short story collection, *The Monster and Other Stories* (1899).

10 Cents a Copy

Kipling's New Poem, "The King"

$1.00 a Year

McCLURE'S MAGAZINE

NOVEMBER

PUBLISHED MONTHLY BY THE S. S. McCLURE CO., 141-155 E. 25TH STREET, NEW YORK CITY
45 Albemarle Street, London, W., Eng.   Copyright, 1899, by The S. S. McClure Co.   Entered at N. Y. Post-Office as Second-Class Mail Matter

Cover of *McClure's Magazine* (November 1899).

While living in England in a rented, run-down manor house near London named Brede Place, Crane drank heavily and kept irregular hours, not only at Brede Place but also during long stays in London and elsewhere. Crane and Stewart's lavish lifestyle led to a sharp deterioration of his economic situation, and in response he worked incessantly to write material that he could try to sell to various periodicals for ready cash.

Unfortunately, Crane's excessive drinking and overwork caused his already poor health—he had contracted malaria, yellow fever, and tuberculosis during his years living in slums and working as a war correspondent—to decline rapidly. In a desperate attempt to improve her husband's health, Stewart took Crane to a sanatorium in Badenweiler, Germany, in May 1900; however, it was too late, and he died from tuberculosis there in June 1900.

"An Experiment in Misery" has an interesting history. While working as a reporter for the *New York Press* newspaper in 1894, Crane dressed as a vagrant and spent the night in a cheap run-down hotel, often called a flophouse. He then related this experience in a story that blended elements of journalism and fiction and which appeared in the *Press* on April 22, 1894, under the flamboyant heading: "AN EXPERIMENT IN MISERY / An Evening, a Night and a Morning with Those Cast Out. / THE TRAMP LIVES LIKE A KING / But His Royalty, to the Novitiate, Has Drawbacks of Smells and Bugs. / LODGED WITH AN ASSASSIN / A Wonderfully Vivid Picture of a Strange Phase of New York Life, / Written for 'The Press' by the Author of 'Maggie.'" In this printing, Crane framed his story with two conversations between the young protagonist (presumably Crane) and an older friend, who reflect on the life of a tramp. Crane removed this frame, though, when he revised the story for inclusion in *The Open Boat and Other Tales of Adventure* (1898). Even though the latter version would appear to represent Crane's final authorial intention, we have chosen to reproduce the *New York Press* version—unknown except among the most dedicated Crane scholars—because of its fascinating frame and the way that this text is thus more deeply embedded in the context of its day.

*Readers should be aware that this story includes some language which, while commonly used during this time period, is no longer considered acceptable because of its offensive nature.

AN EXPERIMENT IN MISERY (1894)

Two men stood regarding a tramp.

"I wonder how he feels," said one, reflectively. "I suppose he is homeless, friendless, and has, at the most, only a few cents in his pocket. And if this is so, I wonder how he feels."

The other being the elder, spoke with an air of authoritative wisdom. "You can tell nothing of it unless you are in that condition yourself. It is idle to speculate about it from this distance."

"I suppose so," said the younger man, and then he added as from an inspiration: "I think I'll try it. Rags and tatters, you know, a couple of dimes, and hungry, too, if possible. Perhaps I could discover his point of view or something near it."

"Well, you might," said the other, and from those words begins this veracious narrative of an experiment in misery.

The youth went to the studio of an artist friend, who, from his store, rigged him out in an aged suit and a brown derby hat[1] that had been made long years before. And then the youth went forth to try to eat as the tramp may eat, and sleep as the wanderers sleep. It was late at night, and a fine rain was swirling softly down, covering the pavements with a bluish luster. He began a weary trudge toward the downtown places, where beds can be hired for coppers.[2] By the time he had reached City Hall Park he was so completely plastered with yells of "bum" and "hobo," and with various unholy epithets that small boys had applied to him at intervals that he was in a state of profound dejection, and looked searchingly for an outcast of high degree that the two might share miseries. But the lights threw a quivering glare over rows and circles of deserted benches that glistened damply, showing patches of wet sod behind them. It seemed that their usual freights of sorry humanity had fled on this night to better things. There were only squads of well dressed Brooklyn people, who swarmed toward the Bridge.[3]

[HE FINDS HIS FIELD.]

The young man loitered about for a time and then went shuffling off down Park Row. In the sudden descent in style of the dress of the crowd he felt relief, and as if he were at last in his own country. He began to see tatters that matched his tatters. In Chatham Square there were aimless men strewn in front of saloons and lodging houses, standing sadly, patiently, reminding one vaguely of the attitudes of chickens in a storm. He aligned himself with these men, and turned slowly to occupy himself with the flowing life of the great street.

Through the mists of the cold and storming night made an intensely blue haze, through which the gaslights in the windows of stores and saloons shone with a golden radiance. The street cars rumbled softly, as if going upon carpet stretched in the aisle made by the pillars of the elevated road. Two interminable processions of people went along the wet pavements, spattered with black mud that made each shoe leave a scar-like impression. The high buildings lurked a-back, shrouded in shadows. Down a side street there were mystic curtains of purple and black, on which lamps dully glittered like embroidered flowers.

A saloon stood with a voracious air on a corner. A sign leaning against the front of the doorpost announced: "Free hot soup to-night." The swing doors snapping to and fro like ravenous lips, made gratified smacks as the saloon gorged itself with plump men.

Caught by the delectable sign, the young man allowed himself to be swallowed. A bartender placed a schooner[4] of dark and portentous beer on the bar.

Its monumental form up-reared until the froth a-top was above the crown of the young man's brown derby.

[HE FINDS HIS SUPPER.]

"Soup over there, gents," said the bartender, affably. A little yellow man in rags and the youth grasped their schooners and went with speed toward a lunch counter, where a man with oily but imposing whiskers ladled genially from a kettle until he had furnished his two mendicants with a soup that was steaming hot, and in which there were little floating suggestions of chicken. The young man, sipping his broth, felt the cordiality expressed by the warmth of the mixture, and he beamed at the man with oily but imposing whiskers, who was presiding like a priest behind an altar. "Have some more, gents?" he inquired of the two sorry figures before him. The little yellow man accepted with a swift gesture, but the youth shook his head and went out, following a man whose wondrous seediness promised that he would have a knowledge of cheap lodging houses.

On the sidewalk he accosted the seedy man. "Say, do you know a cheap place t' sleep?"

The other hesitated for a time, gazing sideways. Finally he nodded in the direction of the street. "I sleep up there," he said, "when I've got th' price."

"How much?"

"Ten cents."

The young man shook his head dolefully. "That's too rich for me."

[ENTER THE ASSASSIN.]

At that moment there approached the two a reeling man in strange garments. His head was a fuddle of bushy hair and whiskers from which his eyes peered with a guilty slant. In a close scrutiny it was possible to distinguish the cruel lines of a mouth, which looked as if its lips had just closed with satisfaction over some tender and piteous morsel. He appeared like an assassin steeped in crimes performed awkwardly.

But at this time his voice was tuned to the coaxing key of an affectionate puppy. He looked at the men with wheedling eyes and began to sing a little melody for charity.

"Say, gents, can't yeh give a poor feller a couple of cents t' git a bed? I got five, an' I gits anudder two I gits me a bed. Now, on th' square, gents, can't yeh jest gimme two cents t' git a bed? Now, yeh know how a respecter'ble gentlem'n feels when he's down on his luck, an' I—"

The seedy man, staring with imperturbable countenance at a train which clattered overhead, interrupted in an expressionless voice: "Ah, go t' h—!"

But the youth spoke to the prayerful assassin in tones of astonishment and inquiry. "Say, you must be crazy! Why don't yeh strike somebody[5] that looks as if they had money?"

The assassin, tottering about on his uncertain legs, and at intervals brushing imaginary obstacles from before his nose, entered into a long explanation of the psychology of the situation. It was so profound that it was unintelligible.

When he had exhausted the subject, the young man said to him: "Let's see th' five cents."

The assassin wore an expression of drunken woe at this sentence, filled with suspicion of him. With a deeply pained air he began to fumble in his clothing, his red hands trembling. Presently he announced in a voice of bitter grief, as if he had been betrayed: "There's on'y four."

[HE FINDS HIS BED.]

"Four," said the young man thoughtfully. "Well, look-a-here, I'm a stranger here, an' if ye'll steer me to your cheap joint I'll find the other three."

The assassin's countenance became instantly radiant with joy. His whiskers quivered with the wealth of his alleged emotions. He seized the young man's hand in a transport of delight and friendliness.

"B'gawd," he cried, "if ye'll do that, b'gawd, I'd say yeh was a damned good fellow, I would, an' I'd remember yeh all m' life, I would, b'gawd, an' if I ever got a chance I'd return th' compliment"—he spoke with drunken dignity—"b'gawd, I'd treat yeh white,[6] I would, an' I'd allus remember yeh—"

The young man drew back, looking at the assassin coldly. "Oh, that's all right," he said. "You show me th' joint—that's all you've got t' do."

The assassin, gesticulating gratitude, led the young man along a dark street. Finally he stopped before a little dusty door. He raised his hand impressively. "Look-a here," he said, and there was a thrill of deep and ancient wisdom upon his face, "I've brought yeh here, an' that's my part, ain't it? If th' place don't suit yeh yeh needn't git mad at me, need yeh? There won't be no bad feelin', will there?"

"No," said the young man.

The assassin waved his arm tragically and led the march up the steep stairway. On the way the young man furnished the assassin with three pennies. At the top a man with benevolent spectacles looked at them through a hole in the board. He collected their money, wrote some names on a register, and speedily was leading the two men along a gloom shrouded corridor.

[A PLACE OF SMELLS.]

Shortly after the beginning of this journey the young man felt his liver turn white, for from the dark and secret places of the building there suddenly came to his nostrils strange and unspeakable odors that assailed him like malignant diseases with wings. They seemed to be from human bodies closely packed in dens; the exhalations from a hundred pairs of reeking lips; the fumes from a thousand bygone debauches;[7] the expression of a thousand present miseries.

A man, naked save for a little snuff colored[8] undershirt, was parading sleepily along the corridor. He rubbed his eyes, and, giving vent to a prodigious yawn, demanded to be told the time.

"Half past one."

The man yawned again. He opened a door, and for a moment his form was outlined against a black, opaque interior. To this door came the three men, and as it was again opened the unholy odors rushed out like released fiends, so that the young man was obliged to struggle as against an overpowering wind.

It was some time before the youth's eyes were good in the intense gloom within, but the man with benevolent spectacles led him skillfully, pausing but a moment to deposit the limp assassin upon a cot. He took the youth to a cot that lay tranquilly by the window, and, showing him a tall locker for clothes that stood near the head with the ominous air of a tombstone, left him.

[TO THE POLITE, HORRORS.]

The youth sat on his cot and peered about him. There was a gas jet in a distant part of the room, that burned a small flickering orange hued flame. It caused vast masses of tumbled shadows in all parts of the place, save where, immediately about it, there was a little gray haze. As the young man's eyes became used to the darkness he could see upon the cots that thickly littered the floor the forms of men sprawled out, lying in death-like silence or heaving and snoring with tremendous effort, like stabbed fish.

The youth locked his derby and his shoes in the mummy case[9] near him and then lay down with his old and familiar coat around his shoulders. A blanket he handled gingerly, drawing it over part of the coat. The cot was leather covered and cold as melting snow. The youth was obliged to shiver for some time on this affair, which was like a slab. Presently, however, his chill gave him peace, and during this period of leisure from it he turned his head to stare at his friend, the assassin, whom he could dimly discern where he lay sprawled on a cot in the abandon of a man filled with drink. He was snoring with incredible vigor. His wet hair and beard dimly glistened and his inflamed nose shone with subdued luster like a red light in a fog.

Within reach of the youth's hand was one who lay with yellow breast and shoulders bare to the cold drafts. One arm hung over the side of the cot and the fingers lay full length upon the wet cement floor of the room. Beneath the inky brows could be seen the eyes of the man exposed by the partly opened lids. To the youth it seemed that he and this corpse-like being were exchanging a prolonged stare and that the other threatened with his eyes. He drew back, watching his neighbor from the shadows of his blanket edge. The man did not move once through the night, but lay in this stillness as of death, like a body stretched out, expectant of the surgeon's knife.

[MEN LAY LIKE THE DEAD.]

And all through the room could be seen the tawny hues of naked flesh, limbs thrust into the darkness, projecting beyond the cots; up-reared knees; arms hanging, long and thin, over the cot edges. For the most part they were statuesque, carven, dead. With the curious lockers standing all about like tombstones there was a strange effect of a graveyard, where bodies were merely flung.

Yet occasionally could be seen limbs wildly tossing in fantastic, nightmare gestures, accompanied by guttural cries, grunts, oaths. And there was one fellow off in a gloomy corner, who in his dreams was oppressed by some frightful calamity, for of a sudden he began to utter long wails that went almost like yells from a hound, echoing wailfully and weird through this chill place of tombstones, where men lay like the dead.

The sound, in its high piercing beginnings that dwindled to final melancholy moans, expressed a red and grim tragedy of the unfathomable possibilities of the man's dreams. But to the youth these were not merely the shrieks of a vision pierced man. They were an utterance of the meaning of the room and its occupants. It was to him the protest of the wretch who feels the touch of the imperturbable granite wheels and who then cries with an impersonal eloquence, with a strength not from him, giving voice to the wail of a whole section, a class, a people. This, weaving into the young man's brain and mingling with his views of these vast and somber shadows that, like mighty black fingers curled around the naked bodies, made the young man so that he did not sleep, but lay carving biographies for these men from his meager experience. At times the fellow in the corner howled in a writhing agony of his imaginations.

[THEN MORNING CAME.]

Finally a long lance point of gray light shot through the dusty panes of the window. Without, the young man could see roofs drearily white in the dawning. The point of light yellowed and grew brighter, until the golden rays of the morning sun came in bravely and strong. They touched with radiant color the form of a small, fat man, who snored in stuttering fashion. His round and shiny bald head glowed suddenly with the valor of a decoration. He sat up, blinked at the sun, swore fretfully and pulled his blanket over the ornamental splendors of his head.

The youth contentedly watched this rout of the shadows before the bright spears of the sun and presently he slumbered. When he awoke he heard the voice of the assassin raised in valiant curses. Putting up his head he perceived his comrade seated on the side of the cot engaged in scratching his neck with long fingernails that rasped like files.

"Hully Jee dis is a new breed.[10] They've got can openers on their feet," he continued in a violent tirade.

The young man hastily unlocked his closet and took out his shoes and hat. As he sat on the side of the cot, lacing his shoes, he glanced about and saw that daylight had made the room comparatively commonplace and uninteresting. The men, whose faces seemed stolid, serene or absent, were engaged in dressing, while a great crackle of bantering conversation arose.

A few were parading in unconcerned nakedness. Here and there were men of brawn, whose skins shone clear and ruddy. They took splendid poses, standing massively, like chiefs. When they had dressed in their ungainly garments there

was an extraordinary change. They then showed bumps and deficiencies of all
kinds.

There were others who exhibited many deformities. Shoulders were slanting,
humped, pulled this way and pulled that way. And notable among these latter
men was the little fat man who had refused to allow his head to be glorified. His
pudgy form, builded like a pear, bustled to and fro, while he swore in fish-wife
fashion. It appeared that some article of his apparel had vanished.

The young man, attired speedily, and went to his friend, the assassin. At first
the latter looked dazed at the sight of the youth. This face seemed to be appealing to him through the cloud wastes of his memory. He scratched his neck and
reflected. At last he grinned, a broad smile gradually spreading until his countenance was a round illumination. "Hello, Willie," he cried cheerily.

"Hello," said the young man "Are yeh ready t' fly?"

"Sure." The assassin tied his shoe carefully with some twine and came ambling.

When he reached the street the young man experienced no sudden relief from
unholy atmospheres. He had forgotten all about them, and had been breathing
naturally and with no sensation of discomfort or distress.

He was thinking of these things as he walked along the street, when he was
suddenly startled by feeling the assassin's hand, trembling with excitement,
clutching his arm, and when the assassin spoke, his voice went into quavers from
a supreme agitation.

"I'll be hully, bloomin' blowed, if there wasn't a feller with a nightshirt on up
there in that joint!"

The youth was bewildered for a moment, but presently he turned to smile
indulgently at the assassin's humor.

"Oh, you're a d—liar," he merely said.

Whereupon the assassin began to gesture extravagantly and take oath by
strange gods. He frantically placed himself at the mercy of remarkable fates if
his tale were not true. "Yes, he did! I cross m' heart thousan' times!" he protested,
and at the time his eyes were large with amazement, his mouth wrinkled in unnatural glee. "Yessir! A nightshirt! A hully white nightshirt!"

"You lie!"

"No, sir! I hope ter die b'fore I kin git anudder ball[11] if there wasn't a jay wid
a hully, bloomin' white nightshirt!"

His face was filled with the infinite wonder of it. "A hully white nightshirt,"
he continually repeated.

The young man saw the dark entrance to a basement restaurant. There was a
sign which read, "No mystery about our hash," and there were other age stained
and world battered legends which told him that the place was within his means.
He stopped before it and spoke to the assassin: "I guess I'll git somethin' t' eat."

[BREAKFAST.]

At this the assassin, for some reason, appeared to be quite embarrassed. He
gazed at the seductive front of the eating place for a moment. Then he started
slowly up the street. "Well, goodby, Willie," he said, bravely.

For an instant the youth studied the departing figure. Then he called out, "Hol' on a minnet." As they came together he spoke in a certain fierce way, as if he feared that the other would think him to be weak. "Look-a here, if yeh wanta git some breakfas' I'll lend yeh three cents t' do it with. But say, look-a here, you've gota git out an' hustle. I ain't goin' t' support yeh, or I'll go broke b'fore night. I ain't no millionaire."

"I take me oath, Willie," said the assassin earnestly, "th' on'y thing I really needs is a ball. Me t'roat feels like a fryin' pan. But as I can't get a ball, why, th' next bes' thing is breakfast, an' if yeh do that for me, b'gawd, I'd say yeh was th' whitest lad[12] I ever see."

They spent a few moments in dexterous exchanges of phrases, in which they each protested that the other was, as the assassin had originally said, "respecter'ble gentlem'n." And they concluded with mutual assurances that they were the souls of intelligence and virtue. Then they went into the restaurant.

There was a long counter, dimly lighted from hidden sources. Two or three men in soiled white aprons rushed here and there.

[A RETROSPECT.]

The youth bought a bowl of coffee for two cents and a roll for one cent. The assassin purchased the same. The bowls were webbed with brown seams, and the tin spoons wore an air of having emerged from the first pyramid.[13] Upon them were black, moss-like encrustations of age, and they were bent and scarred from the attacks of long forgotten teeth. But over their repast the wanderers waxed warm and mellow. The assassin grew affable as the hot mixture went soothingly down his parched throat, and the young man felt courage flow in his veins.

Memories began to throng in on the assassin, and he brought forth long tales, intricate, incoherent, delivered with a chattering swiftness as from an old woman. "—great job out 'n Orange.[14] Boss keep yeh hustlin', though, all time. I was there three days, and then I went an' ask'im t' lend me a dollar. 'G-g-go ter the devil,' he says, an' I lose me job.

—"South no good. Damn niggers[15] work for twenty-five an' thirty cents a day. Run white man out. Good grub, though. Easy livin'.

—"Yas; useter work little in Toledo, raftin' logs.[16] Make two or three dollars er day in the spring. Lived high. Cold as ice, though, in the winter—

"I was raised in northern N'York. O-o-o-oh, yeh jest oughto live there. No beer ner whisky, though, 'way off in the woods. But all th' good hot grub yeh can eat. B'gawd, I hung around there long as I could till th' ol' man fired me. 'Git t'hell outa here, yeh wuthless skunk, git t'hell outa here, an' go die,' he ses. 'You're a hell of a father,' I ses, 'you are,' an' I quit 'im."

As they were passing from the dim eating place they encountered an old man who was trying to steal forth with a tiny package of food, but a tall man with an indomitable moustache stood dragon fashion, barring the way of escape. They heard the old man raise a plaintive protest. "Ah, you always want to know what I take out, and you never see that I usually bring a package in here from my place of business."

[THE LIFE OF A KING.]

As the wanderers trudged slowly along Park Row, the assassin began to expand and grow blithe. "B'gawd, we've been livin' like kings," he said, smacking appreciative lips.

"Look out, or we'll have t' pay fer it t' night," said the youth, with gloomy warning.

But the assassin refused to turn his gaze toward the future. He went with a limping step, into which he injected a suggestion of lamb-like gambols. His mouth was wreathed in a red grin.

In City Hall Park the two wanderers sat down in the little circle of benches sanctified by traditions of their class. They huddled in their old garments, slumbrously conscious of the march of the hours which for them had no meaning.

The people of the street hurrying hither and thither made a blend of black figures, changing, yet frieze-like. They walked in their good clothes as upon important missions, giving no gaze to the two wanderers seated upon the benches. They expressed to the young man his infinite distance from all that he valued. Social position, comfort, the pleasures of living were unconquerable kingdoms. He felt a sudden awe.

And in the background a multitude of buildings, of pitiless hues and sternly high, were to him emblematic of a nation forcing its regal head into the clouds, throwing no downward glances; in the sublimity of its aspirations ignoring the wretches who may flounder at its feet. The roar of the city in his ear was to him the confusion of strange tongues, babbling heedlessly; it was the clink of coin, the voice of the city's hopes, which were to him no hopes.

He confessed himself an outcast, and his eyes from under the lowered rim of his hat began to glance guiltily, wearing the criminal expression that comes with certain convictions.

"Well," said the friend, "did you discover his point of view?"

"I don't know that I did," replied the young man; "but at any rate I think mine own has undergone a considerable alteration."

NOTES

1. A style of popular men's hats with a rounded crown and hard brim, usually made of wool felt.
2. Pennies, which at that time were made of copper.
3. This story takes place on the Lower East Side of Manhattan, which is connected to another New York City borough, Brooklyn, by the Brooklyn Bridge.
4. A large beer glass.
5. To approach a person and ask for something.
6. This racist expression was used by White people to mean "to treat someone fairly or honorably"; it incorrectly insinuates that people of other races would not treat him as kindly as a White person would.

7. Periods of excessive indulgence in sensual pleasures, including eating, drinking, and sex.
8. Dark yellowish brown.
9. In ancient Egypt, mummy cases were used to contain dead bodies; here it is slang for a storage locker.
10. Vernacular for the exclamation "Holy Jesus!" The "assassin" here is referring to particularly aggressive lice or bedbugs.
11. Shortened version of "ball of fire," nineteenth-century slang for a glass of brandy.
12. Similar to note 6 above. This incorrectly insinuates that only someone who is White will treat people honestly.
13. Pyramids are large edifices constructed in ancient Egypt thousands of years ago to contain the remains—and often belongings—of royal family members.
14. The city of Orange, New Jersey, is located approximately seventeen miles west of Lower Manhattan, where this story takes place.
15. An extremely offensive term sometimes used by non-Black people to refer to Black people. While sometimes used among Black people to refer to other Black people, in both the past and the present this term was and is usually intended to be derogatory and hurtful when used by non-Black people; it is thus deeply offensive and should not be used.
16. A city in Ohio. "Raftin' logs" involved helping guide large trees to float down a river to a mill, where they could be transformed into lumber or paper.

REBECCA HARDING DAVIS

(1831–1910)

Rebecca Harding was born on June 24, 1831, in Washington, Pennsylvania; in 1836 her family moved to the nearby industrial city of Wheeling, which at that time was still part of the state of Virginia. In 1848 she graduated with honors from the Washington Female Seminary, a Presbyterian school for women, and subsequently she worked as a reporter for the *Wheeling Intelligencer* newspaper, carrying out duties that at that time were quite unusual for a woman.

Davis's most well-known work, her novella *Life in the Iron Mills; or, The Korl Woman*, appeared anonymously in the *Atlantic Monthly* in April 1861. Heavily influenced by what she had witnessed as a newspaper reporter in Wheeling, it was widely acclaimed and subsequently commended by literary figures such as Louisa May Alcott, Emily Dickinson, Ralph Waldo Emerson, and Nathaniel Hawthorne. Not long after the publication of her excellent full-length novel *Margret Howth: A Story of To-Day* (1862), she married L. Clarke Davis in 1863 and the next year gave birth to a son, Richard Harding Davis, whose celebrity as a writer and journalist would eclipse his mother's during the later years of her life; Davis also had two other children. Due to her husband's lack of success as a lawyer, Davis was forced to focus on writing popular novels that would earn

ready income, as well as to engage in extensive editorial work, including serving
as a contributing editor to the *New York Tribune* from 1869 to 1889. Her later
book *Silhouettes of American Life* (1892) found some popularity, but it was her last.
Davis died at her son's home in Mount Kisco, New York, in 1910 at the age of
seventy-nine.

After Davis's death, all of her work fell into relative obscurity for many years.
However, thanks to the ardent advocacy of writer and activist Tillie Olsen
(1912–2007), the Feminist Press republished *Life in the Iron Mills* in 1972 and
thereby brought this pioneering woman author to the attention of modern
readers and scholars. Researchers have subsequently discovered many excellent
works, including a great number that examine the conflict women faced at the
time between commitments to their families, themselves, and the wider world;
one of these is "A Day with Doctor Sarah," which originally appeared in *Harper's
Monthly* in 1878.

*Readers should be aware that this story includes some language which, while
commonly used during this time period, is no longer considered acceptable because of its offensive nature.

A DAY WITH DOCTOR SARAH (1878)

A dozen ladies were taking luncheon with Mrs. Harry Epps, of Murray Hill.[1]
That little matron's luncheons are always ideal woman's parties. This especial
morning, for example.

There was plenty of space and sunshine in the pretty pale-tinted rooms. No
great pictures nor distracting array of bric-à-brac. Nobody wanted to climb into
regions of high art, or to admire—the day was too warm. There were flowers instead, flowers everywhere; a vine waving in at the bay-window. From the
other windows you could hear the rustle of the trees of Central Park, and catch
glimpses of slopes of grass there, of a clump of dark cedars at the base of a
sunny hill, of a hedge of wistaria—a mass of snaky black arms holding up purple blooms.

Inside there was a clear feminine softness in the very atmosphere; the dishes
on the table were feebly sweetish in flavor, and so was the talk. There was much
good feeling and culture shown in the conversation of these delicate, low-voiced
women; but an idea, naked and freshly born into the world, would have been as
out of place if dragged into sight at Mrs. Epps's luncheon table as a man, or a
greasy joint, or the Archangel Michael with his flaming sword.[2]

At least that was Doctor Sarah Coyt's opinion as she sat in moody silence, listening to the soft ripple of talk about her. If there was one thing of which Doctor
Sarah had a full supply, it was ideas. She kept a stock of them, as David did of
pebbles, and was perpetually slinging them at the head of one Goliath of custom
or another.[3] The aged giants were hard to kill; indeed, her best friends hinted that
her pebbles were only mud. But she fired them with desperate courage—there
was no doubt of that. She had fought her way into her profession, and out of the

Christian Church, and now she had clinched with Law, Religion, and Society in a hand-to-hand fight because of their treatment of women.

When Maria Epps introduced Doctor Coyt to her friends, they felt a shock as from an electric battery, and then they all roused into pleasurable excitement. It was such a treat to see this famous creature face to face!

"I do like this sort of thing, mamma," said Margaret Whyte to her mother. "You know I went to see Jem Mace as the prizefighter in *As You Like it*,[4] and this woman is accounted a kind of intellectual Heenan or Morrissey[5] by the newspapers. So nice in Maria to bring her!"

"It must be true that Maria Epps is going to join the woman's rights people," said her mother, thoughtfully. "She is always aiming at the *bizarre*. You remember she was the first to drive three ponies *à la Russe*[6] in the Park; and she went to those Moody meetings.[7] But I did *not* think she would carry her freaks as far as this."

But they were all courteous to Doctor Sarah. The courtesy, indeed, became oppressive. The very air grew clammy and heavy; all the ease, the pleasant repose, had faded out of it. The man, the greasy joint, were upon the stage now.

Visibly, Doctor Sarah was only a thin little woman in purple silk, sitting painfully erect on a straight-backed chair, her eyes glancing from one woman to another as though she were an officer, and they troops about to be drilled. Her features were delicate though worn, her eyes were sincere, sad brown eyes naturally, but they had learned a fierce trick of challenge in the rough-and-tumble fight which she had chosen to make of life. She had not said a word as yet except about her drive and the dust, but something in the flat, quivering nostril made every woman stand on guard. They felt that they were no longer Maria Epps's chance guests, lazily sipping chocolate; they were human beings—to be, to do, and to suffer.

Mrs. Epps took some pains to draw Doctor Sarah out, just as she had been careful that nobody should miss the flavor of the new salad. A novelty always gave *goût*[8] to a luncheon or dinner.

"This talk of pictures and music must seem horribly trivial to you, doctor," she said. "We are such mere butterflies, compared to a woman with a great object in life."

Doctor Sarah smiled good-humoredly. "I find great help in music," she said, "and I paint pictures—poor ones, but they help me too. Nature and art give me a better insight into the needs of my sex."

"Doctor Coyt's object, you know," explained Mrs. Epps, beaming around the table, "is to emancipate women."

There was a low murmur of polite assent. Mrs. Marmaduke Huff raised her eyeglasses, and courteously inspected Doctor Sarah with a gentle wonder, precisely as she had done the devil-fish that morning in the Aquarium.

"I have never had the pleasure of meeting a woman of your—your party before," said pretty Miss Purcell, softly.

"Oh, I saw several of them in London," cried Mrs. Hipple, who dressed hideously and drank beer since she came home, and fancied herself wholly English. "It is quite a very favorite *fad* with some very respectable people over there."

Then there was a sudden embarrassed pause, for every body expected Doctor Coyt to begin to defend her *fad*. But she sat silent, looking at a bit of honeysuckle which had crept in at the window. The angry red burned up into her thin cheek. Why should these people look at her as though she were the woman with the iron jaw, or some other such monster! No doubt they thought she had holes in her stockings, and went swaggering about at grog-shops. Why, her home was more womanly and fanciful than this, and she herself—

"I was in hopes, madam," said Miss Purcell, gently, "that you would give us some insight into your plans. It is we, after all, whom you should convert."

"I am no proselyter," said Doctor Sarah, with an acrid smile. She felt, as she often did, that the cause was hopeless. These frothy creatures to comprehend its great principles! Even suppose they had suffrage, what would they know of politics, of their fellow-men outside of a ball-room, or even of the money which they squandered?

In which the soured woman made the mistake which we all make when we judge of a chimpanzee, not being of chimpanzee blood. This Maria Epps, with the baby face, had manipulated half a dozen bills through Congress last session. There was not a party wire which she did not know how to work. She had matters in train now to get Epps a foreign mission. There was not a shrewder dealer in stocks in New York than the little blonde widow, Mrs. Huff, on the other side of the table. She had made a snug fortune for herself since Marmaduke died, and had given the boys a fair start in the tobacco trade. While, as for the classes outside of society, that good Fanny Purcell had spent more time last winter in the prisons and hospitals than Doctor Sarah had done in a lifetime. Yet they all wore dresses which framed them into pictures, and they haunted curio shops, cackling about old Satsuma ware.[9]

When they found that Doctor Sarah would not consent to be exhibited that afternoon, they went away one by one.

"Now, dear Maria," said Miss Purcell, as she kissed her hostess outside of the drawing-room door, "don't allow yourself to be entangled with that dreadful woman's set. Infidels, free-lovers—"

"Sarah Coyt is as chaste and clean-minded a woman as there is in New York," said Mrs. Epps, tartly. "Do have some charity with your religion, Fanny." Mrs. Huff hurried Fanny away.

"It is only one of Maria's political manœvres," she said, as she seated herself in her phaeton.[10] "Some of these woman's rights people have influence which she needs to gain Major Epps his appointment. The house will be overrun with radicals until she has secured her point, and then—Oh, we all know Maria!"

Mrs. Epps meanwhile went darting about, re-arranging the flowers, while Doctor Sarah, in her aggressive purple gown, sat bolt-upright, watching her with a quizzical smile. Maria reminded her of a dragon-fly, with its little flutter and shine and buzz, with its poisoned sting underneath, too. She was too hard on Maria, being, like most radicals, intolerant. The little woman inside of her finesse had a hot heart and hot temper; she was just now vehemently minded to side with Doctor Sarah, because the other women had snubbed her.

"I am glad they are all gone before the business meeting commenced," she said. "You asked all the leaders of the cause to be here this afternoon?"

"Yes."

"And you go down to Washington tonight to plead the cause before a Congressional committee? Alone?"

"Yes."

"Wouldn't it be better to have a deputation—for effect, now?"

"No," she said, sharply. "I am in earnest in this matter. Who else is? I've given up my profession for it. There's not another woman in the field who gives more than half her time and energy to the cause." She talked on as if to herself, her black brows contracted, her nostrils drawn in, her eyes fixed in a fierce abstraction. "There's always an obstacle. This one must make her living by writing slipshod novels or lecturing, that one has a baby, another a dead lover to mope over. Some of our leaders have taken up the cause to gain notoriety, and some for even meaner purposes," glaring suspiciously at Maria.

"Oh dear, yes, I suppose so," said that arch little hypocrite. "And you are going to meet the committee to-morrow?" her head on one side, scanning Doctor Sarah critically. "Might I hint?—your mind is so engrossed with high matters—but you must pay some attention to your costume. I know the chairman, Colonel Hoyt, very well. A pretty woman, well dressed, can do as she pleases with him. All men are influenced by dress when women are in question. You're not offended?—it's only poor little me. But I would suggest now black velvet with a hint of scarlet. So much depends on it! I would not spare the scarlet, either."

"Yes. I did not know how much depended on it," said Doctor Sarah, smiling. It was a bitter smile. *She* had not taken up the cause to make money or notoriety out of it. Many of her colleagues laughed and fought for it as for a jolly. She never laughed. She was in as desperate earnest as ever was Luther or Patrick Henry.[11] The newspapers all over the country jeered at her; her own sex held her off at arms-length: being a womanish woman, every jeer and snub had cut deep. But her sex, she had thought, were in as perilous a strait as was ever church or slave. She would give up every thing for them. And now that her cause was coming to a final issue, the verdict depended on a gown and its trimmings!

Two or three of the defenders of the cause had arrived by this time, and were talking apart with Maria; they held Doctor Sarah in a certain reverent awe. She never fraternized with the rest of her party, never accepted invitations to women's clubs, or posed at their public dinners.

"She is more like a wonderful machine than a human being," whispered one of her colleagues. "She makes no friends, leans on nobody, cares for nothing but the cause. Eh? Where is she going now?" For Doctor Sarah had suddenly crossed the room, and was stooping over a table. Mrs. Epps joined her, curiously. The doctor's long nervous fingers were fidgeting over a dish of mignonette[12] and sweet-peas.

"My old-fashioned 'bow-pot," said Maria, smiling.

"Yes; the perfume brought me over to it. I have not seen the flowers together for many years. I used to know a man who always kept a pot of them in his room."

"It was a man that arranged these—the Reverend Matthew Niles. A poor clergyman whom we knew in Maryland. I have him up for a week's vacation, and to fit him out with some new clothes. A good creature!"

A half-quizzical, half-sad smile flickered over Doctor Sarah's sharp face. "Matthew was arranging dishes of peas and mignonette still, eh? A beggar for Major Epps's old clothes? Sentimental, effeminate, boneless creature! And I used to tremble and turn cold when the pretty fellow spoke to me. I suppose that was the disease of love. Well, I had it pretty thoroughly then," she thought. She pulled out a pea and held it to her nose. Her blood ran cold now, and her fingers shook. She could have struck them, with a rage of contempt. Why, it was twenty years ago! She had cast the man off as her inferior when she was a girl, and she had been growing ever since. What subtle physical power had this limping creature still upon her which shook her in this way? "It is my youth—my youth, which takes hold of me in him," thought the doctor, stiffening herself in her purple silk; and marching over to the table, she called for the report of the meeting in Boston.

Surely she had tested this folly of marriage, and knew what it was worth! For the doctor, as the female pioneer of the cause in the West, had married Simon Coyt, the male pioneer, and it had not been a successful partnership. Mental qualities had balanced exactly; yet now that Simon was dead, his widow had not the slightest wish to meet him again any where on the other side of the grave.

Friend Eli Sowerby was on his feet. He was a practical, zealous little man. "We have made a wise choice in selecting Sarah Coyt to lay this matter before the committee. Yet it would be proper, in my judgement, if she would state briefly the arguments by which she will support it, that we may know precisely how she will represent us."

"I shall be guided by the suggestions of the moment in the bulk of my remarks," said the doctor; "but I can give you the principal points which I mean to make. It is only fair you should know to what I bind you."

She stood up, her hands resting on the back of a chair. She always spoke with fluency and decision, and she knew her arguments now by heart. Her thin body after a while began to glow with fiery exaltation. She rose on tiptoe, flourished her lean arms. At last the battle was at hand. She was going out alone to fight it. She was going out, like David, in the face of the conflicting hosts, her nation looking on. (Only David took his sling in the name of the Lord, and she unslung hers in the name of Sarah Coyt.)

"The American is just, reasonable in the hearing of every cause but this," she shouted, shrilly, wondering to herself at the same time what thumping noise that was in the hall, and why Mrs. Epps did not quiet it. "A woman," more vehemently, "is, first of all, a citizen. She loves, marries, by accident, but she is a citizen by inalienable right. It is her highest—"

The thumping was evidently made by a crutch. The doctor had the physician's instinct. Still gesticulating, her eye wandered to the door to see the cripple who should enter.

"She holds a legal place in the social body as a wife—a mother. But as a citizen—"

It was a child—a half-starved, shabbily dressed girl who came limping in.

"You render her—a nullity. Will nobody give that child a chair?"

The child tripped and fell headlong.

"All right," said Eli, picking her up. "Go on, doctor."

But the doctor already had the child in her lap, and was fingering her leg. "I was only about to say that the duties of a woman to the state far outweighed those which she owed as wife and mother, the latter being comparatively selfish, partial, and trivial. This child has had an attack of paraplegia,[13] and it never has been attended to."

"What has paraplegia to do with woman's suffrage?" said Eli.

"Whose child is she? There has been the grossest neglect," continued Doctor Sarah, sharply. She rose and walked out of the room in her usual decisive fashion, the little girl in her arms. She never had entire control of herself when she had a child in her arms. When she was in the dining-room she sat down, uncovered the withered limb, and patted the thin watchful face on her breast.

"What is your name, my dear?"

"Winny Niles."

"Matthew's daughter? She might have been my child," thought Doctor Sarah. It was not her old fancy for the silly young clergyman which brought that change slowly in the expression of her sharp features as she sat holding the girl. It was the remembrance of the dead-born baby which had never lain there. The breast had been full of milk then, but the dead little lips had never touched it, and the breast had shrivelled slowly and grown hard. As Sarah held the child closer to it she remembered how hard it was, as became the mongrel creature which the newspapers called an Advanced Female.

"Bah! They know nothing about us," she broke out, hugging Winny. "You poor, patient little soul, has nothing been done for you? What has your father been about?"

"Papa has only his salary, and he helps the poor a great deal," said Winny, with dignity.

"The poor! And his child looking in this fashion! Idiot!" muttered the doctor. "Well, your mother—where was she?"

"She is dead."

A sudden heat overspread Sarah's face; she was not sorry that this woman was dead, yet assuredly she did not wish to take her place. "How many are there of you?" she said, gently.

"Four—the two boys and baby and me."

"A baby and boys," thought Sarah. "And their father as fit to govern them as a mooncalf. Well, it's none of my business. That is your father's step coming up the stairs," she said, aloud, putting the child hurriedly down. A Venetian mirror hung near them. The little doctor glanced in it quickly; there was in it a wiry, muddy-skinned, high-nosed woman in purple silk. She saw suddenly beside her a vision of a shy, rose-tinted girl, watching a young divinity student as he arranged mignonette in a pot, and she laughed to herself with a keen sense of absurdity.

The door opened, and the Reverent Matthew stood on the threshold, plump, neat, precise, from the tip of his low shoes to the folds of his lawn cravat. Above the folds of the cravat was an apple-cheeked face, full of mild good humor and feeble obstinacy. Coming up the stairs, he had met the retiring delegates to the meeting, and Mrs. Epps, who told him who was with Winny. He heard the name of the great reformer with a little conscious chuckle.

"Doctor Sarah Coyt? Tut! tut! Now, would you believe it, Mrs. Epps, that that lady was an old flame of mine? Fact! A callow fancy—calf-love, you know; had not cut my wisdom-teeth. Sarah Fetridge, she was then. But I have watched her course since with interest, in consequence. With reprobation, of course, but still with interest. I never have any thing to do with that kind of people, but I should like to see her, I confess. *Doctor* Coyt, eh? Tut! tut! Poor creature!"

Then he opened the door, and looked at her with an amused, curious smile.

"Ah, Matthew, how do you do?" Doctor Sarah nodded curtly. "Haven't seen you for twenty years, I believe. We've both grown old, eh?" holding out her hand. It shook; she could not quiet it. His was cool and soft and limp. How well she remembered the touch of it!

"On the contrary," he said, civilly, "I don't know when I have seen a woman as well preserved."

She winced. She had seen hideous caricatures of herself in illustrated papers, and laughed; why should she care when this man of all men called her "well preserved?" But she did care. The hot tears of mortification came in spite of herself to her eyes. What did it mean? Why did she quake as if with ague since he came into the room? She had no regard, no respect, for the man; he was weak, ridiculous—

Mr. Niles, who had a shrewd knack of observing trifles, saw her agitation, and began to quake in his turn. She remembered the past. She would begin to hint at love's young dream. What if she should propose to him? There was nothing which these unsexed women would not do.

Mrs. Epps came in at the moment, and he turned to her with a sense of escape. Maria began to chatter, glancing curiously at them both. She fancied that the doctor's sudden interest in Winny was explained by her old love affair with her father. But Maria was wrong. Nature adapts women to be either wives or mothers; the best of one class are not often the best of the other. Doctor Sarah, with her thin lips and broad forehead, had very few of the qualities which go to make a happy marriage; but she was a born mother. Besides, she had reached the age when the motherly instinct is strongest in any woman. She might have married Matthew now, not from love, but a protective pity—to take care of him. It was the age when Maintenon married Louis, and Margaret Fuller the Italian lad.[14]

She sat silent while Mrs. Epps and the clergyman talked of the weather, and then rose abruptly and tied on her hat; then she came up to him. A mild alarm gathered in his face: he stood on guard.

"About this child of yours, Matthew? I'm a physician, you know."

"So I have understood," repressing a smile. She eyed him a moment in silence.

"Whether I deserve the name or not," she said, calmly, "matters nothing. I know enough to assure you that the child's disease is curable if taken in time, but that, if neglected much longer, she will be a helpless invalid for life. I have given up practice. But I should like to examine her again. I have taken a fancy to the little thing. Will you bring her to my house on Tuesday?"

Mr. Niles hesitated: he blushed, stammered. "Mrs.—Doctor—Coyt, I must consider the matter. I am mother and father both to the children, and, to be candid," gathering courage, "I doubt whether my wife would have risked Winny's case in the hands of so—so irregular a practitioner."

The doctor smiled—a smile which lasted a trifle too long. "I understand. I am sorry. I had taken a fancy to the child," she repeated. "Good-morning." Mrs. Epps followed her down the stairs.

"Don't mind it, doctor. He is a bigoted little man," she said, soothingly.

"Oh, it's nothing!" Doctor Sarah replied, hurriedly. "The objection really came from his wife. Many mothers used to object to me as a practitioner because I never had a child."

When Mr. Niles and his little girl took their seats in the train that evening to return to his parish in Maryland, he saw Doctor Sarah at the other end of the car. The Rev. Mr. Abbott, one of the leaders of his Church, came in, and, much to Matthew's surprise, stopped to speak to her, and did it with marked deference. He took a seat presently beside Matthew.

"That is Sarah Coyt," he whispered. "The little woman with the strong, fine face."

"Oh yes," said Mr. Niles, giggling, "I know. One of the strong-minded sisterhood."

"She has an exceptionally clear head for business, if that is what you mean," replied Mr. Abbott. "Rides the suffrage hobby hard, I believe; but childless women must have some such outlet. But she has amassed a considerable fortune by her business tact."

"Indeed?" said Matthew, gravely. He looked at Sarah with altered eyes. He had a respectful awe of any body who could make money.

The train rolled swiftly on. Doctor Sarah talked to Eli, who accompanied her as far as Philadelphia, of her argument on the sixteenth amendment,[15] but her eyes under her veil scanned deliberately her old lover and his child. How miserably poor they must be! Matthew did not wear now the new suit which Mrs. Epps had given him, and the child's clothes, her hair, her manner, all showed the lack of a mother's care.

"But it is no business of mine," she said.

"I leave the cause in thy hands," said Eli, parting with her at Philadelphia. "The eyes of the country will be upon thee tomorrow."

Evening was falling. The train rolled smoothly on in the soft twilight through the drowsy Maryland villages, with negroes[16] lounging in crowds about the stations, through rich pastures crimson with clover, and the old apple orchards; over long bridges, with stretches of gray lapping water beneath, and here and there a filmy sail moving dim and spectral in the faint shine of the rising moon.

Doctor Sarah pointed them out to Matthew, who now sat behind her. "Surely a ghost sits at the rudder yonder. It might be Charon[17] coming for us in his boat," she said.

Matthew smiled. Women were all silly and fantastic alike! But it was a kindly smile. The little man's affectionate heart smote him for his rudeness. She had meant kindness, and he had snubbed her brutally. She could not be a bad woman, when Mr. Abbott thought so well of her. He was glad when Winny went over and sat down by her. The lonely neglected child had understood the meaning in the woman's eyes. Presently she fell asleep, and Sarah put her arm about her and drew her down on to her shoulder. Then Matthew came over to them, and the doctor nodded and smiled and pointed out Charon and his boat. After all it was comfortable to be in accord with his old friend again. It was a friendly world! That little Mrs. Epps, now, was a good Christian soul, though she had her whims. Matthew, although conscious that he was the only entirely sane person in the world, felt to-night a sense of the beauty and good-will and happiness in it as never before. Usually his little mind was kept acerb and restless by the stringent want of money. But this evening he needed nothing. He looked at the nodding passengers in the silent car with a good-humored smile, and then at the sleeping valley flooded now with the light of the risen moon. It was the time when, if he had been at home, he would have had prayers with the children. He always had the feeling, as they knelt, that their mother was near them. "The Lord is our shepherd," said the devout little man, silently. "He leadeth us beside the still waters."[18]

The valley before him wavered giddily; there was a deafening roar, a hot rush of vapor, and then he was lying in the wet grass, the moon going out in darkness.

Doctor Sarah was unhurt. She gathered her legs and arms out of the mass of struggling bodies, and then, without a word, began to tug at Winny. The child did not move. Doctor Sarah presently caught at the arm of a burly fellow who was shouting out terrified oaths and questions.

"Try and compose yourself," she said, grimly. "We have run into a freight train, and half of us are killed. Take hold of this child. She is a cripple."

"Cripple? God help us! She's done for, then. I believe I'm not hurt," shaking himself. He drew Winny out with exceeding gentleness, and carried her to the field, followed by Sarah. "It's too late, ma'am," as he laid her down.

The doctor's practiced hands were at work. "No; she is alive, but her other leg is broken. What village is that?" For the people from the next station were crowding about the train.

It proved to be Matthew's parish. In half an hour he was carried to his own house by some of his parishioners, who seemed very fond of the little man. He was conscious, and the physicians could find no external injury.

"It is the steam which he has swallowed," said Doctor Sarah. "Bring the other children to him. It will be too late in a few minutes."

It was such a bare little house! Her keen eye took note of every mark of poverty even while she stirred a draught for the dying man. The village doctors were busy with Winny.

"It is a compound fracture," one of them said. "A case for months."

"Have these children no kinsfolk?" demanded Sarah.

"None. Poor Mr. Niles has scratched along as he could for them alone."

"And what is to become of them now, God only knows!" groaned a despondent fat mother in Israel,[19] who held the bandages.

"The Lord will provide. He always does," said the village doctor.

The boys, ugly, manly little fellows, were brought in, terrified and half asleep. Doctor Sarah carried the baby in its night-gown, and laid her on the bed beside Matthew. But he was scarcely conscious now. "Is that you, Dot?" he said. "Papa can't romp this morning." Presently he passed his hand gropingly over her face. "Poor little Dot! O God! who is there to take care of them?"

Sarah hesitated. She remembered the cause to which she had given her life. She had been in earnest when she gave it. Then she stooped and took his hand. "I am here, Matthew," she said, quietly.

The Congressional committee met, according to appointment, and waited in vain for Doctor Sarah.

Friend Eli Sowerby was naturally indignant when he heard of it. "There is always an obstacle in the way with women," he said. "But why must it always be a man or a baby?"

NOTES

1. A neighborhood of the Upper East Side of Manhattan, New York City.
2. In the Bible (Revelation 12:7–9), the archangel Michael defeats Satan in the guise of a dragon; while no "flaming sword" is mentioned here, many paintings and statues of Michael feature him wielding his sword.
3. In the Bible's book of 1 Samuel (chapter 17), the Israelite David defeats the Philistine giant Goliath by hitting him in the forehead with a rock from his slingshot; this story is frequently invoked as a reminder of how a much smaller, seemingly weaker person can defeat an ostensibly more powerful opponent.
4. Jem Mace (1831–1910) was an English professional boxer; in 1870 he won the title of world heavyweight champion and had a small role as a wrestler in William Shakespeare's *As You Like It* at Niblo's Garden, a theater on Broadway in New York City.
5. John Camel Heenan (1834–73) was an American bare-knuckle prize fighter; John Morrissey (1831–78) was an Irish American bare-knuckle prize fighter, politician, and mob boss.
6. To use a troika, or traditional Russian harness, in which three horses are abreast pulling a sleigh or carriage.
7. Christian evangelist meetings led by Dwight Moody (1837–99), founder of the Moody Church in Massachusetts.
8. Taste or flavor (French).
9. Fine pottery from the Japanese province of Satsuma.

10. A light horse-drawn carriage with one or two seats.
11. German monk and Protestant reformer Martin Luther (1483–1546); American founding father Patrick Henry (1736–99).
12. A reddish-brown variety of lettuce.
13. Paralysis.
14. "Maintenon" refers to French noblewoman Françoise d'Aubigné (1635–1719), who secretly married King Louis XIV (1638–1715) when she was approximately forty-eight years old. American author and women's rights advocate Margaret Fuller (1810–50) was believed to have married Italian marquis Giovanni Angelo Ossoli when she was approximately thirty-eight years old. (It is unclear if there was a formal, official marriage, but Fuller and Ossoli lived and had a child together.)
15. The last amendment to the United States Constitution to be ratified before "A Day with Doctor Sarah" was published in 1878 was the Fifteenth Amendment, which became law in 1870 and prohibits the federal government and the states from denying any male citizen the right to vote based on his "race, color, or previous condition of servitude." Women's rights activists hoped the Sixteenth Amendment would extend the vote to women as well; they were disappointed, however, for the Sixteenth Amendment, ratified in 1913, gave Congress the power to impose an income tax. Women would not be guaranteed a constitutional right to vote until the Nineteenth Amendment, ratified in 1920.
16. A term commonly used at the time to refer to African Americans. It is now generally considered offensive and is no longer acceptable.
17. In Greek and Roman mythology, Charon (or Kharon) is a ferryman who helps newly deceased souls cross the river Styx into Hades.
18. Psalm 23:1 (KJV) states, "The Lord is my shepherd; I shall not want."
19. Likely a reference to the prophetess Deborah and the female warrior Jael, who in the biblical Song of Deborah (Judges 5:2–31) act as strong and heroic figures.

SAMUEL POST DAVIS

(1850–1918)

Samuel Post Davis was born in Connecticut, the son of an Episcopal priest, but due to his father's frequent reassignments, he lived in many different communities during his youth, gradually moving farther west. Davis began his journalism career around 1870 by writing for newspapers in Brownville, Nebraska. When his father relocated to California in 1872, Davis went with him. In 1875, Davis moved on his own to the mining town of Virginia City, Nevada, where he edited the *Territorial Enterprise* and *Virginia Evening Chronicle* newspapers until 1879; he then moved to Carson City, Nevada, and became both the editor and proprietor of the *Morning Appeal*, positions he held until his death. Davis is best known today as one of the foremost writers in what is loosely known as the Sagebrush school, a group of writers in the far West who witnessed, and wrote about, their experiences during the days when the West loomed large in many Americans' imagination as a place full of romantic, idiosyncratic characters such as cowboys, gamblers, cattle rustlers, gunfighters, and swindlers.

"A Christmas Carol" was first published in the *Virginia Evening Chronicle*, probably during the late 1870s, when Davis was its editor, and was widely reprinted; it later appeared under the title "The First Piano in Camp." Although this humorous story, like so many other productions by Sagebrush writers published in local newspapers, would have originally been read chiefly by miners who had flooded the area in search of silver, it also contains many elements that would have appealed to readers farther east, for it included a cast of rough-around-the-edges miners, a saloon keeper, and a sharp con man. In addition, the prominence of a piano was fraught with significance for such readers, as it symbolized middle-class domesticity and "civilized" life for many Americans. It is not surprising, given these stock elements, that the story was not only reprinted numerous times in other nineteenth-century American and British newspapers but also widely translated and published in many European publications as well.

A CHRISTMAS CAROL (LATE 1870s)

In 1858—it might have been five years earlier or later, this is not history for the public schools—there was a little camp about ten miles from Pioche,[1] occupied by upwards of three hundred miners, every one of whom might have packed his prospecting implements and left for more inviting fields any time before sunset. When the day was over, these men did not rest from their labors, like the honest New England agriculturist, but sang, danced, gambled, and shot each other, as the mood seized them.

One evening the report spread along the main street (which was the only street) that three men had been killed at Silver Reef, and that the bodies were coming in. Presently a lumbering old conveyance labored up the hill, drawn by a couple of horses, well worn out with their pull. The cart contained a good-sized box, and no sooner did its outlines become visible through the glimmer of a stray light here and there, than it began to affect the idlers. Death always enforces respect, and even though no one had caught sight of the remains, the crowd gradually became subdued, and when the horses came to a stand-still, the cart was immediately surrounded. The driver, however, was not in the least impressed with the solemnity of his commission.

"All there?" asked one.

"Haven't examined. Guess so."

The driver filled his pipe and lit it as he continued:

"Wish the bones and load had gone over the grade."

A man who had been looking on stepped up to the man at once.

"I don't know who you have in that box, but if they happen to be any friends of mine, I'll lay you alongside."

"We can mighty soon see," said the teamster,[2] coolly. "Just burst the lid off, and if they happen to be the men you want, I'm here."

The two looked at each other for a moment, and the crowd gathered a little closer, anticipating trouble.

"I believe that dead men are entitled to good treatment, and when you talk about hoping to see corpses go over a bank, all I have to say is, that it will be better for you if the late lamented ain't my friends."

"We'll open the box. I don't take back what I've said, and if my language don't suit your ways of thinking, I guess I can stand it."

With these words the teamster began to pry up the lid. He got a board off, and then pulled out some old rags. A strip of something dark, like rosewood, presented itself.

"Eastern coffins, by thunder!" said several, and the crowd looked quite astonished.

Some more boards flew up, and the man who was ready to defend his friend's memory shifted his weapon a little. The cool manner of the teamster had so irritated him that he had made up his mind to pull his weapon at the first sight of the dead, even if the deceased was his worst and oldest enemy. Presently the whole of the box cover was off, and the teamster, clearing away the packing, revealed to the astonished group the top of something which puzzled all alike.

"Boys," said he, "this is a pianner."

A general shout of laughter went up, and the man who had been so anxious to enforce respect for the dead muttered something about feeling dry, and the keeper of the nearest bar was several ounces better off[3] by the time the boys had given the joke all the attention it called for.

Had a dozen men been in the box, their presence in the camp could not have occasioned half the excitement that the arrival of that lovely piano caused. By the next morning it was known that the instrument was to grace a hurdy-gurdy saloon, owned by Tom Goskin, the leading gambler in the place. It took nearly a week to get this wonder on its legs, and the owner was the proudest individual in the State. It rose gradually from a recumbent to an upright position, amid a confusion of tongues, after the manner of the tower of Babel.[4]

Of course everybody knew just how such an instrument should be put up. One knew where the "off hind leg"[5] should go, and another was posted on the "front piece."

Scores of men came to the place every day to assist.

"I'll put the bones in good order."

"If you want the wires tuned up, I'm the boy."

"I've got music to feed it for a month."

Another brought a pair of blankets for a cover, and all took the liveliest interest in it. It was at last in a condition for business.

"It's been showin' its teeth all the week. We'd like to have it spit out something."

Alas! There wasn't a man to be found who could play upon the instrument. Goskin began to realize that he had a losing speculation on his hands. He had a fiddler, and a Mexican who thrummed a guitar. A pianist would have made his orchestra complete. One day a three-card monte player told a friend confidentially that he could "knock any amount of music out of the piano, if he only had it alone a few hours to get his hand in." This report spread about the camp, but on being questioned he vowed that he didn't know a note of music. It was noted, however, as a suspicious circumstance, that he often hung about the instrument, and looked upon it longingly, like a hungry man gloating over a beefsteak in a restaurant window. There was no doubt but that this man had music in his soul, perhaps in his fingers'-ends, but did not dare to make trial of his strength after the rules of harmony had suffered so many years of neglect. So the fiddler kept on with his jigs, and the greasy Mexican pawed his discordant guitar, but no man had the nerve to touch that piano. There were, doubtless, scores of men in the camp who would have given ten ounces of gold-dust to have been half an hour alone with it, but every man's nerve shrank from the jeers which the crowd would shower upon him should his first attempt prove a failure. It got to be generally understood that the hand which first essayed to draw music from the keys must not slouch its work.

It was Christmas Eve, and Goskin, according to his custom, had decorated his gambling hall with sprigs of mountain cedar and a shrub whose crimson berries did not seem a bad imitation of English holly. The piano was covered with evergreens, and all that was wanting to completely fill the cup of Goskin's contentment was a man to play that piano.

"Christmas night, and no piano-pounder," he said. "This is a nice country for a Christian to live in."

Getting a piece of paper, he scrawled the words:

> $20 Reward
> To a compitant Pianner Player.

This he stuck up on the music-rack, and though the inscription glared at the frequenters of the room until midnight, it failed to draw any musician from his shell.

So the merry-making went on; the hilarity grew apace. Men danced and sang to the music of the squeaky fiddle and worn-out guitar, as the jolly crowd within tried to drown the howling of the storm without. Suddenly, they became aware of the presence of a white-haired man, crouching near the fire-place. His garments—such as were left—were wet with melting snow, and he had a half-starved, half-crazed expression. He held his thin, trembling hands toward the fire, and the light of the blazing wood made them almost transparent. He looked about him once in a while, as if in search of something, and his presence cast such a chill over the place that gradually the sound of the revelry was hushed, and it seemed that this waif of the storm had brought in with it all of the gloom and coldness of the warring elements. Goskin, mixing up a copy of hot egg-nogg, advanced and remarked cheerily:

"Here, stranger, brace up! This is the real stuff."

The man drained the cup, smacked his lips, and seemed more at home.

"Been prospecting, eh? Out in the mountains—caught in the storm? Lively night, this!"

"Pretty bad," said the man.

"Must feel pretty dry?"

The man looked at his streaming clothes and laughed, as if Goskin's remark was a sarcasm.

"How long out?"

"Four days."

"Hungry?"

The man rose up, and walking over to the lunch counter, fell to work upon some roast bear, devouring it like any wild animal would have done. As meat and drink and warmth began to permeate the stranger, he seemed to expand and lighten up. His features lost their pallor, and he grew more and more content with the idea that he was not in the grave. As he underwent these changes, the people about him got merrier and happier, and threw off the temporary feeling of depression which he had laid upon them.

"Do you always have your place decorated like this?" he finally asked of Goskin.

"This is Christmas Eve," was the reply.

The stranger was startled.

"December twenty-fourth, sure enough."

"That's the way I put it up, pard."

"When I was in England I always kept Christmas. But I had forgotten that this was the night. I've been wandering about in the mountains until I've lost track of the feasts of the church."

Presently his eye fell upon the piano.

"Where's the player?" he asked.

"Never had any," said Goskin, blushing at the expression.

"I used to play when I was young."

Goskin almost fainted at the admission.

"Stranger, do tackle it, and give us a tune! Nary a man in this camp ever had the nerve to wrestle with that music-box." His pulse beat faster, for he feared that the man would refuse.

"I'll do the best I can," he said.

There was no stool, but seizing a candle-box, he drew it up and seated himself before the instrument. It only required a few seconds for a hush to come over the room.

"That old coon is going to give the thing a rattle."

The sight of a man at the piano was something so unusual that even the faro-dealer,[6] who was about to take in a fifty-dollar bet on the try, paused, and did not reach for the money. Men stopped drinking, with the glasses at their lips. Conversation appeared to have been struck with a sort of paralysis, and cards were no longer shuffled.

The old man brushed back his long, white locks, looked up to the ceiling, half closed his eyes, and in a mystic sort of reverie passed his fingers over the keys. He touched but a single note, yet the sound thrilled the room. It was the key to his improvisation, and as he wove his chords together the music laid its spell upon every ear and heart. He felt his way along the keys, like a man treading uncertain paths; but he gained confidence as he progressed, and presently bent to his work like a master. The instrument was not in exact tune, but the ears of his audience, through long disuse, did not detect anything radically wrong. They heard a succession of grand chords, a suggestion of paradise, melodies here and there, and it was enough.

"See him counter with his left!"[7] said an old rough, enraptured.

"He calls the turn every time on the upper end of the board,"[8] responded a man with a stack of chips in his hand.

The player wandered off into the old ballads they had heard at home. All the sad and melancholy, and touching songs that came up like dreams of childhood, this unknown player drew from the keys. His hands kneaded their hearts like dough, and squeezed out the tears as from a wet sponge. As the strains flowed one upon the other, they saw their homes of the long ago reared again; they were playing once more where the apple blossoms sank through the soft air to join the violets on the green turf of the old New England States; they saw the glories of the Wisconsin maples and the haze of the Indian summer, blending their hues together; they recalled the heather of Scottish hills, the white cliffs of Britain, and heard the sullen roar of the sea, as it beat upon their memories, vaguely. Then came all the old Christmas carols, such as they had sung in church thirty years before; the subtle music that brings up the glimmer of wax tapers, the solemn shrines, the evergreen, holly, mistletoe, and surpliced choirs. Then the remorseless performer planted his final stab in every heart with "Home, Sweet Home."

When the player ceased, the crowd slunk away from him. There was no more revelry and devilment left in his audience. Each man wanted to sneak off to his cabin and write the old folks a letter. The day was breaking as the last man left the place, and the player, laying his head down on the piano, fell asleep.

"I say, pard," said Goskin, "don't you want a little rest?"

"I feel tired," the old man said. "Perhaps you'll let me rest here for the matter of a day or so."

He walked behind the bar where some old blankets were lying, and stretched himself upon them.

"I feel pretty sick. I guess I won't last long. I've got a brother down in the ravine—his name's Driscoll. He don't know I'm here. Can you get him before morning. I'd like to see his face once before I die."

Goskin started up at the mention of the name. He knew Driscoll well.

"He your brother? I'll have him here in half an hour."

As he dashed out into the storm the musician pressed his hand to his side and groaned. Goskin heard the word "Hurry!" and sped down the ravine to Driscoll's cabin. It was quite light in the room when the two men returned. Driscoll was pale as death.

"My God! I hope he's alive! I wronged him when we lived in England, twenty years ago."

They saw the old man had drawn the blankets over his face. The two stood a moment, awed by the thought that he might be dead. Goskin lifted the blanket, and pulled it down astonished. There was no one there!

"Gone!" cried Driscoll, wildly.

"Gone!" echoed Goskin, pulling out his cash-drawer. "Ten thousand dollars in the sack, and the Lord knows how much loose change in the drawer!"

The next day the boys got out, followed a horse's tracks through the snow, and lost them in the trail leading toward Pioche.

There was a man missing from the camp. It was the three-card monte man, who used to deny point-blank that he could play the scale. One day they found a wig of white hair, and called to mind when the "stranger" had pushed those locks back when he looked toward the ceiling for inspiration, on the night of December 24, 1861.[9]

NOTES

1. A Nevada mining town founded in 1864, located 180 miles northeast of Las Vegas.
2. A person who owns or drives a "team" of horses or oxen pulling a wagon.
3. Several ounces of gold dust. In mining communities, one could often pay with gold rather than currency.
4. In the Bible's book of Genesis (chapters 6–9), God sends a flood to cleanse the world of its corruption; the only survivors are Noah and those people and animals on his ark. In Genesis 11:1–9, those humans who had survived the flood erect a tower (only later termed the "Tower of Babel") to avoid being deluged in a second flood; God punishes them by making different groups speak languages unintelligible to each other and by scattering them across the world.
5. The "off hind leg" of a horse is, as one views it from behind, the animal's right rear leg; this comment suggests that the people putting the piano together know more about animals than about musical instruments.
6. Faro was a very popular card game among gamblers in the nineteenth century, especially in the American West.
7. This boxing term suggests that the player is fighting with the piano, and simultaneously highlights how little the observers know of piano playing.
8. A "turn" in Faro is one pair, and to "call the turn" simply means to turn the cards over to see which bettor has won; again, the observers' analogy between a card dealer's hand motions and a piano player's movements on the keyboard highlights their lack of refinement and knowledge about piano playing.
9. In the first line of the story, the date of the recounted events is given as 1858, so 1861 would appear to be a misprint; to fix what many took as a "mistake," in

some later printings of this story the final date was changed to 1858. Both dates precede the founding of Pioche in 1864, and so possibly this mix-up of dates was made intentionally to emphasize that this tale is not history but legend; after all, the narrator states in the first line that he is unsure of the date 1858: "It might have been five years earlier or later, this is not history for the public schools."

THEODORE DREISER

(1871–1945)

Born in Terre Haute, Indiana, on August 27, 1871, Theodore Dreiser was part of a large family that was constantly in financial difficulty. The experience of growing up very poor with a strict German immigrant father would make Dreiser acutely sensitive for the rest of his life to the deprivations caused by poverty.

Dreiser graduated from high school in Warsaw, Indiana, but his family was unable to afford tuition for him to attend college; nevertheless, one of his high school teachers paid for Dreiser to enroll at Indiana University in 1889. Dreiser left after only one year, disenchanted with the type of social prejudice he encountered there. Not long after leaving college, Dreiser moved to Chicago and began pursuing a career in journalism; he subsequently worked at newspapers such as the *Chicago Globe,* the *St. Louis Globe-Democrat,* and the *St. Louis Republic.* While on assignment at the 1893 World's Columbian Exposition in Chicago, Dreiser met his first wife, Sara Osborne White, whom he would eventually marry in 1898. Before then, however, in 1894, Dreiser left the Midwest to try his chances in New York City. Initially, he had no success and sank into poverty. Fortunately, his older brother Paul Dresser (born Johann Paul Dreiser) had become a successful songwriter. Paul saved his younger brother by making him editor of a magazine, *Ev'ry Month,* whose chief objective was to promote songs published by Dresser's company. After resigning from this editorship in 1897, Dreiser tried his hand at freelance writing, with limited success. In the fall of 1899, Dreiser undertook the larger task of starting to write a novel, which he entitled *Sister Carrie,* based loosely on the life of his sister Emma. When the New York publishing firm of Doubleday, Page, accepted it in the spring of 1900 (on the recommendation of its manuscript reader, Frank Norris), it appeared that Dreiser had finally achieved his long-sought-after breakthrough. However, the firm had second thoughts about publishing a novel about a young female character, Carrie Meeber, who defies various social mores, uses sex when necessary to obtain food and housing or advance her career, and, rather than being punished for her actions, thrives and finds success as an actress. As a result, the firm published fewer than a thousand copies and refused to promote it. Discouraged, Dreiser suffered a nervous breakdown and became destitute. By 1904, however, again with the help of his brother Paul, Dreiser had recovered and resumed his career as an editor.

Buoyed by the republication of *Sister Carrie* in 1907 and the subsequent critical acclaim it garnered, Dreiser eventually resumed work on his second novel, *Jennie Gerhardt*, which was published in 1911. His most famous novel, after *Sister Carrie*, is *An American Tragedy* (1925), which was based on the 1906 murder trial of a man in upstate New York who murdered a young woman who he felt threatened his climb up the socioeconomic ladder.

Dreiser also frequently critiqued the limitations of conventional moral codes, especially those related to marriage. Certainly, in his own life his relationships with women were anything but conventional. Almost from the beginning of his first marriage in 1898, he began to show interest in other women. Not long after separating from his wife in 1909 (they never divorced), Dreiser entered into a relationship with the actress and painter Kyra Markham. Then in 1919 he began an affair with his much younger cousin, Helen Patges Richardson, which lasted for twenty-five years. During their entire relationship, Dreiser openly engaged in numerous affairs, which Helen reportedly tolerated. She and Dreiser did, however, eventually marry in 1944, shortly before his death on December 28, 1945, in Los Angeles.

The story included here, "Free," which first appeared in the March 16, 1918, issue of the extremely popular and mainstream *Saturday Evening Post* magazine, when Dreiser was only forty-six years old, offers an intriguing psychological exploration of an aging man's feelings about personal freedom, monogamy, fatherhood, and marriage.

FREE (1918)

The large and rather comfortable apartment of Rufus Haymaker, architect, in Central Park West,[1] was very silent. It was scarcely dawn yet, and at the edge of the park, over the way, looking out from the front windows which graced this abode and gave it its charm, a stately line of poplars was still shrouded in a gray morning mist. From his bedroom at one end of the hall, where, also, a glimpse of the park was to be had, came Mr. Haymaker at this early hour to sit by one of these broader windows and contemplate these trees and a small lake beyond. He was very fond of Nature in its manifold art forms—quite poetic, in fact.

He was a tall and spare man of about sixty, not ungraceful, though slightly stoop-shouldered, with heavy overhanging eyebrows and hair, and a short, professionally cut gray mustache and beard, which gave him a severe and yet agreeable presence. For the present he was clad in a light blue dressing gown with silver cords, which enveloped him completely. He had thin, pale, long-fingered hands, wrinkled at the back and slightly knotted at the joints, which bespoke the artist, in mood at least, and his eyes had a weary and yet restless look in them.

For only yesterday Doctor Storm, the family physician, who was in attendance on his wife, ill now for these three weeks past with a combination of heart lesion, kidney poisoning and neuritis, had taken him aside and said very softly and affectionately, as though he were trying to spare his feelings: "Tomorrow, Mr. Haymaker, if your wife is no better I will call in my friend, Doctor Grainger, whom you know, for a consultation. He is more of an expert in these matters of the heart"—the heart, Mr. Haymaker had time to note ironically—"than I am. Together we will make a thorough examination, and then I hope we shall be better able to say what the possibilities of her recovery really are. It's been a very trying case, a very stubborn one, I might say. Still, she has a great deal of vitality and is doing as well as could be expected, all things considered. At the same time, though I don't wish to alarm you unnecessarily—and there is no occasion for great alarm yet—still I feel it my duty to warn you that her condition is very serious indeed. Not that I wish you to feel that she is certain to die. I don't think she is. Not at all. Just the contrary. She may get well, and probably will, and live all of twenty years more." Mentally Mr. Haymaker sighed a purely spiritual sigh. "She has fine recuperative powers, so far as I can judge, but she has a bad heart, and this kidney trouble has not helped it any. Just now, when her heart should have the least strain, it has the most.

"She is just at that point where, as I may say, things are in the balance. A day or two, or three or four at the most, ought to show which way things will go. But, as I have said before, I do not wish to alarm you unnecessarily. We are not nearly at the end of our tether. We haven't tried blood transfusion yet, and there are several arrows to that bow. Besides, at any moment she may respond more vigorously to medication than she has heretofore—especially in connection with her kidneys. In that case the situation would be greatly relieved at once.

"However, as I say, I feel it my duty to speak to you in this way in order that you may be mentally prepared for any event, because in such an odd combination as this the worst may happen at any time. We never can tell. As an old friend of yours and Mrs. Haymaker's, and knowing how much you two mean to each other"—Mr. Haymaker merely stared at him vacantly—"I feel it my duty to prepare you in this way. We all of us have to face these things. Only last year I lost my dear Matilda, my youngest child, as you know. Just the same, as I say, I have the feeling that Mrs. Haymaker is not really likely to die soon, and that we—Doctor Grainger and myself—shall still be able to pull her through. I really do."

Doctor Storm looked at Mr. Haymaker as though he were very sorry for him—an old man long accustomed to his wife's ways and likely to be made very unhappy by her untimely end; whereas Mr. Haymaker, though staring in an almost sculptural way, was really thinking what a farce it all was, what a dull mixture of error and illusion on the part of all. Here he was, sixty years of age, weary of all this, of life really—a man who had never been really happy in all the time that he had been married; and yet here was his wife, who from conventional reasons believed that he was or should be, and who on account of this was serenely happy herself, or nearly so. And this doctor, who imagined that he was old and weak and therefore in need of this loving woman's care and sympathy and understanding! Unconsciously he raised a deprecating hand.

Also his children, who thought him dependent on her and happy with her; his servants and her and his friends thinking the same thing, and yet he really was not. It was all a lie. He was unhappy. Always he had been unhappy, it seemed, ever since he had been married—for over thirty-one years now. Never in all that time, for even so much as a single day, had he ever done anything but long, long, long, in a dark, constrained way—for what, he scarcely dared think—not to be married anymore—to be free—to be as he was before ever he saw Mrs. Haymaker. And yet being conventional in mood and training and utterly domesticated by time and conditions over which he seemed not to have much control—nature, customs, public opinion, and the like, coming into play as forces—he had drifted, had not taken any drastic action. No, he had merely drifted, wondering if time, accident or something might not interfere and straighten out his life for him, but it never had. Now weary, old, or rapidly becoming so, he condemned himself for his inaction.

Why hadn't he done something about it years before? Why hadn't he broken it up before it was too late, and saved his own soul, his longing for life, color? But no, he had not. Why complain so bitterly now?

All the time the doctor had talked the day before he had wanted to smile a wry, dry, cynical smile, for in reality he did not want Mrs. Haymaker to live—or at least at the moment he thought so. He was too miserably tired of it all.

And so now, after nearly twenty-four hours of the same unhappy thought, sitting by this window looking at a not distant building which shone faintly in the haze, he ran his fingers through his hair as he gazed, and sighed.

How often in these weary months, and even years past—ever since he and his wife had been living here, and before—had he come to these or similar windows while she was still asleep, to sit and dream! For some years now they had not even roomed together, so indifferent had the whole state become, though she did not seem to consider that significant, either. Life had become more or less of a practical problem to her, one of position, place, prestige. And yet how often, viewing his life in retrospect, had he wished that his life had been as sweet as his dreams—that his dreams had come true.

After a time on this early morning—for it was still gray, with the faintest touch of pink in the east—he shook his head solemnly and sadly, then rose and returned along the hall to his wife's bedroom, at the door of which he paused to look where she lay seriously ill, and beside her in an armchair, fast asleep, a trained nurse who was supposedly keeping the night vigil ordered by the doctor, but who no doubt was now very weary. His wife was sleeping also—very pale, very thin now, and very weak. He felt sorry for her at times, in spite of his own weariness; now, for instance. Why need he have made so great a mistake so long ago? Perhaps it was his own fault for not having been wiser in his youth. Then he went quietly on to his own room, to lie down and think.

Always these days, now that she was so very ill and the problem of her living was so very acute, the creeping dawn thus roused him—to think. It seemed as though he could not really sleep soundly anymore, so stirred and distrait was he.

He was not so much tired or physically worn as mentally bored or disappointed. Life had treated him so badly, he kept thinking to himself over and over. He had never had the woman he had really wanted, though he had been married so long, had been faithful, respectable and loved by her, in her way. "In her way," he half quoted to himself as he lay there.

Presently he would get up, dress and go down to his office as usual if his wife were not worse. But—but, he asked himself—would she be? Would that slim and yet so durable organism of hers—quite as old as his own, or nearly so—break under the strain of this really severe illness? That would set him free again, and nicely, without blame or comment on him. He could then go where he chose once more, do as he pleased—think of that—without let or hindrance. For she was ill at last, so very ill, the first and really great illness she had endured since their marriage. For weeks now she had been lying so, hovering, as it were, between life and death, one day better, the next day worse, and yet not dying, and with no certainty that she would, and yet not getting better either. Doctor Storm insisted that it was a leak in her heart which had suddenly manifested itself that was causing all the real trouble. He was apparently greatly troubled as to how to control it.

During all this period Mr. Haymaker had been, as usual, most sympathetic. His manner toward her was always soft, kindly, apparently tender. He had never really begrudged her anything—nothing certainly that he could afford. He was always glad to see her and the children humanly happy—though they, too, largely on account of her, he thought, had proved a disappointment to him—because he sympathized with her somewhat unhappy youth—narrow and stinted; and yet he had never been happy himself, never, in all the time that he had been married. She also had endured much, he kept telling himself when he was most unhappy—he was always willing to admit that—only she had had his love, or thought she had—an actual spiritual peace, which he had never had. She knew she had a faithful husband. He felt that he had never really had a wife at all, not one that he could love as he knew a wife should be loved. His dreams as to that!

Going to his office later in the day—it was in one of those tall buildings that face Madison Square—he had looked first, in passing, at the trees that line Central Park West, and then at the bright wall of apartment houses facing it, and meditated sadly, heavily. Here the sidewalks were crowded with nursemaids and children at play, and in between them, of course, the occasional citizen loitering or going about his errands. The day was so fine, so youthful, as spring clays will seem. As he looked, especially at the children, and the young men bustling office-ward, mostly in new spring suits, he sighed and wished that he were young once more. Think how brisk and hopeful they were! Everything was before them. They could still pick and choose—no age or established conditions to stay them. Were any of them, he asked himself for the thousandth time, it seemed to him, as wearily connected as he had been at their age? Did they each have a charming young wife to love—one of whom they were passionately fond—such a one as he had never had, or did they not?

Wondering, he reached his office on one of the topmost floors of one of those highest buildings commanding a wide view of the city, and surveyed it wearily. Here were visible the two great rivers of the city, its towers and spires and far-flung walls. From these sometimes, even yet, he seemed to gain a patience to live, to hope. How in his youth all this had inspired him—or that other city that was then! Even now he was always at peace here, so much more so than in his own home, pleasant as it was. Here he could look out over this great scene and dream or he could lose the memory in his work that his love-life had been a failure. The great city, the buildings he could plan or supervise, the efficient help that always surrounded him—his help, not hers—aided to take his mind off himself and that deep-seated inner ache or loss.

The care of Mr. Haymaker's apartment during his wife's illness and his present absence throughout the day devolved upon a middle-aged woman of great seriousness, Mrs. Elfridge by name, whom Mr. Haymaker had employed years before; and under her a maid of all work, Hester, who waited on table, opened the door, and the like; and also at present two trained nurses, one for night and one for day service, who were in charge of Mrs. Haymaker. The nurses were both bright, healthy, blue-eyed girls, who attracted Mr. Haymaker and suggested all the youth he had lost—without really disturbing his poise. It would seem as though that could never be done.

In addition, of course, there was the loving interest of his son Wesley and his daughter Ethelberta—whom his wife had named so in spite of him—both of whom had long since married and had children of their own and were living in different parts of the great city. In this crisis both of them came daily to learn how things were, and occasionally to stay for the entire afternoon or evening, or both. Ethelberta had wanted to come and take charge of the apartment entirely during her mother's illness, only Mrs. Haymaker, who was still able to direct, and fond of doing so, would not hear of it. She was not so ill but that she could still speak, and in this way could inquire and direct. Besides, Mrs. Elfridge was as good as Mrs. Haymaker in all things that related to Mr. Haymaker's physical comfort, or so she thought.

If the truth will come out—as it will in so many pathetic cases—it was never his physical so much as his spiritual or affections' comfort that Mr. Haymaker craved. As said before, he had never loved Mrs. Haymaker, or certainly not since that now long-distant period back in Muskegon, Michigan, where both had been born and where they had lived and met at the ages, she of fifteen, he of seventeen. It had been, strange as it might seem now, a love match at first sight with them. She had seemed so sweet, a girl of his own age or a little younger, the daughter of a local chemist. Later, when he had been forced by poverty to go out into the world to make his own way, he had written her much, and imagined her to be all that she had seemed at fifteen, and more—a dream among fair women.

But Fortune, slow in coming to his aid and fickle in fulfilling his dreams, had brought it about that for several years more he had been compelled to stay away nearly all of the time, unable to marry her; during which period, unknown to himself really, his own point of view had altered. How it had happened he could never tell really, but so it was. The great city, larger experiences—while she was still enduring the smaller ones—other faces, dreams of larger things, had all combined to destroy it or her; only he had not quite realized it then. He was always so slow in realizing the full import of the immediate thing, he thought.

That was the time, as he had afterward told himself—how often!—that he should have discovered his mistake and stopped. Later it always seemed to become more and more impossible. Then, in spite of some heartache to her and some distress to himself, no doubt, all would be well for him now. But no; he had been too inexperienced, too ignorant, too bound by all the conventions and punctilios of his simple Western world. He thought an engagement, however unsatisfactory it might come to seem afterward, was an engagement, and binding. An honorable man would not break one—or so his country moralists argued.

He might have written her, he might have told her, then. But he had been too sensitive and kindly to speak of it. Afterward it was too late. He feared to wound her, to undo her life. But now—now—look at his! He had gone back on several occasions before marriage, and might have seen and done and been free if he had had but courage and wisdom. But no; duty, order, the beliefs of the region in which he had been reared, and of America—what it expected and what she expected and was entitled to—had done for him completely. He had not spoken. Instead, he had gone on and married her without speaking of the change in himself, without letting her know how worse than ashes it had all become. What a fool he had been! he had since told himself over and over.

Well, having made a mistake it was his duty perhaps, at least according to current beliefs, to stick by it and make the best of it; but still that had never prevented him from being unhappy. He could not prevent that himself. During all these long years, therefore, owing to these same conventions—what people would think and say—he had been compelled to live with her, to cherish her, to pretend to be happy with her—"another perfect union," as he sometimes said to himself. He had been unhappy, horribly so. Even her face wearied him at times, and her presence, her mannerisms. Only yesterday morning Doctor Storm had seemed to indicate by his manner that he thought him lonely, in danger of being left all alone and desperately sad and neglected in case she died. Who would take care of him? his eyes had seemed to say—and yet he himself wanted nothing so much as to be alone for a time, at least in this life, to think for himself, to do for himself, to forget this long, dreary period in which he had pretended to be something that he was not.

Was he never to be rid of the dull round of it, he asked himself now—never before he himself died? And yet shortly afterward he would reproach himself for these very thoughts, as being wrong, hard, unkind—thoughts that would certainly condemn him in the eyes of the general public, that public which made reputations and one's general standing before the world.

During all this time he had never even let her know—no, not once—of the tremendous and soul-crushing sacrifice he had made. Like the Spartan boy, he had concealed the fox gnawing at his vitals.[2] He had not complained. He had been, indeed, the model husband, as such things go in conventional walks. If you doubted it, look at his position; or that of his children; or his wife—her mental and physical comfort, even in her illness, her unfailing belief that he was all he should be! Never once apparently, during all these years, had she doubted his love or felt him to be unduly unhappy—or, if not that exactly, if not fully accepting his love as something that was still at a fever heat, the thing it once was—still believing that he found pleasure and happiness in being with her, and a comfort in knowing that it would endure to the end! To the end! During all these years she had gone on molding his and her lives—as much as that was possible in his case—to suit herself; and thinking all the time that she was doing what he wanted or at least what was best for him.

How she adored convention! What did she not think she knew in regard to how things ought to be—mainly what her old home surroundings had taught her, the American idea of this, that and the other! Her theories in regard to friends, education of the children, and so on, had in the main prevailed, even when he did not quite agree with her; her desires for certain types of pleasure and amusement, of companionship, and so on, were conventional types always. There had been little quarrels, of course, always had been—what happy home is free of them?—but still he had always given in, or nearly always, and had acted as though he were satisfied in so doing.

Why, therefore, should he complain now, or she ever have imagined that he was unhappy? She did not. Like all their relatives and friends of the region from which they sprang, and here also—and she had been most careful to regulate that, courting whom she pleased and ignoring all others—she still believed most firmly, more so than ever, that she knew what was best for him, what he really thought and wanted. It made him smile most wearily at times.

For in her eyes—in regard to him, at least, not always so with others, he had found—marriage was a sacrament, sacrosanct, never to be dissolved. One life, one love. Once one had accepted the yoke or even asked a girl to marry, it was every man's duty to abide by it. To break an engagement, to be unfaithful to a wife, even unkind to her—what a crime, in her eyes! Such people ought to be drummed out of the world. They were not fit to live—dogs, brutes!

And yet, look at himself—what of him? What of one who had made a mistake in regard to all this? Where was his compensation to come from, his peace and happiness? Here on earth or only in some mythical heaven—that odd, angelic heaven that she still believed in? What a farce! And all her friends and his would think he would be so miserable now if she died, or at least ought to be. So far had asinine convention and belief in custom carried the world. Think of it!

But even that was not the worst. No; that was not the worst, either. It had been the gradual realization coming along through the years that he had married an essentially small, narrow woman who could never really grasp his point of view—or, rather, the significance of his dreams or emotions—and yet with whom, nevertheless, because of this original promise or mistake, he was compelled to live. Grant her every quality of goodness, energy, industry, intent—as he did freely—still there was this; and it could never be adjusted—never. Essentially, as he had long since discovered, she was narrow, ultra-conventional, whereas he was an artist by nature, brooding and dreaming strange dreams and thinking of far-off things which she did not or could not understand or did not sympathize with, save in a general and very remote way. The nuances of his craft, the wonders and subtleties of forms and angles—had she ever realized how significant these were to him, let alone to herself? No, never. She had not the least true appreciation of them—never had had. And he could not now go elsewhere to discover that sympathy. No. He had never really wanted to, since the public and she would object, and thinking it half evil himself.

Still, how was it, he often asked himself, that Nature could thus allow one conditioned or equipped with emotions and seekings such as his, not of an utterly conventional order, to seek out and pursue one like Ernestine, who was not fitted to understand him or to care what his personal moods might be? Was love truly blind, as the old saw insisted, or did Nature really plan, and cleverly, to torture the artist mind—as it did the pearl-bearing oyster with a grain of sand—with something seemingly inimical, in order that it might produce beauty? Sometimes he thought so. Perhaps the many interesting and beautiful buildings he had planned—the world called them so, at least—had been due to the loving care he lavished on them, being shut out from love and beauty elsewhere. Cruel Nature, that cared so little for the dreams of man—the individual man or woman!

At the time he had married Ernestine he was really too young to know exactly what it was he wanted to do or how it was he was going to feel in the years to come; and yet there was no one to guide him, to stop him. The custom of the time was all in favor of this dread disaster. Nature herself seemed to desire it—mere children being the be-all and the end-all of everything. Think of that as a theory! Later, when it became so clear to him what he had done, and in spite of all the conventional thoughts and conditions that seemed to bind him to this fixed condition, he had grown restless and weary, but never really irritable.

He had concealed it all from her; only this hankering after beauty of mind and body in ways not represented by her had hurt so—grown finally almost too painful to bear. He had dreamed and dreamed of something different until it had become almost an obsession. Was it never to be, that something different—never, anywhere, in all time? What a tragedy! Soon he would be dead, and then it would never be anywhere—anywhere! Ernestine was charming, he would admit, or had been at first, though time had proved that she was not charming to him either mentally or physically in any compelling way; but how did that help him now? He had actually found himself bored by her for more than twenty-seven years now, and this other dream growing, growing, growing—until—But now he was old, and she was dying, or might be, and it could not make so much difference what happened; only it could, too, because he wanted to be free for a little while, just for a little while, before he died.

One of the things that had always irritated him about Mrs. Haymaker was this: In spite of his determination never to offend the social code in any way—he had felt for so many reasons, emotional as well as practical, that he could not afford so to do—and also in spite of the fact that he had been tortured by this show of beauty in the eyes and bodies of others, his wife, fearing perhaps in some strange psychic way that he might change, had always tried to make him feel or believe—premeditatedly and of a purpose, he thought—that he was not the kind of man who would be attractive to women; that he lacked some physical fitness, some charm that other men had, which would cause all young and really charming women to turn away from him. Think of it! He to whom so many women had turned with questioning eyes!

Also that she had married him largely because she had felt sorry for him! He chose to let her believe that, because he was sorry for her. Because other women had seemed to draw near to him at times in some appealing or seductive way, she had insisted that he was not even a cavalier, let alone a Lothario;[3] that he was ungainly, slow, uninteresting—to all women but her!

Persistently, he thought, and without any real need, she had harped on this, fighting chimeras,[4] a chance danger in the future, though he had never given her any real reason, and had never even planned to sin against her in any way—never. She had thus tried to poison his own mind in regard to himself and his art. And yet—and yet—Ah, those eyes of other women, their haunting beauty, the flitting something they said to him of infinite, inexpressible delight! Why had his life been so very hard?

One of the disturbing things about all this was the iron truth that it had driven home, that Nature, unless it were expressed or represented by some fierce determination from within, cared no whit for him or any other, man or woman. Unless one acted for oneself, upon some stern conclusion nurtured within, one might rot and die spiritually. Nature did not care. "Blessed be the meek"—yes. Blessed be the strong, rather, for they made their own happiness. All these years in which he had dwelt and worked in this knowledge, nothing had happened, except to him, and that in an unsatisfactory way. All along he had seen what was happening to him; and yet held by convention he had refused to act always, because somehow he was not hard enough to act. Almost like a bird in a cage, an animal peeping out from behind bars, he had viewed the world of free thought and freer action. In many a drawing room, on the street, or in his own home even, he had looked into an eye, the face of someone who seemed to offer understanding, to know, to sympathize, though she might not have, of course; and yet religiously and moralistically, like an anchorite, because of duty and current belief and what people would say and think, Ernestine's position and faith, his career and that of the children—he had put them all aside, out of his mind, forgotten them almost, as best he might. It had been hard at times, and sad, but so it had been.

And look at him now, old, not exactly feeble yet—no, not that yet, not quite!—but life-weary and almost indifferent. All these years he had wanted,

wanted—wanted—an understanding mind, a tender heart, the some one woman—she must exist somewhere—who would have sympathized with all the delicate shades and meanings of his own character, his art, his spiritual as well as his material dreams—And yet look at him! Mrs. Haymaker had always been with him, present in the flesh or the spirit, and—so—

Though he could not ever say that she was disagreeable to him in a material way—he could not say that she had ever been that exactly—still she did not correspond to his idea of what he needed, and so—Form had meant so much to him, color; the glorious perfectness of a glorious woman's body, for instance, the color of her thoughts, moods—exquisite they must be, like his own at times; but no, he had never had the opportunity to know one intimately. No, not one, though he had dreamed of her so long. He had never even dared whisper this to anyone, scarcely to himself. It was not wise, not socially fit. Thoughts like this would tend to social ostracism in his circle, or rather, hers—for had she not made the circle?

And here was the rub with Mr. Haymaker, at least, that he could not make up his mind whether in his restlessness and private mental complaints he were not even now guilty of a great moral crime in so thinking. Was it not true that men and women should be faithful in marriage whether they were happy or not? Was there not some psychic law governing this matter of union—one life, one love—which made the thoughts and the pains and the subsequent sufferings and hardships of the individual, whatever they might be, seem unimportant? The churches said so. Public opinion and the law seemed to accept this. There were so many problems, so much order to be disrupted, so much pain caused, many insoluble problems where children were concerned—if people did not stick. Was it not best, more blessed—socially, morally, and in every other way important—for him to stand by a bad bargain rather than to cause so much disorder and pain, even though he lost his own soul emotionally? He had thought so—or at least he had acted as though he thought so—and yet—How often had he wondered over this!

Take, now, some other phases. Granting first that Mrs. Haymaker had, according to the current code, measured up to the requirements of a wife, good and true, and that at first after marriage there had been just enough of physical and social charm about her to keep his state from becoming intolerable, still there was this old ache; and then newer things which came with the birth of the several children: First Elwell—named after a cousin of hers—who had died only two years after he was born; and then Wesley; and then Ethelberta—how he had always disliked that name!—largely because he had hoped to call her Ottilie, a favorite name of his; or Janet, after his mother.

Curiously the arrival of these children and the death of poor little Elwell at two had somehow, in spite of his unrest, bound him to this matrimonial state and filled him with a sense of duty, and pleasure even—almost entirely apart from her, he was sorry to say—in these young lives; though if there had not been children, as he sometimes told himself, he surely would have broken away from her; he could not have stood it. They were so odd in their infancy, those little ones, so troublesome and yet so amusing—little Elwell, for instance, whose nose used to crinkle with delight when he would pretend to bite his neck, and whose gurgle of pleasure was so sweet and heart-filling that it positively thrilled and lured him. In spite of his thoughts concerning Ernestine—and always in those days they were rigidly put down as unmoral and even evil, a certain unsocial streak in him perhaps which was against law and order and well-being—he came to have a deep and abiding feeling for Elwell. The latter, in some chemic, almost unconscious way, seemed to have arrived as a balm to his misery, a bandage for his growing wound—sent by whom, by what, how? He had seized upon his imagination, and so his heartstrings—had come, indeed, to make him feel understanding and sympathy there in that little child; to supply, or seem to at least, what he lacked in the way of love and affection from one whom he could truly love. Elwell was never so happy apparently as when snuggling in his arms, not Ernestine's, or lying against his neck. And when he went for a walk or elsewhere there was Elwell always ready, arms up, to cling to his neck. He seemed, strangely enough, inordinately fond of his father, rather than his mother, and never happy without him. On his part, Haymaker came to be wildly fond of him—that queer little lump of a face, suggesting a little of himself and of his own mother, not so much of Ernestine; or so he thought, though he would not have objected to that. Not at all. He was not so small as that. Toward the end of the second year, when Elwell was just beginning to be able to utter a word or two, he had taught him that silly old rhyme which ran "There were three kittens," and when it came to "and they shall have no—" he would stop and say to Elwell, "What now?" and the latter would gurgle "puh!"—meaning, of course, pie.

Ah, those happy days with little Elwell, those walks with him over his shoulder or on his arm, those hours in which of an evening he would rock him to sleep in his arms! Always Ernestine was there, and happy in the thought of his love for little Elwell and her—her more than anything else perhaps; but it was an illusion—that latter part. He did not care for her even then as she thought he did.

All his fondness was for Elwell, only she took it as evidence of his growing or enduring affection for her—another evidence of the peculiar working of her mind.

And then came that dreadful fever, due to some invading microbe which the doctors could not diagnose or isolate—infantile paralysis perhaps; and little Elwell had finally ceased to be as flesh and was eventually carried forth to the lorn, disagreeable graveyard near Woodlawn. How he had groaned internally, indulged in sad, despondent thoughts concerning the futility of all things human, when this had happened! It seemed for the time being as if all color and beauty had really gone out of his life for good.

"Man born of woman is of few days and full of troubles," the preacher whom Mrs. Haymaker had insisted upon having into the house at the time of the funeral had read. "He fleeth also as a shadow and continueth not."

Yes; so little Elwell had fled, as a shadow, and in his own deep sorrow at the time he had come to feel the first and only sad, deep sympathy for Ernestine that he had ever felt since marriage; and that because she had suffered so much—had lain in his arms after the funeral and cried so bitterly. It was terrible, her sorrow. Terrible—a mother grieving for her firstborn! Why was it, he had thought at the time, that he had never been able to think or make her all she ought to be to him? Ernestine at this time had seemed better, softer, kinder, wiser, sweeter than she had ever seemed; more worthy, more interesting than ever he had thought her before. She had slaved so during the child's illness, stayed awake night after night, watched over him with such loving care—done everything, in short, that a loving human heart could do to rescue her young from the depths; and yet even then he had not really been able to love her. No, sad and unkind as it might seem, he had not. He had just pitied her and thought her better, worthier! What cursed stars disordered the minds and moods of people so? Why was it that these virtues of people, their good qualities, did not make you love them, did not really bind them to you, as against the things you could not like? Why? He had resolved to do better in his thoughts, but somehow, in spite of himself, he had never been able so to do.

Nevertheless, at that time he seemed to realize more keenly than ever her order, industry, frugality, a sense of beauty within limits, a certain laudable am-bition to do something and be somebody—only, only he could not sympathize with her ambitions, could not see that she had anything but a hopelessly com-monplace and always unimportant point of view. There was never any flair to her, never any true distinction of mind or soul. She seemed always, in spite of anything he might say or do, hopelessly to identify doing and being with money and current opinion—neighborhood public opinion, almost—and local social position, whereas he knew that distinguished doing might as well be connected with poverty and shame and disgrace as with these other things—wealth and station, for instance; things which she could never quite understand apparently, though he often tried to tell her, much against her mood always.

Look at the cases of the great artists! Some of the greatest architects right here in the city, or in history, were of peculiar, almost disagreeable, history. But no, Mrs. Haymaker could not understand anything like that, anything connected with history, indeed—she hardly believed in history, its dark, sad pages, and would never read it, or at least did not care to. And as for art and artists—she would never have believed that wisdom and art understanding and true distinc-tion might take their rise out of things necessarily low and evil—never.

Take now the case of young Zingara. Zingara was an architect like himself, whom he had met more than thirty years before, here in New York, when he had first arrived, a young man struggling to become an architect of significance, only he was very poor and rather unkempt and disreputable looking. Haymaker had found him several years before his marriage to Ernestine in the dark old offices of Pyne & Starboard, Architects, and had been drawn to him definitely; but because he smoked all the time and was shabby as to his clothes and had no money—why, Mrs. Haymaker, after he had married her, and though he had known Zingara nearly four years, would have none of him. To her he was low, and a failure, one who would never succeed. Once she had seen him in some cheap restaurant that she chanced to be passing, in company with a drabby-looking maid, and that was the end.

"I wish you wouldn't bring him here anymore, dear," she had insisted; and to have peace he had complied—only, now look. Zingara had since become a great architect, but now of course, owing to Mrs. Haymaker, he was definitely alienated. He was the man who had since designed the Æsculapian Club, and Symphony Hall with its delicate facade, as well as the tower of the Wells Building, sending its sweet lines so high, like a poetic thought or dream. But Zingara was now a dreamy recluse like himself, very exclusive, as Haymaker had long since come to know, and indifferent as to what people thought or said.

But perhaps it was not just obtuseness to certain of the finer shades and meanings of life, but an irritating aggressiveness at times, backed only by her limited understanding, which caused her to seek and wish to be here, there and the other place; wherever, in her mind, the truly successful—which meant nearly always the materially successful of a second or third rate character—were, which irritated him most of all. How often had he tried to point out the difference between true and shoddy distinction—the former rarely connected with great wealth.

But no. So often she seemed to imagine such queer people to be truly successful, when they were really not—usually people with just money, or a very little more.

And in the matter of rearing and educating and marrying their two children, Wesley and Ethelberta, who had come after Elwell. What peculiar pains and feelings had not been involved in all this for him. In infancy both of these had seemed sweet enough, and so close to him, though never quite so wonderful as Elwell. But, as they grew, it seemed somehow as though Ernestine had come between him and them. First, it was the way she had raised them, the very stiff and formal manner in which they were supposed to move and be, copied from the few new-rich whom she had chanced to meet through him—and admired in spite of his warnings. That was the irony of architecture as a profession—it was always bringing such queer people close to one, and for the sake of one's profession, sometimes, particularly in the case of the young architect, one had to be nice to them. Later, it was the kind of school they should attend. He had half imagined at first that it would be the public school, because they both had begun as simple people; but no, since they were prospering it had to be a private school for each, and not one of his selection, either—or hers, really—but one to which the Barlows and the Westervelts, two families of means with whom Ernestine had become intimate, sent their children and therefore thought excellent!

The Barlows! Wealthy, but, to him, gross and mediocre people who had made a great deal of money in the manufacture of patent medicines out West, and who had then come to New York to splurge, and had been attracted to Ernestine—not him particularly, he imagined—because Haymaker had built a town house for them, and also because he was gaining a fine reputation. They were dreadful really, so *gauche*,[5] so truly dull; and yet somehow they seemed to suit Ernestine's sense of fitness and worth at the time, because, as she said, they were good and kind—like her Western home folks; only they were not really. She just imagined so. They were worthy enough people in their way, though with no taste. Young Fred Barlow had been sent to an expensive school for boys, near Morristown, where they were taught manners and airs, and little else, as Haymaker always thought, though Ernestine insisted that they were given a religious training as well. And so Wesley had to go there—for a time, anyhow. It was the best school.

And similarly, because Mercedes Westervelt, senseless, vain little thing, was sent to a big school, near White Plains, Ethelberta had to go there. Think of it! It was all so silly, so pushing. How well he remembered the long, delicate campaign which preceded this, the logic and tactics employed, the importance of it socially to Ethelberta, the tears and cajolery. Mrs. Haymaker could always cry so easily, or seem to be on the verge of it, when she wanted anything; and somehow, in spite of the fact that he knew her tears were unimportant, or timed and for a purpose, he could never stand out against them, and she knew it. Always he felt moved or weakened in spite of himself. He had no weapon wherewith to fight them, though he resented them as a part of the argument. Positively Mrs. Haymaker could be as sly and as ruthless as Machiavelli himself at times, and yet believe all the while that she was tender, loving, self-sacrificing, generous, moral and a dozen other things, all of which led to the final achievement of her own aims. Perhaps this was admirable from one point of view, but it irritated him always. But if one were unable to see himself—or herself—his actual disturbing inconsistencies, what were you to do?

And again, he had by then been married so long that it was almost impossible to think of throwing her over, or so it seemed at the time. They had reached the place then where they had supposedly achieved position together, though in reality it was all his—and not such position as he was entitled to, at that. Ernestine—and he was thinking this in all kindness—could never attract the ideal sort. And anyhow, the mere breath of a scandal between them, separation or unfaithfulness, which he never really contemplated, would have led to endless bickering and social and commercial injury, or so he thought. All her strong friends—and his, in a way—those who had originally been his clients, would have deserted him. Their wives, their own social fears, would have compelled them to ostracize him! He would have been a scandal-marked architect, a brute for objecting to so kind and faithful and loving a wife. And perhaps he would have been, at that. He could never quite tell—it was all so mixed and tangled.

Take, again, the marriage of his son Wesley into the De Gaud family—George de Gaud *père*[6] being nothing more than a retired real-estate speculator and promoter who had money, but nothing more; and Irma de Gaud, the daughter, being a gross, coarse, sensuous girl, physically attractive no doubt, and financially reasonably secure, or so she had seemed; but what else? Nothing, literally nothing; and his son had seemed to have at least some spiritual ideals at first. Ernestine had taken up with Mrs. George de Gaud—a miserable, narrow creature, so Haymaker thought—largely for Wesley's sake, he presumed. Anyhow,

everything had been done to encourage Wesley in his suit and Irma in her toleration, and now look at them! De Gaud *père* had since failed and left his daughter
practically nothing. Irma had been interested in anything but Wesley's career,
had followed what she considered the smart among the new-rich—a smarter,
wilder, newer new-rich than ever Ernestine had fancied, or could. Today she was
without a thought for anything besides teas and country clubs and theaters—and
what else?

And long since Wesley had begun to realize it himself. He was an engineer
now, in the employ of one of the great construction companies, a moderately
successful man. But even Ernestine, who had engineered the match and thought
it wonderful, was now down on her. She had begun to see through her some years
ago, when Irma had begun to ignore her; only before it was always the De Gauds
here and the De Gauds there. Good gracious, what more could anyone want
than the De Gauds—Irma de Gaud, for instance? Then came the concealed dis-
sension between Irma and Wesley, and now Mrs. Haymaker insisted that Irma
had held, and was holding, Wesley back. She was not the right woman for him.
Almost—against all her prejudices—she was willing that he should leave her.
Only, if Haymaker had broached anything like that in connection with himself!

And yet Mrs. Haymaker had been determined, because of what she considered the position of the De Gauds at that time, that Wesley should marry Irma.
Wesley now had to slave at mediocre tasks in order to have enough to allow Irma
to run in so-called fast society of a second or third rate. And even at that she was
not faithful to him—or so Haymaker believed. There were so many strange evidences. And yet Haymaker felt that he did not care to interfere now. How could
he? Irma was tired of Wesley, and that was all there was to it. She was looking
elsewhere, he was sure.

Take but one more case, that of Ethelberta. What a name! In spite of all Ernestine's determination to make her so successful and thereby reflect some credit
on, her, had she really succeeded in so doing? To be sure, Ethelberta's marriage
was somewhat more successful financially than Wesley's had proved to be, but
was she any better placed in other ways? John Kelso "Jack," as she always called
him—with his light ways and lighter mind, was he really anyone—anything
more than a waster? His parents stood by him, no doubt, but that was all; and so
much the worse for him. According to Mrs. Haymaker at the time, he, too, was
an ideal boy, admirable, just the man for Ethelberta, because the Kelsos, *père* and
mère,[7] had money. Horner Kelso had made a kind of fortune in Chicago in the
banknote business, and had settled in New York, about the time that Ethelberta
was fifteen, to spend it. Ethelberta had met Grace Kelso at school.

And now see! She was not unattractive, and had some pleasant, albeit highly
affected, social ways; she had money, and a comfortable apartment in Park Avenue; but what had it all come to? John Kelso had never done anything really,
nothing. His parents' money and indulgence and his early training for a better
social state had ruined him if he had ever had a mind that amounted to anything.
He was idle, pleasure-loving, mentally indolent, like Irma de Gaud. Those two

should have met and married, only they could never have endured each other. But how Mrs. Haymaker had courted the Kelsos in her eager and yet diplomatic way, giving teas and receptions and theater parties; and yet he had never been able to exchange ten significant words with either of them, or the younger Kelsos either. Think of it!

And somehow in the process Ethelberta, for all his early affection and tenderness and his still kindly feeling for her, had been weaned away from him and had proved a limited and conventional girl, somewhat like her mother, and more inclined to listen to her than to him—though he had not minded that really. It had been the same with Wesley before her. Perhaps, however, a child was entitled to its likes and dislikes, regardless.

But why had he stood for it all, he now kept asking himself. Why? What grand results, if any, had been achieved? Were their children so wonderful—their lives? Would he not have been better off without her—his children better, even, by a different woman? Wouldn't it have been better if he had destroyed it all, broken away? There would have been pain, of course, terrible consequences, but even so he would have been free to go, to do, to reorganize his life on another basis. Zingara had avoided marriage entirely—wise man. But no, no; always convention, that long list of reasons and terrors he was always reciting to himself. He had allowed himself to be pulled round by the nose, God only knows why, and that was all there was to it. Weakness, if you will, perhaps; fear of convention; fear of what people would think and say.

Always now he found himself brooding over the dire results to him of all this respect on his part for convention, moral order, the duty of keeping society on an even keel, of not bringing disgrace to his children and himself and her, and yet ruining his own life emotionally by so doing. To be respectable had been so important that it had resulted in spiritual failure for him. But now all that was over with him, and Mrs. Haymaker was ill, near to death, and he was expected to wish her to get well, and be happy with her for a long time yet! Be happy! In spite of anything he might wish or think he ought to do, he couldn't. He couldn't even wish her to get well.

It was too much to ask. There was actually a haunting satisfaction in the thought that she might die now. It wouldn't be much, but it would be something—a few years of freedom. That was something. He was not utterly old yet, and he might have a few years of peace and comfort to himself still—and—and—That dream—that dream—though it might never come true now—it couldn't really still—still—He wanted to be free to go his own way once more, to do as he pleased, to walk, to think, to brood over what he had not had—to brood over what he had not had! Only, only, whenever he looked into her pale sick face and felt her damp limp hands he could not quite wish that, either; not quite, not even now. It seemed too hard, too brutal—only only—So he wavered.

No; in spite of her long-past struggle over foolish things and in spite of himself and all he had endured or thought he had, he was still willing that she should live; only he couldn't wish it exactly. Yes, let her live if she could. What matter to him now whether she lived or died? Whenever he looked at her he could not help thinking how helpless she would be without him, what a failure at her age, and so on. And all along, as he wryly repeated to himself, she had been thinking and feeling that she was doing the very best for him and her and the children—that she was really the ideal wife for him, making every dollar go as far as it would, every enjoyment yield the last drop for them all, every move seeming to have been made to their general advantage! Yes, that was true. There was a pathos about it, wasn't there? But as for the actual results—

The next morning found him sitting once more beside his front window in the early dawn, and so much of all this, and more, was coming back to him, as before. For the thousandth or the ten-thousandth time, as it seemed to him, in all the years that had gone, he was concluding again that his life was a failure. If only he were free for a little while just to be alone and think, perhaps to discover what life might bring him yet; only on this occasion his thoughts were colored by a new turn in the situation. Yesterday afternoon, because Mrs. Haymaker's condition had grown worse, the consultation between Grainger and Storm was held earlier, and today sometime transfusion was to be tried, that last grim stand taken by physicians in distress over a case; blood taken from a strong ex-cavalryman out of a position, in this case, and the best to be hoped for, but not assured. In this instance his thoughts were, as before, wavering. Now supposing she really died, in spite of this? What would he think of himself then? He went back after a time and looked in on his wife, who was still sleeping. Now she was not so strong as before, or so the nurse said; her pulse was not so good. And now, as before, his mood changed in her favor, but only for a little while. She seemed to look better.

Later he came up to the dining room, where the nurse was taking her breakfast, and seating himself, asked: "How do you think she is today?"

He and the night nurse had thus had their breakfasts together for days. This nurse, Miss Filson, was such a smooth, pink, graceful creature, with light hair and blue eyes, the kind of eyes and color that of late, and in earlier years, had suggested to him the youth that he had missed.

She looked grave, as though she really feared the worst but was concealing it.

"No worse, I think, and possibly a little better," she replied, eying him sympathetically. He could see that she, too, felt that he was old and in danger of being neglected. "Her pulse is a little stronger, nearly normal now, and she is resting easily. Doctor Storm and Doctor Grainger are coming, though, at ten. Then they'll decide what's to be done. I think if she's worse that they are going to try transfusion. The man has been engaged. Doctor Storm said that when she woke today she was to be given strong beef tea. Mrs. Elfridge is making it now. The fact that she is not much worse, though, is a good sign in itself, I think."

Haymaker merely stared at her from under his heavy gray eyebrows. He was so tired and gloomy, not only because he had not slept much of late himself but because of this sawing to and fro between his varying moods. Was he never to be able to decide for himself what he really wished? Was he never to be done with this interminable moral or spiritual problem? Miss Filson pattered on about

other heart cases, how so many people lived years and years after they were supposed to die of heart lesion; and he meditated as to the grayness and strangeness
of it all, the worthlessness of his own life, the variability of his own moods. Why
was he so? How queer—how almost evil, sinister—he had become at times; how
weak at others. Last night as he had looked at Ernestine lying in bed, and this
morning before he had seen her, he had thought if she only would die—if he
were only really free once more, even at this late date. But then when he saw
her again this morning, and now when Miss Filson spoke of transfusion, he felt
sorry again. What good would it do him now? Why should he want to kill her?
Could such evil ideas go unpunished either in this world or the next? Supposing
his children could guess! Supposing she did die now—and he had wished it so
fervently only this morning—how would he feel? After all, Ernestine had not
been so bad. She had tried, hadn't she?—only she had not been able to make a
success of things, as he saw it, and he had not been able to love her, that was all.
He reproached himself once more now with the hardness and the cruelty of his
thoughts.

The opinion of the two physicians was that Mrs. Haymaker was not much
better, and that this first form of blood transfusion must be resorted to—injected
straight via a pump; which should restore her greatly if her heart did not bleed
it out too freely. Before doing so, however, both men spoke to Haymaker, who in
an excess of self-condemnation insisted that no expense must be spared. If her
life was in danger, save it by any means—all. It was precious to her, to him and to
her children. Thus he could lend every force aside from fervently wishing for her
recovery, which, even now, in spite of himself, he could not do. He was too weary
of it all, the conventional round of duties and obligations. But if she recovered,
as her physicians seemed to think she might if transfusion were tried, and she
gained, it would mean that he would have to take her away for the summer to
some quiet mountain resort—to be with her hourly during the long period in
which she would be recovering. Well, he would not complain now. That was all
right. He would do it. He would be bored of course as usual, but it would be too
bad to have her die when she could be saved. And yet—

He went down to his office now, and in the meantime this first form of transfusion was tried, and proved a great success apparently. She was much better, so
the day nurse phoned at three; very much better. At five-thirty Mr. Haymaker
returned, no unsatisfactory word having come in the interim, and there she was,
resting on a raised pillow, if you please, and looking so cheerful, and more like
her old self than he had seen her in some time.

At once his mood changed again. They were amazing—these variations in
his own thoughts, almost chemic, not volitional, decidedly peculiar for a man
who was supposed to know his own mind—only did one, ever? Now she would
not die. Now the whole thing would go on as before. Well, he might as well resign
himself to the old sense of failure. He would never be free now. Everything
would go on as before—terrible; and the next day it was the same. Though he
seemed glad—really grateful, in a way, seeing her cheerful and hopeful once

more—still the obsession of failure and being bound returned now, and in his own bed at midnight he said to himself: "Now she will really get well. All will be as before. Shall I never be free? Shall I never have a day—a day?"

But the next morning, to his surprise and fear or comfort, as his moods varied, she was worse again; and then once more he reproached himself for his black thoughts. Was he not really killing her by what he thought? he asked himself—these constant changes in his mood. Did not his dark wishes have power? Think, if he had always to feel from now on that he had killed her by wishing so! Would not that be dreadful—an awful thing really? Why was he this way? Could he not be kind, human?

When Doctor Storm came at nine-thirty, after a telephone call from the nurse, and looked grave and spoke of horse's blood as being better, thicker than human blood—not so easily bled out of the heart when injected as a serum, Haymaker was beside himself with self-reproaches and sad, disturbing fear. Why had he wished last night that she would die? Her case must be very desperate. Was he really a murderer at heart, a dark criminal, plotting her death?—and for what?

"You must do your best," he said to Doctor Storm. "Whatever is needful—she must not die if you can help it."

"No, Mr. Haymaker," returned the latter sympathetically. "All that can be done will be done. You need not fear. I have an idea that we didn't inject enough yesterday. She responded, but not enough. We will see what we can do today."

Haymaker, pressed with duties, went away sadly, subdued. Now once more he decided that he must not tolerate these dark ideas anymore; he must rid himself of these black wishes, whatever he might feel. It was evil. They would eventually come back to him in some evil way, he might be sure. They might be influencing her. She must be allowed to recover if she could. He must now make a further sacrifice of his own life, whatever it cost. It was only decent, only human. Why should he complain now, anyhow, after all these years? What difference would a few more years make? He returned at evening, consoled by his own good thoughts and a telephone message at three to the effect that his wife was much better. This second injection had proved much more effective. Horse's blood was plainly better for her. She was stronger, and sitting up again. He entered at five, and found her lying there pale and weak, but still with a better light in her eye—or so he thought—more force, and a very faint smile for him, as well as a touch of color in her cheeks, so marked had been the change. How great and kind Doctor Storm really was! If she would only get well now! If this dread siege would only abate! Doctor Storm was coming again at eight.

"Well, how are you, dear?" she asked, looking at him sweetly and lovingly, and taking his hand in hers.

He bent and kissed her forehead—a Judas kiss,[8] he had thought up to now, but not so tonight. Tonight he was kind, generous—anxious, even, for her to live.

"All right, dearest; very good indeed. And how are you? It's such a fine evening out. You ought to get well soon so as to enjoy these spring days."

"I'm going to," she replied softly. "I feel so much better. And how have you been? Has your work gone all right?"

He nodded and smiled and told her bits of news. Ethelberta had phoned that she was coming, bringing violets. Wesley had said he would be here at six, with Irma! Such-and-such people had asked after her. How could he have been so evil, he now asked himself, as to wish her to die? She was not so bad—really quite charming in her way, an ideal wife for someone if not him. She was as much entitled to live and enjoy her life as he was; and after all she was the mother of his children, had been with him all these years. Besides, the day had been so fine—it was now—a wondrous May evening. The air and sky were simply delicious. The telephone bell now ringing brought still another of a long series of inquiries as to her condition. There had been so many of these during the last few days, the maid said, and especially today and she gave Mr. Haymaker a list of names. See, he thought, she had even more friends than he, being so good, faithful, worthy. Why should he wish her ill?

He sat down to dinner with Ethelberta and Wesley when they arrived, and chatted quite gayly—more hopefully than he had in weeks. His own varying thoughts no longer depressing him, for the moment he was happy. How were they? What were the children all doing? At eight-thirty Doctor Storm came again, and announced that he thought Mrs. Haymaker was doing very well indeed, all things considered.

"Her condition is fairly promising, I must say," he said. "If she gets through another night or two comfortably without falling back I think she'll do very well from now on. Her strength seems to be increasing a fraction. Tomorrow we'll see how she feels, whether she needs any more blood."

He went away, and at ten Ethelberta and Wesley left for the night, leaving him alone once more. Then he sat and meditated. At eleven, after a few moments at his wife's bedside—absolute quiet had been the doctor's instructions these many days—he himself went to bed. He was very tired. His varying thoughts had afflicted him so much that he was always tired, it seemed—his evil conscience, he called it—but tonight he was sure he would sleep. He felt better about himself, about life. He should never have tolerated such dark thoughts. And yet—and yet—and yet—

He lay on his bed near a window which commanded a view of a small angle of the park, and looked out. There were the spring trees, as usual, silvered now by the light, a bit of lake showing at one end. In his youth he had been so fond of water, any small lake or stream or pond. In his youth, also, he had loved the moon, and to walk in the dark. It had all, always, been so suggestive of love and happiness, and he had so craved love and happiness. Once he had designed a yacht club, the base of which suggested waves. Once, years ago, he had thought of designing a lovely cottage or country house for himself and some new love—that wonderful one—if ever she came and he were free. How wonderful it would all have been. Now—now—the thought at such an hour and especially when it was too late, seemed sacrilegious, hard, cold, unmoral, evil. He turned his face away from the moonlight and sighed, deciding to sleep and shut out these older and darker and sweeter thoughts if he could, and did.

Presently he dreamed, and it was as if some lovely spirit of beauty—that wondrous thing he had always been seeking—came and took him by the hand and led him out, out by dimpling streams and clear rippling lakes and a great, noble highway where were temples and towers and figures in white marble. And it seemed, as he walked, as if something had been, or were, promised him—a lovely fruition to something which he craved—only the world toward which he walked was still dark or shadowy, with something sad and repressing about it, a haunting sense of a still darker distance. He was going toward beauty apparently, but he was still seeking, seeking, when—

"Mr. Haymaker! Mr. Haymaker!" came a voice—soft, almost mystical at first, and then clearer and more disturbing afterward, as a hand was laid on him. "Will you come at once? It's Mrs. Haymaker!"

On the instant he was on his feet, seizing the blue silk dressing gown hanging at his bed's head and adjusting it as he hurried. Mrs. Elfridge and the nurse were behind him, very pale and distrait, wringing their hands. When he reached the bedroom—her bedroom—there she lay as in life—still, peaceful, already limp, as though she were sleeping. Her thin, and as he sometimes thought cold, lips were now parted in a kind of faint, gracious smile, or trace of one. He had seen her look that way, too, at times, a really gracious smile, and wise, wiser than she was. The long, thin, graceful hands were open, the fingers spread slightly apart as though she were tired, very tired. The eyelids, too, rested wearily on tired eyes. Her form, spare as always, was outlined clearly under the thin coverlets. Miss Filson, the night nurse, was saying something about having fallen asleep for a moment, and waked only to find her so. She was terribly depressed and disturbed, possibly because of Doctor Storm.

Haymaker paused, greatly shocked and moved by the sight—more so than by anything since the death of little Elwell. After all, she had tried, according to her light. But now she was dead—and they had been together so long! He came forward, tears of sympathy springing to his eyes, then sank down beside the bed on his knees so as not to disturb her right hand where it lay.

"Ernie, dear," he said gently, "Ernie—are you really gone?" His voice was full of sorrow; but to himself it sounded mean, traitorous.

He lifted the hand and put it to his lips sadly, then leaned his head against her,—thinking of his long, mixed thoughts these many days, while both Mrs. Elfridge and the nurse began wiping their eyes. They were so sorry for him, he was so old now!

After a while he got up—they came forward to persuade him at last—looking tremendously sad and distrait, and asked Mrs. Elfridge and the nurse not to disturb his children. They could not aid her now. Let them rest until morning. Then he went back to his own room and sat down on the bed for a moment, gazing out on the same silvery scene that had attracted him before. So then his dark wishing had come true at last? It was dreadful. Possibly his black thoughts had killed her after all. Was that possible? Had his voiceless prayers been answered in this grim way? And did she know now what he had really thought? Dark thought. Where was she now? What was she thinking now if she knew? Would she hate him—haunt him? It was not dawn yet, only two or three in the morning, and the moon was still bright. And in the next room she was lying, pale and cool, gone forever now out of his life.

He got up after a time and went forward into that pleasant front room where he had loved to sit so often, then back into her room to view the body again. Now that she was gone, here more than elsewhere, in her dead presence, he seemed better able to collect his scattered thoughts. She might see or she might not—might know or not. It was all over now. Only he could not help but feel a little evil. She had been so faithful, if nothing more, so earnest in behalf of him and of his children. His feelings were so jumbled that he could not place them half the time. But at the same time the ethics of the past, of his own irritated feelings and moods in regard to her, had to be adjusted somehow before he could have peace. They must be adjusted; only how—how?

After a time he came forward once more to the front room to sit and gaze at the park. Here, perhaps, he could solve these mysteries for himself, think them out, find out what he did feel. He was evil for wishing all he had—that he knew and felt. The dawn was breaking by now; a faint grayness shaded the east and dimly lightened this room. A tall pier mirror between two windows now revealed him to himself—spare, angular, disheveled, his beard and hair astray and his eyes weary. The figure he made here as against his dreams of a happier life, once he were free, now struck him forcibly. What a farce! What a failure! Why should he, of all people, think of further happiness in love, even if he were free? Look at his reflection here in this mirror. What a picture—old, grizzled, done for! Had he not known that for so long? Was it not too ridiculous. No thing of beauty would have him now. Of course not. That glorious dream of his youth was gone forever. His wife might just as well have lived as died, for all the difference it would or could make to him. Only he was really free just the same almost as it were in spite of his varying moods. But he was old, weary, done for, a recluse and ungainly.

He stared first at his dark wrinkled skin; the crow's-feet at the sides of his eyes; the wrinkles across his forehead and between the eyes; his long, dark, wrinkled hands—handsome hands they once were, he thought; his angular, stiff body. Once he had been very much of a personage, he thought, striking, forceful, dynamic—but now! He turned and looked out over the park where the young trees were, and the lake, to the pinking dawn—just a trace now—a significant thing in itself at this hour surely—then back at himself. What could he wish for now—what hope for?

As he did so his dream came back to him—that strange dream of seeking and being led and promised and yet always being led forward into a dimmer, darker land. What did that mean? Had it any real significance? Was it all to be dimmer, darker still? Was it typical of his life? He pondered.

"Free!" he said after a time. "Free! I know now how that is. I am free now, at last! Free! . . . Free! . . . Yes—free . . . to die!" So he stood there ruminating and smoothing his beard.

NOTES

1. This location situates the story in New York City.
2. In a story recorded by Plutarch, circa 100 CE, some boys from the Greek city of Sparta were engaged in a game of stealing to prove their bravery to one another; one boy concealed a young fox under his coat, never flinching as it attacked and mauled him, because for Spartans experiencing physical pain yet remaining silent was preferable to the mental pain and public disgrace of showing "weakness."
3. A man who frequently seduces women. The character of Lothario originally appeared in a story entitled "El Curioso Impertinente" ("The Impertinently Curious Man"), found in book 1 of Miguel de Cervantes's famous novel *The Ingenious Gentleman Don Quixote of La Mancha* (published in two parts in 1605 and 1615).
4. In Greek mythology, a chimera is a fire-breathing female monster composed of parts from a lion, goat, and serpent; the term can also refer more generally to imaginary beasts who are similarly implausible.
5. Unsophisticated (French).
6. Father (French)
7. Mother (French)
8. In all four canonical Gospels of the Bible, Judas Iscariot kisses Jesus in order to identify him to those who will arrest him and lead him to his death; it has come to represent more generally an act of betrayal by a trusted friend.

PAUL LAURENCE DUNBAR

(1872–1906)

For a long time after his death, Paul Laurence Dunbar was remembered chiefly as the author of numerous highly popular poems written in what is known today as African American Vernacular English. In fact, the popularity among White readers of this dialect poetry—which often included Black characters who longed for the "happy" days of pre–Civil War slavery or who lazily wasted their days in all kinds of ways—made him the first African American poet to achieve national and international fame. Yet some critics have charged that Dunbar, in order to publish his work and make a living as a writer, "sold out" to White editors and readers by giving them the type of demeaning, stereotypical images of African Americans they wanted. Largely because of these criticisms, most literary academics ignored Dunbar not only in the 1970s, when they began actively seeking out works by early African American authors to include in anthologies, but also in the decades afterward.

In recent years, however, this conception of Dunbar and his writing has begun to change as scholars have looked more closely at his work, especially his later short stories and one of his novels, *The Sport of the Gods* (1902). It is now clear that after he had achieved strong name recognition, Dunbar broke away from the constraints of what White editors and audiences wanted in order to write works that detailed in powerful terms how poorly he felt African Americans had been treated by White American society. For instance, some of his poems, most notably the widely anthologized "We Wear the Mask" (1895), "Sympathy" (1899), and "The Haunted Oak" (1900), portray in blistering detail the pain and suffering of African Americans. A great many of his short stories, too, criticized African Americans' treatment by White society; unfortunately, these were not accepted by mainstream periodicals for publication, which negatively affected Dunbar's income. He was forced to instead include them in various less remunerative short story collections that had comparatively smaller audiences; "One Man's Fortunes," for instance, appeared in *The Strength of Gideon and Other Stories* (1900), and "The Lynching of Jube Benson" was included in *The Heart of Happy Hollow* (1904).

The final years of Dunbar's life, despite his numerous publications and fame, were not happy ones. Diagnosed with tuberculosis in 1900, he was told by doctors to begin drinking whiskey in order to ease the pain. He became an alcoholic and developed a highly mercurial temperament, which caused great friction with his wife, Alice, a poet and writer whom he had married in March 1898, and they separated in 1902. Toward the end of Dunbar's life, when he needed to make money to support himself and his mother, he was forced to return to writing dialect poetry. Dunbar spent his final years in severely diminished health, living in his hometown of Dayton, Ohio, where he died at the age of thirty-three.

*Readers should be aware that both of the Dunbar stories included here include some language which, while commonly used during this time period, is no longer considered acceptable because of its offensive nature.

ONE MAN'S FORTUNES (1900)

PART I

When Bertram Halliday left the institution which, in the particular part of the middle west where he was born, was called the state university, he did not believe, as young graduates are reputed to, that he had conquered the world and had only to come into his kingdom. He knew that the battle of life was, in reality, just beginning and, with a common sense unusual to his twenty-three years but born out of the exigencies of a none-too-easy life, he recognized that for him the battle would be harder than for his white comrades.

Looking at his own position, he saw himself the member of a race dragged from complacent savagery into the very heat and turmoil of a civilization for which it was in nowise prepared; bowed beneath a yoke to which its shoulders were not fitted, and then, without warning, thrust forth into a freedom as absurd as it was startling and overwhelming. And yet, he felt, as most young men must feel, an individual strength that would exempt him from the workings of the general law. His outlook on life was calm and unfrightened. Because he knew the dangers that beset his way, he feared them less. He felt assured because with so clear an eye he saw the weak places in his armor which the world he was going to meet would attack, and these he was prepared to strengthen. Was it not the fault of youth and self-confessed weakness, he thought, to go into the world always thinking of it as a foe? Was not this great Cosmopolis, this dragon of a thousand talons kind as well as cruel? Had it not friends as well as enemies? Yes. That was it: the outlook of young men, of colored[1] young men in particular, was all wrong,—they had gone at the world in the wrong spirit. They had looked upon it as a terrible foeman and forced it to be one. He would do it, oh, so differently. He would take the world as a friend. He would even take the old, old world under his wing.

They sat in the room talking that night, he and Webb Davis and Charlie McLean. It was the last night they were to be together in so close a relation. The commencement was over. They had their sheepskins.[2] They were pitched there on the bed very carelessly to be the important things they were,—the reward of four years digging in Greek and Mathematics.

They had stayed after the exercises of the day just where they had first stopped. This was at McLean's rooms, dismantled and topsy-turvy with the business of packing. The pipes were going and the talk kept pace. Old men smoke slowly and in great whiffs with long intervals of silence between their observations. Young men draw fast and say many and bright things, for young men are wise,—while they are young.

"Now, it's just like this," Davis was saying to McLean, "Here we are, all three of us turned out into the world like a lot of little sparrows pitched out of the nest, and what are we going to do? Of course it's easy enough for you, McLean, but what are my grave friend with the nasty black briar, and I, your humble servant, to do? In what wilderness are we to pitch our tents and where is our manna coming from?"

"Oh, well, the world owes us all a living," said McLean.

"Hackneyed, but true. Of course it does; but every time a colored man goes around to collect, the world throws up its hands and yells 'insolvent'—eh, Halliday?"

Halliday took his pipe from his mouth as if he were going to say something. Then he put it back without speaking and looked meditatively through the blue smoke.

"I'm right," Davis went on, "to begin with, we colored people haven't any show here. Now, if we could go to Central or South America, or some place like that,—but hang it all, who wants to go thousands of miles away from home to earn a little bread and butter?"

"There's India and the young Englishmen, if I remember rightly," said McLean.

"Oh, yes, that's all right, with the Cabots and Drake and Sir John Franklin[3] behind them. Their traditions, their blood, all that they know makes them willing to go 'where there ain't no ten commandments and a man can raise a thirst,'[4] but for me, home, if I can call it home."

"Well, then, stick it out."

"That's easy enough to say, McLean; but ten to one you've got some snap picked out for you already, now 'fess up, ain't you?"

"Well, of course I'm going in with my father, I can't help that, but I've got—"

"To be sure," broke in Davis, "you go in with your father. Well, if all I had to do was to step right out of college into my father's business with an assured salary, however small, I shouldn't be falling on my own neck and weeping to-night. But that's just the trouble with us; we haven't got fathers before us or behind us, if you'd rather."

"More luck to you, you'll be a father before or behind some one else; you'll be an ancestor."

"It's more profitable being a descendant, I find."

A glow came into McLean's face and his eyes sparkled as he replied: "Why, man, if I could, I'd change places with you. You don't deserve your fate. What is before you? Hardships, perhaps, and long waiting. But then, you have the zest of the fight, the joy of the action and the chance of conquering. Now what is before me,—me, whom you are envying? I go out of here into a dull counting-room. The way is prepared for me. Perhaps I shall have no hardships, but neither have I the joy that comes from pains endured. Perhaps I shall have no battle, but even so, I lose the pleasure of the fight and the glory of winning. Your fate is infinitely to be preferred to mine."

"Ah, now you talk with the voluminous voice of the centuries," bantered Davis. "You are but echoing the breath of your Nelsons, your Cabots, your Drakes and your Franklins. Why, can't you see, you sentimental idiot, that it's all different and has to be different with us? The Anglo-Saxon race has been producing that fine frenzy in you for seven centuries and more. You come, with the blood of merchants, pioneers and heroes in your veins, to a normal battle. But for me, my forebears were savages two hundred years ago. My people learn to know civilization by the lowest and most degrading contact with it, and thus equipped or unequipped I tempt, an abnormal contest. Can't you see the disproportion?"

"If I do, I can also see the advantage of it."

"For the sake of common sense, Halliday," said Davis, turning to his companion, "don't sit there like a clam; open up and say something to convince this Don Quixote[5] who, because he himself, sees only windmills, cannot be persuaded that we have real dragons to fight."

"Do you fellows know Henley?"[6] asked Halliday, with apparent irrelevance.

"I know him as a critic," said McLean.

"I know him as a name," echoed the worldly Davis, "but—"

"I mean his poems," resumed Halliday, "he is the most virile of the present-day poets. Kipling is virile, but he gives you the man in hot blood with the brute in him to the fore; but the strong masculinity of Henley is essentially intellectual. It is the mind that is conquering always."

"Well, now that you have settled the relative place in English letters of Kipling and Henley, might I be allowed humbly to ask what in the name of all that is good has that to do with the question before the house?"

"I don't know your man's poetry," said McLean, "but I do believe that I can see what you are driving at."

"Wonderful perspicacity, oh, youth!"

"If Webb will agree not to run, I'll spring on you the poem that seems to me to strike the keynote of the matter in hand."

"Oh, well, curiosity will keep me. I want to get your position, and I want to see McLean annihilated."

In a low, even tone, but without attempt at dramatic effect, Halliday began to recite:

> *"Out of the night that covers me,*
> *Black as the pit from pole to pole,*
> *I thank whatever gods there be*
> *For my unconquerable soul!*
> *"In the fell clutch of circumstance,*
> *I have not winced nor cried aloud.*
> *Under the bludgeonings of chance,*
> *My head is bloody, but unbowed.*
> *"Beyond this place of wrath and tears*
> *Looms but the horror of the shade,*
> *And yet the menace of the years*
> *Finds, and shall find me unafraid.*
> *"It matters not how strait the gate,*
> *How charged with punishments the scroll,*
> *I am the master of my fate,*
> *I am the captain of my soul."*[7]

"That's it," exclaimed McLean, leaping to his feet, "that's what I mean. That's the sort of a stand for a man to take."

Davis rose and knocked the ashes from his pipe against the window-sill. "Well, for two poetry-spouting, poetry-consuming, sentimental idiots, commend me to you fellows. 'Master of my fate,' 'captain of my soul,' be dashed! Old Jujube, with his bone-pointed hunting spear, began determining a couple of hundred years ago what I should be in this year of our Lord one thousand eight hundred and ninety-four. J. Webb Davis, senior, added another brick to this structure, when he was picking cotton on his master's plantation forty years ago."

"And now," said Halliday, also rising, "don't you think it fair that you should start out with the idea of adding a few bricks of your own, and all of a better make than those of your remote ancestor, Jujube, or that nearer one, your father?"

"Spoken like a man," said McLean.

"Oh, you two are so hopelessly young," laughed Davis.

PART II

After the two weeks' rest which he thought he needed, and consequently promised himself, Halliday began to look about him for some means of making a start
for that success in life which he felt so sure of winning.

With this end in view he returned to the town where he was born. He had
settled upon the law as a profession, and had studied it for a year or two while at
college. He would go back to Broughton now to pursue his studies, but of course,
he needed money. No difficulty, however, presented itself in the getting of this for
he knew several fellows who had been able to go into offices, and by collecting
and similar duties make something while they studied. Webb Davis would have
said, "but they were white," but Halliday knew what his own reply would have
been: "What a white man can do, I can do."

Even if he could not go to studying at once, he could go to work and save
enough money to go on with his course in a year or two. He had lots of time before him, and he only needed a little start. What better place then, to go to than
Broughton, where he had first seen the light? Broughton, that had known him,
boy and man. Broughton that had watched him through the common school and
the high school, and had seen him go off to college with some pride and a good
deal of curiosity. For even in middle west towns of such a size, that is, between
seventy and eighty thousand souls, a "smart negro" was still a freak.

So Halliday went back home because the people knew him there and would
respect his struggles and encourage his ambitions.

He had been home two days, and the old town had begun to take on its remembered aspect as he wandered through the streets and along the river banks.
On this second day he was going up Main street deep in a brown study when he
heard his name called by a young man who was approaching him, and saw an
outstretched hand.

"Why, how de do, Bert, how are you? Glad to see you back. I hear you have
been astonishing them up at college."

Halliday's reverie had been so suddenly broken into that for a moment, the
young fellow's identity wavered elusively before his mind and then it materi-
alized, and his consciousness took hold of it. He remembered him, not as an
intimate, but as an acquaintance whom he had often met upon the football and
baseball fields.

"How do you do? It's Bob Dickson," he said, shaking the proffered hand,
which at the mention of the name, had grown unaccountably cold in his grasp.

"Yes, I'm Mr. Dickson," said the young man, patronizingly. "You seem to
have developed wonderfully, you hardly seem like the same Bert Halliday I used
to know."

"Yes, but I'm the same Mr. Halliday."

"Oh—ah—yes," said the young man, "well, I'm glad to have seen you.
Ah—good-bye, Bert."

"Good-bye, Bob."

"Presumptuous darky!"[8] murmured Mr. Dickson.

"Insolent puppy!" said Mr. Halliday to himself.

But the incident made no impression on his mind as bearing upon his status in the public eye. He only thought the fellow a cad, and went hopefully on. He was rather amused than otherwise. In this frame of mind, he turned into one of the large office-buildings that lined the street and made his way to a business suite over whose door was the inscription, "H. G. Featherton, Counsellor and Attorney-at-Law." Mr. Featherton had shown considerable interest in Bert in his school days, and he hoped much from him.

As he entered the public office, a man sitting at the large desk in the centre of the room turned and faced him. He was a fair man of an indeterminate age, for you could not tell whether those were streaks of grey shining in his light hair, or only the glint which it took on in the sun. His face was dry, lean and intellectual. He smiled now and then, and his smile was like a flash of winter lightning, so cold and quick it was. It went as suddenly as it came, leaving the face as marbly cold and impassive as ever. He rose and extended his hand, "Why—why—ah—Bert, how de do, how are you?"

"Very well, I thank you, Mr. Featherton."

"Hum, I'm glad to see you back, sit down. Going to stay with us, you think?"

"I'm not sure, Mr. Featherton; it all depends upon my getting something to do."

"You want to go to work, do you? Hum, well, that's right. It's work makes the man. What do you propose to do, now since you've graduated?"

Bert warmed at the evident interest of his old friend. "Well, in the first place, Mr. Featherton," he replied, "I must get to work and make some money. I have heard of fellows studying and supporting themselves at the same time, but I musn't expect too much. I'm going to study law."

The attorney had schooled his face into hiding any emotion he might feel, and it did not betray him now. He only flashed one of his quick cold smiles and asked,

"Don't you think you've taken rather a hard profession to get on in?"

"No doubt. But anything I should take would be hard. It's just like this, Mr. Featherton," he went on, "I am willing to work and to work hard, and I am not looking for any snap."

Mr. Featherton was so unresponsive to this outburst that Bert was ashamed of it the minute it left his lips. He wished this man would not be so cold and polite and he wished he would stop putting the ends of his white fingers together as carefully as if something depended upon it.

"I say the law is a hard profession to get on in, and as a friend I say that it will be harder for you. Your people have not the money to spend in litigation of any kind."

"I should not cater for the patronage of my own people alone."

"Yes, but the time has not come when a white person will employ a colored attorney."

"Do you mean to say that the prejudice here at home is such that if I were as competent as a white lawyer a white person would not employ me?"

"I say nothing about prejudice at all. It's nature. They have their own lawyers; why should they go outside of their own to employ a colored man?"

"But I am of their own. I am an American citizen, there should be no thought of color about it."

"Oh, my boy, that theory is very nice, but State University democracy doesn't obtain in real life."

"More's the pity, then, for real life."

"Perhaps, but we must take things as we find them, not as we think they ought to be. You people are having and will have for the next ten or a dozen years the hardest fight of your lives. The sentiment of remorse and the desire for atoning which actuated so many white men to help negroes right after the war has passed off without being replaced by that sense of plain justice which gives a black man his due, not because of, nor in spite of, but without consideration of his color."

"I wonder if it can be true, as my friend Davis says, that a colored man must do twice as much and twice as well as a white man before he can hope for even equal chances with him? That white mediocrity demands black genius to cope with it?"

"I am afraid your friend has philosophized the situation about right."

"Well, we have dealt in generalities," said Bert, smiling, "let us take up the particular and personal part of this matter. Is there any way you could help me to a situation?"

"Well,—I should be glad to see you get on, Bert, but as you see, I have nothing in my office that you could do. Now, if you don't mind beginning at the bottom—"

"That's just what I expected to do."

"—Why I could speak to the head-waiter of the hotel where I stay. He's a very nice colored man and I have some influence with him. No doubt Charlie could give you a place."

"But that's a work I abhor."

"Yes, but you must begin at the bottom, you know. All young men must."

"To be sure, but would you have recommended the same thing to your nephew on his leaving college?"

"Ah—ah—that's different."

"Yes," said Halliday, rising, "it is different. There's a different bottom at which black and white young men should begin, and by a logical sequence, a different top to which they should aspire. However, Mr. Featherton, I'll ask you to hold your offer in abeyance. If I can find nothing else, I'll ask you to speak to the head-waiter. Good-morning."

"I'll do so with pleasure," said Mr. Featherton, "and good-morning."

As the young man went up the street, an announcement card in the window of a publishing house caught his eye. It was the announcement of the next Sunday's number in a series of addresses which the local business men were giving before the Y. M. C. A. It read, "'How a Christian young man can get on in the law'—an address by a Christian lawyer—H. G. Featherton."

Bert laughed. "I should like to hear that address," he said. "I wonder if he'll recommend them to his head-waiter. No, 'that's different.' All the addresses and all the books written on how to get on, are written for white men. We blacks must solve the question for ourselves."

He had lost some of the ardor with which he had started out but he was still full of hope. He refused to accept Mr. Featherton's point of view as general or final. So he hailed a passing car that in the course of a half hour set him down at the door of the great factory which, with its improvements, its army of clerks and employees, had built up one whole section of the town. He felt especially hopeful in attacking this citadel, because they were constantly advertising for clerks and their placards plainly stated that preference would be given to graduates of the local high school. The owners were philanthropists in their way. Well, what better chance could there be before him? He had graduated there and stood well in his classes, and besides, he knew that a number of his classmates were holding good positions in the factory. So his voice was cheerful as he asked to see Mr. Stockard, who had charge of the clerical department.

Mr. Stockard was a fat, wheezy young man, with a reputation for humor based entirely upon his size and his rubicund face, for he had really never said anything humorous in his life. He came panting into the room now with a "Well, what can I do for you?"

"I wanted to see you about a situation"—began Halliday.

"Oh, no, no, you don't want to see me," broke in Stockard, "you want to see the head janitor."

"But I don't want to see the head janitor. l want to see the head of the clerical department."

"You want to see the head of the clerical department!"

"Yes, sir, I see you are advertising for clerks with preference given to the high school boys. Well, I am an old high school boy, but have been away for a few years at college."

Mr. Stockard opened his eyes to their widest extent, and his jaw dropped. Evidently he had never come across such presumption before.

"We have nothing for you," he wheezed after awhile.

"Very well, I should be glad to drop in again and see you," said Halliday, moving to the door. "I hope you will remember me if anything opens."

Mr. Stockard did not reply to this or to Bert's good-bye. He stood in the middle of the floor and stared at the door through which the colored man had gone, then he dropped into a chair with a gasp.

"Well, I'm dumbed!" he said.

A doubt had begun to arise in Bertram Halliday's mind that turned him cold and then hot with a burning indignation. He could try nothing more that morning. It had brought him nothing but rebuffs. He hastened home and threw himself down on the sofa to try and think out his situation.

"Do they still require of us bricks without straw?[9] I thought all that was over. Well, I suspect that I will have to ask Mr. Featherton to speak to his head-waiter in my behalf. I wonder if the head-waiter will demand my diploma. Webb Davis, you were nearer right than I thought."

He spent the day in the house thinking and planning.

PART III

Halliday was not a man to be discouraged easily, and for the next few weeks he kept up an unflagging search for work. He found that there were more Feathertons and Stockards than he had ever looked to find. Everywhere that he turned his face, anything but the most menial work was denied him. He thought once of going away from Broughton, but would he find it any better anywhere else, he asked himself? He determined to stay and fight it out there for two reasons. First, because he held that it would be cowardice to run away, and secondly, because he felt that he was not fighting a local disease, but was bringing the force of his life to bear upon a national evil. Broughton was as good a place to begin curative measures as elsewhere.

There was one refuge which was open to him, and which he fought against with all his might. For years now, from as far back as he could remember, the colored graduates had "gone South to teach." This course was now recommended to him. Indeed, his own family quite approved of it, and when he still stood out against the scheme, people began to say that Bertram Halliday did not want work; he wanted to be a gentleman.

But Halliday knew that the South had plenty of material, and year by year was raising and training her own teachers. He knew that the time would come, if it were not present when it would be impossible to go South to teach, and he felt it to be essential that the North should be trained in a manner looking to the employment of her own negroes. So he stayed. But he was only human, and when the tide of talk anent his indolence began to ebb and flow about him, he availed himself of the only expedient that could arrest it.

When he went back to the great factory where he had seen and talked with Mr. Stockard, he went around to another door and this time asked for the head janitor. This individual, a genial Irishman, took stock of Halliday at a glance.

"But what do ye want to be doin' sich wurruk for, whin ye've been through school?" he asked.

"I am doing the only thing I can get to do," was the answer.

"Well," said the Irishman, "ye've got sinse, anyhow."

Bert found himself employed as an under janitor at the factory at a wage of nine dollars a week. At this, he could pay his share to keep the house going, and save a little for the period of study he still looked forward to. The people who had accused him of laziness now made a martyr of him, and said what a pity it was for a man with such an education and with so much talent to be so employed menially.

He did not neglect his studies, but read at night, whenever the day's work had not made both brain and body too weary for the task.

In this way his life went along for over a year when one morning a note from Mr. Featherton summoned him to that gentleman's office. It is true that Halliday read the note with some trepidation. His bitter experience had not yet taught him how not to dream. He was not yet old enough for that. "Maybe," he thought, "Mr. Featherton has relented, and is going to give me a chance anyway. Or perhaps he wanted me to prove my metal before he consented to take me up. Well, I've tried to do it, and if that's what he wanted, I hope he's satisfied." The note which seemed written all over with joyful tidings shook in his hand.

The genial manner with which Mr. Featherton met him reaffirmed in his mind the belief that at last the lawyer had determined to give him a chance. He was almost deferential as he asked Bert into his private office, and shoved a chair forward for him.

"Well, you've been getting on, I see," he began.

"Oh, yes," replied Bert, "l have been getting on by hook and crook."

"Hum, done any studying lately?"

"Yes, but not as much as I wish to. Coke and Wharton[10] aren't any clearer to a head grown dizzy with bending over mops, brooms and heavy trucks all day."

"No, I should think not. Ah—oh—well, Bert, how should you like to come into my office and help around, do such errands as I need and help copy my papers?"

"I should be delighted."

"It would only pay you five dollars a week, less than what you are getting now, I suppose, but it will be more genteel."

"Oh, now, that I have had to do it, I don't care so much about the lack of gentility of my present work, but I prefer what you offer because I shall have a greater chance to study."

"Well, then, you may as well come in on Monday. The office will be often in your charge, as I am going to be away a great deal in the next few months. You know I am going to make the fight for nomination to the seat on the bench which is vacant this fall."

"Indeed. I have not so far taken much interest in politics, but I will do all in my power to help you with both nomination and election."

"Thank you," said Mr. Featherton, "I am sure you can be of great service to me as the vote of your people is pretty heavy in Broughton. l have always been a friend to them, and I believe I can depend upon their support. I shall be glad of any good you can do me with them."

Bert laughed when he was out on the street again. "For value received," he said. He thought less of Mr. Featherton's generosity since he saw it was actuated by self-interest alone, but that in no wise destroyed the real worth of the opportunity that was now given into his hands. Featherton, he believed, would make an excellent judge, and he was glad that in working for his nomination his convictions so aptly fell in with his inclinations.

His work at the factory had put him in touch with a larger number of his people than he could have possibly met had he gone into the office at once. Over them, his naturally bright mind exerted some influence. As a simple laborer he had fellowshipped with them but they acknowledged and availed themselves of his leadership, because they felt instinctively in him a power which they did not have. Among them now he worked sedulously. He held that the greater part of the battle would be in the primaries, and on the night when they convened, he had his friends out in force in every ward which went to make me up the third judicial district. Men who had never seen the inside of a primary meeting before were there actively engaged in this.

The *Diurnal* said next morning that the active interest of the hard-working, church-going colored voters, who wanted to see a Christian judge on the bench had had much to do with the nomination of Mr. Featherton.

The success at the primaries did not tempt Halliday to relinquish his efforts on his employer's behalf. He was indefatigable in his cause. On the west side where the colored population had largely colonized, he made speeches and held meetings clear up to election day. The fight had been between two factions of the party and after the nomination it was feared that the defection of the part defeated in the primaries might prevent the ratification of the nominee at the polls. But before the contest was half over all fears for him were laid. What he had lost in the districts where the skulking faction was strong, he made up in the wards where the colored vote was large. He was overwhelmingly elected.

Halliday smiled as he sat in the office and heard the congratulations poured in upon Judge Featherton.

"Well, it's wonderful," said one of his visitors, "how the colored boys stood by you."

"Yes, I have been a friend to the colored people, and they know it," said Featherton.

It would be some months before His Honor would take his seat on the bench, and during that time, Halliday hoped to finish his office course.

He was surprised when Featherton came to him a couple of weeks after the election and said, "Well, Bert, I guess I can get along now. I'll be shutting up this office pretty soon. Here are your wages and here is a little gift I wish to add out of respect to you for your kindness during my run for office."

Bert took the wages, but the added ten dollar note he waved aside. "No, I thank you, Mr. Featherton," he said, "what I did, I did from a belief in your fitness for the place, and out of loyalty to my employer. I don't want any money for it."

"Then let us say that I have raised your wages to this amount."

"No, that would only be evasion. I want no more than you promised to give me."

"Very well, then accept my thanks, anyway." What things he had at the office Halliday took away that night. A couple of days later he remembered a book which he had failed to get and returned for it. The office was as usual. Mr. Featherton was a little embarrassed and nervous. At Halliday's desk sat a young white man about his own age. He was copying a deed for Mr. Featherton.

PART IV

Bertram Halliday went home, burning with indignation at the treatment he had received at the hands of the Christian judge.

"He has used me as a housemaid would use a lemon," he said, "squeezed all out of me he could get, and then flung me into the street. Well, Webb was nearer right than I thought."

He was now out of everything. His place at the factory had been filled, and no new door opened to him. He knew what reward a search for work brought a man of his color in Broughton, so he did not bestir himself to go over the old track again. He thanked his stars that he, at least, had money enough to carry him away from the place and he determined to go. His spirit was quelled, but not broken.

Just before leaving, he wrote to Davis.

"My dear Webb!" the letter ran, "you, after all, were right. We have little or no show in the fight for life among these people. I have struggled for two years here at Broughton, and now find myself back where I was when I first stepped out of school with a foolish faith in being equipped for something. One thing, my eyes have been opened anyway, and I no longer judge so harshly the shiftless and unambitious among my people. I hardly see how a people, who have so much to contend with and so little to hope for, can go on striving and aspiring. But the very fact that they do, breeds in me a respect for them. I now see why so many promising young men, class orators, valedictorians and the like fall by the wayside and are never heard from after commencement day. I now see why the sleeping and dining-car companies are supplied by men with better educations than half the passengers whom they serve. They get tired of swimming always against the tide, as who would not? and are content to drift.

"I know that a good many of my friends would say that I am whining. Well, suppose I am, that's the business of a whipped cur. The dog on top can bark, but the under dog must howl.

"Nothing so breaks a man's spirit as defeat, constant, unaltering, hopeless defeat. That's what I've experienced. I am still studying law in a half-hearted way for I don't know what I am going to do with it when l have been admitted. Diplomas don't draw clients. We have been taught that merit wins. But I have learned that the adages, as well as the books and the formulas were made by and for others than us of the black race.

"They say, too, that our brother Americans sympathize with us, and will help us when we help ourselves. Bah! The only sympathy that l have ever seen on the part of the white man was not for the negro himself, but for some portion of white blood that the colored man had got tangled up in his veins.

"But there, perhaps my disappointment has made me sour, so think no more of what I have said. I am going now to do what I abhor. Going South to try to find a school. It's awful. But I don't want any one to pity me. There are several thousands of us in the same position.

"I am glad you are prospering. You were better equipped than I was with a deal of materialism and a dearth of ideals. Give us a line when you are in good heart.

"Yours, HALLIDAY.

"P. S.—Just as I finished writing I had a note from Judge Featherton offering me the court messengership at five dollars a week. I am twenty-five. The place was held before by a white boy of fifteen. I declined. 'Southward Ho!'"

Davis was not without sympathy as he read his friend's letter in a city some distance away. He had worked in a hotel, saved money enough to start a barbershop and was prospering. His white customers joked with him and patted him on the back, and he was already known to have political influence. Yes, he sympathized with Bert, but he laughed over the letter and jingled the coins in his pockets.

"Thank heaven," he said, "that I have no ideals to be knocked into a cocked hat. A colored man has no business with ideals—not in *this* nineteenth century!"

NOTES

1. A term commonly used at this time to refer to African Americans. It is now generally considered offensive and is no longer used.
2. Diplomas. In medieval Europe, traveling scholars had their credentials printed on sheepskin parchments because they could be rolled and unrolled multiple times without damage.
3. John Cabot (ca. 1450–ca. 1498), whose real name was Giovanni Caboto, was an Italian who explored the globe for Great Britain; Sir Francis Drake (ca. 1540–96) was the first Englishman to go around the world in a ship, and in 1588, as a vice admiral of the British Navy, helped defeat the Spanish Armada; and Sir John Franklin (1786–1847) was a British Royal Navy officer and Arctic explorer.
4. From the poem "Mandalay" (1890), by British author Rudyard Kipling (1865–1936). In it the narrator speaks nostalgically of his time in Burma (then part of colonial British India and now known as Myanmar), where he felt free of Western societal constraints such as those embodied in the Ten Commandments dictated by the Christian god.
5. In the classic text *The Ingenious Gentleman Don Quixote of La Mancha* (published in two parts in 1605 and 1615), by Spanish author Miguel de Cervantes, the protagonist imagines himself to be on a quest like those of knights from the stories he reads. He believes that some windmills he sees are giants, which he proceeds to "fight." "Tilting at windmills" is an expression that has come to mean one is attacking imaginary enemies.
6. English poet William Ernest Henley (1849–1903).
7. This is a poem written by Henley in 1875 and published in 1888 in his first volume of poems, *A Book of Verses*, which was extremely popular and reprinted numerous times. In 1900 an editor gave the poem the title "Invictus," Latin for "unconquered."
8. Another derogatory and offensive term some White people used to refer to African Americans. In this passage "Mr." Dickson feels Bert has been "presumptuous"

in calling him by his first name, because at this time, African Americans were expected to always use the title of a White person, such as "Mr." or "Mrs." or "Miss," in order to show respect. The same was not true in reverse: Bob Dickson conspicuously avoids addressing Bert Halliday as "Mr. Halliday."

9. In the book of Exodus 5:7 (King James Version), Pharaoh commands that the enslaved Israelites in Egypt no longer be given the straw needed to produce bricks but must continue making the same number of bricks as before; being expected to make "bricks without straw" constitutes an impossible demand.

10. Sir Edward Coke (1552–1634) was the author of *The Institutes of the Lawes of England*, a series of highly influential legal treatises published between 1628 and 1644, and Francis Wharton (1820–89) was a prominent American lawyer and author of many important books on various aspects of law; at the time this story was written, works by Coke and Wharton would have been included in the course of study for any aspiring lawyer.

THE LYNCHING OF JUBE BENSON (1904)

Gordon Fairfax's library held but three men, but the air was dense with clouds of smoke. The talk had drifted from one topic to another much as the smoke wreaths had puffed, floated, and thinned away. Then Handon Gay, who was an ambitious young reporter, spoke of a lynching story in a recent magazine, and the matter of punishment without trial put new life into the conversation.

"I should like to see a real lynching," said Gay rather callously.

"Well, I should hardly express it that way," said Fairfax, "but if a real, live lynching were to come my way, I should not avoid it."

"I should," spoke the other from the depths of his chair, where he had been puffing in moody silence. Judged by his hair, which was freely sprinkled with gray, the speaker might have been a man of forty-five or fifty, but his face, though lined and serious, was youthful, the face of a man hardly past thirty.

"What, you, Dr. Melville? Why, I thought that you physicians wouldn't weaken at anything."

"I have seen one such affair," said the doctor gravely, "in fact, I took a prominent part in it."

"Tell us about it," said the reporter, feeling for his pencil and note-book, which he was, nevertheless, careful to hide from the speaker.

The men drew their chairs eagerly up to the doctor's, but for a minute he did not seem to see them, but sat gazing abstractedly into the fire, then he took a long draw upon his cigar and began:

"I can see it all very vividly now. It was in the summer time and about seven years ago. I was practising at the time down in the little town of Bradford. It was a small and primitive place, just the location for an impecunious medical man, recently out of college.

"In lieu of a regular office, I attended to business in the first of two rooms which I rented from Hiram Daly, one of the more prosperous of the townsmen.

Here I boarded and here also came my patients—white and black—whites from every section, and blacks from 'nigger town,' as the west portion of the place was called.[1]

"The people about me were most of them coarse and rough, but they were simple and generous, and as time passed on I had about abandoned my intention of seeking distinction in wider fields and determined to settle into the place of a modest country doctor. This was rather a strange conclusion for a young man to arrive at, and I will not deny that the presence in the house of my host's beautiful young daughter, Annie, had something to do with my decision. She was a beautiful young girl of seventeen or eighteen, and very far superior to her surroundings. She had a native grace and a pleasing way about her that made everybody that came under her spell her abject slave. White and black who knew her loved her, and none, I thought, more deeply and respectfully than Jube Benson, the black man of all work about the place.

"He was a fellow whom everybody trusted; an apparently steady-going, grinning sort, as we used to call him. Well, he was completely under Miss Annie's thumb, and would fetch and carry for her like a faithful dog. As soon as he saw that I began to care for Annie, and anybody could see that, he transferred some of his allegiance to me and became my faithful servitor also. Never did a man have a more devoted adherent in his wooing than did I, and many a one of Annie's tasks which he volunteered to do gave her an extra hour with me. You can imagine that I liked the boy and you need not wonder any more that as both wooing and my practice waxed apace, I was content to give up my great ambitions and stay just where I was.

"It wasn't a very pleasant thing, then, to have an epidemic of typhoid break out in the town that kept me going so that I hardly had time for the courting that a fellow wants to carry on with his sweetheart while he is still young enough to call her his girl. I fumed, but duty was duty, and I kept to my work night and day. It was now that Jube proved how invaluable he was as a coadjutor. He not only took messages to Annie, but brought sometimes little ones from her to me, and he would tell me little secret things that he had overheard her say that made me throb with joy and swear at him for repeating his mistress' conversation. But best of all, Jube was a perfect Cerberus,[2] and no one on earth could have been more effective in keeping away or deluding the other young fellows who visited the Dalys. He would tell me of it afterwards, chuckling softly to himself. 'An', Doctah, I say to Mistah Hemp Stevens, '"Scuse us, Mistah Stevens, but Miss Annie, she des gone out," an' den he go outer de gate lookin' moughty lonesome. When Sam Elkins come, I say, "Sh, Mistah Elkins, Miss Annie, she done tuk down," an' he say, "What, Jube, you don' reckon hit de—" Den he stop an' look skeert, an' I say, "I feared hit is, Mistah Elkins," an' sheks my haid ez solemn. He goes outer de gate lookin' lak his bes' frien' done daid, an' all de time Miss Annie behine de cu'tain ovah de po'ch des' a laffin' fit to kill.'

"Jube was a most admirable liar, but what could I do? He knew that I was a young fool of a hypocrite, and when I would rebuke him for these deceptions, he would give way and roll on the floor in an excess of delighted laughter until from very contagion I had to join him—and, well, there was no need of my preaching when there had been no beginning to his repentance and when there must ensue a continuance of his wrong-doing.

"This thing went on for over three months, and then, pouf! I was down like a shot. My patients were nearly all up, but the reaction from overwork made me an easy victim of the lurking germs. Then Jube loomed up as a nurse. He put everyone else aside, and with the doctor, a friend of mine from a neighbouring town, took entire charge of me. Even Annie herself was put aside, and I was cared for as tenderly as a baby. Tom, that was my physician and friend, told me all about it afterward with tears in his eyes. Only he was a big, blunt man and his expressions did not convey all that he meant. He told me how my nigger[3] had nursed me as if I were a sick kitten and he my mother. Of how fiercely he guarded his right to be the sole one to 'do' for me, as he called it, and how, when the crisis came, he hovered, weeping, but hopeful, at my bedside, until it was safely passed, when they drove him, weak and exhausted, from the room. As for me, I knew little about it at the time, and cared less. I was too busy in my fight with death. To my chimerical vision there was only a black but gentle demon that came and went, alternating with a white fairy, who would insist on coming in on her head, growing larger and larger and then dissolving. But the pathos and devotion in the story lost nothing in my blunt friend's telling.

"It was during the period of a long convalescence, however, that I came to know my humble ally as he really was, devoted to the point of abjectness. There were times when for very shame at his goodness to me, I would beg him to go away, to do something else. He would go, but before I had time to realise that I was not being ministered to, he would be back at my side, grinning and pottering just the same. He manufactured duties for the joy of performing them. He pretended to see desires in me that I never had, because he liked to pander to them, and when I became entirely exasperated, and ripped out a good round oath, he chuckled with the remark, 'Dah, now, you sholy is gittin' well. Nevah did hyeah a man anywhaih nigh Jo'dan's sho'[4] cuss lak dat.'

"Why, I grew to love him, love him, oh, yes, I loved him as well—oh, what am I saying? All human love and gratitude are damned poor things; excuse me, gentlemen, this isn't a pleasant story. The truth is usually a nasty thing to stand.

"It was not six months after that that my friendship to Jube, which he had been at such great pains to win, was put to too severe a test.

"It was in the summer time again, and as business was slack, I had ridden over to see my friend, Dr. Tom. I had spent a good part of the day there, and it was past four o'clock when I rode leisurely into Bradford. I was in a particularly joyous mood and no premonition of the impending catastrophe oppressed me. No sense of sorrow, present or to come, forced itself upon me, even when I saw men hurrying through the almost deserted streets. When I got within sight of my home and saw a crowd surrounding it, I was only interested sufficiently to spur my horse into a jog trot, which brought me up to the throng, when something in the sullen, settled horror in the men's faces gave me a sudden, sick thrill. They whispered a word to me, and without a thought, save for Annie, the girl who had been so surely growing into my heart, I leaped from the saddle and tore my way through the people to the house.

"It was Annie, poor girl, bruised and bleeding, her face and dress torn from struggling. They were gathered round her with white faces, and, oh, with what terrible patience they were trying to gain from her fluttering lips the name of her murderer. They made way for me and I knelt at her side. She was beyond my skill, and my will merged with theirs. One thought was in our minds.

"'Who?' I asked.

"Her eyes half opened, 'That black—' She fell back into my arms dead.

"We turned and looked at each other. The mother had broken down and was weeping, but the face of the father was like iron.

"'It is enough,' he said; 'Jube has disappeared.' He went to the door and said to the expectant crowd, 'She is dead.'

"I heard the angry roar without swelling up like the noise of a flood, and then I heard the sudden movement of many feet as the men separated into searching parties, and laying the dead girl back upon her couch, I took my rifle and went out to join them.

"As if by intuition the knowledge had passed among the men that Jube Benson had disappeared, and he, by common consent, was to be the object of our search. Fully a dozen of the citizens had seen him hastening toward the woods and noted his skulking air, but as he had grinned in his old good-natured way they had, at the time, thought nothing of it. Now, however, the diabolical reason of his slyness was apparent. He had been shrewd enough to disarm suspicion, and by now was far away. Even Mrs. Daly, who was visiting with a neighbour, had seen him stepping out by a back way, and had said with a laugh, 'I reckon that black rascal's a-running off somewhere.' Oh, if she had only known.

"'To the woods! To the woods!' that was the cry, and away we went, each with the determination not to shoot, but to bring the culprit alive into town, and then to deal with him as his crime deserved.

"I cannot describe the feelings I experienced as I went out that night to beat the woods for this human tiger. My heart smouldered within me like a coal, and I went forward under the impulse of a will that was half my own, half some more malignant power's. My throat throbbed drily, but water nor whiskey would not have quenched my thirst. The thought has come to me since that now I could interpret the panther's desire for blood and sympathise with it, but then I thought nothing. I simply went forward, and watched, watched with burning eyes for a familiar form that I had looked for as often before with such different emotions.

"Luck or ill-luck, which you will, was with our party, and just as dawn was graying the sky, we came upon our quarry crouched in the corner of a fence. It was only half light, and we might have passed, but my eyes had caught sight of him, and I raised the cry. We levelled our guns and he rose and came toward us.

"'I t'ought you wa'n't gwine see me,' he said sullenly, 'I didn't mean no harm.'

"'Harm!'

"Some of the men took the word up with oaths, others were ominously silent.

"We gathered around him like hungry beasts, and I began to see terror dawning in his eyes. He turned to me, 'I's moughty glad you's hyeah, doc,' he said, 'you ain't gwine let 'em whup me.'

"'Whip you, you hound,' I said,' I'm going to see you hanged,' and in the excess of my passion I struck him full on the mouth. He made a motion as if to resent the blow against even such great odds, but controlled himself.

"'W'y, doctah,' he exclaimed in the saddest voice I have ever heard, 'w'y, doctah! I ain't stole nuffin' o' yo'n, an' I was comin' back. I only run off to see my gal, Lucy, ovah to de Centah.'

"'You lie!' I said, and my hands were busy helping the others bind him upon a horse. Why did I do it? I don't know. A false education, I reckon, one false from the beginning. I saw his black face glooming there in the half light, and I could only think of him as a monster. It's tradition. At first I was told that the black man would catch me, and when I got over that, they taught me that the devil was black, and when I had recovered from the sickness of that belief, here were Jube and his fellows with faces of menacing blackness. There was only one conclusion: This black man stood for all the powers of evil, the result of whose machinations had been gathering in my mind from childhood up. But this has nothing to do with what happened.

"After firing a few shots to announce our capture, we rode back into town with Jube. The ingathering parties from all directions met us as we made our way up to the house. All was very quiet and orderly. There was no doubt that it was as the papers would have said, a gathering of the best citizens. It was a gathering of stern, determined men, bent on a terrible vengeance.

"We took Jube into the house, into the room where the corpse lay. At sight of it, he gave a scream like an animal's and his face went the colour of storm-blown water. This was enough to condemn him. We divined, rather than heard, his cry of 'Miss Ann, Miss Ann, oh, my God, doc, you don't t'ink I done it?'

"Hungry hands were ready. We hurried him out into the yard. A rope was ready. A tree was at hand. Well, that part was the least of it, save that Hiram Daly stepped aside to let me be the first to pull upon the rope. It was lax at first. Then it tightened, and I felt the quivering soft weight resist my muscles. Other hands joined, and Jube swung off his feet.

"No one was masked. We knew each other. Not even the culprit's face was covered,[5] and the last I remember of him as he went into the air was a look of sad reproach that will remain with me until I meet him face to face again.

"We were tying the end of the rope to a tree, where the dead man might hang as a warning to his fellows, when a terrible cry chilled us to the marrow.

"'Cut 'im down, cut 'im down, he ain't guilty. We got de one. Cut him down, fu' Gawd's sake. Here's de man, we foun' him hidin' in de barn!'

"Jube's brother, Ben, and another Negro,[6] came rushing toward us, half dragging, half carrying a miserable-looking wretch between them. Someone cut the rope and Jube dropped lifeless to the ground.

"'Oh, my Gawd, he's daid, he's daid!' wailed the brother, but with blazing eyes he brought his captive into the centre of the group, and we saw in the full light the scratched face of Tom Skinner—the worst white ruffian in the town—but the face we saw was not as we were accustomed to see it, merely smeared with dirt. It was blackened to imitate a Negro's.

"God forgive me; I could not wait to try to resuscitate Jube. I knew he was already past help, so I rushed into the house and to the dead girl's side. In the excitement they had not yet washed or laid her out. Carefully, carefully, I searched underneath her broken finger nails. There was skin there. I took it out, the little curled pieces, and went with it to my office.

"There, determinedly, I examined it under a powerful glass, and read my own doom. It was the skin of a white man, and in it were embedded strands of short, brown hair or beard.

"How I went out to tell the waiting crowd I do not know, for something kept crying in my ears, 'Blood guilty! Blood guilty!'

"The men went away stricken into silence and awe. The new prisoner attempted neither denial nor plea. When they were gone I would have helped Ben carry his brother in, but he waved me away fiercely, 'You he'ped murder my brotha, you dat was *his* frien', go 'way, go 'way! I'll tek him home myse'f.' I could only respect his wish, and he and his comrade took up the dead man and between them bore him up the street on which the sun was now shining full.

"I saw the few men who had not skulked indoors uncover as they passed, and I—I—stood there between the two murdered ones, while all the while something in my ears kept crying, 'Blood guilty! Blood guilty!'"

The doctor's head dropped into his hands and he sat for some time in silence, which was broken by neither of the men, then he rose, saying, "Gentlemen, that was my last lynching."

NOTES

1. Many towns and cities in the South at this time forced African Americans to live only in certain areas; the name given here for Bradford's segregated area includes a highly derogatory and offensive racial slur.
2. In Greek mythology, Cerberus is a large hound with three heads who guards Hades to keep the dead from trying to escape; here the reference implies that Jube did an excellent job keeping other suitors away from Miss Annie.
3. An extremely offensive term used by some non-Black people to refer to Black people. While sometimes used among Black people to refer to other Black people, in both the past and the present this term was and is usually intended to be derogatory and hurtful when used by non-Black people; it is thus deeply offensive and should not be used.

4. In Joshua 3:10–13, the Israelites are able to cross the Jordan River because God stops its waters so they can proceed by land; this miracle is often referred to as a demonstration of God's power. Here, though, being near the shore of the Jordan means being close to death, and "crossing Jordan" means to die.

5. Often during lynchings, victims had their heads covered, but here Jube (ironically named as the "culprit") does not have such a covering. During lynchings, too, those perpetrating the act typically wore masks of some kind to keep from later being identified to law enforcement; it is partially for this reason that members of the Ku Klux Klan, a group involved in many lynchings of African Americans throughout the South, typically wore white robes and masks with holes only for their eyes. The fact that these White men are not masked is an indication that they are confident none in the mob will ever tell legal authorities about this criminal act or that they will be punished for it.

6. A term commonly used by many people at the time to refer to an African American person. It is now generally considered offensive and is no longer acceptable.

ALICE DUNBAR NELSON

(1875–1935)

Alice Ruth Moore was born in New Orleans and spent the first twenty years of her life there, graduating from a local teachers' training college (Straight University) in 1892; however, she spent most of her life in the North, not only as a graduate student (both at Cornell University and the University of Pennsylvania) but also as a teacher in New York City and Delaware.

Before she met and married her famous first husband, poet and author Paul Laurence Dunbar, Moore herself was an aspiring poet and writer. Her first book, *Violets and Other Tales* (1895), a compendium of poems, stories, and essays, was brought out by a minor Boston publisher. It was the appearance of one of these poems alongside a picture of her, in the *Boston Review* in 1895, that prompted Dunbar to start writing to her. Their letters to each other continued for two years, until finally Alice and Paul met in person in February 1897; they became engaged that same day. Before marrying in March 1898, Moore worked as a teacher at the White Rose Mission in New York City's Harlem neighborhood, an experience that gave her a great deal of familiarity with economically disadvantaged families of many different races and ethnicities. After her marriage, Dunbar Nelson moved to Washington, DC, where her husband resided. Unfortunately, their relationship was fraught with tension and other difficulties, including Dunbar's tuberculosis, diagnosed in 1900, and his alcoholism (doctors prescribed drinking as a way to combat the pain of tuberculosis). They separated in 1902 and never reconciled. Dunbar Nelson then moved to Delaware and became a teacher, later working as an advocate for numerous progressive African

American organizations. In 1916, she married journalist Robert J. Nelson and remained married to him until her death in 1935.

During her brief marriage to Paul Laurence Dunbar, Dunbar Nelson continued to pursue her own writing career. In 1899 she published a well-received short story collection (dedicated to "my best Comrade, my Husband") entitled *The Goodness of St. Rocque and Other Stories*, which includes her best-known and most commonly anthologized fictions. All the works in this volume take as their subject life in New Orleans toward the end of the nineteenth century, and significantly—given that Moore's father was Creole and her mother African American—they are chiefly about Creole life and contain no African American main characters. The fair-skinned Dunbar Nelson, who could often pass in real life for White and disliked it when her darker-skinned husband made racial issues the central topics of his poetry and fiction, rarely dealt directly with anti-Black racism in her fiction or published nonfiction.

The two stories included here, "Titee" and "When the Bayou Overflows," are definitely not among Dunbar Nelson's better-known works. "Titee" first appeared in *Violets and Other Tales*, published in 1895. In the introduction to this volume, Dunbar Nelson is quite self-deprecating about its contents, writing, "If perchance this collection of idle thoughts may serve to while away an hour or two, or lift for a brief space the load of care from someone's mind, their purpose has been served—the author is satisfied." However, this story about an impoverished boy and his self-sacrifice represents much more than "idle thoughts," for it prompts the reader to reconsider many common assumptions about such young men. Dunbar Nelson revised this story for inclusion in *The Goodness of St. Rocque and Other Stories* (1899), but some of the changes make it a weaker work. For instance, Dunbar Nelson makes Titee less sympathetic by no longer referring to him as "little," adds in more French phrases to make her characters more "exotic" and thus marketable to a national readership, and completely changes the ending. The second story included here, "When the Bayou Overflows," originally published in *The Goodness of St. Rocque*, also defies expectations in a number of ways, particularly in the way it does not portray the North as the "promised land" that so many African Americans believed it to be at this time.

According to Sylvanie F. Williams, who wrote a preface for *Violets and Other Tales*, Dunbar Nelson belonged "to that type of the 'brave new woman who scorns to sigh,' but feels that she has something to say, and says it to the best of her ability, and leaves the verdict in the hands of the public." Unfortunately, some of her best stories remained unpublished at her death, for as scholar Gloria T. Hull notes in her introduction to volume 3 of *The Works of Alice Dunbar-Nelson* (1988), magazine editors would not accept her more realistic stories, preferring instead the type of Romantic Local Color stories about Louisiana she had published earlier. In addition, because Dunbar Nelson's earlier collections were not reprinted, for many years the public had little access to her work. Fortunately, however, Dunbar Nelson's oeuvre became much more easily accessible to readers with the publication of a three-volume series, *The Works of Alice Dunbar-Nelson*, in 1988. Like the stories included in the present anthology, many of the pieces included in these volumes deserve further exploration and appreciation.

TITEE (1895)

It was cold that day; the great sharp north wind swept out Elysian Fields Street[1] in blasts that made men shiver, and bent everything in its track. The skies hung lowering and gloomy; the usually quiet street was more than deserted, it was dismal.

Titee leaned against one of the brown freight cars for protection against the shrill norther, and warmed his little chapped hands at a blaze of chips and dry grass. "May be it'll snow," he muttered, casting a glance at the sky that would have done credit to a practised seaman. "Then *won't* I have fun! Ugh, but the wind blows!"

It was Saturday, or Titee would have been in school—the big yellow school on Marigny Street, where he went every day when its bell boomed nine o'clock. Went with a run and a joyous whoop, presumably to imbibe knowledge, ostensibly to make his teacher's life a burden.

Idle, lazy, dirty, troublesome boy, she called him, to herself, as day by day wore on, and Titee improved not, but let his whole class pass him on its way to a higher grade. A practical joke he relished infinitely more than a practical problem, and a good game at pinsticking was far more entertaining than a language lesson. Moreover, he was always hungry, and *would* eat in school before the half-past ten intermission,[2] thereby losing much good play-time for his voracious appetite.

But there was nothing in natural history that Titee didn't know. He could dissect a butterfly or a mosquito-hawk and describe their parts as accurately as a spectacled student with a scalpel and microscope could talk about a cadaver. The entire Third District,[3] with its swamps and canals and commons and railroad sections, and its wondrous, crooked, tortuous streets was as an open book to Titee. There was not a nook or corner that he did not know or could tell of. There was not a bit of gossip among the gamins, little Creole and Spanish fellows,[4] with dark skins and lovely eyes like Spaniels, that Titee could not tell of. He knew just exactly when it was time for crawfish to be plentiful down in the Claiborne and Marigny canals;[5] just when a poor, breadless fellow might get a job in the big bone-yard and fertilizing factory out on the railroad track; and as for the levee,[6] with its ships and schooners and sailors—Oh, how he could revel among them! The wondrous ships, the pretty little schooners, where the foreign-looking sailors lay on long moon-lit nights, singing gay bar carols to the tinkle of a guitar and mandolin. All these things, and more, could Titee tell of. He had been down to the Gulf,[7] and out on its treacherous waters through Eads Jetties[8] on a fishing smack[9] with some jolly, brown sailors, and could interest the whole school-room in the "talk lessons," if he chose.

Titee shivered as the wind swept round the freight cars. There isn't much warmth in a bit of a jersey coat.[10]

"Wish 'twas summer," he murmured, casting another sailor's glance at the sky. "Don't believe I like snow; it's too wet and cold." And, with a last parting caress at the little fire he had built for a minute's warmth, he plunged his hands in his pockets, shut his teeth, and started manfully on his mission out the railroad track toward the swamps.

It was late when Titee came home, to such a home as it was, and he had but illy[11] performed his errand, so his mother beat him, and sent him to bed supperless. A sharp strap stings in cold weather, and long walks in the teeth of a biting wind creates a keen appetite. But if Titee cried himself to sleep that night, he was up bright and early next morning, and had been to early mass, devoutly kneeling on the cold floor, blowing his fingers to keep them warm, and was home almost before the rest of the family were awake.

There was evidently some great matter of business on the young man's mind, for he scarcely ate his breakfast, and had left the table, eagerly cramming the remainder of his meal in his pockets.

"I wonder what he's up to now?" mused his mother as she watched his little form sturdily trudging the track in the face of the wind, his head, with the rimless cap thrust close on the shock of black hair, bent low, his hands thrust deep in the bulging pockets.

"A new snake, perhaps," ventured the father; "he's a queer child."

But the next day Titee was late for school. It was something unusual, for he was always the first on hand to fix some plan of mechanism to make the teacher miserable. She looked reprovingly at him this morning, when he came in during arithmetic class, his hair all wind-blown, his cheeks rosy from a hard fight with the sharp blasts. But he made up for his tardiness by his extreme goodness all day; just think, Titee didn't even eat in school. A something unparalleled in the entire previous history of his school-life.

When the lunch-hour came, and all the yard was a scene of feast and fun, one of the boys found him standing by one of the posts, disconsolately watching a ham sandwich as it rapidly disappeared down the throat of a sturdy, square-headed little fellow.

"Hello, Edgar,"[12] he said, "What yer got fer lunch?"

"Nothin'," was the mournful reply.

"Ah, why don't yer stop eatin' in school, fer a change? You don't ever have nothin' to eat."

"I didn't eat to-day," said Titee, blazing up.

"You did!"

"I tell you I didn't!" and Titee's hard little fist planted a punctuation mark on his comrade's eye.

A fight in the school-yard! Poor Titee in disgrace again. But in spite of his battered appearance, a severe scolding from the principal, lines to write,[13] and a further punishment from his mother, Titee scarcely remained for his dinner, but was off, down the railroad track, with his pockets partly stuffed with the remnants of his scanty meal.

And the next day Titee was tardy again, and lunchless, too, and the next, and the next, until the teacher in despair sent a nicely printed note to his mother about him, which might have done some good, had not Titee taken great pains to tear it up on the way home.

But one day it rained, whole bucketful of water, that poured in torrents from a miserable angry sky. Too wet a day for bits of boys to be trudging to school, so Titee's mother thought, so kept him home to watch the weather through the window, fretting and fuming, like a regular storm-cloud in miniature. As the day wore on, and the storm did not abate, his mother had to keep a strong watch upon him, or he would have slipped away.

At last dinner came and went, and the gray soddenness of the skies deepened into the blackness of coming night. Someone called Titee to go to bed—and Titee was nowhere to be found.

Under the beds, in corners and closets, through the yard, and in such impossible places as the soap-dish and the water-pitcher even; but he had gone as completely as if he had been spirited away. It was of no use to call up the neighbors; he had never been near their houses, they affirmed, so there was nothing to do but to go to the rail-road track, where little Titee had been seen so often trudging in the shrill north wind.

So with lanterns and sticks, and his little yellow dog, the rescuing party started out the track. The rain had ceased falling, but the wind blew a tremendous gale, scurrying great, gray clouds over a fierce sky. It was not exactly dark, though in this part of the city, there was neither gas nor electricity, and surely on such a night as this, neither moon nor stars dared show their faces in such a grayness of sky; but a sort of all-diffused luminosity was in the air, as though the sea of atmosphere was charged with an ethereal phosphorescence.

Search as they would, there were no signs of poor little Titee. The soft earth between the railroad ties crumbled beneath their feet without showing any small tracks or foot-prints.

"Let us return," said the big brother, "he can't be here anyway."

"No, no," urged the mother, "I feel that he is; let's go on."

So on they went, slipping on the wet earth, stumbling over the loose rocks, until a sudden wild yelp from Tiger[14] brought them to a standstill. He had rushed ahead of them, and his voice could be heard in the distance, howling piteously.

With a fresh impetus the little muddy party hurried forward. Tiger's yelps could be heard plainer and plainer, mingled now with a muffled wail, as of some one in pain.

And then, after a while they found a pitiful little heap of wet and sodden rags, lying at the foot of a mound of earth and stones thrown upon the side of the track. It was little Titee with a broken leg, all wet and miserable, and moaning.

They picked him up tenderly, and started to carry him home. But he cried and clung to the mother, and begged not to go.

"He's got fever," wailed his mother.

"No, no, it's my old man. He's hungry," sobbed Titee, holding out a little package. It was the remnants of his dinner, all wet and rain washed.

"What old man?" asked the big brother.

"My old man, oh, please, please don't go home until I see him, I'm not hurting much, I can go."

So, yielding to his whim, they carried him further away, down the sides of the track up to an embankment or levee by the sides of the Marigny canal. Then Titee's brother, suddenly stopping, exclaimed:

"Why, here's a cave, a regular Robinson Cruso affair?"[15]

"It's my old man's cave," cried Titee; "oh, please go in, maybe he's dead."

There can't be much ceremony in entering a cave, there is but one thing to do, walk in. This they did, and holding high the lantern, beheld a weird sight. On a bed of straw and paper in one corner lay a withered, wizened, white-bearded old man, with wide eyes staring at the unaccustomed sight. In the corner lay a cow.

"It's my old man!" cried Titee, joyfully. "Oh, please, grandpa,[16] I couldn't get here to-day, it rained all morning, and when I ran away this evening, I slipped down and broke something, and oh, grandpa, I'm so tired an' hurty, and I'm so afraid you're hungry."

So the secret of Titee's jaunts out the railroad was out. In one of his trips around the swamp-land, he had discovered the old man dying from cold and hunger in the fields. Together they had found this cave, and Titee had gathered the straw and brush that scattered itself over the ground and made the bed. A poor old cow turned adrift by an ungrateful master, had crept in and shared the damp dwelling. And thither Titee had trudged twice a day, carrying his luncheon in the morning, and his dinner in the afternoon, the sole support of a half-dead cripple.[17]

"There's a crown in Heaven for that child,"[18] said the officer to whom the case was referred.

And so there was, for we scattered winter roses on his little grave down in old St. Rocque's cemetery. The cold and rain, and the broken leg had told their tale.[19]

NOTES

1. Now known as Elysian Fields Avenue, which runs north from the Mississippi River in central New Orleans to Lake Pontchartrain. The neighborhood of Elysian Fields was later made famous as the setting of Tennessee Willliams's play *A Streetcar Named Desire* (1947).
2. Recess.
3. An area of north New Orleans just west of Elysian Fields Avenue.
4. Children generally left to roam the streets. Creoles were regarded as White descendants of early French or Spanish settlers of the area.
5. The city of New Orleans is crisscrossed by many canals such as these, which were commonly used for transportation.

6. An earthen embankment meant to hold back water from a river or other body of water. These are very important in New Orleans, which lies below sea level next to the Mississippi River and is thus very susceptible to flooding.
7. The Gulf of Mexico, only a few miles from New Orleans.
8. A jetty is a structure—usually made up of rocks or concrete blocks—that extends from shore out into the ocean and is intended to protect an area from strong waves and winds; the Eads jetties (named after their designer, James Eads), constructed where the Mississippi River meets the Gulf of Mexico, were completed in 1879.
9. A small boat.
10. Made of thin cotton.
11. Poorly.
12. Edgar is Titee's actual name.
13. To punish bad behavior, teachers at this time would often make students write out particular lines of text multiple times.
14. Titee's dog.
15. Robinson Crusoe is the main character of Daniel Defoe's famous early novel, *The Life and Strange Surprising Adventures of Robinson Crusoe, of York, Mariner* (1719), and was shipwrecked on a deserted island for twenty-eight years; the spelling of "Cruso" was corrected in later versions of "Titee."
16. This person is not actually Titee's grandfather, but it is significant that Titee refers to him with this familial term.
17. A term used in the past to denote a physically handicapped person. It is no longer acceptable to use.
18. Many devout Christians believe that one can, if one's faith is strong enough and one's conduct in life good enough, be rewarded with a "crown in heaven"; the New Testament of the Bible refers to five possible heavenly crowns: the incorruptible crown, the crown of rejoicing, the crown of righteousness, the crown of glory, and the crown of life.
19. In the revised version of "Titee" that appeared in *The Goodness of St. Rocque and Other Stories* (1899), Dunbar Nelson replaced these final two sentences with a single sentence that concluded the story on a happier note, likely in order to please prospective readers: "But as for Titee, when the leg was well, he went his way as before."

WHEN THE BAYOU OVERFLOWS (1899)

When the sun goes down behind the great oaks along the Bayou Teche near Franklin,[1] it throws red needles of light into the dark woods, and leaves a great glow on the still bayou. Ma'am Mouton[2] paused at her gate and cast a contemplative look at the red sky.

"Hit will rain to-morrow, sho'. I mus' git in my t'ings."

Ma'am Mouton's remark must have been addressed to herself or to the lean dog, for no one else was visible. She moved briskly about the yard, taking things from the line, when Louisette's voice called cheerily:

"Ah, Ma'am Mouton, can I help?"

Louisette was petite and plump and black-haired. Louisette's eyes danced, and her lips were red and tempting. Ma'am Mouton's face relaxed as the small brown hands relieved hers of their burden.

"Sylves', has he come yet?" asked the red mouth.

"Mais non, ma chère," said Ma'am Mouton, sadly, "I can' tell fo' w'y he no come home soon dese day. Ah me, I feel lak' somet'ing goin' happen. He so strange."[3]

Even as she spoke a quick nervous step was heard crunching up the brick walk. Sylves' paused an instant without the kitchen door, his face turned to the setting sun. He was tall and slim and agile; a true 'cajan.

"Bon jour, Louisette," he laughed. "Eh, maman!"

"Ah, my son, you are ver' late."

Sylves' frowned, but said nothing. It was a silent supper that followed. Louisette was sad, Ma'am Mouton sighed now and then, Sylves' was constrained.

"Maman," he said at length, "I am goin' away."

Ma'am Mouton dropped her fork and stared at him with unseeing eyes; then, as she comprehended his remark, she put her hand out to him with a pitiful gesture.

"Sylves'!" cried Louisette, springing to her feet.

"Maman, don't, don't!" he said weakly; then gathering strength from the silence, he burst forth:

"Yaas, I'm goin' away to work. I'm tired of dis, jus' dig, dig, work in de fiel', nothin' to see but de cloud, de tree, de bayou. I don't lak' New Orleans; it too near here, dere no mo' money dere. I go up fo' Mardi Gras,[4] an' de same people, de same strit'. I'm goin' to Chicago!"

"Sylves'!" screamed both women at once. Chicago! That vast, far-off city that seemed in another world.

Chicago! A name to conjure with for wickedness.

"W'y, yaas," continued Sylves', "lots of boys I know dere. Henri an' Joseph Lascaud an' Arthur, dey write me what money dey mek' in cigar. I can mek' a livin' too. I can mek' fine cigar.[5] See how I do in New Orleans in de winter."

"Oh, Sylves'," wailed Louisette, "den you'll forget me!"

"Non, non, ma chère," he answered tenderly. "I will come back when the bayou overflows again,[6] an' maman an' Louisette will have fine present."

Ma'am Mouton had bowed her head on her hands, and was rocking to and fro in an agony of dry-eyed misery.

Sylves' went to her side and knelt. "Maman," he said softly, "maman, you mus' not cry. All de boys go 'way, an' I will come back reech, an' you won't have fo' to work no mo'."

But Ma'am Mouton was inconsolable.

It was even as Sylves' had said. In the summer-time the boys of the Bayou Teche would work in the field or in the town of Franklin, hack-driving[7] and doing odd jobs. When winter came, there was a general exodus to New Orleans, a hundred miles away, where work was to be had as cigar-makers. There is money, plenty of it, in cigar-making, if one can get in the right place. Of late, however, there had been a general slackness of the trade. Last winter oftentimes Sylves' had walked the streets out of work. Many were the Creole[8] boys who had gone to Chicago to earn a living, for the cigar-making trade flourishes there wonderfully. Friends of Sylves' had gone, and written home glowing accounts of the money to be had almost for the asking. When one's blood leaps for new scenes, new adventures, and one needs money, what is the use of frittering away time alternately between the Bayou Teche and New Orleans? Sylves' had brooded all summer, and now that September had come, he was determined to go.

Louisette, the orphan, the girl-lover, whom everyone in Franklin knew would some day be Ma'am Mouton's daughter-in-law, wept and pleaded in vain. Sylves' kissed her quivering lips.

"Ma chère," he would say, "t'ink, I will bring you one fine diamon' ring, nex' spring, when de bayou overflows again."

Louisette would fain be content with this promise. As for Ma'am Mouton, she seemed to have grown ages older. Her Sylves' was going from her; Sylves', whose trips to New Orleans had been a yearly source of heart-break, was going far away for months to that mistily wicked city, a thousand miles away.

October came, and Sylves' had gone. Ma'am Mouton had kept up bravely until the last, when with one final cry she extended her arms to the pitiless train bearing him northward. Then she and Louisette went home drearily, the one leaning upon the other.

Ah, that was a great day when the first letter came from Chicago! Louisette came running in breathlessly from the post-office, and together they read it again and again. Chicago was such a wonderful city, said Sylves'. Why, it was always like New Orleans at Mardi Gras with the people. He had seen Joseph Lascaud, and he had a place to work promised him. He was well, but he wanted, oh, so much, to see maman and Louisette. But then, he could wait.

Was ever such a wonderful letter? Louisette sat for an hour afterwards building gorgeous air-castles,[9] while Ma'am Mouton fingered the paper and murmured prayers to the Virgin[10] for Sylves'. When the bayou overflowed again? That would be in April. Then Louisette caught herself looking critically at her slender brown fingers, and blushed furiously, though Ma'am Mouton could not see her in the gathering twilight.

Next week there was another letter, even more wonderful than the first. Sylves' had found work. He was making cigars, and was earning two dollars a day. Such wages! Ma'am Mouton and Louisette began to plan pretty things for the brown cottage on the Teche.

That was a pleasant winter, after all. True, there was no Sylves', but then he was always in New Orleans for a few months any way. There were his letters, full of wondrous tales of the great queer city, where cars went by ropes underground,[11] and where there was no Mardi Gras and the people did not mind Lent.[12] Now and then there would be a present, a keepsake for Louisette, and some money for maman. They would plan improvements for the cottage, and

Louisette began to do sewing and dainty crochet, which she would hide with a blush if anyone hinted at a trousseau.[13]

It was March now, and Spring-time. The bayou began to sweep down between its banks less sluggishly than before; it was rising, and soon would spread over its tiny levees. The doors could be left open now, though the trees were not yet green; but then down here the trees do not swell and bud slowly and tease you for weeks with promises of greenness. Dear no, they simply look mysterious, and their twigs shake against each other and tell secrets of the leaves that will soon be born. Then one morning you awake, and lo, it is a green world! The boughs have suddenly clothed themselves all in a wondrous garment, and you feel the blood run riot in your veins out of pure sympathy.

One day in March, it was warm and sweet. Underfoot were violets, and wee white star flowers peering through the baby-grass. The sky was blue, with flecks of white clouds reflecting themselves in the brown bayou. Louisette tripped up the red brick walk with the Chicago letter in her hand, and paused a minute at the door to look upon the leaping waters, her eyes dancing.

"I know the bayou must be ready to overflow," went the letter in the carefully phrased French that the brothers taught at the parochial school,[14] "and I am glad, for I want to see the dear maman and my Louisette. I am not so well, and Monsieur le docteur says it is well for me to go to the South again."

Monsieur le docteur! Sylves' not well! The thought struck a chill to the hearts of Ma'am Mouton and Louisette, but not for long. Of course, Sylves' was not well, he needed some of maman's tisanes.[15] Then he was homesick; it was to be expected.

At last the great day came, Sylves' would be home. The brown waters of the bayou had spread until they were seemingly trying to rival the Mississippi in width. The little house was scrubbed and cleaned until it shone again. Louisette had looked her dainty little dress over and over to be sure that there was not a flaw to be found wherein Sylves' could compare her unfavourably to the stylish Chicago girls.

The train rumbled in on the platform, and two pair of eyes opened wide for the first glimpse of Sylves'. The porter, all officiousness and brass buttons, bustled up to Ma'am Mouton.

"This is Mrs. Mouton?" he inquired deferentially.

Ma'am Mouton nodded, her heart sinking. "Where is Sylves'?"

"He is here, madam."

There appeared Joseph Lascaud, then some men bearing Something. Louisette put her hands up to her eyes to hide the sight, but Ma'am Mouton was rigid.

"It was too cold for him," Joseph was saying to almost deaf ears, "and he took the consumption.[16] He thought he could get well when he come home. He talk all the way down about the bayou, and about you and Louisette. Just three hours ago he had a bad hemorrhage, and he died from weakness. Just three hours ago. He said he wanted to get home and give Louisette her diamond ring, when the bayou overflowed."

NOTES

1. The Bayou Têche (properly rendered with a French circumflex over the *e*) is a 125-mile-long waterway in south-central Louisiana; a bayou can be a slow-moving stream or river in a flat landscape or it can be a marshy area. Franklin is a small town on this bayou, approximately 100 miles due west of New Orleans.

2. An informal pronunciation of "Madame Mouton."

3. The mixture of French ("Mais non, ma chère," meaning "But no, my dear") and dialect here was common in Louisiana among people known as Cajuns, which is a dialect pronunciation of the word "'Cadian," referring to someone who is of Acadian heritage. The Acadians in Louisiana were descended from chiefly French-speaking settlers expelled from Nova Scotia (Canada) by the British between 1755 and 1764 and who, after being treated harshly by people in the British colonies along the East Coast of what is now the United States, moved west in the late eighteenth century; they were generally regarded in Louisiana as White, yet quite low in class status. Fiction authors of this time period used such vernacular language not only to be realistic but also to highlight the "exotic" nature of their regional characters and thereby satisfy northern readers' desire for "traveling" through literature.

4. In the New Orleans area, Mardi Gras (French for "Fat Tuesday") refers to the religious holiday celebrated during the days before Ash Wednesday; the actual Fat Tuesday is the last day on which devout Christians can eat rich foods before Lent, a time when many Christians sacrifice certain pleasures and/or sins to demonstrate their religious faith.

5. During the time when this story was written, cigars were rolled by hand.

6. A reference to springtime flooding due to seasonal rains.

7. A hack was a horse-drawn carriage for hire; it functioned much as a taxi or rideshare service does today.

8. At this time period in Louisiana history, people known as Creoles were regarded as White descendants of early French or Spanish settlers of the area. Sylvester is Cajun and thus lower in class status than those Creoles he says succeeded in Chicago.

9. The practice of making grand plans unlikely to be achieved.

10. The Virgin Mary, mother of Jesus, who is often regarded as someone who answers people's prayers.

11. Streetcars pulled by cables under the tracks and connected to a central powerhouse. Such streetcars are still in use in San Francisco.

12. For most Christians, Lent is the period between Ash Wednesday and Easter; because it is intended to represent the forty days Jesus spent fasting in the Judean desert, many Christians promise to forego certain pleasures to show their religious devotion. That people in Chicago "did not mind Lent" signifies that they are not observant Christians.

13. A bride's outfit of clothes.

14. Male teachers at a Catholic school, commonly known as "brothers" because of their association with the Roman Catholic Institute of the Brothers of the Christian Schools, founded by St. John Baptist de la Salle in France in 1684.

15. Herbal teas.

16. Either a general wasting away of the body or, more specifically, tuberculosis.

SUI SIN FAR (EDITH MAUDE EATON)

(1865–1914)

Sui Sin Far, which translates from Chinese to mean "water lily" or "narcissus" in English, was the pen name used by author Edith Maude Eaton. Now recognized as the first Asian American to publish fiction in the United States, Eaton was born in Macclesfield, England, on March 15, 1865, the daughter of a British father and Chinese mother. When Eaton was six years old, her family immigrated to the United States and lived briefly in the New York City area before settling in Montreal, Canada.

Eaton's father struggled to make ends meet for his very large family, and Eaton herself left school at the age of eleven to earn money. As a teen, Eaton worked in offices and as a typesetter for the *Montreal Star* newspaper. The field of journalism appealed to Eaton, and in the mid-1880s she began writing—and selling—fiction and nonfiction pieces to various periodicals, most notably the Canadian publication *Dominion Illustrated*. Beginning in 1896, she drew on her experiences as a person of Chinese heritage and was quite successful in having her resulting works accepted by midlevel periodicals. After less than a year working as a journalist in Jamaica, Eaton returned briefly to Montreal in 1898 before heading west on doctor's orders, eventually settling in San Francisco, hoping to find better weather for her health and more job opportunities.

For the next decade, Eaton moved between the major cities of the West Coast—Los Angeles, San Francisco, and Seattle—and earned her living as a stenographer, journalist, and fiction writer. As she became increasingly familiar with the Chinese communities of these western cities, she both reported on their inhabitants' concerns and depicted their experiences in her fiction. Her short stories appeared in a broad range of regional and national newspapers and literary magazines, including *Good Housekeeping* (New York); the *Land of Sunshine* (Los Angeles), which published "Sweet Sin. A Chinese-American Story" in 1898; the *Los Angeles Express;* the *Montreal Daily Witness;* the *New York Evening Post;* and Seattle's *Westerner* magazine, in which "The Success of a Mistake" appeared in 1908. In 1909, after finally placing her work in some major American magazines, Eaton relocated to Boston. Her only book-length publication, *Mrs. Spring Fragrance,* which includes many of her best-known short stories, was published in 1912. Suffering from poor health, Eaton, who never married, returned home to her family in Montreal shortly afterwards and died there in 1914.

To fully appreciate Eaton's insights into the lives of Chinese people in both Canada and the United States during the turn of the twentieth century, it is helpful to note the political environment in which she was writing. Many Chinese immigrants came to the United States, particularly the West Coast, during the second half of the nineteenth century. They provided an important labor force for booming industries—including lumber, railroads, and fishing—in addition to building businesses that supported the neighborhoods in which they lived. However, even though Chinese people made significant contributions to the economic growth and development of the region, they faced a great deal of prejudice. For instance, the Chinese Exclusion Act of 1882 severely restricted immigration to the United States and was renewed multiple times; it was not repealed until 1943, and Chinese immigrants were not allowed to become naturalized US citizens until 1954.

Eaton occupies an important, albeit complex, place in the history of American literature. She spent most of her life in Canada—yet she also was the first Asian writer to publish fiction about the Chinese experience in the United States. Eaton and her works first attracted the attention of literary critics in the 1970s, but the most significant boost to her reputation came in 1995 with the publication of *Mrs. Spring Fragrance and Other Writings,* a collection coedited by Amy Ling and Annette White-Parks. Despite this groundbreaking work, for many years after this it was difficult for modern scholars to properly assess her work and career, because some of her writings were published without attribution, others appeared under various pseudonyms (besides "Sui Sin Far"), and a great many were published in lesser-known (and thus less accessible) periodicals.

Some scholars have suggested that even in her efforts to combat stigma and stereotypes, Eaton reinforced them through her use of dialect (pidgin English) or her depictions of seemingly one-dimensional Chinese characters. However, if one looks beneath the surface, one can see that in all her works Eaton interrogated North American readers' preconceptions about Chinese people and presented them in complex ways, as can be seen in both "Sweet Sin" and "The Success of a Mistake."

SWEET SIN. A CHINESE-AMERICAN STORY (1898)[1]

"CHINESE! Chinese!"

A small form darted across the street, threw itself upon the boys from whom the derisive cry had arisen, and began kicking and thumping and scratching and shaking, so furiously that a companion cried in fright, "Sweet Sin! Oh, Sweet Sin! Come away, you will kill them!"

But Sweet Sin was deaf to all sounds save "Chinese! Chinese!" Before her eyes was a fiery mist.

A quarter of an hour later Sweet Sin with a bandaged head was being led to her home by a couple of much scandalized Sunday-school teachers, her little friend following with a very pale face.

Sweet Sin was the child of a Chinese merchant and his American wife. She had been baptized Wilhelmina, but for reasons apart from the fact that her father was Hwuy Sin, a medical student had, in her babyhood, dubbed her Sweet Sin, and the name had clung.

On arrival at the house, they were met by the mother, who was much perturbed at the sight of her offspring.

The Sunday-school teachers explained the case and departed. The mother bathed Sweet Sin's face. The child liked the feeling of the cool water; her head was feverish and so was her heart.

"I'm so sorry that this happened," said the mother. "I wanted you to go to Mrs. Goodwin's party tonight, and now you are not fit to be seen."

"I'm glad," answered Sweet Sin. "I don't want to go."

"Why not?" queried the mother. "I'm surprised, she is so kind to you."

"I do not think so," replied Sweet Sin, "and I don't want her toys and candies. It's just because I'm half Chinese and a sort of curiosity that she likes to have me there. When I'm in her parlor, she whispers to the other people and they try to make me talk and examine me from head to toe as if I were a wild animal—I'd rather be killed than be a show."

"Sweet Sin, you must not speak so about your friends," remonstrated the mother.

"I don't care!" defiantly asserted Sweet Sin. "Last week, when I was at her house for tea, she came up with an old gentleman with white hair and gold-rimmed glasses. I heard the old gentleman say, 'Oh, indeed, you don't say so! her father a Chinaman!' and then he stared at me with all his might. Mrs. Goodman said, 'Do you not notice the peculiar cast of features?' and he said 'Ah, yes! and such bright eyes—very peculiar little girl.'"

"Well, and what did you do then?"

"Oh, I jumped up and cried: 'And you're a very peculiar, mean old man,' and ran out of the house."

"They must have thought you a little Chinese savage," said the mother, but her cheek glowed.

"They can think what they like! Besides, it isn't the Chinese half of me that makes me feel like this—it's the American half. My Chinese half is good and patient, like all the Chinese people we know, but it's my American half that feels insulted for the Chinese half and wants to fight. Oh, mother, mother, you don't know what it is to be half one thing and half another, like I am! I feel all torn to pieces. I don't know what I am, and I don't seem to have any place in the world."

Sweet Sin had been brought up in the Methodist Church and her mother sent her to Sunday-school regularly. Sometimes she felt a missionary spirit. One day, to an old laundryman, she told the story of the creation of Adam and Eve, the first man and woman. The old man listened attentively, but when she had finished, said:

"No, no, I tell you something better than that, and more true. The first man and woman were made like this: Long, long time ago, two brooms were sent down from the sky. They were brooms while they were in the air, but as soon as they touched earth, one became a man, the other a woman—the first man and woman."

Sweet Sin was greatly shocked, and for several days could think of little else than the broom theory. At last, she asked her father if he would not, as a special favor, enlighten Li Chung as to his true descent, but her father merely smiled and said:

"You had better leave Li Chung alone; his theory serves him as well as your Sunday-school teacher's serves her. Each is as reasonable as the other."

"Father!" exclaimed Sweet Sin, "are you a heathen?"

"That is a matter of opinion, my daughter."

II.

"Forget me," commanded Sweet Sin.

"Not while I have breath and blood."

"You must; I tell you to."

"But one always remembers what one's told to forget."

Dick Farrell's grey eyes looked pleadingly into Sweet Sin's. She was seventeen now. California sunshine and the balmy freshness of Pacific breezes had helped to make her a bewitching woman.

"I thought you liked me, Sweet Sin."

"So I do."

"But I thought you cared for me as I do for you."

Sweet Sin turned her face aside. She would not let him know.

"I like, but I do not love. As to you, why, next week there will be somebody else to whom you will be telling the same old tale. Don't interrupt. I know all about it. Besides, even if you did love me, as you say, the life of love is short—like all that's lovely. Yesterday, we hailed its birth, today we mourn it—dead."

"Sweet Sin, come to me—don't be wicked!"

"I told you I did not care for you."

"I will not believe it."

"Well, whether you believe it or not, I must leave you now, as I have something to do for father. Dick, do you remember once asking me if my father was a Chinaman; and when I replied yes, you said, 'Doesn't your flesh creep all over when you go near him?' You were about twelve then and I ten."

"I cannot recall the things I said so long ago," replied the young fellow, flushing up.

"No! Well, you see this is the day when I remember—the day when you forget."

III.

They were all there—the fiddler with his fiddle, the flutist with his flute, the banjo man with his banjo, and the kettledrummer with his kettledrum. All the Chinese talent in that California city were assembled together, and right merrily was the company entertained.

Hwuy Sin was giving a farewell banquet to his Chinese friends. He was about to return to China after an exile of about twenty-five years, and Sweet Sin, the child of the American woman, now dead two years, was to accompany him. His daughter was of a full marriageable age, and like every good Chinese father, what he desired for her was a husband—a husband such as could be found only amongst his cousins in China.

Hwuy Sin thought tenderly of his child; she had been a good daughter—a little more talkative and inquisitive perhaps than a woman should be, but always loving to him. Suddenly he arose from his seat; he had not seen her that evening and there were some instructions about the packing of his caps which he would like to give before the night closed.

Rat, tat, tat. Hwuy Sin stood outside Sweet Sin's door and waited. As it was not opened to him, he called softly, "My child, it is your father."

But Sweet Sin heard him not.

IV.

When Hwuy Sin returned to his guests he walked heavily.

"My daughter has gone to the land of spirits; mourn with me," he said.

And in Chinese fashion they mourned with him.

Hwuy Sin went back to China, and the mid-ocean received a casket containing what had once been called Sweet Sin. As he watched it sink, he said, "In all between the four seas, there was none like her. She belonged neither to her mother's country, nor to mine. Therefore, let her rest where no curious eyes may gaze."

Sweet Sin's farewell he carefully laid away. It was written in the beautiful Chinese characters he himself had taught her, and the words were:

"Father, so dear: I am not tired of life, and I dislike death, but though life to me is sweet, yet if I cannot have both it and honor, I will let life go. Father, stand up for me, and no matter what others may say, do not feel hard against me. My Christian friends will shake their heads and say, 'Ah, Sweet Sin!' their faces will become long and melancholy, and if you ask them to give me Christian burial, for my mother's sake, probably they will refuse. They will talk about right and wrong, and say that I have gone before my Maker with a crime on my soul. But for that I do not care, as what is right and what is wrong, who knows? The Chinese teachers say that the conscience tells us and they teach the practice of virtue for virtue's sake. The Christians point to the Bible as a guide, saying that if we live according to its lessons, we will be rewarded in an after life. I have puzzled much over these things, seeking as it were for a lost mind.

"Father, I cannot marry a Chinaman, as you wish, because my heart belongs to an American—an American who loves me and wishes to make me his wife. But, Father, though I cannot marry a Chinaman, who would despise me for being an American, yet I will not marry an American, for the Americans have made me feel so that I will save the children of the man I love from being called 'Chinese! Chinese!'

"Farewell, father. I hope God will forgive me for being what He made me.

"Sweet Sin."

NOTE

1. This story was originally published in the *Land of Sunshine* magazine with the author's name printed as "Sui Seen Far." During her career, Eaton's work appeared under many variations of her chosen pen name, "Sui Sin Far"; these included "Sui Seen Far," "Sui Sin Fah," and "Sue Seen Far."

THE SUCCESS OF A MISTAKE (1908)

In answer to the reporter's knock the door of the Chinese Mission swung open and a good-looking Chinaman appeared.

"Good morning, Wah Lee," said the reporter. "Have you any news for me today?"

"I not know, but I got something to tell you, and perhaps you call it news," returned the Chinaman.

"Well, I'll come in and hear what it is," and the young woman stepped within the Mission. It was a good-sized room, furnished with half a dozen long tables, around which were ranged wooden benches. There was matting on the floor, a few biblical pictures on the wall, and scattered on the tables were Bibles and text books. At the further end of the room, facing the door, was an alcove, the floor of which was raised so that it could be used as a platform. On the back wall of the alcove was an illuminated card on which was printed The Lord's Prayer in Chinese characters.

The reporter had visited the school on other occasions, so she did not waste any time in asking questions, but with notebook and pencil in hand waited for the Chinaman to speak.

"I think now perhaps I better not tell you," he said after some hesitation.

"Why, Wah Lee, of course you will."

"All right. I think what I say. You know Mrs. Wong Lee. She live on Jackson street. She very smart woman, all same American woman and Chinese woman too—and all same lawyer. Well, she have ten children, seven girl and three boy. The name of the eldest boy it is Charlie, and the name of her eldest girl it is Anna. They have Chinese name, too. All the children of the Wong family they born in this country. The eldest daughter she very pretty girl, her skin it smooth and white as rice, her face shaped like a melon seed, her mouth same as red leaf of vine, her nose fine carved piece of jade stone, her eye long and black, and her hair most plenty and shiny and dressed in the first Chinese style. See!"

"Yes, I see, Wah."

The Chinaman, who seemed to have lost himself in his description of his young countrywoman, became suddenly embarrassed.

"That's all right, Wah," encouraged the reporter, removing from him the scrutiny of her eyes. "I like to hear you. It is the first time I have heard a Chinaman acknowledge that he paid any attention to things feminine. I remember that when I called upon Tsing Leang soon after his wife came to America and inquired as to how she was, what she looked like, how old, if she dressed in American or Chinese clothes, and so forth, that his answer to each and every question was 'I don't know.'"

"That so, Miss Lund. Perhaps you ask same question of American man, he says he not know, too."

The reporter flushed, but answered good naturedly:

"True! But you understand, Wah, that when we Americans ask questions of Chinese people that it is because we want you to enlighten us on subjects about which we are ignorant, and not with the intention of being rude."

"Sure that your case," returned the Chinaman. "I think you very kind lady. Now I complete what I say," and he concluded his remarks with an interesting item of news concerning the Wong family.

"A CHINESE BETROTHAL."

"Mrs. Wong, the wife of Wong Chow, well-known Chinese merchant of Jackson street, has gone to San Francisco to find a suitable husband for her eldest daughter, Anna. Mrs. Wong is a Chinese lady of education and refinement, and is resolved to betroth her daughter to none but a man of ability and character. Miss Anna is said to be a very pretty girl, and great festivities and rejoicings will take place at her wedding."

The above, followed by a description of Chinese betrothal and marriage customs, appeared in Miss Lund's paper the evening of her interview with Wah Lee.

Shortly after its appearance Miss Lund met with an accident which confined her to her room for several weeks. When she was able to move around again she wended her way to the Wong family's residence in Chinatown, with the intention of finding out when the wedding would take place.

Mrs. Wong, who took for granted that her visitor was connected with some missionary work, invited her into the sitting-room, furnished in Chinese-American fashion. The reporter made a few remarks about the weather and the pretty little girl clinging to Mrs. Wong's skirts, then began:

"I hear that your eldest daughter is to be married soon. Won't you tell me when the wedding will be? I should very much like to be present."

The Chinese woman's face darkened and her voice was deep with passion as she answered:

"My daughter's wedding! Huh! Speak not of that. It can never be."

"Oh, why?" exclaimed the reporter, gazing in astonishment at the stout, quivering figure of the Chinese matron.

"Because—my daughter—she is ruined for life—and so also all my girls."

Miss Lund did not feel very comfortable, but her newspaper instinct told her that here might be a good story, so she sympathetically enquired as to what had happened.

"What happen?" returned the angry woman. "Well, my husband he have a friend come to America long time gone by. His name Ju Chu and he have no wife, but he have good business in Seattle and he be very industrious and smart man. He tell my husband that he want marry and he send to China for a wife, and my husband he come tell me what his friend say and I reply, 'What for he send to China for wife?' Why not he marry our eldest daughter? She be eighteen years old and she be well brought up, and as we got six other daughters to be married it would be very excellent thing to make arrangement with your friend to marry the eldest of our daughters.' My husband, he say, 'You be wise woman and I am in accord with what you think with regard to our daughter. When a girl is grown to be a woman it is proper that a husband should be found for her.' So, as is the custom of our people, my husband sent a go-between to see Ju Chu's uncle, and ask him to consider the betrothal of our daughter to his nephew, and Ju Chu's uncle he seem very pleased, and Ju Chu pleased too, for one day when he come see my husband, my daughter she pass by the room they be in and he see her, and he tell my husband that he think she be very good to look at."

"If she takes after her mother she certainly must be," said Miss Lund, and Mrs. Wong continued:

"Now, my son Charlie, he also be of age to marry, so I decide that I take trip to San Francisco to find good wife for him at the Mission school. I brought up at Baptist Mission[1] so I want find Baptist girl to be my son Charlie's wife. I leave arrangements for my daughter's betrothal in the hands of my husband and I go to San Francisco. Just before I leave, my husband tell me that Ju Chu, he have the engagement card ready very soon, so I feel satisfied that all is right and I go to San Francisco with peaceful mind. When I get there I find nice little girl to betroth to my son and I arrange that she come here to be marry next month. Then I come back to Seattle. Now, what you think I find when I come home. That all the negotiation my husband and myself make to engage my daughter all come to no good, and Ju Chu he go away for some month and he tell all the Chinese people that he not want to have anything to do with my family. For why? Because the newspaper publish wicked lying story about me go to San Francisco to find husband for my daughter."

Mrs. Wong paused to take breath. Miss Lund, feeling like a criminal, faintly murmured.

"Well, well!"

"What man in Los Angeles want one of my daughters if he think I want go to San Francisco to find husband for her? And it be not true, it be most wicked lie. I not need go look for husband for my daughters. They be nice looking girls and I teach them all that the Chinese woman should know and at the American school they learn all that the American girl know. Plenty Chinaman make offer for them before the bad story appear, but we particular, we not common class Chinese people, so I say to my husband, 'Wait,' and then come Ju Chu. Now, the Chinamen in Seattle, they not want have anything more to do with our family. My girls they all be ruined—no man here take them for wife."

"But you went to get a wife for your son, did you not?" said Miss Lund, feeling that she must say something.

"That much different," replied the Chinese woman. "There be few Chinese girls in Seattle—and it is not the same to write that I go to get wife for son as to say I go for husband for daughter. It is not the same when we live in America and we hear that the American people think shame for to do such a thing as for a mother to go to a city where she not live to find husband for her daughter. The Chinese people have same feelings as the American people, only the

American people they not seem to understand that. The Chinese men in San Francisco, when they hear what in the paper, say 'What for Wong family want to find husband for their daughter in San Francisco? There be plenty Chinamen in Seattle. Sure there must be something not right with the daughters if the Seattle Chinamen not want them.' I say to my husband this morning, 'Find me the man that wrote that most wicked lie and I pluck his heart out.'"

"I think I must go now. I am very sorry that you are in trouble, Mrs. Wong. Perhaps it is not as bad as you imagine."

After reaching the street Miss Lund walked absently along. Her mind was much perturbed by what she had heard. She was a good-hearted young woman and that she should have brought misfortune to the house of Wong was not a pleasant thought. "If I had only made some enquiries of the Chinese mother as I would have of an American mother before sending in the article, this mightn't have happened," she remorsefully mused. She was angry with Wah Lee, too. "That wicked Wah to tell me such a story," she mentally exclaimed and promised herself that she would punish him.

Nevertheless, the situation appealed to her sense of humor and she could scarcely repress an hysterical giggle when in answer to her rap at the Mission door, the Missionary, Miss Hastings, appeared.

"What's the matter?" asked that little woman, drawing her friend into the room.

The reporter's interview with Mrs. Wong was briefly but vividly described. Miss Hastings looked serious.

"I can hardly believe it of Wah Lee," said she, "He is such a good honest fellow."

"He has always appeared so to me," returned the other. "I have depended upon him for my Chinese news for over a year and he has given me some very good points. I consider him really cleverer than most of the educated Chinamen I have met."

"Yes, poor lad! He has considerable ability and despite the fact that he has no 'cousins' in America, as most of the other Chinamen have, seems able to make his little laundry yield him an independence. He makes something as well by looking after this place for us."

"How is it he doesn't get married?" asked the reporter.

"I'm not sure, but I think I know why. It is said amongst the Chinese here that were he to return to China he would be a slave. He ran away from the family to which he belonged when but twelve years old and came to America with a company of strolling actors. The Chinese have ideas of caste.[2] A freeborn Chinaman will not give his daughter to a slave. This applies as well to the Chinese here as to those in their own country. You see, if Wah Lee is a slave, his wife and children would also be slaves in China."

"But Wah says that he has no intention of returning there."

"Perhaps not; but the father of the Chinese girl he might seek for a wife would not consider a man who had turned his back for good upon his own country."

he not want to have anything to do with my family. For why? Because the newspaper publish wicked lying story about me go to San Francisco to find husband for my daughter."

Mrs. Wong paused to take breath. Miss Lund, feeling like a criminal, faintly murmured.

"Well, well!"

"What man in Los Angeles want one of my daughters if he think I want go to San Francisco to find husband for her? And it be not true, it be most wicked lie. I not need go look for husband for my daughters. They be nice looking girls and I teach them all that the Chinese woman should know and at the American school they learn all that the American girl know. Plenty Chinaman make offer for them before the bad story appear, but we particular, we not common class Chinese people, so I say to my husband, "Wait," and then come Ju Chu. Now, the Chinamen in Seattle, they not want have anything more to do with our family. My girls they all be ruined—no man here take them for wife."

"But you went to get a wife for your son, did you not?" said Miss Lund, feeling that she must say something.

"That much different," replied the Chinese woman. "There be few Chinese girls in Seattle—and it is not the same to write that I go to get wife for son as to say I go for husband for daughter. It is not the same when we live in America and we hear that the American people think shame for to do such a thing as for a mother to go to a city where she not live to find husband for her daughter. The Chinese people have same feelings as the American people, only the American people they not seem to understand that. The Chinese men in San Francisco, when they hear what in the paper, say 'What for Wong family want to find husband for their daughter in San Francisco? There be plenty Chinamen in Seattle. Sure there must be something not right with the daughters if the Seattle Chinamen not want them.' I say to my husband this morning, 'Find me the man that wrote that most wicked lie and I pluck his heart out."

"I think I must go now. I am very sorry that you are in trouble, Mrs. Wong. Perhaps it is not as bad as you imagine."

After reaching the street Miss Lund walked absently along. Her mind was much perturbed by what she had heard. She was a good-hearted young woman and that she should have brought misfortune to the house of Wong was not a pleasant thought. "If I had only made some enquiries of the Chinese mother as I would have of an American mother before sending in the article, this mightn't have happened," she remorsefully mused. She was angry with Wah Lee, too. "That wicked Wah to tell me such a story," she mentally exclaimed and promised herself that she would punish him.

"How is it he does'nt get married?" asked the reporter.

Nevertheless, the situation appealed to her sense of humor and she could scarcely repress an hysterical giggle when in answer to her rap at the Mission door, the Missionary, Miss Hastings, appeared.

"What's the matter?" asked that little woman, drawing her friend into the room.

The reporter's interview with Mrs. Wong was briefly but vividly described. Miss Hastings looked serious.

"I can hardly believe it of Wah Lee," said she, "He is such a good honest fellow."

"He has always appeared so to me," returned the other. "I have depended upon him for my Chinese news for over a year and he has given me some very good points, I consider him really cleverer than most of the educated Chinamen I have met."

"Yes, poor lad! He has considerable ability and despite the fact that he has no "cousins" in America, as most of the other Chinamen have, seems able to make his little laundry yield him an independence. He makes something as well by looking after this place for us."

"How is it he doesn't get married?" asked the reporter.

"I'm not sure, but I think I know why. It is said amongst the Chinese here that were he to return to China he would be a slave. He ran away from the family to which he belonged when but twelve years old and came to America with a company of strolling actors. The Chinese have ideas of caste. A freeborn Chinaman will not give his daughter to a slave. This applies as well to the Chinese here as to those in their own country. You see, if Wah Lee is a slave, his wife and children would also be slaves in China."

"But Wah says that he has no intention of returning there."

"Perhaps not; but the father of the Chinese girl he might seek for a wife would not consider a man who had turned his back for good upon his own country."

"Too bad for Wah Lee."

"I'm sorry for him," said Miss Hastings.

"I'm not," returned her friend emphatically. "That story he told me deprives him of my sympathy. I thought he was such a splendid Chinaman."

"I did think that he had embraced Christianity in all sincerity; but if he could do what you say he has done I have been mistaken," sighed Miss Hastings.

"Would the embracing of Christianity interfere with a Chinaman's other actions?"

"You heathen!"

"There's one that I do feel sorry for. That is the girl who was so nearly betrothed," said Miss Lund, ignoring the epithet bestowed upon her.

Miss Hastings smiled.

"She does not seem to be very sorry for herself," said she. "She's a dear bright little thing and was in here yesterday to tell me all about it. She said she felt that

Illustration from Sui Sin Far [Edith Maude Eaton], "Success of a Mistake," *Westerner* 8 (1908).

"Too bad for Wah Lee."

"I'm sorry for him," said Miss Hastings.

"I'm not," returned her friend emphatically. "That story he told me deprives him of my sympathy. I thought he was such a splendid Chinaman."

"I did think that he had embraced Christianity in all sincerity; but if he could do what you say he has done I have been mistaken," sighed Miss Hastings.

"Would the embracing of Christianity interfere with a Chinaman's other actions?"

"You heathen!"

"There's one that I do feel sorry for. That is the girl who was so nearly betrothed," said Miss Lund, ignoring the epithet bestowed upon her.

Miss Hastings smiled.

"She does not seem to be very sorry for herself," said she. "She's a dear bright little thing and was in here yesterday to tell me all about it. She said she felt that the person who wrote that story about her mother's trip to San Francisco and its object is one of her best friends, as the article had certainly driven away from her a man she abhorred. 'You know, teacher,' said she, 'Mother and father cannot make me marry a man who does not want me, and I am so happy as a bird, only put on sad face before my parents.'"

"The cute little thing. I am so glad. My conscience is quite relieved."

Miss Lund laughed heartily. Miss Hastings laughed too, then tried to be serious.

"I don't approve of anything like deception," said she.

"I would like to meet this little Anna," Miss Lund was saying, when the door was pushed open and Wah Lee entered. He came towards the young woman with head bared.

"Wah Lee, you are a very bad Chinaman. What do you mean by telling me stories which are not true and causing so much mischief?" was the greeting he received. It in no wise, however, perturbed him, for he answered calmly and respectfully:

"If you say I am a bad Chinaman, Miss Lund, then a bad Chinaman I be, but I not tell you any stories that not be true."

"What about Mrs. Wong's trip to San Francisco?"

"Yes, I hear about that; plenty Chinamen talk about it," said Wah Lee, "and I intend first time I see you to tell you that you make mistake. I not say that Mrs. Wong go find husband for her daughter. I say she go find wife for her son Charlie."

"Did you tell me that, Wah?"

"Yes, Miss Lund."

"It may be, dear," said Miss Hastings with a little twinkle in her eye, "that someone else has made a mistake—not Wah Lee."

"Nonsense, it is impossible. You told me just what I wrote, Wah, otherwise it would not have been written."

"Yes, I told you that what you wrote in your book," assented the Chinaman, "but not what you wrote in the paper." "Perhaps the printer make mistake," he added brightly.

"No, no," said Miss Lund, "it's either you or I, Wah. However, here's the proof. As you say, I put down what you told me in my notes."

She hurriedly turned over the pages of the book referred to until she reached one dated the day she had last been at the Mission, then read aloud:

"Mrs. Wong has gone to San Francisco to find a wife for her son, Charlie———"

She threw the book on the table.

"I knew Wah was all right," exclaimed Miss Hastings.

"Indeed he is and I humbly beg his pardon," said the reporter, extending her hand to the Chinaman, who shook it calmly, a smile on his face.

"Wah has appeared to be very happy these last few days," remarked Miss Hastings.

"That be on account of that story. I be very grateful to you Miss Lund."

The young women laughed at what they took to be a joke and feeling better than when she entered the Mission Miss Lund departed. She had reached the corner of the street when a timid pull at her dress from behind arrested her, and turning she beheld a pretty young Chinese girl.

"Did you wish to speak to me?" asked the reporter.

"I—I Lady, will you be so kind as to tell me if you write for the papers?"

"Why, yes—sometimes."

"I thought so," said the girl, her face brightening. "I have seen you going into the mission across the street and Wah Lee has told me that you visit him to get news of the Chinese."

"Oh, indeed! Are you one of Wah Lee's friends?"

"I am Anna Wong. That is my American name. My Chinese name is Mai Gwi Far, which means a rose."

"Anna Wong! Why, you are just the little girl I have wanted to meet."

"How glad I am. I have been wanting to speak to you for some time. Please don't think I mean to be bold, but may I ask you if you wrote that article in the paper—about my mother."

"I did."

"Ah! I was right then that I had you to thank for saving me from much misery."

"No need to thank me, poor child!"

"Yes, you and Wah Lee, for I know he told you. Wah Lee and I are friends, though my parents do not know. If they did, they would be very angry, for they keep to all the Chinese customs and think it is not proper for a man and a maid to become friends with one another until after they are married."

"And you think differently!"

"Lady," said she, "When a Chinese girl is born in America and learns in an American school, how can be the same as a Chinese girl who is born and brought up in China?"

"I see," said Miss Lund, "You were born and brought up here. That accounts for your American tongue, I suppose. Wah Lee is a clever boy, but he does not speak as well you do."

"That is because he has had to work all day while I have been at school."

"Come with me to Leschi Park?[3] I would like to have a chat with you," proposed the American girl. The Chinese girl assented, a passing car was hailed and the two were soon out in the open, the blue sky above them, the mountains in the distance, the still lake before them, and peace and pleasantness around.

Miss Lund drew in a big breath of the sweet invigorating air, then turned to her young companion.

"Does Wah Lee love you?" she enquired.

Anna started, then answered happily enough, "He has not said so, but as he told you to write that in the paper I am sure that he does. I suppose he thought when Ju Chu heard about it that he would give up the idea of marrying me."

"Here's another mistake to be rectified," thought the reporter, but kept her silence. "Sometimes I have thought that he did not care, but this proves I was wrong, does it not?"

"From what Wah Lee has said to me I am sure that he cares for you," replied Miss Lund, remembering Wah Lee's thanks, and Anna continued:

"Mother did go to San Francisco to see about a wife for my brother, Charlie, so it was not all untrue—what Wah Lee said. Don't you think a story like that can be excused? It was just to save me from Ju Chu."

"But your mother doesn't approve of your being saved, does she?"

"No! poor mother and father! They say no Chinaman will want me now. But I think one will, don't you?"

This question was put most anxiously.

"I know one who will," answered Miss Lund, contemplating the red vine leaf mouth, the long black eyes and pretty form Wah Lee had so admirably described.

The Chinese girl smiled a happy smile.

"You are most sweet to say that," lisped she.

"Do you love Wah Lee?"

"I have not let him know."

"But you will now that he has let you know, will you not?"

"Do you think that would be wise?"

"Certainly."

"But my father and mother—they would not approve of my marrying a man who is a slave in China."

"He is not a slave here, and you are an American girl."

"No, I am Chinese and so is Wah Lee."

"Yes, but you have always lived in this country and can have no wish to live in China."

"Oh, lady, that has been the fear of my life—that my parents would marry me to some Chinaman who would take me away from America. This is the country in which I was born. I know no other."

"If you marry Wah Lee, you can stay here always, for he tells me he will never return to China."

"But my parents!"

"No matter what they have said, I do not think they will object to Wah Lee now. Have you not just now told me that their great fear is that no man will take you from them."

"Ah, yes."

"Naturally then they will be very glad if Wah Lee makes an offer. And when you are safely married other Chinamen will come forward for your sisters. You will help your family by becoming Wah Lee's wife."

"Do you really think so?"

"Of course. The thing now to be done is to let Wah Lee understand that you care for him."

"And it will be all right—it will not be bold."

"It will be all right."

"You will not tell my mother that it was Wah Lee who said that she had gone to San Francisco to find a husband for me."

"How could I tell such a story about Wah Lee?"

* * * * * * * *

Miss Lund and Miss Hastings were discussing the event of the day to them.

"It is the prettiest wedding that has ever taken place here," murmured Miss Hastings. "If all mistakes turned out as happily as did this one of yours, there would be little to regret."

"Oh," replied Miss Lund, laughing mischievously, "There were more mistakes than mine. Little Anna took for granted that Wah got the article published in order to drive Ju Chu away, and thereupon came to the conclusion that Wah was in love with her."

"You don't mean to say that you allowed Anna to believe that and encouraged her to reveal her love for the man before he had spoken himself."

"I acknowledge my transgression. My sin is ever before me."

"You wicked girl!"

"I only wish it were true that Wah had manufactured the tale to gain his ends. It would have been so much more romantic."

"I don't care for romance; I like a man I can trust."

"Then, as he still remains a man after your own heart, you need not scold, Fan. It was plain to me that those two children loved one another. Wah would never have dared to reveal what he felt had he not received some encouragement. As to Anna—how could I rob her of the proof to her of her lover's love?"

"I'm afraid you allow your good nature to override your principles."

"So would you in my place. Now, own up that 'All's well that ends well,'[4] and be glad over the success of my mistake."

Even as she said this, Wah Lee and Mai Gwi Far were telling one another that their coming together had surely been ordained by Heaven.

NOTES

1. In the nineteenth century, Baptist missionaries both in China and in Chinese communities along the West Coast of the United States exerted great effort to convert Chinese people to Christianity. In some cities, missionary churches were built for immigrant laborers; later, many congregations were founded by American-born Chinese Christians.
2. Castes are a form of social hierarchy in which one's position is hereditary and based on factors such as occupation and perceived importance to the community.
3. Leschi Park in Seattle is located east of the city's Chinatown-International District, on the shore of Lake Washington.
4. Reference to William Shakespeare's *All's Well That Ends Well* (1623), a comedy that poses ethical dilemmas with no easy solutions. It ends, like this story, with a marriage.

MARY E. WILKINS FREEMAN

(1852–1930)

Mary E. Wilkins was born on October 31, 1852, in Randolph, Massachusetts; only after her marriage in 1902 was she known as Mary Wilkins Freeman. Her parents were devout Congregationalists, and her childhood was heavily influenced by their strict religious views. When Freeman was fifteen years old, her family moved to Brattleboro, Vermont. The Wilkins family struggled financially, and her father encouraged Mary to get married as soon as possible to achieve economic security; nonetheless, she remained single until the age of forty-nine. Despite the family's minimal resources, Freeman was able to attend Mount Holyoke Female Seminary (now Mount Holyoke College) in Massachusetts for one academic year, from 1870 to 1871; whether she withdrew because her family could no longer afford the fees or because of her dislike for the institution's rules is unknown.

After her sister Anna died in 1876 and her mother died in 1880, Freeman began to write in order to support herself and her father. In 1882 she experienced her first major success when her story "The Shadow Family" won a fifty-dollar prize from the *Boston Sunday Budget* newspaper; shortly thereafter *Harper's Bazar* magazine published her short story "Two Old Lovers." When Freeman's father, Warren Edward Wilkins, passed away in 1883, he left a meager estate of less than a thousand dollars. Without family or income on which to rely, Freeman had no choice but to move back to Randolph and live with her childhood friend, Mary John Wales, and her parents. Fortunately, living with the Waleses afforded Freeman time to focus on her writing. During the almost two decades that Freeman lived with the Wales family, she produced most of the works for which she is best known. Her fictions proved extremely popular with readers and critics alike; they were in great demand from the major magazines and publishers of the day, and W. D. Howells and Henry James were among the many notable literary figures who lauded Freeman's talent. Her two most prominent collections, *A Humble Romance and Other Stories* (1887) and *A New England Nun and Other Stories* (1891), depict life in mostly small New England towns, highlighting the tensions between modernity and tradition, the struggles of poor people in the face of adversity, and the limitations placed on women. Many of her female characters challenge conventional gender expectations, as seen in two of her most frequently anthologized stories, "A New England Nun" (1887) and "The Revolt of 'Mother'" (1890).

In 1892, while visiting New Jersey, she met Dr. Charles Manning Freeman, a nonpracticing doctor who was seven years her junior. After a courtship that lasted close to a decade, the couple married on January 1, 1902, and set up house in Metuchen, New Jersey. Unfortunately, the Freemans' marriage was not a happy one, for Charles proved to be an alcoholic, drug addict, and womanizer. Mary Wilkins Freeman's attention was increasingly directed toward these difficulties in her personal life, making it difficult for her to focus on her writing as much as she would have liked. Eventually, Freeman had her husband committed to the New Jersey State Hospital for the Insane and in 1922 the two were officially separated. Charles Freeman died in 1923, spitefully leaving only one dollar of his estate to his ex-wife and most of the remainder to his chauffeur.

During the course of her career, Freeman was a remarkably prolific writer whose publications included fourteen novels, twenty-two volumes of short stories and essays, a number of plays, and a few volumes of poetry. Over a hundred of her stories, first published in various periodicals, also remained uncollected in volume form. Freeman's works are often described as belonging to the Local Color or Regionalist literary traditions due to the effort she made to faithfully represent her New England settings and characters, including detailed descriptions of nature and attempts to accurately render local dialects. Although American literary culture was slow to consider women as serious authors of merit, Freeman received a number of notable accolades late in her life. In 1925, for instance, she was the first-ever recipient of the William Dean Howells Medal for distinction in fiction, presented by the American Academy of Arts and Letters, and she was among the first women admitted to the National Institute of Arts and Letters. She died of a heart attack in 1930 at the age of seventy-seven.

"One Good Time" first appeared in *Harper's Monthly* in January 1897, at the height of Freeman's popularity, and it well represents many of her most important themes, especially the question of what society expects from unmarried older women. As is obvious from the title of the other story presented here, "Old Woman Magoun" also prominently features an older woman, but it is the fate of her much younger granddaughter, Lily, that provides the central drama. First published in *Harper's Monthly* in October 1905 and later included in *The Winning*

Lady and Others (1909), this complex tale refutes the perception of many that the quality of Freeman's writing sharply declined after her marriage.

*Readers should be aware that the following story includes language which, while commonly used during this time period, is no longer considered acceptable because of its offensive nature.

ONE GOOD TIME (1897)

Richard Stone was nearly seventy-five years old when he died, his wife was over sixty, and his daughter Narcissa past middle age. Narcissa Stone had been very pretty, and would have been pretty still had it not been for those lines, as distinctly garrulous of discontent and worry as any words of mouth, which come so easily in the face of a nervous, delicate-skinned woman. They were around Narcissa's blue eyes, her firmly closed lips, her thin nose; a frown like a crying repetition of some old anxiety and indecision was on her forehead; and she had turned her long neck so much to look over her shoulder for new troubles on her track that the lines of fearful expectation had settled there. Narcissa had yet her beautiful thick hair, which the people in the village had never quite liked because it was red; her cheeks were still pink, and she stooped only a little from her slender height when she walked. Some people said that Narcissa Stone would be quite good-looking now if she had a decent dress and bonnet. Neither she nor her mother had any clothes which were not deemed shabby, even by the humbly attired women in the little mountain village. "Mis' Richard Stone, she ain't had a new silk dress since Narcissa was born," they said; "and as for Narcissa, she ain't never had anything that looked fit to wear to meeting."[1]

When Richard Stone died, people wondered if his widow and Narcissa would not have something new. Mrs. Nathan Wheat, who was a third cousin to Richard Stone, went, the day before the funeral, a half mile down the brook road to see Hannah Turbin, the dressmaker. The road was little traveled; she walked through an undergrowth of late autumn flowers, and when she reached the Turbins' house her black thibet[2] gown was gold-powdered and white-flecked to the knees with pollen and winged seeds of passed flowers.

Hannah Turbin's arm, brown and wrinkled like a monkey's, in its woolen sleeve, described arcs of jerky energy past the window, and never ceased when Mrs. Wheat came up the path and entered the house. Hannah herself scarcely raised her seamy brown face from her work.

"Good afternoon," said Mrs. Wheat.

Hannah nodded. "Good afternoon," she responded then, as if words were an after-thought.

Mrs. Wheat shook her black skirts vigorously. "I'm all over dust from them yaller weeds," said she. "Well, I don't care about this old thibet." She pulled a rocking-chair forward and seated herself. "Warm for this time of year," said she.

Hannah drew her thread through her work. "Yes, 'tis," she returned, with a certain pucker of scorn, as if the utter foolishness of allusions to obvious conditions of nature struck her. Hannah Turbin was not a favorite in the village, but she was credited with having much common sense, and people held her in somewhat distant respect.

"Guess it's Injun summer,"[3] remarked Mrs. Wheat.

Hannah Turbin said nothing at all to that. Mrs. Wheat cast furtive glances around the room as she swayed in her rocking-chair. Everything was very tidy and there were few indications of its owner's calling. A number of fashion papers were neatly piled on a bureau in the corner, and some nicely folded breadths of silk lay beside them. There was not a scrap or shred of cloth upon the floor; not a thread, even. Hannah was basting a brown silk basque.[4] Mrs. Wheat could see nowhere the slightest evidence of what she had come to ascertain, so was finally driven to inquiry, still, however, by devious windings.

"Seems sad about Richard," she said.

"Yes," returned Hannah, with a sudden contraction of her brown face, which seemed to flash a light over a recollection in Mrs. Wheat's mind. She remembered that there was a time, years ago, when Richard Stone had paid some attention to Hannah Turbin, and people had thought he might marry her instead of Jane Basset. However, it had happened so long ago that she did not really believe that Hannah dwelt upon it, and it faded immediately from her own mind.

"Well," said she, with a sigh, "it is a happy release, after all; he's been such a sufferer so long. It's better for him, and it's better for Jane and Narcissa. He's left 'em comfortable; they've got the farm, and his life's insured, you know. Besides, I suppose Narcissa'll marry William Crane now. Most likely they'll rent the farm, and Jane will go and live with Narcissa when she's married. I want to know——"

Hannah Turbin sewed.

"I was wondering," continued Mrs. Wheat, "if Jane and Narcissa wasn't going to have some new black dresses for the funeral. They ain't got a thing that's fit to wear, I know. I don't suppose they've got much money on hand now except what little Richard saved up for his funeral expenses. I know he had a little for that because he told me so, but the life insurance is coming in, and anybody would trust them. There's a nice piece of black cashmere down to the store, a dollar a yard. I didn't know but they'd get dresses off it; but Jane she never tells me anything—anybody'd think she might, seeing as I was poor Richard's cousin; and as for Narcissa, she's as close as her mother."

Hannah Turbin sewed.

"'Ain't Jane and Narcissa said anything to you about making them any new black dresses to wear to the funeral?" asked Mrs. Wheat, with desperate directness.

"No, they 'ain't," replied Hannah Turbin.

"Well, then, all I've got to say is they'd ought to be ashamed of themselves. There they've got fourteen if not fifteen hundred dollars coming in from poor Richard's insurance money, and they ain't even going to get decent clothes to wear to his funeral out of it. They 'ain't made any plans for new bonnets, I know. It ain't showing proper respect to the poor man. Don't you say so?"

"I suppose folks are their own best judges," said Hannah Turbin, in her conclusive, half-surly fashion, which intimidated most of their neighbors. Mrs. Wheat did not stay much longer. When she went home through the ghostly weeds and grasses of the country road she was almost as indignant with Hannah Turbin as with Jane Stone and Narcissa. "Never saw anybody so close in my life," said she to herself. "Needn't talk if she don't want to. Dun'no' as thar's any harm in my wanting to know if my own third cousin is going to have mourning wore for him."

Mrs. Wheat, when she reached home, got a black shawl which had belonged to her mother out of the chest, where it had lain in camphor, and hung it on the clothesline to air. She also removed a spray of bright velvet flowers from her bonnet, and sewed in its place a black ostrich feather. She found an old crape[5] veil, too, and steamed it into stiffness. "I'm going to go to that funeral looking decent, if his own wife and daughter ain't," she told her husband.

"If I wa'n't along, folks would take you for the widder," said Nathan Wheat with a chuckle. Nathan Wheat was rather inclined to be facetious with his wife.

However, Mrs. Wheat was not the only person who attended poor Richard Stone's funeral in suitable attire. Hannah Turbin was black from head to foot; the material, it is true, was not of the conventional mourning kind, but the color was. She wore a black silk gown, a black ladies'-cloth mantle, a black velvet bonnet trimmed with black flowers, and a black lace veil.

"Hannah Turbin looked as if she was dressed in second mourning," Mrs. Wheat said to her husband after the funeral. "I should have thought she'd most have worn some color, seeing as some folks might remember she was disappointed about Richard Stone; but, anyway, it was better than to go looking the way Jane and Narcissa did. There was Jane in that old brown dress, and Narcissa in her green, with a blue flower in her bonnet. I think it was dreadful, and poor Richard leaving them all that money through his dying, too."

In truth, all the village was scandalized at the strange attire of the widow and daughter of Richard Stone at his funeral, except William Crane. He could not have told what Mrs. Stone wore, through scarcely admitting her in any guise into his inmost consciousness, and as for Narcissa, he admitted her so fully that he could not see her robes at all in such a dazzlement of vision.

"William Crane never took his eyes off Narcissa Stone all through the funeral; shouldn't be surprised if he married her in a month or six weeks," people said.

William Crane took Jane and Narcissa to the grave in his covered wagon, keeping his old white horse at a decorous jog behind the hearse in the little funeral procession, and people noted that. They wondered if he would go over to the Stones' that evening, and watched, but he did not. He left the mother and daughter to their closer communion of grief that night, but the next the neighbors saw him in his best suit going down the road before dark. "Must have done up his chores early to get started soon as this," they said.

William Crane was about Narcissa's age but he looked older. His gait was shuffling, his hair scanty and gray, and, moreover, he had that expression of patience which comes only from long abiding, both of body and of soul. He went through the south yard to the side door of the house, stepping between the rocks. The yard abounded in mossy slopes of half-sunken rocks, as did the entire farm. Folks often remarked of Richard Stone's place, as well as himself, "Stone by name, and stone by nature." Underneath nearly all his fields, cropping plentifully to the surface, were rock ledges. The grass could be mown only by hand. As for this south yard, it required skilful maneuvering to drive a team through it. When William Crane knocked that evening, Narcissa opened the door. "Oh, it's you!" she said. "How do you do?"

"How do you do, Narcissa?" William responded, and walked in. He could have kissed his old love in the gloom of the little entry, but he did not think of that. He looked at her anxiously with his soft, patient eyes. "How are you gettin' on?" he asked.

"Well as can be expected," replied Narcissa.

"How's your mother?"

"She's as well as can be expected."

William followed Narcissa, who led the way, not into the parlor as he had hoped, but into the kitchen. The kitchen's great interior of smoky gloom was very familiar to him, but tonight it looked strange. For one thing, the armchair to which Richard Stone had been bound with his rheumatism for the last fifteen years was vacant, and pushed away into a corner. William looked at it, and it seemed to him that he must see the crooked, stern old figure in it, and hear again the peremptory tap of the stick which he kept always at his side to summon assistance. After his first involuntary glance at the dead man's chair, William saw his widow coming forward out of her bedroom with a great quilt over her arm.

"Good-evenin', William," she said, with faint melancholy, then lapsed into feeble weeping.

"Now, mother, you said you wouldn't; you know it don't do any good, and you'll be sick," Narcissa cried out, impatiently.

"I know it, Narcissa, but I can't help it, I can't. I'm dreadful upset! Oh, William, I'm dreadful upset! It ain't his death alone—it's—"

"Mother, I'd rather tell him myself," interrupted Narcissa. She took the quilt from her mother, and drew the rocking chair toward her. "Do sit down and keep calm, mother," said she.

But it was not easy for the older woman, in her bewilderment of grief and change, to keep calm.

"Oh, William, do you know what we're goin' to do?" she wailed, yet seating herself obediently in the rocking chair. "We're goin' to New York. Narcissa says so. We're goin' to take the insurance money, when we get it, an' we're goin' to New York. I tell her we hadn't ought to, but she won't listen to it! There's the trunk. Look at there, William! She dragged it down from the garret this forenoon. Look at there, William!"

William's startled eyes followed the direction of Mrs. Stone's wavering index finger, and saw a great ancient trunk, lined with blue-and-white wall-paper, standing open against the opposite wall.

"She dragged it down from the garret this forenoon," continued Mrs. Stone, in the same tone of unfaltering tragedy, while Narcissa, her delicate lips pursed tightly, folded up the bedquilt which her mother had brought. "It bumped so hard on those garret stairs I thought she'd break it, or fall herself, but she wouldn't let me help her. Then she cleaned it, an' made some paste, an' lined it with some of the parlor paper. There ain't any key to it—I never remember none. The trunk was in this house when I come here. Richard had it when he went West before we were married. Narcissa she says she is goin' to tie it up with the clothes-line. William, can't you talk to her? Seems to me I can't go to New York nohow."

William turned then to Narcissa, who was laying the folded bed quilt in the trunk. He looked pale and bewildered, and his voice trembled when he spoke. "This ain't true, is it, Narcissa?" he said.

"Yes, it is," she replied, shortly, still bending over the trunk.

"We ain't goin' for a month," interposed her mother again; "we can't get the insurance money before then, Lawyer Maxham says; but she says she's goin' to have the trunk standin' there, an' put things in when she thinks of it, so she won't forget nothin'. She says we'd better take one bedquilt with us, in case they don't have 'nough clothes on the bed. We've got to stay to a hotel. Oh, William, can't you say anything to stop her?"

"This ain't true, Narcissa?" William repeated, helplessly.

Narcissa raised herself and faced him. Her cheeks were red, her blue eyes glowing, her hair tossing over her temples in loose waves. She looked as she had when he first courted her. "Yes, it is, William Crane," she cried. "Yes, it is."

William looked at her so strangely and piteously that she softened a little. "I've got my reasons," said she. "Maybe I owe it to you to tell them. I suppose you were expecting something different." She hesitated a minute, looking at her mother, who cried out again:

"Oh, William, say somethin' to stop her! Can't you say somethin' to stop her?"

Then Narcissa motioned to him resolutely. "Come into the parlor, William," said she, and he followed her out across the entry. The parlor was chilly; the chairs stood as they had done at the funeral, primly against the walls glimmering faintly in the dusk with blue and white paper like the trunk lining. Narcissa stood before William and talked with feverish haste. "I'm going," said she—"I'm going to take that money and go with mother to New York, and you mustn't try to stop me, William. I know what you've been expecting. I know, now father's gone, you think there ain't anything to hinder our getting married; you think we'll rent this house, and mother and me will settle down in yours for the rest of our lives. I know you ain't counting on that insurance money; it ain't like you."

"The Lord knows it ain't, Narcissa," William broke out with pathetic pride.

"I know that as well as you do. You thought we'd put it in the bank for a rainy day, in case mother got feeble, or anything, and that is all you did think. Maybe I'd ought to. I s'pose I had, but I ain't going to. I ain't never done anything my whole life that I thought I ought not to do, but now I'm going to. I'm going to if it's wicked. I've made up my mind. I ain't never had one good time in my whole life, and now I'm going to even if I have to suffer for it afterwards.

"I 'ain't never had anything like other women. I've never had any clothes nor gone anywhere. I've just staid at home here and drudged. I've done a man's work on the farm. I've milked and made butter and cheese; I've waited on father; I've got up early and gone to bed late. I've just drudged, drudged, ever since I can remember. I don't know anything about the world nor life. I don't know anything but my own old tracks, and—I'm going to get out of them for a while, whether or no."

"How long are you calculating to stay?"

"I don't know."

"I've been thinking," said William, "I'd have some new gilt paper on the sitting room at my house, and a new stove in the kitchen. I thought—"

"I know what you thought," interrupted Narcissa, still trembling and glowing with nervous fervor. "And you're real good, William. It ain't many men would have waited for me as you've done, when father wouldn't let me get married as long as he lived. I know by good rights I hadn't ought to keep you waiting, but I'm going to, and it ain't because I don't think enough of you—it ain't that; I can't help it. If you give up having me at all, if you think you'd rather marry somebody else, I can't help it; I won't blame you—"

"Maybe you want me to, Narcissa," said William, with a sad dignity. "If you do, if you want to get rid of me, if that's it—"

Narcissa started. "That ain't it," said she. She hesitated, and added, with formal embarrassment—she had the usual reticence of a New England village woman about expressions of affection, and had never even told her lover in actual words that she loved him—"My feelings toward you are the same as they have always been, William."

It was almost dark in the parlor. They could see only each other's faces gleaming as with pale light. "It would be a blow to me if I thought they wa'n't, Narcissa," William returned, simply.

"They are."

William put his arm around her waist, and they stood close together for a moment. He stroked back her tumbled red hair with clumsy tenderness. "You have had a hard time, Narcissa," he whispered, brokenly. "If you want to go, I ain't going to say anything against it. I ain't going to deny I'm kind of disappointed. I've been living alone so long, and I feel kind of sore sometimes with waitin' but—"

"I shouldn't make you any kind of a wife if I married you now, without waiting," Narcissa said, in a voice at once stern and tender. She stood apart from him, and put up her hand with a sort of involuntary maiden primness to smooth her hair where his had stroked it awry. "If," she went on, "I had to settle down in your house, as I have done in father's, and see the years stretching ahead like a long road without any turn, and nothing but the same old dog trot of washing and ironing and scrubbing and cooking and sewing and washing dishes till I drop into my grave, I should hate you, William Crane."

"I could fetch an' carry all the water for the washin', Narcissa, and I could wash the dishes," said William, with humble beseeching.

"It ain't that. I know you'd do all you could. It's—Oh, William! I've got to have a break; I've got to have one good time. I—like you, and—I liked father; but love ain't enough sometimes when it ties anybody. Everybody has got their own feet and their own wanting to use 'em, and sometimes when love comes in the way of that, it ain't anything but a dead wall. Once we had a black heifer[6] that would jump all the walls; we had to sell her. She always made me think of myself. I tell you, William, I've got to jump my wall, and I've got to have one good time."

William Crane nodded his gray head in patient acquiescence. His forehead was knitted helplessly; he could not in the least understand what his sweetheart meant; in her present mood she was in altogether a foreign language for him, but still the unintelligible sound of her was sweet as a song to his ears. This poor village lover had at least gained the crown of absolute faith through his weary years of waiting; the woman he loved was still a star, and her rays not yet resolved into human reachings and graspings.

"How long do you calculate to be gone, Narcissa?" he asked again.

"I don't know," she replied. "Fifteen hundred dollars is a good deal of money. I s'pose it'll take us quite a while to spend it, even if we ain't very saving."

"You ain't goin' to spend it all, Narcissa!" William gave a little dismayed gasp in spite of himself.

"Land, no! we couldn't, unless we stayed three years, an' I ain't calculating to be gone as long as that. I'm going to bring home what we don't want, and put it in the bank; but—I shouldn't be surprised if it took 'most a year to spend what I've laid out to."

"'Most a year!"

"Yes; I've got to buy us both new clothes for one thing. We ain't neither of us got anything fit to wear, and 'ain't had for years. We didn't go to the funeral lookin' decent, and I know folks talked. Mother felt bad about it, but I couldn't help it. I wa'n't goin' to lay out money foolish and get things here when I was going to New York and could have others the way they ought to be. I'm going to buy us some jewelry, too; I 'ain't never had a good breastpin even; and as for mother, father never even bought her a ring when they were married. I ain't saying anything against him; it wa'n't the fashion so much in those days."

"I was calculatin'—" William stammered, blushing. "I always meant to, Narcissa."

"Yes, I know you have; but you mustn't lay out too much on it, and I don't care anything about a stone ring—just a plain gold one. There's another thing I'm going to have, too, an' that's a gold watch. I've wanted one all my life."

"Mebbe—" began William, painfully.

"No!" cried Narcissa, peremptorily. "I don't want you to buy me one. I ain't ever thought of it. I'm going to buy it myself. I'm going to buy mother a real cashmere shawl, too, like the one that New York lady had that came to visit

Lawyer Maxham's wife. I've got a list of things written down on paper. I guess I'll have to buy another trunk in New York to put them in."

"Well," said William, with a great sigh, "I guess I'd better be goin'. I hope you'll have as good a time as you're countin' on, Narcissa."

"It's the first good time I ever did count on, and I'd ought to," said Narcissa. "I'm going to take mother to the theatre, too. I don't know but it's wicked,[7] but I'm going to." Narcissa fluttered out of the parlor and William shuffled after her. He would not go into the kitchen again.

"Well, good-night," said Narcissa, and William also said good night, with another heavy sigh. "Look out for them rocks going out of the yard, an' don't tumble over 'em," she called after him.

"I'm used to 'em," he answered back, sadly, from the darkness.

Narcissa shut and bolted the door. "He don't like it; he feels real bad about it; but I can't help it—I'm going."

Through the next few weeks Narcissa Stone's face looked strange to those who had known her from childhood. While the features were the same, her soul informed them with a new purpose, which overlighted all the old ones of her life, and even the simple village folks saw the effect, though with no understanding. Soon the news that Narcissa and her mother were going to New York was abroad. On the morning they started, in the three-seated open wagon which served as stage to connect the little village with the railroad ten miles away, all the windows were set with furtively peering faces.

"There they go," the women told one another. "Narcissa an' her mother an' the trunk. Wonder if Narcissa's got that money put away safe? They're wearin' the same old clothes. S'pose we sha'n't know 'em when they get back. Heard they was goin' to stay a year. Guess old Mr. Stone would rise up in his grave if he knew it. Lizzy saw William Crane a-helpin' Narcissa h'ist the trunk out ready for the stage. I wouldn't stan' it if I was him. Ten chances to one Narcissa'll pick up somebody down to New York, with all that money. She's good-lookin', and she looks better since her father died."

Narcissa, riding out of her native village to those unknown fields in which her imagination had laid the scene of the one good time of her life, regarded nothing around her. She sat straight, her slender body resisting stiffly the jolt of the stage. She said not a word, but looked ahead with shining eyes. Her mother wept, a fold of her old shawl before her face. Now and then she lamented aloud, but softly, lest the driver hear. "Goin' away from the place where I was born an' married an' have lived ever since I knew anything, to stay a year. I can't stan' it, I can't."

"Hush, mother! You'll have a real good time."

"No, I sha'n't, I sha'n't. Goin'—to stay a whole—year. I—can't, nohow."

"S'pose we sha'n't see you back in these parts for some time," the stage driver said, when he helped them out at the railroad station. He was an old man, and had known Narcissa since her childhood.

"Most likely not," she replied. Her mother's face was quite stiff with repressed emotion when the stage driver lifted her out. She did not want him to report in the village that she was crying when she started for New York. She had some pride in spite of her distress.

"Well, I'll be on the lookout for ye a year from to-day," said the stage driver, with a jocular twist of his face. There were no passengers for his village on the in-coming train, so he had to drive home alone through the melancholy autumn woods. The sky hung low with pale, freezing clouds; over everything was that strange hush which prevails before snow. The stage driver, holding the reins loosely over his tramping team, settled forward with elbows on his knees, and old brows bent with aimless brooding. Over and over again his brain worked the thought, like a peaceful cud of contemplation. "They're goin' to be gone a year. Narcissa Stone an' her mother are goin' to be gone a year afore I'll drive 'em home."

So little imagination had the routine of his life fostered that he speculated not, even upon the possible weather of that far-off day, or the chances of his living to see it. It was simply, "They're goin' to be gone a year afore I'll drive 'em home."

So fixed was his mind upon that one outcome of the situation that when Narcissa and her mother reappeared in less than one week—in six days—he could not for a moment bring his mind intelligently to bear upon it. The old stage-driver may have grown something like his own horses through his long sojourn in their company, and his intelligence, like theirs, been given to only the halts and gaits of its first breaking.

For a second he had a bewildered feeling that time had flown fast, that a week was a year. Everybody in the village had said the travelers would not return for a year. He hoisted the ancient paper-lined trunk into his stage, then a fine new one, nailed and clamped with shining brass, then a number of packages, all the time with puzzled eyes askant upon Narcissa and her mother. He would scarcely have known them, as far as their dress was concerned. Mrs. Stone wore a fine black satin gown; her perturbed old face looked out of luxurious environments of fur and lace and rich black plumage. As for Narcissa, she was almost regal. The old stage driver backed and ducked awkwardly, as if she were a stranger, when she approached. Her fine skirts flared imposingly and rustled with unseen silk; her slender shoulders were made shapely by the graceful spread of rich fur; her red hair shone under a hat fit for a princess, and there was about her a faint perfume of violets which made the stage driver gaze confusedly at the snowy ground under the trees when they had started on the homeward road. "Seems as if I smelt posies, but I know there ain't none hereabouts this time of year," he remarked, finally, in a tone of mild ingratiation, as if more to himself than to his passengers.

"It's some perfumery Narcissa's got on her pocket-handkerchief that she bought in New York," said Mrs. Stone, with a sort of sad pride. She looked worn and bewildered, ready to weep at the sight of familiar things, and yet distinctly superior to all such weakness. As for Narcissa, she looked like a child thrilled with scared triumph at getting its own way, who rejoices even in the midst of correction at its own assertion of freedom.

"That so?" said the stage-driver, admiringly. Then he added, doubtfully, bringing one white-browed eye to bear over his shoulder, "Didn't stay quite so long as you calculated on?"

"No, we didn't," replied Narcissa, calmly. She nudged her mother with a stealthy, firm elbow, and her mother understood well that she was to maintain silence.

"I ain't going to tell a living soul about it but William Crane; I owe it to him," Narcissa had said to her mother before they started on their homeward journey. "The other folks sha'n't know. They can guess and surmise all they want to, but they sha'n't know. I sha'n't tell; and William, he's as close-mouthed as a rock; and as for you, mother, you always did know enough to hold your tongue when you made up your mind to it."

Mrs. Stone had compressed her mouth until it looked like her daughter's. She nodded. "Yes," said she; "I know some things that I 'ain't never told you, Narcissa."

The stage passed William Crane's house. He was shuffling around to the side door from the barn, with a milk-pail in each hand, when they reached it.

"Stop a minute," Narcissa said to the driver. She beckoned to William, who stared, standing stock-still, holding his pails. Narcissa beckoned again imperatively. Then William set the pails down on the snowy ground and came to the fence. He looked over it, quite pale, and gaping.

"We've got home," said Narcissa.

William nodded; he could not speak.

"Come over by-and-by," said Narcissa.

William nodded.

"I'm ready to go now," Narcissa said to the stage driver. "That's all."

That evening, when William Crane reached his sweetheart's house, a bright light shone on the road from the parlor windows. Narcissa opened the door. He stared at her open-mouthed. She wore a gown the like of which he had never seen before—soft lengths of blue silk and lace trailed about her; blue ribbons fluttered.

"How do you do?" said she.

William nodded solemnly.

"Come in."

William followed her into the parlor, with a wary eye upon his feet, lest they trample her trailing draperies. Narcissa settled gracefully into the rocking-chair; William sat opposite and looked at her. Narcissa was a little pale, still her face wore that look of insistent triumph.

"Home quicker'n you expected," William said, at length.

"Yes," said Narcissa. There was a wonderful twist on her red hair, and she wore a high shell comb. William's dazzled eyes noted something sparkling in the laces at her throat; she moved her hand, and something on that flashed like a point of white flame. William remembered vaguely how, often in the summertime when he had opened his house door in the sunny morning, the dewdrops on the grass had flashed in his eyes. He had never seen diamonds.

"What started you home so much sooner than you expected?" he asked, after a little.

"I spent—all the money—"

"All—that money?"

"Yes."

"Fifteen hundred dollars in less 'n a week?"

"I spent more'n that."

"More'n that?" William could scarcely bring out the words. He was very white.

"Yes," said Narcissa. She was paler than when he had entered, but she spoke quite decidedly. "I'm going to tell you all about it, William. I ain't going to make a long story of it. If after you've heard it you think you'd rather not marry me, I sha'n't blame you. I sha'n't have anything to say against it. I'm going to tell you just what I've been doing; then you can make up your mind.

"Today's Tuesday, and we went away last Thursday. We've been gone just six days. Mother an' me got to New York Thursday night, an' when we got out of the cars the men come round hollering this hotel an' that hotel. I picked out a man that looked as if he didn't drink and would drive straight, an' he took us to an elegant carriage, an' mother an' me got in. Then we waited till he got the trunk an' put it up on the seat with him where he drove. Mother, she hollered to him not to let it fall off.

"We went to a beautiful hotel. There was a parlor with a red velvet carpet and red stuffed furniture, and a green sitting-room and a blue one. The ceilin' had pictures on it. There was a handsome young gentleman downstairs at a counter in the room where we went first, and mother asked him, before I could stop her, if the folks in the hotel was all honest. She'd been worrying all the way for fear somebody'd steal the money.

"The gentleman said—he was real polite—if we had any money or valuables, we had better leave them with him, and he would put them in the safe. So we did. Then a young man with brass buttons on his coat took us to the elevator and showed us our rooms. We had a parlor with a velvet carpet an' stuffed furniture and a gilt clock on the mantel shelf, two bedrooms, and a bathroom. There ain't anything in town equal to it. Lawyer Maxham ain't got anything to come up to it. The young man offered to untie the rope on the trunk, so I let him. He seemed real kind about it.

"Soon's the young man went I says to mother, 'We ain't going down to get any tea to-night.'

"'Why not?' says she.

"'I ain't going down a step in this old dress,' says I, 'an' you ain't going in yours.'

"Mother didn't like it very well. She said she was faint to her stomach, and wanted some tea, but I made her eat some gingerbread we'd brought from home, an' get along. The young man with the brass buttons come again after a while, an' asked if there was anything we wanted, but I thanked him an' told him there wasn't.

"I would have asked him to bring up mother some tea and a hot biscuit, but I didn't know but what it would put 'em out; it was after seven o'clock then. So we got along till morning.

"The next morning mother an' me went out real early, an' went into a bakery an' bought some cookies. We ate 'em as we went down the street, just to stay our stomachs; then we went to buying. I'd taken some of the money in my purse, an' I got mother an' me, first of all, two handsome black silk dresses, and we put 'em on as soon as we got back to the hotel, and went down to breakfast.

"You never see anythin' like the dining-room, and the kinds of things to eat. We couldn't begin to eat 'em all. There were men standin' behind our chairs to wait on us all the time.

"Right after breakfast mother an' me put our rooms to rights; then we went out again and bought things at the stores. Everybody was buying Christmas presents, an' the stores were all trimmed with evergreen—you never see anything like that. Mother an' me never had any Christmas presents, an' I told her we'd begin, an' buy 'em for each other. When the money I'd taken with us was gone, I sent things to the hotel for the gentleman at the counter to pay, the way he'd told me to. That day we bought our breastpins and this ring, an' mother's and my gold watches, an'—I got one for you, too, William. Don't you say anything—it's your Christmas present. That afternoon we went to Central Park, an' that evenin' we went to the theatre. The next day we went to the stores again, an' I bought mother a black satin dress, and me a green one. I got this I've got on, too. It's what they call a tea-gown. I always wore it to tea in the hotel after I got it. I got a hat, too, an' mother a bonnet; an' I got a fur cape, and mother a cloak with fur on the neck an' all around it. That evening mother an' me went to the opera; we sat in something they call a box. I wore my new green silk and breastpin, an' mother wore her black satin. We both of us took our bonnets off. The music was splendid, but I wouldn't have young folks go to it much.

"The next day was Sunday. Mother an' me went to meeting in a splendid church, and wore our new black silks. They gave us seats way up in front, an' there was a real good sermon, though mother thought it wa'n't very practical, an' folks got up an' sat down more'n we do. Mother an' me set still, for fear we'd get up an' down in the wrong place. That evening we went to a sacred concert. Everywhere we went we rode in a carriage. They invited us to at the hotel, an' I s'posed it was free, but it wa'n't, I found out afterward.

"The next day was Monday—that's yesterday. Mother an' me went out to the stores again. I bought a silk bed-quilt, an' some handsome vases, an' some green an' gilt teacups setting in a tray to match. I've got 'em home without breaking. We got some silk stockings, too, an' some shoes, an' some gold-bowed spectacles for mother, an' two more silk dresses, an' mother a real Cashmere shawl. Then we went to see some wax-works, and the pictures and curiosities in the Art Museum; then in the afternoon we went to ride again, and we were goin' to the theatre in the evening; but the gentleman at the counter called out to me when I was going past an' said he wanted to speak to me a minute.

"Then I found out we'd spent all that fifteen hundred dollars, an' more, too. We owed 'em 'most ten dollars at the hotel; an' that wa'n't the worst of it—we didn't have enough money to take us home.

"Mother, she broke right down an' cried, an' said it was all we had in the world besides the farm, an' it was poor father's insurance money, an' we couldn't get home, an' we'd have to go to prison.

"Folks come crowding round, an' I couldn't stop her. I don't know what I did do myself; I felt kind of dizzy, an' things looked dark. A lady come an' held a smelling bottle to my nose, an' the gentleman at the counter sent a man with brass buttons for some wine.

"After I felt better an' could talk steady they questioned me up pretty sharp, an' I told 'em the whole story—about father an' his rheumatism, an' everything, just how I was situated, an' I must say they treated us like Christian folks, though, after all, I don't know as we were much beholden to 'em. We never begun to eat all there was on the list, an' we were real careful of the furniture; we didn't really get our money's worth after all was said. But they said the rest of our bill to them was no matter, an' they gave us our tickets to come home."

There was a pause. William looked at Narcissa in her blue gown as if she were a riddle whose answer was lost in his memory. His honest eyes were fairly pitiful from excess of questioning.

"Well," said Narcissa, "I've come back, an' I've spent all that money. I've been wasteful an' extravagant an'—There was a gentleman beautifully dressed who sat at our table, an' he talked real pleasant about the weather, an'—I got to thinking about him a little. Of course I didn't like him as well as you, William, for what comes first comes last with all our folks, but somehow he seemed to be kind of a part of the good time. I sha'n't never see him again, an' all there was betwixt us was his saying twice it was a pleasant day, an' once it was cold, an' me saying yes; but I'm going to tell you the whole. I've been an' wasted fifteen hundred dollars; I've let my thoughts wander from you; an' that ain't all. I've had a good time an' I can't say I 'ain't. I've had one good time, an'—I ain't sorry. You can—do just what you think best, William, an'—I won't blame you."

William Crane went over to the window. When he turned round and looked at Narcissa his eyes were full of tears and his wide mouth was trembling. "Do you think you can be contented to—stay on my side of the wall now, Narcissa?" he said, with a sweet and pathetic dignity.

Narcissa in her blue robes went over to him and put, for the first time of her own accord, an arm around his faithful neck. "I wouldn't go out again if the bars were down," said she.

"'I WOULDN'T GO OUT AGAIN IF THE BARS WERE DOWN'"

Illustration from Mary E. Wilkins [Freeman], "One Good Time," *Harper's Monthly* 94 (January 1897).

NOTES

1. A church service. In New England, Congregational churches were often referred to as "meeting houses."
2. A fine woolen fabric used for dresses.
3. An "Indian summer" is a period in the Northern Hemisphere of unseasonably warm weather during October or November; it is thought to have originated among early settlers in New England, who saw such milder weather as encouraging attacks from Native Americans in the area. The term "Injun" was a derogatory and offensive slang term for "Indian" commonly used by some non-Native people at this time to refer to a person who would now be known as Native American.
4. "Basting" refers to the act of loosely, and temporarily, stitching pieces of fabric together for later finishing; a basque is a piece of fabric that forms a loose decorative flap on the front of a woman's dress
5. A thin type of silk cloth, typically used for clothing worn to funerals.
6. A young cow.
7. Among many devoted Christians during this time period, attending theater productions was regarded as sinful, not only because it was seen as a distraction from more serious activities, such as prayer and religious devotion, but also because it supposedly encouraged all kinds of un-Christian beliefs and practices.

OLD WOMAN MAGOUN (1905)

The hamlet of Barry's Ford is situated in a sort of high valley among the mountains. Below it the hills lie in moveless curves like a petrified ocean; above it they rise in green-cresting waves which never break. It is *Barry's* Ford because at one time the Barry family was the most important in the place; and *Ford* because just at the beginning of the hamlet the little turbulent Barry River is fordable. There is, however, now a rude bridge across the river.

Old Woman Magoun was largely instrumental in bringing the bridge to pass. She haunted the miserable little grocery, wherein whiskey and hands of tobacco[1] were the most salient features of the stock in trade, and she talked much. She would elbow herself into the midst of a knot of idlers and talk.

"That bridge ought to be built this very summer," said Old Woman Magoun. She spread her strong arms like wings, and sent the loafers, half laughing, half angry, flying in every direction. "If I were a *man*," said she, "I'd go out this very minute and lay the fust[2] log. If I were a passel of lazy men layin' round, I'd start up for once in my life, I would." The men cowered visibly—all except Nelson Barry; he swore under his breath and strode over to the counter.

Old Woman Magoun looked after him majestically. "You can cuss all you want to, Nelson Barry," said she; "I ain't afraid of you. I don't expect you to lay ary log of the bridge, but I'm goin' to have it built this very summer." She did. The weakness of the masculine element in Barry's Ford was laid low before such strenuous feminine assertion.

Old Woman Magoun and some other women planned a treat—two sucking pigs,[3] and pies, and sweet cake—for a reward after the bridge should be finished. They even viewed leniently the increased consumption of ardent spirits.[4]

"It seems queer to me," Old Woman Magoun said to Sally Jinks, "that men can't do nothin' without havin' to drink and chew[5] to keep their sperits up. Lord! I've worked all my life and never done nuther."

"Men is different," said Sally Jinks.

"Yes, they be," assented Old Woman Magoun, with open contempt.

The two women sat on a bench in front of Old Woman Magoun's house, and little Lily Barry, her granddaughter, sat holding her doll on a small mossy stone near by. From where they sat they could see the men at work on the new bridge. It was the last day of the work.

Lily clasped her doll—a poor old rag thing—close to her childish bosom, like a little mother, and her face, round which curled her long yellow hair, was fixed upon the men at work. Little Lily had never been allowed to run with the other children of Barry's Ford. Her grandmother had taught her everything she knew—which was not much, but tending at least to a certain measure of spiritual growth—for she, as it were, poured the goodness of her own soul into this little receptive vase of another. Lily was firmly grounded in her knowledge that it was wrong to lie or steal or disobey her grandmother. She had also learned that one should be very industrious. It was seldom that Lily sat idly holding her doll-baby, but this was a holiday because of the bridge. She looked only a child, although she was nearly fourteen; her mother had been married at sixteen. That is, Old Woman Magoun said that her daughter, Lily's mother, had married at sixteen; there had been rumors, but no one had dared openly gainsay[6] the old woman. She said that her daughter had married Nelson Barry, and he had deserted her. She had lived in her mother's house, and Lily had been born there, and she had died when the baby was only a week old. Lily's father, Nelson Barry, was the fairly dangerous degenerate of a good old family. Nelson's father before him had been bad. He was now the last of the family, with the exception of a sister of feeble intellect, with whom he lived in the old Barry house. He was a middle-aged man, still handsome. The shiftless population of Barry's Ford looked up to him as to an evil deity. They wondered how Old Woman Magoun dared brave him as she did. But Old Woman Magoun had within her a mighty sense of reliance upon herself as being on the right track in the midst of a maze of evil, which gave her courage. Nelson Barry had manifested no interest whatever in his daughter. Lily seldom saw her father. She did not often go to the store which was his favorite haunt. Her grandmother took care that she should not do so.

However, that afternoon she departed from her usual custom and sent Lily to the store. She came in from the kitchen, whither she had been to baste the roasting pig. "There's no use talkin'," said she, "I've got to have some more salt. I've jest used the very last I had to dredge over that pig. I've got to go to the store."

Sally Jinks looked at Lily. "Why don't you send her?" she asked.

"MEN IS DIFFERENT," SAID SALLY JINKS

Half-tone plate engraved by F. A. Pettit

Illustration from Mary E. Wilkins Freeman, "Old Woman Magoun," *Harper's Monthly* 111 (October 1, 1905).

Old Woman Magoun gazed irresolutely at the girl. She was herself very tired. It did not seem to her that she could drag herself up the dusty hill to the store. She glanced with covert resentment at Sally Jinks. She thought that she might offer to go. But Sally Jinks said again, "Why don't you let her go?" and looked with a languid eye at Lily holding her doll on the stone.

Lily was watching the men at work on the bridge, with her childish delight in a spectacle of any kind, when her grandmother addressed her.

"Guess I'll let you go down to the store an' git some salt, Lily," said she.

The girl turned uncomprehending eyes upon her grandmother at the sound of her voice. She had been filled with one of the innocent reveries of childhood. Lily had in her the making of an artist or a poet. Her prolonged childhood went to prove it, and also her retrospective eyes, as clear and blue as blue light itself, which seemed to see past all that she looked upon. She had not come of the old Barry family for nothing. The best of the strain was in her, along with the splendid staunchness in humble lines which she had acquired from her grandmother.

"Put on your hat," said Old Woman Magoun; "the sun is hot, and you might git a headache." She called the girl to her, and put back the shower of fair curls under the rubber band which confined the hat. She gave Lily some money, and watched her knot it into a corner of her little cotton handkerchief. "Be careful you don't lose it," said she, "and don't stop to talk to anybody, for I am in a hurry for that salt. Of course, if anybody speaks to you, answer them polite, and then come right along."

Lily started, her pocket-handkerchief weighted with the small silver dangling from one hand, and her rag doll carried over her shoulder like a baby. The absurd travesty of a face peeped forth from Lily's yellow curls. Sally Jinks looked after her with a sniff.

"She ain't goin' to carry that rag doll to the store?" said she.

"She likes to," replied Old Woman Magoun, in a half-shamed yet defiantly extenuating voice.

"Some girls at her age is thinkin' about beaux[7] instead of rag dolls" said Sally Jinks.

The grandmother bristled. "Lily ain't big nor old for her age," said she. "I ain't in any hurry to have her git married. She ain't none too strong."

"She's got a good color," said Sally Jinks. She was crocheting white cotton lace, making her thick fingers fly. She really knew how to do scarcely anything except to crochet that coarse lace; somehow her heavy brain or her fingers had mastered that.

"I know she's got a beautiful color," replied Old Woman Magoun, with an odd mixture of pride and anxiety, "but it comes an' goes."

"I've heard that was a bad sign," remarked Sally Jinks, loosening some thread from her spool.

"Yes, it is," said the grandmother. "She's nothin' but a baby, though she's quicker than most to learn."

Lily Barry went on her way to the store. She was clad in a scanty short frock of blue cotton; her hat was tipped back, forming an oval frame for her innocent face. She was very small, and walked like a child, with the clap-clap of little feet of babyhood. She might have been considered, from her looks, under ten.

Presently she heard footsteps behind her; she turned around a little timidly to see who was coming. When she saw a handsome, well-dressed man, she felt reassured. The man came alongside and glanced down carelessly at first, then his look deepened. He smiled, and Lily saw he was very handsome indeed, and that his smile was not only reassuring but wonderfully sweet and compelling.

"Well, little one," said the man, "where are you bound, you and your dolly?"

"I am going to the store to buy some salt for grandma," replied Lily, in her sweet treble. She looked up in the man's face, and he fairly started at the revelation of its innocent beauty. He regulated his pace by hers, and the two went on together. The man did not speak again at once. Lily kept glancing timidly up at him, and every time that she did so the man smiled and her confidence increased. Presently when the man's hand grasped her little childish one hanging by her side, she felt a complete trust in him. Then she smiled up at him. She felt glad that this nice man had come along, for just here the road was lonely.

After a while the man spoke. "What is your name, little one?" he asked, caressingly.

"Lily Barry."

The man started. "What is your father's name?"

"Nelson Barry," replied Lily.

The man whistled. "Is your mother dead?"

"Yes, sir."

"How old are you, my dear?"

"Fourteen," replied Lily.

The man looked at her with surprise. "As old as that?"

Lily suddenly shrank from the man. She could not have told why. She pulled her little hand from his, and he let it go with no remonstrance. She clasped both her arms around her rag doll, in order that her hand should not be free for him to grasp again.

She walked a little farther away from the man, and he looked amused.

"You still play with your doll?" he said, in a soft voice.

"Yes, sir," replied Lily. She quickened her pace and reached the store.

When Lily entered the store, Hiram Gates, the owner, was behind the counter. The only man besides in the store was Nelson Barry. He sat tipping his chair back against the wall; he was half asleep, and his handsome face was bristling with a beard of several days' growth, and darkly flushed. He opened his eyes when Lily entered, the strange man following. He brought his chair down on all fours, and he looked at the man—not noticing Lily at all—with a look compounded of defiance and uneasiness.

"Hullo, Jim!" he said.

"Hullo, old man!" returned the stranger.

Lily went over to the counter and asked for the salt, in her pretty little voice. When she had paid for it and was crossing the store, Nelson Barry was on his feet.

"Well, how are you, Lily? It is Lily, isn't it?" he said.

"Yes, sir," replied Lily, faintly.

Her father bent down and, for the first time in her life, kissed her, and the whiskey odour of his breath came into her face.

Lily involuntarily started, and shrank away from him. Then she rubbed her mouth violently with her little cotton handkerchief, which she held gathered up with the rag doll.

"Damn it all! I believe she is afraid of me," said Nelson Barry, in a thick voice.

"Looks a little like it," said the other man, laughing.

"It's that damned old woman," said Nelson Barry. Then he smiled again at Lily. "I didn't know what a pretty little daughter I was blessed with," said he, and he softly stroked Lily's pink cheek under her hat.

Now Lily did not shrink from him. Hereditary instincts and nature itself were asserting themselves in the child's innocent, receptive breast.

Nelson Barry looked curiously at Lily. "How old are you, anyway, child?" he asked.

"I'll be fourteen in September," replied Lily.

"But you still play with your doll?" said Barry, laughing kindly down at her.

Lily hugged her doll more tightly, in spite of her father's kind voice. "Yes, sir," she replied.

Nelson glanced across at some glass jars filled with sticks of candy. "See here, little Lily, do you like candy?" said he.

"Yes, sir."

"Wait a minute."

Lily waited while her father went over to the counter. Soon he returned with a package of the candy.

"I don't see how you are going to carry so much," he said, smiling. "Suppose you throw away your doll?"

Lily gazed at her father and hugged the doll tightly, and there was all at once in the child's expression something mature. It became the reproach of a woman. Nelson's face sobered.

"Oh, it's all right, Lily," he said; "keep your doll. Here, I guess you can carry this candy under your arm."

Lily could not resist the candy. She obeyed Nelson's instructions for carrying it, and left the store laden. The two men also left, and walked in the opposite direction, talking busily.

When Lily reached home, her grandmother, who was watching for her, spied at once the package of candy.

"What's that?" she asked, sharply.

"My father gave it to me," answered Lily, in a faltering voice. Sally regarded her with something like alertness.

"Your father?"

"Yes, ma'am."

"Where did you see him?"

"In the store."

"He gave you this candy?"

"Yes, ma'am."

"What did he say?"

"He asked me how old I was, and—"

"And what?"

"I don't know," replied Lily; and it really seemed to her that she did not know, she was so frightened and bewildered by it all, and, more than anything else, by her grandmother's face as she questioned her.

Old Woman Magoun's face was that of one upon whom a long-anticipated blow had fallen. Sally Jinks gazed at her with a sort of stupid alarm.

Old Woman Magoun continued to gaze at her grandchild with that look of terrible solicitude, as if she saw the girl in the clutch of a tiger. "You can't remember what else he said?" she asked, fiercely, and the child began to whimper softly.

"No, ma'am," she sobbed. "I—don't know, and—"

"And what? Answer me."

"There was another man there. A real handsome man."

"Did he speak to you?" asked Old Woman Magoun.

"Yes, ma'am; he walked along with me a piece," confessed Lily, with a sob of terror and bewilderment.

"What did *he* say to you?" asked Old Woman Magoun, with a sort of despair.

Lily told, in her little, faltering, frightened voice, all of the conversation which she could recall. It sounded harmless enough, but the look of the realization of a long-expected blow never left her grandmother's face.

The sun was getting low, and the bridge was nearing completion. Soon the workmen would be crowding into the cabin for their promised supper. There became visible in the distance, far up the road, the heavily plodding figure of another woman who had agreed to come and help. Old Woman Magoun turned again to Lily.

"You go right up-stairs to your own chamber now," said she.

"Good land! ain't you goin' to let that poor child stay up and see the fun?" said Sally Jinks.

"You jest mind your own business," said Old Woman Magoun, forcibly, and Sally Jinks shrank. "You go right up there now, Lily," said the grandmother, in a softer tone, "and grandma will bring you up a nice plate of supper."

"When be you goin' to let that girl grow up?" asked Sally Jinks, when Lily had disappeared.

"She'll grow up in the Lord's good time," replied Old Woman Magoun, and there was in her voice something both sad and threatening. Sally Jinks again shrank a little.

Soon the workmen came flocking noisily into the house. Old Woman Magoun and her two helpers served the bountiful supper. Most of the men had drunk as much as, and more than, was good for them, and Old Woman Magoun had stipulated that there was to be no drinking of anything except coffee during supper.

"I'll git you as good a meal as I know how," she said, "but if I see ary one of you drinkin' a drop, I'll run you all out. If you want anything to drink, you can go up to the store afterward. That's the place for you to go to, if you've got to make hogs of yourselves. I ain't goin' to have no hogs in my house."

Old Woman Magoun was implicitly obeyed. She had a curious authority over most people when she chose to exercise it. When the supper was in full swing, she quietly stole up-stairs and carried some food to Lily. She found the girl, with the rag doll in her arms, crouching by the window in her little rocking-chair—a relic of her infancy, which she still used.

"What a noise they are makin', grandma!" she said, in a terrified whisper, as her grandmother placed the plate before her on a chair.

"They've 'most all of 'em been drinkin'. They air a passel of hogs," replied the old woman.

"Is the man that was with—with my father down there?" asked Lily, in a timid fashion. Then she fairly cowered before the look in her grandmother's eyes.

"No, he ain't; and what's more, he never will be down there if I can help it," said Old Woman Magoun, in a fierce whisper. "I know who he is. They can't cheat me. He's one of them Willises—that family the Barrys married into. They're worse than the Barrys, ef they *have* got money. Eat your supper, and put him out of your mind, child."

It was after Lily was asleep, when Old Woman Magoun was alone, clearing away her supper dishes, that Lily's father came. The door was closed, and he knocked, and the old woman knew at once who was there. The sound of that knock meant as much to her as the whir of a bomb to the defender of a fortress. She opened the door and Nelson Barry stood there.

"Good-evening, Mrs. Magoun," he said.

Old Woman Magoun stood before him, filling up the doorway with her firm bulk.

"Good-evening, Mrs. Magoun," said Nelson Barry again.

"I ain't got no time to waste," replied the old woman, harshly. "I've got my supper dishes to clean up after them men."

She stood there and looked at him as she might have looked at a rebellious animal which she was trying to tame. The man laughed.

"It's no use," said he. "You know me of old.[8] No human being can turn me from my way when I am once started in it. You may as well let me come in."

Old Woman Magoun entered the house, and Barry followed her.

Barry began without any preface. "Where is the child?" asked he.

"Up-stairs. She has gone to bed."

"She goes to bed early."

"Children ought to," returned the old woman, polishing a plate.

Barry laughed. "You are keeping her a child a long while," he remarked, in a soft voice which had a sting in it.

"She *is* a child," returned the old woman, defiantly.

"Her mother was only three years older when Lily was born."

The old woman made a sudden motion toward the man which seemed fairly menacing. Then she turned again to her dish-washing.

"I want her," said Barry.

"You can't have her," replied the old woman, in a still stern voice.

"I don't see how you can help yourself. You have always acknowledged that she was my child."

The old woman continued her task, but her strong back heaved. Barry regarded her with an entirely pitiless expression.

"I am going to have the girl, that is the long and short of it," he said, "and it is for her best good, too. You are a fool, or you would see it."

"Her best good?" muttered the old woman.

"Yes, her best good. What are you going to do with her, anyway? The girl is a beauty, and almost a woman grown, although you try to make out that she is a baby. You can't live forever."

"The Lord will take care of her," replied the old woman, and again she turned and faced him, and her expression was that of a prophetess.

"Very well, let Him," said Barry, easily. "All the same I'm going to have her, and I tell you it is for her best good. Jim Willis saw her this afternoon, and—"

Old Woman Magoun looked at him. "Jim Willis!" she fairly shrieked.

"Well, what of it?"

"One of them Willises!" repeated the old woman, and this time her voice was thick. It seemed almost as if she were stricken with paralysis. She did not enunciate clearly.

The man shrank a little. "Now what is the need of your making such a fuss?" he said. "I will take her and Isabel will look out for her."

"Your half-witted sister?" said Old Woman Magoun.

"Yes, my half-witted sister. She knows more than you think."

"More wickedness."

"Perhaps. Well, a knowledge of evil is a useful thing. How are you going to avoid evil if you don't know what it is like? My sister and I will take care of my daughter."

The old woman continued to look at the man, but his eyes never fell. Suddenly her gaze grew inconceivably keen. It was as if she saw through all externals.

"I know what it is!" she cried. "You have been playing cards and you lost, and this is the way you will pay him."

Then the man's face reddened, and he swore under his breath.

"Oh, my God!" said the old woman; and she really spoke with her eyes aloft as if addressing something outside of them both. Then she turned again to her dish-washing.

The man cast a dogged look at her back. "Well, there is no use talking. I have made up my mind," said he, "and you know me and what that means. I am going to have the girl."

"When?" said the old woman, without turning around.

"Well, I am willing to give you a week. Put her clothes in good order before she comes."

The old woman made no reply. She continued washing dishes. She even handled them so carefully that they did not rattle.

"You understand," said Barry. "Have her ready a week from to-day."

"Yes," said Old Woman Magoun, "I understand."

Nelson Barry, going up the mountain road, reflected that Old Woman Magoun had a strong character, that she understood much better than her sex in general the futility of withstanding the inevitable.

"Well," he said to Jim Willis when he reached home, "the old woman did not make such a fuss as I expected."

"Are you going to have the girl?"

"Yes; a week from to-day. Look here, Jim; you've got to stick to your promise."

"All right," said Willis. "Go you one better."

The two were playing at cards in the old parlor, once magnificent, now squalid, of the Barry house. Isabel, the half-witted sister, entered, bringing some glasses on a tray. She had learned with her feeble intellect some tricks, like a dog. One of them was the mixing of sundry drinks. She set the tray on a little stand near the two men, and watched them with her silly simper.

"Clear out now and go to bed," her brother said to her, and she obeyed.

Early the next morning Old Woman Magoun went up to Lily's little sleeping-chamber, and watched her a second as she lay asleep, with her yellow locks spread over the pillow. Then she spoke. "Lily," said she—"Lily, wake up. I am going to Greenham across the new bridge, and you can go with me."

Lily immediately sat up in bed and smiled at her grandmother. Her eyes were still misty, but the light of awakening was in them.

"Get right up," said the old woman. "You can wear your new dress if you want to."

Lily gurgled with pleasure like a baby. "And my new hat?" asked she.

"I don't care."

Old Woman Magoun and Lily started for Greenham before Barry's Ford, which kept late hours, was fairly awake. It was three miles to Greenham. The old woman said that, since the horse was a little lame, they would walk. It was a beautiful morning, with a diamond radiance of dew over everything. Her grandmother had curled Lily's hair more punctiliously than usual. The little face peeped like a rose out of two rows of golden spirals. Lily wore her new muslin dress with a pink sash, and her best hat of a fine white straw trimmed with a wreath of rosebuds; also the neatest black open-work stockings and pretty shoes. She even had white cotton gloves. When they set out, the old, heavily stepping woman, in her black gown and cape and bonnet, looked down at the little pink fluttering figure. Her face was full of the tenderest love and admiration, and yet there was something terrible about it. They crossed the new bridge—a primitive structure built of logs in a slovenly fashion. Old Woman Magoun pointed to a gap.

"Jest see that," said she. "That's the way men work."

"Men ain't very nice, be they?" said Lily, in her sweet little voice.

"No, they ain't, take them all together," replied her grandmother.

"That man that walked to the store with me was nicer than some, I guess," Lily said, in a wishful fashion. Her grandmother reached down and took the child's hand in its small cotton glove. "You hurt me, holding my hand so tight," Lily said presently, in a deprecatory little voice.

The old woman loosened her grasp. "Grandma didn't know how tight she was holding your hand," said she. "She wouldn't hurt you for nothin', except it was to save your life, or somethin' like that." She spoke with an undertone of tremendous meaning which the girl was too childish to grasp. They walked along the country road. Just before they reached Greenham they passed a stone wall overgrown with blackberry-vines, and, an unusual thing in that vicinity, a lusty spread of deadly nightshade full of berries.

"Those berries look good to eat, grandma," Lily said.

At that instant the old woman's face became something terrible to see. "You can't have any now," she said, and hurried Lily along.

"They look real nice," said Lily.

When they reached Greenham, Old Woman Magoun took her way straight to the most pretentious house there, the residence of the lawyer, whose name was Mason. Old Woman Magoun bade Lily wait in the yard for a few moments, and Lily ventured to seat herself on a bench beneath an oak-tree; then she watched with some wonder her grandmother enter the lawyer's office door at the right of the house. Presently the lawyer's wife came out and spoke to Lily under the tree. She had in her hand a little tray containing a plate of cake, a glass of milk, and an early apple. She spoke very kindly to Lily; she even kissed her, and offered her the tray of refreshments, which Lily accepted gratefully. She sat eating, with Mrs. Mason watching her, when Old Woman Magoun came out of the lawyer's office with a ghastly face.

"What are you eatin'?" she asked Lily, sharply. "Is that a sour apple?"

"I thought she might be hungry," said the lawyer's wife, with loving, melancholy eyes upon the girl.

Lily had almost finished the apple. "It's real sour, but I like it; it's real nice, grandma," she said.

"You ain't been drinkin' milk with a sour apple?"

"It was real nice milk, grandma."

"You ought never to have drunk milk and eat a sour apple," said her grandmother. "Your stomach was all out of order this mornin', an' sour apples and milk is always apt to hurt anybody."

"I don't know but they are," Mrs. Mason said, apologetically, as she stood on the green lawn with her lavender muslin sweeping around her. "I am real sorry, Mrs. Magoun. I ought to have thought. Let me get some soda for her."

"Soda never agrees with her," replied the old woman, in a harsh voice. "Come," she said to Lily, "it's time we were goin' home."

After Lily and her grandmother had disappeared down the road, Lawyer Mason came out of his office and joined his wife, who had seated herself on the bench beneath the tree. She was idle, and her face wore the expression of those who review joys forever past. She had lost a little girl, her only child, years ago, and her husband always knew when she was thinking about her. Lawyer Mason looked older than his wife; he had a dry, shrewd, slightly one-sided face.

"What do you think, Maria?" he said. "That old woman came to me with the most pressing entreaty to adopt that little girl."

"She is a beautiful little girl," said Mrs. Mason, in a slightly husky voice.

"Yes, she is a pretty child," assented the lawyer, looking pityingly at his wife; "but it is out of the question, my dear. Adopting a child is a serious measure, and in this case a child who comes from Barry's Ford."

"But the grandmother seems a very good woman," said Mrs. Mason.

"I rather think she is. I never heard a word against her. But the father! No, Maria, we cannot take a child with Barry blood in her veins. The stock has run out; it is vitiated[9] physically and morally. It won't do, my dear."

"Her grandmother had her dressed up as pretty as a little girl could be," said Mrs. Mason, and this time the tears welled into her faithful, wistful eyes.

"Well, we can't help that," said the lawyer, as he went back to his office.

Old Woman Magoun and Lily returned, going slowly along the road to Barry's Ford. When they came to the stone wall where the blackberry-vines and the deadly nightshade grew, Lily said she was tired, and asked if she could not sit down for a few minutes. The strange look on her grandmother's face had deepened. Now and then Lily glanced at her and had a feeling as if she were looking at a stranger.

"Yes, you can set down if you want to," said Old Woman Magoun, deeply and harshly.

Lily started and looked at her, as if to make sure that it was her grandmother who spoke. Then she sat down on a stone which was comparatively free of the vines.

"Ain't you goin' to set down, grandma?" Lily asked, timidly.

"No; I don't want to get into that mess," replied her grandmother. "I ain't tired, I'll stand here."

Lily sat still; her delicate little face was flushed with heat. She extended her tiny feet in her best shoes and gazed at them. "My shoes are all over dust," said she.

"It will brush off," said her grandmother, still in that strange voice.

Lily looked around. An elm-tree in the field behind her cast a spray of branches over her head; a little cool puff of wind came on her face. She gazed at the low mountains on the horizon, in the midst of which she lived, and she sighed, for no reason that she knew. She began idly picking at the blackberry-vines; there were no berries on them; then she put her little fingers on the berries of the deadly nightshade. "These look like nice berries," she said.

Old Woman Magoun, standing stiff and straight in the road, said nothing.

"They look good to eat," said Lily.

Old Woman Magoun still said nothing, but she looked up into the ineffable blue of the sky, over which spread at intervals great white clouds shaped like wings.

Lily picked some of the deadly nightshade berries and ate them. "Why, they are real sweet," said she. "They are nice." She picked some more and ate them.

Presently her grandmother spoke. "Come," she said, "it is time we were going. I guess you have set long enough."

Lily was still eating the berries when she slipped down from the wall and followed her grandmother obediently up the road.

Before they reached home, Lily complained of being very thirsty. She stopped and made a little cup of a leaf and drank long at a mountain brook. "I am dreadful dry, but it hurts me to swallow," she said to her grandmother when she stopped drinking and joined the old woman waiting for her in the road. Her grandmother's face seemed strangely dim to her. She took hold of Lily's hand as they went on. "My stomach burns," said Lily, presently. "I want some more water."

"There is another brook a little farther on," said Old Woman Magoun, in a dull voice.

When they reached that brook, Lily stopped and drank again, but she whimpered a little over her difficulty in swallowing. "My stomach burns, too," she said, walking on, "and my throat is so dry, grandma." Old Woman Magoun held Lily's hand more tightly. "You hurt me holding my hand so tight, grandma," said Lily, looking up at her grandmother, whose face she seemed to see through a mist, and the old woman loosened her grasp.

When at last they reached home, Lily was very ill. Old Woman Magoun put her on her own bed in the little bedroom out of the kitchen. Lily lay there and moaned, and Sally Jinks came in.

"Why, what ails her?" she asked. "She looks feverish."

Lily unexpectedly answered for herself. "I ate some sour apples and drank some milk," she moaned.

"Sour apples and milk are dreadful apt to hurt anybody," said Sally Jinks. She told several people on her way home that Old Woman Magoun was dreadful careless to let Lily eat such things.

Meanwhile Lily grew worse. She suffered cruelly from the burning in her stomach, the vertigo,[10] and the deadly nausea. "I am so sick, I am so sick, grandma," she kept moaning. She could no longer see her grandmother as she bent over her, but she could hear her talk.

Old Woman Magoun talked as Lily had never heard her talk before, as nobody had ever heard her talk before. She spoke from the depths of her soul; her voice was as tender as the coo of a dove, and it was grand and exalted. "You'll feel better very soon, little Lily," said she.

"I am so sick, grandma."

MARY E. WILKINS FREEMAN

"You will feel better very soon, and then—"

"I am sick."

"You shall go to a beautiful place."

Lily moaned.

"You shall go to a beautiful place," the old woman went on.

"Where?" asked Lily, groping feebly with her cold little hands. Then she moaned again.

"A beautiful place, where the flowers grow tall."

"What color? Oh, grandma, I am so sick."

"A blue color," replied the old woman. Blue was Lily's favourite color. "A beautiful blue color, and as tall as your knees, and the flowers always stay there, and they never fade."

"Not if you pick them, grandma? Oh!"

"No, not if you pick them; they never fade, and they are so sweet you can smell them a mile off; and there are birds that sing, and all the roads have gold stones in them, and the stone walls are made of gold."

"Like the ring grandpa gave you? I am so sick, grandma."

"Yes, gold like that. And all the houses are built of silver and gold, and the people all have wings, so when they get tired walking they can fly, and—"

"I am so sick, grandma."

"And all the dolls are alive," said Old Woman Magoun. "Dolls like yours can run, and talk, and love you back again."

Lily had her poor old rag doll in bed with her, clasped close to her agonized little heart. She tried very hard with her eyes, whose pupils were so dilated that they looked black, to see her grandmother's face when she said that, but she could not. "It is dark," she moaned feebly.

"There where you are going it is always light," said the grandmother, "and the commonest things shine like that breast-pin Mrs. Lawyer Mason had on to-day."

Lily moaned pitifully, and said something incoherent. Delirium was commencing. Presently she sat straight up in bed and raved; but even then her grandmother's wonderful compelling voice had an influence over her.

"You will come to a gate with all the colors of the rainbow," said her grandmother; "and it will open, and you will go right in and walk up the gold street, and cross the field where the blue flowers come up to your knees, until you find your mother and she will take you home where you are going to live. She has a little white room all ready for you, white curtains at the windows, and a little white looking-glass, and when you look in it you will see—"

"What will I see? I am so sick, grandma."

"You will see a face like yours, only it's an angel's; and there will be a little white bed, and you can lay down an' rest."

"Won't I be sick, grandma?" asked Lily. Then she moaned and babbled wildly, although she seemed to understand through it all what her grandmother said.

"No, you will never be sick any more. Talkin' about sickness won't mean anything to you."

It continued. Lily talked on wildly, and her grandmother's great voice of soothing never ceased, until the child fell into a deep sleep, or what resembled sleep; but she lay stiffly in that sleep, and a candle flashed before her eyes made no impression on them.

Then it was that Nelson Barry came. Jim Willis waited outside the door. When Nelson entered he found Old Woman Magoun on her knees beside the bed, weeping with dry eyes and a might of agony which fairly shook Nelson Barry, the degenerate of a fine old race.

"Is she sick?" he asked, in a hushed voice.

Old Woman Magoun gave another terrible sob, which sounded like the gasp of one dying.

"Sally Jinks said that Lily was sick from eating milk and sour apples," said Barry, in a tremulous voice. "I remember that her mother was very sick once from eating them."

Lily lay still, and her grandmother on her knees shook with her terrible sobs.

Suddenly Nelson Barry started. "I guess I had better go to Greenham for a doctor if she's as bad as that," he said. He went close to the bed and looked at the sick child. He gave a great start. Then he felt of her hands and reached down under the bedclothes for her little feet. "Her hands and feet are like ice," he cried out. "Good God! why didn't you send for some one—for me—before? Why, she's dying; she's almost gone!"

Barry rushed out and spoke to Jim Willis, who turned pale and came in and stood by the bedside.

"She's almost gone," he said, in a hushed whisper.

"There's no use going for the doctor; she'd be dead before he got here," said Nelson, and he stood regarding the passing child with a strange sad face—unutterably sad, because of his incapability of the truest sadness.

"Poor little thing, she's past suffering, anyhow," said the other man, and his own face also was sad with a puzzled, mystified sadness.

Lily died that night. There was quite a commotion in Barry's Ford until after the funeral, it was all so sudden, and then everything went on as usual. Old Woman Magoun continued to live as she had done before. She supported herself by the produce of her tiny farm; she was very industrious, but people said that she was a trifle touched, since every time she went over the log bridge with her eggs or her garden vegetables to sell in Greenham, she carried with her, as one might have carried an infant, Lily's old rag doll.

NOTES

1. A small bunch of dried tobacco leaves.
2. First. This is Freeman's representation of New Englanders' speech.
3. An unweaned piglet or young pig, thought to have particularly tender meat. Typically they are called "suckling" pigs.
4. Alcohol.
5. Chew tobacco.

6. Contradict.
7. Plural of "beau," French for a male admirer.
8. "You've known me for a long time."
9. Morally debased.
10. Dizziness.

HAMLIN GARLAND

(1860–1940)

Like many Regionalist writers of this time period, Hamlin Garland was continually conflicted between loyalty to his home region—in this case, the upper Midwest—and a desire to achieve success and acceptance among editors, publishers, critics, and readers from urban areas on the East and West Coasts. Born into a farming family that lived in Wisconsin and then Iowa, Garland, as a teenager and young adult, experienced rural life, and at the age of twenty-three he spent one year farming in Dakota Territory. Unhappy with all these locales and seeking to escape an agricultural-based future to pursue a different kind of life, Garland moved to Boston in 1884, where he supported himself for the next decade by patching together various writing, teaching, and lecturing jobs.

Somewhat ironically, what finally set Garland on the path of success were two trips home to his parents in Dakota Territory during the summers of 1887 and 1888. These visits made him realize that no one had as yet told, in a realistic manner, about the difficulties and hardships of pioneer and farm life. Returning to Boston, he began writing short stories set in what Garland called the "Middle Border"; he also became an ardent supporter of, and speaker for, a number of different political organizations that were striving to improve conditions for farmers and their families. At this time he fortuitously met Benjamin Flower, who in 1890 had founded *Arena* magazine in Boston and dedicated it to promoting social and political reform. Before this meeting, Garland had been discouraged by the rejection of many of his grittier, harder-hitting stories of life in the Midwest by editors at various mainstream magazines. When Flower bought one such rejected story, "A Prairie Heroine," paid well for it, and wrote Garland a letter of encouragement, the latter felt as if he had finally started on the road to success.

"Up the Coulé. A Story of Wisconsin" was another story Garland had a difficult time getting accepted by a major magazine, but possibly not only because of its subject matter. In a letter to *Century Magazine* editor Richard Watson Gilder dated November 1, 1890, he stated that he was writing "Up the Coulé" for the *Century;* however, it likely was turned down because of its length, for at approximately fifteen thousand words, it was too long to be published in one issue and not long enough to run for multiple issues as a serial. Fortunately for Garland, a suitable publication venue presented itself in late 1890. In September of that year Flower had begun publishing books through the Arena Publishing

Co., and soon after this date he asked Garland to collect some of his stories for a book. Garland gathered four previously published stories plus two hitherto unpublished works, including "Up the Coulé," and these appeared together in June 1891 under the title *Main-Travelled Roads: Six Mississippi Valley Stories*. The book's pressrun was quite small, but fortunately for Garland, one copy found its way into the hands of the highly influential editor of *Harper's Monthly*, William Dean Howells, who praised it in a review.

Flush with this success, Garland began to have more of his short fictions accepted by major magazines and was able to publish a number of books in the next five years, including a significant collection of critical essays arguing for a new type of "veritist" American literature (*Crumbling Idols*, 1894) and a boundary-pushing novel about a liberated farm girl forging a modern life in Chicago (*Rose of Dutcher's Coolly*, 1895). After these successes, Garland turned away from writing starkly realistic fictions about midwestern farm life and began writing a string of Romantic adventure novels set in the Rocky Mountains, many of which sold (and thus paid) quite well. He continued in this vein until 1917, when he published his memoir, *A Son of the Middle Border*. It proved enormously popular among readers, leading Garland to follow up with *A Daughter of the Middle Border* (1921), which won the Pulitzer Prize for Biography. After this point, Garland, who moved to Southern California in 1929, spent most of the rest of his career penning various reminiscences; the only significant work from these years was *The Book of the American Indian* (1923), a collection of his short stories that displayed—for its time—a relatively sympathetic view of Native Americans.

"Up the Coulé," like many of Garland's best early fictions, was grounded solidly in personal experience. Like the story's narrator, Garland felt guilty for having "deserted" his parents (and especially his mother) when he left for Boston and for having had a number of advantages growing up that his brother Franklin did not (the latter did not, however, remain in the Midwest and become a farmer, as the character Grant does). Similar to Garland's more widely known stories, such as "Under the Lion's Paw" (1889), "Up the Coulé" offers a detailed, un-Romantic insider's account of farming life in this region during an era when America was rapidly becoming a more urban and industrialized country.

*Readers should be aware that this story includes some language which, while commonly used during this time period, is no longer considered acceptable because of its offensive nature.

UP THE COULÉ. A STORY OF WISCONSIN (1891)

"Keep the main-travelled road up the Coolly[1]*—it's the second house after crossin' the crick."*

The ride from Milwaukee to the Mississippi is a fine ride at any time, superb in summer. To lean back in a reclining-chair and whirl away in a breezy July day, past lakes, groves of oak, past fields of barley being reaped, past hay-fields, where the heavy grass is toppling before the swift sickle, is a panorama of delight, a road full of delicious surprises, where down a sudden vista lakes open, or a distant wooded hill looms darkly blue, or swift streams, foaming deep down the solid rock, send whiffs of cool breezes in at the window.

It has majesty, breadth. The farming has nothing apparently petty about it. All seems vigorous, youthful, and prosperous. Mr. Howard McLane in his chair let his newspaper fall on his lap and gazed out upon it with dreaming eyes. It had a certain mysterious glamour to him; the lakes were cooler and brighter to his eye, the greens fresher, and the grain more golden than to anyone else, for he was coming back to it all after an absence of ten years. It was, besides, *his* West. He still took pride in being a Western man.

His mind all day flew ahead of the train to the little town, far on toward the Mississippi, where he had spent his boyhood and youth. As the train passed the Wisconsin River, with its curiously carved cliffs, its cold, dark, swift-swirling water eating slowly under cedar-clothed banks, Howard began to feel curious little movements of the heart, like those of a lover nearing his sweetheart.

The hills changed in character, growing more intimately recognizable. They rose higher as the train left the ridge and passed down into the Black River valley, and specifically into the La Crosse valley. They ceased to have any hint of upheavals of rock, and became simply parts of the ancient level left standing after the water had practically given up its post-glacial, scooping action.

It was about six o'clock as he caught sight of the dear broken line of hills on which his baby eyes had looked thirty-five years ago. A few minutes later and the train drew up at the grimy little station set in at the hillside, and, giving him just time to leap off, plunged on again toward the West. Howard felt a ridiculous weakness in his legs as he stepped out upon the broiling-hot splintery planks of the station and faced the few idlers lounging about. He simply stood and gazed with the same intensity and absorption one of the idlers might show standing before the Brooklyn Bridge.

The town caught and held his eyes first. How poor and dull and sleepy and squalid it seemed! The one main street ended at the hillside at his left, and stretched away to the north, between two rows of the usual village stores, unrelieved by a tree or a touch of beauty. An unpaved street, drab-colored, miserable, rotting wooden buildings, with the inevitable battlements; the same—only worse, and more squalid—was the town.

The same, only more beautiful still, was the majestic amphitheater of green wooded hills that circled the horizon, and toward which he lifted his eyes. He thrilled at the sight.

"Glorious!" he cried involuntarily.

Accustomed to the White Mountains, to the Alleghenies,[2] he had wondered if these hills would retain their old-time charm. They did. He took off his hat to them as he stood there. Richly wooded, with gently sloping green sides, rising to massive square or rounded tops with dim vistas, they glowed down upon the squalid town, gracious, lofty in their greeting, immortal in their vivid and delicate beauty.

He was a goodly figure of a man as he stood there beside his valise. Portly, erect, handsomely dressed, and with something unusually winning in his brown mustache and blue eyes, something scholarly suggested by the pinch-nose glasses, something strong in the repose of the head. He smiled as he saw how unchanged was the grouping of the old loafers on the salt-barrels and nail-kegs. He recognized most of them—a little dirtier, a little more bent, and a little grayer.

They sat in the same attitudes, spat tobacco with the same calm delight, and joked each other, breaking into short and sudden fits of laughter, and pounded each other on the back, just as when he was a student at the La Crosse Seminary[3] and going to and fro daily on the train.

They ruminated on him as he passed, speculating in a perfectly audible way upon his business.

"Looks like a drummer."[4]

"No, he ain't no drummer. See them Boston glasses?"

"That's so. Guess he's a teacher."

"Looks like a moneyed cuss."

"Bos'n, I *guess.*"

He knew the one who spoke last—Freeme Cole, a man who was the fighting wonder of Howard's boyhood, now degenerated into a stoop-shouldered, faded, garrulous, and quarrelsome old man. Yet there was something epic in the old man's stories, something enthralling in the dramatic power of recital.

Over by the blacksmith shop the usual game of "quaits"[5] was in progress, and the drug-clerk on the corner was chasing a crony with the squirt-pump, with which he was about to wash the windows. A few teams stood ankle-deep in the mud, tied to the fantastically gnawed pine pillars of the wooden awnings. A man on a load of hay was "jawing" with the attendant of the platform scales, who stood below, pad and pencil in hand.

"Hit 'im! hit 'im! Jump off and knock 'im!" suggested a bystander, jovially.

Howard knew the voice.

"Talk's cheap. Takes money t' buy whiskey," he said when the man on the load repeated his threat of getting off and whipping the scales-man.

"You're William McTurg," Howard said, coming up to him.

"I am, sir," replied the soft-voiced giant, turning and looking down on the stranger, with an amused twinkle in his deep brown eyes. He stood as erect as an Indian,[6] though his hair and beard were white.

"I'm Howard McLane."

"Ye begin t' look it," said McTurg, removing his right hand from his pocket. "How are yeh?"

"I'm first-rate. How's mother and Grant?"

"Saw 'm plowing corn as I came down. Guess he's all right. Want a boost?"

"Well, yes. Are you down with a team?"

"Yep. 'Bout goin' home. Climb right in. That's my rig, right there," nodding at a sleek bay colt hitched in a covered buggy. "Heave y'r grip[7] under the seat."

They climbed into the seat after William had lowered the buggy-top and unhitched the horse from the post. The loafers were mildly curious. Guessed Bill had got hooked onto by a lightnin'-rod peddler, or somethin' o' that kind.

"Want to go by river, or 'round by the hills?"

"Hills, I guess."

The whole matter began to seem trivial, as if he had only been away for a month or two.

William McTurg was a man little given to talk. Even the coming back of a nephew did not cause any flow of questions or reminiscences. They rode in silence. He sat a little bent forward, the lines held carelessly in his hands, his great lion-like head swaying to and fro with the movement of the buggy.

As they passed familiar spots, the younger man broke the silence with a question.

"That's old man McElvaine's place, ain't it?"

"Yep."

"Old man living?"

"I *guess* he is. Husk more corn 'n any man he c'n hire."

On the edge of the village they passed an open lot on the left, marked with circus-rings of different eras.

"There's the old ball-ground. Do they have circuses on it just the same as ever?"

"Just the same."

"What fun that field calls up! The games of ball we used to have! Do you play yet?"

"Sometimes. Can't stoop as well as I used to." He smiled a little. "Too much fat."

It all swept back upon Howard in a flood of names and faces and sights and sounds; something sweet and stirring somehow, though it had little of esthetic charms at the time. They were passing along lanes now, between superb fields of corn, wherein plowmen were at work. Kingbirds flew from post to post ahead of them; the insects called from the grass. The valley slowly outspread below them. The workmen in the fields were "turning out" for the night; they all had a word of chaff with McTurg.

Over the western wall of the circling amphitheatre the sun was setting. A few scattering clouds were drifting on the west wind, their shadows sliding down the green and purple slopes. The dazzling sunlight flamed along the luscious velvety grass, and shot amid the rounded, distant purple peaks, and streamed in bars of gold and crimson across the blue mist of the narrower upper Coulés.

The heart of the young man swelled with pleasure almost like pain, and the eyes of the silent older man took on a far-off, dreaming look, as he gazed at the scene which had repeated itself a thousand times in his life, but of whose beauty he never spoke.

Far down to the left was the break in the wall through which the river ran on its way to join the Mississippi. They climbed slowly among the hills, and the valley they had left grew still more beautiful as the squalor of the little town was hid by the dusk of distance. Both men were silent for a long time. Howard knew the peculiarities of his companion too well to make any remarks or ask any questions, and besides it was a genuine pleasure to ride with one who understood that silence was the only speech amid such splendors.

Once they passed a little brook singing in a mournfully sweet way its eternal song over its pebbles. It called back to Howard the days when he and Grant, his younger brother, had fished in this little brook for trout, with trousers rolled above the knee and wrecks of hats upon their heads.

"Any trout left?" he asked.

"Not many. Little fellers." Finding the silence broken, William asked the first question since he met Howard. "Le' 's see: you're a show feller now? B'long to a troupe?"

"Yes, yes; I'm an actor."

"Pay much?"

"Pretty well."

That seemed to end William's curiosity about the matter.

"Ah, there's our old house, ain't it?" Howard broke out, pointing to one of the houses farther up the coulé. "It'll be a surprise to them, won't it?"

"Yep; only they don't live there."

"What! They don't!"

"Who does?"

"Dutchman."

Howard was silent for some moments. "Who lives on the Dunlap place?"

"'Nother Dutchman."

"Where's Grant living, anyhow?"

"Farther up the Coolly."

"Well, then I'd better get out here, hadn't I?"

"Oh, I'll drive yeh up."

"No, I'd rather walk."

The sun had set, and the Coulé was getting dusk when Howard got out of Mc-Turg's carriage and set off up the winding lane toward his brother's house. He walked slowly to absorb the coolness and fragrance and color of the hour. The katydids sang a rhythmic song of welcome to him. Fireflies were in the grass. A whippoorwill in the deep of the wood was calling weirdly, and an occasional night-hawk, flying high, gave his grating shriek, or hollow boom, suggestive and resounding.

He had been wonderfully successful, and yet had carried into his success as a dramatic author as well as actor a certain puritanism that made him a paradox to his fellows. He was one of those actors who are always in luck, and the best of it was he kept and made use of his luck. Jovial as he appeared, he was inflexible as granite against drink and tobacco. He retained through it all a certain fresh-ness of enjoyment that made him one of the best companions in the profession;

and now as he walked on, the hour and the place appealed to him with great power. It seemed to sweep away the life that came between.

How close it all was to him, after all! In his restless life, surrounded by the glare of electric lights, painted canvas, hot colors, creak of machinery, mock trees, stones, and brooks, he had not lost, but gained appreciation for the coolness, quiet and low tones, the shyness of the wood and field.

In the farmhouse ahead of him a light was shining as he peered ahead, and his heart gave another painful movement. His brother was awaiting him there, and his mother, whom he had not seen for ten years and who had lost the power to write. And when Grant wrote, which had been more and more seldom of late, his letters had been cold and curt.

He began to feel that in the pleasure and excitement of his life he had grown away from his mother and brother. Each summer he had said, "Well, now I'll go home *this* year sure." But a new play to be produced, or a new yachting trip, or a tour of Europe, had put the home-coming off; and now it was with a distinct consciousness of neglect of duty that he walked up to the fence and looked into the yard, where William had told him his brother lived.

It was humble enough—a small white house, story-and-a-half structure, with a wing set in the midst of a few locust-trees; a small drab-colored barn, with a sagging ridge-pole; a barnyard full of mud, in which a few cows were standing, fighting the flies and waiting to be milked. An old man was pumping water at the well; the pigs were squealing from a pen nearby; a child was crying.

Instantly the beautiful, peaceful valley was forgotten. A sickening chill struck into Howard's soul as he looked at it all. In the dim light he could see a figure milking a cow. Leaving his valise at the gate, he entered and walked up to the old man, who had finished pumping and was about to go to feed the hogs.

"Good-evening," Howard began. "Does Mr. Grant McLane live here?"

"Yes, sir, he does. He's right over there milkin'."

"I'll go over there an—"

"Don't b'lieve I would. It's darn muddy over there. It's been turrible rainy. He'll be done in a minute, anyway."

"Very well; I'll wait."

As he waited, he could hear a woman's fretful voice and the impatient jerk and jar of kitchen things, indicative of ill-temper or worry. The longer he stood absorbing this farm-scene, with all its sordidness, dullness, triviality, and its endless drudgeries, the lower his heart sank. All the joy of the home-coming was gone, when the figure arose from the cow and approached the gate, and put the pail of milk down on the platform by the pump.

"Good-evening," said Howard out of the dusk.

Grant stared a moment. "Good-evening."

Howard knew the voice, though it was older and deeper and more sullen. "Don't you know me, Grant? I am Howard."

The man approached him, gazing intently at his face. "You are?" after a pause. "Well, I'm glad to see you, but I can't shake hands. That damned cow had laid down in the mud."

They stood and looked at each other. Howard's cuffs, collar, and shirt, alien in their elegance, showed through the dusk, and a glint of light shot out from the jewel of his necktie, as the light from the house caught it at the right angle. As they gazed in silence at each other, Howard divined something of the hard, bitter feeling which came into Grant's heart, as he stood there, ragged, ankle-deep in muck, his sleeves rolled up, a shapeless old straw hat on his head.

The gleam of Howard's white hands angered him. When he spoke, it was in a hard, gruff tone, full of rebellion.

"Well, go in the house and set down. I'll be in soon's I strain the milk and wash the dirt off my hands."

"But Mother—"

"She's 'round somewhere. Just knock on the door under the porch 'round there."

Howard went slowly around the corner of the house, past a vilely smelling rain-barrel, toward the west. A gray-haired woman was sitting in a rocking-chair on the porch, her hands in her lap, her eyes fixed on the faintly yellow sky, against which the hills stood, dim purple silhouettes, and on which the locust trees were etched as fine as lace. There was sorrow, resignation, and a sort of dumb despair in her attitude.

Howard stood, his throat swelling till it seemed as if he would suffocate. This was his mother—the woman who bore him, the being who had taken her life in her hand for him; and he, in his excited and pleasurable life, had neglected her!

He stepped into the faint light before her. She turned and looked at him without fear. "Mother!" he said. She uttered one little, breathing, gasping cry, called his name, rose, and stood still. He bounded up the steps, and took her in his arms.

"Mother! Dear old mother!"

In the silence, almost painful, which followed, an angry woman's voice could be heard inside: "I don't care. I ain't goin' to wear myself out fer him. He c'n eat out here with us, or else—"

Mrs. McLane began speaking. "Oh, I've longed to see yeh, Howard. I was afraid you wouldn't come till—too late."

"What do you mean, mother? Ain't you well?"

"I don't seem to be able to do much now 'cept sit around and knit a little. I tried to pick some berries the other day, and I got so dizzy I had to give it up."

"You mustn't work. You *needn't* work. Why didn't you write to me how you were?" Howard asked, in an agony of remorse.

"Well, we felt as if you probably had all you could do to take care of yourself."

"Are you married, Howard?" she broke off to ask.

"No, mother; and there ain't any excuse for me—not a bit," he said, dropping back into her colloquialisms. "I'm ashamed when I think of how long it's been since I saw you. I could have come."

"It don't matter now," she interrupted gently. "It's the way things go. Our boys grow up and leave us."

"Well, come in to supper," said Grant's ungracious voice from the doorway. "Come, mother."

Mrs. McLane moved with difficulty. Howard sprang to her aid, and, leaning on his arm, she went through the little sitting room, which was unlighted, out into the kitchen, where the supper table stood near the cook-stove.

"How.—this is my wife," said Grant, in a cold, peculiar tone.

Howard bowed toward a remarkably handsome young woman, on whose forehead was a scowl, which did not change as she looked at him and the old lady.

"Set down, anywhere," was the young woman's cordial invitation.

Howard sat down next his mother, and facing the wife, who had a small, fretful child in her arms. At Howard's left was the old man, Lewis. The supper was spread upon a gay-colored oil-cloth, and consisted of a pan of milk, set in the midst, with bowls at each plate. Beside the pan was a dipper and a large plate of bread, and at one end of the table was a dish of fine honey.

A boy of about fourteen leaned upon the table, his bent shoulders making him look like an old man. His hickory shirt,[8] like Grant's, was still wet with sweat, and discolored here and there with grease, or green from grass. His hair, freshly wet and combed, was smoothed away from his face, and shone in the light of the kerosene lamp. As he ate, he stared at Howard, as if he would make an inventory of each thread of the visitor's clothing.

"Did I look like that at his age?" thought Howard.

"You see we live jest about the same as ever," said Grant, as they began eating, speaking with a grim, almost challenging inflection.

The two brothers studied each other curiously, as they talked of neighborhood scenes. Howard seemed incredibly elegant and handsome to them all, with his rich, soft clothing, his spotless linen, and his exquisite enunciation and ease of speech. He had always been "smooth-spoken," and he had become "elegantly persuasive," as his friends said of him, and it was a large factor in his success.

Every detail of the kitchen, the heat, the flies buzzing aloft, the poor furniture, the dress of the people—all smote him like the lash of a wire whip. His brother was a man of great character. He could see that now. His deep-set, gray eyes and rugged face showed at thirty a man of great natural ability. He had more of the Scotch in his face than Howard, and he looked much older.

He was dressed, like the old man and the boy, in a checked shirt, without vest. His suspenders, once gay-colored, had given most of their color to his shirt, and had marked irregular broad bands of pink and brown and green over his shoulders. His hair was uncombed, merely pushed away from his face. He wore a mustache only, though his face was covered with a week's growth of beard. His face was rather gaunt, and was brown as leather.

Howard could not eat much. He was disturbed by his mother's strange silence and oppression, and sickened by the long-drawn gasps with which the old man ate his bread and milk, and by the way the boy ate. He had his knife gripped tightly in his fist, knuckles up, and was scooping honey upon his bread.

The baby, having ceased to be afraid, was curious, gazing silently at the stranger.

"Hello, little one! Come and see your uncle. Eh? 'Course 'e will," cooed Howard, in the attempt to escape the depressing atmosphere. The little one listened to his inflections as a kitten does, and at last lifted its arms in sign of surrender.

The mother's face cleared up a little. "I declare, she wants to go to you."

"'Course she does. Dogs and kittens always come to me when I call 'em. Why shouldn't my own niece come?"

He took the little one and began walking up and down the kitchen with her, while she pulled at his beard and nose. "I ought to have you, my lady, in my new comedy. You'd bring down the house."

"You don't mean to say you put babies on the stage, Howard," said his mother in surprise.

"Oh, yes. Domestic comedy must have a baby these days."

"Well, that's another way of makin' a livin', sure," said Grant. The baby had cleared the atmosphere a little. "I s'pose you fellers make a pile of money."

"Sometimes we make a thousand a week; oftener we don't."

"A thousand dollars!" They all stared.

"A thousand dollars sometimes, and then lose it all the next week in another town. The dramatic business is a good deal like gambling—you take your chances."

"I wish you weren't in it, Howard. I don't like to have my son—"

"I wish I was in somethin' that paid better'n farmin'. Anything under God's heavens is better'n farmin'," said Grant.

"No, I ain't laid up much," Howard went on, as if explaining why he hadn't helped them. "Costs me a good deal to live, and I need about ten thousand dollars leeway to work on. I've made a good living, but I—I ain't made any money."

Grant looked at him, darkly meditative.

Howard went on:

"How'd ye come to sell the old farm? I was in hopes—"

"How'd we come to sell it?" said Grant with terrible bitterness. "We had something on it that didn't leave anything to sell. You probably don't remember anything about it, but there was a mortgage on it that eat us up in just four years by the almanac. 'Most killed Mother to leave it. We wrote to you for money, but I don't s'pose you remember *that*."

"No, you didn't."

"Yes, I did."

"When was it? I don't—why, it's—I never received it. It must have been that summer I went with Bob Manning to Europe." Howard put the baby down and faced his brother. "Why, Grant, you didn't think I refused to help?"

"Well, it looked that way. We never heard a word from yeh all summer, and when y' did write, it was all about yerself 'n plays 'n things we didn't know anything about. I swore to God I'd never write to you again, and I won't."

"But, good heavens! I never got it."

"Suppose you didn't. You might of known we were poor as Job's off-ox.[9] Everybody is that earns a living. We fellers on the farm have to earn a livin' for ourselves and you fellers that don't work. I don't blame yeh. I'd do it if I could."

"Grant, don't talk so! Howard didn't realize——"

"I tell yeh I don't blame 'im! Only I don't want him to come the brotherly business over me, after livin' as he has—that's all." There was a bitter accusation in the man's voice.

Howard leaped to his feet, his face twitching. "By God, I'll go back tomorrow morning!" he threatened.

"Go, an' be damned! I don't care what yeh do," Grant growled, rising and going out.

"Boys," called the mother, piteously, "it's terrible to see you quarrel."

"But I'm not to blame, Mother," cried Howard in a sickness that made him white as chalk. "The man is a savage. I came home to help you all, not to quarrel."

"Grant's got one o' his fits on," said the young wife, speaking for the first time. "Don't pay any attention to him. He'll be all right in the morning."

"If it wasn't for you, Mother, I'd leave now and never see that savage again."

He lashed himself up and down in the room, in horrible disgust and hate of his brother and of this home in his heart. He remembered his tender anticipations of the home-coming with a kind of self-pity and disgust. This was his greeting!

He went to bed, to toss about on the hard, straw-filled mattress in the stuffy little best room. Tossing, writhing under the bludgeoning of his brother's accusing inflections, a dozen times he said, with a half-articulate snarl:

"He can go to hell! I'll not try to do anything more for him. I don't care if he *is* my brother; he has no right to jump on me like that. On the night of my return, too. My God! he is a brute, a savage!"

He thought of the presents in his trunk and valise, which he couldn't show to him that night, after what had been said. He had intended to have such a happy evening of it, such a tender reunion! It was to be so bright and cheery!

In the midst of his cursings—his hot indignation—would come visions of himself in his own modest rooms. He seemed to be yawning and stretching in his beautiful bed, the sun shining in, his books, foils, pictures around him, to say good morning and tempt him to rise, while the squat little clock on the mantel struck eleven warningly.

He could see the olive walls, the unique copper-and-crimson arabesque frieze (his own selection), and the delicate draperies; an open grate full of glowing coals, to temper the sea winds; and in the midst of it, between a landscape by Enneking and an Indian in a canoe in a cañon, by Brush, he saw a somber landscape by a master greater than Millet, a melancholy subject, treated with pitiless fidelity.

A farm in the valley! Over the mountains swept jagged, gray, angry, sprawling clouds, sending a freezing, thin drizzle of rain, as they passed, upon a man following a plow. The horses had a sullen and weary look, and their manes and tails streamed sidewise in the blast. The plowman, clad in a ragged gray coat, with uncouth, muddy boots upon his feet, walked with his head inclined toward the sleet, to shield his face from the cold and sting of it. The soil rolled away, black and sticky and with a dull sheen upon it. Nearby, a boy with tears on his cheeks was watching cattle, a dog seated near, his back to the gale.

As he looked at this picture, his heart softened. He looked down at the sleeve of his soft and fleecy night-shirt, at his white, rounded arm, muscular, yet fine as a woman's, and when he looked for the picture it was gone. Then came again the assertive odor of stagnant air, laden with camphor; he felt the springless bed under him, and caught dimly a few soap-advertising lithographs on the walls. He thought of his brother, in his still more in hospitable bedroom, disturbed by the child, condemned to rise at five o'clock and begin another day's pitiless labor. His heart shrank and quivered, and the tears started to his eyes.

"I forgive him, poor fellow! He's not to blame."

II

He woke, however, with a dull, languid pulse and an oppressive melancholy on his heart. He looked around the little room, clean enough, but oh, how poor! how barren! Cold plaster walls, a cheap wash-stand, a wash-set of three pieces, with a blue band around each; the windows rectangular, and fitted with fantastic green shades.

Outside he could hear the bees humming. Chickens were merrily moving about. Cow-bells far up the road were sounding irregularly. A jay came by and yelled an insolent reveille, and Howard sat up. He could hear nothing in the house but the rattle of pans on the back side of the kitchen. He looked at his watch, which indicated half-past seven. Grant was already in the field, after milking, currying the horses, and eating breakfast—had been at work two hours and a half.

He dressed himself hurriedly in a negligé shirt, with a Windsor scarf, light-colored, serviceable trousers with a belt, russet shoes, and a tennis hat—a knock-about costume, he considered.[10] His mother, good soul, thought it a special suit put on for her benefit, and admired it through her glasses.

He kissed her with a bright smile, nodded at Laura, the young wife, and tossed the baby, all in a breath, and with the manner, as he himself saw, of the returned captain in the war dramas of the day.

"Been to breakfast?" He frowned reproachfully. "Why didn't you call me? I wanted to get up, just as I used to, at sunrise."

"We thought you was tired, and so we didn't—"

"Tired! Just wait till you see me help Grant pitch hay or something. Hasn't finished his haying yet, has he?"

"No, I guess not. He will to-day if it don't rain again."

"Well, breakfast is all ready—Howard," said Laura, hesitating a little on his name.

"Good! I am ready for it. Bacon and eggs, as I'm a jay![11] Just what I was wanting. I was saying to myself, 'Now if they'll only get bacon and eggs and hot biscuits and honey—' Oh, say, mother, I heard the bees humming this morning; same noise they used to make when I was a boy, exactly. Must be the same bees,—Hey, you young rascal! come here and have some breakfast with your uncle."

"I never saw her take to anyone so quick," Laura said, emphasizing the baby's sex. She had on a clean calico dress and a gingham apron, and she looked strong and fresh and handsome. Her head was intellectual, her eyes full of power. She seemed anxious to remove the impression of her unpleasant looks and words the night before. Indeed, it would have been hard to resist Howard's sunny good-nature.

The baby laughed and crowed. The old mother could not take her dim eyes off the face of her son, but sat smiling at him as he ate and rattled on. When he rose from the table at last, after eating heartily and praising it all, he said with a smile:

"Well, now I'll just telephone down to the express and have my trunk brought up. I've got a few little things in there you'll enjoy seeing. But this fellow," indicating the baby, "I didn't take into account. But never mind; Uncle How'll make that all right."

"You ain't goin' to lay it up agin Grant, be you, my son?" Mrs. McLane faltered, as they went out into the best room.

"Of course not! He didn't mean it. Now, can't you send word down and have my trunk brought up? Or shall I have to walk down?"

"I guess I'll see somebody goin' down," said Laura.

"All right. Now for the hay-field," he smiled and went out into the glorious morning.

The circling hills the same, yet not the same as at night, a cooler, tenderer, more subdued cloak of color upon them. Far down the valley a cool, deep, impalpable, blue mist hung, under which one divined the river ran, under its elms and basswoods and wild grapevines. On the shaven slopes of the hills cattle and sheep were feeding, their cries and bells coming to the ear with a sweet suggestiveness. There was something immemorial in the sunny slopes dotted with red and brown and gray cattle.

Walking toward the haymakers, Howard felt a twinge of pain and distrust. Would he ignore it all and smile—

He stopped short. He had not seen Grant smile in so long—he couldn't quite see him smiling. He had been cold and bitter for years. When he came up to them, Grant was pitching on; the old man was loading, and the boy was raking after.

"Good-morning," Howard cried cheerily; the old man nodded, the boy stared. Grant growled something, without looking up. These "finical" things of saying good morning and good night are not much practiced in such homes as Grant McLane's.

"Need some help? I'm ready to take a hand. Got on my regimentals[12] this morning."

Grant looked at him a moment. "You look it."

Howard smiled. "Gimme a hold on that fork, and I'll show you. I'm not so soft as I look, now you bet."

He laid hold upon the fork in Grant's hands, who released it sullenly and stood back sneering. Howard struck the fork into the pile in the old way, threw his left hand to the end of the polished handle, brought it down into the hollow of his thigh, and laid out his strength till the handle bent like a bow. "Oop she rises!" he called laughingly, as the whole pile began slowly to rise, and finally rolled upon the high load.

"Oh, I ain't forgot how to do it," he laughed as he looked around at the boy, who was eyeing the tennis suit with a devouring gaze.

Grant was studying him, too, but not in admiration.

"I shouldn't say you had," said the old man, tugging at the forkful.

"Mighty funny to come out here and do a little of this. But if you had to come here and do it all the while, you wouldn't look so white and soft in the hands," Grant said, as they moved on to another pile. "Give me that fork. You'll be spoiling your fine clothes."

"Oh, these don't matter. They're made for this kind of thing."

"Oh, are they? I guess I'll dress in that kind of a rig. What did that shirt cost? I need one."

"Six dollars a pair; but then it's old."

"And them pants," he pursued; "they cost six dollars, too, didn't they?"

Howard's face darkened. He saw his brother's purpose. He resented it. "They cost fifteen dollars, if you want to know, and the shoes cost six-fifty. This ring on my cravat cost sixty dollars, and the suit I had on last night cost eighty-five. My suits are made by Breckstein, on Fifth Avenue, if you want to patronize him," he ended brutally, spurred on by the sneer in his brother's eyes. "I'll introduce you."

"Good idea," said Grant with a forced, mocking smile.

"I need just such a get-up for haying and corn-plowing. Singular I never thought of it. Now my pants cost eighty-five cents, s'penders fifteen, hat twenty, shoes one-fifty; stockin's I don't bother about."

He had his brother at a disadvantage, and he grew fluent and caustic as he went on, almost changing places with Howard, who took the rake out of the boy's hands and followed, raking up the scatterings.

"Singular we fellers here are discontented and mulish, am't it? Singular we don't believe your letters when you write, sayin', 'I just about make a live of it'? Singular we think the country's goin' to hell, we fellers, in a two-dollar suit, wadin' around in the mud or sweatin' around in the hay-field, while you fellers lay around New York and smoke and wear good clothes and toady to millionaires?"

Howard threw down the rake and folded his arms. "My God! you're enough to make a man forget the same mother bore us!"

"I guess it wouldn't take much to make you forget that. You ain't put much thought on me nor her for ten years."

The old man cackled, the boy grinned, and Howard, sick and weak with anger and sorrow, turned away and walked down toward the brook. He had tried once more to get near his brother, and had failed. Oh, God! how miserably, pitiably! The hot blood gushed all over him as he thought of the shame and disgrace of it.

He, a man associating with poets, artists, sought after by brilliant women, accustomed to deference even from such people, to be sneered at, outfaced, shamed, shoved aside, by a man in a stained hickory shirt and patched overalls, and that man his brother! He lay down on the bright grass, with the sheep all around him, and writhed and groaned with the agony and despair of it.

And worst of all, underneath it was a consciousness that Grant was right in distrusting him. He *had* neglected him; he *had* said, "I guess they're getting along all right." He had put them behind him when the invitation to spend summer on the Mediterranean or in the Adirondacks,[13] came.

"What can I do? What can I do?" he groaned.

The sheep nibbled the grass near him, the jays called pertly, "Shame, shame," a quail piped somewhere on the hillside, and the brook sung a soft, soothing melody that took away at last the sharp edge of his pain, and he sat up and gazed down the valley, bright with the sun and apparently filled with happy and prosperous people.

Suddenly a thought seized him. He stood up so suddenly that the sheep fled in affright. He leaped the brook, crossed the flat, and began searching in the bushes on the hillside. "Hurrah!" he said with a smile.

He had found an old road which he used to travel when a boy—a road that skirted the edge of the valley, now grown up to brush, but still passable for footmen. As he ran lightly along down the beautiful path, under oaks and hickories, past masses of poison-ivy, under hanging grapevines, through clumps of splendid hazelnut bushes loaded with great sticky, rough, green burrs, his heart threw off part of its load.

How it all came back to him! How many days, when the autumn sun burned the frost off the bushes, had he gathered hazel-nuts here with his boy and girl friends—Hugh and Shelley McTurg, Rome Sawyer, Orrin McIlvaine, and the rest! What had become of them all? How he had forgotten them!

This thought stopped him again, and he fell into a deep muse, leaning against an oak tree, and gazing into the vast fleckless space above. The thrilling, inscrutable mystery of life fell upon him like a blinding light. Why was he living in the crush and thunder and mental unrest of a great city, while his companions, seemingly his equal in powers, were milking cows, making butter, and growing corn and wheat in the silence and drear monotony of the farm?

His boyish sweethearts! Their names came back to his ear now with a dull, sweet sound as of faint bells. He saw their faces, their pink sunbonnets tipped back upon their necks, their brown ankles flying with the swift action of the scurrying partridge. His eyes softened, he took off his hat. The sound of the wind and the leaves moved him almost to tears.

A woodpecker gave a shrill, high-keyed, sustained cry "Ki, ki, ki!" and he started from his revery, the dapples of sun and shade falling upon his lithe figure as he hurried on down the path.

He came at last to a field of corn that ran to the very wall of a large weather-beaten house, the sight of which made his breathing quicker. It was the place where he was born. The mystery of his life began there. In the branches of those poplar and hickory trees he had swung and sung in the rushing breeze, fearless as a squirrel. Here was the brook where, like a larger kildee,[14] he with Grant had waded after crawfish, or had stolen upon some wary trout, rough-cut pole in hand.

Seeing someone in the garden, he went down along the corn-row through the rustling ranks of green leaves. An old woman was picking berries, a squat and shapeless figure.

"Good morning," he called cheerily.

"Morgen," she said, looklng up at him with a startled and very red face. She was German in every line of her body.

"Ich bin Herr McLane," he said after a pause.

"So?" she replied with a questioning inflection.

"Yah; ich bin Herr Grant's bruder."

"Ach, So!" she said with a downward inflection. "Ich no spick Inglish. No spick Inglis."

"Ich bin durstig," he said. Leaving her pans, she went with him to the house, which was what he really wanted to see.

"Ich bin hier geboren."[15]

"Ach, so!" She recognized the little bit of sentiment, and said some sentences in German whose general meaning was sympathy. She took him to the cool cellar where the spring had been trained to run into a tank containing pans of cream and milk; she gave him a cool draught from a large tin cup, and then at his request went with him upstairs. The house was the same, but somehow seemed cold and empty. It was clean and sweet, but it had so little evidence of being lived in. The old part, which was built of logs, was used as best room, and modelled after the best rooms of the neighboring "Yankee" homes, only it was emptier, without the cabinet organ and the rag carpet and the chromos.

The old fireplace was bricked up and plastered—the fireplace beside which in the far-off days, he had lain on winter nights, to hear his uncles tell tales of hunting, or to hear them play the violin, great dreaming giants that they were.

The old woman went out and left him sitting there, the center of a swarm of memories, coming and going like so many ghostly birds and butterflies.

A curious heartache and listlessness, a nerveless mood came on him. What was it worth, anyhow—success? Struggle, strife, trampling on someone else. His play crowding out some other poor fellow's hope. The hawk eats the partridge, the partridge eats the flies and bugs, the bugs eat each other, and the hawk, when he in his turn is shot by man. So in the world of business, the life of one man seemed to him to be drawn from the life of another man, each success to spring from other failures.

He was like a man from whom all motives had been withdrawn. He was sick, sick to the heart. Oh, to be a boy again! An ignorant baby, pleased with a block and string, with no knowledge and no care of the great unknown! To lay his head again on his mother's bosom and rest! To watch the flames on the hearth!—

Why not? Was not that the very thing to do? To buy back the old farm? It would cripple him a little for the next season, but he could do it. Think of it! To see his mother back in the old home, with the fireplace restored, the old furniture in the sitting room around her, and fine new things in the parlor!

His spirits rose again. Grant couldn't stand out when he brought to him a deed of the farm. Surely his debt would be canceled when he had seen them all back in the wide old kitchen. He began to plan and to dream. He went to the windows, and looked out on the yard to see how much it had changed.

He'd build a new barn and buy them a new carriage. His heart glowed again, and his lips softened into their usual feminine grace—lips a little full and falling easily into curves.

The old German woman came in at length, bringing some cakes and a bowl of milk, smiling broadly and hospitably as she waddled forward.

"Ach! Goot!" he said, smacking his lips over the pleasant draught.

"Wo ist ihre goot mann?"[16] he inquired, ready for business.

III

When Grant came in at noon, Mrs. McLane met him at the door with a tender smile on her face.

"Where's Howard, Grant?"

"I don't know," he replied in a tone that implied "I don't care."

The dim eyes clouded with quick tears.

"Ain't you seen him?"

"Not since nine o'clock."

"Where do you think he is?"

"I tell yeh I don't know. He'll take care of himself; don't worry."

He flung off his hat and plunged into the wash-basin. His shirt was wet with sweat and covered with dust of the hay and fragments of leaves. He splashed his burning face with the water, paying no further attention to his mother. She spoke again, very gently, in reproof:

"Grant, why do you stand out against Howard so?"

"I don't stand out against him," he replied harshly, pausing with the towel in his hands. His eyes were hard and piercing. "But if he expects me to gush over his coming back, he's fooled, that's all. He's left us to paddle our own canoe all this while, and, so far as *I'm* concerned, he can leave us alone hereafter. He looked

out for his precious hide mighty well, and now he comes back here to play big
gun and pat us on the head. I don't propose to let him come that over me."

Mrs. McLane knew too well the temper of her son to say any more, but she
inquired about Howard of the old hired man.

"He went off down the valley. He 'n' Grant had s'm words, and he pulled out
down toward the old farm. That's the last I see of 'im."

Laura took Howard's part at the table. "Pity you can't be decent," she said,
brutally direct as usual "You treat Howard as if he was a—a—I do' know what."

"Will you let me alone?"

"No, I won't. If you think I'm going to set by an' agree to your bullyraggin'
him, you're mistaken. It's a shame! You're mad 'cause he's succeeded and you
ain't. He ain't to blame for his brains. If you and I'd had any, we'd 'a' succeeded,
too. It ain't our fault, and it ain't his; so what's the use?"

There was a look came into Grant's face that the wife knew. It meant bitter
and terrible silence. He ate his dinner without another word.

It was beginning to cloud up. A thin, whitish, all-pervasive vapor which meant
rain was dimming the sky, and Grant forced his hands to their utmost during the
afternoon, in order to get most of the down hay in before the rain came. He was
pitching hay up into the barn when Howard came by just before one o'clock.

It was windless there. The sun fell through the white mist with undiminished
fury, and the fragrant hay sent up a breath that was hot as an oven-draught.
Grant was a powerful man, and there was something majestic in his action as he
rolled the huge flakes of hay through the door. The sweat poured from his face
like rain, and he was forced to draw his dripping sleeve across his face to clear
away the blinding sweat that poured into his eyes.

Howard stood and looked at him in silence, remembering how often he had
worked there in that furnace heat, his muscles quivering, cold chills running over
his flesh, red shadows dancing before his eyes.

His mother met him at the door anxiously, but smiled as she saw his pleasant
face and cheerful eyes.

"You're a little late, m' son."

Howard spent most of the afternoon sitting with his mother on the porch, or
under the trees, lying sprawled out like a boy, resting at times with sweet forgetfulness of the whole world, but feeling a dull pain whenever he remembered the
stern, silent man pitching hay in the hot sun on the torrid side of the barn.

His mother did not say anything about the quarrel; she feared to reopen it.
She talked mainly of old times in a gentle monotone of reminiscence, while he
listened, looking up into her patient face.

The heat slowly lessened as the sun sank down toward the dun clouds rising
like a more distant and majestic line of mountains beyond the western hills. The
sound of cow-bells came irregularly to the ear, and the voices and sounds of the
haying-fields had a jocund, thrilling effect on the ear of the city-dweller.

He was very tender. Everything conspired to make him simple, direct, and
honest.

"Mother, if you'll only forgive me for staying away so long, I'll surely come to see you every summer."

She had nothing to forgive. She was so glad to have him there at her feet—her great, handsome, successful boy! She could only love him and enjoy him every moment of the precious days. If Grant would only reconcile himself to Howard! That was the great thorn in her flesh.

Howard told her how he had succeeded.

"It was luck, mother. First I met Cook, and he introduced me to Jake Saulsman of Chicago. Jake asked me to go to New York with him, and—I don't know why—took a fancy to me some way. He introduced me to a lot of the fellows in New York, and they all helped me along. I did nothing to merit it. Everybody helps me. Anybody can succeed in that way."

The doting mother thought it not at all strange that they all helped him.

At the supper table Grant was gloomily silent, ignoring Howard completely. Mrs. McLane sat and grieved silently, not daring to say a word in protest. Laura and the baby tried to amuse Howard, and under cover of their talk the meal was eaten.

The boy fascinated Howard. He "sawed wood" with a rapidity and uninterruptedness which gave alarm. He had the air of coaling up for a long voyage.

"At that age," Howard thought, "I must have gripped my knife in my right hand so, and poured my tea into my saucer so. I must have buttered and bit into a huge slice of bread just so, and chewed at it with a smacking sound in just that way. I must have gone to the length of scooping up honey with my knife-blade."

The sky was magically beautiful over all this squalor and toil and bitterness, from five till seven—a moving hour. Again the falling sun streamed in broad banners across the valleys; again the blue mist lay far down the Coolly over the river; the cattle called from the hills in the moistening, sonorous air; the bells came in a pleasant tangle of sound; the air pulsed with the deepening chorus of katydids and other nocturnal singers.

Sweet and deep as the very springs of his life was all this to the soul of the elder brother; but in the midst of it, the younger man, in ill-smelling clothes and great boots that chafed his feet, went out to milk the cows,—on whose legs the flies and mosquitoes swarmed, bloated with blood,—to sit by the hot side of the cow and be lashed with her tail as she tried frantically to keep the savage insects from eating her raw.

"The poet who writes of milking the cows does it from the hammock, looking on," Howard soliloquized, as he watched the old man Lewis racing around the filthy yard after one of the young heifers that had kicked over the pail in her agony with the flies and was unwilling to stand still and be eaten alive.

"So, *so!* you beast!" roared the old man as he finally cornered the shrinking, nearly frantic creature.

"Don't you want to look at the garden?" asked Mrs. McLane of Howard; and they went out among the vegetables and berries.

The bees were coming home heavily laden and crawling slowly into the hives. The level, red light streamed through the trees, blazed along the grass, and lighted a few old-fashioned flowers into red and gold flame. It was beautiful, and Howard looked at it through his half-shut eyes as the painters do, and turned away with a sigh at the sound of blows where the wet and grimy men were assailing the frantic cows.

"There's Wesley with your trunk," Mrs. McLane said, recalling him to himself. Wesley helped him carry the trunk in and waved off thanks.

"Oh, that's all right," he said; and Howard knew the Western man too well to press the matter of pay.

As he went in an hour later and stood by the trunk, the dull ache came back into his heart. How he had failed! It seemed like a bitter mockery now to show his gifts.

Grant had come in from his work, and with his feet released from his chafing boots, in his wet shirt and milk-splashed overalls, sat at the kitchen table reading a newspaper which he held close to a small kerosene lamp. He paid no attention to anyone. His attitude, curiously like his father's, was perfectly definite to Howard. It meant that from that time forward there were to be no words of any sort between them. It meant that they were no longer brothers, not even acquaintances. "How inexorable that face!" thought Howard.

He turned sick with disgust and despair, and would have closed his trunk without showing any of the presents, only for the childish expectancy of his mother and Laura.

"Here's something for you, Mother," he said, assuming a cheerful voice as he took a fold of fine silk from the trunk and held it up. "All the way from Paris." He laid it on his mother's lap and stooped and kissed her, and then turned hastily away to hide the tears that came to his own eyes as he saw her keen pleasure.

"And here's a parasol for Laura. I don't know how I came to have that in here. And here's General Grant's autobiography[17] for his namesake," he said with an effort at carelessness, and waited to hear Grant rise.

"Grant, won't you come in?" asked his mother, quiveringly.

Grant did not reply nor move. Laura took the handsome volumes out and laid them beside him on the table. He simply pushed them to one side and went on with his reading.

Again that horrible anger swept hot as flame over Howard. He could have cursed him. His hands shook as he handed out other presents to his mother and Laura and the baby. He tried to joke.

"I didn't know how old the baby was, so she'll have to grow to some of these things."

But the pleasure was all gone for him and for the rest. His heart swelled almost to a feeling of pain as he looked at his mother. There she sat with the presents in her lap. The shining silk came too late for her. It threw into appalling relief her age, her poverty, her work-weary frame. "My God!" he almost cried aloud, "how little it would have taken to lighten her life!"

Upon this moment, when it seemed as if he could endure no more, came the smooth voice of William McTurg:

"Hello, folkses!"

"Hello, Uncle Bill! Come in."

"That's what we came for," laughed a woman's voice.

"Is that you, Rose?" asked Laura.

"It's me—Rose," replied the laughing girl as she bounced into the room and greeted everybody in a breathless sort of way.

"You don't mean little Rosy?"

"Big Rosy now," said William.

Howard looked at the handsome girl and smiled, saying in a nasal sort of tone, "Wal, wal! Rosy, how you've growed since I saw yeh!"

"Oh, look at all this purple and fine linen! Am I left out?"

Rose was a large girl of twenty-five or thereabouts, and was called an old maid. She radiated good-nature from every line of her buxom self. Her black eyes were full of drollery, and she was on the best of terms with Howard at once. She had been a teacher, but that did not prevent her from assuming a peculiar directness of speech. Of course they talked about old friends.

"Where's Rachel?" Howard inquired. Her smile faded away.

"Shellie married Orrin McIlvaine. They're way out in Dakota. Shellie's havin' a hard row of stumps."

There was a little silence.

"And Tommy?"

"Gone West. Most all the boys have gone West. That's the reason there's so many old maids."

"You don't mean to say—"

"I don't *need* to say—I'm an old maid. Lots of the girls are. It don't pay to marry these days. Are you married?"

"Not *yet.*" His eyes lighted up again in a humorous way.

"Not yet! That's good! That's the way old maids all talk."

"You don't mean to tell me that no young fellow comes prowling around—"

"Oh, a young Dutchman or Norwegian once in a while. Nobody that counts.[18] Fact is, we're getting like Boston—four women to one man; and when you consider that we're getting more particular each year, the outlook is—well, it's dreadful!"

"It certainly is."

"Marriage is a failure these days for most of us. We can't live on a farm, and can't get a living in the city, and there we are." She laid her hand on his arm. "I declare, Howard, you're the same boy you used to be. I ain't a bit afraid of you, for all your success."

"And you're the same girl? No, I can't say that. It seems to me you've grown more than I have—I don't mean physically, I mean mentally," he explained as he saw her smile in the defensive way a fleshy girl has, alert to ward off a joke.

They were in the midst of talk, Howard telling one of his funny stories, when a wagon clattered up to the door and merry voices called loudly:

"Whoa, there, Sampson!"

"Hullo, the house!"

Rose looked at her father with a smile in her black eyes exactly like his. They went to the door.

"Hullo! What's wanted?"

"Grant McLane live here?"

"Yup. Right here."

A moment later there came a laughing, chatting squad of women to the door. Mrs. McLane and Laura stared at each other in amazement. Grant went outdoors.

Rose stood at the door as if she were hostess.

"Come in, Nettie. Glad to see yeh—glad to see yeh! Mrs. McIlvaine, come right in! Take a seat. Make yerself to home, *do!* And Mrs. Peavey! Wal, I never! This must be a surprise party. Well, I swan! How many more o' ye air they?"

All was confusion, merriment, hand-shakings as Rose introduced them in her roguish way.

"Folks, this is Mr. Howard McLane of New York. He's an actor, but it hain't spoiled him a bit as *I* can see. How., this is Nettie McIlvaine—Wilson that was."

Howard shook hands with Nettie, a tall, plain girl with prominent teeth.

"This is Ma McIlvaine."

"She looks just the same," said Howard, shaking her hand and feeling how hard and work-worn it was.

And so amid bustle, chatter, and invitations "to lay off y'r things an' stay awhile," the women got disposed about the room at last. Those that had rocking-chairs rocked vigorously to and fro to hide their embarrassment. They all talked in loud voices.

Howard felt nervous under this furtive scrutiny. He wished that his clothes didn't look so confoundedly dressy. Why didn't he have sense enough to go and buy a fifteen-dollar suit of diagonals for everyday wear.

Rose was the life of the party. Her tongue rattled on m the most delightful way.

"It's all Rose an' Bill's doin's," Mrs. McIlvaine explained. "They told us to come over an' pick up anybody we see on the road. So we did."

Howard winced a little at her familiarity of tone. He couldn't help it for the life of him.

"Well, I wanted to come to-night because I'm going away next week, and I wanted to see how he'd act at a surprise-party again," Rose explained.

"Married, I s'pose?" said Mrs. McIlvaine abruptly.

"No, not yet."

"Good land! Why, y' mus' be thirty-five, How. Must a dis'p'inted y'r mam not to have a young 'un to call 'er granny."

The men came clumping in, talking about haying and horses. Some of the older ones Howard knew and greeted, but the younger ones were mainly too much changed. They were all very ill at ease. Most of them were in compromise dress—something lying between working "rig" and Sunday dress. Some of them had on clean shirts and paper collars, and wore their Sunday coats (thick woollen garments) over rough trousers. Most of them crossed their legs at once, and all of them sought the wall and leaned back perilously upon the hind legs of their chairs, eyeing Howard slowly.

For the first few minutes the presents were the subjects of conversation. The women especially spent a good deal of talk upon them.

Howard found himself forced to taking the initiative, so he inquired about the crops and about the farms.

"I see you don't plow the hills as we used to. And reap! *What* a job it used to be. It makes the hills more beautiful to have them covered with smooth grass and cattle."

There was only dead silence to this touching upon the idea of beauty.

"I s'pose it pays reasonably."

"Not enough to kill," said one of the younger men. "You c'n see that by the houses we live in—that is, most of us. A few that came in early an' got land cheap, like McIlvaine, here—he got a lift that the rest of us can't get."

"I'm a free trader, myself,"[19] said one young fellow, blushing and looking away as Howard turned and said cheerily:

"So'm I."

The rest seemed to feel that this was a tabooed subject—a subject to be talked out of doors, where a man could prance about and yell and do justice to it.

Grant sat silently in the kitchen doorway, not saying a word, not looking at his brother.

"Well, I don't never use hot vinegar for mine," Mrs. McIlvaine was heard to say. "I jest use hot water, an' I rinse 'em out good, and set 'em bottom-side up in the sun. I do' know but what hot vinegar *would* be more cleansin'."

Rose had the younger folks in a giggle with a droll telling of a joke on herself.

"How'd y' stop 'em from laffin'?"

"I let 'em laugh. Oh, my school is a disgrace—so one director says. But I like to see children laugh. It broadens their cheeks."

"Yes, that's all hand-work." Laura was showing the baby's Sunday clothes.

"Goodness Peter! How do you find time to do so much?"

"I take time."

Howard, being the lion of the evening, tried his best to be agreeable. He kept near his mother, because it afforded her so much pride and satisfaction, and because he was obliged to keep away from Grant, who had begun to talk to the men. Howard talked mainly about their affairs, but still was forced more and more into talking of life in the city. As he told of the theater and the concerts, a sudden change fell upon them; they grew sober, and he felt deep down in the hearts of these people a melancholy which was expressed only illusively with little tones or sighs. Their gayety was fitful.

They were hungry for the world, for life—these young people. Discontented, and yet hardly daring to acknowledge it; indeed, few of them could have made definite statement of their dissatisfaction. The older people felt it less. They practically said, with a sigh of pathetic resignation:

"Well, I don't expect ever to see these things *now*."

A casual observer would have said, "What a pleasant bucolic—this little surprise-party of welcome!" But Howard, with his native ear and eye, had no such pleasing illusion. He knew too well these suggestions of despair and bitterness. He knew that, like the smile of the slave, this cheerfulness was self-defense; deep down was another unsatisfied ego.

Seeing Grant talking with a group of men over by the kitchen door, he crossed over slowly and stood listening. Wesley Cosgrove—a tall, raw-boned young fellow with a grave, almost tragic face—was saying:

"Of course I ain't. Who is? A man that's satisfied to live as we do is a fool."

"The worst of it is," said Grant without seeing Howard, "a man can't get out of it during his lifetime, and *I* don't know that he'll have any chance in the next—the speculator'll be there ahead of us."

The rest laughed, but Grant went on grimly:

"Ten years ago Wess, here, could have got land in Dakota pretty easy, but now it's about all a feller's life's worth to try it. I tell you things seem shuttin' down on us fellers."

"Plenty o' land to rent," suggested someone.

"Yes, in terms that skin a man alive. More than that, farmin' ain't so free a life as it used to be. This cattle-raisin' and butter-makin' makes a nigger[20] of a man. Binds him right down to the grindstone and he gets nothin' out of it—that's what rubs it in. He simply wallers around in the manure for somebody else. I'd like to know what a man's life is worth who lives as we do? How much higher is it than the lives the niggers used to live?"

These brutally bald words made Howard thrill with emotion like some great tragic poem. A silence fell on the group.

"That's the God's truth, Grant," said young Cosgrove after a pause.

"A man like me is helpless," Grant was saying. "Just like a fly in a pan of molasses. There ain't any escape for him. The more he tears around the more liable he is to rip his legs off."

"What can he do?"

"Nothin'."

The men listened in silence.

"Oh, come, don't talk politics all night!" cried Rose, breaking in. "Come, let's have a dance. Where's that fiddle?"

"Fiddle!" cried Howard, glad of a chance to laugh. "Well, now! Bring out that fiddle. Is it William's?"

"Yes, pap's old fiddle."

"Oh, gosh! he don't want to hear me play," protested William. "He's heard s' many fiddlers."

"Fiddlers! I've heard a thousand violinists, but not fiddlers. Come, give us 'Honest John.'"

William took the fiddle in his work-calloused and crooked hands and began tuning it. The group at the kitchen door turned to listen, their faces lighting up a little. Rose tried to get a "set" on the floor.[21]

"Oh, good land!" said some. "We're all tuckered out. What makes you so anxious?"

"She wants a chance to dance with the New Yorker."

"That's it, exactly," Rose admitted.

"Wal, if you'd churned and mopped and cooked for hayin' hands as I have today, you wouldn't be so full o' nonsense."

"Oh, bother! Life's short. Come, quick, get Bettie out. Come, Wess, never mind your hobby-horse."

By incredible exertion she got a set on the floor, and William got the fiddle in tune. Howard looked across at Wesley, and thought the change in him splendidly dramatic. His face had lighted up into a kind of deprecating, boyish smile. Rose could do anything with him.

William played some of the old tunes that had a thousand associated memories in Howard's brain, memories of harvest-moons, of melon-feasts, and of clear, cold winter nights. As he danced, his eyes filled with a tender light. He came closer to them all than he had been able to do before. Grant had gone out into the kitchen.

After two or three sets had been danced, the company took seats and could not be stirred again. So Laura and Rose disappeared for a few moments, and returning, served strawberries and cream, which Laura said she "just happened to have in the house."

And then William played again. His fingers, now grown more supple, brought out clearer, firmer tones. As he played, silence fell on these people. The magic of music sobered every face; the women looked older and more careworn, the men slouched sullenly in their chairs, or leaned back against the wall.

It seemed to Howard as if the spirit of tragedy had entered this house. Music had always been William's unconscious expression of his unsatisfied desires. He was never melancholy except when he played. Then his eyes grew somber, his drooping face full of shadows.

He played on slowly, softly, wailing Scotch tunes and mournful Irish love songs. He seemed to find in these melodies, and especially in a wild, sweet, low-keyed Negro[22] song, some expression for his indefinable inner melancholy.

He played on, forgetful of everybody, his long beard sweeping the violin, his toil-worn hands marvelously obedient to his will.

At last he stopped, looked up with a faint, deprecating smile, and said with a sigh:

"Well, folkses, time to go home."

The going was quiet. Not much laughing. Howard stood at the door and said good-night to them all, his heart very tender.

"Come and see us," they said.

"I will," he replied cordially. "I'll try and get around to see everybody, and talk over old times, before I go back."

After the wagons had driven out of the yard, Howard turned and put his arm about his mother's neck.

"Tired?"

"A little."

"Well, now, good night. I'm going for a little stroll."

His brain was too active to sleep. He kissed his mother good-night and went out into the road, his hat in his hand, the cool, moist wind on his hair.

It was very dark, the stars being partly hidden by a thin vapor. On each side the hills rose, every line familiar as the face of an old friend. A whippoorwill called occasionally from the hillside, and the spasmodic jangle of a bell now and then told of some cow's battle with the mosquitoes.

As he walked, he pondered upon the tragedy he had rediscovered in these people's lives. Out here under the inexorable spaces of the sky, a deep distaste of his own life took possession of him. He felt like giving it all up. He thought of the infinite tragedy of these lives which the world loves to call peaceful and pastoral. His mind went out in the aim to help them. What could he do to make life better worth living? Nothing.

They must live and die practically as he saw them to-night.

And yet he knew this was a mood, and that in a few hours the love and the habit of life would come back upon him and upon them; that he would go back to the city in a few days; that these people would live on and make the best of it.

"*I'll* make the best of it," he said at last, and his thought came back to his mother and Grant.

I V

The next day was a rainy day; not a shower, but a steady rain—an unusual thing in midsummer in the West. A cold, dismal day in the fireless, colorless farm-houses. It came to Howard in that peculiar reaction which surely comes during a visit of this character, when thought is a weariness, when the visitor longs for his own familiar walls and pictures and books, and longs to meet his friends, feeling at the same time the tragedy of life which makes friends nearer and more congenial than blood-relations.

Howard ate his breakfast alone, save Baby and Laura its mother going about the room. Baby and mother alike insisted on feeding him to death. Already dyspeptic pangs were setting in.

"Now ain't there something more I can—"

"Good heavens! No!" he cried in dismay. "I'm likely to die of dyspepsia[23] now. This honey and milk, and these delicious hot biscuits—"

"I'm afraid it ain't much like the breakfasts you have in the city."

"Well, no, it ain't," he confessed. "But this is the kind a man needs when he lives in the open air."

She sat down opposite him, with her elbows on the table, her chin in her palm, her eyes full of shadows.

"I'd like to go to a city once. I never saw a town bigger'n La Crosse. I've never seen a play, but I've read of 'em in the magazines. It must be wonderful; they say they have wharves and real ships coming up to the wharf, and people getting off and on. How do they do it?"

"Oh, that's too long a story to tell. It's a lot of machinery and paint and canvas. If I told you how it was done, you wouldn't enjoy it so well when you come on and see it."

"Do you ever expect to see me in New York?"

"Why, yes. Why not? I expect Grant to come on and bring you all some day, especially Tonikins here. Tonikins, you hear, sir? I expect you to come on you' forf birfday, sure." He tried thus to stop the woman's gloomy confidence.

"I hate farm-life," she went on with a bitter inflection. "It's nothing but fret, fret and work the whole time, never going any place, never seeing anybody but a lot of neighbors just as big fools as you are. I spend my time fighting flies and washing dishes and churning. I'm sick of it all."

Howard was silent. What could he say to such an indictment? The ceiling swarmed with flies which the cold rain had driven to seek the warmth of the kitchen. The gray rain was falling with a dreary sound outside, and down the kitchen stove-pipe an occasional drop fell on the stove with a hissing, angry sound.

The young wife went on with a deeper note:

"I lived in La Crosse two years, going to school, and I know a little something of what city life is. If I was a man, I bet I wouldn't wear my life out on a farm, as Grant does. I'd get away and I'd do something. I wouldn't care what, but I'd get away."

There was a certain volcanic energy back of all the woman said that made Howard feel she'd make the attempt. She didn't know that the struggle for a place to stand on this planet was eating the heart and soul out of men and women in the city, just as in the country. But he could say nothing. If be had said in conventional phrase, sitting there in his soft clothing, "We must make the best of it all," the woman could justly have thrown the dish-cloth in his face. He could say nothing.

"I was a fool for ever marrying," she went on, while the baby pushed a chair across the room. "I made a decent living teaching, I was free to come and go, my money was my own. Now I'm tied right down to a churn or a dishpan, I never have a cent of my own. *He's* growlin' round half the time, and there's no chance of his ever being different."

She stopped with a bitter sob in her throat. She forgot she was talking to her husband's brother. She was conscious only of his sympathy.

As if a great black cloud had settled down upon him, Howard felt it all—the horror, hopelessness, imminent tragedy of it all. The glory of nature, the bounty and splendor of the sky, only made it the more benumbing. He thought of a sentence Millet[24] once wrote:

"I see very well the aureole of the dandelions, and the sun also, far down there behind the hills, flinging his glory upon the clouds. But not alone that—I see in the plains the smoke of the tired horses at the plough, or, on a stony-hearted spot of ground, a back-broken man trying to raise himself upright for a moment to breathe. The tragedy is surrounded by glories—that is no invention of mine."

Howard arose abruptly and went back to his little bedroom, where he walked up and down the floor till he was calm enough to write, and then he sat down and poured it all out to "Dearest Margaret," and his first sentence was this:

"If it were not for you (just to let you know the mood I'm in)—if it were not *for* you, and I had the world in my hands, I'd crush it like a puff-ball; evil so predominates, suffering is so universal and persistent, happiness so fleeting and so infrequent."

He wrote on for two hours, and by the time he had sealed and directed several letters he felt calmer, but still terribly depressed. The rain was still falling, sweeping down from the half-seen hills, wreathing the wooded peaks with a gray garment of mist and filling the valley with a whitish cloud.

It fell around the house drearily. It ran down into the tubs placed to catch it, dripped from the mossy pump, and drummed on the upturned milk-pails, and upon the brown and yellow beehives under the maple trees. The chickens seemed depressed, but the irrepressible bluejay screamed amid it all, with the same insolent spirit, his plumage untarnished by the wet. The barnyard showed a horrible mixture of mud and mire, through which Howard caught glimpses of the men, slumping to and fro without more additional protection than a ragged coat and a shapeless felt hat.

In the sitting room where his mother sat sewing there was not an ornament, save the etching he had brought. The clock stood on a small shelf, its dial so much defaced that one could not tell the time of day; and when it struck, it was with noticeably disproportionate deliberation, as if it wished to correct any mistake into which the family might have fallen by reason of its illegible dial.

The paper on the walls showed the first concession of the Puritans to the Spirit of Beauty, and was made up of a heterogeneous mixture of flowers of unheard-of-shapes and colors, arranged in four different ways along the wall. There were no books, no music, and only a few newspapers in sight—a bare, blank, cold, drab-colored shelter from the rain, not a home. Nothing cozy, nothing heartwarming; a grim and horrible shed.

"What are they doing? It can't be they're at work such a day as this," Howard said, standing at the window.

"They find plenty to do, even on rainy days," answered his mother. "Grant always has some job to set the men at. It's the only way to live."

"I'll go out and see them." He turned suddenly. "Mother, why should Grant treat me so? Have I deserved it?"

Mrs. McLane sighed in pathetic hopelessness. "I don't know, Howard. I'm worried about Grant. He gets more an' more down-hearted an' gloomy every day. Seems if he'd go crazy. He don't care how he looks any more, won't dress up on Sunday. Days an' days he'll go aroun' not sayin' a word. I was in hopes you could help him, Howard."

"My coming seems to have had an opposite effect. He hasn't spoken a word to me, except when he had to, since I came. Mother, what do you say to going home with me to New York?"

"Oh, I couldn't do that!" she cried in terror. "I couldn't live in a big city—never!"

"There speaks the truly rural mind," smiled Howard at his mother, who was looking up at him through her glasses with a pathetic forlornness which sobered him again. "Why, Mother, you could live in Orange, New Jersey, or out in Connecticut, and be just as lonesome as you are here. You wouldn't need to live in the city. I could see you then every day or two."

"Well, I couldn't leave Grant an' the baby, anyway," she replied, not realizing how one could live in New Jersey and do business daily in New York.

"Well, then, how would you like to go back into the old house?" he said, facing her.

The patient hands fell to the lap, the dim eyes fixed in searching glance on his face. There was a wistful cry in the voice.

"Oh, Howard! Do you mean——"

He came and sat down by her, and put his arm about her and hugged her hard. "I mean, you dear, good, patient, work-weary old mother, I'm going to buy back the old farm and put you in it."

There was no refuge for her now except in tears, and she put up her thin, trembling old hands about his neck, and cried in that easy, placid, restful way age has.

Howard could not speak. His throat ached with remorse and pity. He saw his forgetfulness of them all once more without relief,—the black thing it was!

"There, there, mother, don't cry!" he said, torn with anguish by her tears. Measured by man's tearlessness, her weeping seemed terrible to him. "I didn't realize how things were going here. It was all my fault—or, at least, most of it. Grant's letter didn't reach me. I thought you were still on the old farm. But no matter; it's all over now. Come, don't cry any more, mother dear. I'm going to take care of you now."

It had been years since the poor, lonely woman had felt such warmth of love. Her sons had been like her husband, chary of expressing their affection; and like most Puritan families, there was little of caressing among them. Sitting there with the rain on the roof and driving through the trees, they planned getting back into the old house. Howard's plan seemed to her full of splendor and audacity. She began to understand his power and wealth now, as he put it into concrete form before her.

"I wish I could eat Thanksgiving dinner there with you," he said at last, "but it can't be thought of. However, I'll have you all in there before I go home. I'm going out now and tell Grant. Now don't worry any more; I'm going to fix it all up with him, sure." He gave her a parting hug.

Laura advised him not to attempt to get to the barn; but as he persisted in going, she hunted up an old rubber coat for him. "You'll mire down and spoil your shoes," she said, glancing at his neat calf gaiters.

"Darn the difference!" he laughed in his old way. "Besides, I've got rubbers."[25]

"Better go round by the fence," she advised as he stepped out into the pouring rain.

How wretchedly familiar it all was! The miry cow yard, with the hollow trampled out around the horse-trough, the disconsolate hens standing under the wagons and sheds, a pig wallowing across its sty, and for atmosphere the desolate, falling rain. It was so familiar he felt a pang of the old rebellious despair which seized him on such days in his boyhood.

Catching up courage, he stepped out on the grass, opened the gate, and entered the barn-yard. A narrow ribbon of turf ran around the fence, on which he could walk by clinging with one hand to the rough boards. In this way he slowly made his way around the periphery, and came at last to the open barn door without much harm.

It was a desolate interior. In the open floorway Grant, seated upon a half-bushel, was mending a harness. The old man was holding the trace in his hard brown hands; the boy was lying on a wisp of hay. It was a small barn, and poor at that. There was a bad smell, as of dead rats, about it, and the rain fell through the shingles here and there. To the right, and below, the horses stood, looking up with their calm and beautiful eyes, in which the whole scene was idealized.

Grant looked up an instant and then went on with his work.

"Did yeh wade through?" grinned Lewis, exposing his broken teeth.

"No, I kinder circumambiated the pond." He sat down on the little tool-box near Grant. "Your barn is good deal like that in 'The Arkansas Traveller.'[26] Needs a new roof, Grant." His voice had a pleasant sound, full of the tenderness of the scene through which he had just been. "In fact, you need a new barn."

"I need a good many things more'n I'll ever get," Grant replied shortly.

"How long did you say you'd been on this farm?"

"Three years this fall."

"I don't s'pose you've been able to think of buying—Now hold on, Grant," he cried, as Grant threw his head back. "For God's sake, don't get mad again! Wait till you see what I'm driving at."

"I don't see what you're drivin' at, and I don't care. All I want you to do is to let us alone. That ought to be easy enough for you."

"I tell you, I didn't get your letter. I didn't know you'd lost the old farm." Howard was determined not to quarrel. "I didn't suppose——"

"You might 'a' come to see."

"Well, I'll admit that. All I can say in excuse is that since I got to managing plays I've kept looking ahead to making a big hit and getting a barrel of money—just as the old miners used to hope and watch. Besides, you don't understand how much pressure there is on me. A hundred different people pulling and hauling to have me go here or go there, or do this or do that. When it isn't yachting, it's canoeing, or——"

He stopped. His heart gave a painful throb, and a shiver ran through him. Again he saw his life, so rich, so bright, so free, set over against the routine life in the little low kitchen, the barren sitting room, and this still more horrible barn. Why should his brother sit there in wet and grimy clothing mending a broken trace, while he enjoyed all the light and civilization of the age?

He looked at Grant's fine figure, his great strong face; recalled his deep, stern, masterful voice. "Am I so much superior to him? Have not circumstances made me and destroyed him?"

"Grant, for God's sake, don't sit there like that! I'll admit I've been negligent and careless. I can't understand it all myself. But let me do something for you now. I've sent to New York for five thousand dollars. I've got terms on the old farm. Let me see you all back there once more before I return."

"I don't want any of your charity."

"It ain't charity. It's only justice to you." He rose. "Come now, let's get at an understanding, Grant. I can't go on this way. I can't go back to New York and leave you here like this."

Grant rose, too. "I tell you, I don't ask your help. You can't fix this thing up with money. If you've got more brains 'n I have, why it's all right. I ain't got any right to take anything that I don't earn."

"But you don't get what you do earn. It ain't your fault. I begin to see it now. Being the oldest, I had the best chance. I was going to town to school while you were plowing and husking corn. Of course I thought you'd be going soon, yourself. I had three years the start of you. If you'd been in my place, *you* might have met a man like Cooke, *you* might have gone to New York and have been where I am."

"Well, it can't be helped now. So drop it."

"But it must be helped!" Howard said, pacing about, his hands in his coat-pockets. Grant had stopped work, and was gloomily looking out of the door at a pig nosing in the mud for stray grains of wheat at the granary door. The old man and the boy quietly withdrew.

"Good God! I see it all now," Howard burst out in an impassioned tone. "I went ahead with *my* education, got *my* start in life, then father died, and you took up his burdens. Circumstances made me and crushed you. That's all there is about that. Luck made me and cheated you. It ain't right."

His voice faltered. Both men were now oblivious of their companions and of the scene. Both were thinking of the days when they both planned great things in the way of an education, two ambitious, dreamful boys.

"I used to think of you, Grant, when I pulled out Monday morning in my best suit—cost fifteen dollars in those days." He smiled a little at the recollection. "While you in overalls and an old 'wammus' was going out into the field to plow, or husk corn in the mud. It made me feel uneasy, but, as I said, I kept saying to myself, 'His turn'll come in a year or two.' But it didn't."

His voice choked. He walked to the door, stood a moment, came back. His eyes were full of tears.

"I tell you, old man, many a time in my boarding-house down to the city, when I thought of the jolly times I was having, my heart hurt me. But I said: 'It's no use to cry. Better go on and do the best you can, and then help them afterward. There'll only be one more miserable member of the family if you stay at home.' Besides, it seemed right to me to have first chance. But I never thought you'd be shut off, Grant. If I had, I never would have gone on. Come, old man, I want you to believe that." His voice was very tender now and almost humble.

"I don't know as I blame yeh for that, How.," said Grant slowly. It was the first time he had called Howard by his boyish nickname. His voice was softer, too, and higher in key. But he looked steadily away.

"I went to New York. People liked my work. I was very successful, Grant; more successful than you realize. I could have helped you at any time. There's no use lying about it. And I ought to have done it; but some way—it's no excuse, I don't mean it for an excuse, only an explanation—some way I got in with the boys. I don't mean I was a drinker and all that. But I bought pictures and kept a horse and a yacht, and of course I had to pay my share of all expeditions, and—oh, what's the use!"

He broke off, turned, and threw his open palms out toward his brother, as if throwing aside the last attempt at an excuse.

"I *did* neglect you, and it's a damned shame! and I ask your forgiveness. Come, old man!"

He held out his hand, and Grant slowly approached and took it. There was a little silence. Then Howard went on, his voice trembling, the tears on his face.

"I want you to let me help you, old man. That's the way to forgive me. Will you?"

"Yes, if you can help me."

Howard squeezed his hand. "That's right, old man. Now you make me a boy again. Course I can help you. I've got ten—"

"I don't mean that, How." Grant's voice was very grave. "Money can't give me a chance now."

"What do you mean?"

"I mean life ain't worth very much to me. I'm too old to take a new start. I'm a dead failure. I've come to the conclusion that life's a failure for ninety-nine per cent of us. You can't help me now. It's too late."

The two men stood there, face to face, hands clasped, the one fair-skinned, full-lipped, handsome in his neat suit; the other tragic, sombre in his softened mood, his large, long, rugged Scotch face bronzed with sun and scarred with wrinkles that had histories, like saber cuts on a veteran, the record of his battles.

NOTES

1. A small ravine created by a stream. Garland referred to this story as "Up the Coulé" in a letter shortly before its publication, and that was its title in the 1891 edition published by the Arena firm; however, elsewhere (even here in the epigraph) Garland used variant spellings such as "coolly" and "coulee."
2. Mountain ranges in New Hampshire and Pennsylvania, respectively. Many summer resorts for city dwellers were located there.
3. An excellent high school located in La Crosse, Wisconsin. Despite being referred to as a "seminary," it was not for training priests.
4. A traveling salesman.

5. Most likely a reference to "quoits," a game played by throwing rings of some type toward a short pole or spike. The winner is the person who gets the most rings over the pole or spike or closest to it.

6. Native Americans were commonly believed by European Americans to have excellent posture.

7. Suitcase.

8. A durable shirt of the type worn by those who work outdoors a great deal.

9. Reference to an ox owned by the biblical figure of Job. This term was commonly used in rural areas at this time to emphasize a person's extreme poverty.

10. These are all clothing items Howard regards as casual, but to his mother and others on the farm they appear very dressy and expensive.

11. A colloquial expression for a provincial, unrefined person.

12. The formal uniform of a particular military regiment. Howard is trying to be lighthearted.

13. A mountain range in New York State, popular among vacationers from New York City.

14. A bird known for its shrill call that sounds like "kill-deer."

15. Howard here speaks simple German to the neighbor. "Ich bin Herr McLane" means "I am Mr. McLane"; "Yah; ich bin Herr Grant's bruder" means "Yes, I am Mr. Grant's brother"; "Ich bin durstig" means "I am thirsty"; and "Ich bin hier geboren" means "I was born here."

16. "Where is your good man/husband?" (German).

17. Ulysses S. Grant (1822–85) was a prominent general during the American Civil War and afterward served as president of the United States (1869–77). *The Personal Memoirs of U. S. Grant* was published in 1885. Quite coincidentally, Garland himself would later publish *Ulysses S. Grant: His Life and Character* in 1898.

18. At this time, native-born Americans often looked down on immigrants, including those from countries such as the Netherlands and Norway.

19. Someone who believes in an unregulated market economy. In this context, it signifies that the young man is an opponent of the Populist Party, founded in 1891, which sought fairer conditions for farmers and workers through government regulation of corporations and large businesses. Like Grant and most of the other men present in this scene, Garland himself was a strong supporter of the Populist Party.

20. Here this term is used to suggest an enslaved Black person who is forced to constantly work, has no freedom, and is less than human; later in the paragraph this term is used to refer specifically to enslaved African Americans before emancipation. While this term is sometimes used among Black people to refer to other Black people, in both the past and the present this term was and is usually intended to be derogatory and hurtful when used by non-Black people; it is thus deeply offensive and should not be used.

21. A group for a square dance, a type of folk dance popular in rural areas at this time.

22. A term commonly used at this time to refer to African Americans. It is now considered offensive and no longer acceptable.

23. A blanket term for a wide variety of digestion disorders, typically involving indigestion, loss of appetite, and weakness.

24. Jean-François Millet (1814–75) was a French painter well known for producing paintings that over-romanticized rural people and scenes, neglecting the harsh realities of agrarian living.
25. Waterproof boots
26. An extremely popular folk song originally composed in the nineteenth century that features a cabin with a leaky roof.

CHARLOTTE PERKINS GILMAN

(1860–1935)

Not long after Charlotte Perkins's birth in 1860, her father deserted the family, leaving her mother alone with two children to raise and no child support. As a result, Charlotte had a difficult childhood. When Charlotte married artist Walter Stetson in 1884 and gave birth to her daughter Katherine less than a year later, she seemed to have overcome her early difficulties and to be fulfilling the conventional role of a middle-class White woman. However, after suffering for an extended period from postpartum depression and realizing she needed to work in order to feel fulfilled, Charlotte Stetson became increasingly unhappy with the traditional expectations of marriage at the time and consequently separated from her husband, who had not encouraged her work. In 1887 she moved to California to pursue a career as a journalist and obtained an official divorce in 1894. Charlotte sent Katherine to live with her ex-husband on the East Coast, believing that he and his new wife would provide a better environment for her daughter than she could. This supposed "abandonment" of her daughter scandalized many people for its rejection of the supposed "natural" bond of mother and child. Charlotte, however, felt called to serve what she believed was a greater, larger purpose of using her writing, editing, and speaking talents to promote greater equality between men and women. She did remarry, in 1900, but this time it was to someone—a first cousin named George Houghton Gilman—who fully supported her work, which involved not only traveling to deliver many public lectures but also, from 1909 to 1916, serving as the sole editor and author of a magazine entitled the *Forerunner*. They remained happily married until his death in May 1934; she, suffering from terminal breast cancer, committed suicide about one year later.

In her fiction as well as in her nonfiction writing, Gilman wished to expose how husbands at the time abused their wives, show how the legal and economic systems established by men worked to oppress women, and promote the benefits of women working outside the home if they wished to. Today, Gilman is almost exclusively known as the author of a single short story she published in 1892: "The Yellow Wall-Paper." Initially read by contemporaries as a horror story, since its rediscovery and republication in 1973 it has been heralded as a loud, vigorous protest against patriarchal domination of women and now regularly appears in almost all major anthologies of American literature. Gilman, though, deserves to be remembered for more than just that one work. Her more than two hundred short stories, innumerable editorials and journalistic writings, novel *Herland* (1915), and magnum opus, *Women and Economics: A Study of the Economic Relation between Men and Women as a Factor in Social Evolution* (1898), stand together as strong testimony of a woman who was at the forefront of the struggle for women's rights in the late nineteenth and early twentieth centuries.

The story reprinted here, "Mrs. Beazley's Deeds," first appeared in the pages of *Woman's World* magazine in March 1911 and engaged many of the issues Gilman often foregrounded in her work; she undoubtedly chose this venue in order to reach a large audience of women who, for the most part, were adhering to traditional gender expectations. Gilman later reprinted this story in the *Forerunner* in June 1913; the text presented here is reproduced from that version.

MRS. BEAZLEY'S DEEDS (1911)

Mrs. William Beazley was crouching on the floor of her living-room over the store in a most peculiar attitude. It was what a doctor would call the "knee-chest position;" and the woman's pale, dragged out appearance quite justified the idea.

She was as one scrubbing a floor and then laying her cheek to it, a rather undignified little pile of bones, albeit discreetly covered with stringy calico.

A hard voice from below suddenly called "Maria!" and when she jumped nervously, and hurried downstairs in answer, the cause of the position became apparent—she had been listening at a stovepipe hole.

In the store sat Mr. Beazley, quite comfortable in his back-tilted chair, enjoying a leisurely pipe and as leisurely a conversation with another smoking, back-tilting man, beside the empty stove.

"This lady wants some cotton elastic," said he; "you know where those dew-dabs are better'n I do."

A customer, also in stringy calico, stood at the counter. Mrs. Beazley waited on her with the swift precision of long practice, and much friendliness besides, going with her to the wagon afterwards, and standing there to chat, her thin little hand on the wheel as if to delay it.

"Maria!" called Mr. Beazley.

"Oh, good land!" said Mrs. Janeway, gathering up the reins.

"Well—good-by, Mrs. Janeway—do come around when you can; I can't seem to get down to Rockwell."

"Maria!" She hurried in. "Ain't supper ready yet?" inquired Mr. Beazley.

"It'll be ready at six, same as it always is," she replied wearily, turning again to the door. But her friend had driven off and she went slowly up-stairs.

Luella was there. Luella was only fourteen, but a big, courageous-looking girl, and prematurely wise from many maternal confidences. "Now you sit down and rest," she said. "I'll set the table and call Willie and everything. Baby's asleep all right."

Willie, shrilly summoned from the window, left his water wheel reluctantly and came in dripping and muddy.

"Never mind, mother," said Luella. "I'll fix him up in no time; supper's all ready."

"I can't eat a thing," said Mrs. Beazley, "I'm so worried!" She vibrated nervously in the wooden rocker by the small front window. Her thin hands gripped the arms; her mouth quivered—a soft little mouth that seemed to miss the smiles naturally belonging to it.

"It's another of them deeds!" she was saying over and over in her mind. "He'll do it. He's no right to do it, but he will; he always does. He don't care what I want—nor the children."

When the supper was over Willie went to bed, and Luella minding the store and the baby, Mr. Beazley tipped back his chair and took to his toothpick. "I've got another deed for you to sign, Mrs. Beazley," said he. "Justice Fielden said he'd be along to-night sometime, and we can fix it before him—save takin' it to town."

"What's it about?" she demanded. "I've signed away enough already. What you sellin' now."

Mr. Beazley eyed her contemptuously. The protest that had no power of resistance won scant consideration from a man like him.

"It's a confounding foolish law," said he, meditatively. "What do women know about business, anyway! You just tell him you're perfectly willin' and under no compulsion, and sign the paper—that's all you have to do!"

"You might as well tell me what you're doin'—I have to read the deed anyhow."

"Much you'll make out of readin' the deed," said he, with some dry amusement, "and Justice Fielden lookin' on and waitin' for you!"

"You're going to sell the Rockford lot—I know it!" said she. "How can you do it, William! The very last piece of what father left me!—and it's mine—you can't sell it—I don't sign!"

Mr. Beazley minded her outcry no more than he minded the squawking of a to-be beheaded hen.

"Seems to me you know a lot," he observed, eyeing her with shrewd scrutiny. Then without a word he rose to his lank height, went out to the woodshed and hunted about, returning with an old piece of tin. This he took up-stairs with him, and a sound of hammering told Mrs. Beasley that one source of information was closed to her completely.

"You'd better not take that up, Mrs. Beazley," said he, returning. "It makes it drafty round your feet up there. I always wondered at them intuitions of yours—guess they wasn't so remarkable after all."

"Now before Mr. Fielden comes, seein' as you are so far on to this business, we may as well talk it out. I suppose you'll admit that you're a woman—and that you don't know anything about business, and that it's a man's place to take care of his family to the best of his ability."

"You just go ahead and say what you want to—you needn't wait for any admits from me! What I know is my father left me a lot o' land—left it to me—to take care of me and the children, and you've sold it all—in spite of me—but this one lot."

"We've sold it, Mrs. Beazley; you've signed the deeds."

"Yes, I know I have—you made me."

"Now, Mrs. Beazley! Haven't you always told Justice Fielden that you were under no compulsion?"

"O yes—I told him so—what's the use of fightin' over everything! But that house in Rockford is mine—where I was brought up—and I want to keep it for the children. If you'd only live there, William, I'd take boarders and be glad to—to keep the old home! And you could sell that water power—or lease it—"

Mr. Beazley's face darkened. "You're talking nonsense, Mrs. Beazley—and too much of it. 'Women are words and men are deeds' is a good sayin'. But what's more to the purpose is Bible sayin'—this fool law is a mere formality—you know the real law—'Wives submit yourselves to your husbands!'"[1]

He lit his pipe and rose to go outside, adding, "Oh, by the way, here 'tis Friday night, and I clean forgot to tell you—there's a boarder comin' to-morrow."

"A boarder—for who?"

"For you, I guess—you'll see more of her than I shall, seein' as it's a woman."

"William Beazley! Have you gone and taken a boarder without even askin' me?" The little woman's hands shook with excitement. Her voice rose in a plaintive crescendo, with a helpless break at the end.

"Saves a lot of trouble, you see; now you'll have no time to worry over it; and yet you've got a day to put her room in order."

"Her room! What room? We've got no room for ourselves over this store. William—I won't have it! I can't—I haven't the strength!"

"Oh, nonsense, Mrs. Beazley! You've got nothin' to do but keep house for a small family—and tend to store now and then when I'm busy. As to room, give her Luella's, of course. She can sleep on the couch, and Willie can sleep in the attic. Why, Morris Whiting's wife has six boarders—down at Ordways' there're eight."

"Yes—and they are near dead, both of them women! It's little they get from their boarders! Just trouble and work and the insultin' manners of those city people—and their husbands pocketing all the money. And now you expect me—in four rooms—to turn my children out of doors to take one—and a woman at that; more trouble'n three men! I won't, I tell you!"

Luella came in at this point and put a sympathetic arm around her. "Bert Fielden was in just now," she told her father. "He says his father had to go to the city and won't be back for some time—left word for you about it."

"Oh, well," said Mr. Beazley philosophically, "a few days more or less won't make much difference, I guess. That bein' the case you better help your mother wash up and then go to bed, both of you," and he took himself off to lounge on the steps of the store, smoking serenely.

Next day at supper time the boarder came. Mr. Beazley met her at the station and brought her and her modest trunk back with him. He took occasion on the journey to inform the lady that one reason for his making to arrangement was that he thought his wife needed company—intelligent company of her own sex.

"She's nervous and notional and kinder dreads it, now it's all arranged," he said; "but I know she'll like you first rate."

He himself was most favorably impressed, for the woman was fairly young, undeniably good looking, and had a sensible, prompt friendliness that was most attractive.

The drive was quite a long one and slower than mere length accounted for, owing to the nature of rural roads in mountain districts; and Mr. Beazley found himself talking more freely than was his habit with strangers, and pointing out the attractive features of the place with fluency.

Miss Lawrence was observant, interested, appreciative.

"There ought to be good water power in that river," she suggested; "what a fine place for a mill. Why, there was a mill, wasn't there?"

"Yes," said he. "That place belonged to my wife's father. Her father had a mill there in the old times when we had tanneries and saw mills all along in this country. They've cut out most of the hemlock now."

"That's a pleasant looking house on it, too. Do you live there?"

"No—we live quite a piece beyond—up at Shade City. This is Rockwell we're going through. It's a growin' place—if the railroad ever gets in here as they talk about."

Mr. Beazley looked wise. He knew a good deal more about that railroad than was worth mentioning to a woman. Meanwhile he speculated inwardly on his companion's probable standing and profession.

"She's Miss, all right, and no chicken," he said to himself, "but looks young enough, too. Can't have much money or she'd not be boardin' with us, up here. Schoolma'am, I guess."

"Find school-teachin' pretty wearin'?" he hazarded.

"School teaching? Oh, there are harder professions than that," she replied lightly. "Do I look so tired?"

"I have a friend in the girl's high school who gets very much exhausted by the summer time," she pursued. "When I am tired I prefer the sea; but this year I wanted a perfectly quiet place—and I believe I've found one. Oh, how pretty, it is!" she cried as they rounded a steep hill shoulder and skirted the river to their destination. Shade City was well named, in part at least, for it stood in a crack of the mountains and saw neither sunrise nor sunset.

The southern sun warmed it at midday, and the north wind cooled it well; there was hardly room for the river and the road; and the "City" consisted of five or six houses, a blacksmith shop and "the store," strung along the narrow banks.

But the little pass had its strategic value for a country trader, lying between wide mountain valleys and concentrating all their local traffic.

"Maria!" called Mr. Beazley. "Here's Miss Lawrence, I'll take her trunk up right now. Luella! Show Miss Lawrence where her room is! You can't miss it, Miss Lawrence—we haven't got so many."

Mrs. Beazley's welcome left much to be desired; Luella wore an air of subdued hostility, and Willie, caught by his father in unobserved derision, was cuffed and warned to behave or he'd be sorry.

But Miss Lawrence took no notice. She came down to supper simply dressed, fresh and cheerful. She talked gaily, approved the food, soon won Luella's interest, and captured Willie by a small mechanical puzzle she brought out of her pocket. Her hostess remained cold, however, and stood out for some days against the constant friendliness of her undesired guest.

"I'll take care of my own room," said Miss Lawrence. "I like to, and then I've so little to do here—and you have so much. What would I prefer to eat? Whatever you have—it's a change I'm after, you know—not just what I get at home."

After a little while, Mrs. Beazley owned to a friend and customer that her boarder was "no more trouble than a man, and a sight more agreeable."

"What does she do all the time?" asked the visitor. "You've got no piazza."

"She ain't the piazza kind," answered Mrs. Beazley. "She's doing what they call nature study. She tramps off with an opera glass and a book—Willie likes to go with her, and she's tellin' him a lot about birds and plants and stones and things. She gets mushrooms, too—and cooks them herself—and eats them. Says they are better than meat and cheaper. I don't like to touch them myself, but it does save money."

In about a week Mrs. Beazley hauled down her flag and capitulated. In two she grew friendly—in three, confidential, and when she heard through Luella and Bert Fielden that his father would soon be back now—her burden of trouble overflowed—the overhanging loss of her last bit of property.

"It's not only because it's our old place and I love it," she said; "and it's not only because it would be so much better for the children—though that's enough—but it would be better business to live there—and I can't make him see it!"

"He thinks he sees way beyond it, doesn't he?"

"Of course—but you know how men are! Oh, no, you don't; you're not married. He's all for buyin' and sellin' and makin' money, and I think half the time he loses and won't let me know."

"The store seems to be popular, doesn't it?"

"Not so much as it would be if he'd attend to it. But he won't stock up as he ought to—and he takes everything he can scrape and puts it into land—and then sells that and gets more. And he swaps horses, and buys up stuff at 'andoos'[2] and sells it again—he's always speculatin'. And he won't let me send Luella to school—nor Willie half the time—and now—but I've no business talkin' to you like this, Miss Lawrence!"

"If it's any relief to your mind, Mrs. Beazley, I wish you would. It is barely possible that I may be of some use. My father is in the real estate business and knows a good deal about these mountain lands."

"Well, it's no great story—I'm not complainin' of Mr. Beazley, understand—only about this property. It does seem as if it was mine—and I do have to sign deeds—but he will sell it off!"

"Why do you let him, if you feel sure he is wrong!"

"Let him!—Oh, well you ain't married! Let him! Miss Lawrence, you don't know men!"

"But still, Mrs. Beazley, if you want to keep your property—"

"O, Miss Lawrence, you don't understand—here am I and here's the children, and none of us can get away, and if I don't do as he says I must, he takes it out of us—that's all. You can't do nothin' with a man like that—and him with the Bible on his side!"

Miss Lawrence meditated for some moments.

"Have you ever thought of leaving him?" she ventured.

"Oh, yes, I've thought of it; my sister's always wantin' me to. But I don't believe in divorce—and if I did, this is New York state and I couldn't get it."[3]

"It's pretty hard on the children, isn't it?"

"That's what I can't get reconciled to. I've had five children, Miss Lawrence. My oldest boy went off when he was only twelve, he couldn't stand his father—he used to punish him so—seems as if he did it to make me give in, So he never had proper schoolin' and can't earn much—he's fifteen now—I don't hear from him very often, and he never was very strong." Mrs. Beazley's eyes filled. "He hates the city, too, and he'd come back to me any day—if it wasn't for his father."

"You had five, you say?"

"Yes, there was a baby between Willie and this one—but it died. We're so far up from a doctor, and he wouldn't hitch up—said it was all my nonsense till it was too late! And this baby's delicate—just the way he was!" The tears ran down now, but the faded little woman wiped them off resignedly and went on.

"It's worst now for Luella. Luella's at an age when she oughtn't to be tendin' store the whole time—she ought to be at a good school. There's too many young fellows hangin' around here already. Luella's large for her age, and pretty. I was good lookin' when I was Luella's age, Miss Lawrence, and I got married not much later—girls don't know nothing!"

Miss Lawrence studied her unhappy little face with attention.

"How old should you think I was, Mrs. Beazley?"

Mrs. Beazley, struggling between politeness and keen observation, guessed twenty-seven.

"Ten years short," she answered cheerfully. "I was thirty-seven this very month."

"What!" cried the worn woman in calico. "You're older'n I am! I'm only thirty-two!"

"Yes, I'm a lot older, you see, and I'm going to presume on my age now, and on some business experience, and commit the unpardonable sin of interfering

between man and wife—in the interest of the children. It seems to me, Mrs. Beazley, that you owe it them to make a stand.

"Think now—before it is too late. If you kept possession of this property in
Rockwell, and had control of your share of what has been sold heretofore—could
you live on it?"

"Why, I guess so. There's the house, my sister's in it now—she takes boarders
and pays us rent—she thinks I get the money. We could make something that
way."

"How much land is there?"

"There's six acres in all. There's the home lot right there in town, and the
strip next to it down to the falls—we own the falls—both sides."

"Isn't that rather valuable? You could lease the water power, I should think."

"There was some talk of a 'lectric company takin' it—but it fell through. He
wouldn't sell to them—said he'd sell nothin' to Sam Hunt—just because he was
an old friend of mine. Sam keeps a good store down to Rockwell, and he was in
that company—got it up, I think. Mr. Beazley was always jealous of Sam—and
'twan't me at all he wanted—'twas my sister."

"But, Mrs. Beazley, think. If you and your sister could keep house together
you could make a home for the children, and your boy would come back to you.
If you leased or sold the falls you could afford to send Luella away to school.
Willie could go to school in town—the baby would do better down there where
there is more sunlight, I'm sure—why do you not make a stand for the children's
sake?"

Mrs. Beazley looked at her with a faint glimmer of hope. "If I only could,"
she said.

"Has Mr. Beazley any property of his own?" pursued Miss Lawrence.

"Property! He's got debts. Old ones and new ones. He was in debt when I
married him—and he's made more."

"But the proceeds of these sales you tell me of?"

"Oh, he has some trick about that. He banks it in my name or something—so
his creditors can't get it. He always gets ahead of everybody."

"M-m-m," said Miss Lawrence.

* * * * * * * *

Mr. Beazley had a long ride before him the next day; he was to drive to Princev-
ille for supplies.

An early breakfast was prepared and consumed, with much fault finding on
his part—and he started off by six o'clock in a bad temper, unrestrained by the
presence of Miss Lawrence, who had not come down.

"Whoa! Hold up!" he cried, stopping the horses with a spiteful yank as they
had just settled into the collar.

"Maria!"

"Well—what you forgotten?"

"Forgot nothin'! I've remembered something; see that you're on hand tonight—don't go gallivantin' down to Rockwell or anywhere just because I'm off. Justice Fielden's comin' up and we've got to settle that business I told you about. See't you're here! Gid ap!"

The big wagon lumbered off across the bridge, around the corner, into the hidden wood road.

When Mr. Beazley returned the late dusk had fallen thickly in the narrow pass. He was angry at being late, for he had counted much on having this legal formality in his own house—where he could keep a sterner hand on his wife.

He was tired, too, and in a cruel temper, as the sweating horses showed.

"Willie!" he shouted. "Here you, Willie! Come and take the horses!" No hurrying, frightened child appeared.

"Maria!" he yelled. "Maria! Where's that young one! Luella! Maria!"

He clambered down, swearing under his breath; and rushed to the closed front door. It was locked.

"What in Halifax!" he muttered, shaking and banging vainly. Then he tried the side door—the back door—the woodshed—all were locked and the windows shut tight with sticks over them. His face darkened with anger.

"They've gone off—the whole of them—and I told her she'd got to be here to-night. Gone to Rockwell, of course, leavin' the store, too. We'll have a nice time when she comes back! That young one needs a lickin'."

He attended to the horses after a while, leaving the loaded wagon in the barn, and then broke a pane of glass in a kitchen window and let himself in.

A damp, clean, soapy smell greeted him. He struck matches and looked for a lamp. There was none. The room was absolutely empty. So were the closet, pantry and cellar. So were the four rooms up-stairs and the attic. So was the store.

"Halifax!" said Mr. Beazley. He was thoroughly mystified now, and his rage died in bewilderment.

A knocking at the door called him.

It was not Justice Fielden, however, but Sam Hunt.

"I heard you brought up a load of goods, today," said he easily; "and I thought you might like to sell 'em. I bought out the rest of the stuff this morning, and the store, and the good-will o' the business—and this lot isn't much by itself."

Mr. Beazley looked at him with a blackening countenance.

"You bought out this store, did you? I'd like to know who you bought it of!"

"Why, the owner, of course! Mrs. Beazley; paid cash on the nail, too. I've bought it, lock, stock and barrel—cows, horses, hens and cats. You don't own the wagon, even. As to your clothes—they're in that trunk yonder. However, keep your stuff—you'll need some capital," with this generous parting shot Mr. Hunt drove off.

Mr. Beazley retired to the barn. He had no wish to consult his neighbors for further knowledge.

Mrs. Beazley had gone to her sister's, no doubt.

And she had dared to take this advantage of him—of the fact that the property stood in her name—Sam Hunt had put her up to it. He'd have the law on them—it was a conspiracy.

Then he went to sleep on the hay, muttering vengeance for the morrow.

The strange atmosphere awoke him early, and he breakfasted on some crackers from his wagon.

Then he grimly set forth on foot for the village, refusing offered lifts from the loads of grinning men who passed him. He presented himself at the door of his wife's house in the village at an early hour. Her sister opened it.

"Well," she said, holding he door-knob in her hand, "What do you want at this time in the morning?"

"I want my family," said he. "I'll have you know a man has some rights in his family at any rate."

"There's no family of yours in this house, William Beazley," said she grimly. "No, I'm not a liar—never had that reputation. You can come in and search the house if you please—after the boarders are up."

"Where is my wife?" he demanded.

"I don't know, thank goodness, and I don't think you'll find her very soon either," she added to herself, as he turned and marched off without further words.

In the course of the morning he presented himself at Justice Fielden's office.

"Gone off, has she?" inquired the Judge genially. "Or just gone visiting, I guess. Forgot to leave word."

"It's not only that, I want to know my rights in this case, Judge. I've been to the bank—and she's drawn every cent. Every cent of my property."

"Wasn't it her property, Mr. Beazley?"

"Some of it was, and some of it wasn't. All I've made since we was married was in there, too. I've speculated quite a bit, you know, buying and selling—there was considerable money."

"How on earth could she get your money out of the bank?" asked Mr. Fielden.

"Why, it was in her name, of course; matter of business, you understand."

"Why, yes; I understand, I guess. Well, I don't see exactly what you can do about it, Mr. Beazley. You technically gave her the property, you see, and she's taken it—that's all there is to it."

"She's sold out the store!" broke in Mr. Beazley, "all the stock, the fixtures—she couldn't do that, could she?"

"Appears as if she had, don't it? It was rather overbearin' I do think, and you can bring suit for compensation for your services—you tended the store, of course?"

"If I knew where she was——" said Mr. Beazley slowly, with a grinding motion of his fingers. "But she's clean gone—and the children, too."

"If she remains away that constitutes desertion, of course," said the Judge briskly, "and your remedy is clear. You can get a separation—in due time. If you cared to live in another state long enough you could get a divorce—not in New York, though. Being in New York, and not knowing where your wife is, I don't just see what you can do about it. Do you care to employ detectives?"

"No," said Mr. Beazley, "not yet."

Suddenly he started up.

"There's Miss Lawrence," said he. "She'll know something," and he darted out after her.

She came into the little office, calm, smiling, daintily arrayed.

"Do you know where my wife is, Miss Lawrence?" he demanded.

"Yes," she replied pleasantly.

"Well—where is she?"

"That I am not at liberty to tell you, Mr. Beazley. But any communication you may wish to make to her you can make through me. And I can attend to any immediate business. She has given me power of attorney."

Justice Fielden's small eyes were twinkling.

"You never knew you had a counsel learned in the law at your place, did you? Miss Lawrence is the best woman lawyer in New York, Mr. Beazley—just going kinder incog[4] for a vacation."

"Are you at the bottom of all this deviltry?" said the angry man, turning upon her fiercely.

"If you mean that Mrs. Beazley is acting under my advice, yes. I found that she had larger business interests than she supposed, and that they were not being well managed. I happened to be informed as to real estate values in this locality, and was able to help her. We needed a good deal of ready money to take advantage of our opportunity, and Mr. Hunt was willing to help us out on the stock."

He set his teeth and looked at her with growing fury, to which she paid no attention whatever.

"I advised Mrs. Beazley to take the children and go away for a complete change and rest, and to leave me to settle this matter. I was of the opinion that you and I could make business arrangements more amiably perhaps."

"What do you mean business arrangements?" he asked.

"We are prepared to make you this offer: If you will sign the deed of separation I have here, agreeing to waive all rights in the children and live out of the state, we will give you five thousand dollars. In case you reappear in the state, you will be liable for debts, and for—you remember that little matter of the wood lot deal?"

"That's a fair offer, I think," said Justice Fielden. "I always told you that wood lot matter would get you into trouble if your wife got on to it—and cared to push it. I think you'd better take up with this proposition."

"What's she going to do—a woman alone? What are the children going to do? A man can't give up his family this way."

"You need not be at all concerned about that," she answered. "Mrs. Beazley's plans are open and aboveboard. She is going to enlarge her house and keep boarders. Her sister is to marry Mr. Hunt, as you doubtless know. The children are to be properly educated. There is nothing you need fear for your family."

"And how about me? I—if I could just talk to her?"

"That is exactly what I advised my client to avoid. She has gone to a quiet, pleasant place for this summer. She needs a long rest, and you and I can settle this little matter without any feeling, you see."

"What with summers in quiet places, and enlarging the house, you seem to have found a good deal more in that property than I did," said he with a sneer.

"That is not improbable," she replied sweetly. "Here is the agreement; take the offer or leave it."

"And if I don't take it? Then what'll you do?"

"Nothing. You may continue to live here if you insist—and pay your debts by your own exertions. You can get employment, no doubt, of your friends and neighbors."

Mr. Beazley looked out of the window. Quite a number of his friends and neighbors were gathered together around Hunt's store, and as each new arrival was told the story, they slapped their thighs and roared with laughter.

Judge Fielden smiling dryly, threw up the sash.

"Clean as a whistle!" he heard Sturgis Black's strident voice. "Not so much as a cat to kick! Nobody to holler at! No young ones to lick! Nothin' whatsomever to eat! You should a heard him bangin' on the door!"

"And him a luggin' in that boarder just to spite her," crowed old Sam Wiley— "that was the last straw I guess."

"Well, he was always an enterprisin' man," said Horace Johnson. "Better at specilatin' with his wife's property than workin' with his hands. Guess he'll have to hunt a job now, though."

"He ain't likely to git one in a hurry—not in this county—unless Sam Hunt'll take him in." Wiley yelled again at this.

"Have you got that deed drawn up?" said Mr. Beazley harshly—"I'll sign."

NOTES

1. In Ephesians 5:22 (King James Version) appears the line "Wives, submit yourselves unto your own husbands, as unto the Lord," and in Colossians 3:18, this appears in a slightly altered form: "Wives, submit yourselves unto your own husbands, as it is fit in the Lord." These lines have commonly been used to justify the belief that wives should obey their husbands.

2. Short for "vandoos," small wagons or carts used by tradespeople to transport their goods.

3. In New York State at this time, a husband's abuse did not provide legal justification for divorce; the only accepted ground for divorce was adultery.

4. Short for "incognito," meaning to have one's identity concealed.

C. C. (CHARLES CARROLL) GOODWIN

(1832–1917)

Like so many writers about the American West in the nineteenth century, C. C. Goodwin was a transplanted easterner, originally from upstate New York. In 1852, at the age of twenty, Goodwin moved to Marysville, California, a small mining community high in the Sierra Nevada mountains. While engaged in various business ventures and serving as a teacher, Goodwin studied law with his brother and began practicing in 1859. The next year, he moved to Nevada and was shortly thereafter elected as a district judge; even though he served as such for a comparatively short time, for the rest of his life he would be referred to as "Judge Goodwin." Around this time, Goodwin also began his career as a newspaper editor, serving in various small-town Nevada communities but eventually moving to Salt Lake City and becoming the editor of the *Salt Lake Tribune* in 1880. From his editorial pulpit, which he occupied until around the turn of the century, he not only opposed women's suffrage but also railed against the Mormon practice of polygamy, which made him many enemies in Utah. During these years, Goodwin also found the time to write two novels, *The Comstock Club* (1891) and *The Wedge of Gold* (1893); he later published a collection of reminiscences about other early figures in Nevada and California entitled *As I Remember Them* (1913), which one advertisement described as "Fascinating Stories of Various Members of the Royal Band That Came to Settle the Great West in the Olden, Golden Days." Toward the end of his life, Goodwin served as editor of *Goodwin's Weekly: A Thinking Paper for Thinking People*, founded in 1902 by his son James; he continued in this position until his death in 1917.

"Sister Celeste" was originally published in the *Salt Lake Tribune* on April 5, 1885, when Goodwin was its editor; this is the version reprinted here. Drawing on his intimate knowledge of early mining communities in the West, it introduces a figure not usually associated with fictions about this region: a Catholic nun. A few years after its original publication, Goodwin had one character in his 1891 novel, *The Comstock Club*, tell Sister Celeste's story—with a slightly different ending—as a narrative intended to comfort a grieving friend.

SISTER CELESTE (1885)

In one of the mountain towns of Northern California, a good many years ago, while yet good women, compared to the number of the men, were so disproportionately few, suddenly one day upon the street, clad in the unattractive garb of a Sister of Charity,[1] appeared a woman whose marvelous loveliness the coarse garments and uncouth hood peculiar to the order could not conceal. There was a Sisters' Hospital in the place, and this nun was one of the devoted women who had come to minister to the sick in that Hospital. She was of medium size and height, and despite her shapeless garments, it was easy to see that her form was beautiful. The hand that carried a basket was a delicate one; under her unsightly hood glimpses of a brow as white as a planet's light could be caught; the coarse shoes upon her feet were three sizes too large. When she raised her eyes, from the inner depths a light like that of kindly stars shone out, and, though a Sister of Charity, there was something about her lips which seemed to say that of all famines, a famine of kisses was hardest to endure. There was a

STATELY, KINDLY DIGNITY

In her mien, but in all her ways there was a dainty grace, which, upon the hungry eyes of the miners of that mountain town, shone like enchantment. She could not have been more than twenty years of age.

It was told that she was known as "Sister Celeste," that she had recently come to the Western Coast, it was believed from France, and that was all that was known of her. When the Mother Superior at the Hospital was questioned about the new Sister, she simply answered: "Sister Celeste is a Sister now, she will be a glorified saint by and by." The first public appearance of Sister Celeste in the town was one Sunday afternoon, when she emerged from the Hospital and started to carry some delicacy to a poor, sick woman—a Mrs. De Lacy, who lived at the opposite end of the town from the Hospital; so to visit her the Nun was obliged to walk almost the whole length of the one long, crooked street which, in the narrow canyon, included all the business portion of the town. When the Nun started out from the Hospital, the town was full of miners, as was the habit in those days on Sunday afternoons, and as the Sister passed along the street

HUNDREDS OF EYES

Were bent upon her. She seemed unconscious of the attention she was attracting; had she been walking in her sleep she could not have been more composed.

Many were the comments made as she passed out of the hearing of different groups of men. One big, rough miner, who had just accepted an invitation to drink, caught sight of the vision, watched the Sister as she passed, and then said to the companion who had asked him: "Excuse me, Bob; I have a feeling as though my soul had just partaken of the Sacrament; no more gin for me today." Said another: "It is a fearful pity. That woman was born to be loved, and to love somebody better than nine hundred and ninety out of every thousand could. Her occupation is, in her case, a sin against nature. Every hour her heart must protest against the starvation which it feels; every day she must feel upon her robes the clasp of little hands which are not to be." One boisterous miner, a little in his cups,[2] watched until the Sister disappeared around a bend in the crooked street, and then cried out: "Did you see her, boys? That is the style of a woman that a man could die for, and smile while dying, Oh! Oh!" Then drawing from his belt a buckskin purse, he held it aloft and shouted: "Here are eighty ounces of the cleanest dust[3] ever mined in Bear Gulch; it's all I have in the world, but I will

GIVE THE LAST GRAIN

To any bruiser in this camp who will look crooked at that Sister when she comes back this way, and let me see him do it. In just a minute and a half there would not be enough left of him for the Coroner to gather in a sack and sit on." After that, daily, for all the following week, Sister Celeste was seen going to and returning from the sick woman's house. It suddenly grew to be a habit with everybody to uncover their heads as Sister Celeste came by.

Sunday came around again, and it was noticed that on that morning the Nun went early to visit her charge, and remained longer than usual. On her return, when just about opposite the main saloon of the place, a kindly, elderly gentleman, who was universally known and respected, ventured to cross the path of the Sister, and addressed her as follows:

"I beg pardon, good Sister, but you are attending upon a sick person. We understand that it is a woman; may I not ask if we can not in some way assist you and your patient?" A faint flush swept over the glorious face of Sister Celeste as she raised her eyes, but simply and frankly, and with a slight French accent, she answered:

"The lady, kind sir, is very ill. Unless, in some way, we can manage to remove her to the Hospital, where she can have an evenly warmed room, and close nursing, I fear she will not live; but she is penniless, and we are very poor, and, moreover, I do not see how she can be moved, for there are no carriages."

She spoke with perfect distinctness, notwithstanding the slight foreign accent. The accent was no impediment; rather, from her lips, it gave her words a rhythm like music.

The man raised his voice, "Boys," he shouted, "there is a suffering woman up the street; she is

VERY DESTITUTE AND VERY ILL,

And must be removed to the Hospital. The first thing required is some money." Then taking off his hat with one hand, with the other he took from his pocket a twenty dollar piece; he put the money in the hat, then he sprang upon a low stump that was standing by the trail, and added: "I start the subscription; those who have a trifle that they can spare, will please pass around this way and drop the trifle, as they pass, into the hat." Then Sister Celeste had a new experience. In an instant she was surrounded by a shouting, surging, struggling crowd, all eager to contribute. There was a babel of voices, but for once a California crowd was awakened to full roar without an oath being heard. The boys could not swear in the presence of Sister Celeste. In a few minutes between seven and eight hundred dollars was raised. It was poured out of the hat into a buckskin purse; the purse was tied, and handed by the man who first addressed her, to Sister Celeste, with the remark that it was for her poor, and that when she needed more the boys would "stand in."

Again the Nun raised her eyes and in a low voice which trembled a little she said: "Please salute the gentlemen, and say to them, that God will keep the account." The man turned around and with an awkward laugh said: "Boys! I am authorized, by one of His angels, to say that, for your contribution, God has taken down your names, and given you credit."

Then a wild fellow cried out from the crowd:

"Three cheers for the angel!"

The cheers rang out like the braying of a thousand trumpets in accord. Then, in hoarse under-tones, a voice shouted "Tiger,"[4] and the deep-toned old-day California "Tiger" rolled up the hillsides like an ocean roar. It would have startled an ordinary woman, but Sister Celeste was looking at the purse, and it is doubtful if she heard it at all. Then, the first speaker called from the crowd eight men by name, and said:

"You were all married men in the States, and for all that I know to the contrary, were decent, respectable gentlemen. As

MASTER OF CEREMONIES,

I delegate you, as there are no carriages in this camp, to go to the sick woman's house, and carry her to the Hospital, while the good Sister proceeds in advance, and makes a place for her." This was agreed to, and the Sister was told that in half an hour she might expect her patient.

Then she turned away, the crowd watching her, and remarking that her usual stately step seemed greatly quickened. Long after, the Mother Superior[5] related that when Sister Celeste reached the Hospital on that day she fell sobbing into the Mother's arms, and when she could command her voice, said: "Those shaggy men, that I thought were all tigers, are all angels disguised. Oh Mother! I have seen them as Moses and Elias were when the Master was transfigured."[6]

The eight men held a brief consultation in the street; then going to a store, they bought a pair of heavy white blankets, an umbrella, and four pick-handles. Borrowing a packer's needle and some twine, they proceeded to sew the pick-handles into the sides of the blankets, first rolling the handles around once or twice in the edges of the blanket. They then proceeded to the sick woman's house; one went in first, and told the woman, gently, what they had come to do, and bade her have no fears: that she was to be moved so gently that, if she would close her eyes, she would not know anything about it. The others were called in; the blanket was laid upon the floor; the bed was lifted with its burden from the bedstead and laid on the blankets, the covers were neatly tucked under the mattress; four men seized the pick-handles at the sides,

LIFTED THE BED,

Woman and all from the floor; a fifth man stepped outside, raised the umbrella, and held it above the woman's face, and so, as gently as ever a mother rocked her babe to sleep, the sick woman was carried the whole length of the street to the Hospital, where Sister Celeste and the Mother Superior received her.

Then all hands went up town and talked the matter over, and I am afraid that some of them drank a little, but the burden of all the talk, and all the toasts, was Sister Celeste.

After that the Nun was often seen going on her errands of mercy, and it is true that some men who had been rough, and who had drank hard for months previous to the coming of the Sister, grew quiet in their lives, and ceased going to the saloons.

One day a most laughable event transpired. Two men got quarreling in the street, which in a moment culminated in a fight. The friends of the respective men joined in, and soon there was a general fight in which perhaps thirty men were engaged. When it was at its height (and such a fight meant something), Sister Celeste suddenly turned the sharp bend of the street, and came into full view not sixty yards from where the melee was raging in full fury. One of the fighters saw her, and made a sound between a hiss and a low whistle, a peculiar sound of alarm and warning, so significant that all looked up.

In an instant the men clapped their hands into their side pockets, and commenced moving away, some of them whistling low, and dancing as they went, as though the whole thing was but

A JOVIAL LARK.

When Sister Celeste reached the spot, a moment afterward, the street was entirely clear. The men washed their faces; some wag began to describe the comical scene which they made when they concluded that the street under certain circumstances was no good place for a fight; good humor was restored, the chief contestants shook hands with perfect cordiality, a drink of reconciliation was ordered all around, and when the glasses were emptied a man cried out: "Fill up once more boys. I want you to drink with me the health of the only capable peace officer that we have ever had in town—'Sister Celeste.'" The health was drunk with enthusiasm.

The winter came on at length, and there was much sickness. Sister Celeste redoubled her exertions; she was seen at all hours of the day, and was met sometimes, as late as midnight, returning from her watch beside a sick bed.

The town was full of rough men; some of them would cut or shoot at a word; but Sister Celeste never felt afraid. Indeed since that Sabbath when the subscription was taken up in the street, she had felt that nothing sinister could ever happen to her in that place. Once, however, she met a jolly miner who had been in town too long, and who had started for home a good deal the worse for liquor. She met him in a lonely place, where the houses had been a few days previous burned down on both sides of the street. Emboldened by rum, the man stepped directly in front of the nun, and said:

"My pretty Sister, I will give your Hospital a thousand dollars for one kiss."

The Sister never wavered; she raised her calm, undaunted eyes to the face of the man; an incandescent whiteness warmed upon her cheek, giving to her striking face unwonted splendor; for a moment she held the man under the spell of her eyes, then stretching her right arm out toward the sky, slowly and with infinite sadness in her tones, said:

"If your mother is watching from there, what will she think of her son?" The man fell on his knees, crying, "Pardon!" and Sister Celeste, with her accustomed stately step, passed slowly on her way.

Next day, an envelope directed to Sister Celeste was received at the Hospital. Within there was nothing but a certificate of deposit from a local bank for

ONE THOUSAND DOLLARS,

Made to the credit of the Hospital.

On another occasion the Nun had a still harder trial to bear. A young man was stricken with typhoid fever, and sent to the Hospital. He was a rich and handsome man. He had come from the East only a few weeks before he was taken down. His business in California was to settle the estate of an uncle who had died some months previous, leaving a large property.

When carried to the Hospital, Sister Celeste was appointed his nurse. The fever ran twenty-one days, and when it left him, finally, he lay helpless as a child and hovering on the very threshold of the grave for days.

With a sick man's whim, no one could do anything for him but Sister Celeste. She had to move him on his pillows, give him his medicines, and such food as he could bear. In lifting him, her arms were often around him, and her bosom was so near his breast that she could feel the throbbing of his heart.

As health slowly returned the young man watched the nurse, with steadily increasing interest. At length the time came when the physician said that the patient would require no further attention, but that he ought, so soon as possible, to go to the seaside, where the salt air would furnish him the tonic that he needed most.

When the physician went away, the young man said: "Sister Celeste, sit down, and let us talk." She obeyed. "Let me hold your hand," he said. "I want to tell you of my mother and my home, and with your hand in mine it will seem as though the dear ones there were by my side." She gave him her hand in silence. Then he told her of his beautiful home in the east, of the love that had always been a benediction in that home; of his mother and little sister, of their daily life, and their unbroken happiness. Insidiously,

THE STORY FLOWED ON,

Until at length he said, with returning health, his business being nearly all arranged, he should return to those who awaited, anxiously, his coming; and before Sister Celeste had any time for preparation or remonstrance, the young man added: "You have been my guardian angel; you have saved my life; the world will be all dark without you; you can serve God and humanity better as my wife, than as a lowly and poor Sister here; some women have higher destinies and nobler spheres to fill on earth than as Sisters of Charity; you were never meant to be a Nun, but a loving wife. Be mine. If it is the poor you wish to serve, a thousand shall bless you where one blesses you here; but come with me, filling my mother's heart with joy, and taking your rightful place as my wife, be my guardian angel forever."

The face of Sister Celeste was white as the pillow on which her hand lay; for a moment she seemed choking, while about her lips and eyes there was a tremulousness as though she was about to break into a storm of uncontrollable sobs. But she rallied under a tremendous effort of self-control, gently disengaged her hand from the hand that held it, rose to her feet and said:

"I ought not to have permitted this—ought not to have heard what you said. However, we must bear our cross. I do not belong to the world; but do not misjudge me. I have not always been as you see me. I can only tell you this. To a woman, now and then there comes a time when either her heart must break, or she must give it to God. I have given mine to Him. I cannot take it back. I would not if I could.

"If you suffer a little now, you will forget it with returning strength. I only ask that when you are strong and well, and far away—you will sometimes remember. The world is full of heart-aches. Comfort as many as you can. And now, God bless you, and fare well." She laid her hand a moment on his brow, then drew it down upon his cheek, where it lingered for a moment like a caress, and then she was gone. After that the Mother Superior became the young man's nurse until he left the Hospital. He tried hard, but he never saw Sister Celeste again. While he remained in the place she ceased to appear on the street.

ANOTHER YEAR PASSED BY

And Sister Celeste grew steadily in the love of the people. With the winter months small pox broke out in the village. The country was new, the people careless and no particular alarm was felt until the breaking out of ten cases in a single day awakened the people to the fact that a contagion was upon them.

Sister Celeste, almost without rest, labored night and day until the violence of the epidemic had passed; then she was stricken. She recovered, but was shockingly pitted[7] by the disease.

She was in a darkened room, and how to break to her the news of her disfigurement was a matter of sore distress to her sister nuns. But one day to a Sister who was watching by her bed side, she suddenly said:

"I am almost well now, Sister; throw back the blinds and bring me a mirror!" and with a gentle gaiety that never forsook her when with her sister nuns, she added: "It is time that I began to admire myself."

The nun opened the blinds, brought the glass, laid it upon the bed, and sat down trembling.

Sister Celeste, without glancing at the mirror, laid one hand upon it, and shading her eyes with the other hand, for a moment was absorbed in silent prayer. Then she picked up the glass and held it before her face. The watching nun, in an agony of suspense and hardly breathing, waited.

After a long, earnest look, without a shade passing over her face, Sister Celeste laid down the glass, clasped her hands and said:

"God be praised! now all is peace; never, never again will my face bring sorrow to my heart."

The watching nun sank sobbing to her knees, but as she did so, she saw, on the face of the stricken woman, a smile which she declared was radiant as an angel's robes.

With the return of health Sister Celeste again took up the work of mercy, and for a few months more her presence

WAS A BENEDICTION

To the place. At last, however, it began to be noticed that her presence on the street was less frequent than formerly, and soon an unwelcome rumor began to circulate that she was ill. The truth of this was soon confirmed. Then, day by day for several weeks, the report was that she was growing weaker and weaker, and finally one morning it was known that she was dead.

A lady of the place who was a beneficiary of the hospital, and to whom Sister Celeste was greatly attached, was permitted to watch by the dying couch of the glorified Nun. Of the closing moment she gave the following account:

For an hour the dying woman had been motionless as though hushed in peaceful sleep. When the first rays of the morning sun struck on the window, a lark lighted on a tree near the window and in a full voice caroled his greeting to the new born day. Then the Sister opened her eyes, already fringed by the death-frost, and in faint and broken sentences said:

"A delicious vision has been sent me, *Deo Gratias!*[8] In the vision, every act meant in kindness that I have ever performed had become a flower giving off an incense ineffable. These had been woven into a diadem for me. Every word said in comfort or sympathy that I have ever spoken had been set to marvelously sweet music which voices and harps, not of this world, were singing and playing while I was being crowned; every tear of mine shed in pity had become a flashing gem. These were woven into the robes of light that they drew around me. A glass was brought and held before me; from face and bosom the cruel scars were all gone; to eye and brow and cheek the luster and enchantment of youth had come back, and near, all radiant"——

The eyes, with a look of inexpressibly joyous surprise and happiness in them, grew fixed, and all was still save that the lark outside the casement once more warbled his morning song.

Among the few effects left by Sister Celeste was found a package addressed to the lady who had watched through the closing hours of her life. This was brought to her by the Mother Superior. On being opened, there was found within it another package tied with a ribbon of black. This, in turn, was opened, and a large double locket was revealed. On one side was the picture of a young man in the uniform of

A FRENCH COLONEL

From the other side a picture had evidently been removed, for there were scratches on the case, which seemed as though made by a too impetuous use of some sharp instrument. On the outer edge of the case was a half round hole, such as bullets make, and there were dark stains on one side of the locket. Below the picture, in the delicate hand-writing of a woman, were the words: "Henri. Died at Magenta."[9]

The lady showed the locket to the Mother Superior. Tears came to the faded eyes of the devoted woman.

"Now God be praised!" said she. "Three nights since, as I watched the poor child, I heard her murmur that name in her fevered sleep, and I was troubled, for I feared she was dreaming of the youth she nursed back to life in the hospital. It was not so; her work was finished on earth; she was nearing the sphere where love never brings sorrow; her soul was already outstretching its wings to join"—the poor nun stopped, breathed short and hard, and incoherently began to tell her beads. The lady, on pretense of looking for the last time on the face of Celeste, slipped the locket beneath the folds of the winding sheet and left it concealed upon the pulseless breast.

The whole population of the place were sorrowing mourners at the obsequies of Sister Celeste, and for years afterward, every morning, in summer and winter, upon her grave a dressing of fresh flowers could be seen.

On the day of the funeral the miners made up a purse and gave it to Mrs. De Lacy, the consideration being that every day for a year the grave of the Sister should be flower-dressed. The contract was renewed yearly until Mrs. De Lacy herself died. In the mean time, a wild rose and a cypress had been planted at the head and foot of the grave, and they keep watch there still, and shield the lowly couch from storm and sun. One who passed there last year heard, from under the rose bush at the head of the grave, a mourning dove calling her mate, and the answer came back, from where the trees grew dense a little way off, and the call and the answer were low and sweet and plaintive, as though there lingered still around the spot a tender sorrow for the beautiful dead.

NOTES

1. A Catholic nun.
2. To be slightly drunk.
3. Gold dust.
4. A special cheer of the time period.
5. The head of a community of nuns.
6. According to the Gospel of Matthew 17:1–9 (King James Version), the Old Testament figures of Moses and Elijah (Elias) were seen speaking with Jesus during his "transfiguration" on a mountain top; here Celeste is emphasizing that she was now able to see the goodness of the men beneath their physical exterior.

7. Those infected with smallpox suffered from blisters that, when they burst, form scabs; when these scabs subsequently fall off, they leave disfiguring scars ("pits") on the skin.
8. "Thanks be to God" (Latin).
9. The Battle of Magenta took place between Austrian and French troops just west of what is now Milan, Italy, on June 4, 1859, during the Second War of Italian Independence.

BRET HARTE

(1836–1902)

Francis Bret Harte was a prolific author whose writing career spanned more than forty years. During that time, he published numerous poems, plays, lectures, book reviews, editorials, magazine sketches, and fictions. However, Harte was—and still is—best known for his fictional depictions of the California gold rush and life in the American West during the mid to late nineteenth century.

When he was eighteen, Harte moved west with his family to Oakland, California. Drifting from job to job—some of which cannot be verified and may be the stuff of self-invented legend—Harte worked as a tutor, typesetter, gold miner, and stagecoach "shotgun" rider who kept lookout for bandits. Eventually, Harte became an editor and writer for many different periodicals in California, including the weekly *Northern Californian,* the *Overland Monthly* magazine, the weekly *Golden Era* (where he published under the pseudonym "the Bohemian"), and the *San Francisco Call,* a paper that also employed Samuel Clemens (Mark Twain). Harte and Twain were in fact close friends and even collaborators from the mid-1860s until 1876, when they had an irreparable falling out; Twain even told friends and colleagues that it was Harte who had taught him some of the most important things about writing. Harte's connections to these various publications afforded him a place to publish and an audience for his work, which helped establish his reputation as a voice for northern California. In fact, his legacy is so tied to this region that there is a town named Bret Harte in that state's Stanislaus County.

However, during the course of his career, Harte repeatedly returned to exploring themes of injustice and cruelty, especially describing abuse perpetuated against minorities by people in positions of power. In his stories, socially dominant figures, such as politicians, ministers, miners, merchants, and sheriffs, are depicted as morally bankrupt, hypocritical, greedy, and self-serving. Conversely, social outsiders, such as gamblers, prostitutes, or minorities, adhere to a code that may deviate from the norm but is nonetheless consistent and transparent. Although Harte's outsiders may break laws, they retain a sense of honor.

The stories included in this anthology, "The Luck of Roaring Camp" (1868) and "Wan Lee, the Pagan" (1874), examine two very different aspects of the West and contain numerous traits considered characteristic of his writing.

Harte, hired in 1868 by publisher Anton Roman to edit the *Overland Monthly*, a San Francisco–based magazine intended to compete with Boston's *Atlantic Monthly* and represent the West positively to a national audience, submitted his own story, "The Luck of Roaring Camp," for the magazine's second issue. The story almost did not make it into print, however, because the magazine's printer found it "indecent, irreligious, and improper" and consequently alerted Roman, who agreed with him. When Harte threatened to resign if the story was not published, Roman backed down. Fortunately for Harte, "Luck" proved extremely popular among readers on the East Coast, the very audience Roman most wanted to reach, and he consequently was quite eager to publish Harte's subsequent Western tales, including the much-anthologized "The Outcasts of Poker Flat" (1869). These were later collected in the extremely popular *The Luck of Roaring Camp, and Other Sketches* (1870), which made Harte nationally famous. Significantly, in his preface to this volume, Harte wrote, "I trust that in the following sketches I have abstained from any positive moral," adding that he only wished "to illustrate an era of which Californian history has preserved the incidents more often than the character of the actors."

Harte also frequently engaged the subject of Chinese immigrants in the United States. This is evident, for example, in his poem entitled "Plain Language from Truthful James," originally published in the *Overland Monthly* in September 1870, which was wildly popular (it was later renamed "The Heathen Chinee"). Unfortunately, Harte's biting satire of White people's prejudiced views against Chinese people in America was lost on the majority of readers, who saw it instead as endorsing anti-Chinese prejudice. Nonetheless, its popularity led him to later collaborate with Mark Twain and turn it into the play *Ah Sin;* this, however, proved a great failure. In our anthology we have chosen to include Harte's short story "Wan Lee, the Pagan," which first appeared in the September 1874 issue of *Scribner's Monthly*, a New York magazine which at that time was very interested in presenting "exotic" American locales and people to its readers. Its final tragic scene, it should be noted, is actually based on a riot that took place in San Francisco's Chinatown over two days in 1869, when the fictional Wan Lee would have been about thirteen years old. Numerous Chinese people were killed or injured, and many Chinese-owned businesses were badly damaged by angry mobs who resented the immigrant population.

Harte's early success led the *Atlantic Monthly* in 1871 to offer him a lucrative contract of $10,000 for all that he would write in the next year. However, Harte failed to produce anything noteworthy, and the contract was consequently canceled. To earn money to support his family yet still have time to write, Harte sought—and won—an appointment as United States consul in Krefeld, Germany, where he stayed from 1878 to 1880. Subsequently, he served as the US consul in Glasgow from 1880 to 1885 and then moved to London and became a

·VOL. IV. N° 3.   SEPTEMBER 1888   PRICE 25 CENTS·

SCRIBNER'S MAGAZINE

SEPTEMBER

PUBLISHED MONTHLY
WITH ILLUSTRATIONS

·CHARLES SCRIBNER'S SONS NEW YORK·
·F. WARNE & C° LONDON·

Cover of *Scribner's Magazine* (September 1888).

full-time writer for the rest of his life. He died of cancer in 1902; his gravestone in Frimley, England, is etched with his poem "Death Shall Reap the Braver Harvest."

*Readers should be aware that both stories by Harte presented here include language which, while commonly used during this time period, is no longer considered acceptable because of its offensive nature.

THE LUCK OF ROARING CAMP (1868)

There was commotion in Roaring Camp. It could not have been a fight, for in 1850 that was not novel enough to have called together the entire settlement. The ditches and claims were not only deserted, but "Tuttle's" grocery had contributed its gamblers, who, it will be remembered, calmly continued their game the day that French Pete and Kanaka[1] Joe shot each other to death over the bar in the front room. The whole camp was collected before a rude cabin on the outer edge of the clearing. Conversation was carried on in a low tone, but the name of a woman was frequently repeated. It was a name familiar enough in the camp: "Cherokee[2] Sal."

Perhaps the less said of her the better. She was a coarse, and, it is to be feared, a very sinful woman. But at that time she was the only woman in Roaring Camp, and was just then lying in[3] sore extremity when she most needed the ministration of her own sex. Dissolute, abandoned and irreclaimable, she was yet suffering a martyrdom—hard enough to bear even in the seclusion and sexual sympathy with which custom veils it—but now terrible in her loneliness. The primal curse[4] had come to her in that original isolation, which must have made the punishment of the first transgression so dreadful. It was, perhaps, part of the expiation of her sin, that at a moment when she most lacked her sex's intuitive sympathy and care, she met only the half-contemptuous faces of her masculine associates. Yet a few of the spectators were, I think, touched by her sufferings. Sandy Tipton thought it was "rough on Sal," and in the contemplation of her condition, for a moment rose superior to the fact that he had an ace and two bowers[5] in his sleeve.

It will be seen, also, that the situation was novel. Deaths were by no means uncommon in Roaring Camp, but a birth was a new thing. People had been dismissed [from] the camp effectively, finally, and with no possibility of return, but this was the first time that anybody had been introduced *ab initio.*[6] Hence the excitement.

"You go in there, Stumpy," said a prominent citizen known as "Kentuck," addressing one of the loungers. "Go in there, and see what you kin do. You've had experience in them things."

Perhaps there was a fitness in the selection. Stumpy, in other climes, had been the putative head of two families; in fact, it was owing to some legal informality in these proceedings that Roaring Camp—a city of refuge—was indebted to his company. The crowd approved the choice, and Stumpy was wise enough to bow to the majority. The door closed on the extempore surgeon and midwife, and Roaring Camp sat down outside, smoked its pipe, and awaited the issue.

The assemblage numbered about a hundred men. One or two of these were actual fugitives from justice, some were criminal, and all were reckless. Physically, they exhibited no indication of their past lives and character. The greatest scamp had a Raphael[7] face, with a profusion of blond hair; Oakhurst, a gambler, had the melancholy air and intellectual abstraction of a Hamlet; the coolest and most courageous man was scarcely over five feet in height, with a soft voice and an embarrassed timid manner. The term "roughs" applied to them was a distinction rather than a definition. Perhaps in the minor details of fingers, toes, ears, etc., the camp may have been deficient, but these slight omissions did not detract from their aggregate force. The strongest man had but three fingers on his right hand; the best shot had but one eye.

Such was the physical aspect of the men that were dispersed around the cabin. The camp lay in a triangular valley, between two hills and a river. The only outlet was a steep trail over the summit of a hill that faced the cabin, now illuminated by the rising moon. The suffering woman might have seen it from the rude bunk whereon she lay—seen it winding like a silver thread until it was lost in the stars above.

A fire of withered pine boughs added sociability to the gathering. By degrees the natural levity of Roaring Camp returned. Bets were freely offered and taken regarding the result. Three to five that "Sal would get through with it;" even, that the child would survive; side bets as to the sex and complexion of the coming stranger. In the midst of an excited discussion an exclamation came from those nearest the door, and the camp stopped to listen. Above the swaying and moaning of the pines, the swift rush of the river and the crackling of the fire, rose a sharp querulous cry—a cry unlike anything heard before in the camp. The pines stopped moaning, the river ceased to rush, and the fire to crackle. It seemed as if Nature had stopped to listen too.

The camp rose to its feet as one man! It was proposed to explode a barrel of gunpowder, but, in consideration of the situation of the mother, better counsels prevailed, and only a few revolvers were discharged; for, whether owing to the rude surgery of the camp, or some other reason, Cherokee Sal was sinking fast. Within an hour she had climbed, as it were, that rugged road that led to the stars, and so passed out of Roaring Camp, its sin and shame forever. I do not think that the announcement disturbed them much, except in speculation as to the fate of the child. "Can he live now?" was asked of Stumpy. The answer was doubtful. The only other being of Cherokee Sal's sex and maternal condition in the set- tlement was an ass. There was some conjecture as to fitness, but the experiment was tried. It was less problematical than the ancient treatment of Romulus and Remus,[8] and apparently as successful.

When these details were completed, which exhausted another hour, the door was opened, and the anxious crowd, which had already formed themselves into a queue, entered single file. Beside the low bunk or shelf, on which the figure of the mother was starkly outlined below the blankets, stood a pine table. On this a candle-box was placed, and within it, swathed in staring red flannel, lay the last arrival at Roaring Camp. Beside the candle-box was placed a hat. Its use was soon indicated. "Gentlemen," said Stumpy, with a singular mixture of authority and *ex officio*[9] complacency—"Gentlemen will please pass in at the front door, round the table, and out at the back door. Them as wishes to contribute anything toward the orphan will find a hat handy." The first man entered with his hat on; he uncovered, however, as he looked about him, and so, unconsciously, set an example to the next. In such communities good and bad actions are catching. As the procession filed in, comments were audible—criticisms addressed, perhaps, rather to Stumpy, in the character of showman: "Is that him?" "mighty small specimen;" "hasn't mor'n got the color;" "ain't bigger nor a derringer."[10] The contributions were as characteristic: A silver tobacco-box; a doubloon; a navy revolver, silver mounted; a gold specimen; a very beautifully embroidered lady's handkerchief (from Oakhurst, the gambler); a diamond breastpin; a diamond ring (suggested by the pin, with the remark from the giver that he "saw that pin and went two diamonds better"); a slung shot; a Bible (contributor not detected); a golden spur; a silver teaspoon (the initials, I regret to say, were not the giver's); a pair of surgeon's shears; a lancet; a Bank of England note for £5; and about $200 in loose gold and silver coin. During these proceedings Stumpy maintained a silence as impassive as the dead on his left—a gravity as inscrutable as that of the newly-born on his right. Only one incident occurred to break the monotony of the curious procession. As Kentuck bent over the candle-box half curiously, the child turned, and, in a spasm of pain, caught at his groping finger, and held it fast for a moment. Kentuck looked foolish and embarrassed. Something like a blush tried to assert itself in his weather-beaten cheek. "The d——d little cuss!" he said, as he extricated his finger, with, perhaps, more tenderness and care than he might have been deemed capable of showing. He held that finger a little apart from its fellows as he went out, and examined it curiously. The examination provoked the same original remark in regard to the child. In fact, he seemed to enjoy repeating it. "He rastled with my finger," he remarked to Tipton, holding up the member, "The d——d little cuss!"

It was four o'clock before the camp sought repose. A light burnt in the cabin where the watchers sat, for Stumpy did not go to bed that night. Nor did Kentuck. He drank quite freely and related with great gusto his experience, invariably ending with his characteristic condemnation of the newcomer. It seemed to relieve him of any unjust implication of sentiment, and Kentuck had the weaknesses of the nobler sex. When everybody else had gone to bed he walked down to the river and whistled, reflectingly. Then he walked up the gulch, past the cabin, still whistling with demonstrative unconcern. At a large redwood tree he paused and retraced his steps, and again passed the cabin. Halfway down to the river's bank he again paused, and then returned and knocked at the door. It was opened by Stumpy. "How goes it?" said Kentuck, looking past Stumpy toward the candle-box. "All serene," replied Stumpy, "Anything up?" "Nothing." There was a pause—an embarrassing one—Stumpy still holding the door. Then Kentuck had recourse to his finger, which he held up to Stumpy. "Rastled with it—the d——d little cuss," he said and retired.

The next day Cherokee Sal had such rude sepulture[11] as Roaring Camp afforded. After her body had been committed to the hill-side, there was a formal meeting of the camp to discuss what should be done with her infant. A resolution to adopt it was unanimous and enthusiastic. But an animated discussion in regard to the manner and feasibility of providing for its wants at once sprung up. It was remarkable that the argument partook of none of those fierce personalities with which discussions were usually conducted at Roaring Camp. Tipton proposed that they should send the child to Red Dog—a distance of forty miles—where female attention could be procured. But the unlucky suggestion met with fierce and unanimous opposition. It was evident that no plan which entailed parting from their new acquisition would for a moment be entertained. "Besides," said Tom Ryder, "them fellows at Red Dog would swap it and ring in somebody else on us." A disbelief in the honesty of other camps prevailed at Roaring Camp as in other places.

The introduction of a female nurse in the camp also met with objection. It was argued that no decent woman could be prevailed to accept Roaring Camp as her home, and the speaker urged that "they did'nt want any more of the other kind." This unkind allusion to the defunct mother, harsh as it may seem, was the first spasm of propriety—the first symptom of the camp's regeneration. Stumpy advanced nothing. Perhaps he felt a certain delicacy in interfering with the selection of a possible successor in office. But when questioned he averred stoutly that he and "Jinny"—the mammal before alluded to—could manage to rear the child. There was something original, independent and heroic about the plan, that pleased the camp. Stumpy was retained. Certain articles were sent for to Sacramento. "Mind," said the treasurer, as he pressed a bag of gold-dust into the express-man's hand, "the best that can be got—lace, you know, and filigree work and frills—d——m the cost!"

Strange to say, the child thrived. Perhaps the invigorating climate of the mountain camp was compensation for material deficiencies. Nature took the foundling to her broader breast. In that rare atmosphere of the Sierra foot-hills—that air pungent with balsamic odor; that etherial cordial, at once bracing and exhilarating, he may have found food and nourishment, or a subtle chemistry that transmuted asses' milk to lime and phosphorus. Stumpy inclined to the belief that it was the latter and good nursing. "Me and that ass," he would say, "has been father and mother to him! Don't you," he would add, apostrophizing the helpless bundle before him, "never go back on us."

By the time he was a month old, the necessity of giving him a name became apparent. He had generally been known as "the Kid," "Stumpy's boy," "the Cayote"—(an allusion to his vocal powers)—and even by Kentuck's endearing diminutive of "the d——d little cuss." But these were felt to be vague and unsatisfactory, and were at last dismissed under another influence. Gamblers and adventurers are generally superstitious, and Oakhurst one day declared that the baby had brought "the luck" to Roaring Camp. It was certain that of late they had been successful. "Luck" was the name agreed upon, with the prefix of Tommy for greater convenience. No allusion was made to the mother, and the father was unknown. "It's better," said the philosophical Oakhurst, "to take a fresh deal all around. Call him Luck, and start him fair." A day was accordingly set apart for the christening. What was meant by this ceremony the reader may imagine, who has already gathered some idea of the reckless irreverence of Roaring Camp. The master of ceremonies was one "Boston," a noted wag,[12] and the occasion seemed to promise the greatest facetiousness. This ingenious satirist had spent two days in preparing a burlesque of the church service, with pointed local allusions. The choir was properly trained, and Sandy Tipton was to stand godfather. But after the procession had marched to the grove with music and banners, and the child had been deposited before a mock altar, Stumpy stepped before the expectant crowd. "It ain't my style to spoil fun, boys," said the little man, stoutly, eyeing the faces around him, "but it strikes me that this thing ain't exactly on the squar. It's playing it pretty low down on this yer baby to ring in fun on him that he ain't going to understand. And ef there's going to be any godfathers round, I'd like to see who's got any better rights than me." A silence followed Stumpy's speech. To the credit of all humorists be it said that the first man to acknowledge its justice was the satirist, thus estopped of his fun. "But," said Stumpy quickly, following up his advantage, "we're here for a christening, and we'll have it. I proclaim you Thomas Luck, according to the laws of the United States and the State of California—So help me God." It was the first time that the name of the Deity had been uttered aught but profanely in the camp. The form of christening was perhaps even more ludicrous than the satirist had conceived, but strangely enough, nobody saw it and nobody laughed. "Tommy" was christened as seriously as he would have been under a christian roof, and cried and was comforted in as orthodox fashion.

And so the work of regeneration began in Roaring Camp. Almost imperceptibly a change came over the settlement. The cabin assigned to "Tommy Luck"—or "The Luck," as he was more frequently called—first showed signs of improvement. It was kept scrupulously clean and whitewashed. Then it was boarded, clothed and papered. The rosewood cradle—packed eighty miles by mule—had, in Stumpy's way of putting it, "sorter killed the rest of the furniture." So the rehabilitation of the cabin became a necessity. The men who were in the habit of lounging in at Stumpy's to see "how The Luck got on" seemed to appreciate the change, and, in self-defence, the rival establishment of "Tuttle's grocery" bestirred itself, and imported a carpet and mirrors. The reflections of the latter on the appearance of Roaring Camp tended to produce stricter habits of personal cleanliness. Again Stumpy imposed a kind of quarantine upon those who aspired to the honor and privilege of holding "The Luck." It was a cruel mortification to Kentuck—who, in the carelessness of a large nature and the habits of frontier life, had begun to regard all garments as a second cuticle, which, like a snake's, only sloughed off through decay—to be debarred this privilege from certain prudential reasons. Yet such was the subtle influence of innovation that he thereafter appeared regularly every afternoon in a clean shirt, and face still shining from his ablutions. Nor were moral and social sanitary laws neglected. "Tommy," who was supposed to spend his whole existence in a persistent attempt to repose, must not be disturbed by noise. The shouting and yelling which had gained the camp its infelicitous title were not permitted within hearing distance of Stumpy's. The men conversed in whispers, or smoked in Indian gravity.[13] Profanity was tacitly given up in these sacred precincts, and throughout the camp a popular form of expletive, known as "D——n the luck!" and "Curse the luck!" was abandoned, as having a new personal bearing. Vocal music was not interdicted, being supposed to have a soothing, tranquillizing quality, and one song, sung by "Man O'War Jack," an English sailor, from Her Majesty's Australian Colonies, was quite popular as a lullaby. It was a lugubrious recital of the exploits of "the Arethusa, Seventy-four," in a muffled minor, ending with a prolonged dying fall at the burden of each verse, "On b-o-o-o-ard of the Arethusa." It was a fine sight to see Jack holding The Luck, rocking from side to side as if with the motion of a ship, and crooning forth this naval ditty. Either through the peculiar rocking of Jack or the length of his song—it contained ninety stanzas, and was continued with conscientious deliberation to the bitter end—the lullaby generally had the desired effect. At such times the men would lie at full length under the trees, in the soft summer twilight, smoking their pipes and drinking in the melodious utterances. An indistinct idea that this was pastoral happiness pervaded the camp. "This ere kind o' think," said the Cockney Simmons, meditatively reclining on his elbow, "is evingly." It reminded him of Greenwich.[14]

On the long summer days The Luck was usually carried to the gulch, from whence the golden store of Roaring Camp was taken. There, on a blanket spread over pine boughs, he would lie while the men were working in the ditches below. Latterly, there was a rude attempt to decorate this bower with flowers and sweet-smelling shrubs, and generally some one would bring him a cluster of wild honeysuckles, azalias, or the painted blossoms of Las Mariposas. The men had suddenly awakened to the fact that there were beauty and significance in these trifles, which they had so long trodden carelessly beneath their feet. A flake of glittering mica, a fragment of variegated quartz, a bright pebble from the bed of the creek, became beautiful to eyes thus cleared and strengthened, and were invariably put aside for "The Luck." It was wonderful how many treasures the woods and hillsides yielded that "would do for Tommy." Surrounded by playthings such as never child out of fairyland had before, it is to be hoped that Tommy was content. He appeared to be securely happy—albeit there was an infantine gravity about him—a contemplative light in his round grey eyes that sometimes worried Stumpy. He was always tractable and quiet, and it is recorded that once, having crept beyond his "corral"—a hedge of tessallated pine boughs, which surrounded his bed—he dropped over the bank on his head in the soft earth, and remained with his mottled legs in the air in that position for at least five minutes with unflinching gravity. He was extricated without a murmur. I hesitate to record the many other instances of his sagacity, which rest, unfortunately, upon the statements of prejudiced friends. Some of them were not without a tinge of superstition. "I crep up the bank just now," said Kentuck one day, in a breathless state of excitement, "and dern my skin if he wasn't a talking to a jay bird as was a-sittin on his lap. There they was, just as free and sociable as anything you please, a-jawin at each other just like two cherry-bums." Howbeit, whether creeping over the pine boughs or lying lazily on his back, blinking at the leaves above him, to him the birds sang, the squirrels chattered, and the flowers bloomed. Nature was his nurse and playfellow. For him she would let slip between the leaves golden shafts of sunlight that fell just within his grasp; she would send wandering breezes to visit him with the balm of bay and resinous gums; to him the tall redwoods nodded familiarly and sleepily, the bumble-bees buzzed, and the rooks cawed a slumbrous accompaniment.

Such was the golden summer of Roaring Camp. They were "flush times"—and the Luck was with them. The claims had yielded enormously. The camp was jealous of its privileges and looked suspiciously on strangers. No encouragement was given to immigration, and to make their seclusion more perfect, the land on either side of the mountain wall that surrounded the camp, they duly preëmpted. This, and a reputation for singular proficiency with the revolver, kept the reserve of Roaring Camp inviolate. The express-man—their only connecting link with the surrounding world—sometimes told wonderful stories of the camp. He would say, "They've a street up there in 'Roaring,' that would lay over any street in Red Dog. They've got vines and flowers round their houses, and they wash themselves twice a day. But they're mighty rough on strangers, and they worship an Ingin[15] baby."

With the prosperity of the camp came a desire for further improvement. It was proposed to build a hotel in the following spring, and to invite one or two decent families to reside there for the sake of "the Luck"—who might perhaps profit by female companionship. The sacrifice that this concession to the sex cost these men, who were fiercely skeptical in regard to its general virtue and usefulness, can only be accounted for by their affection for Tommy. A few still held out. But the resolve could not be carried into effect for three months, and the minority meekly yielded in the hope that something might turn up to prevent it. And it did.

The winter of '51 will long be remembered in the foot-hills. The snow lay deep on the Sierras, and every mountain creek became a river, and every river a lake. Each gorge and gulch was transformed into a tumultuous water-course that descended the hill-sides, tearing down giant trees and scattering its drift and debris along the plain. Red Dog had been twice under water, and Roaring Camp had been forewarned. "Water put the gold into them gulches," said Stumpy, "It's been here once and will be here again!" And that night the North Fork suddenly leaped over its banks, and swept up the triangular valley of Roaring Camp.

In the confusion of rushing water, crushing trees and crackling timber, and the darkness which seemed to flow with the water and blot out the fair valley, but little could be done to collect the scattered camp. When the morning broke, the cabin of Stumpy nearest the river bank was gone. Higher up the gulch they found the body of its unlucky owner, but the pride—the hope—the joy—the Luck—of Roaring Camp had disappeared. They were returning with sad hearts when a shout from the bank recalled them.

It was a relief boat from down the river. They had picked up, they said, a man and an infant, nearly exhausted, about two miles below. Did anybody know them, and did they belong here? It needed but a glance to show them Kentuck lying there, cruelly crushed and bruised, but still holding the Luck of Roaring Camp in his arms. As they bent over the strangely assorted pair, they saw that the child was cold and pulseless. "He is dead," said one. Kentuck opened his eyes. "Dead?" he repeated feebly. "Yes, my man, and you are dying too." A smile lit the eyes the expiring Kentuck. "Dying," he repeated, "he's a taking me with him—tell the boys I've got the Luck with me, now;" and the strong man clinging to the frail babe as a drowning man is said to cling to a straw, drifted away into the shadowy river that flows forever to the unknown sea.

NOTES

1. An adjective used at this time to describe someone from Hawaii or the Pacific Islands. It is now considered offensive and no longer used.
2. A Native American tribe from the southeastern United States. It is unclear if Sal is actually a member of this tribe or if the term is being used by Whites to generically signify a Native American, for if Sal were truly a member of this tribe, she would be a long way from her homeland, since the story takes place in California.
3. "Lying in" describes a period during pregnancy and after childbirth when, at the time of this story, women were kept secluded from society.
4. The punishment God places on Eve in Genesis 3:16 (King James Version): "Unto the woman he said, I will greatly multiply thy sorrow and thy conception; in sorrow thou shalt bring forth children; and thy desire shall be to thy husband, and he shall rule over thee."
5. Playing cards, specifically "jacks." He is playing poker and potentially cheating.
6. From the beginning (Latin).
7. Beautiful. The allusion is to depictions of archangel Raphael or to portraits by Italian painter Raffaello Sanzio da Urbino (1483–1520).
8. In Roman mythology, twin brothers Romulus and Remus were fed by nursing from a wolf; here, the baby is to be fed milk from the ass (a donkey).
9. To assume a position due to proximity (Latin).
10. A very small pistol.
11. Burial.
12. Someone who exhibits great wit.
13. White writers of the time often described Native Americans as being somber in their actions.

14. Greenwich, England—likely his home.
15. A derogatory and offensive slang term for "Indian" that was commonly used by some non-Native people at this time to refer to a person who would now be known as Native American.

WAN LEE, THE PAGAN (1874)

As I opened Hop Sing's letter, there fluttered to the ground a square strip of yellow paper covered with hieroglyphics which at first glance I innocently took to be the label from a pack of Chinese fire-crackers. But the same envelope also contained a smaller strip of rice paper, with two Chinese characters traced in India ink, that I at once knew to be Hop Sing's visiting card.[1] The whole, as afterwards literally translated, ran as follows:

> "*To the stranger the gates of my house are not*
> *closed; the rice-jar is on the left, and the*
> *sweetmeats[2] on the right as you enter.*
> *Two sayings of the Master:*
> *Hospitality is the virtue of the son and the*
> *wisdom of the ancestor.*
> *The Superior man is light hearted after the*
> *crop-gathering; he makes a festival.*
> *When the stranger is in your melon patch observe*
> *him not too closely; inattention is often*
> *the highest form of civility.*
> *Happiness, Peace, and Prosperity.*
> HOP SING.*"

Admirable, certainly, as was this morality and proverbial wisdom, and although this last axiom was very characteristic of my friend Hop Sing, who was that most sombre of all humorists, a Chinese philosopher, I must confess that, even after a very free translation, I was at a loss to make any immediate application of the message. Luckily I discovered a third enclosure in the shape of a little note in English, and Hop Sing's own commercial hand. It ran thus:

"THE pleasure of your company is requested at No.—Sacramento St., on Friday Evening at 8 o'clock. A cup of tea at 9—sharp.

"HOP SING."

This explained all. It meant a visit to Hop Sing's warehouse, the opening and exhibition of some rare Chinese novelties and *curios*, a chat in the back office, a cup of tea of a perfection unknown beyond these sacred precincts, cigars, and a visit to the Chinese Theater or Temple. This was in fact the favorite programme of Hop Sing when he exercised his functions of hospitality as the chief factor or superintendent of the Ning Foo Company.

At eight o'clock on Friday evening I entered the warehouse of Hop Sing. There was that deliciously commingled mysterious foreign odor that I had so often noticed; there was the old array of uncouth looking objects, the long procession of jars and crockery, the same singular blending of the grotesque and the mathematically neat and exact, the same endless suggestions of frivolity and fragility, the same want of harmony in colors that were each, in themselves, beautiful and rare. Kites in the shape of enormous dragons and gigantic butterflies; kites so ingeniously arranged as to utter at intervals, when facing the wind, the cry of a hawk; kites so large as to be beyond any boy's power of restraint—so large that you understood why kite-flying in China was an amusement for adults; gods of china and bronze so gratuitously ugly as to be beyond any human interest or sympathy from their very impossibility; jars of sweetmeats covered all over with moral sentiments from Confucius;[3] hats that looked like baskets, and baskets that looked like hats; silks so light that I hesitate to record the incredible number of square yards that you might pass through the ring on your little finger—these and a great many other indescribable objects were all familiar to me. I pushed my way through the dimly-lighted warehouse until I reached the back office or parlor, where I found Hop Sing waiting to receive me.

Before I describe him I want the average reader to discharge from his mind any idea of a Chinaman that he may have gathered from the pantomime.[4] He did not wear beautifully scalloped drawers[5] fringed with little bells—I never met a Chinaman who did; he did not habitually carry his forefinger extended before him at right angles with his body, nor did I ever hear him utter the mysterious sentence "Ching a ring a ring chaw,"[6] nor dance under any provocation. He was on the whole, a rather grave, decorous, handsome gentleman. His complexion, which extended all over his head, except where his long pig-tail[7] grew, was like a very nice piece of glazed brown paper-muslin. His eyes were black and bright, and his eye-lids set at an angle of $15°$; his nose straight and delicately formed; his mouth small, and his teeth white and clean. He wore a dark blue silk blouse; and in the streets on cold days, a short jacket of astrackan[8] fur. He wore also a pair of drawers of blue brocade gathered tightly over his calves and ankles, offering a general sort of suggestion that he had forgotten his trousers that morning, but, that so gentlemanly were his manners, his friends had forborne to mention the fact to him. His manner was urbane, although quite serious. He spoke French and English fluently. In brief, I doubt if you could have found the equal of this Pagan[9] shop-keeper among the Christian traders of San Francisco.

There were a few others present: a Judge of the Federal Court, an editor, a high government official, and a prominent merchant. After we had drunk our tea, and tasted a few sweetmeats from a mysterious jar, that looked as if it might contain a preserved mouse among its other nondescript treasures, Hop Sing arose and, gravely beckoning us to follow him, began to descend to the basement. When we got there, we were amazed at finding it brilliantly lighted, and that a number of chairs were arranged in a half-circle on the asphalt pavement. When he had courteously seated us he said:

"I have invited you to witness a performance which I can at least promise you no other foreigners but yourselves have ever seen. Wang, the court juggler,[10] arrived here yesterday morning. He has never given a performance outside of the palace before. I have asked him to entertain my friends this evening. He requires no theater, stage accessories, or any confederate—nothing more than you see here. Will you be pleased to examine the ground yourselves, gentlemen."

Of course we examined the premises. It was the ordinary basement or cellar of the San Francisco store-house, cemented to keep out the damp. We poked our sticks into the pavement and rapped on the walls to satisfy our polite host, but for no other purpose. We were quite content to be the victims of any clever deception. For myself, I knew I was ready to be deluded to any extent, and if I had been offered an explanation of what followed, I should have probably declined it.

Although I am satisfied that Wang's general performance was the first of that kind ever given on American soil, it has probably since become so familiar to many of my readers that I shall not bore them with it here. He began by setting to flight, with the aid of his fan, the usual number of butterflies made before our eyes of little bits of tissue paper, and kept them in the air during the remainder of the performance. I have a vivid recollection of the Judge trying to catch one that had lit on his knee, and of its evading him with the pertinacity of a living insect. And even at this time Wang, still plying his fan, was taking chickens out of hats, making oranges disappear, pulling endless yards of silk from his sleeve, apparently filling the whole area of the basement with goods that appeared mysteriously from the ground, from his own sleeves, from nowhere! He swallowed knives to the ruin of his digestion for years to come, he dislocated every limb of his body, he reclined in the air, apparently upon nothing. But his crowning performance, which I have never yet seen repeated, was the most weird, mysterious and astounding. It is my apology for this long introduction, my sole excuse for writing this article, the genesis of this veracious history.

He cleared the ground of its encumbering articles for a space of about fifteen feet square, and then invited us all to walk forward and again examine it. We did so gravely; there was nothing but the cemented pavement below to be seen or felt. He then asked for the loan of a handkerchief, and, as I chanced to be nearest him, I offered mine. He took it, and spread it open upon the floor. Over this he spread a large square of silk, and over this again a large shawl nearly covering the space he had cleared. He then took a position at one of the points of this rectangle, and began a monotonous chant, rocking his body to and fro in time with the somewhat lugubrious air.

We sat still and waited. Above the chant we could hear the striking of the city clocks, and the occasional rattle of a cart in the street overhead. The absolute watchfulness and expectation, the dim mysterious half-light of the cellar falling in a grewsome[11] way upon the misshapen bulk of a Chinese deity in the back ground, a faint smell of opium smoke mingling with spice, and the dreadful uncertainty of what we were really waiting for, sent an uncomfortable thrill down our backs, and made us look at each other with a forced and unnatural smile. This feeling was heightened when Hop Sing slowly rose, and, without a word, pointed with his finger to the center of the shawl.

There was something beneath the shawl. Surely—and something that was not there before. At first a mere suggestion in relief, a faint outline, but growing more and more distinct and visible every moment. The chant still continued, the perspiration began to roll from the singer's face, gradually the hidden object took upon itself a shape and bulk that raised the shawl in its center some five or six inches. It was now unmistakably the outline of a small but perfect human figure, with extended arms and legs. One or two of us turned pale, there was a feeling of general uneasiness, until the editor broke the silence by a gibe that, poor as it was, was received with spontaneous enthusiasm. Then the chant suddenly ceased, Wang arose, and, with a quick, dexterous movement, stripped both shawl and silk away, and discovered, sleeping peacefully upon my handkerchief, a tiny Chinese baby!

The applause and uproar which followed this revelation ought to have satisfied Wang, even if his audience was a small one; it was loud enough to awaken the baby—a pretty little boy about a year old, looking like a Cupid cut out of sandalwood. He was whisked away almost as mysteriously as he appeared. When Hop Sing returned my handkerchief to me with a bow, I asked if the juggler was the father of the baby. "No sabe!"[12] said the imperturbable Hop Sing, taking refuge in that Spanish form of non-committalism so common in California.

"But does he have a new baby for every performance?" I asked. "Perhaps; who knows?" "But what will become of this one?" "Whatever you choose, gentlemen," replied Hop Sing, with a courteous inclination, "it was born here,—you are its godfathers."

There were two characteristic peculiarities of any Californian assemblage in 1856; it was quick to take a hint, and generous to the point of prodigality in its response to any charitable appeal. No matter how sordid or avaricious the individual, he could not resist the infection of sympathy. I doubled the points of my handkerchief into a bag, dropped a coin into it, and, without a word, passed it to the Judge. He quietly added a twenty dollar gold-piece, and passed it to the next; when it was returned to me it contained over a hundred dollars. I knotted the money in the handkerchief, and gave it to Hop Sing.

"For the baby, from its godfathers."

"But what name?" said the Judge. There was a running fire of "Erebus," "Nox," "Plutus," "Terra Cotta," "Antaeus," etc., etc. Finally the question was referred to our host.

"Why not keep his own name?" he said quietly—"Wan Lee." And he did.

And thus was Wan Lee, on the night of Friday, the 5th of March, 1856, born into this veracious chronicle.

The last form of "The Northern Star" for the 19th of July, 1865,—the only daily paper published in Klamath County,—had just gone to press;[13] and at three A.M. I was putting aside my proofs and manuscripts, preparatory to going home, when I discovered a letter lying under some sheets of paper, which I must have overlooked. The envelope was considerably soiled, it had no post-mark; but I had no difficulty in recognizing the hand of my friend Hop Sing. I opened it hurriedly, and read as follows:

"MY DEAR SIR: I do not know whether the bearer will suit you; but, unless the office of 'devil'[14] in your newspaper is a purely technical one, I think he has all the qualities required. He is very quick, active, and intelligent; understands English better than he speaks it, and makes up for any defect by his habits of observation and imitation. You have only to show him how to do a thing once, and he will repeat it, whether it is an offence or a virtue. But you certainly know him already; you are one of his god-fathers, for is he not Wan Lee, the reputed son of Wang the Conjurer, to whose performances I had the honor to introduce you? But perhaps you have forgotten it.

"I shall send him with a gang of coolies[15] to Stockton,[16] thence by express to your town. If you can use him there, you will do me a favor, and probably save his life, which is at present in great peril from the hands of the younger members of your Christian and highly civilized race who attend the enlightened schools in San Francisco.

"He has acquired some singular habits and customs from his experience of Wang's profession, which he followed for some years, until he became too large to go in a hat, or be produced from his father's sleeve. The money you left with me has been expended on his education; he has gone through the Tri-literal Classics,[17] but, I think, without much benefit. He knows but little of Confucius and absolutely nothing of Mencius.[18] Owing to the negligence of his father, he associated, perhaps, too much with American children.

"I should have answered your letter before, by post; but I thought that Wan Lee himself would be a better messenger for this.

"Yours respectfully,

"HOP SING."

And this was the long-delayed answer to my letter to Hop Sing. But where was "the bearer"? How was the letter delivered? I summoned hastily the foreman, printers, and office-boy, but without eliciting anything; no one had seen the letter delivered, nor knew anything of the bearer. A few days later, I had a visit from my laundry-man, Ah Ri.

"You wantee debbil? All lightee: me catchee him."[19]

He returned in a few moments with a bright-looking Chinese boy, about ten years old, with whose appearance and general intelligence I was so greatly impressed that I engaged him on the spot. When the business was concluded, I asked his name.

"Wan Lee," said the boy.

"What! Are you the boy sent out by Hop Sing? What the devil do you mean by not coming here before, and how did you deliver that letter?"

Wan Lee looked at me and laughed. "Me pitchee in top side window."

I did not understand. He looked for a moment perplexed, and then snatching the letter out of my hand, ran down the stairs. After a moment's pause, to my great astonishment, the letter came flying in the window, circled twice around the room, and then dropped gently like a bird upon my table. Before I had got over my surprise Wan Lee reappeared, smiled, looked at the letter and then at me, said, "So, John," and then remained gravely silent. I said nothing further; but it was understood that this was his first official act.

His next performance, I grieve to say, was not attended with equal success. One of our regular paper-carriers fell sick, and, at a pinch, Wan Lee was ordered to fill his place. To prevent mistakes, he was shown over the route the previous evening, and supplied at about daylight with the usual number of subscribers' copies. He returned after an hour, in good spirits and without the papers. He had delivered them all, he said.

Unfortunately for Wan Lee, at about eight o'clock, indignant subscribers began to arrive at the office. They had received their copies; but how? In the form of hard-pressed cannon balls, delivered by a single shot and a mere *tour de force*, through the glass of bed-room windows. They had received them full in the face, like a base ball, if they happened to be up and stirring; they had received them in quarter sheets, tucked in at separate windows; they had found them in the chimney, pinned against the door, shot through attic windows, delivered in long slips through convenient keyholes, stuffed into ventilators, and occupying the same can with the morning's milk. One subscriber, who waited for some time at the office door, to have a personal interview with Wan Lee (then comfortably locked in my bed-room), told me, with tears of rage in his eyes, that he had been awakened at five o'clock by a most hideous yelling below his windows; that on rising, in great agitation, he was startled by the sudden appearance of "The Northern Star," rolled hard, and bent into the form of a boomerang or East Indian club,[20] that sailed into the window, described a number of fiendish circles in the room, knocked over the light, slapped the baby's face, "took" him (the subscriber) "in the jaw," and then returned out of the window, and dropped helplessly in the area. During the rest of the day wads and strips of soiled paper, purporting to be copies of "The Northern Star" of that morning's issue, were brought indignantly to the office. An admirable editorial on "The Resources of Humboldt County," which I had constructed the evening before, and which, I had reason to believe, might have changed the whole balance of trade during the ensuing year, and left San Francisco bankrupt at her wharves, was in this way lost to the public.

It was deemed advisable for the next three weeks to keep Wan Lee closely confined to the printing-office and the purely mechanical part of the business. Here he developed a surprising quickness and adaptability, winning even the favor and good will of the printers and foreman, who at first looked upon his introduction into the secrets of their trade as fraught with the gravest political significance.[21] He learned to set type readily and neatly, his wonderful skill in manipulation aiding him in the mere mechanical act, and his ignorance of the language confining him simply to the mechanical effort—confirming the print-er's axiom that the printer who considers or follows the ideas of his copy makes a poor compositor. He would set up deliberately long diatribes against himself, composed by his fellow-printers, and hung on his hook as copy, and even such short sentences as "Wan Lee is the devil's own imp," "Wan Lee is a Mongolian[22] rascal," and bring the proof to me with happiness beaming from every tooth and satisfaction shining in his huckleberry eyes.

It was not long, however, before he learned to retaliate on his mischievous persecutors. I remember one instance in which his reprisal came very near involving me in a serious misunderstanding. Our foreman's name was Webster, and Wan Lee presently learned to know and recognize the individual and com-bined letters of his name. It was during a political campaign, and the eloquent and fiery Col. Starbottle of Siskyou,[23] had delivered an effective speech, which was reported especially for "The Northern Star." In a very sublime perora-tion, Col. Starbottle had said, "In the language of the godlike Webster,[24] I repeat,"—and here followed the quotation, which I have forgotten. Now, it chanced that Wan Lee, looking over the galley[25] after it had been revised, saw the name of his chief persecutor, and, of course, imagined the quotation his. After the form was locked up, Wan Lee took advantage of Webster's absence to remove the quotation, and substitute a thin piece of lead, of the same size as the type, engraved with Chinese characters, making a sentence which, I had reason to believe, was an utter and abject confession of the incapacity and offensiveness of the Webster family generally, and exceedingly eulogistic of Wan Lee himself personally.

The next morning's paper contained Col. Starbottle's speech in full, in which it appeared that the "god-like" Webster had on one occasion uttered his thoughts in excellent but perfectly enigmatical Chinese. The rage of Col. Starbottle knew no bounds. I have a vivid recollection of that admirable man walking into my office and demanding a retraction of the statement.

"But my dear sir," I asked, "are you willing to deny, over your own signature, that Webster ever uttered such a sentence? Dare you deny, that, with Mr. Web-ster's well-known attainments, a knowledge of Chinese might not have been among the number? Are you willing to submit a translation suitable to the ca-pacity of our readers, and deny, upon your honor as a gentleman, that the late Mr. Webster ever uttered such a sentiment? If you are, sir, I am willing to publish your denial."

The Col. was not, and left, highly indignant.

Webster, the foreman, took it more coolly. Happily, he was unaware, that, for two days after, Chinamen from the laundries, from the gulches, from the kitch-ens, looked in the front office door with faces beaming with sardonic delight; that three hundred extra copies of the "Star" were ordered for the wash-houses on the river. He only knew that during the day Wan Lee occasionally went off into convulsive spasms and that he was obliged to kick him into consciousness again. A week after the occurrence I called Wan Lee into my office.

"Wan," I said gravely, "I should like you to give me, for my own personal satisfaction, a translation of that Chinese sentence which my gifted countryman, the late god-like Webster, uttered upon a public occasion." Wan Lee looked at me intently, and then the slightest possible twinkle crept into his black eyes. Then he replied with equal gravity:

"Mishtel Webstel,—he say: 'China boy makee me belly much foolee. China boy makee me heap sick.'" Which I have reason to think was true.

But I fear I am giving but one side, and not the best, of Wan Lee's character. As he imparted it to me, his had been a hard life. He had known scarcely any childhood—he had no recollection of a father or mother. The conjurer Wang had brought him up. He had spent the first seven years of his life in appearing from baskets, in dropping out of hats, in climbing ladders, in putting his little limbs out of joint in posturing. He had lived in an atmosphere of trickery and deception; he had learned to look upon mankind as dupes of their senses; in fine, if he had thought at all, he would have been a sceptic, if he had been a little older, he would have been a cynic, if he had been older still, he would have been a philosopher. As it was, he was a little imp! A good-natured imp it was, too—an imp whose moral nature had never been awakened, an imp up for a holiday, and willing to try virtue as a diversion. I don't know that he had any spiritual nature; he was very superstitious: he carried about with him a hideous little porcelain god, which he was in the habit of alternately reviling and propitiating. He was too intelligent for the commoner Chinese vices of stealing or gratuitous lying.[26] Whatever discipline he practiced was taught by his intellect.

I am inclined to think that his feelings were not altogether unimpressible,—although it was almost impossible to extract an expression from him,—and I conscientiously believe he became attached to those that were good to him. What he might have become under more favorable conditions than the bondsman of an over-worked, under-paid, literary man, I don't know; I only know that the scant, irregular, impulsive kindnesses that I showed him were gratefully received. He was very loyal and patient—two qualities rare in the average American servant. He was like Malvolio,[27] "sad and civil" with me; only once, and then under great provocation, do I remember of his exhibiting any impatience. It was my habit, after leaving the office at night, to take him with me to my rooms, as the bearer of any supplemental or happy after-thought in the editorial way, that might occur to me before the paper went to press. One night I had been scribbling away past the usual hour of dismissing Wan Lee, and had become quite oblivious of his presence in a chair near my door, when suddenly I became aware of a voice saying, in plaintive accents, something that sounded like "Chy Lee."

I faced around sternly.

"What did you say?"

"Me say, 'Chy Lee.'"

"Well?" I said impatiently.

"You sabe, 'How do, John?'"

"Yes."

"You sabe, 'So long, John'?"

"Yes."

"Well, 'Chy Lee' allee same!"

I understood him quite plainly. It appeared that "Chy Lee" was a form of "good-night," and that Wan Lee was anxious to go home. But an instinct of mischief which I fear I possessed in common with him, impelled me to act as if oblivious of the hint. I muttered something about not understanding him, and again bent over my work. In a few minutes I heard his wooden shoes pattering pathetically over the floor. I looked up. He was standing near the door.

"You no sabe, 'Chy Lee'?"

"No," I said sternly.

"You sabe muchee big foolee!—allee same!"

And, with this audacity upon his lips, he fled. The next morning, however, he was as meek and patient as before, and I did not recall his offense. As a probable peace-offering, he blacked all my boots,—a duty never required of him,—including a pair of buff deer-skin slippers and an immense pair of horseman's jack-boots, on which he indulged his remorse for two hours.

I have spoken of his honesty as being a quality of his intellect rather than his principle, but I recall about this time two exceptions to the rule. I was anxious to get some fresh eggs, as a change to the heavy diet of a mining-town, and, knowing that Wan Lee's countrymen were great poultry raisers, I applied to him. He furnished me with them regularly every morning, but refused to take any pay, saying that the man did not sell them,—a remarkable instance of self-abnegation, as eggs were then worth half a dollar apiece. One morning my neighbor, Forster, dropped in upon me at breakfast, and took occasion to bewail his own ill fortune, as his hens had lately stopped laying, or wandered off in the bush. Wan Lee, who was present during our colloquy, preserved his characteristic sad taciturnity. When my neighbor had gone, he turned to me with a slight chuckle: "Flostel's hens—Wan Lee's hens—allee same!" His other offense was more serious and ambitious. It was a season of great irregularities in the mails, and Wan Lee had heard me deplore the delay in the delivery of my letters and newspapers. On arriving at my office one day, I was amazed to find my table covered with letters, evidently just from the post-office, but unfortunately not one addressed to me. I turned to Wan Lee, who was surveying them with a calm satisfaction, and demanded an explanation. To my horror he pointed to an empty mail-bag in the corner, and said, "Postman he say, 'No lettee, John—no lettee, John.' Postman plentee lie! Postman no good. Me catchee lettee last night—allee same!" Luckily it was still early; the mails had not been distributed; I had a hurried interview with the Postmaster, and Wan Lee's bold attempt at robbing the U. S. Mail was finally condoned, by the purchase of a new mail bag, and the whole affair thus kept a secret.

If my liking for my little Pagan page had not been sufficient, my duty to Hop Sing was enough to cause me to take Wan Lee with me when I returned to San Francisco, after my two years' experience with "The Northern Star." I do not think he contemplated the change with pleasure. I attributed his feelings to a nervous dread of crowded public streets—when he had to go across town for me on an errand, he always made a circuit of the outskirts—to his dislike for the discipline of the Chinese and English school to which I proposed to send him, to his fondness for the free, vagrant life of the mines, to sheer willfulness! That it might have been a superstitious premonition did not occur to me until long after.

Nevertheless it really seemed as if the opportunity I had long looked for and confidently expected had come—the opportunity of placing Wan Lee under gently restraining influences, of subjecting him to a life and experience that would draw out of him what good my superficial care and ill-regulated kindness could not reach. Wan Lee was placed at the school of a Chinese Missionary,[28]—an intelligent and kind-hearted clergyman, who had shown great interest in the boy, and who, better than all, had a wonderful faith in him. A home was found for him in the family of a widow, who had a bright and interesting daughter about two years younger than Wan Lee. It was this bright, cheery, innocent, and artless child that touched and reached a depth in the boy's nature that hitherto had been unsuspected—that awakened a moral susceptibility which had lain for years insensible alike to the teachings of society or the ethics of the theologian.

These few brief months, bright with a promise that we never saw fulfilled, must have been happy ones to Wan Lee. He worshipped his little friend with something of the same superstition, but without any of the caprice that he bestowed upon his porcelain pagan god. It was his delight to walk behind her to school, carrying her books—a service always fraught with danger to him from the little hands of his Caucasian Christian brothers. He made her the most marvelous toys, he would cut out of carrots and turnips the most astonishing roses and tulips; he made life-like chickens out of melon-seeds, he constructed fans and kites, and was singularly proficient in the making of dolls' paper dresses. On the other hand, she played and sang to him, taught him a thousand little prettinesses and refinements only known to girls, gave him a yellow ribbon for his pig-tail, as best suiting his complexion, read to him, showed him wherein he was original and valuable, took him to Sunday school with her, against the precedents of the school, and, small-woman-like, triumphed. I wish I could add here, that she effected his conversion, and made him give up his porcelain idol, but I am telling a true story, and this little girl was quite content to fill him with her own Christian goodness, without letting him know that he was changed. So they got along very well together—this little Christian girl with her shining cross hanging around her plump, white, little neck; and this dark little Pagan, with his hideous porcelain god hidden away in his blouse.

There were two days of that eventful year which will long be remembered in San Francisco—two days when a mob of her citizens set upon and killed unarmed, defenseless foreigners, because they were foreigners and of another race, religion and color, and worked for what wages they could get. There were some public men so timid, that, seeing this, they thought that the end of the world had come; there were some eminent statesmen whose names I am ashamed to write here, who began to think that the passage in the Constitution which guarantees civil and religious liberty to every citizen or foreigner was a mistake. But there were also some men who were not so easily frightened, and in twenty-four hours we had things so arranged that the timid men could wring their hands in safety, and the eminent statesmen utter their doubts without hurting anybody or anything. And in the midst of this I got a note from Hop Sing, asking me to come to him immediately.

I found his warehouse closed and strongly guarded by the police against any possible attack of the rioters. Hop Sing admitted me through a barred grating with his usual imperturbable calm, but, as it seemed to me, with more than his usual seriousness. Without a word he took my hand, and led me to the rear of the room, and thence down stairs into the basement. It was dimly lighted, but there was something lying on the floor covered by a shawl. As I approached he drew the shawl away with a sudden gesture, and revealed Wan Lee, the Pagan, lying there dead.

Dead, my reverend friends, dead! Stoned to death in the streets of San Francisco, in the year of grace, eighteen hundred and sixty-nine, by a mob of half-grown boys and Christian school children!

As I put my hand reverently upon his breast, I felt something crumbling beneath his blouse. I looked inquiringly at Hop Sing. He put his hand between the folds of silk and drew out something with the first bitter smile I had ever seen on the face of that pagan gentleman.

It was Wan Lee's porcelain god, crushed by a stone from the hands of those Christian iconoclasts!

NOTES

1. A "visiting card" typically contained a person's name and perhaps a small image or quotation; it could also function as a notecard. Visitors left cards at a house after social visits, sent them to request a visit, or sent them when they could not personally attend a gathering.
2. Confection, such as candied fruit.
3. A Chinese philosopher and politician (551–479 BCE) who is highly revered for his teachings.
4. Pantomime is a genre of theatrical production intended to be broadly melodramatic and comical; here the narrator is referring to what must have been well-known pantomime productions in which people of Chinese origin were portrayed in the stereotypical ways enumerated here.
5. Underwear.
6. "Ching-a-Ring Chaw" was an early minstrel song, performed by White singers wearing blackface; these songs often portrayed African Americans in very demeaning ways. Here the narrator displays his racism against both African Americans as well as against a person of Chinese origin in the way he incorrectly assumes that people from China would utter such a phrase.
7. During the Qing dynasty in China (1644–1912), men were required to shave the front of their scalps, grow their hair long in back, and braid that hair in order

to indicate submission to Qing rule; this was known as the "Manchu hairstyle," and if a Chinese man did not wear his hair this way, he was executed for treason. In the United States, Chinese men's braids were derogatorily referred to as "pig-tails."

8. Curly wool or "fur" from young lambs, originally from Astrakhan, in southern Russia.

9. In general, "pagan" refers to a person who does not subscribe to any formal religion; in the United States the term has typically been used to refer to anyone who is not a Christian. Here the term is used ironically.

10. A juggler who performs regularly for a noble person. In this case, Wang is understood to have served as a juggler for such a noble person in China.

11. An antiquated spelling of the word "gruesome."

12. I don't know (Spanish).

13. Here the narrator refers to the "form" of a newspaper, consisting of a frame and the type, which was to be used for the printing; to make sure the type would not move during the printing process, it would be "locked up" with spacing blocks between the frame and type. Klamath County, California, from 1851 to 1874, was located in a rural area along the Pacific Ocean and on the border with Oregon; it was disestablished in 1874 and its territory divided between Siskiyou and Humboldt Counties.

14. The "printer's devil" was a name given to apprentices in newspaper composing rooms, where the type was set. Responsibilities ranged from preparing and cleaning the presses to running errands for the printer.

15. A derogatory slang term formerly used to refer to unskilled laborers from Asian countries, such as China or India. Because of its offensive nature, it is no longer acceptable to use this term.

16. Stockton is a city in the Central Valley of California.

17. Most likely this is a reference to a classic thirteenth-century Chinese text known as *San Zi Jing*, typically translated in English as the *Trimetric Classic* or *Three Character Classic*; written in relatively easy-to-understand triplets of Chinese characters, it was used chiefly by parents to teach Chinese characters to young children.

18. Chinese Confucian philosopher (ca. 372–289 BCE), sometimes spelled "Mengzi."

19. This is an example of "eye dialect," a literary device that involves the author rendering speech patterns unknown to readers by spelling familiar words phonetically, as they might be pronounced by the speaker. American writers commonly used this device to try to reproduce what was known as "pidgin English," used by Chinese immigrants; it was usually employed to suggest a Chinese person's simplicity and lack of intelligence.

20. Named by nineteenth-century British colonists who encountered them on the Indian subcontinent, so-called Indian clubs are bowling pin–shaped clubs weighing up to a hundred pounds and usually made of wood that are used as exercise equipment to build strength and dexterity.

21. It is implied here that the printers are worried that if they teach their trade to a Chinese person, they will be let go in favor of someone who will work for lower wages; many times in American history, the threat of losing jobs to immigrants has been used to justify anti-immigrant violence.

22. The Mongol Empire of the thirteenth and fourteenth centuries stretched from what is now Eastern Europe all the way to the Sea of Japan; at this time many Americans incorrectly conflated the term "Mongol" and "Chinese."

23. Probably a printer's misspelling of "Siskiyou," a county of California located east of Klamath County, on the border with Oregon.

24. Noah Webster Jr. (1758–1843) was a prominent leader during the early years of the United States; he was especially known for his work as a lexicographer, and his *An American Dictionary of the English Language* (1828) was a milestone in establishing standardized American spellings.

25. "Galley proofs" are the first printings from type that has been set up; these sheets of paper are intended for review by editors and proofreaders before "locking up" the type for final printing.

26. These were both common, and insulting, stereotypes of Chinese behavior.

27. A character from William Shakespeare's *Twelfth Night*, Malvolio is an ambitious and puritanical servant who sees himself as superior to other characters in the comedy; contemporary interpretations of the play describe him as an antagonist, rather than as a "civil" presence.

28. Along with White settlers and prospectors, Christian missionaries came to California in the late nineteenth century, but their object was to convert Native Americans and Chinese immigrants to their religion; many of these missionaries established schools as part of their project of not only converting members of these groups to Christianity but also forcing them to leave their own respective cultural heritages and languages behind in order to become "American."

LAFCADIO HEARN

(1850–1904)

Lafcadio Hearn's complicated personal history makes it somewhat difficult to definitively classify him as an "American author." Born to a Greek mother and an Irish father on a Greek island, Hearn grew up chiefly in Ireland but also later attended schools in France and England. In 1869 he emigrated to the United States, where he lived for two years in New York City, six years in Cincinnati, and then thirteen years in New Orleans. During his time in the latter two cities, Hearn supported himself with his writing, chiefly for local newspapers.

Always seeking new adventures and exciting locales to write about, Hearn left New Orleans in 1890 for Japan, where he lived the rest of his life. At a time when Japan was gradually opening itself up to the outside world, Hearn was able to make a living by serving as an English literature teacher and professor in a number of different Japanese institutions. Much of his time, however, was spent writing articles explaining Japanese culture to Westerners, which he published in the United States, as well as researching and translating Japanese folktales and legends that were quickly being forgotten by the Japanese themselves during their rush to modernize. Even to this day he is highly regarded by many Japanese for the significant role he played in preserving these elements of their traditional culture. Although Hearn did regard himself primarily as an American, he was no superficial tourist of Japan who offered only an outsider's perspective; indeed, he married a Japanese woman, had four children with her, and became a Japanese citizen. Ironically, just after the turn of the century, Hearn was pushed out of his teaching position at the Imperial University of Tokyo because of antiforeigner sentiment, and this might have contributed to the stroke that killed him in 1904.

"In the Twilight of the Gods" originally appeared in the prestigious American magazine *Atlantic Monthly* (June 1895) and deftly blends a reportorial style with a fiction writer's attention to symbolic significance. It also exhibits a rare self-awareness of how little most Westerners understood or appreciated the Asian cultures that their commercial and imperialistic projects were fast destroying. This piece was later included in Hearn's third collection of stories and essays about Japan, *Kokoro: Hints and Echoes of Japanese Inner Life* (1896).

IN THE TWILIGHT OF THE GODS (1895)

"Do you know anything about josses?"

"Josses?"

"Yes; idols, Japanese idols,—josses."

"Something," I answered, "but not very much."

"Well, come and look at my collection, won't you? I've been collecting josses for twenty years, and I've got some worth seeing. They're not for sale, though, except to the British Museum."[1]

I followed the curio dealer through the bric-à-brac of his shop, and across a paved yard into an unusually large go-down.[2] Like all go-downs it was dark: I could barely discern a stairway sloping up through gloom. He paused at the foot.

"You'll be able to see better in a moment," he said. "I had this place built expressly for them; but now it is scarcely big enough. They're all in the second story. Go right up; only be careful,—the steps are bad."

I climbed, and reached a sort of gloaming, under a very high roof, and found myself face to face with the gods.

In the dusk of the great go-down the spectacle was more than weird: it was apparitional. Arhats and Buddhas and Bodhisattvas,[3] and the shapes of a mythology older than they, filled all the shadowy space; not ranked by hierarchies, as in a temple, but mingled without order, as in a silent panic. Out of the wilderness of multiple heads and broken aureoles and hands uplifted in menace or in prayer, a shimmering confusion of dusty gold half lighted by cobwebbed air-holes in the heavy walls, I could at first discern little; then, as the dimness cleared, I began to distinguish personalities. I saw Kwannon, of many forms; Jizō, of many names; Shaka, Yaakushi, Amida, the Buddhas and their disciples.[4] They were very old; and their art was not all of Japan, nor of any one place or time:

there were shapes from Korea, China, India,—treasures brought over sea in the rich days of the early Buddhist missions. Some were seated upon lotos flowers, the lotos flowers of the Apparitional Birth.[5] Some rode leopards, tigers, lions, or monsters mystical, typifying lightning, typifying death. One, triple-headed and many-handed, sinister and splendid, seemed moving through the gloom on a throne of gold, uplifted by a phalanx of elephants. Fudō I saw, shrouded and shrined in fire, and Maya-Fujin, riding her celestial peacock; and strangely mingling with these Buddhist visions, as in the anachronism of a Limbo, armored effigies of daimyō and images of the Chinese sages. There were huge forms of wrath, grasping thunderbolts, and rising to the roof: the Deva-kings, like impersonations of hurricane power; the Ni-O, guardians of long-vanished temple gates.[6] Also there were forms voluptuously feminine: the light grace of the limbs folded within their lotos cups, the suppleness of the fingers numbering the numbers of the Good Law,[7] were ideals possibly inspired in some forgotten time by the charm of an Indian dancing-girl. Shelved against the naked brickwork above, I could perceive multitudes of lesser shapes: demon figures with eyes that burned through the dark like the eyes of a black cat, and figures half man, half bird, winged and beaked like eagles,—the *Tengu* of Japanese fancy.

"Well?" queried the curio dealer, with a chuckle of satisfaction at my evident surprise.

"It is a very great collection," I responded.

He clapped his hand on my shoulder, and exclaimed triumphantly in my ear, "Cost me fifty thousand dollars."

But the images themselves told me how much more was their cost to forgotten piety, notwithstanding the cheapness of artistic labor in the East. Also they told me of the dead millions whose pilgrim feet had worn hollow the steps leading to their shrines, of the buried mothers who used to suspend little baby-dresses before their altars, of the generations of children taught to murmur prayers to them, of the countless sorrows and hopes confided to them. Ghosts of the worship of centuries had followed them into exile; a thin, sweet odor of incense haunted all the dusty place.

"What would you call that?" asked the voice of the curio dealer. "I've been told it's the best of the lot."

He pointed to a figure resting upon a triple golden lotos,—Avalokitesvara: she "who looketh down above the sound of prayer."[8] . . . *Storms and hate give way to her name. Fire is quenched by her name. Demons vanish at the sound of her name. By her name one may stand firm in the sky, like a sun.* . . . The delicacy of the limbs, the tenderness of the smile, were dreams of the Indian paradise.

"It is a Kwannon," I made reply, "and very beautiful."

"Somebody will have to pay me a very beautiful price for it," he said, with a shrewd wink. "It cost me enough! As a rule, though, I get these things pretty cheap. There are few people who care to buy them, and they have to be sold privately, you know: that gives me an advantage. See that joss in the corner,—the big black fellow? What is it?"

"Emmei-Jizō," I answered,—"Jizō, the giver of long life. It must be very old."

"Well," he said, again taking me by the shoulder, "the man from whom I got that piece was put in prison for selling it to me."

Then he burst into a hearty laugh,—whether at the recollection of his own cleverness in the transaction, or at the unfortunate simplicity of the person who had sold the statue contrary to law. I could not decide.

"Afterwards," he resumed, "they wanted to get it back again, and offered me more than I had given for it. But I held on. I don't know everything about josses, but I do know what they are worth. There isn't another idol like that in the whole country. The British Museum will be glad to get it."

"When do you intend to offer the collection to the British Museum?" I presumed to ask.

"Well, I first want to get up a show," he replied. "There's money to be made by a show of josses in London. London people never saw anything like this in their lives. Then the church folks help that sort of a show, if you manage them properly; it advertises the missions. 'Heathen idols from Japan!' . . . How do you like the baby?"

I was looking at a small gold-colored image of a naked child, standing, one tiny hand pointing upward, and the other downward,—representing the Buddha newly born. *Sparkling with light he came from the womb, as when the Sun first rises in the east. . . . Upright he took deliberately seven steps; and the prints of his feet upon the ground remained burning as seven stars. And he spoke with clearest utterance, saying, "This birth is a Buddha birth. Rebirth is not for me. Only this last time am I born for the salvation of all on earth and in heaven."*

"That is what they call a Tanjō-Shakia,"[9] I said. "It looks like bronze."

"Bronze it is," he responded, tapping it with his knuckles to make the metal ring. "The bronze alone is worth more than the price I paid."

I looked at the four Devas[10] whose heads almost touched the roof, and thought of the story of their apparition told in the Mahavagga.[11] *On a beautiful night the Four Great Kings entered the holy grove, filling all the place with light; and having respectfully saluted the Blessed One, they stood in the four directions, like four great firebrands.*

"How did you ever manage to get those big figures upstairs?" I asked.

"Oh, hauled them up! We've got a hatchway. The real trouble was getting them here by train. It was the first railroad trip they ever made. . . . But look at these here: *they* will make the sensation of the show!"

I looked, and saw two small wooden images, about three feet high.

"Why do you think they will make a sensation?" I inquired innocently.

"Don't you see what they are? They date from the time of the persecutions. *Japanese devils trampling on the Cross!*"

They were small temple guardians only; but their feet rested upon X-shaped supports.

"Did any person tell you these were devils trampling on the cross?" I made bold to ask.

"What else are they doing?" he answered evasively. "Look at the crosses under their feet."

"But they are not devils," I insisted; "and those cross-pieces were put under their feet simply to give equilibrium."

He said nothing, but looked disappointed, and I felt a little sorry for him. *Devils trampling on the Cross*, as a display line in some London poster announcing the arrival of "josses from Japan," might certainly have been relied on to catch the public eye.

"This is more wonderful," I said, pointing to a beautiful group,—Maya with the infant Buddha issuing from her side,[12] according to tradition. *Painlessly the Bodhisattva was born from her right side. It was the eighth day of the fourth moon.*

"That's bronze, too," he remarked, tapping it. "Bronze josses are getting rare. We used to buy them up and sell them for old metal. Wish I'd kept some of them. You ought to have seen the bronzes, in those days, coming in from the temples,—bells and vases and josses! That was the time we tried to buy the Daibutsu at Kamakura."[13]

"For old bronze?" I queried.

"Yes. We calculated the weight of the metal, and formed a syndicate. Our first offer was thirty thousand. We could have made a big profit, for there's a good deal of gold and silver in that work. The priests wanted to sell, but the people wouldn't let them."

"It's one of the world's wonders," I said. "Would you really have broken it up?"

"Certainly. Why not? What else could you do with it? . . . That one there looks just like a Virgin Mary,[14] doesn't it?"

He pointed to the gilded image of a female clasping a child to her breast.

"Yes," I replied; "but it is Kishibōjin, the goddess who loves little children."

"People talk about idolatry," he went on musingly. "I've seen things like many of these in Roman Catholic chapels. Seems to me religion is pretty much the same the world over."

"I think you are right," I said.

"Why, the story of Buddha is like the story of Christ, isn't it?"

"To some degree," I assented.

"Only, he wasn't crucified."

I did not answer; thinking of the text, *In all the world there is not one spot even so large as a mustard-seed where he has not surrendered his body for the sake of creatures.* Then it suddenly seemed to me that this was absolutely true. For the Buddha of the deeper Buddhism is not Gautama, nor yet any one Tathagata,[15] but simply the divine in man. Chrysalides[16] of the infinite we all are: each contains a ghostly Buddha, and the millions are but one. All humanity is potentially the Buddha-to-come, dreaming through the ages in Illusion; and the teacher's smile will make beautiful the world again when selfishness shall die. Every noble sacrifice brings nearer the hour of his awakening; and who may justly doubt—remembering the myriads of the centuries of man—that even now there does not remain one place on earth where life has not been freely given for love or duty?

I felt the curio dealer's hand on my shoulder again.

"At all events," he cried in a cheery tone, "they'll be appreciated in the British Museum—eh?"

"I hope so. They ought to be."

Then I fancied them immured somewhere in that vast necropolis of dead gods, under the gloom of a pea-soup fog, chambered with forgotten divinities of Egypt or Babylon, and trembling faintly at the roar of London,—all to what end? Perhaps to aid another Alma Tadema[17] to paint the beauty of another vanished civilization; perhaps to assist the illustration of an English Dictionary of Buddhism; perhaps to inspire some future laureate with a metaphor startling as Tennyson's figure of the "oiled and curled Assyrian bull."[18] Assuredly they would not be preserved in vain. The thinkers of a less conventional and selfish era would teach new reverence for them. Each eidolon[19] shaped by human faith remains the shell of a truth eternally divine; and even the shell itself may hold a ghostly power. The soft serenity, the passionless tenderness, of these Buddha faces might yet give peace of soul to a West weary of creeds transformed into conventions, eager for the coming of another teacher to proclaim, "*I have the same feeling for the high as for the low, for the moral as for the immoral, for the depraved as for the virtuous, for those holding sectarian views and false opinions as for those whose beliefs are good and true.*"[20]

NOTES

1. During the time of the British Empire, representatives of the British Museum in London avidly acquired items from far-off lands in various ways; in recent years many of those acquisitions have been challenged as unethical and illegal.

2. According to the footnote in the original *Atlantic Monthly* appearance, "go-down" is "a name given to fireproof storehouses in the open ports of the Far East. The word is derived from the Malay *gâdong*."

3. Statues of various figures important to Buddhism. An "arhat" is someone who understands the true nature of human existence and has thus achieved nirvana; Buddhist temples are often decorated with statues or other representations of the sixteen original arhat disciples of Buddha. The term "buddha" can refer to any person who has achieved enlightenment from ignorance or specifically to the historical figure Gautama Buddha, a monk who lived in what is now northeastern India sometime between the sixth and fourth centuries BCE and whose writings and teachings subsequently became the basis of Buddhism. A "bodhisattva" is one who forgoes nirvana in order to serve others on earth.

4. "Kwannon" is an anglicized form of "Guanyin," a female Chinese bodhisattva revered for her compassion toward others; Jizō Bosatsu was a bodhisattva known for his protection of travelers, women, and children (both born and unborn); Shaka Nyorai is the Japanese name for Gautama Buddha; Yakushi Nyorai is known as the buddha of medicine and healing; and Amitābha Buddha is regarded as a savior in Mahayana Buddhism.

5. According to chapter 8 of the sacred Buddhist text the Lotus Sutra, in a more perfected future "all beings in that Buddha-field shall be pure and lead a spiritual life. Springing into existence by apparitional birth, they shall all be gold-colored and display the thirty-two characteristic signs."

6. The names given in this passage are all various Buddhist figures who are frequently depicted in statuary.
7. A probable reference to the Five Precepts of Buddhism: no killing, no stealing, no committing sexual misconduct, no lying, and no taking intoxicants.
8. Avalokiteśvara, well known for his compassion, is also known as Guanyin or Kwannon.
9. Most likely a figure from the Tanjō region of Japan that depicts a member of the Shakya people, whose most famous representative was Gautama Buddha.
10. The Four Heavenly Kings of Buddhism watch over the four directions (north, south, east, and west).
11. The Mahāvagga is a sacred Buddhist text that contains, among other things, narratives about the spiritual awakenings of Gautama Buddha and of his ten principal disciples.
12. Maya was Buddha's mother.
13. A "daibutsu" is a large statue of Buddha; the Daibutsu at Kamakura is a forty-four-foot-tall hollow bronze statue completed in 1252.
14. The dealer's ethnocentrism is again emphasized by the way his frame of reference is limited to Christianity, for here he compares a Buddhist figure to the Virgin Mary, mother of Jesus.
15. "Tathāgata" is a general term for any buddha.
16. Plural of "chrysalis," the stage between larva and birth for most insects.
17. Sir Lawrence Alma-Tadema (1836–1912) was a Dutch-born painter who lived most of his adult life in Britain; he was most famous for his depictions of scenes from the Roman Empire.
18. In the poem "Maud" (1855), the English poet Alfred, Lord Tennyson (1809–92), refers to Maud's brother with this metaphor.
19. A specter or insubstantial being.
20. These words are commonly ascribed to Gautama Buddha.

O. HENRY (WILLIAM SYDNEY PORTER)

(1862–1910)

O. Henry (the pen name of William Sydney Porter) was one of America's most beloved and prolific short story authors at the turn of the nineteenth and into the twentieth century. Not long after his death, in fact, the hundreds of short stories he had published were gathered into a fourteen-volume edition entitled *The Complete Writings of O. Henry* (1917). Before he began his career as a writer, though, O. Henry, who moved from his native North Carolina to Texas in 1882, worked at a number of jobs, including pharmacist, shepherd, ranch hand, cook, and accountant. While serving in this last capacity at a bank in Austin, he was charged with, and convicted of, embezzlement; after first fleeing to Honduras to avoid sentencing, he returned to be with his young daughter and dying wife. Subsequently, he served a three-year term in the penitentiary, during which time

he began writing short stories and having a friend on the outside submit them to
magazines for publication. He wrote under a number of different pseudonyms
and saw his work accepted at, and published in, some of the leading magazines
of the day. After his release from prison in 1901, he began a full-time writing
career and settled on "O. Henry" as his sole nom de plume; there is no definitive
answer as to where this name came from. His stories, set variously in the West, the
Midwest, and New York City, depicted the nation's diversity; they also were well-
known for their surprise endings. A few of his stories have become classics, most
notably "The Gift of the Magi" (1905) and "The Ransom of Red Chief" (1907).

For many years academic critics considered O. Henry's stories insufficiently artistic to merit inclusion in literary anthologies, often categorizing them as juvenile
fiction. However, the severity of these judgments, and the general dismissal that
resulted, deserves to be interrogated by modern readers. "A Municipal Report"
(first published in his 1910 collection, *Strictly Business*) is a good example of what
has unfairly been overlooked in O. Henry's oeuvre. Significantly preceded by quotations from Rudyard Kipling and Frank Norris, two well-known contemporary
authors who, like O. Henry, frequently blended Realistic and Romantic elements
in their fictions, the collection defies many expectations readers would have had
for a work usually placed in the category of Regionalist Realism. Such works
typically presented cities, towns, and rural areas outside the urban Northeast
as "quaint" locales where nothing of importance happened besides visits from
more sophisticated city dwellers, thereby satisfying most contemporary readers,
who would have identified with such visitors and looked down on the inhabitants
and cultures of these locales. Yet this sophisticated tale deploys an experimental
narrative form and subtly prompts readers to question their expectations. Why,
for instance, does O. Henry intersperse snippets of "factual" writing throughout
his fictional narrative? Does "nothing important" occur, or does the story reveal
a complex reality underneath what the narrator believes he understands? Is the
"hero" (the one with the most humanity) the narrator/outsider from the big city,
as in so many works of this genre? Finally, one must ask how the narrator's being
a self-proclaimed southerner, just like O. Henry, might affect his portrayal of certain characters and of racial relations in a southern state during Reconstruction?

*Readers should be aware that this story includes some language which, while
commonly used during this time period, is no longer considered acceptable because of its offensive nature.

A MUNICIPAL REPORT (1910)

> The cities are full of pride,
> Challenging each to each—
> This from her mountainside,
> That from her burthened beach.
>
>   R[udyard] Kipling

Fancy a novel about Chicago or Buffalo, let us say, of Nashville,
Tennessee! There are just three big cities in the United States that are
"story cities"—New York, of course, New Orleans, and, best of the
lot, San Francisco.

Frank Norris

East is East, and West is San Francisco, according to Californians. Californians
are a race of people; they are not merely inhabitants of a State. They are the
Southerners of the West. Now, Chicagoans are no less loyal to their city; but
when you ask them why, they stammer and speak of lake fish and the new Odd
Fellows Building. But Californians go into detail.

Of course they have, in the climate, an argument that is good for half an hour
while you are thinking of your coal bills and heavy underwear. But as soon as
they come to mistake your silence for conviction, madness comes upon them, and
they picture the city of the Golden Gate as the Bagdad of the New World. So
far, as a matter of opinion, no refutation is necessary. But dear cousins all (from
Adam and Eve descended), it is a rash one who will lay his finger on the map and
say: "In this town there can be no romance—what could happen here?" Yes, it is
a bold and a rash deed to challenge in one sentence history, romance, and Rand
and McNally.[1]

NASHVILLE.—A city, port of delivery, and the capital of the State of Tennessee,
is on the Cumberland River and on the N. C. & St. L. and the L. & N. railroads.
This city is regarded as the most important educational centre in the South.

I stepped off the train at 8 P. M. Having searched thesaurus in vain for adjectives, I must, as a substitution, hie me to comparison in the form of a recipe.

Take of London fog 30 parts; malaria 10 parts; gas leaks 20 parts; dew-drops
gathered in a brick yard at sunrise, 25 parts; odor of honeysuckle 15 parts. Mix.

The mixture will give you an approximate conception of a Nashville drizzle.
It is not so fragrant as a moth-ball nor as thick as pea-soup; but 'tis enough—
'twill serve.[2]

I went to a hotel in a tumbril.[3] It required strong self-suppression for me to
keep from climbing to the top of it and giving an imitation of Sidney Carton.[4]
The vehicle was drawn by beasts of a bygone era and driven by something dark
and emancipated.[5]

I was sleepy and tired, so when I got to the hotel I hurriedly paid it the fifty
cents it demanded (with approximate lagniappe,[6] I assure you). I knew its habits;
and I did not want to hear it prate about its old "marster" or anything that
happened "befo' de wah."

The hotel was one of the kind described as "renovated." That means $20,000
worth of new marble pillars, tiling, electric lights and brass cuspidors in the lobby,
and a new L. & N. time table and a lithograph of Lookout Mountain in each
one of the great rooms above. The management was without reproach, the attention full of exquisite Southern courtesy, the service as slow as the progress of
a snail and as good-humored as Rip Van Winkle.[7] The food was worth traveling

a thousand miles for. There is no other hotel in the world where you can get such chicken livers *en brochette*.[8]

At the dinner I asked a Negro[9] waiter if there was anything doing in town. He pondered gravely for a minute, and then replied: "Well, boss, I don't really reckon there's anything at all doin' after sundown."

Sundown had been accomplished; it had been drowned in the drizzle long before. So that spectacle was denied me. But I went forth upon the streets in the drizzle to see what might be there.

It is built on undulating grounds; and the streets are lighted by electricity at a cost of $32,470 per annum.

As I left the hotel there was a race riot. Down upon me charged a company of freedmen, or Arabs, or Zulus, armed with—no, I saw with relief that they were not rifles, but whips.[10] And I saw dimly a caravan of black, clumsy vehicles; and at the reassuring shouts, "Kyar you anywhere in the town, boss, fuh fifty cents," I reasoned that I was merely a "fare" instead of a victim.

I walked through long streets, all leading uphill. I wondered how those streets ever came down again. Perhaps they didn't until they were "graded." On a few of the "main streets" I saw lights in stores here and there; saw street cars go by conveying worthy burghers hither and yon; saw people pass engaged in the art of conversation, and heard a burst of semi-lively laughter issuing from a soda-water and ice-cream parlor. The streets other than "main" seemed to have enticed upon their borders houses consecrated to peace and domesticity. In many of them lights shone behind discreetly drawn window shades, in a few pianos tinkled orderly and irreproachable music. There was, indeed, little "doing." I wished I had come before sundown. So I returned to my hotel.

In November, 1864, the Confederate General Hood advanced against Nashville, where he shut up a National force under General Thomas. The latter then sallied forth and defeated the Confederates in a terrible conflict.

All my life I have heard of, admired, and witnessed the fine marksmanship of the South in its peaceful conflicts in the tobacco-chewing regions. But in my hotel a surprise awaited me. There were twelve bright, new, imposing, capacious brass cuspidors[11] in the great lobby, tall enough to be called urns and so wide-mouthed that the crack pitcher of a lady baseball team should have been able to throw a ball into one of them at five paces distant. But, although a terrible battle had raged and was still raging, the enemy had not suffered. Bright, new, imposing, capacious, untouched, they stood. But, shades of Jefferson Brick![12] the tile floor—the beautiful tile floor! I could not avoid thinking of the battle of Nashville, and trying to draw, as is my foolish habit, some deductions about hereditary marksmanship.

Here I first saw Major (by misplaced courtesy) Wentworth Caswell.[13] I knew him for a type the moment my eyes suffered from the sight of him. A rat has no geographical habitat. My old friend, A. Tennyson, said, as he so well said almost everything:

Prophet, curse me the blabbing lip,
  And curse me the British vermin, the rat.[14]

Let us regard the word "British" as interchangeable *ad lib.* A rat is a rat.

This man was hunting about the hotel lobby like a starved dog that had forgotten where he had buried a bone. He had a face of great acreage, red, pulpy, and with a kind of sleepy massiveness like that of Buddha. He possessed one single virtue—he was very smoothly shaven. The mark of the beast is not indelible upon a man until he goes about with a stubble. I think that if he had not used his razor that day I would have repulsed his advances, and the criminal calendar of the world would have been spared the addition of one murder.

I happened to be standing within five feet of a cuspidor when Major Caswell opened fire upon it. I had been observant enough to perceive that the attacking force was using Gatlings instead of squirrel rifles,[15] so I sidestepped so promptly that the major seized the opportunity to apologize to a noncombatant. He had the blabbing lip. In four minutes he had become my friend and had dragged me to the bar.

I desire to interpolate here that I am a Southerner. But I am not one by profession or trade. I eschew the string tie, the slouch hat, the Prince Albert,[16] the number of bales of cotton destroyed by Sherman,[17] and plug chewing. When the orchestra plays "Dixie"[18] I do not cheer. I slide a little lower on the leather-cornered seat and, well, order another Würzburger[19] and wish that Longstreet[20] had—but what's the use?

Major Caswell banged the bar with his fist, and the first gun at Fort Sumter re-echoed. When he fired the last one at Appomattox I began to hope.[21] But then he began on family trees, and demonstrated that Adam was only a third cousin of a collateral branch of the Caswell family. Genealogy disposed of, he took up, to my distaste, his private family matters. He spoke of his wife, traced her descent back to Eve, and profanely denied any possible rumor that she may have had relations in the land of Nod.[22]

By this time I began to suspect that he was trying to obscure by noise the fact that he had ordered the drinks, on the chance that I would be bewildered into paying for them. But when they were down he crashed a silver dollar loudly upon the bar. Then, of course, another serving was obligatory. And when I had paid for that I took leave of him brusquely; for I wanted no more of him. But before I had obtained my release he had prated loudly of an income that his wife received, and showed a handful of silver money.

When I got my key at the desk the clerk said to me courteously: "If that man Caswell has annoyed you, and if you would like to make a complaint, we will have him ejected. He is a nuisance, a loafer, and without any known means of support, although he seems to have some money most the time. But we don't seem to be able to hit upon any means of throwing him out legally."

"Why, no," said I, after some reflection; "I don't see my way clear to making a complaint. But I would like to place myself on record as asserting that I do not care for his company. Your town," I continued, "seems to be a quiet one. What manner of entertainment, adventure, or excitement, have you to offer to the stranger within your gates?"

"Well, sir," said the clerk, "there will be a show here next Thursday. It is—I'll look it up and have the announcement sent up to your room with the ice water. Good-night."

After I went up to my room I looked out the window. It was only about ten o'clock, but I looked upon a silent town. The drizzle continued, spangled with dim lights, as far apart as currants in a cake sold at the Ladies' Exchange.

"A quiet place," I said to myself, as my first shoe struck the ceiling of the occupant of the room beneath mine. "Nothing of the life here that gives color and good variety to the cities in the East and West. Just a good, ordinary, hum-drum, business town."

Nashville occupies a foremost place among the manufacturing centres of the country. It is the fifth boot and shoe market in the United States, the largest candy and cracker manufacturing city in the South, and does an enormous wholesale drygoods, grocery, and drug business.

I must tell you how I came to be in Nashville, and I assure you the digression brings as much tedium to me as it does to you. I was traveling elsewhere on my own business, but I had a commission from a Northern literary magazine to stop over there and establish a personal connection between the publication and one of its contributors, Azalea Adair.

Adair (there was no clue to the personality except the handwriting) had sent in some essays (lost art!) and poems that had made the editors swear approvingly over their one o'clock luncheon. So they had commissioned me to round up said Adair and corner by contract his or her output at two cents a word before some other publisher offered her ten or twenty.

At nine o'clock the next morning, after my chicken livers *en brochette* (try them if you can find the hotel), I strayed out into the drizzle, which was still on for an unlimited run. At the first corner I came upon Uncle Caesar. He was a stalwart Negro, older than the pyramids, with gray wool and a face that reminded me of Brutus, and a second afterwards of the late King Cettiwayo.[23] He wore the most remarkable coat that I ever had seen or expect to see. It reached to his ankles and had once been a Confederate gray in colors. But rain and sun and age had so variegated it that Joseph's coat,[24] beside it, would have faded to a pale monochrome. I must linger with that coat, for it has to do with the story—the story that is so long in coming, because you can hardly expect anything to happen in Nashville.

Once it must have been the military coat of an officer. The cape of it had vanished, but all adown its front it had been frogged[25] and tasseled magnificently. But now the frogs and tassels were gone. In their stead had been patiently stitched (I surmised by some surviving "black mammy"[26]) new frogs made of cunningly twisted common hempen twine. This twine was frayed and disheveled. It must have been added to the coat as a substitute for vanished splendors, with tasteless but painstaking devotion, for it followed faithfully the curves of the long-missing frogs. And, to complete the comedy and pathos of the garment, all its buttons were gone save one. The second button from the top alone remained. The coat was fastened by other twine strings tied through the buttonholes and other holes rudely pierced in the opposite side. There was never such a weird garment so fantastically bedecked and of so many mottled hues. The lone button was the size of a half-dollar, made of yellow horn and sewed on with coarse twine.

This Negro stood by a carriage so old that Ham himself[27] might have started a hack line with it after he left the ark with the two animals hitched to it. As I approached he threw open the door, drew out a feather duster, waved it without using it, and said in deep, rumbling tones:

"Step right in, suh; ain't a speck of dost in it—jus' got back from a funeral, suh."

I inferred that on such gala occasions carriages were given an extra cleaning. I looked up and down the street and perceived that there was little choice among the vehicles for hire that lined the curb. I looked in my memorandum book for the address of Azalea Adair.

"I want to go to 861 Jessamine Street," I said, and was about to step into the hack. But for an instant the thick, long, gorilla-like arm of the Negro barred me.[28] On his massive and saturnine face a look of sudden suspicion and enmity flashed for a moment. Then, with quickly returning conviction, he asked, blandishingly: "What are you gwine there for, boss?"

"What is that to you?" I asked, a little sharply.

"Nothin', suh, jus' nothin'. Only it's a lonesome kind of part of town and few folks ever has business out there. Step right in. The seats is clean—jes' got back from a funeral, suh."

A mile and a half it must have been to our journey's end. I could hear nothing but the fearful rattle of the ancient hack over the uneven brick paving; I could smell nothing but the drizzle, now further flavored with coal smoke and something like a mixture of tar and oleander blossoms. All I could see through the streaming windows were two rows of dim houses.

The city has an area of 10 square miles; 181 miles of streets, of which 137 miles are paved; a system of waterworks that cost $2,000,000, with 77 miles of mains.

Eight-sixty-one Jessamine Street was a decayed mansion. Thirty yards back from the street it stood, outmerged in a splendid grove of trees and untrimmed shrubbery. A row of box bushes overflowed and almost hid the paling fence from sight; the gate was kept closed by a rope noose that encircled the gate post and the first paling of the gate. But when you got inside you saw that 861 was a shell, a shadow, a ghost of former grandeur and excellence. But in the story, I have not yet got inside.

When the hack had ceased from rattling and the weary quadrupeds came to a rest I handed my jehu[29] his fifty cents with an additional quarter, feeling a glow of conscious generosity as I did so. He refused it.

"It's two dollars, suh," he said.

"How's that?" I asked. "I plainly heard you call out at the hotel. 'Fifty cents to any part of the town.'"

"It's two dollars, suh," he repeated obstinately. "It's a long ways from the hotel."

"It is within the city limits and well within them," I argued. "Don't think that you have picked up a greenhorn Yankee. Do you see those hills over there?" I went on, pointing toward the east (I could not see them, myself, for the drizzle); "well, I was born and raised on their other side. You old fool nigger,[30] can't you tell people from other people when you see 'em?"

The grim face of King Cettiwayo softened. "Is you from the South, suh? I reckon it was them shoes of yourn fooled me. They is somethin' sharp in the toes for a Southern gen'l'man to wear."

"Then the charge is fifty cents, I suppose?" said I, inexorably.

His former expression, a mingling of cupidity and hostility, returned, remained ten seconds, and vanished.

"Boss," he said, "fifty cents is right; but I *needs* two dollars, suh; I'm *obleeged* to have two dollars. I ain't *demandin'* it now, suh; after I knows whar you's from; I'm jus sayin' that I *has* to have two dollars to-night and business is mighty po'."

Peace and confidence settled upon his heavy features. He had been luckier than he had hoped. Instead of having picked up a greenhorn, ignorant of rates, he had come upon an inheritance.

"You confounded old rascal," I said, reaching down to my pocket, "you ought to be turned over to the police."

For the first time I saw him smile. He knew; *he knew*; HE KNEW.

I gave him two one-dollar bills. As I handed them over I noticed that one of them had seen parlous times. Its upper right-hand corner was missing, and it had been torn through in the middle, but joined again. A strip of blue tissue paper, pasted over the split, preserved its negotiability.

Enough of the African bandit for the present: I left him happy, lifted the rope, and opened the creaky gate.

The house, as I said, was a shell. A paint brush had not touched it in twenty years. I could not see why a strong wind should not have bowled it over like a house of cards until I looked again at the trees that hugged it close—the trees that saw the battle of Nashville and still drew their protecting branches around it against storm and enemy and cold.

Azalea Adair, fifty years old, white-haired, a descendant of the cavaliers,[31] as thin and frail as the house she lived in, robed in the cheapest and cleanest dress I ever saw, with an air as simple as a queen's, received me.

The reception room seemed a mile square, because there was nothing in it except some rows of books, on unpainted white-pine bookshelves, a cracked marble-topped table, a rag rug, a hairless horsehair sofa, and two or three chairs. Yes, there was a picture on the wall, a colored crayon drawing of a cluster of pansies. I looked around for the portrait of Andrew Jackson[32] and the pine-cone hanging basket but they were not there.

Azalea Adair and I had conversation, a little of which will be repeated to you. She was a product of the old South, gently nurtured in the sheltered life. Her learning was not broad, but was deep and of splendid originality in its somewhat narrow scope. She had been educated at home, and her knowledge of the world was derived from inference and by inspiration. Of such is the precious, small group of essayists made. While she talked to me I kept brushing my fingers, trying, unconsciously, to rid them guiltily of the absent dust from the half-calf backs of Lamb, Chaucer, Hazlitt, Marcus Aurelius, Montaigne, and Hood.[33] She was exquisite, she was a valuable discovery. Nearly everybody nowadays knows too much—oh, so much too much—of real life.

I could perceive clearly that Azalea Adair was very poor. A house and a dress she had, not much else, I fancied. So, divided between my duty to the magazine and my loyalty to the poets and essayists who fought Thomas in the valley of the Cumberland,[34] I listened to her voice which was like a harpsichord's, and found that I could not speak of contracts. In the presence of the nine Muses and the three Graces[35] one hesitated to lower the topic to two cents. There would have to be another colloquy after I had regained my commercialism. But I spoke of my mission, and three o'clock of the next afternoon was set for the discussion of the business proposition.

"Your town," I said, as I began to make ready to depart (which is the time for smooth generalities) "seems to be a quiet, sedate place. A home town, I could say, where few things out of the ordinary ever happen."

It carries on an extensive trade in stoves and hollow ware with the West and South, and its flouring mills have a daily capacity of more than 2,000 barrels.

Azalea Adair seemed to reflect.

"I have never thought of it that way," she said, with a kind of sincere intensity that seemed to belong to her. "Isn't it in the still, quiet places that things do happen? I fancy that when God began to create the earth on the first Monday morning one could have leaned out one's window and heard the drops of mud splashing from His trowel as He built up the everlasting hills. What did the nois-iest project in the world—I mean the building of the tower of Babel—result in finally?[36] A page and a half of Esperanto in the *North American Review.*"[37]

"Of course," said I, platitudinously, "human nature is the same everywhere; but there is more color—er—more drama and movement and—er—romance in some cities than in others."

"On the surface," said Azalea Adair. "I have traveled many times around the world in a golden airship wafted on two wings—print and dreams. I have seen (on one of my imaginary tours) the Sultan of Turkey bowstring[38] with his own hands one of his wives who had uncovered her face in public. I have seen a man in Nashville tear up his theatre tickets because his wife was going out with her face covered—with rice powder. In San Francisco's Chinatown I saw the slave girl Sing Yee dipped slowly, inch by inch, in boiling almond oil to make her swear she would never see her American lover again. She gave in when the boiling oil had reached three inches above her knee. At a euchre[39] party in East Nashville the other night I saw Kitty Morgan cut dead[40] by seven of her schoolmates and lifelong friends because she had married a house painter. The boiling oil was sizzling as high as her heart; but I wish you could have seen the fine little smile that she carried from table to table. Oh, yes, it is a humdrum town. Just a few miles of red brick houses and mud and stores and lumber yards."

Some one had knocked hollowly at the back of the house. Azalea Adair breathed a soft apology and went to investigate the sound. She came back in three minutes with brightened eyes, a faint flush on her cheeks, and ten years lifted from her shoulders.

"You must have a cup of tea before you go," she said, "and a sugar cake."

She reached and shook a little iron bell. In shuffled a small Negro girl about twelve, barefoot, not very tidy, glowering at me with thumb in mouth and bulging eyes.

Azalea Adair opened a tiny, worn purse and drew out a dollar bill, a dollar bill with the upper right-hand corner missing, torn in two pieces and pasted together again with a strip of blue tissue paper. It was one of those bills I had given the piratical Negro—there was no doubt of it.

"Go up to Mr. Baker's store on the corner, Impy," she said, handing the girl the dollar bill, "and get a quarter of a pound of tea—the kind he always sends me—and ten cents' worth of sugar cakes. Now, hurry. The supply of tea in the house happens to be exhausted," she explained to me.

Impy left by the back way. Before the scrape of her hard, bare feet had died away on the back porch, a wild shriek—I was sure it was hers—filled the hollow house. Then the deep, gruff tones of an angry man's voice mingled with the girl's further squeals and unintelligible words.

Azalea Adair rose without surprise or emotion and disappeared. For two minutes I heard the hoarse rumble of the man's voice, then something like an oath and a small scuffle, and she returned calmly to her chair.

"This is a roomy house," she said, "and I have a tenant for part of it. I am sorry to have to rescind my invitation to tea. It is impossible to get the kind I always use at the store. Perhaps to-morrow Mr. Baker will be able to supply me."

I was sure that Impy had not had time to leave the house. I inquired concerning streeet-car lines and took my leave. After I was well on my way I remembered that I had not learned Azalea Adair's name. But to-morrow would do.

That same day I started in on the course of iniquity that this uneventful city forced upon me. I was in the town only two days, but in that time I managed to lie shamelessly by telegraph, and to be an accomplice—after the fact, if that is the correct legal term—to a murder.

As I rounded the corner nearest my hotel the Afrite coachman of the polychromatic, nonpareil coat seized me, swung open the dungeony door of his peripatetic sarcophagus, flirted his feather duster and began his ritual: "Step right in, boss. Carriage is clean—jus' got back from a funeral. Fifty cents to any—"

And then he knew me and grinned broadly. "'Scuse me, boss; you is de gen'l'man what rid out with me dis mawnin'. Thank you kindly, suh."

"I am going out to 861 again to-morrow afternoon at three," said I, "and if you will be here, I'll let you drive me. So you know Miss Adair?" I concluded, thinking of my dollar bill.

"I belonged to her father, Judge Adair, suh," he replied.

"I judge that she is pretty poor," I said. "She hasn't much money to speak of, has she?"

For an instant I looked again at the fierce countenance of King Cettiwayo, and then he changed back to an extortionate old Negro hack driver.

"She ain't gwine to starve, suh," he said, slowly. "She has reso'ces, suh; she has reso'ces."

"I shall pay you fifty cents for the trip," said I.

"Dat is puffeckly correct, suh," he answered, humbly. "I jus' *had* to have dat two dollars dis mawnin', boss."

I went to the hotel and lied by electricity. I wired the magazine: "A. Adair holds out for eight cents a word."

The answer that came back was: "Give it to her quick, you duffer."[41]

Just before dinner "Major" Wentworth Caswell bore down upon me with the greetings of a long-lost friend. I have seen few men whom I have so instantaneously hated, and of whom it was so difficult to be rid. I was standing at the bar when he invaded me; therefore I could not wave the white ribbon in his face. I would have paid gladly for the drinks, hoping thereby, to escape another; but he was one of those despicable, roaring, advertising bibbers who must have brass bands and fireworks attend upon every cent that they waste in their follies.

With an air of producing millions he drew two one-dollar bills from a pocket and dashed one of them upon the bar. I looked once more at the dollar bill with the upper right-hand corner missing, torn through the middle, and patched with a strip of blue tissue paper. It was my dollar again. It could have been no other.

I went up to my room. The drizzle and the monotony of a dreary, eventless Southern town had made me tired and listless. I remember that just before I went to bed I mentally disposed of the mysterious dollar bill (which might have formed the clue to a tremendously fine detective story of San Francisco) by saying to myself sleepily: "Seems as if a lot of people here own stock in the Hack-Drivers' Trust. Pays dividends promptly, too. Wonder if—" Then I fell asleep.

King Cettiwayo was at his post the next day, and rattled my bones over the stones out to 861. He was to wait and rattle me back again when I was ready.

Azalea Adair looked paler and cleaner and frailer than she had looked on the day before. After she had signed the contract at eight cents per word she grew still paler and began to slip out of her chair. Without much trouble I managed to get her up on the antediluvian horsehair sofa and then I ran out to the sidewalk and yelled to the coffee-colored Pirate to bring a doctor. With a wisdom that I had not suspected in him, he abandoned his team and struck off up the street afoot, realizing the value of speed. In ten minutes he returned with a grave, gray-haired, and capable man of medicine. In a few words (worth much less than eight cents each) I explained to him my presence in the hollow house of mystery.

He bowed with stately understanding, and turned to the old Negro.

"Uncle Caesar," he said, calmly, "run up to my house and ask Miss Lucy to give you a cream pitcher full of fresh milk and half a tumbler of port wine. And hurry back. Don't drive—run. I want you to get back sometime this week."

It occurred to me that Dr. Merriman also felt a distrust as to the speeding powers of the land-pirate's steeds. After Uncle Caesar was gone, lumberingly, but swiftly, up the street, the doctor looked me over with great politeness and as much careful calculation until he had decided that I might do.

"It is only a case of insufficient nutrition," he said. "In other words, the result of poverty, pride, and starvation. Mrs. Caswell has many devoted friends who would be glad to aid her, but she will accept nothing except from that old Negro, Uncle Caesar, who was once owned by her family."

"Mrs. Caswell!" said I, in surprise. And then I looked at the contract and saw that she had signed it "Azalea Adair Caswell."

"I thought she was Miss Adair," I said.

"Married to a drunken, worthless loafer, sir," said the doctor. "It is said that he robs her even of the small sums that her old servant contributes toward her support."

When the milk and wine had been brought the doctor soon revived Azalea Adair. She sat up and talked of the beauty of the autumn leaves that were then in season and their height of color. She referred lightly to her fainting seizure as the outcome of an old palpitation of the heart. Impy fanned her as she lay on the sofa. The doctor was due elsewhere, and I followed him to the door. I told him that it was within my power and intentions to make a reasonable advance of money to Azalea Adair on future contributions to the magazine, and he seemed pleased.

"By the way," he said, "perhaps you would like to know that you had royalty for a coachman. Old Caesar's grandfather was a king in Congo. Caesar himself has royal ways, as you may have observed."

As the doctor was moving off I heard Uncle Caesar's voice inside: "Did he git bofe of dem two dollars from you, Mis' Zalea?"

"Yes, Caesar," I heard Azalea Adair answer, weakly. And then I went in and concluded business negotiations with our contributor. I assumed the responsibility of advancing fifty dollars, putting it as a necessary formality in binding our bargain. And then Uncle Caesar drove me back to the hotel.

Here ends all of the story as far as I can testify as a witness. The rest must be only bare statements of facts.

At about six o'clock I went out for a stroll. Uncle Caesar was at his corner. He threw open the door of his carriage, flourished his duster, and began his depressing formula: "Step right in, suh. Fifty cents to anywhere in the city—hack's puffickly clean, suh—jus' got back from a funeral—"

And then he recognized me. I think his eyesight was getting bad. His coat had taken on a few more faded shades of color, the twine strings were more frayed and ragged, the last remaining button—the button of yellow horn—was gone. A motley descendant of kings was Uncle Caesar!

About two hours later I saw an excited crowd besieging the front of the drug store. In a desert where nothing happens this was manna; so I wedged my way inside. On an extemporized couch of empty boxes and chairs was stretched the mortal corporeality of Major Wentworth Caswell. A doctor was testing him for the mortal ingredient. His decision was that it was conspicuous by its absence.

The erstwhile Major had been found dead on a dark street and brought by curious and ennuied citizens to the drug store. The late human being had been engaged in terrific battle—the details showed that. Loafer and reprobate though he had been, he had also been a warrior. But he had lost. His hands were yet clinched so tightly that his fingers would not be opened. The gentle citizens who had known him stood about and searched their vocabularies to find some good words, if it were possible, to speak of him. One kind-looking man said, after much thought: "When 'Cas' was about fo'teen he was one of the best spellers in the school."

While I stood there the fingers of the right hand of "the man that was," which hung down the side of a white pine box, relaxed, and dropped something at my feet. I covered it with one foot quietly, and a little later on I picked it up and pocketed it. I reasoned that in his last struggle his hand must have seized that object unwittingly and held it in a death grip.

At the hotel that night the main topic of conversation, with the possible exceptions of politics and prohibition, was the demise of Major Caswell. I heard one man say to a group of listeners:

"In my opinion, gentlemen, Caswell was murdered by some of these no-account niggars for his money. He had fifty dollars this afternoon which he showed to several gentlemen in the hotel. When he was found the money was not on his person."

I left the city the next morning at nine, and as the train was crossing the bridge over the Cumberland River I took out of my pocket a yellow horn overcoat button the size of a fifty-cent piece, with frayed ends of coarse twine hanging from it, and cast it out of the window into the slow, muddy waters below.

I wonder what's doing in Buffalo!

NOTES

1. A well-known publisher of atlases.
2. See *Romeo and Juliet*, act 3, scene 1, lines 99–100.
3. An open, unfinished horse-drawn cart for hauling freight.
4. In *A Tale of Two Cities* (1859), by British author Charles Dickens (1812–70), the protagonist, Sydney Carton, is transported in a tumbril to his death at the guillotine.
5. This reference to the African American driver as a "something" and, in the next line, "it" is extremely derogatory in the way it dehumanizes him, and it reflects both the narrator's ignorance and his racism.
6. A tip, or gratuity.
7. The genial main character of a short story entitled "Rip Van Winkle" (1819), by American author Washington Irving (1783–1859).

8. Cooked on a skewer (French).
9. A term commonly used during this time period to refer to African Americans. It is now considered offensive and is no longer used.
10. The narrator is here insultingly comparing formerly enslaved African American wagon drivers (freedmen) competing for his business to peoples he believes his White readers would stereotypically regard as "savage."
11. A receptacle typically placed on the floor during this era into which people were supposed to spit their tobacco juice. The running joke here is that some people miss the opening.
12. A fictional American journalist in Charles Dickens's novel *Martin Chuzzlewit* (1844) known for his wild behavior.
13. Caswell is not an authentic major; it was common practice in the South at this time to honor a White man in authority with an officer's title even if he had never served in the military.
14. An excerpt from part 5 of the 1855 poem "Maud," by the very famous British poet Alfred, Lord Tennyson (1809–92).
15. "Gatlings" were machine guns that fired from multiple barrels joined together in a circle. Their rate of fire was, for the time, very rapid; unlike a "squirrel rifle," however, they were not very accurate.
16. A type of knee-length men's coat popular in the nineteenth century. It was named after the British queen Victoria's husband.
17. William T. Sherman (1820–91) was a Union general during the Civil War whose troops decimated a large swath of the South, from Atlanta to the Atlantic Ocean.
18. A song first popularized by minstrel singers in the 1850s. It became the unofficial anthem of the Confederacy during the Civil War. For what were known as "minstrel shows," White performers would put on theatrical makeup to make their faces black and their lips white; these caricatures of African Americans, and the mocking, inaccurate portrayals involved in the shows, were very racist and, except in the South, mostly disappeared after approximately 1910.
19. A brand of German beer.
20. James Longstreet (1821–1904) was a leading Confederate general.
21. Fort Sumter, in South Carolina, is where the Civil War began in April 1861; it ended when Confederate general Robert E. Lee (1807–70) surrendered at Appomattox, Virginia, in April 1865. The narrator here appears to hope that Major Caswell will stop talking when he gets to this point, but he does not.
22. In Genesis 4:16–26, Cain finds other descendants of Adam and Eve. Caswell claims "profanely" that his wife is descended directly from Eve and not from subsequent generations; he also disputes rumors that Eve might have had sexual relations with those living in the land of Nod, which according to Genesis was located east of Eden.
23. A king of the Zulu tribe in southern Africa, which inflicted heavy casualties on colonial British army units in 1879.
24. In Genesis 37:3, Joseph is given a brightly colored coat by his father, Jacob; many saw this as a sign that Jacob deemed Joseph his rightful successor.
25. Here a "frog" refers to a braided loop and a button on opposite sides of a coat; one secures a closed coat by putting the loop over the button.
26. A term that refers to a stereotypical portrayal of African American women, both before and after the Civil War, as overweight, desexualized, and always cheerfully

servile to the Whites who enslaved or employed her. It was frequently used by Whites as "proof" of how happy enslaved Black people were and thus as justification for slavery.

27. In the Bible, Ham is one of Noah's sons and survives the Flood; he is later cursed, and many White Christians have long considered him the progenitor of Black people and used his example to justify the enslavement and oppression of Black people.

28. The comparison here of the African American driver to a gorilla is further evidence of the narrator's racism.

29. A joking reference to Jehu, who was a king of the northern kingdom of Israel.

30. An extremely denigrating and offensive term used by some non-Black people to refer to African Americans. While sometimes used among Black people to refer to other Black people, in both the past and the present this term was and is usually intended to be derogatory and hurtful when used by non-Black people; it is thus deeply offensive and should not be used.

31. The Cavaliers were wealthy royalists who supported the British kings Charles I and Charles II between 1642 and 1679.

32. Andrew Jackson (1767–1845) was president of the United States from 1829 to 1837; his large plantation, the Hermitage, was located approximately ten miles east of Nashville.

33. Famous classic authors whose works were often published in fancy, leather-bound ("half-calf") editions.

34. George Henry Thomas (1816–70) was a Union general in the Civil War. The Cumberland Valley is in eastern Tennessee.

35. According to Greek mythology, the Muses are the inspirational goddesses of literature, science, and the arts, and the Three Graces are goddesses of such things as charm, beauty, and creativity.

36. The Tower of Babel appears in Genesis 11:1–9, where humans try to construct a very tall tower to avoid a second Flood.

37. "Esperanto" is an artificial language composed of elements from various European languages and intended to be "universally" understood. The *North American Review* was a high-class nineteenth-century magazine respected for its scholarly essays.

38. Turkish executioners sometimes strangled their victims with bow strings.

39. A popular four-handed card game.

40. "To cut dead" was a nineteenth-century term that meant "to snub."

41. Someone who is incompetent.

WILLIAM DEAN HOWELLS

(1837–1920)

William Dean Howells was an author, editor, and literary critic who played an extremely important role in shaping the path of American literature at the turn of the twentieth century. Born in Martinsville, Ohio (now Martins Ferry), in 1837, Howells was the second of eight children. His father, William Cooper

Howells, was a printer and a publisher, and his son worked for him as a typesetter and printer's apprentice, occupations that allowed him to read extensively.

As a young man, after a short time as city editor of the *Ohio State Journal* in Columbus, Howells began to publish stories, poems, and reviews in a number of different magazines, including the *Atlantic Monthly.* In 1860, Howells published *Life of Abraham Lincoln,* a presidential campaign biography; the profits from that book helped him fund a trip to New England, during which he met many literary luminaries of the day, including Ralph Waldo Emerson, Nathaniel Hawthorne, Henry David Thoreau, and Walt Whitman. As a reward for his contribution to Lincoln's election as president, Howells was appointed as the American consul to Venice, serving there from 1861 to 1865. In 1862, at the American embassy in Paris, he married Elinor Mead; the couple would go on to have three children.

Upon returning to the United States in 1866, Howells was hired as the assistant editor of the *Atlantic Monthly* and subsequently served as its editor from 1871 to 1881. "A Romance of Real Life," the Howells story included here, was published during his tenure as assistant editor, and it offers a fascinating rumination on what he believed constituted Realism at this time. It should be further noted that during his time as *Atlantic* editor, Howells promoted many different kinds of Realism by publishing fictions not only by his friends Mark Twain and Henry James but also by a large number of emerging American authors. These new voices offered a wide variety of perspectives on American society during this era, including Charles W. Chesnutt, Stephen Crane, Paul Laurence Dunbar, Mary E. Wilkins Freeman, Abraham Cahan, Edith Wharton, Hamlin Garland, Sarah Orne Jewett, and Frank Norris. Howells also later used his regular Editor's Study (1886–92) and Editor's Easy Chair (1900–1920) columns in *Harper's Monthly* magazine to direct the course of the genre's development.

During the course of his career, Howells wrote over a hundred books, including novels, poetry, plays, travel writing, memoir, and literary criticism. Howells is best known for his novels *A Modern Instance* (1881), *The Rise of Silas Lapham* (1885), and *A Hazard of New Fortunes* (1890), in all of which his keen interest in the social and political developments of his age is clearly evident. Some of the most prominent reoccurring topics he examined were divorce, the ethical dilemmas facing American businessmen pursuing "success," and the problems associated with unbridled capitalism, including the exploitation of ordinary workers.

Howells's importance to American literary culture was widely acknowledged by his contemporaries, and he earned the nickname "Dean of American Letters." In 1908 that moniker became somewhat more official when the American Academy of Arts and Letters elected Howells to be its first president, and in 1915 it created the Howells Medal for exceptional fiction. After Howells's death in May 1920, the new generation of Modernist writers that succeeded his generation generally felt Howells and his works had not been sufficiently "realistic." Sinclair Lewis, for instance, in his acceptance speech for the Nobel Prize in Literature in 1931, stated, "It was with the emergence of William Dean Howells that we first began to have something like a standard, and a very bad standard it was. Mr. Howells was one of the gentlest, sweetest, and most honest of men, but he had the code of a pious old maid whose greatest delight was to have tea at the vicarage. He abhorred not only profanity and obscenity but all of what H. G. Wells called 'the jolly coarsenesses of life.'" Later generations of readers and critics, however, have come to appreciate Howells as a major figure whose indefatigable advocacy of Realism played a major role in making American literature a significant presence in the world.

A ROMANCE OF REAL LIFE (1870)

It was long past the twilight hour, which has been already mentioned as so oppressive in suburban places, and it was even too late for visitors, when a resident, whom I shall briefly describe as the Contributor, was startled by a ring at his door, in the vicinity of one of our great maritime cities,—say Plymouth or Manchester. As any thoughtful person would have done upon the like occasion, he ran over his acquaintance in his mind, speculating whether it were such or such a one, and dismissing the whole list of improbabilities, before laying down the book he was reading, and answering the bell. When at last he did this, he was rewarded by the apparition of an utter stranger on his threshold,—a gaunt figure of forlorn and curious smartness towering far above him, that jerked him a nod of the head, and asked if Mr. Hapford lived there. The face which the lamp-light revealed was remarkable for a harsh two days' growth of beard, and a single bloodshot eye; yet it was not otherwise a sinister countenance, and there was something in the strange presence that appealed and touched. The contributor, revolving the facts vaguely in his mind, was not sure, after all, that it was not the man's clothes rather than his expression that softened him toward the rugged visage: they were so tragically cheap, and the misery of helpless needlewomen, and the poverty and ignorance of the purchaser, were so apparent in their shabby newness, of which they appeared still conscious enough to have led the way to the very window, in the Semitic quarter of the city,[1] where they had lain ticketed, "This nobby suit for $15."

But the stranger's manner put both his face and his clothes out of mind, and claimed a deeper interest when, being answered that the person for whom he asked did not live there, he set his bristling lips hard together, and sighed heavily.

"They told me," he said, in a hopeless way, "that he lived on this street, and I've been to every other house. I'm very anxious to find him, Cap'n,"—the contributor, of course, had no claim to the title with which he was thus decorated,—"for I've a daughter living with him, and I want to see her; I've just got home from a two years' voyage, and"—there was a struggle of the Adam's-apple in the man's gaunt throat—"I find she's about all there is left of my family."

How complex is every human motive! This contributor had been lately thinking, whenever he turned the pages of some foolish traveller,—some empty prattler of Southern or Eastern lands, where all sensation was long ago exhausted, and the oxygen has perished from every sentiment, so has it been breathed and breathed again,—that nowadays the wise adventurer sat down beside his own register and waited for incidents to seek him out. It seemed to him that the cultivation of a patient and receptive spirit was the sole condition needed to insure the occurrence of all manner of surprising facts within the range of one's own personal knowledge; that not only the Greeks were at our doors, but the fairies and the genii, and all the people of romance, who had but to be hospitably treated in order to develop the deepest interest of fiction, and to become the characters of plots so ingenious that the most cunning invention were poor beside them. I myself am not so confident of this, and would rather trust Mr. Charles Reade,[2] say, for my amusement than any chance combination of events. But I should be afraid to say how much his pride in the character of the stranger's sorrows, as proof of the correctness of his theory, prevailed with the contributor to ask him to come in and sit down; though I hope that some abstract impulse of humanity, some compassionate and unselfish care for the man's misfortunes as misfortunes, was not wholly wanting. Indeed, the helpless simplicity with which he had confided his case might have touched a harder heart. "Thank you," said the poor fellow, after a moment's hesitation. "I believe I will come in. I've been on foot all day, and after such a long voyage it makes a man dreadfully sore to walk about so much. Perhaps you can think of a Mr. Hapford living somewhere in the neighborhood."

He sat down, and, after a pondering silence, in which he had remained with his head fallen upon his breast, "My name is Jonathan Tinker," he said, with the unaffected air which had already impressed the contributor, and as if he felt that some form of introduction was necessary, "and the girl that I want to find is Julia Tinker." Then he said, resuming the eventful personal history which the listener exulted while he regretted to hear: "You see, I shipped first to Liverpool, and there I heard from my family; and then I shipped again for Hong-Kong, and after that I never heard a word: I seemed to miss the letters everywhere. This morning, at four o'clock, I left my ship as soon as she had hauled into the dock, and hurried up home. The house was shut, and not a soul in it; and I didn't know what to do, and I sat down on the doorstep to wait till the neighbors woke up, to ask them what had become of my family. And the first one come out he told me my wife had been dead a year and a half, and the baby I'd never seen, with her; and one of my boys was dead; and he didn't know where the rest of the children was, but he'd heard two of the little ones was with a family in the city."

The man mentioned these things with the half-apologetic air observable in a certain kind of Americans when some accident obliges them to confess the infirmity of the natural feelings. They do not ask your sympathy, and you offer it quite at your own risk, with a chance of having it thrown back upon your hands. The contributor assumed the risk so far as to say, "Pretty rough!" when the stranger paused; and perhaps these homely words were best suited to reach the homely heart. The man's quavering lips closed hard again, a kind of spasm passed over his dark face, and then two very small drops of brine shone upon his weather-worn cheeks. This demonstration, into which he had been surprised, seemed to stand for the passion of tears into which the emotional races fall at such times. He opened his lips with a kind of dry click, and went on:—

"I hunted about the whole forenoon in the city, and at last I found the children. I'd been gone so long they didn't know me, and somehow I thought the people they were with weren't over-glad I'd turned up. Finally the oldest child told me that Julia was living with a Mr. Hapford on this street, and I started out here to-night to look her up. If I can find her, I'm all right. I can get the family together, then, and start new."

"It seems rather odd," mused the listener aloud, "that the neighbors let them break up so, and that they should all scatter as they did."

"Well, it ain't so curious as it seems, Cap'n. There was money for them at the owners', all the time; I'd left part of my wages when I sailed; but they didn't know how to get at it, and what could a parcel of children do? Julia's a good girl, and when I find her I'm all right."

The writer could only repeat that there was no Mr. Hapford living on that street, and never had been, so far as he knew. Yet there might be such a person in the neighborhood; and they would go out together, and ask at some of the houses about. But the stranger must first take a glass of wine; for he looked used up.

The sailor awkwardly but civilly enough protested that he did not want to give so much trouble, but took the glass, and, as he put it to his lips, said formally, as if it were a toast or a kind of grace, "I hope I may have the opportunity of returning the compliment." The contributor thanked him; though, as he thought of all the circumstances of the case, and considered the cost at which the stranger had come to enjoy his politeness, he felt little eagerness to secure the return of the compliment at the same price, and added, with the consequence of another set phrase, "Not at all." But the thought had made him the more anxious to befriend the luckless soul fortune had cast in his way; and so the two sallied out together, and rang door-bells wherever lights were still seen burning in the windows, and asked the astonished people who answered their summons whether any Mr. Hapford were known to live in the neighborhood.

And although the search for this gentleman proved vain, the contributor could not feel that an expedition which set familiar objects in such novel lights? was altogether a failure. He entered so intimately into the cares and anxieties of his *protégé*[3] that at times he felt himself in some inexplicable sort a shipmate of Jonathan Tinker, and almost personally a partner of his calamities. The estrangement of all things which takes place, within doors and without, about midnight may have helped to cast this doubt upon his identity;—he seemed to be visiting now for the first time the streets and neighborhoods nearest his own, and his feet stumbled over the accustomed walks. In his quality of houseless wanderer, and—so far as appeared to others—possibly worthless vagabond, he also got a new and instructive effect upon the faces which, in his real character, he knew so well by their looks of neighborly greeting; and it is his belief that the first hospitable prompting of the human heart is to shut the door in the eyes of homeless strangers who present themselves after eleven o'clock. By that time the servants are all abed, and the gentleman of the house answers the bell, and looks out with a loath and bewildered face, which gradually changes to one of suspicion, and of wonder as to what those fellows can possibly want of *him*, till at last the prevailing expression is one of contrite desire to atone for the first reluctance by any sort of service. The contributor professes to have observed these changing phases in the visages of those whom he that night called from their dreams, or arrested in the act of going to bed; and he drew the conclusion—very proper for his imaginable connection with the garroting and other adventurous brotherhoods—that the most flattering moment for knocking on the head people who answer a late ring at night is either in their first selfish bewilderment, or their final self-abandonment to their better impulses. It does not seem to have occurred to him that he would himself have been a much more favorable subject for the predatory arts that any of his neighbors, if his shipmate, the unknown companion of his researches for Mr. Hapford, had been at all so minded. But the faith of the gaunt giant upon which he reposed was good, and the contributor continued to wander about with him in perfect safety. Not a soul among those they asked had ever heard of a Mr. Hapford,—far less of a Julia Tinker living with him. But they all listened to the contributor's explanation with interest and eventual sympathy; and in truth,—briefly told, with a word now and then thrown in by Jonathan Tinker, who kept at the bottom of the steps, showing like a gloomy spectre in the night, or, in his grotesque length and gauntness, like the other's shadow cast there by the lamplight,—it was a story which could hardly fail to awaken pity.

At last, after ringing several bells where there were no lights, in the mere wantonness of good-will, and going away before they could be answered (it would be entertaining to know what dreams they caused the sleepers within), there seemed to be nothing for it but to give up the search till morning, and go to the main street and wait for the last horse-car to the city.

There, seated upon the curbstone, Jonathan Tinker, being plied with a few leading questions, told in hints and scraps the story of his hard life, which was at present that of a second mate, and had been that of a cabin-boy and of a seaman before the mast. The second mate's place he held to be the hardest aboard ship. You got only a few dollars more than the men, and you did not rank with the officers; you took your meals alone, and in everything you belonged by yourself. The men did not respect you, and sometimes the captain abused you awfully before the passengers. The hardest captain that Jonathan Tinker ever sailed with was Captain Gooding of the Cape. It had got to be so that no man would ship second mate under Captain Gooding; and Jonathan Tinker was with him only one voyage. When he had been home awhile, he saw an advertisement for a second mate, and he went round to the owners'. They had kept it secret who the captain was; but there was Captain Gooding in the owners' office. "Why, here's the man, now, that I want for a second mate," said he, when Jonathan Tinker entered; "he knows me." "Captain Gooding, I know you 'most too well to want to sail under you," answered Jonathan. "I might go if I hadn't been with you one voyage too many already."

"And then the men!" said Jonathan, "the men coming aboard drunk, and having to be pounded sober! And the hardest of the fight falls on the second mate! Why, there isn't an inch of me that hasn't been cut over or smashed into a jell. I've had three ribs broken; I've got a scar from a knife on my cheek; and I've been stabbed bad enough, half a dozen times, to lay me up."

Here he gave a sort of desperate laugh, as if the notion of so much misery and such various mutilation were too grotesque not to be amusing. "Well, what can you do?" he went on. "If you don't strike, the men think you're afraid of them; and so you have to begin hard and go on hard. I always tell a man, 'Now, my man, I always begin with a man the way I mean to keep on. You do your duty and you're all right. But if you don't—' Well, the men ain't Americans any more,—Dutch, Spaniards, Chinese, Portuguee,[4]—and it ain't like abusing a white man."[5]

Jonathan Tinker was plainly part of the horrible tyranny which we all know exists on shipboard; and his listener respected him the more that, though he had heart enough to be ashamed of it, he was too honest not to own it.

Why did he still follow the sea? Because he did not know what else to do. When he was younger, he used to love it, but now he hated it. Yet there was not a prettier life in the world if you got to be captain. He used to hope for that once, but not now; though he *thought* he could navigate a ship. Only let him get his family together again, and he would—yes, he would—try to do something ashore.

No car had yet come in sight, and so the contributor suggested that they should walk to the car-office, and look in the Directory, which is kept there for the name of Hapford, in search of whom it had already been arranged that they should renew their acquaintance on the morrow. Jonathan Tinker, when they had reached the office, heard with constitutional phlegm that the name of the Hapford, for whom he inquired was not in the Directory. "Never mind," said the other; "come round to my house in the morning. We'll find him yet." So they parted with a shake of the hand, the second mate saying that he believed he should go down to the vessel and sleep aboard,—if he could sleep,—and murmuring at the last moment the hope of returning the compliment, while the other walked homeward, weary as to the flesh, but, in spite of his sympathy for Jonathan Tinker, very elate in spirit. The truth is,—and however disgraceful to human nature, let the truth still be told,—he had recurred to his primal satisfaction in the man as calamity capable of being used for such and such literary ends, and, while he pitied him, rejoiced in him as an episode of real life quite as striking and complete as anything in fiction. It was literature made to his hand. Nothing could be better, he mused; and once more he passed the details of the story in review, and beheld all those pictures which the poor fellow's artless words had so vividly conjured up: he saw him leaping ashore in the gray summer dawn as soon as the ship hauled into the dock, and making his way, with his vague sea-legs unaccustomed to the pavements, up through the silent and empty city streets; he imagined the tumult of fear and hope which the sight of the man's home must have caused in him, and the benumbing shock of finding it blind and deaf to all his appeals; he saw him sitting down upon what had been his own threshold, and waiting in a sort of bewildered patience till the neighbors should be awake, while the noises of the streets gradually arose, and the wheels began to rattle over the stones, and the milkman and the ice-man came and went, and the waiting figure began to be stared at, and to challenge the curiosity of the passing policeman; he fancied the opening of the neighbor's door, and the slow, cold understanding of the case; the manner, whatever it was, in which the sailor was told that one year before his wife had died, with her babe, and that his children were scattered, none knew where. As the contributor dwelt pityingly upon these things, but at the same time estimated their aesthetic value one by one, he drew near the head of his street, and found himself a few paces behind a boy slouching onward through the night, to whom he called out, adventurously, and with no real hope of information,—

"Do you happen to know anybody on this street by the name of Hapford?"

"Why no, not in this town," said the boy; but he added that there was a street of the same name in a neighboring suburb, and that there was a Hapford living on it.

"By Jove!" thought the contributor, "this is more like literature than ever;" and he hardly knew whether to be more provoked at his own stupidity in not thinking of a street of the same name in the next village, or delighted at the element of fatality which the fact introduced into the story; for Tinker, according to his own account, must have landed from the cars a few rods from the very door he was seeking, and so walked farther and farther from it every moment. He thought the case so curious, that he laid it briefly before the boy, who, however he might have been inwardly affected, was sufficiently true to the national traditions not to make the smallest conceivable outward sign of concern in it.

At home, however, the contributor related his adventures and the story of Tinker's life, adding the fact that he had just found out where Mr. Hapford lived. "It was the only touch wanting," said he; "the whole thing is now perfect."

"It's *too* perfect," was answered from a sad enthusiasm. "Don't speak of it! I can't take it in."

"But the question is," said the contributor, penitently taking himself to task for forgetting the hero of these excellent misfortunes in his delight at their perfection, "how am I to sleep to-night, thinking of that poor soul's suspense and uncertainty? Never mind,—I'll be up early, and run over and make sure that it is Tinker's Hapford, before he gets out here, and have a pleasant surprise for him. Would it not be a justifiable *coup de théâtre*[6] to fetch his daughter here, and let her answer his ring at the door when he comes in the morning?"

This plan was discouraged. "No, no; let them meet in their own way. Just take him to Hapford's house and leave him."

"Very well. But he's too good a character to lose sight of. He's got to come back here and tell us what he intends to do."

The birds, next morning, not having had the second mate on their minds either as an unhappy man or a most fortunate episode, but having slept long and soundly, were singing in a very sprightly way in the wayside trees; and the sweetness of their notes made the contributor's heart light as he climbed the hill and rang at Mr. Hapford's door.

The door was opened by a young girl of fifteen or sixteen, whom he knew at a glance for the second mate's daughter, but of whom, for form's sake, he asked if there were a girl named Julia Tinker living there.

"My name's Julia Tinker," answered the maid, who had rather a disappointing face.

"Well," said the contributor, "your father's got back from his Hong-Kong voyage."

"Hong-Kong voyage?" echoed the girl, with a stare of helpless inquiry, but no other visible emotion.

"Yes. He had never heard of your mother's death. He came home yesterday morning, and was looking for you all day."

Julia Tinker remained open-mouthed but mute; and the other was puzzled at the want of feeling shown, which he could not account for even as a national trait. "Perhaps there's some mistake," he said.

"There must be," answered Julia: "my father hasn't been to sea for a good many years. *My* father," she added, with a diffidence indescribably mingled with a sense of distinction,—"*my* father's in State's Prison. What kind of looking man was this?"

The contributor mechanically described him.

Julia Tinker broke into a loud, hoarse laugh. "Yes, it's him, sure enough." And then, as if the joke were too good to keep: "Miss Hapford, Miss Hapford, father's got out. Do come here!" she called into a back room.

When Mrs. Hapford appeared, Julia fell back, and, having deftly caught a fly on the door-post, occupied herself in plucking it to pieces, while she listened to the conversation of the others.

"It's all true enough," said Mrs. Hapford, when the writer had recounted the moving story of Jonathan Tinker, "so far as the death of his wife and baby goes. But he hasn't been to sea for a good many years, and he must have just come out of State's Prison, where he was put for bigamy. There's always two sides to a story, you know; but they say it broke his first wife's heart, and she died. His friends don't want him to find his children, and this girl especially."

"He's found his children in the city," said the contributor, gloomily, being at a loss what to do or say, in view of the wreck of his romance.

"O, he's found 'em has he?" cried Julia, with heightened amusement. "Then he'll have me next, if I don't pack and go."

"I'm very, very sorry," said the contributor, secretly resolved never to do another good deed, no matter how temptingly the opportunity presented itself. "But you may depend he won't find out from *me* where you are. Of course I had no earthly reason for supposing his story was not true."

"Of course," said kind-hearted Mrs. Hapford, mingling a drop of honey with the gall in the contributor's soul, "you only did your duty."

And indeed, as he turned away he did not feel altogether without compensation. However Jonathan Tinker had fallen in his esteem as a man, he had even risen as literature. The episode which had appeared so perfect in its pathetic phases did not seem less finished as a farce; and this person, to whom all things of every-day life presented themselves in periods more or less rounded, and capable of use as facts or illustrations, could not but rejoice in these new incidents, as dramatically fashioned as the rest. It occurred to him that, wrought into a story, even better use might be made of the facts now than before, for they had developed questions of character and of human nature which could not fail to interest. The more he pondered upon his acquaintance with Jonathan Tinker, the more fascinating the erring mariner became, in his complex truth and falsehood, his delicately blending shades of artifice and *naïveté.*[7] He must, it was felt, have believed to a certain point in his own inventions: nay, starting with that groundwork of truth,—the fact that his wife was really dead, and that he had not seen his family for two years,—why should he not place implicit faith in all the fictions reared upon it? It was probable that he felt a real sorrow for her loss, and that he found a fantastic consolation in depicting the circumstances of her death so that they should look like his inevitable misfortunes rather than his faults. He might well have repented his offence during those two years of prison; and why should he not now cast their dreariness and shame out of his memory, and replace them with the freedom and adventure of a two years' voyage to China,—so probable, in all respects, that the fact should appear an impossible nightmare? In the experiences of his life he had abundant material to furnish forth the facts of such a voyage, and in the weariness and lassitude that should follow a day's walking equally after a two years' voyage and two years' imprisonment, he had as much physical proof in favor of one hypothesis as the other. It was doubtless true, also, as he said, that he had gone to his house at dawn, and sat down on the threshold of his ruined home; and perhaps he felt the desire he had expressed to see his daughter, with a purpose of beginning life anew; and it may have cost him a veritable pang when he found that his little ones did not know him. All the sentiments of the situation were such as might persuade a lively fancy of the truth of its own inventions; and as he heard these continually repeated by the contributor in their search for Mr. Hapford, they must have acquired an objective force and repute scarcely to be resisted. At the same time, there were touches of nature throughout Jonathan Tinker's narrative which could not fail to take the faith of another. The contributor, in reviewing it, thought it particularly charming that his mariner had not overdrawn himself, or attempted to paint his character otherwise than as it probably was; that he had shown his ideas and practices of life to be those of a second mate, nor more nor less, without the gloss of regret or the pretenses to refinement that might be pleasing to the supposed philanthropist with whom he had fallen in. Captain Gooding was of course a true portrait; and there was nothing in Jonathan

Tinker's statement of the relations of a second mate to his superiors and his inferiors which did not agree perfectly with what the contributor had just read in "Two Years before the Mast,"[8]—a book which had possibly cast its glamour upon the adventure. He admired also the just and perfectly characteristic air of grief in the bereaved husband and father,—those occasional escapes from the sense of loss into a brief hilarity and forgetfulness, and those relapses into the hovering gloom, which every one has observed in this poor, crazy human nature when oppressed by sorrow, and which it would have been hard to simulate. But, above all, he exulted in that supreme stroke of the imagination given by the second mate when, at parting, he said he believed he would go down and sleep on board the vessel. In view of this, the State's Prison theory almost appeared a malign and foolish scandal.

Yet even if this theory were correct, was the second mate wholly answerable for beginning his life again with the imposture he had practiced? The contributor had either so fallen in love with the literary advantages of his forlorn deceiver that he would see no moral obliquity in him, or he had touched a subtler verity at last in pondering the affair. It seemed now no longer a farce, but had a pathos which, though very different from that of its first aspect, was hardly less tragical. Knowing with what coldness, or, at the best, uncandor, he (representing Society in its attitude toward convicted Error) would have met the fact had it been owned to him at first, he had not virtue enough to condemn the illusory stranger, who must have been helpless to make at once evident any repentance he felt or good purpose he cherished. Was it not one of the saddest consequences of the man's past,—a dark necessity of misdoing,—that, even with the best will in the world to retrieve himself, his first endeavor must involve a wrong? Might he not, indeed, be considered a martyr, in some sort, to his own admirable impulses? I can see clearly enough where the contributor was astray in this reasoning, but I can also understand how one accustomed to value realities only as they resembled fables should be won with such pensive sophistry; and I can certainly sympathize with his feeling that the mariner's failure to reappear according to appointment added its final and most agreeable charm to the whole affair, and completed the mystery from which the man emerged and which swallowed him up again.

NOTES

1. Refers to a "Jewish quarter," or neighborhood. Due to anti-Semitism, many American cities at this time unfairly restricted Jewish people to particular residential areas.
2. A popular nineteenth-century British author of adventure novels.
3. Someone who is tutored by a more experienced individual (French).
4. Portuguese.
5. Jonathan's racism and ethnocentrism is evident here in his implication that Americans—presumably White—deserve better treatment than people from these other countries.

6. A sudden or sensational turn of events in a play (French).
7. Inexperience (French).
8. *Two Years before the Mast* (1840) was a seafaring memoir by American author Richard Henry Dana Jr. (1815–82).

HENRY JAMES

(1843–1916)

A key figure of American literature, Henry James was born in New York City on April 15, 1843, to an intellectual family of substantial wealth and prominence. Throughout his lifetime, James would often move between the United States and Europe, engaging with some of the greatest writers and thinkers of his day. These experiences uniquely enabled him to synthesize in his work many of the most important social and cultural issues of his time. Indeed, James wrote from a rare vantage point, one that influenced many other artists, and today he is widely recognized as one of the greatest prose stylists of the late nineteenth and early twentieth centuries.

Henry James's grandfather William James immigrated to the United States from Ireland in 1789 and through various business ventures, including the development of salt refining, amassed a significant fortune—one of the largest of his day. His son, Henry James Sr., strongly believed that travel and education were essential for his children's development, and thus he and his family spent a great deal of time abroad, with the James children studying under many different tutors and attending schools both in Europe and the United States. Because of his father's many connections, Henry James, as a child, came in contact with many significant literary and intellectual figures who were family friends, including Ralph Waldo Emerson and Nathaniel Hawthorne. In 1862, James followed his older brother William (who later became a very well-known philosopher and psychologist) to Harvard, ostensibly to study law. However, James—much to the disappointment of his father—chose to spend most of his time there writing, and left after only one year.

In 1869, Henry James went abroad alone for the first time. During this trip, he became acquainted with many notable English thinkers and writers, including Charles Darwin, George Eliot, Dante Gabriel Rossetti, and John Ruskin. James's early introduction to artistic and intellectual circles both abroad and at home inspired him to begin writing about some of the subjects that would occupy him for the rest of his career: the artist's role in modern society and Americans' interactions with European culture. Indeed, his first significant novella, *A Passionate Pilgrim* (1871), depicts an eager American navigating the complexities of European society, and his second novel, *Roderick Hudson* (1875), explores the development of a young American sculptor in Italy.

James returned to his family's home in Cambridge, Massachusetts, in May 1870, but he soon grew tired of life in the United States. For the next several years he lived and worked in Cambridge, London, Paris, Rome, and Florence. This was a period of great productivity for James: in 1877, he published his novel *The American*, followed in 1878 by his most famous work, the novella *Daisy Miller: A Study*, as well as another novel, *The Europeans*. Soon thereafter, James produced the novels *Washington Square* (1880) and *The Portrait of a Lady* (1881), the latter often considered the first of James's masterpieces.

James's parents both died in 1882. He spent over a year in the United States to mourn them, settle their affairs, spend time with his siblings, and visit familiar places, but in August 1883 he left the country for England, not to return for over two decades. In the 1880s and early 1890s, James wrote and published many short stories and novels that both exemplified what would later be termed "Genteel Realism." However, while literary critics and learned readers embraced James's work, his increasingly obtuse writing style led many readers and editors to become less interested in his productions; as a result he often found it difficult to place his writing in magazines, and sales of his books sharply declined.

At the turn of the century, James began writing in a mode that would later be recognized as anticipating the literary genre of Modernism. Some of the most important representatives of this period are his major novels *The Sacred Fount* (1901), *The Wings of the Dove* (1902), *The Ambassadors* (1903), and *The Golden Bowl* (1904). Unfortunately for James, while a number of critics recognized the great skill it took to write these works, most readers found them puzzling, and James's audience shrank even further.

Late in the summer of 1904, James returned to the United States for the first time since 1883. For the next ten months he toured the country, from New England through the middle states, to Florida, west to Los Angeles, north to Seattle, and back again to New York. During these travels he gave numerous talks, which, because of his iconic status, were fairly well attended, but he also recorded extensive notes about his perceptions of what he was seeing. After his return to England in July 1905, James began to write *The American Scene* (1907), a collection of essays reflecting on his impressions of America after having lived abroad for so long; most were extremely critical of the country and its inhabitants, especially of its slums, its architecture, and its (in James's view) greatly debased English language.

In late 1910, James made his final trip to the United States and stayed until August 1911. After World War I erupted in August 1914, James was torn between a sentimental affection for his home country and his adopted England. He was extremely disappointed at the United States' reluctance to enter the war and support the Allies, which led him to, on July 26, 1915, renounce his American citizenship and become a British subject. His physical health continued to decline, and he suffered a series of strokes in December 1915; in January 1916, though, shortly before his death, James was awarded the Order of Merit, the highest honor bestowed on British citizens by the monarchy. On February 28,

1916, James died at his flat in London; his cremated ashes were returned to the United States and buried in the family plot in Cambridge.

It was after James's trip to the United States in 1904–5 that he began writing "The Jolly Corner," the short story included here. It is narrated by a character who returns to his family home and properties in New York City after having lived in Europe for many years and who ruminates at length on his old life in America, Europe's influence on him, and the greatly changed New York he encounters now. These thoughts prompt him to wonder what his life might have been like had he never left his home country. Many of these issues would obviously have been at the forefront of James's own mind during and after his own recent trip to the United States. Leaving aside its biographical aspects, though, "The Jolly Corner" is a highly engaging and suspenseful story on its own, for in it James deftly weaves the tortuous windings of the narrator's psychological fears with the possibly supernatural aspects of his experience in an empty old house. "The Jolly Corner" originally appeared in the first issue of the London-based *English Review* magazine in December 1908, but within months James had extensively revised it for republication in volume 17 of the New York Edition of his collected works. The text reproduced here is from the *English Review.*

THE JOLLY CORNER (1908)

I

"Every one asks me what I 'think' of everything," said Spencer Brydon; "and I make answer as I can—begging or dodging the question, putting them off with any nonsense. It wouldn't matter to any of them really," he went on, "for, even were it possible to meet in that stand-and-deliver way so silly a demand on so big a subject, my 'thoughts' would still be almost altogether about something that concerns only myself." He was talking to Miss Staverton, with whom for a couple of months now he had availed himself of every possible occasion to talk; this disposition and this resource, this comfort and support, as the matter in fact presented itself, having promptly enough taken the first place among the surprises, as he would have called them, attending his so strangely belated return to America. Everything was somehow a surprise; and that might be natural when one had so long and so consistently neglected everything, taken pains to give surprises so much margin for play. He had given them more than thirty years—thirty-three, to be exact; and they now seemed to him to have organised their performance quite on the scale of that licence. He had been twenty-three on leaving New York—he was fifty-six to-day: unless indeed he were to reckon as he had sometimes, since his repatriation, found himself feeling, in which case he would have lived longer than is often allotted to man. It would have taken a century, he repeatedly said to himself, and said also to Alice Staverton, it would have taken a longer absence and a more averted mind than those even of which he had been guilty, to pile up the differences, the newnesses, the queernesses, above all the bignesses, for the better or the worse, that at present assaulted his vision wherever he looked.

The great fact all the while, however, had been the incalculability; since he *had* supposed himself, from decade to decade, to be allowing, and in the most liberal and intelligent manner, for brilliancy of change. He actually saw that he had allowed for nothing; he missed what he would have been sure of finding, he found what he would never have imagined. Proportions and values were upside-down; the ugly things he had expected, the ugly things of his far-away youth, when he had too promptly waked up to a sense of the ugly—these uncanny phenomena placed him rather, as it happened, under the charm; whereas the "swagger"[1] things, the modern, the monstrous, the famous things, those he had more particularly, like thousands of ingenuous inquirers every year, come over to see, were exactly his sources of dismay. They were as so many set traps for displeasure, above all for reaction, of which his restless tread was constantly pressing the spring. It was interesting, doubtless, the whole show, but it would have been too disconcerting had not a certain finer truth saved the situation. He had distinctly not, in this steadier light, come over *all* for the monstrosities; he had come, not only in the last analysis but quite on the face of the act, under an impulse with which they had nothing to do. He had come (putting the thing pompously) to look at his "property," which he had thus, for a third of a century, not been within four thousand miles of; or, expressing it less sordidly, he had yielded to the humour of seeing again his house on the jolly corner, as he usually, and quite fondly, described it—the one in which he had first seen the light, in which various members of his family had lived and had died, in which the holi-days of his overschooled boyhood had been passed and the few social flowers of his chilled adolescence gathered, and which, alienated then for so long a period, had, through the successive deaths of his two brothers and the termination of old arrangements, come wholly into his hands. He was the owner of another, not quite so "good"—the jolly corner having been, from far back, superlatively ex-tended and consecrated; and the value of the pair represented his main capital, with an income consisting, in these later years, of their respective rents, which (thanks precisely to their original excellent type) had never been depressingly low. He could live in "Europe," as he had been in the habit of living, on the product of these flourishing New York leases, and all the better since that of the second structure, the mere number in its long row, having within a twelvemonth fallen in[2] renovation at a high advance had proved beautifully possible.

These were items of property indeed, but he had found himself since his arrival distinguishing more than ever between them. The house within the street, two bristling stretches westward, was already in course of reconstruction as a tall mass of flats; he had acceded some time before to overtures for this conversion—in which, now that it was going forward, it had been not the least of his astonishments to find himself able, on the spot and though without an ounce of such experience, to participate with a certain intelligence, almost with

a certain competence. He had lived his life with his back so turned to such concerns and his face addressed to those of so different an order, that he scarce
knew what to make of this lively stir, in a compartment of his mind never yet
penetrated, of a capacity for business and a sense for construction. These virtues,
so common all round him now, had been dormant in his own organism—where
it might be said of them perhaps that they had slept the sleep of the just. At
present, in the splendid autumn weather—the autumn at least *was* a pure boon
in the terrible place—he loafed about his "work" undeterred, secretly agitated;
not in the least "minding" that the whole proposition, as they said, was vulgar
and sordid, and ready to climb ladders, to walk the plank, to handle materials
and look wise about them, to ask questions, in fine, and challenge explanations
and really "go into" figures.

It amused, it verily quite charmed him; and, by the same stroke, it amused,
and even more, Alice Staverton, though perhaps charming her perceptibly less.
She wasn't, however, going to be better off for it, as *he* was—and so astonish-
ingly much: nothing was now likely, he knew, ever to make her better off than
she found herself, in the afternoon of life, as the delicately frugal possessor and
tenant of the small house in Irving Place to which she had subtly managed to
cling through her almost unbroken New York career. If he knew the way to it
now better than to any other address among the dreadful multiplied numberings
which seemed to him to reduce the whole place to some vast ledger-page, overgrown, fantastic, of ruled and criss-crossed lines and figures—if he had formed,
for his consolation, that habit, it was really not a little because of the charm of
his having encountered and recognised in the vast wilderness of the wholesale,
breaking through the mere gross generalisation of wealth and force and success,
a small, still scene where items and shades, all delicate things, kept the sharpness
of the notes of a high voice perfectly trained, and where economy hung about
like the scent of a garden. His old friend lived with one maid and herself dusted
her relics and trimmed her lamps and polished her silver; she stood oft, in the
awful modern crush, when she could, but she sallied forth and did battle when
the challenge was really to "spirit," the spirit she after all confessed to, proudly
and a little shyly, as to that of the better time, that of *their* common, their quite
far-away and antediluvian social period and order. She made use of the streetcars when need be, the terrible things that people scrambled for as the panic-
stricken at sea scramble for the boats; she affronted inscrutably, under stress, all
the public concussions and ordeals; and yet with that slim mystifying grace of her
appearance, which defied you to say if she were a fair young woman who looked
older through trouble, or a fine smooth older one who looked young through
successful indifference; with her precious reference, above all, to memories and
histories into which he could enter, she was exquisite for him like some pale
pressed flower (a rarity to begin with), and, failing other sweetnesses, she was
a sufficient reward of his effort. They had communities of knowledge, "their"
knowledge (this discriminating possessive was always on her lips) of presences of
the other age, presences all overlaid, in his case, by the experience of a man and

the freedom of a wanderer, overlaid by pleasure, by infidelity, by passages of life that were strange and dim to her, just by "Europe" in short, but still unobscured, still exposed and cherished, under that pious visitation of the spirit from which she had never been diverted.

She had come with him one day to see how his "apartment-house" was rising; he had helped her over gaps and explained to her plans, and while they were there had happened to have, before her, a brief but lively discussion with the man in charge, the representative of the building firm that had undertaken his work. He had found himself quite "standing up" to this personage over a failure on the latter's part to observe some detail of one of their noted conditions, and had so lucidly argued his case that, besides ever so prettily flushing, at the time, for sympathy in his triumph, she had afterwards said to him (though to a slightly greater effect of irony) that he had clearly for too many years neglected a real gift. If he had but stayed at home he would have anticipated the inventor of the sky-scraper. If he had but stayed at home he would have discovered his genius in time really to develop streets and to harvest a fortune. He was to remember these words, while the weeks elapsed, for the little silver ring with which he might feel that they had died away in the queerest and deepest of his own lately most disguised and most muffled vibrations.

It had begun to be present to him after the first fortnight, it had broken out with the oddest abruptness, this particular wanton wonderment: it met him there—and this was the image under which he himself judged the matter, or at least, not a little, thrilled and flushed with it—very much as he might have been met by some strange figure, some unexpected occupant, at a turn of one of the dim passages of an empty house. The quaint analogy quite hauntingly remained with him, when he didn't indeed rather improve it by a still intenser form: that of his opening a door behind which he would have made sure of finding nothing, a door into a room shuttered and void, and yet so coming, with a great suppressed start, on some quite erect confronting presence, something planted in the middle of the place and facing him through the dusk. After that visit to the house in construction he walked with his companion to see the other and always so much the better one, which, in the eastward direction, formed one of the corners of the street now so generally dishonoured and disfigured in its westward reaches and of the comparatively conservative Avenue.[3] The Avenue still had pretensions, as Miss Staverton said, to decency; the old people had mostly gone, mostly, the old names were unknown, and here and there an old association seemed to stray, all vaguely, like some very aged person, out too late, whom you might meet and feel the impulse to watch or follow, in kindness, for safe restoration to shelter.

They went in together, our friends; he admitted himself with his key, as he kept no one there, he explained, preferring, for his reasons, to leave the place empty, under a simple arrangement with a good woman living in the neighbourhood and who came for a daily hour to open windows and dust and sweep. Spencer Brydon had his reasons and was growingly aware of them; they seemed to him better each time he was there, though he didn't name them all to his companion, any more than he told her as yet how often, how quite absurdly often, he himself came. He only let her see for the present, while they walked through the great blank rooms, that absolute vacancy reigned and that, from top to bottom, there was nothing but Mrs. Muldoody's broomstick, in a corner, to tempt the burglar. Mrs. Muldoody was then on the premises, and she loquaciously attended the visitors, preceding them from room to room and pushing back shutters and throwing up sashes—all to show them, as she remarked, how little there was to see. There was little indeed to see in the great gaunt shell where the main dispositions and the general apportionment of space, the style of an age of ampler allowances, had nevertheless for its master their honest pleading message, affecting him as some good old servant's, some lifelong retainer's appeal for a character, or even for a retiring-pension; yet it was also a remark of Mrs. Muldoody's that, glad as she was to oblige him by her noonday round, there was a request she greatly hoped he would never make of her. If he should wish her for any reason to come in after dark she would just tell him, if he "plased,"[4] that he must ask it of somebody else.

The fact that there was nothing to see didn't militate for the worthy woman against what one *might* see, and she put it frankly to Miss Staverton that no lady could be expected to like, could she?—"craping up to thim top storeys in the ayvil hours."[5] The gas and the electric light were off the house, and she fairly evoked a gruesome vision of her march through the great grey rooms—so many of them as there were too!—with her glimmering taper.[6] Miss Staverton met her honest glare with a smile and the profession that she herself certainly would recoil from such an adventure. Spencer Brydon meanwhile held his peace—for the moment; the question of the "evil" hours in his old home had already become too grave for him. He had begun some time since to "crape," and he knew just why a packet of candles addressed to that pursuit had been stowed by his own hand, three weeks before, at the back of a drawer of the fine old sideboard that occupied, as a "fixture," the deep recess in the dining-room. Just now he laughed at his companions—quickly however changing the subject; for the reason that, in the first place, his laugh struck him even at that moment as starting the odd echo, the conscious human resonance (he scarce knew how to qualify it) that sounds made while he was there alone sent back to his ear or his fancy; and that, in the second, he imagined Alice Staverton for the instant on the point of asking him, with a divination, if he ever so prowled. There were divinations he was unprepared for, and he had at all events averted enquiry by the time Mrs. Muldoon had left them, passing on to other parts.

There was happily enough to say, on so consecrated a spot, that could be said freely and fairly; so that a whole train of declarations was precipitated by his friend's having herself broken out, after a yearning look round: "But I hope you don't mean they want you to pull *this* to pieces!" His answer came, promptly, with his re-awakened wrath: it was of course exactly what they wanted, and what they were "at" him for, daily, with the iteration of people who couldn't for their life understand a man's liability to decent feelings. He had found the place, just as it stood and beyond what he could express, an interest and a joy. There were values other than the beastly rent-values, and in short, in short———! But it was thus Miss Staverton took him up. "In short you're to make so good a thing of your sky-scraper that, living in luxury on *those* ill-gotten gains, you can afford for a while to be sentimental here!" Her smile had for him, with the words, the particular mild irony with which he found half her talk suffused; an irony without bitterness and that came, exactly, from her having so much imagination—not, like the cheap sarcasms with which one heard most people, about the world of "society," bid for the reputation of cleverness, from nobody's really having any. It was agreeable to him at this very moment to be sure that when he had answered, after a brief demur, "Well, yes; so, precisely, you may put it!" her imagination would still do him justice. He explained that even if never a dollar were to come to him from the other house he would nevertheless cherish this one; and he dwelt, further, while they lingered and wandered, on the fact of the stupefaction he was already exciting, the positive mystification he felt himself create.

He spoke of the value of all he read into it, into the mere sight of the walls, mere shapes of the rooms, mere sound of the floors, mere feel, in his hand, of the old silver-plated knobs of the several mahogany doors, which suggested the pressure of the palms of the dead the seventy years of the past in fine that these things represented, the annals of nearly three generations, counting his grandfather's, the one that had ended there, and the impalpable ashes of his long-extinct youth, afloat in the very air like microscopic motes. She listened to everything; she was a woman who answered intimately but who utterly didn't chatter. She scattered abroad therefore no cloud of words; she could assent, she could agree, above all she could encourage, without doing that. Only at the last she went a little further than he had done himself. "And then how do you know? You may still, after all, want to live here." It rather indeed pulled him up, for it wasn't what he had been thinking, at least in her sense of the words, "You mean I may decide to stay on for the sake of it?"

"Well, *with* such a home———!" But, quite beautifully, she had too much tact to dot so monstrous an *i*, and it was precisely an illustration of the way she didn't rattle. How could any one—of any wit—insist on any one else's "wanting" to live in New York?

"Oh," he said, "I *might* have lived here (since I had my opportunity early in life); I might have put in here all these years. Then everything would have been different enough—and, I daresay, 'funny' enough. But that's another matter. And then the beauty of it—I mean of my perversity, of my refusal to agree to a 'deal'—is just in the total absence of a reason. Don't you see that if I had a reason about the matter at all it would *have* to be the other way, and would then be inevitably a reason of dollars? There are no reasons here *but* of dollars. Let us therefore have none whatever—not the ghost of one."

They were back in the hall then for departure, but from where they stood the vista was large, through an open door, into the great square main saloon,[7] with its almost antique felicity of brave intervals between windows. Her eyes quitted that long reach and met his own a moment. "Are you very sure the 'ghost' of one doesn't much rather serve——?"

He had a positive sense of turning pale. But it was as near as they were then to come. For he made answer, he believed, between a glare and a grin: "Oh, ghosts—of course the place must swarm with them! I should be ashamed of it if it didn't. Poor Mrs. Muldoody's right, and it's why I haven't asked her to do more than look in."

Miss Staverton's gaze again lost itself, and things that she didn't utter, it was clear, came and went in her mind. She might even for the minute, off there in the fine room, have imagined some element dimly gathering. Simplified like the death-mask of a handsome face, it perhaps produced for her just then an effect akin to the stir of an expression in the "set" commemorative plaster. Yet whatever her impression may have been she uttered instead of it a vague platitude. "Well, if it were only furnished and lived in——!"

She appeared to imply that in case of its being still furnished he might have been a little less opposed to the idea of a return. But she passed straight into the vestibule, as if to leave her words behind her, and the next moment he had opened the house-door and was standing with her on the steps. He closed the door and while he repocketed his key, looking up and down, they took in the comparatively harsh actuality of the Avenue, which reminded him of the assault of the outer light of the Desert on the traveller emerging from an Egyptian tomb. But he risked before they stepped into the street his gathered answer to her speech. "For me it *is* lived in. For me it *is* furnished." At which it was easy for her to sigh "Ah yes——!" very vaguely and discreetly, since his parents and his favourite sister, to say nothing of other kin, in numbers, had run their course and met their end there. That represented, within the walls, ineffaceable life.

It was a few days after this that, during an hour passed with her again, he had expressed his impatience of the too flattering curiosity—among the people he met—about his appreciation of New York. He had arrived at none at all that was socially producible, and as for that matter of his "thinking" (thinking the better or the worse of anything there) he was wholly taken up with one subject of thought. It was mere vain egoism, and it was moreover, if she liked, a morbid obsession. He found all things come back to the question of what he personally might have been, how he might have led his life and "turned out," if he had not so at the outset given it up. And confessing for the first time to the intensity within him of this absurd speculation—which but proved too, no doubt, the habit of selfishly thinking—he affirmed the impotence there of any other source of interest, any other local appeal. "What would it have made of me, what would it have made of me? I keep for ever wondering, all idiotically; as if I could possibly know! I see what it has made of dozens of others, those I meet, and it positively aches within me, to the point of exasperation, that it would have made something of me as well. Only I can't make out *what*, and the worry of it, the small rage of curiosity, never to be satisfied, brings back what I remember to have felt once or twice after judging best, for reasons, to burn some important letter unopened. I've been sorry, I've hated it—I've never known what was in the letter. You may of course say it's a trifle——!"

"I don't say it's a trifle," Miss Staverton gravely interrupted.

She was seated by her fire, and before her, on his feet and restless, he turned to and fro between this intensity of his idea and a fitful and unseeing inspection, through his single eye-glass, of the dear little old objects on her chimneypiece. Her interruption made him for an instant look at her harder. "I shouldn't care if you did!" he laughed, however; "and it's only a figure, at any rate, for the way I now feel. *Not* to have followed my perverse young course—and almost in the teeth of my father's curse, as I may say; not to have kept it up so, 'over there,' from that day to this, without a doubt or a pang; not, above all, to have liked it, to have loved it, so much, loved it, naturally, with such an abysmal *conceit* of my own preference; some variation from *that,* I say, must have produced some different effect for my life and for my 'form.' I should have stuck here—if it had been possible; and I was too young, at twenty-three, to judge, *pour deux sous,*[8] whether it *were* possible. If I had waited I might have seen it was, and then I might have been, by staying here, something nearer to one of these types who have been hammered so hard and made so keen by their conditions. It isn't that I admire them so much—the question of any charm in them, or of any charm beyond that of the rank money-passion exerted by their conditions *for* them, has nothing to do with the matter; it's only a question of what fantastic, yet perfectly possible, development of my own nature I may not have missed. It comes over me that I had then a strange *alter ego*[9] deep down somewhere within me, as the full-blown flower is in the small tight bud, and that I just took the course, I just transferred him to the climate, that blighted him at once and for ever."

"And you wonder about the flower," Miss Staverton said. "So do I, if you want to know; and so I've been wondering these several weeks. I believe in the flower," she continued. "I feel that it would have been quite splendid, quite huge and monstrous."

"Monstrous above all!" her visitor echoed; "and I imagine, by the same stroke, quite hideous and offensive."

"You don't believe that," she returned; "if you did you wouldn't wonder. You'd know, and that would be enough for you. What you feel—and what I feel for you—is that you'd have had power."

"You'd have liked me that way?" he asked.

She barely hung fire.[10] "How should I not have liked you?"

"I see. You'd have liked me, have preferred me, a billionaire!"

"How should I not have liked you?" she simply again asked.

He stood before her still—her question kept him motionless. He took it in, so much there was of it; and indeed his not otherwise meeting it testified to that. "I know at least what I am," he simply went on; "the other side of the medal is clear enough. I've not been edifying—I believe I'm thought in a hundred quarters to have been barely decent. I've followed strange paths and worshipped strange gods; it must have come to you again and again—in fact you've admitted to me as much—that I was leading, at any time these thirty years, a selfish, frivolous, scandalous life. And you see what it has made of me."

She just waited, smiling at him. "You see what it has made of *me.*"

"Oh, you're a person whom nothing can have altered. You were born to be what you are, anywhere, anyway: you've the perfection nothing else could have touched. And don't you see how, without my exile, I shouldn't have been waiting till now——?" But he pulled up for the strange pang.

"The great thing to see," she presently said, "seems to me to be that it has spoiled nothing. It hasn't spoiled your being here at last. It hasn't spoiled this. It hasn't spoiled your speaking——" She also, however, faltered.

He wondered at everything her controlled emotion might mean. "Do you believe then—too dreadfully!—that I *am* as good as I might ever have been?"

"Oh no! Far from it!" With which she got up from her chair and was nearer him. "But I don't care," she smiled.

"You mean I'm good enough?"

She considered a little. "Will you believe it if I say so? I mean will you let that settle your question for you?" And then as if making out in his face that he drew back from this, that he had some idea which, however absurd, he couldn't yet bargain away: "Oh, you don't care either—but very differently: you don't care for anything but yourself."

Spencer Brydon recognised it—it was in fact what he had absolutely professed. Yet he importantly qualified. "*He* isn't myself. He's the just so totally other person. But I do want to see him," he added. "And I can. And I shall."

Their eyes met for a minute while he guessed from something in hers that she divined his strange sense. But neither of them otherwise expressed it, and her apparent understanding, with no protesting shock, no easy derision, touched him more deeply than anything yet, constituting for his stifled perversity, on the spot, an element that was like breathable air. What she said, however, was unexpected. "Well, *I've* seen him."

"You—?"

"I've seen him in a dream."

"Oh, a 'dream'——!" It let him down.

"But twice over," she continued. "I saw him as I see you now."

"You've dreamed the same dream——?"

"Twice over," she repeated. "The very same."

This did somehow a little speak to him, as it also pleased him. "You dream about me at that rate?"

"Ah, about *him!*" she smiled.

His eyes again sounded her. "Then you know all about him."

And as she said nothing more: "What's the wretch like?"

She hesitated, and it was as if he were pressing her so hard that, resisting for reasons of her own, she had to turn away. "I'll tell you some other time!"

II

It was after this that there was most of a virtue for him most of a cultivated charm, most of a preposterous secret thrill, in the particular form of surrender to his obsession and of address to what he more and more believed to be his privilege. It was what in these weeks he was living for—since he really felt life to begin but after Mrs. Muldoody had retired from the scene and, visiting the ample house from attic to cellar, making sure he was alone, he knew himself in safe possession and, as he tacitly expressed it, let himself go. He sometimes came twice in the twenty-four hours; the moments he liked best were those of gathering dusk, of the short autumn twilight; this was the time of which, again and again, he found himself hoping most. Then he could, as seemed to him, most intimately wander and wait, linger and listen, feel his fine attention, never in his life before so fine, on the pulse of the great vague place: he preferred the lampless hour and only wished he might have prolonged, each day, the deep crepuscular[11] magic. Later—rarely much before midnight, but then for a considerable vigil—he watched with his glimmering light; moving slowly, holding it high, playing it far, rejoicing above all, as much as he might, in open vistas, reaches of communication between rooms and along passages; the long, straight chance or show, as he would have called it, for the revelation he pretended to invite. It was a practice he found he could perfectly "work" without exciting remark; no one was in the least the wiser for it; even Alice Staverton, who was moreover a well of discretion, didn't quite fully imagine.

He let himself in and let himself out with the assurance of calm proprietorship; and accident so far favoured him that if a fat Avenue "officer" had happened on occasion to see him entering at eleven-thirty, he had never yet, to the best of his belief, been noticed as emerging at two. He walked there on the crisp November nights, arrived regularly at the evening's end; it was as easy to do this after dining out as to take his way to a club[12] or to his hotel. When he left his club, if he had not been dining out, it was ostensibly to go to his hotel; and when he left his hotel, if he had spent a part of the evening there, it was ostensibly to go to his club. Everything was easy in fine; everything conspired and promoted: there was truly even in the quality of his experience something that glossed over, something that salved and simplified all the rest of consciousness. He circulated, talked, renewed, loosely and pleasantly, old relations—met indeed, so far as he could, new expectations and seemed to make out on the whole that in spite of the career, of such different contacts, which he had spoken of to Miss Staverton as ministering so little, for those who might have watched it, to edification, he was positively rather liked than not. He was a dim secondary social success—and all with people who had truly not an idea of him. It was all mere surface sound, this murmur of their welcome, this popping of their corks—just as his gestures of response were the extravagant shadows, emphatic in proportion as they meant little, of some game of *ombres chinoises*.[13] He projected himself all day, in thought, straight over the bristling line of hard unconscious heads and into the other, the real, the waiting life; the life that, as soon as he had heard behind him the click of his great housedoor, began for him as beguilingly as the slow opening bars of some rich music follows the tap of the conductor's wand.

He always caught the first effect of the steel point of his stick on the old marble of the hall pavement, large black and white squares that he remembered as the admiration of his childhood and that had then made in him, as he now saw, for the growth of an early conception of style. This effect was the thin reverberating tinkle as of some far-off bell hung who should say where?—in the depths of the house, in the past of that mystical other world that might have been for him had he not, for weal or woe, abandoned it. On this impression he did ever the same thing; he put his stick all noiselessly away in a corner—feeling the place once more in the likeness of some great glass bowl, all precious concave crystal, set delicately humming by the play of a moist finger round its edge. The concave crystal held, as it were, this mystical other world, and the indescribably fine murmur of its rim was the sigh there, the scarce audible pathetic wail, to his strained ear, of all the old baffled forsworn possibilities. What he did therefore by this appeal of his hushed presence was to wake them into such measure of ghostly life as they might still enjoy. They were shy, all but unappeasably shy, but they weren't really sinister; at least they weren't as he had hitherto felt them—before they had taken the Form he so yearned to make them take, the Form he at moments saw himself in the light of fairly hunting, on tiptoe, the points of his evening-shoes, from room to room and from storey to storey.

That was the essence of his vision—which was all rank folly, if one would, while he was out of the house and otherwise occupied, but which took on the last verisimilitude as soon as he was isolated. He knew what he meant and what he wanted; it was as clear as the figure on a cheque presented in demand for cash. His *alter ego* "walked"—that was the note of his image of him, and his image of his motive for his own odd pastime was the desire to waylay him and meet him. He roamed slowly, warily, but all restlessly, he himself did—Mrs. Muldoody had been absolutely right with her figure of their "craping"; and the presence he watched for would roam restlessly too. But it would be as cautious and as shifty; the conviction of its probable, in fact its already quite sensible, quite audible evasion of pursuit grew for him from night to night, laying on him finally a spell to which nothing in his life had been comparable. It had been the theory of many superficially judging persons, he knew, that he was wasting that life in a surrender to sensations; but he had tasted of no pleasure as fine as his actual tension, had been introduced to no sport that demanded at once the patience and the nerve of this stalking of a creature more subtle, yet at bay perhaps more formidable, than any beast of the forest. The terms, the comparisons, the very practices of the chase came again positively into play; there were even moments when passages of his occasional experience as a sportsman, stirred memories, from his younger time, of moor and mountain and desert, revived for him—and to the increase of his keenness—by the tremendous force of analogy. He found himself at moments—once he had placed his single light on some mantelshelf or in some recess—stepping back into shelter or shade, effacing himself behind a door or in an embrasure as he had sought of old the vantage of rock and tree; he found himself holding his breath and living in the joy of the instant, the supreme suspense created by big game alone.

He wasn't afraid (though putting himself the question as he believed gentlemen on Bengal tiger-shoots or in close quarters with the great bear of the Rockies had been known to confess to having put it); and this indeed—since here at least he might be frank!—because of the impression, so intimate and so strange, that he himself produced as yet a dread, produced certainly a strain, beyond the liveliest he was likely to feel. They fell for him into categories, they fairly became familiar, the signs, for his own perception, of the alarm his presence and his vigilance created; though leaving him always to remark portentously on his probably having formed a relation, his probably enjoying a consciousness, unique in the experience of man. People enough, first and last, had been in terror of apparitions, but who had ever before so turned the tables and become himself, in the apparitional world, an incalculable terror? He might have found this sublime had he quite dared to think of it; but he didn't too much insist, truly, on that side of his privilege. With habit and repetition he gained to an extraordinary degree the power to penetrate the dusk of distances and the darkness of corners, to resolve back into their innocence the treacheries of uncertain light, the evil-looking forms taken in the gloom by mere shadows, by accidents of the air, by shifting effects of perspective; putting down his dim luminary, he could still wander on without it, pass into other rooms and, only knowing it was there behind him in case of need, see his way about, project visually, for his purpose, a comparative clearness. It made him feel, this acquired faculty, like some monstrous stealthy cat; he wondered if he would have appeared to have at these moments large shining yellow eyes, and what it mightn't verily be for the poor hard-pressed *alter ego* to be confronted with such a face.

He liked, however, the open shutters; he opened everywhere those Mrs. Muldoody had closed, closing them as carefully afterwards, so that she shouldn't notice; he liked—oh this he did like and above all in the upper rooms!—the sense of the hard silver of the autumn stars through the window-panes, and scarcely less the flare of the street-lamps below, the white electric lustre which it would have taken curtains to keep out. This was human, actual, social; this was of the world he had lived in, and he was more at his ease certainly for the countenance, coldly general and impersonal, that, all the while and in spite of his detachment, it seemed to give him. He had support of course mostly in the rooms at the wide front and the prolonged side; it failed him considerably in the parts of the back. But if he sometimes, on his rounds, was glad of his optical reach, so none the less often the rear of the house affected him as the very jungle of his prey. The place was there more subdivided, a large "extension," in particular, where small rooms for servants had been multiplied, abounded in nooks and corners, in closets and passages, in the ramifications especially of an ample back-staircase over which he leaned, many a time, to look far down—not deterred from his gravity even while aware that he might for a spectator have figured some solemn simpleton playing at hide-and-seek. He himself, outside, might in fact make that ironic *rapprochement*;[14] but within the walls, and in spite of the clear windows, his consistency was proof against the cynical light of New York.

It had been in the nature of that measure of the exasperated consciousness of his victim to become a real test for him; since he had quite put it to himself from the first that, oh distinctly! he could "cultivate" his whole perception. He had felt it as above all open to cultivation—which indeed was but another name for his manner of spending his time. He was bringing it on, bringing it to perfection, by practice, the expenditure by which it had grown so fine that he was now aware of impressions, attestations of his general postulate, that couldn't have broken upon him at once. This was the case more specifically with a phenomenon at last quite frequent for him in the upper rooms, the recognition—absolutely unmistakable and by a turn dating from a particular hour, his resumption of his campaign after a diplomatic drop, a calculated absence of three nights—of his being followed at a distance carefully taken and to the express end that he should the less confidently, less arrogantly, appear to himself merely to pursue. It worried, it finally quite broke him up, for it proved, of all the conceivable impressions, the one that least suited his book. He was kept in sight while remaining himself—as regards the essence of his position—sightless, and his only recourse then was in abrupt turns, rapid recoveries of ground. He wheeled about, retracing his steps, as if he might so catch in his face at least the stirred air of some other quick revolution. It was indeed true that his fully dislocalised thought of these manoeuvres recalled to him Pantaloon, at the Christmas farce, buffeted and tricked from behind by ubiquitous Harlequin;[15] but it remained wholly without prejudice to the influence of the conditions themselves, each time he was re-exposed to them, so that in fact this association, had he suffered it to become constant, would on a certain side have but ministered to his intenser gravity. He had made, as I have said, to create on the premises the baseless sense of a reprieve, his three absences; and the result of the third was to confirm the after-effect of the second.

On his return, that night—the night succeeding his last intermission—he stood in the hall and looked up the staircase with a certainty more intimate than any he had yet known. "He's *there*, at the top, and waiting—not, as in general, falling back for disappearance. He's holding his ground, and it's the first time—which is a proof, isn't it? that something has happened for him." So Brydon argued with his hand on the banister and his foot on the lowest stair; in which position he felt, as never before, the air chilled by his logic. He himself turned cold in it, for he seemed of a sudden to know what now was involved. "Harder pressed?—yes, he takes it in, with its thus making clear to him that I've come, as they say, 'to stay.' He doesn't like it, at last: in the sense, I mean, that his wrath, his menaced interest, now balances with his dread. I've hunted him till he has 'turned': that, up there, is what has happened—he's the fanged or the antlered animal brought at last to bay." There came to him, as I say—but determined by an influence beyond my notation!—the acuteness of this certainty; under which, however, the

next moment, he had broken into a sweat that he would as little have consented
to attribute to fear as he would have dared immediately to act upon it for a sign
of exaltation. It marked none the less a prodigious thrill, a thrill that represented
sudden dismay, no doubt, but also represented, and with the selfsame throb,
the strangest, the most joyous, possibly the next minute almost the proudest,
duplication of consciousness.

"He has been dodging, retreating, hiding, but now, worked up to anger, he'll
fight!"—this intense impression made a single mouthful as it were, of terror and
applause. But what was wondrous was that the applause, for the felt fact, was so
eager, since if it was his other self he was running to earth this ineffable identity
was thus in the last resort not unworthy of him. It bristled there—somewhere
near at hand, however unseen still—as the hunted thing, even as the trodden
worm of the adage,[16] *must* at last bristle; and Brydon at this instant tasted probably of a sensation more complex than had ever before found itself consistent
with sanity. It was as if it would have shamed him that a character so associated
with his own should triumphantly succeed in just skulking, should to the end
not dare to face him; so that the drop of this danger was, on the spot, a great
lift of the whole situation. Yet by another rare shift of the same subtlety he was
already trying to ascertain how much more he himself might now be in peril of
fear; rejoicing thus that he could, in another form, actively inspire that fear, and
simultaneously quaking for the form in which he might passively know it.

The apprehension of knowing it must after a little have grown in him, and
the strangest moment of his adventure perhaps, the most memorable or really
most interesting, afterwards, of his crisis, was the lapse of a sharp spasm of
concentrated conscious *combat*, the sense of a need to hold on to something, even
after the manner of a man slipping and slipping on some awful incline; the vivid
impulse, above all, to move, to act, to charge somehow and upon something—to
show himself, in a word, that he wasn't afraid. The state of "holding-on" was
thus the state to which he was momentarily reduced; if there had been anything
in the great vacancy to seize he would have been presently aware of having
clutched it as, under a shock at home, he might have clutched the nearest chair-
back. He had been surprised at any rate—of this he *was* aware—into something
unprecedented since his original appropriation of the place; he had closed his
eyes, held them tight for a long minute, as with that instinct of dismay and that
terror of vision. When he opened them the room, the other contiguous rooms,
extraordinarily, seemed lighter—so light, almost, that at first he thought it was
day. He stood firm, however that might be, just where he had paused; his resistance had helped him—it was as if there were something he had tided over. He
knew after a little what this was—it had been in the imminent danger of flight.
He had stiffened his will against going, without which he would have made for
the stairs; and it seemed to him that, still with his eyes closed, he would have
descended them, would have known how, straight and swiftly to the bottom.

Well, as he had held out here he was—still at the top, among the more intricate upper rooms and with the gauntlet of the others, of all the rest of the house,

still to run when it should be his time to go. He would go at his time—only at
his time: didn't he go every night at very much the same hour? He took out his
watch—there was light for that: it was scarcely a quarter past one, and he had
never retreated so soon. He reached his lodgings for the most part at two—with
his walk of a quarter of an hour. He would wait for the last quarter—he wouldn't
stir till then; and he kept his watch there with his eyes on it, reflecting while
he held it that this deliberate wait, a wait with an effort which he recognised,
would serve perfectly for the attestation he desired to make. It would prove his
courage—unless indeed the latter might most be proved by his budging at last
from his place. What he mainly felt now was that, since he hadn't originally
scuttled, he had his dignities—which had never in his life seemed so many—all
to preserve and to carry aloft. This was before him in truth as a physical image,
an image almost worthy of an age of greater romance. That remark indeed
glimmered for him only to glow the next instant with a finer light; since what age
of romance, after all, could have matched either the state of his mind or, "objectively" as they said, the wonder of his situation? The only difference would
have been that, brandishing his dignities over his head as in a parchment scroll,
he might then—that is in the heroic time—have proceeded downstairs with a
drawn sword in his other grasp.

At present, really, the light he had set down on the mantel of the next room
would have to figure his sword; which utensil, in the course of a minute, he had
taken the requisite number of steps to possess himself of. The door between the
rooms was open, and from the second another door opened to a third. These
rooms, as he remembered, gave all three upon a common corridor as well, but
there was a fourth beyond them without issue save through the preceding. To
have moved, to have heard his step again, was appreciably a help; though even in
recognising this he lingered once more a little by the chimney-piece on which his
light had rested. When he next moved, hesitating a little where to turn, he found
himself considering a circumstance that, after his first and comparatively vague
apprehension of it, produced in him the start that often attends some pang of
recollection, the violent shock of having ceased happily to forget. He had come
into sight of the door in which the brief chain of communication ended, and
which he now looked at from the nearer threshold, the one not directly facing
it. Placed at some distance to the left of this point, it would have admitted him
to the last room of the four, the room without other approach or egress, had it
not, to his intimate conviction, been closed *since* his former visitation, the matter
probably of a quarter of an hour before. He stared with all his eyes at the wonder
of the fact, arrested again where he stood and again holding his breath while he
sounded its sense. Surely it had *been* closed—that is it had been on his previous
passage indubitably open!

He took it full in the face that something had happened between—that he
couldn't have noticed before (by which he meant on his original tour of all the
rooms that evening) that such a barrier had exceptionally presented itself. He
had indeed since that moment undergone an agitation so extraordinary that

it might have muddled for him any earlier view; and he tried to think that he might perhaps have then gone into the room and inadvertently, automatically, on coming out, have drawn the door after him. The difficulty was that this, exactly, was what he never did; it was against his whole policy as he might have said, the essence of which was to keep vistas clear. He had had them from the first, he was well aware, quite on the brain: the strange apparition, at the far end of one of them, of his baffled "prey" (which had become by so sharp an irony so little the term now to apply) was the form of success his imagination had most cherished, projecting into it always a refinement of beauty. He had known fifty times the start of perception that had afterwards dropped; had fifty times gasped to himself "There!" under some fond brief hallucination. The house, as the case stood, admirably lent itself; he might wonder at the taste, the native architecture of the particular time, which could rejoice so in the multiplication of doors—the opposite extreme to the modern, the actual, almost complete proscription of them; but it had fairly contributed to provoke this obsession of the presence encountered telescopically, as he might say, focussed and studied in diminishing perspective and as by a rest for the elbow.

It was with these considerations that his present attention was charged—they perfectly availed to make what he saw portentous. He *couldn't* by any lapse have blocked that aperture; and if he hadn't, if it was unthinkable, why what else was clear but that there had been another agent? Another agent?—he had been catching, as he felt a moment back, the very breath of him; but when had he been so close as in this simple, this logical, this completely personal act? It was so logical, that is, that one might have *taken* it for personal; yet for what did Brydon take it, he asked himself while, softly panting, he felt his eyes almost leave their sockets. Ah this time at last they *were*, the two, the opposed projections of him, in presence; and this time, as much as one would, the question of danger loomed. With it rose as not before the question of courage—for what he knew the blank face of the door to say to him was "Show us how much you have!" It stared, it glared back at him with that challenge; it put to him the two alternatives: should he just push it open or not? Oh, to have this consciousness was to *think*—and to think, Brydon knew as he stood there, was, with the lapsing moments, not to have acted! Not to have acted—that was the misery and the pang—was even still not to act; was in fact *all* to feel the thing in another, in a new and terrible way. How long did he pause and how long did he debate? There was presently nothing to measure it; for his vibration had already changed—as just by the effect of its intensity. Shut up there, at bay, defiant, and with the prodigy of the thing palpably, provably *done* thus giving notice like some stark signboard—under that accession of accent the situation itself had turned; and Brydon at last remarkably made up his mind on what it had turned to.

It had turned altogether to a different admonition; to a supreme hint for him of the value of Discretion! This slowly dawned, no doubt—for it could take its time; so perfectly, on his threshold, had he been stayed, so little, as yet, had he either advanced or retreated. It was the strangest of all things that now when, by his taking ten steps and applying his hand to a latch, or even his shoulder and his knee, if necessary, to a panel, all the hunger of his prime need might have been met, his high curiosity crowned, his unrest assuaged—it was amazing, but it was also exquisite and rare, that insistence should have, at a touch, quite dropped from him. Discretion—he jumped at that; and yet not, verily, at such a pitch, because it saved his nerves or his skin, but because, much more valuably, it saved the situation. When I say he "jumped" at it I feel the consonance of this term with the fact that—at the end indeed of I know not how long—he did move again, he crossed straight to the door. He wouldn't touch it—it seemed now that he might *if* he would: he would only just wait there a little to show, to prove that he wouldn't. He had thus another station close to the thin partition by which revelation was denied him; but with his eyes bent and his hands held off in a mere intensity of stillness. He listened as if there had been something to hear, but this attitude, while it lasted, was his own communication. "If you won't then—good: I spare you and I give up. You affect me as by the appeal, positively, for pity: you convince me that, for reasons rigid and sublime—what do I know?—we both of us should have suffered. I respect them then, and, though moved and privileged as, I believe, it has never been given to man, I retire, I renounce—and never, on my honour, to try again. So rest for ever—and let *me!*"

That, for Brydon, was the deep sense of this last demonstration—solemn, measured, directed as he felt it to be. He brought it to a close, he turned away; and now verily he knew how deeply he had been stirred. He retraced his steps, taking up his candle, burnt, he observed, well-nigh to the socket, and marking again, lighten it as he would, the distinctness of his footfall; after which he in a moment knew himself at the other side of the house. He did here what he had not yet done at these hours—he opened half a casement, one of those in the front, and let in the air of the night; a thing he would have taken at any time previous for a sharp rupture of his spell. His spell was broken now, and it didn't matter—broken by his concession and his surrender, which made it idle henceforth that he should ever come back. The empty street, with its other life so marked even by the great lamplit vacancy, was within call, within touch; he stayed there as to be in it again, high above it though he was still perched; he watched as for some comforting common fact, some vulgar human note, the passage of a scavenger or a thief, some night-bird however base. He would have blessed that sign of life; he would have welcomed, positively, the slow approach of his friend the policeman, whom he had hitherto only sought to avoid, and wasn't sure that if the patrol had come into sight he mightn't have felt the impulse to get into relation with it, to hail it on some pretext from his fourth floor.

The pretext that wouldn't have been too silly or too compromising, the explanation that would have saved his dignity and kept his name, in such a case, out of the papers, was not definite to him: he was so occupied with the thought of recording his Discretion—as an effect of the vow he had just uttered to his intimate adversary—that the importance of this loomed large and something had overtaken, all ironically, his sense of proportion. If there had been a ladder applied to the front of the house, even one of the vertiginous perpendiculars em-ployed by painters and roofers and sometimes left standing overnight, he would have managed somehow, astride of the window-sill, to compass by outstretched leg and arm that mode of descent. If there had been some such uncanny thing as he had found in his room at hotels, a workable fire-escape in the form of notched cable or canvas shoot, he would have availed himself of it as a proof—well, of his present delicacy. He nursed that sentiment, as the question stood, a little in vain, and even—at the end of he scarce knew once more how long—found it, as by the action on his mind of the failure of response of the outer world, sinking back to vague anguish. It seemed to him he had waited an age for some stir of the great grim hush; the life of the town was itself under a spell—so unnaturally, up and down the whole prospect of known and rather ugly objects, the blankness and the silence lasted. Had they ever, he asked himself, the hard-faced houses which had begun to look livid in the dim dawn, had they ever spoken so little to any need of his spirit? Great builded voids, great crowded stillnesses put on often, in the heart of cities, for the small hours, a sort of sinister mask, and it was of this large collective negation that Brydon presently became conscious—all the more that the break of day was, almost incredibly, now at hand, proving to him what a night he had made of it.

He looked again at his watch, saw what had become of his time-values (he had taken hours for minutes—not, as in other tense situations, minutes for hours) and the strange air of the streets was but the weak, the sullen flush of a dawn in which everything was still locked up. His choked appeal from his own open window had been the sole note of life, and he could but break off at last as for a worse despair. Yet while so deeply demoralised he was capable again of an impulse denoting—at least by his present measure—extraordinary resolution; of retracing his steps to the spot where he had turned cold with the extinction of his last pulse of doubt as to there being in the place another presence than his own. This required an effort strong enough to sicken him; but he had his reason, which over-mastered for the moment everything else. There was the whole of the rest of the house to traverse, and how should he screw himself to that if the door he had seen closed were at present open? He could hold to the idea that the closing had practically been for him an act of mercy, a chance offered him to descend, depart, get off the ground and never again profane it. This conception held together, it worked; but what it meant for him depended now clearly on the amount of forbearance his recent action, or rather his recent inaction, had engendered. The image of the "presence," whatever it was, waiting there for him to go—this image had not yet been so concrete for his nerves as when he stopped short of the point at which certainty would have come to him. For with all his resolution, or more exactly with all his dread, he did stop short—he hung back from really seeing. The risk was too great and his fear too definite: it took at this moment an awful specific form.

He knew—yes, as he had never known anything—that, *should* he see the door open it would all too abjectly be the end of him. It would mean that the agent of his shame—his shame being the deep abjection—was once more at large and in general possession; and what glared him thus in the face was the act that this would determine for him. It would send him straight about to the window he had left open, and by that window, be the long ladder or the dangling rope as absent as it would, he saw himself uncontrollably, insanely, fatally take his way to the street. The hideous chance of this he at least could avert; but he could only avert it by recoiling in time from assurance. He had the whole house to traverse—this fact was still there; only he now knew that uncertainty alone could start him. He stole back from where he had checked himself—merely to do so was suddenly like safety—and, making blindly for the greater staircase, left gaping rooms and sounding passages behind. Here was the top of the stairs, with a fine large dim descent and three spacious landings to deal with. His instinct was all for mildness, but his feet were harsh on the floors, and, strangely, when he had in a couple of minutes become aware of this, it counted somehow for help. He couldn't have spoken, the tone of his voice would have scared him and the common conceit or resource of "whistling in the dark"[17] (whether literally or figuratively) have appeared basely vulgar; yet he liked none the less to hear himself go, and when he had reached his first landing—taking it all with no rush, but quite steadily—that stage of success drew from him a gasp of relief.

The house withal seemed immense, the scale of space again inordinate; the open rooms, to no one of which his eyes deflected, gloomed in their shuttered state like mouths of caverns; only the high skylight that formed the crown of the deep well created for him a medium in which he could advance but which might have been, for queerness of colour, some watery underworld. He tried to think of something noble, as that his property was really grand, a splendid possession; but this nobleness took the form too of the clear delight with which he was finally to sacrifice it. They might come in now, the builders, the destroyers—they might come as soon as they would. At the end of two flights he had dropped to another zone, and from the middle of the third, with only one more left, he recognised the influence of the lower windows, of half-drawn blinds, of the occasional gleam of street-lamps, of the glazed spaces of the vestibule. This was the bottom of the sea, which showed an illumination of its own and which he even saw paved—when at a given moment he drew up to sink a long look over the banisters—with the marble squares of his childhood. By that time, indubitably, he felt, as he might have said in a commoner cause, better; it had allowed him to stop and take breath, and the ease increased with the sight of the old black-and-white slabs. But what he most felt was that now surely, with the element of impunity moving him on as by hard firm hands, the case was settled for what he might have seen above had he dared that last look. The closed door, blessedly remote now, was still closed—and he had only in short to reach that of the house.

He came down further, he crossed the passage forming the access to the last flight; and if here again he stopped an instant it was almost for the sharpness of the thrill of assured escape. It made him shut his eyes—which opened again to the straight descent of the remainder of the stairs. Here was impunity still, but impunity almost excessive; inasmuch as the sidelights and the high fan-tracery of the entrance were glimmering straight into the hall; an appearance produced, he the next instant saw, by the fact that the vestibule gaped wide, that the hinged halves of the inner door had been thrown far back. Out of that again the *question* sprang at him, making his eyes, as he felt, half start from his head as they had done at the top of the house before the sign of the other door. If he had left that one open hadn't he left this one closed, and wasn't he now in *most* immediate presence of some inconceivable occult activity? It was as sharp, the question, as a knife in his side, but the answer hung fire still and seemed to lose itself in the vague darkness to which the thin admitted dawn, glimmering archwise over the whole outer door, made a semicircular margin, a cold, silvery nimbus that seemed to play a little as he looked, to shift and expand and contract.

It was as if there had been something within it protected by indistinctness and corresponding in extent with the opaque surface behind, the painted panels of the last barrier to his escape, of which the key was in his pocket. The indistinct-ness mocked him even while he stared, affected him as somehow shrouding or challenging certitude, so that after faltering an instant on his step he let himself go with the sense that here *was* at last something to meet, to touch, to take, to know—something all unnatural and dreadful, but to advance upon which was the condition for him either of liberation or of supreme defeat. The penumbra, dense and dark, was the virtual screen of a figure which stood in it as still as some image erect in a niche or as some black-vizored sentinel guarding a trea-sure. Brydon was to know afterwards, was to recall and make out, the particular thing he had believed during the rest of his descent. He saw, in its great grey glimmering margin, the central vagueness diminish, and he felt it to be taking the very form toward which for so many days the passion of his curiosity had yearned. It gloomed, it loomed, it was something, it was somebody, the prodigy of a personal presence.

Rigid and conscious, spectral yet human, a man of his own substance and stature waited there to measure himself with his power to dismay. This only could it be—this only till he recognised, with his advance, that what made the face dim was the pair of raised hands that covered it and in which, so far from being offered in defiance, it was buried as for dark deprecation. So Brydon, be-fore him, took him in; with every fact of him now, in the higher light, hard and acute—his planted stillness, his vivid truth, his grizzled bent head and white masking hands, his queer actuality of evening-dress, of dangling double eyeglass, of gleaming silk lappet and white linen, of pearl button and gold watchguard and polished shoe. No portrait by a great modern master could have presented him with more intensity, thrust him out of his frame with more art, as if there had been "treatment," of the consummate sort, in his every shade and salience. The revulsion, for our friend, had become, before he knew it, immense—this drop, in the act of apprehension, to the sense of his adversary's inscrutable ma-noeuvre. That meaning at least, while he gaped, it offered him; for he could but gape at his other self in this other anguish, gape as a proof that *he*, standing there for the achieved, the enjoyed, the triumphant life, couldn't be faced in his triumph. Wasn't the proof in the splendid covering hands, strong and completely spread?—so spread and so intentional that, in spite of a special verity that surpassed every other, the fact that one of these hands had lost two fingers, which were reduced to stumps, as if accidentally shot away, the face was effectually guarded and saved.

"Saved," though, *would* it be?—Brydon breathed his wonder till the very impunity of his attitude and the very insistence of his eyes produced, as he felt, a sudden stir which showed, the next instant, for a deeper portent, while the head raised itself, the betrayal of a braver purpose. The hands, as he looked, began to move, to open; then, as if deciding in a flash, dropped from the face and left it uncovered and presented. Horror, with the sight, had leaped into Brydon's throat, gasping there in a sound he couldn't utter; for the bared identity was too hideous as *his*, and his glare was the passion of his protest. The face, *that* face, Spencer Brydon's?—he searched it still, but looking away from it in dismay and denial, falling straight from his height of sublimity. It was unknown, inconceivable, awful, disconnected from any possibility——! He had been "sold,"[18] he inwardly moaned, stalking such game as this: the presence before him was a presence, the horror within him was a horror, but the waste of his nights had been only grotesque and the success of his adventure an irony. Such an identity fitted his at *no* point, made its alternative monstrous. A thousand times yes, as it came upon him nearer now—the face was the face of a stranger. It came upon him nearer now, quite as one of those expanding fantastic images projected by the magic-lantern of childhood; for the stranger, whoever he might be, evil, odious, blatant, vulgar, had advanced as for aggression, and he knew himself give ground. Then harder pressed still, sick with the force of his shock and falling back as under the hot breath and the roused passion of a life larger than his own, a rage of personality before which his own collapsed, he felt the whole vision turn to darkness and his very feet give way. His head went round; he was going; he had gone.

III

What had next brought him back, clearly—though after how long?—was Mrs. Muldoody's voice, coming to him from quite near, from so near that he seemed presently to see her as kneeling on the ground before him while he lay looking up at her; himself not wholly on the ground, but half raised and upheld—conscious, yes, of tenderness of support and more particularly of a head pillowed in extraordinary softness and faintly refreshing fragrance. He considered, he wondered, his wit but half at his service; then another face intervened, bending more directly over him, and he finally knew that Alice Staverton had made her lap an ample and perfect cushion to him, and that she had to this end seated herself on the lowest degree of the staircase, the rest of his long person remaining stretched on his old black and white slabs. They were cold, these marble squares of his youth; but *he* somehow was not, in this rich return of consciousness—the most wonderful hour, little by little, that he had ever known, leaving him, as it did, so gratefully, so abysmally passive, and yet as with a treasure of intelligence waiting, all round him, for quiet appropriation; dissolved, he might call it, in the air of the place and producing the golden glow of a late autumn afternoon. He had come back, yes—come back from further away than any man but himself had ever travelled; yet it was strange how, with this sense, what he had come back *to* seemed really the great thing, and as if his prodigious journey had been all for the sake of it. Slowly and surely his consciousness grew, his vision of his state thus completing itself: he had been miraculously *carried* back—lifted and carefully borne as from where he had been picked up, the uttermost end of an interminable grey passage. Even with this he had been suffered to rest, and what had now brought him to knowledge was the break in the long, mild motion.

It had brought him to knowledge, to knowledge—yes, this was the beauty of his state; which came to resemble more and more that of a man who, going to sleep on some news of a great inheritance, has then, after dreaming it away, after profaning it with matters strange to it, waked up again to full serenity of certitude and has only to lie and see it shine. This was the drift of his patience—that he had only to let it shine steadily. He must moreover, with intermissions, still have been lifted and borne; since why and how else should he have known himself, later on, with the afternoon glow intenser, no longer at the foot of his stairs—situated as these now seemed at that dark other end of his tunnel—but on a deep window-bench of his high saloon, over which had been spread, couch-fashion, a mantle of soft stuff lined with grey fur that was familiar to his eyes and that one of his hands kept fondly feeling as if for its pledge of truth. Mrs. Muldoody's face had gone, but the other, the second he had recognised, hung over him in a way that showed how he was still propped and pillowed. He took it all in, and the more he took it the more it seemed to suffice: he was as much at peace as if he had had food and drink. It was the two women who had found him, on Mrs. Muldoody's having plied, at her usual hour, her latch-key—and on her having above all arrived while Miss Staverton still lingered near the house. She had been turning away, all anxiety, from worrying the vain bell-handle—her calculation having been of the hour of the good woman's visit; but the latter, blessedly, had come up in time not to miss her, and they had entered together. He had then lain, beyond the vestibule, very much as he was lying now—quite, that is, as he appeared to have fallen, but all so wondrously without bruise or gash; only in a depth of stupor. What he most took in, however, at present, with the steadier clearance, was that Alice Staverton had, for a long unspeakable moment, not doubted he was dead.

"It must have been that I *was*." He made it out as she held him. "Yes—I can only have died. You brought me literally to life. Only," he wondered, his eyes rising to her, "only, in the name of all the benedictions,[19] how?"

It took her but an instant to bend her face and kiss him, and something in the manner of it, and in the way her hands clasped and locked his head while he felt the cool charity and virtue of her lips, something in all this beatitude somehow answered everything. "And now I keep you," she said.

"Oh keep me, keep me!" he pleaded while her face still hung over him; in response to which it dropped again and stayed close, clingingly close. It was the seal of their situation—of which he tasted the impress for a long blissful moment in silence. But he came back. "Yet how did you know——?"

"I was uneasy. You were to have come, you remember—and you had sent no word."

"Yes, I remember—I was to have gone to you at one to-day." It caught on to their "old" life and relation—which were so near and so far. "I was still out there in my strange darkness—where was it, what was it? I must have stayed there so long." He could but wonder at the depth and the duration of his swoon.

"Since last night?" she asked with a shade of fear for her possible indiscretion.

"Since this morning—it must have been: the cold dim dawn of to-day. Where have I been," he vaguely wailed, "where have I been?" He felt her hold him close, and it was as if this helped him now to make in all security his mild moan. "What a long dark day!"

All in her tenderness she had waited a moment. "In the cold dim dawn?" she quavered.

But he had already gone on, piecing together the parts of the whole prodigy. "As I didn't turn up, you came straight——?"

She barely hesitated. "I went first to your hotel—where they told me of your absence. You had dined out last evening and had not been back since. But they appeared to know you had been at your club."

"So you had the idea of *this*——?"

"Of what?" she asked in a moment.

"Well—of what has happened."

"I believed at least you'd have been here. I've known, all along," she said, "that you've been coming."

"'Known' it——?"

"Well, I've believed it. I said nothing to you after that talk we had a month ago—but I felt sure. I knew you *would*," she declared.

"That I would persist, you mean?"

"That you'd see him."

"Ah, but I didn't!" cried Brydon with his long wail. "There's somebody—an awful beast; whom I brought, too horribly, to bay. But it's not me."

At this she bent over him again, and her eyes were in his eyes. "No—it's not you." And it was as if, while her face hovered, he might have made out in it, had it not been so near, some particular meaning blurred by a smile. "No, thank heaven," she repeated—"it's not you! Of course it wasn't to have been."

"Ah, but it *was*" he gently insisted. And he stared before him now as he had been staring for so many weeks. "I was to have known myself."

"You couldn't!" she returned consolingly. And then reverting, and as if to account further for what she had herself done, "But it wasn't only *that*, that you hadn't been at home," she went on. "I waited till the hour at which we had found Mrs. Muldoody that day of your bringing me; and she arrived, as I've told you, while, failing to bring any one to the door, I waited, in my despair, on the steps. After a little, if she hadn't come by such a mercy, I should have found means to hunt her up. But it wasn't," said Alice Staverton, as if once more with her fine intention—"it wasn't only that."

His eyes, as he lay, turned back to her. "What more then?"

She met it, the wonder she had stirred. "In the cold dim dawn, you say? Well, in the cold dim dawn of this morning I too saw you."

"Saw *me*——?"

"Saw *him*," said Alice Staverton. "It must have been at the same moment."

He lay an instant taking it in—as if he wished to be quite reasonable. "At the same moment?"

"Yes—in my dream again, the same one I've named to you. He came back to me. Then I knew it for a sign. He had come to you."

At this Brydon raised himself; he had to see her better. She helped him when she understood his movement, and he sat up, steadying himself beside her there on the window-bench and with his right hand grasping her left. "He didn't come to me."

"You came to yourself," she beautifully smiled.

"Ah, I've come to myself now—thanks to you, dearest. But this brute, with his awful face—this brute's a black stranger. He's none of *me*, even as I *might* have been," Brydon sturdily contended.

But she kept her clearness. "Isn't the whole point that you'd have been different?"

He almost scowled for it. "As different as that——?"

Her lucid look seemed to bathe him. "Haven't you exactly wanted to know *how* different? So this morning," she said, "you appeared to me."

"Like *him*?"

"A black stranger!"

"Then how did you know it was I?"

"Because, as I told you weeks ago, my mind, my imagination, had worked so over what you might, what you mightn't have been—to show you, you see, how I've thought of you. In the midst of that you came to me—that my wonder might be answered. So I knew," she went on; "and believed that, since the question held you too so fast, as you told me that day, you too would see for yourself. And when this morning I again saw I knew it would be because you had—and also then, from the first moment, because you somehow wanted me. *He* seemed to tell me of that. So why," she strangely smiled, "shouldn't I like him?"

It brought Spencer Brydon to his feet. "You 'like' that horror——?"

"I *could* have liked him. And to me," she said, "he was no horror. I had accepted him."

"'Accepted'———?" Brydon oddly sounded.

"Before, for the interest of his difference—yes. And as I didn't disown him, as *I* knew him—which you at last, confronted with him in his difference, so cruelly didn't, my dear—well, he must have been, you see, less dreadful to me. And it may have pleased him that I pitied him."

She was beside him on her feet, but still holding his hand—still with her arm supporting him. Yet though it all brought for him thus a dim light, "You 'pitied' him?" he grudgingly, resentfully asked.

"He has been unhappy, he has been ravaged," she said.

"And haven't I been unhappy? Am not I—you've only to look at me!—ravaged?"

"Ah I don't say I like him *better*" she granted after a thought. "But he's grim, he's worn—and things have happened to him. He doesn't make shift, for sight, with your charming monocle."

"No"—it struck Brydon: "I couldn't have sported mine 'down town.' They'd have guyed[20] me there."

"His great convex pince-nez—I saw it, I recognised the kind—is for his poor ruined sight. And his poor right hand———!"

"Aie!" Brydon winced—whether for his proved identity or for his lost fingers. Then "He has a million a year," he lucidly added. "But he hasn't you."

"And he isn't—no, he isn't—*you!*" she murmured as he drew her to his breast.

NOTES

1. Prominent, or fashionable.
2. Meaning that, for some unstated reason, the lease on this property has terminated. Later in the story it is clear that the renovations will include adding extra stories to the structure.
3. Fifth Avenue in New York City. The story is set in an area of Lower Manhattan where Henry James lived for much of his childhood.
4. Pleased. This is James's attempt to represent Mrs. Muldoody's Irish brogue.
5. Again, this is James's attempt at replicating Mrs. Muldoody's pronunciation; the "evil hours" are generally regarded as a time late at night when supernatural beings are more likely to be present.
6. A candle. The house has no electric lighting.
7. A reception room.
8. For two sous (French). A sou was a French coin of little value, only a few cents.
9. Alternate personality (Latin).
10. To delay an action. This idiom originated in the eighteenth century to describe when a musket's priming powder ignited but the gun either delayed or did not fire.
11. Pertaining to the periods around dawn and twilight.
12. Social clubs, where men could dine, drink, and smoke together, were very popular in New York City and London at the turn of the century; membership was usually extended only to a select group of men as a way to maintain exclusivity.
13. Chinese shadows (French), or shadow puppets.
14. Reconciliation (French).

15. Brydon is comparing himself to the character Pantaloon from the Italian, then British, dramatic genre the Harlequinade; in these light slapstick comedies Harlequin, who is in love with Pantaloon's daughter Columbine, is often portrayed as sneaking up behind Pantaloon and playing tricks on him.

16. A reference to the English proverb "Tread a worm on the tail, and it turnest again," first attributed to John Heywood (1497–1580), although versions later appear in multiple places, including Shakespeare's *Henry VI* (1591). Sometimes shortened to "Even the worm will turn," the proverb implies that even a small creature will defend itself or fight when pushed to the limit.

17. To act brave so as to conceal one's sense of fear.

18. To have been fooled.

19. Blessings often used to conclude a Christian worship service

20. To mock or ridicule.

SARAH ORNE JEWETT

(1849–1909)

Short story writer, novelist, and poet Theodora Sarah Orne Jewett was born on September 3, 1849, in South Berwick, Maine, the second daughter of Dr. Theodore H. Jewett and Caroline Perry Jewett. Both her maternal and paternal predecessors had lived in New England for many generations, and much of Jewett's writing reflects her close association with this region and its people. Although she did travel extensively in the United States, Canada, and Europe, and later spent much of each year in and around Boston, Jewett lived most of her life, and died in, South Berwick, in the same colonial house owned by her grandfather.

As a child, Jewett suffered from rheumatoid arthritis, a disorder that affects joints with stiffness and swelling. Daily walks were recommended as part of her treatment, and the time spent outside deepened Jewett's love of nature. With her formal education often interrupted by poor health, Jewett supplemented her learning by delving into her family's library. She also frequently accompanied her father on his rounds as he drove to visit patients throughout the countryside.

The first of many publications that would secure Jewett's reputation as an important practitioner of the Regionalist genre was "Mr. Bruce," which appeared in the prominent *Atlantic Monthly* magazine of Boston in 1869. Works of Regionalist fiction are generally characterized by an emphasis on the importance of accurately reflecting the unique characteristics of a place through techniques such as the use of dialect, the inclusion of characters who may not be often represented in literary fiction (for example, those who are poor), and an effort to faithfully depict the environment with detailed descriptions of flora and fauna. Jewett's contemporaries lauded her ability to both create nuanced, sympathetic New England characters and depict the region's natural beauty.

A major step forward in Jewett's career was the publication in 1877 of her first book, *Deephaven*, a collection of previously published yet interconnected sketches about various characters in a fictional Maine town. Another major event took place in 1880, when Jewett made the acquaintance of *Atlantic Monthly* editor James T. Fields and his wife, Annie Adams Fields. James died shortly thereafter, in 1881, but Jewett and Annie remained lifelong companions, living together for extended periods in Fields's Massachusetts residences and also taking many trips together. Although there is much debate as to whether the women were romantically involved, they can most certainly be described as partners in what was called a "Boston marriage," a living arrangement in which two women co-habitated without the support of a man.

Jewett enjoyed her greatest success during the 1880s and 1890s, when her short stories were highly sought-after by editors of the nation's most prominent magazines and newspapers. Her best-known and most widely read and studied book, *The Country of the Pointed Firs* (1896), is, similar to *Deephaven*, a series of in-terrelated sketches, most of them previously published in the *Atlantic Monthly*, that capture life in a small, declining Maine seaport. Since the book's rediscovery in the 1970s, feminist scholars in particular have championed it as one of the best examples of American women's writing, citing both its original structure and its complex and detailed depictions of women's lives. Unfortunately, Jewett's career ended prematurely on her fifty-third birthday, in 1902, when she was injured in a carriage accident and was left unable to write professionally; she died in 1909 after a series of strokes.

Like so many other women authors of this period, Jewett's work was mostly forgotten between her death and the 1970s, when a new generation of scholars began to appreciate its excellence, especially how her fictions reflected a female sensibility quite different than the male viewpoints that had previously been almost exclusively represented. The stories included here, "Tom's Husband" (1882) and "Stolen Pleasures" (1885), are excellent examples of Jewett's writing style and prevalent themes, especially her interest in portraying the relations between women and men. "Tom's Husband" was first published in the *Atlantic Monthly* in February 1882, and "Stolen Pleasures" reached a much more hetero-geneous audience by virtue of its being originally syndicated in a large number of newspapers in October 1885.

TOM'S HUSBAND (1882)

I shall not dwell long upon the circumstances that led to the marriage of my hero and heroine; though their courtship was, to them, the only one ideal, it had many aspects in which it was entirely commonplace in other people's eyes. While the world in general smiles at lovers with kindly approval and sympathy, it refuses to be aware of the unprecedented delight which is amazing to the lovers themselves.

But, as has been true in many other cases, when they were at last married, the most ideal of situations was found to have been changed to the most practical. Instead of having shared their original duties, and, as school-boys would say, going halves, they discovered that the cares of life had been doubled. This led to some distressing moments for both our friends; they understood suddenly that instead of dwelling in heaven they were still upon earth, and had made themselves slaves to new laws and limitations. Instead of being freer and happier than ever before, they had assumed new responsibilities; they had established a new household, and must fulfill in some way or another the obligations of it. They looked back with affection to their engagement; they had been longing to have each other to themselves, apart from the world, but it seemed that they never felt so keenly that they were still units in modern society. Since Adam and Eve were in Paradise, before the devil joined them, nobody has had a chance to imitate that unlucky couple. In some respects they told the truth when, twenty times a day, they said that life had never been so pleasant before; but there were mental reservations on either side which might have subjected them to the accusation of lying. Somehow, there was a little feeling of disappointment, and they caught themselves wondering—though they would have died sooner than confess it—whether they were quite so happy as they had expected. The truth was, they were much happier than people usually are, for they had an uncommon capacity for enjoyment. For a little while they were like a sail-boat that is beating and has to drift a few minutes before it can catch the wind and start off on the other tack. And they had the same feeling, too, that any one is likely to have who has been long pursuing some object of his ambition or desire. Whether it is a coin, or a picture, or a stray volume of some old edition of Shakespeare, or whether it is an office under government or a lover, when it is fairly in one's grasp there is a loss of the eagerness that was felt in pursuit. Satisfaction, even after one has dined well, is not so interesting and eager a feeling as hunger.

My hero and heroine were reasonably well established to begin with: they each had some money, though Mr. Wilson had most. His father had at one time been a rich man, but with the decline, a few years before, of manufacturing interests, he had become, mostly through the fault of others, somewhat involved;[1] and at the time of his death his affairs were in such a condition that it was still a question whether a very large sum or a modestly large one would represent his estate. Mrs. Wilson, Tom's step-mother, was somewhat of an invalid; she suffered severely at times with asthma, but she was almost entirely relieved by living in another part of the country. While her husband lived, she had accepted her illness as inevitable, and had rarely left home; but during the last few years she had lived in Philadelphia with her own people, making short and wheezing visits only from time to time, and had not undergone a voluntary period of suffering since the occasion of Tom's marriage, which she had entirely approved. She had a sufficient property of her own, and she and Tom were independent of each other in that way. Her only other step-child was a daughter, who had married a navy officer, and had at this time gone out to spend three years (or less) with her husband, who had been ordered to Japan.

It is not infrequently noticed that in many marriages one of the persons who choose each other as partners for life is said to have thrown himself or herself away, and the relatives and friends look on with dismal forebodings and ill-concealed submission. In this case it was the wife who might have done so much better, according to public opinion. She did not think so herself, luckily, either before marriage or afterward, and I do not think it occurred to her to picture to herself the sort of career which would have been her alternative. She had been an only child, and had usually taken her own way. Some one once said that it was a great pity that she had not been obliged to work for her living, for she had inherited a most uncommon business talent, and, without being disreputably keen at a bargain, her insight into the practical working of affairs was very clear and far-reaching. Her father, who had also been a manufacturer, like Tom's, had often said it had been a mistake that she was a girl instead of a boy. Such executive ability as hers is often wasted in the more contracted sphere of women, and is apt to be more a disadvantage than a help. She was too independent and self-reliant for a wife; it would seem at first thought that she needed a wife herself more than she did a husband. Most men like best the women whose natures cling and appeal to theirs for protection. But Tom Wilson, while he did not wish to be protected himself, liked these very qualities in his wife which would have displeased some other men; to tell the truth, he was very much in love with his wife just as she was. He was a successful collector of almost everything but money, and during a great part of his life he had been an invalid, and he had grown, as he laughingly confessed, very old-womanish. He had been badly lamed, when a boy, by being caught in some machinery in his father's mill, near which he was idling one afternoon, and though he had almost entirely outgrown the effect of his injury, it had not been until after many years. He had been in college, but his eyes had given out there, and he had been obliged to leave in the middle of his junior year, though he had kept up a pleasant intercourse with the members of his class, with whom he had been a great favorite. He was a good deal of an idler in the world. I do not think his ambition, except in the case of securing Mary Dunn for his wife, had ever been distinct; he seemed to make the most he could of each day as it came, without making all his days' works tend toward some grand result, and go toward the upbuilding of some grand plan and purpose. He consequently gave no promise of being either distinguished or great. When his eyes would allow, he was an indefatigable reader; and although he would have said that he read only for amusement, yet he amused himself with books that were well worth the time he spent over them.

The house where he lived nominally belonged to his step-mother, but she had taken for granted that Tom would bring his wife home to it, and assured him that it should be to all intents and purposes his. Tom was deeply attached to the old place, which was altogether the pleasantest in town. He had kept bachelor's hall there most of the time since his father's death, and he had taken great pleasure, before his marriage, in refitting it to some extent, though it was already comfortable and furnished in remarkably good taste. People said of him that if it had not been for his illnesses, and if he had been a poor boy, he probably would have made something of himself. As it was, he was not very well known by the townspeople, being somewhat reserved, and not taking much interest in their every-day subjects of conversation. Nobody liked him so well as they liked his wife, yet there was no reason why he should be disliked enough to have much said about it.

After our friends had been married for some time, and had outlived the first strangeness of the new order of things, and had done their duty to their neighbors with so much apparent willingness and generosity that even Tom himself was liked a great deal better than he ever had been before, they were sitting together one stormy evening in the library, before the fire. Mrs. Wilson had been reading Tom the letters which had come to him by the night's mail. There was a long one from his sister in Nagasaki, which had been written with a good deal of ill-disguised reproach. She complained of the smallness of the income of her share in her father's estate, and said that she had been assured by American friends that the smaller mills were starting up everywhere, and beginning to do well again. Since so much of their money was invested in the factory, she had been surprised and sorry to find by Tom's last letters that he had seemed to have no idea of putting in a proper person as superintendent, and going to work again. Four per cent. on her other property, instead of eight, which she had been told she must soon expect, would make a great difference to her. A navy captain in a foreign port was obliged to entertain a great deal, and Tom must know that it cost them much more to live than it did him, and ought to think of their interest. She hoped he would talk over what was best to be done with their mother (who had been made executor, with Tom, of his father's will).

Tom laughed a little, but looked disturbed. His wife had said something to the same effect, and his mother had spoken once or twice in her letters of the prospect of starting the mill again. He was not a bit of a business man, and he did not feel certain, with the theories which he had arrived at of the state of the country, that it was safe yet to spend the money which would have to be spent in putting the mill in order. "They think that the minute it is going again we shall be making money hand over hand, just as father did when we were children," he said. "It is going to cost us no end of money before we can make anything. Before father died he meant to put in a good deal of new machinery, I remember. I don't know anything about the business myself, and I would have sold out long ago if I had had an offer that came anywhere near the value. The larger mills are the only ones that are good for anything now, and we should have to bring a crowd of French Canadians here; the day is past for the people who live in this part of the country to go into the factory again. Even the Irish all go West when they come into the country, and don't come to places like this any more."

"But there are a good many of the old work-people down in the village," said Mrs. Wilson. "Jack Towne asked me the other day if you weren't going to start up in the spring."

Tom moved uneasily in his chair. "I'll put you in for superintendent, if you like," he said, half angrily, whereupon Mary threw the newspaper at him; but by the time he had thrown it back he was in good humor again.

"Do you know, Tom," she said, with amazing seriousness, "that I believe I should like nothing in the world so much as to be the head of a large business? I hate keeping house,—I always did; and I never did so much of it in all my life put together as I have since I have been married. I suppose it isn't womanly to say so, but it I could escape from the whole thing I believe I should be perfectly happy. If you get rich when the mill is going again, I shall beg for a housekeeper, and shift everything. I give you fair warning. I don't believe I keep this house half so well as you did before I came here."

Tom's eyes twinkled. "I am going to have that glory,—I don't think you do, Polly; but you can't say that I have not been forbearing. I certainly have not told you more than twice how we used to have things cooked. I'm not going to be your kitchen-colonel."

"Of course it seemed the proper thing to do," said his wife, meditatively; "but I think we should have been even happier than we have if I had been spared it. I have had some days of wretchedness that I shudder to think of. I never know what to have for breakfast; and I ought not to say it, but I don't mind the sight of dust. I look upon housekeeping as my life's great discipline;" and at this pathetic confession they both laughed heartily.

"I've a great mind to take it off your hands," said Tom. "I always rather liked it, to tell the truth, and I ought to be a better housekeeper,—I have been at it for five years; though housekeeping for one is different from what it is for two, and one of them a woman. You see you have brought a different element into my family. Luckily, the servants are pretty well drilled. I do think you upset them a good deal at first!"

Mary Wilson smiled as if she only half heard what he was saying. She drummed with her foot on the floor and looked intently at the fire, and presently gave it a vigorous poking. "Well?" said Tom, after he had waited patiently as long as he could.

"Tom! I'm going to propose something to you. I wish you would really do as you said, and take all the home affairs under your care, and let me start the mill. I am certain I could manage it. Of course I should get people who understood the thing to teach me. I believe I was made for it; I should like it above all things. And this is what I will do: I will bear the cost of starting it, myself,—I think I have money enough, or can get it; and if I have not enough, or can get it; and if I have not put affairs in the right trim at the end of a year I will stop, and you may make some other arrangement. If I have, you and your mother and sister can pay me back."

"So I am going to be the wife, and you the husband," said Tom, a little indignantly; "at least, that is what people will say. It's a regular Darby and Joan[2] affair, and you think you can do more work in a day than I can do in three. Do you know that you must go to town to buy cotton? And do you know there are a thousand things about it that you don't know?"

"And never will?" said Mary, with perfect good humor. "Why, Tom, I can learn as well as you, and a good deal better, for I like business, and you don't. You forget that I was always father's right-hand man after I was a dozen years old, and that you have let me invest my money and some of you own, and I haven't made a blunder yet."

Tom thought that his wife had never looked so handsome or so happy. "I don't care, I should rather like the fun of knowing what people will say. It is a new departure, at any rate. Women think they can do everything better than men in these days, but I'm the first man, apparently, who has wished he were a woman."

"Of course people will laugh," said Mary, "but they will say that it's just like me, and think I am fortunate to have married a man who will let me do as I choose. I don't see why it isn't sensible: you will be living exactly as you were before you married, as to home affairs; and since it was a good thing for you to know something about housekeeping then, I can't imagine why you shouldn't go on with it now, since it makes me miserable, and I am wasting a fine business talent while I do it. What do we care for people's talking about it?"

"It seems to me that it is something like women's smoking: it isn't wicked, but it isn't the custom of the country. And I don't like the idea of your going among business men. Of course I should be above going with you, and having people think I must be an idiot; they would say that you married a manufacturing interest, and I was thrown in. I can foresee that my pride is going to be humbled to the dust in every way," Tom declared in mournful tones, and began to shake with laughter. "It is one of your lovely castles in the air, dear Polly, but an old brick mill needs a better foundation that the clouds. No, I'll look around, and get an honest man with a few select brains for agent. I suppose it's the best thing we can do, for the machinery ought not to lie still any longer; but I mean to sell the factory as soon as I can. I devoutly wish it would take fire, for the insurance would be the best price we are likely to get. That is a famous letter from Alice! I am afraid the captain has been growling over his pay, or they have been giving too many little dinners on board ship. If we were rid of the mill, you and I might go out there this winter. It would be capital fun."

Mary smiled again in an absent-minded way. Tom had an uneasy feeling that he had not heard the end of it yet, but nothing more was said for a day or two. When Mrs. Tom Wilson announced, with no apparent thought of being contradicted, that she had entirely made up her mind, and she meant to see those men who had been overseers of the different departments, who still lived in the village, and have the mill put in order at once, Tom looked disturbed, but made no opposition; and soon after breakfast his wife formally presented him with a handful of keys, and told him there was meat enough in the house for dinner; and presently he heard the wheels of her little phaeton[3] rattling off down the road. I should be untruthful if I tried to persuade any one that he was not provoked; he thought she would at least have waited for his formal permission, and at first he meant to take another horse, and chase her, and bring her back in disgrace, and put a stop to the whole thing. But something assured him that she knew what she was about, and he determined to let her have her own way. If she failed, it might do no harm, and this was the only ungallant thought he gave her. He was sure that she would do nothing unladylike, or be unmindful of his dignity; and he believed it would be looked upon as one of her odd, independent freaks, which always had won respect in the end, however much they had been laughed at in the beginning. "Susan," said he, as that estimable person went by the door with the dust-pan, "you may tell Catherine to come to me for orders about the house, and you may do so yourself. I am going to take charge again, as I did before I was married. It is no trouble to me, and Mrs. Wilson dislikes it. Besides she is going into business, and will have a great deal else to think of."

"Yes, sir; very well, sir," said Susan, who was suddenly moved to ask so many questions that she was utterly silent. But her master looked very happy; there was evidently no disapproval of his wife; and she went on up the stairs, and began to sweep them down, knocking the dust-brush about excitedly, as if she were trying to kill a descending colony of insects.

Tom went out to the stable and mounted his horse, which had been waiting for him to take his customary after-breakfast ride to the post-office, and he galloped down the road in quest of the phaeton. He saw Mary talking with Jack Towne, who had been an overseer and a valued workman of his father's. He was looking much surprised and pleased.

"I wasn't caring so much about getting work, myself," he explained; "I've got what will carry me and my wife through; but it'll be better for the young folks about here to work near home. My nephews are wanting something to do; they were going to Lynn[4] next week. I don't say but I should like to be to work in the old place again. I've sort of missed it, since we shut down."

"I'm sorry I was so long in overtaking you," said Tom, politely, to his wife. "Well, Jack, did Mrs. Wilson tell you she's going to start the mill? You must give her all the help you can."

"'Deed I will," said Mr. Towne, gallantly, without a bit of astonishment.

"I don't know much about the business yet," said Mrs. Wilson, who had been a little overcome at Jack Towne's lingo of the different rooms and machinery, and who felt an overpowering sense of having a great deal before her in the next few weeks. "By the time the mill is ready, I will be ready, too," she said, taking heart a little; and Tom, who was quick to understand her moods, could not help laughing, as he rode alongside. "We want a new barrel of flour, Tom, dear," she said, by way of punishment for his untimely mirth.

If she lost courage in the long delay, or was disheartened at the steady call for funds, she made no sign; and after a while the mill started up, and her cares were lightened, so that she told Tom that before next pay day she would like to go to Boston for a few days, and go to the theatre, and have a frolic and a rest. She really looked pale and thin, and she said she never worked so hard in all her life; but nobody knew how happy she was, and she was so glad she had married Tom, for some men would have laughed at it.

"I laughed at it," said Tom, meekly. "All is, if I don't cry by and by, because I am a beggar, I shall be lucky." But Mary looked fearlessly serene, and said that there was no danger at present.

It would have been ridiculous to expect a dividend[5] the first year, though the Nagasaki people were pacified with difficulty. All the business letters came to Tom's address, and everybody who was not directly concerned thought that he was the motive power of the reawakened enterprise. Sometimes business people came to the mill, and were amazed at having to confer with Mrs. Wilson, but they soon had to respect her talents and her success. She was helped by the old clerk, who had been promptly recalled and reinstated, and she certainly did capitally well. She was laughed at, as she had expected to be, and people said they should think Tom would be ashamed of himself; but it soon appeared that he was not to blame, and what reproach was offered was on the score of his wife's oddity. There was nothing about the mill that she did not understand before very long, and at the end of the second year she declared a small dividend with great pride and triumph. And she was congratulated on her success, and every one thought of her project in a different way from the way they had thought of it in the beginning. She had singularly good fortune: at the end of the third year she was making money for herself and her friends faster than most people were, and approving letters began to come from Nagasaki. The Ashtons had been ordered to stay in that region, and it was evident that they were continually being obliged to entertain more instead of less. Their children were growing fast too, and constantly becoming more expensive. The captain and his wife had already begun to congratulate themselves secretly that their two sons would in all probability come into possession, one day, of their uncle Tom's handsome property.

For a good while Tom enjoyed life, and went on his quiet way serenely. He was anxious at first, for he thought that Mary was going to make ducks and drakes[6] of his money and her own. And then he did not exactly like the looks of the thing, either; he feared that his wife was growing successful as a business person at the risk of losing her womanliness. But as time went on, and he found there was no fear of that, he accepted the situation philosophically. He gave up his collection of engravings, having become more interested in one of coins and medals, which took up most of his leisure time. He often went to the city in pursuit of such treasures, and gained much renown in certain quarters as a numismatologist of great skill and experience. But at last his house (which had almost kept itself, and had given him little to do beside ordering the dinners, while faithful old Catherine and her niece Susan were his aids) suddenly became a great care to him. Catherine, who had been the main-stay of the family for many years, died after a short illness, and Susan must needs choose that time, of all others, for being married to one of the second hands in the mill. There followed a long and dismal season of experimenting, and for a time there was a procession of incapable creatures going in at one kitchen door and out of the other. His wife would not have liked to say so, but it seemed to her that Tom was growing fussy about the house affairs, and took more notice of those minor details than he used. She wished more than once, when she was tired, that he would not talk so much about the housekeeping; he seemed sometimes to have no other thought.

In the first of Mrs. Wilson's connection with manufacturing, she had made it a rule to consult Tom on every subject of importance; but it had speedily proved to be a formality. He tried manfully to show a deep interest which he did not feel, and his wife gave up, little by little, telling him much about her affairs. She said that she liked to drop business when she came home in the evening; and at last she fell into the habit of taking a nap on the library sofa, while Tom, who could not use his eyes much by lamp-light, sat smoking or in utter idleness before the fire. When they were first married his wife had made it a rule that she should always read him the evening papers, and afterward they had always gone on with some book of history or philosophy, in which they were both interested. These evenings of their early married life had been charming to both of them, and from time to time one would say to the other that they ought to take up again the habit of reading together. Mary was so unaffectedly tired in the evening that Tom never liked to propose a walk; for, though he was not a man of peculiarly social nature, he had always been accustomed to pay an occasional evening visit to his neighbors in the village. And though he had little interest in the business world, and still less knowledge of it, after a while he wished that his wife would have more to say about what she was planning and doing, or how things were getting on. He thought that her chief aid, old Mr. Jackson, was far more in her thoughts than he. She was forever quoting Jackson's opinions. He did not like to find that she took in for granted that he was not interested in the welfare of his own property; it made him feel like a sort of pensioner and dependent, though, when they had guests at the house, which was by no means seldom, there was nothing in her manner that would imply that she thought herself in any way the head of the family. It was hard work to find fault with his wife in any way, though, to give him his due, he rarely tried.

But, this being a wholly unnatural state of things, the reader must expect to hear of its change at last, and the first blow from the enemy was dealt by an old woman, who lived near by, and who called to Tom one morning, as he was driving down to the village in a great hurry (to post a letter, which ordered his agent to secure a long-wished-for ancient copper coin, at any price), to ask him if they had made yeast that week, and if she could borrow a cupful, as her own had met with some misfortune. Tom was instantly in a rage, and he mentally condemned her to some undesired fate, but told her aloud to go and see the cook. This slight delay, besides being killing to his dignity, caused him to lose the mail, and in the end his much-desired copper coin. It was a hard day for him, altogether; it was Wednesday, and the first days of the week having been stormy the washing was very late. And Mary came home to dinner provokingly good-natured. She had met an old school-mate and her husband driving home from the mountains, and had first taken them over her factory, to their great amusement and delight, and then had brought them home to dinner. Tom greeted them cordially, and manifested his usual graceful hospitality; but the minute he saw his wife alone he said in a plaintive tone of rebuke, "I should think you might have remembered that the girls are unusually busy to-day. I do wish you would take a little interest in things at home. The girls have been washing, and I'm sure I don't know what sort of a dinner we can give your friends. I wish you had thought to bring home some steak. I have been busy myself, and couldn't go down to the village. I thought we would only have a lunch."

Mary was hungry, but she said nothing, except that it would be all right,—she didn't mind; and perhaps they could have some canned soup.

She often went to town to buy or look at cotton, or to see some improvement in machinery, and she brought home beautiful bits of furniture and new pictures for the house, and showed a touching thoughtfulness in remembering Tom's fancies; but somehow he had an uneasy suspicion that she could get along pretty well without him when it came to the deeper wishes and hopes of her life, and that her most important concerns were all matters in which he had no share. He seemed to himself to have merged his life in his wife's; he lost his interest in things outside the house and grounds; he felt himself fast growing rusty and behind the times, and to have somehow missed a good deal in life; he felt that he was a failure. One day the thought rushed over him that his had been almost exactly the experience of most women, and he wondered if it really was any more disappointing and ignominious to him than it was to women themselves. "Some of them may be contented with it," he said to himself, soberly. "People think women are designed for such careers by nature, but I don't know why I ever made such a fool of myself."

Having once seen his situation in life from such a stand-point, he felt it day by day to be more degrading, and he wondered what he should do about it; and once, drawn by a new, strange sympathy, he went to the little family burying-ground. It was one of the mild, dim days that come sometimes in early November, when the pale sunlight is like the pathetic smile of a sad face, and he sat for a long time on the limp, frostbitten grass beside his mother's grave.

But when he went home in the twilight his step-mother, who just then was making them a little visit, mentioned that she had been looking through some boxes of hers that had been packed long before and stowed away in the garret. "Everything looks very nice up there," she said, in her wheezing voice (which, worse than usual that day, always made him nervous); and added without any intentional slight to his feelings, "I do think you have always been a most excellent housekeeper."

"I'm tired of such nonsense!" he exclaimed, with surprising indignation. "Mary, I wish you to arrange your affairs so that you can leave them for six months at least. I am going to spend this winter in Europe."

"Why, Tom, dear!" said his wife, appealingly. "I couldn't leave my business any way in the"—

But she caught sight of a look on his usually placid countenance that was something more than decision, and refrained from saying anything more.

And three weeks from that day they sailed.

NOTES

1. In debt.
2. Darby and Joan are characters in "The Joys of Love Never Forgot" (1735), a poem by Henry Woodfall (ca. 1686–1747); they also appeared in a popular song and subsequent poems. Their names became synonymous with the image of a contentedly married couple, usually elderly.
3. A lightweight, open horse-drawn carriage.
4. A manufacturing town near Boston.
5. Profit.
6. "Ducks and drakes" is a game of skipping flat stones across water, but also refers to squandering money.

STOLEN PLEASURES (1885)

John Webber passed a group of his fellow workmen who loitered on the sidewalk outside the gate of the Zenith Machine Company's works one Thursday evening, with a quick business-like step. It had been a very hot day, the sun had not yet set and was pouring its last level rays along the street, making the dust look gold-coloured, and dazzling the eyes of everybody that faced that way. The air seemed closer and warmer than ever, and the men scolded about it, and wiped their grimy faces with an impatient, half indignant gesture as if they felt a sense of personal injustice after such an August day.

"Where are you racin' to now, Webber?" somebody asked our hero, and several of his friends in the complaining group, turned to look at him.

"Goin' home," responded Webber cheerfully, as he paused for a minute, and when somebody said, "Give our love to the baby!" in a tone that was meant to be provoking, he only shook his head with mock resentment.

"Hold on!" called the first speaker, "We're gettin' together to see how many of us want to hire Jones' barge for Sunday and go down to the beach. Start late Saturday, quick 's we're out of the shop, and get back some time Sunday night. Jones'll take us for a dollar-ten apiece if we can get twenty-four to say they'll go."

"Well, I ain't one," answered Webber moving off. "The only time I ever tried such a spree I came home worse off than I went. Ride all night and scorch all day, that ain't my idea o' fun," and he disappeared round the corner, smiling with all his might as if he knew of something a great deal better than any such foolish plans.

He was a delicate-looking, boyish, young man. Everybody liked Johnny Webber, for with all his quick temper and satisfaction with his own way of doing things, he was friendly and generous and always ready to do anybody a good turn. His acquaintances had laughed at him and taxed him over and over again for his habit of telling long stories about his own affairs. He seemed to think that everybody was as much interested as he when something pleasant happened to him—it was not brag on his part and he had no idea of outshining anybody else, but to use the oft repeated saying, "Johnny Webber thinks he must go halves with everybody." It was deplored among the wisest of his comrades that he should have fallen in love with a selfish, complaining sort of girl, a pretty girl enough but vain, and not of the sort that John Webber deserved.

But he was apparently satisfied, and never seemed to be troubled when things went wrong; he was always ready to make excuses for everybody else, and when his wife fretted he blamed the weather or her ill health or the house work which she did not like, or the care of the baby which, to be sure, he always tried to take upon himself at night.

As he walked along this evening he whistled and felt an unusual pride in his success and well being; then he hummed a tune, and occasionally slipped his hand into his side pocket to feel his purse. This was the second Thursday in the month, and consequently pay day. For the last four weeks he had been doing double work, and there was the pay for it folded away safe and sound, and in his heart was a secret just ready to be told. He was as tired as a hard-working man could be, but he forgot his aching back and hurried as fast as he could go toward home along the dusty, half-built streets that made the outskirts of the town.

The evening grew hotter and hotter, but he did not mind it, and he felt as if he could not wait another minute before he turned into the new bit of street where there was a row of eight small houses all alike and looking as if they were set in there in the sand to be sold and carried away elsewhere and established among trees and made homes of—only one had a bit of garden already in this temporary looking spot, and it was toward that door that John Webber went. With all the sand, and no fence for shelter except a row of stakes made from a split dry-goods box, he had managed to make some flowers grow like those his mother had in her little front yard when he was a boy. There was an invisible wall about this plain, dull, little dwelling which separated it from all the rest of the world. As he glanced at the rest of the houses as he passed them, they all looked inferior to his own, which really belonged to him and his wife and baby. He had chosen it because there was a tree in the small back yard, a silver poplar that had persisted in growing in spite of many discouragements. John Webber had felt much disappointed because his wife had complained that it cut off her view of another road, which was a thoroughfare, from the kitchen window.

The master of this little house looked eagerly up at that window as he came along, because when Hattie was good natured and felt like it, she used to stand there and watch for him and hold the baby up for him to see. Anybody else must have been forced to recognize the fact that the baby was not a beauty, but there was nothing in the world so lovely, the young father thought, and he mistook the round, fat, pinkish face and imperceptible whitish hair and faded blue eyes for the best good looks that any baby in the world could have. His own eyes were beaming full of love and pride, and changed sadly at the moment when he made sure that nobody was looking out for him that evening. Somehow a foreboding sense of disappointment filled his heart as he mounted the step to the back door and found it—*locked?*

Yes; and when he rapped the house echoed the sound from its empty corners. There is a difference between the sound of a knock that somebody hears, and that beats against the recognized ears of some housekeeper and an unanswered summons like this. What could have become of Hattie and the baby? John Webber stopped to think. She would not have locked the door and shut the windows if she had only gone to see one of the neighbours. Ah! perhaps she had gone to her sister's, two miles further out in the country, thinking it might be cooler there. They had been meaning to go out to spend a day or two, though John himself had protested craftily, being proudly conscious of another plan which he had been keeping secret. It was too far away from his work, and he had pleaded that and his real tiredness in this dog-day weather. He lived too far away from the works already, but he knew the air here was so much better for Hattie and the baby than it would be in the heart of the town. That very morning Hattie had been complaining of various maladies, and said that she felt too ill to be out of her bed—perhaps her sister had come in and insisted on taking her home. John did not like this sister; she was always making Hattie see faults and failings in people and things, and wondered why he had bought a house just here; in fact she seemed to question everything he did. Hattie had seemed dreadfully dissatisfied lately, but perhaps it was only the hot weather.

He had found the key under the door mat, and gone into the deserted, cheerless, hot little house; he put away his dinner pail and sat down in the rocking chair. He was tired and hungry, and he did not know whether to go out and join his wife or not. There was nobody to tell his secret to, and he had been counting for weeks upon the happiness he would have this very evening. Well, he must cool off awhile anyhow, and then he would take the rest of his long walk. How still it seemed without the baby! The little fellow took up more room than anybody in the house already, and John reached to the table for a rubber rattle that lay there, and held it in his hand a minute before he began to strike his knee with it and make the bell ring as if the baby were there to hear.

II.

Hallo! there is a folded piece of white paper pinned to the table cloth, which he had not observed before, and he springs for it and takes it over to the window where the light is better. Hattie writes a faint, cramped little school girlish hand that is not easy to read, but John Webber's heart sinks as he spells out the note:—

"I didn't see any chance of your going to the beach or any wheres like other folks, and Nell Stince urged me and the baby to start right off with her this morning. She has got part of a house for two weeks down to West Harborside and invited me to make a visit so twont[1] be any expense to you, but I don't expect I can be gone but a few days. Mrs. Stince felt as if the baby needed change very bad. She hopes you will come down for Sunday anyway—Can't you get a week off? I know you wouldn't say no if you was here. You are most always so dear, don't be cross, Johnny."

"She knew I would say no," muttered John Webber, his good nature stirred at last like a smooth, deep sea in a great storm. Then he covered his face with his hands and cried. The darkness fell; he sat there still in the rocking chair facing the fact of his wife's thoughtlessness and his own disappointment. She had been so pretty, so merry and trim and neat when he first knew her. She did not wear flaunting colors like many other girls. Hattie looked like a little lady, he had told himself many times, and was proud to notice how many people turned to look at her as she went along the streets. It had been hard work to win her, for she had many other admirers, and John Webber was a plain fellow who had more money in the bank than some young men, but who would not spend any more than he could help on new cravats or cheap shows and needless nonsense. Nell Stince for one had said he was stingy, and wondered why he did not give his promised wife all sorts of gilt jewelry, and one particular feather fan, which winked its spangles enticingly from a jeweler's window. Nell Stince sneered at the presents this honest lover did buy; she even railed at his foolishness in buying a house and paying for it before he married. She would rather have paid rent and spent all that money for something worth having. She and her husband were both deep in debt already, but it mattered nothing to them. "A short life and a merry one," Jim Stince was fond of saying to his admiring audiences on the street corners. They had one girl, a little monkey of a thing, rigged in greasy silk and draggled feathers. Nell Stince was Hattie's evil genius. They had worked in the same shop together before they were married, and Hattie would be worth twice as much if he could keep her to himself, poor John thought. Hattie had married because she loved him—he reminded himself of that proudly. He was not a dandy like the other fellows, but alas, Hattie seemed to be getting tired of him lately and of her small house which they had put in order so lovingly in the early days of their married life. She was fretful and dissatisfied, and when John sat there in the dark and remembered his mother and their dear, old-fashioned, simple, country life—the farm, the honest, friendly neighbors—he grew bitterly impatient of all the shams and makeshifts of the town—the life that was all for show and made "what other folks would say" its only conscience. The sauciness of the first part of his wife's letter and the cajoling of the end gave him equal pain. "She ought to know me better than that," he told himself over and over. Go down to spend Sunday with the Stinces—he would die first.

Poor boy, he had waited so patiently for his own holiday; he had never worked harder in his life than through this last month, and it was to make sure of a good time with his wife and baby at the end. He had found the year's expenses a hard pull anyway; the doctor's bill had been very heavy, but this extra work would make everything square. The extras of every month always counted about the same, and he tried to save a little as he went along,—he had always been used to saving. This very night when he asked the boss if he could take his vacation, he had been given a hearty permission. "Take two weeks while you are about it, Johnny," said one of the owners who stood by. "I guess we can get along; you deserve it, and I wish we could scare up a dozen fellows like you!"

Two whole weeks! what couldn't he do in that time? The baby should go up to the old farm and see his grandmother who had never taken him into her arms yet—he should roll in the grass where his father used to roll and get solid and strong, poor little beggar! his round, weak face didn't have the look that John Webber believed that a baby's ought to have, though he didn't know much about babies. "Mother'll know how to cosset[2] him," said John more than once; "and she'll get Hattie on her feet too, and make some of those old herb teas for her that she used to set so much by. Wormwood;[3] that'll make her hungry!" and Hattie should go down to Harborside and they would find a snug place to board, the first few days, and go out to sail once or twice, and dear me how good it would all be! Hattie should not know a word about it until they were ready to start the next day—it should be a surprise. "You always want your own way," she had accused him more than once of late; now he would joke her well and see if his way wasn't a good one, sometimes! Oh, poor Hattie! how could she have gone away?

That was a long, sad evening for kind-hearted Johnny Webber to spend alone. It was not only his wife's going away on a stolen holiday that troubled him, he had lost his truest faith in the woman to whom he had given his best love. The little house and its furnishings seemed so pitiful and trivial as he went through the rooms with a light that night. The life had gone out of everything, and it was untidy and uncared for. "I learned my trade," said poor Webber once, savagely. "I learned my trade, and I know how to do the things I have to do. It isn't so with women. If I kept a school for 'em hang me if I wouldn't turn 'em out to be good for something!" And then he caught sight of a little frock which the baby had worn that very day while he crept about the floor. Poor baby, poor Hattie!—they must both be taken care of—one was as much a child as the other.

The best people in the world are the surest to have enemies, and so here was our hero, hindered and worried by that worthless member of society, Nell Stince. She cared very little for the poor little wife whom she teased into more or less willing acquiescence to her own foolish ideas. Johnny Webber was such a pattern of propriety, was he? Then nothing would content her but letting the world see that he was no better than anybody else—and any way she knew of mocking and shaming him must be tried. Hattie was well enough, but as weak as a straw, and so by flattery and challenge of a foolish pride the well being and prosperity of this new household were brought into danger. And the young wife's eyes were blinded more and more.

The journey to the seashore had been very hot and tiresome; the baby had cried pitifully, and even the Stince child had forgotten the satisfaction of her best clothes and was fretful and provoking. The dust blew after the hard springed wagon in white stifling clouds; the country roads were unshaded and the fourteen mile drive seemed likely never to come to an end. Nell Stince's brother, a saucy, half-grown boy, frightened poor little Mrs. Webber by his reckless driving, and his beating of the thin horse which stumbled every little while and was hardly equal to such a load. When they reached the beach there was no cool breeze—in fact the glare made it seem hotter than it did at home. Even the despised poplar tree in the yard was remembered with affection, and later, when the depressed little company sat down to their evening meal, an uncomfortable fly-beset lunch—the repentant wife said that she would have given anything if she had thought to get Johnny's supper ready for him. Nell Stince gave a mocking laugh which somehow grated upon the listener's nerves. Toward night there was a delightful breath of sea wind and the baby stopped his crying and grew drowsy at last and went to sleep. Nell Stince was triumphant and wondered how they should have lived through another hot night at home, but her guest thought of John Webber all the time and wondered what he said when he came home, and if he were angry and wished over and over again that he were there with her at Harborside in the rough house which seemed very shelterless and uncomfortable. And John Webber's silly little wife cried herself to sleep. Running away did not seem like a joke at all from this point of view, though her hostess was merry enough down stairs with some new and old acquaintances whom she had picked up during the evening.

III.

When John Webber waked up next day from an uneasy sleep, he felt as if some enchantment had worked a miserable change in him. No words could say how lonely and wretched and angry he was, for, like most good-humored, equable people, his temper was very sullen, and hard to manage when it was once roused. This was a sad beginning to the vacation he had looked forward to with such high hopes; he could not go back to the works and face anybody's jeers and curious questioning, neither would he follow Nell Stince's lead and join the household at Harborside. Yes, this would be the best thing; he would go off by himself, too; he would go to see his dear old mother. She was very feeble this year, and he would not disappoint her of her promised visit. Oh, if he could only have taken his baby! But there was nothing to do but go alone, and so he shut the house and left the key at a neighbor's and hurried away to the train. As he was rushing across the green inland country and the fresh air blew in at the car window, his anger faded a little. "Poor Hattie," he said once or twice softly, as if he understood that she had felt the need of getting out of the hot town, and had known no better way to act.

He hardly felt like himself until he was nearing his old home on a high Vermont hillside, and after a long walk from the station there came in view the little red house and barn which looked as if they had slipped part way down the long, lonely hill slope. Then he felt like a boy again, the very boy who had gone years ago from that quiet spot out into the busy world to seek his fortune. Alas! he was bringing back a heavy, disappointed heart; he began to wish that he had gone after his wife and brought her with him. That would have been the square thing, and he grew afraid to look his mother in the face.

There she was, dear soul, at the little side door—coming out to pick up some chips to boil the tea-kettle—kettle for supper, but she stopped first and shaded her eyes with her hand as she looked along the horizon, and then as if urged by some instinct of what was going to happen cast an eager glance down the long lane that led to the main road. Could it be Johnny? Oh no, not without his wife and baby. Johnny, after three long years, when she had tried to fancy him married and living in his own house, and being a father. He had sent her many a five-dollar bill, and short, dull, little letter, and nobody knew how much they loved each other, this mother and her youngest boy.

The troubled young man and anxious, tender-hearted woman were soon face to face—they were both undemonstrative after the fashion of their kind. Their eyes were a half startled brightness as they reached out their hands to each other, and then John turned away and took the dull axe and began to split some wood while his mother stood watching him. He knew that she expected an explanation of his coming alone, and felt his face and even the very tips of his ears grow scarlet as he hewed away at the knotty sticks of pine in the gathering twilight. But one cannot split kindling wood all night, and at last John Webber threw down his axe and told his story. It was no use to spare himself, for the hard-worked patient woman was as just a soul as ever lived, and she would not excuse him because he himself made excuses.

"Yes, 'twas hard on you," she said at last, "I can see how you felt, but you needn't have done wrong, Johnny. Now you go right back an' get her. I'm glad it's so that you won't mind the expense as much as some other times. I'm urgent about it because I don't know 's I shall be here another summer and I feel's though I wanted to see your folks—winters go dreadful hard with me. * * * I've got a good many things to talk over and get you to see about. Austin's folks have as much as they can carry and the girls too. I've been a kind o' feelin' as if you were the only child I'd got this summer, and I should ha' took it hard if you hadn't come."

So, early the next morning, before day, John Webber went back lighter-hearted than he came and found his wife at the Harborside shanty, having anything but a pleasant time. The baby had taken cold in the night and been very sick. The doctor had been sent for and the little patient was out of danger, and even a great deal better, but his mother, unstrung and pathetically remorseful, threw herself into her husband's ready arms. Nell Stince sniffed a little; she had not made trouble between them after all; they loved each other a great deal better than ever before. The illusion of freedom and seeing something of the world had lost its charm for the poor little woman, she had had time to think over things—and as for John Webber he had made up his mind anew and could not forget some wise words that his dear old mother had spoken, "I guess your woman wants a little old-fashioned mothering," she said. "And I never saw no good of secrets between husbands and wives or of their doing things apart. You might have let her have all the month's pleasure of thinking of it beforehand same's you had, an' settlin' what she would do. You take right holt o' hands, and look at life together just as 'tis. Don't you think everything's as *you* say. She's got rights an' you've been too good sometimes, and treated her an' the baby just the same way other times. You mean well, Johnny, but we all need experience."

And two or three days later the young people went together to the hillside farm; and spent the rest of their fortnight—and wished it had been a month. They never had such a good time in their lives, any of them, and the grandmother promised that if everything went well she would come down another year, and make them a visit. "I'll treat you like a queen," said Hattie, "and you won't know me, I shall be such a smart housekeeper, your doughnuts and huckleberry bread won't be worth speakin' of."

"Yes, they will, too!" maintained John, stoutly. And they all laughed together, while the baby, not to be outdone, beat his plate with his spoon and shouted some unintelligible remark.

That evening, while John Webber and his wife came strolling up the lane picking blackberries after he had showed her the big nut trees he used to climb and the hole where he had killed a big fox when he was a boy, they both said that it seemed like their courting days, only better, and as if they were really going to be married and begin life all over again when they went back to town.

NOTES

1. It won't.
2. Pamper, spoil, or care for in an indulgent manner.
3. A woody shrub used in many herbal remedies; also an ingredient in absinthe liqueur.

GRACE KING

(1852–1932)

Like a number of other southern writers, such as Ruth McEnery Stuart, King has not received much critical attention since her death or had her works frequently anthologized by the literary establishment, which over the years has most highly valued Realism and liberal values. In large part the neglect of King is due to her works' strong tinges of Romanticism and her often negative depictions of African American characters. That King wrote this way should come as no surprise given her background. Born in New Orleans to a quite wealthy, cotton-plantation-owning New Orleans family before the Civil War, King experienced firsthand how this conflict had not only altered the power structure that had traditionally governed Louisiana life but also negatively affected her family's fortunes. In fact, King became an author largely because she wished to counteract the negative depictions of Louisiana's ruling Whites, especially those penned by fellow Louisianian fiction writer George Washington Cable.

In the mid-1880s, encouraged by two northern editors, Richard Watson Gilder and Charles Dudley Warner, King began writing and publishing stories

about New Orleans during Reconstruction, with her first story appearing in the
New Princeton Review in 1886. The first collection of her stories, *Tales of a Time
and Place,* was published in 1892, and the second, *Balcony Stories,* was issued the
following year. King's works typically depicted White southern women dealing
with the loss of money and status due to the Civil War; usually, these women,
persevering despite great challenges, are shown to be stronger and more resilient
than the defeated and weak surviving men. To some extent these pieces represent King's wish fulfillment, for after her father's death in 1881, her brothers
failed to prosper and she had been forced to work harder as a writer in order to
support herself, her mother, and her sisters. King never married.

Around the turn of the century, as the nation's interest in Regionalist fiction waned, so, too, did King's literary career, and she turned instead to writing
books about various aspects of southern history. The present story, "Making
Progress," came at the tail end of King's fiction-writing career, in 1901, and
was the last piece King ever published in the prestigious *Harper's Monthly;* it was
never collected in book form during her lifetime. Its intriguing glimpse into the
family dynamics and gender roles of a New Orleans family striving to "make it"
in a world that was rapidly adopting the "northern" definitions of "success" and
"progress" makes it an important complement to other fictional portrayals of
southern life during this period.

MAKING PROGRESS (1901)

Walking rapidly along upon some quest of momentary importance that absorbed my thought and dulled observation, I was suddenly stopped by a crowd
on the sidewalk in front of me: a compact, eager, curious crowd, not to be
threaded, and using its elbows viciously against pushing. No wonder! A cart
of the Little Sisters of the Poor[1] stood backed up against the curbing, and
four men were just in the act of pushing a stretcher into it. To see such a sight
was well worth the while of a whole neighborhood of shopkeepers, for I was
in the thickest shopkeeping quarter of the city. Practically speaking, there was
very little to be seen: a slight form covered by a sheet, and the outline of a
head on a low pillow. Every precaution had, as usual, been taken to ensure
concealment, the only privacy possible. But as the stretcher slid into the wagon
a murmur passed through the crowd, an involuntary shiver. The woman upon
the stretcher slowly raised her head, opened her eyes, and gave a look upon the
gazers. What a look! Woe! woe! woe!

The horses jerked forward; the head fell back; the cart rattled away.

I felt my elbow plucked, then grasped, and still looking after the cart, with
the rest of the crowd, I was forcibly dragged into a doorway. It was my friend
Madame Jacob, the second-hand dealer, who had hold of me, and I perceived
now that it was her shop that had furnished the excitement to the street. It always
seemed to be furnishing an excitement to the street. I never passed along there

A MURMUR PASSED THROUGH THE CROWD

Illustration from Grace King, "Making Progress," *Harper's Monthly* 102 (February 1901).

without noticing a turmoil: Madame Jacob putting her assistant, her nephew, out upon the banquette with cuffs and harder words, or hauling her husband in from a drinking-shop, or railing against a cautious customer, or assaulting the four corners of the heavens with voluble French, English, and German declamations upon some other misadventure. It was shrewdly suspected by some, and I believed it, that Madame Jacob used her noise and excitement as an auctioneer's drum, to call a crowd together, and so get at people. One could not help slacking one's pace to listen to her, nor, while one listened, glancing into her shop, and every glance of mine into that mysterious interior had, as I calculated it, cost me fifty cents. Others, of course, could get off cheaper, but they were not after bric-à-brac, or, to be more specific, old cut glass.

My eye hastily glanced around now, taking in the prospect of a bargain, as I was still pulled forward through the piled-up junk to a little recess behind the shop, the landing-place of the stairs, where I was thrust into a chair. Madame Jacob squatted on a low stool in the doorway, whence she could dominate her business and watch her nephew; and whenever she saw a customer edging away without buying anything, she would rush at the boy, box his ears, sell something, and come back to her stool, and her story, before the interruption was noticed.

Of course she wanted to tell me the story of the girl just carried away to the Little Sisters of the Poor: the young girl, she called her, although that gray-haired, ashen-faced head could by no means be called young, except in the sense of unmarried.

The story after all is not much, perhaps hardly worth writing down; but when it comes to that, what true stories are worth writing down? They are like natural flowers in comparison with the artificial—good only for the day, not for permanent show. The girl's name was Achard, Volsy Achard. When Madame Jacob first rented her shop, some thirty years before, the Achard family were living in the rooms above; they owned the building, rented the downstairs, and retained the upstairs—two rooms, a large one, and a small one adjoining. Madame Achard and Volsy slept in the large room. Paul, the boy, in the small one.

The family had been well-to-do shopkeepers in that very house, and in that very business. Madame Jacob intimated, for with a curious delicacy she would not say it outright, that Achard made his start with a sack over his back and a broom-handle with a crooked nail at the end of it.[2] At any rate, when he died and Madame Achard became the head of the family, and sold his business and collected all his profits together, she found that she had enough to invest in two houses—that one and the one next to it—which she rented at, in a round sum, fifty dollars a month apiece. And so, as Madame Jacob said, we see them, rich enough for anybody, with the boy going to the public school, the little girl to the day school of the convent. The family could not have been any more comfortable anywhere, nor happier: close to the market, under the very spire of the Cathedral, and with the opera-house at the end of their foot, so to speak. The little daughter, Volsy, "was so good, so good; . . . and Paul, he was 'smart,' 'smart.'" There was no American in his school who was smarter than he—to quote Madame Jacob's own words. The mother adored her son; the daughter was devoted to the mother. When Paul left school, he said he would be a lawyer, that and nothing else.

Every day the boy would go to his law study, and every day Volsy and her mother would sit together and sew and talk, and watch the soup simmering on the furnace. They went a great deal to church, and Volsy had a particular devotion to the Infant Jesus: the mother with the Infant, or the Infant alone, was all she cared to have on her little altar, and her picture cards; never the Virgin alone, or any of the saints. Paul read law in the office of a low-born but very well known lawyer—one who had a great practice in the shopkeeping class.

When Paul was admitted to the bar, this same lawyer gave him a desk in his office. This was a great advance for Paul, in one way, although in another, as the young man was good-looking, well-mannered, spoke French and English, and was, in short, more than usually intelligent, he was not a bad investment of the sort that older lawyers are ever on the alert to make from among the younger ones. Many a young lawyer, so picked up, has been known in the course of time to carry an old patron on his shoulders and seat him on the bench of the Suptreme Court for the reversion of his business, and marrying his daughter to boot. Going ahead means, necessarily, leaving behind, and Paul's advance caused the little family of three to change its rank. It did not, as of yore, march three abreast . . . Paul stepped on in front; the two women came together after him.

Paul dressed better and better, and associating with lawyers and imitating them, he, in the course of a few years, was not to be distinguished from any gentleman among them. This was the radiant time of life for his mother and sister. They talked of nothing else but Paul, thought of nothing else, lived for nothing else, and in their gratitude to Heaven they devoted themselves more and more to the church, and spent more and more of their money in votive offerings—to ensure the continuance of favors, or patronage, as Madame Jacob put it. And according to Madame Jacob's superior judgment in such business, it is always well to wait awhile and be sure about your blessing before you go into excess of gratitude, for in her experience the greatest blessings, apparently, had turned out to be the most unmitigated curses, and one's prayers and money were thus thrown away.

As if in the course of nature, Paul, marching always farther and farther ahead, advanced beyond coming home to his dinner,—beyond going to church Sunday morning, beyond going to the opera Sunday night, beyond going to picnics in the spring, given by his mother's benevolent society, or the balls in winter, given by the society to which his defunct father had always belonged, beyond going on little excursions of summer evenings to music places, beyond passing even an evening at home,—beyond everything of the past, in fact, except taking the cup of coffee that his mother made for him in the morning and eating with it the roll fetched from the market for him by his sister.

But the farther he advanced the better he pleased the two women, and the more devoted they became to him, if that were possible. Volsy's first communion dress, white muslin, year after year had been taken out, enlarged, washed, ironed, and fluted. It lay the year through freshly done up, unworn, with the string of pearl beads she always wore with it, and the wreath of pink roses that Madame Jacob herself had presented when Volsy went to some extraordinary event of a ball somewhere. Her brother did not think of her; her mother did not think of her; she did not think of herself. All were too busy thinking of one person—Paul.

Then Paul advanced beyond his little room, and went to live in other quarters—advanced, in plain fact, out of the women's lives; but they, gazing in to the place whence he disappeared, were still happy, and praised God all the more. He came at first every Sunday to see them, then every other Sunday, then once a month. They did not seem to mind his not coming—in truth, they did not mind it any more than they did the sun's not shining on a cloudy day. Serenely they awaited Paul's next advancement. It came, and even they had not expected so handsome an answer to their prayers. Paul announced that he was engaged to be married, and not to a nobody, but to the daughter of his patron. They—Madame Jacob, the mother, the sister—did not even know the old lawyer had a daughter! Judge what a miracle it was to them! . . . A young lady who lived in the rich American quarter of the city,[3] who went into the fine society up there, and gave entertainments that the newspapers described. It was astounding! And then there was inaugurated in that upstairs room a boom of industry and enterprise and "making of economies," to furnish Paul's wedding-present. Table and bed linen, silken and lace coverlets, curtains, cut glass. The second-hand dealer did her part in ferreting out bargains—and indeed some of her triumphs in that line were well worth the pride she took in recounting them. And this, in Madame Jacob's opinion, was the greatest pleasure Paul ever gave his family in his life—the opportunity of complete devotion and self-sacrifice: they could have kept it up forever and never known otherwise but that they were in paradise.

Paul never brought his bride to see his family, never took his family to see his bride. The young lady went away, and the marriage took place in the North, so of course the mother and sister could not be at the wedding. When the young couple returned, it was arranged that Paul would be met by the mother and sister. Paul was to take them on a Sunday. It was a month after his return before Paul found the right Sunday. Then he came for them. Madame Jacob watched them depart, and counted the moments until they returned, when . . . She did not recognize the mother! . . . Head up in the air, eyes shining, cheeks glowing, and tongue—talking at both ends. The fine house! The servant-man! The grand madame! Her elegant dress, and her elegant manners! Like a queen, yes, like a queen in the opera! . . .

In his mother's eyes, Paul had risen so high by his marriage that, as Madame Jacob said, he was to her like the picture of the Saviour in the transfiguration.[4] Volsy had nothing to say; she went quietly up stairs.

Shortly after this there was another boom of energy and industry in the room upstairs, another furious making of economies. Laces and linens, piqués and flannels. Madame Achard shopped from morning till night; Volsy never left her seat at the window, but sewed and embroidered, sewed and embroidered, from daylight till dark, and sewed and embroidered on after that by lamp-light. Oh no! The mother's eyes were not good enough for this work. Volsy's even were not good enough, nor her hands, for Madame Jacob never heard the mother say now, as she used to, that Volsy had the eyes and hands to embroider for the saints in heaven,—and Madame Jacob seemed to hear everything that was said upstairs. Volsy grew tired and worn, but not the mother; she looked happier and happier. She lived not in a honey-moon, but in honey-moons.

When she became a grandmother she talked and laughed and boasted about Paul just the same as when she became a mother. She did not have to wait for Paul now, and she and Volsy raced up to the house, laden with their bundles, and you may imagine how well they were received, bringing so beautiful a present, the layette for a prince.

And now ensued another change in the marching order of the family. It was no longer abreast, no longer one close behind the other. Either Madame Achard stepped ahead or Volsy lagged behind, with a growing space between them; that was the way they went now. Volsy always had an excuse not to go to see her sister-in-law; Madame Achard always had an excuse to go and see her daughter-in-law. Volsy's excuses cost nothing, but her mother's—they cost not only money but work; always something new and pretty; a cap or a bib trimmed with real Valenciennes, a cloak with real Cluny,[5] a silk-embroidered petticoat, dresses tucked to the waist, or hem-stitched in inch-wide insertings[6]—all made by hand, by the hand of Volsy, working still from morning to night, and after. There was no time for cooking,—sometimes the soup simmered in the pot, but sometimes, too, the fire in the furnace went out, and staid out as long as Madame Achard did in the street. The coffee in the morning was often the only regular meal that Paul and his baby allowed them. And then Madame Jacob, who saw as much as she heard upstairs, observed that the soup meat in the pot began to diminish in size—from ten cents to five cents, from five cents to a quartee (half of five cents) bone, and the soup was saved over longer and longer. Nothing was spent for clothing, nothing for pleasure or comfort. What money did not go for the bare daily fare, went in presents to that baby, and after a while toys were added to clothing, not cheap, common toys, but toys such as the rich American children uptown played with.

Volsy was one of those persons that no one ever notices particularly. She was neither tall nor short, fat nor thin, fair nor dark, pretty nor ugly, sad nor gay. But after two years of her beautiful work Madame Jacob did notice her one day as she passed through the shop on her way from church. She was tall and thin, dark and sad, and Madame Jacob reflected to herself that girls become women, and women become old. And this reflection of hers made so great an impression upon Madame Jacob that she kept it not to herself, but repeated it to everybody she talked to in the shop for a week, and she repeated it to Madame Achard.

"Ay! ay! La! la! la!" . . . What a song she was singing! without a word of common-sense in it! Volsy! bah! bah! And then Madame Achard started off to talk about her grandson, showing his photograph.

Now we may believe it or not, Madame Jacob gives formal permission for the alternative—from that day the mother began to pout against her daughter, ... to sigh, as Madame Jacob expressed it, and to raise her eyes to heaven against her. Why? Because Volsy did not love her nephew as she should. In vain the girl protested, in vain she worked harder than ever, in vain she volunteered special gifts of her own, in vain she carried them herself to the altar of her mother's divinity. The mother remained firm to her "tic," as the Jacob woman called it, and the "tic" changed her completely. In not a very long time she would not mention Paul, or his wife, or the baby, to the girl. She withdrew her confidence on this subject from her; she took to deceiving her about them. She let her do no more work for the baby; she hid its photograph from her; she made a secret of her visits uptown, slipping out of the house as if on an errand in the neighborhood, slipping in again with lips tight shut. But before she took the cars she always slipped into some shop or other and bought a present, which was as far as Madame Jacob's observations went, but the rest was easily inferred.

Volsy attempted an explanation once or twice, but the mother would lose her temper, raise her voice, and say things to the poor girl that were pitiful to the listener. There was no doubt the mother's feelings had changed absolutely, were turned, as the listener said, wrong side out.

Well, the girl changed too, naturally. No one would have said that she was the young girl who had worn the white muslin dress and pearl beads and pink flowers to balls, and laughed and danced there.

She seemed afraid of people; she never spoke to any one if she could avoid it. She never spoke at all, first.

At last, when one did not know what was going to happen next, Madame Achard fell ill with one of those little complaints that seem nothing at first, but which last until they kill.

And now, with Volsy nursing her, like an angel, with such tenderness and patience, and a strength that never gave out, and always so cheerful and bright, talking, laughing, singing ever—things from the opera that they used to like in old times—to amuse her, that flea-bitten mother's heart had to feel good again—and Volsy became her daughter again. But the old woman (to Madame Jacob any woman past fifty is old)—the old woman did not get strong; she got well—that is, she got out of bed, but always when she thought she would be able to go out she would fall sick again, and have to go to bed, and she could not leave the house, and naturally could not go to the other house. And Volsy began to see that she was pining for the sight of her son and grandson. The son—oh, that she knew was impossible—a man in his position, you understand; for his position was now out of sight of his people; but the grandson, he was not old enough to remember; that was possible. So Volsy began to lay her plans. If she had not made plans before, it was not because she had not sense enough. She had just as much sense as her mother and her brother. Oh, she showed it now! She was shrewd! She bought presents too, but presents for the mother, not for the child. And every time she went to see her sister-in-law, and brought the child to see the grandmother, he took home with him a piece of silver, a crystal decanter, a piece of porcelain, a piece of old lace to make your mouth water. Madame Jacob knew, for she bought them all, of course, as Volsy left her mother but for the one purpose of fetching the child and taking him home again. The old lady did not know anything, except that the child came to see her, and that was enough to give her happiness; but she fretted after he was gone, because she could not go out and buy presents for him, and so Volsy saw herself obliged to provide her mother with pretty play-things, but of the expensive kind, for, as has been said, Madame Achard would have none other. And the iller she became and the more desperate her condition, the oftener would Volsy bring the child to her, to ease her. But it cost! It cost! And the doctors had to be paid too, and medicine bought, and fine wine. Volsy would not have had the money for it without borrowing.

One night, in the most unexpected manner, Madame Achard died. A messenger was sent for Paul. He came, and arranged for the funeral early the next morning from the church.

Volsy came back alone from the cemetery, and went up stairs without saying a word, to her room, which in her absence Madame Jacob herself had put in order. At three o'clock Madame Jacob went up stairs to take her some dinner. She was still sitting in the same chair, with her bonnet and gloves on. At nine o'clock she was still there. She would not eat; she would not talk; she seemed to be thinking, thinking. Madame Jacob, however, forced her to bed, in the little chamber, in Paul's old bed. The next morning she was up early and at work, and in a week she had accepted the new routine of life. Perhaps she had thought it out as the best way. When the first of the month came, Madame Jacob, before any other business, went up stairs and paid her rent, as she had done for over twenty years.

The money did not stay in Volsy's hand long enough to warm it. In that class, dealers do not send their bills delicately through the mail, they bring them, and stand and wait until they are paid. Some people, like Madame Jacob, when they have no money, or want to hold on to their money for a while, pay with their tongue. But Volsy, though she had little money, only her month's rent, had less tongue. She paid and paid, and borrowed to pay, borrowing from her very debtors to pay her debts—a transaction that only a tongue such as Madame Jacob possessed can properly qualify.

Before the month was out, Volsy asked Madame Jacob to find lodgers for the front room. She moved out into one of the little rooms on the gallery—the lodgings of the "*crasse*,"[7] as madame described them. And in addition she did embroidery and sewing for pay. So she could look forward to facing the next first of the month like an honest woman. But there was no first of the month again for her, at least in regard to receiving rent. The mother's estate had to be settled. Madame Jacob had forgotten that—the opening and reading of the will.

When Volsy came back from her brother's office, the day of this ceremony, she motioned to Madame Jacob to follow her up stairs. In brief, and not to dwell upon a poor girl's pain and grief, the mother's will left a special legacy of a thousand dollars to the grandson, and the rest of what she possessed to be divided between her children. The rest of her possessions! "But, sacred Heaven!" exclaimed

Madame Jacob. She had no more possessions! The papers signed at the time of the brother's marriage, signed by all three, mother, daughter, son—what were they but a mortgage on her property? Volsy knew it now, well enough! and the money for what? To give Paul to marry his rich wife on, to play the rich gentleman with . . . And where did the old woman get the money to play the rich grandmother on? She borrowed it. As Volsy in her emergency had borrowed it. . . . For, said Madame Jacob, her voice hoarse and face red with the vehemence of her anger, "the rich love only the rich, as the poor old woman knew. They have no heart"; or, as Madame put it more vigorously in French—they have no *entrailles.*[8] "Money, money," rubbing her fingers together, "that is their heart, their soul, their body. May God choke them in purgatory with money!" Her temper was to conceal her emotion—any one could discern that. Well, what was there to say? Nothing by Volsy, much by Madame Jacob; and Madame Jacob found much that could be done by a lawyer. But Volsy, who had absolutely nothing, found nothing to do, except to try and make her living by sewing.

And now, just as before, when one was wondering what would happen next, Paul's father-in-law died, and so soon as his estate was settled and his fortune put into the possession of his daughter, Paul decided to go to Europe with wife and child. He was a rich lawyer now, and did not have to stay at home to look for business. He left in the spring. Volsy went to his office to say good-by. She did not cry then, but she cried when she came home, and Madame Jacob found her crying often after that.

When Volsy's fête[9] came, on the 15th of August, Madame Jacob took up to her room a little present, such as she had always given, and Volsy had been delighted to receive, ever since she was a little girl—an image of the Virgin and Son, this time in porcelain, and much prettier than ever before, on account of the poor girl's troubles. But when Volsy saw it she could only shake her head, and tremble. Madame Jacob, to take her eyes away, looked around the room. What she had not noticed before, she saw now: there was not a Holy Mother and Child in the room; there was not even one on the altar! And Volsy had always been so pious! and the little Child had been her soul's devotion!

Madame Jacob crossed herself, as though washing her hands of the responsibility of that part of her narrative.

As the summer wore on, Volsy fell ill. She tried and tried to get well, to make her living, but impossible! She could not. And there was the doctor again for her, and the medicines. There was no other way. She herself sent for the Little Sisters of the Poor, . . . and Madame Jacob made a gesture to indicate what I had seen on the sidewalk.

The doctor had given her something to put her asleep, and keep her so as long as possible. The grating of the stretcher as it slid into the wagon had roused her. Perhaps she thought she was in her room, in bed, when she lifted herself up, . . . and then she saw; she knew all.

Madame Jacob's last words were, "Paul has made progress—that is, he has made money."

NOTES

1. An organization of Roman Catholic women, similar to nuns, dedicated to caring for elderly poor people.
2. This suggests that the father Achard began as a traveling salesman who sold wares that he carried in a sack attached to a broom handle, which rested on his shoulder.
3. The note appearing in the original serialized version of the story states: "New Orleans is divided into 'up' town and 'down' town—the new, or American quarter, and the old, or French quarter." The latter was inhabited mostly by Creole descendants of the area's French settlers, who arrived previous to the Louisiana Purchase of 1803, which had precipitated an influx of many Americans from other parts of the country. Beginning in the 1840s, the French Quarter started to decline and became the more decrepit, poorer part of the city; the American sector, at the time this story was written, was the richer part.
4. In three of the Gospels included in the Bible, Jesus takes a group of his apostles up a mountain with him, where they have a glorious vision of Jesus "transfigured," with his clothes turned blindingly white; this scene was commonly depicted in religious paintings.
5. Different types of expensive lace.
6. A band of material stitched to a dress all around the circumference of its hem.
7. Grime (French). Figuratively, it refers to "dirty" people of the lower classes.
8. Entrails or guts (French). Here it suggests the English term "inner core."
9. A person's "name day." In predominantly Catholic countries, most people are named after saints, and people often celebrate the feast day of their saint instead of celebrating their birthday. August 15 is a special day in the liturgical calendar, corresponding to the Assumption of Mary, and it is also the name day for people with names such as Mary, Marie, or Maria, suggesting that Volsy's given name is Marie.

JACK LONDON

(1876–1916)

Jack London was born in very humble circumstances on January 12, 1876, in San Francisco. Forced to start working at a young age due to his family's poverty, London would eventually live a life of extreme highs and lows, marked by hard physical labor, economic struggle, adventure, travel, and eventually wealth and fame. Because much of his best-known writing is set in rural California, Alaska, and the Yukon Territory of Canada, London has frequently been associated with a rugged spirit of outdoor adventure and exploration. Yet he was also a literary innovator who broke new ground by frequently blending various genres, including Realism, Naturalism, science fiction, dystopian fiction, and political activist fiction—the last often infused with his socialist beliefs. On the page and in life, London was compelled to explore. And clearly those explorations resonated with large numbers of readers, for he was one of the first American authors to achieve great wealth from his writing.

At the time of London's birth his mother, Flora Wellman, was unmarried, but she identified his father as William Chaney, an impecunious and self-proclaimed "Professor of Astrology" who denied paternity of the child. In September 1876, Wellman's son gained the surname "London" when she married John London, a Civil War veteran and widower. Unfortunately, his stepfather suffered a series of failed business ventures, and London had to work part-time at the age of nine while only intermittently attending school. At thirteen, London graduated from elementary school and immediately went to work full-time in a canning factory. Two years later, he and a group of fellow hoodlums spent months poaching oysters from other people's oyster beds on San Francisco Bay. Soon thereafter, London joined a Pacific seal-hunting expedition as a seaman, and his time at sea provided inspiration for his first publication, "Story of a Typhoon off the Coast of Japan" (1893), as well as his much later popular adventure novel *The Sea-Wolf* (1904).

Upon his return to the United States, London worked at a number of physically demanding blue-collar jobs. As he became increasingly disillusioned about the prospects of improving his circumstances through hard physical work alone, he began to read more about socialism as a possible recourse for working people who wished to secure a decent life. At the age of eighteen, determined to obtain an education and lift himself above the ranks of exploited laborers, London enrolled at Oakland High School. After graduation, he was accepted to the University of California, Berkeley, and spent a semester there before financial difficulty forced him to withdraw. Hoping to support himself in some way not requiring manual labor, London around this time began writing and submitting stories to various periodicals. However, as he later related in the highly autobiographical novel *Martin Eden* (1909), submission after submission was rejected and, once again, London had to rely on income from manual labor.

Always one to keep an eye out for escape and opportunity, in July 1897 London joined the Klondike gold rush and left for Alaska. Although it was ultimately a transformative experience for London, his health suffered in the harsh climate and he left after less than a year due to scurvy. He brought home less than five dollars in gold dust, but along the way he had acquired material for some of his most famous literary works, set in that inhospitable place, ones that would prove very popular and remunerative for their author. After his return from the Yukon, London pursued his literary aspirations with great zeal. Editors of major East Coast magazines, whose readers thirsted for vicarious adventure through print, now hastened to accept London's fictions set in Alaska and the Yukon. Some of his best-known works of this type are *The Son of the Wolf: Tales of the Far North* (1900), *The Call of the Wild* (1903), and *White Fang* (1906).

At the same time London's career was taking off, his personal life was full of conflict. In 1900 he married Bessie Mae Maddern, and they had two children together; however, they became increasingly unhappy with each other. Their strife was exacerbated by London's affair with Charmian Kittredge, an independent woman who matched London's interest in art, literature, philosophy, and social change. London and Bessie divorced in November 1905; he married Kittredge two days later.

Before that occurred, however, in the summer of 1902, London had taken a major career step by traveling to England and spending six weeks living in the East End, London's infamous slums, staying with a poor family and sleeping on the streets or in workhouses. The resulting book was *The People of the Abyss* (1903), a nonfiction account of the impoverished lives of those he had encountered. London's immersive approach to journalistic research and writing, combined with social activism, inspired many future authors, including George Orwell. Most readers, however, preferred when London wrote about different subjects; indeed, it was London's next novel, *The Call of the Wild,* set in California and the Yukon and dealing with dogs, wolves, and colorful human characters, that finally brought him international fame.

Eventually, celebrity began to wear on London, and he pursued a number of different ventures in hopes of reinvigorating himself. Possibly the endeavor that most engrossed him during the last decade of his life was the development of Beauty Ranch, a property London had purchased in 1905 in the Sonoma Valley, north of San Francisco. London died in a cottage on the grounds of Beauty Ranch on November 22, 1916, at the age of forty; years of alcoholism and the lingering effects of various diseases acquired abroad contributed to the failure of London's kidneys.

The two stories presented here offer just a glimpse of London's extensive range and enormous talent. "The League of the Old Men," originally published in the short-lived *Brandur Magazine* in 1902 and subsequently reprinted in his book collection *The Children of the Frost* later that same year, offers a very different perspective on the Klondike gold rush than most readers are accustomed to: that of a Canadian First Nations person named Imber—or more accurately, the viewpoint of such a person as imagined by London. The influx of tens of thousands of non-Indigenous people to the Yukon in search of gold affected First Nations people in many negative ways and severely impacted their traditional ways of living; London in this story indicates his awareness of this fact and his desire to make others know about it too. Possibly due to its negative portrayal of White civilization, "The League of the Old Men" was rejected by three magazines before it was accepted by *Brandur.* While other London short stories, including "The Law of Life" (1901) and "To Build a Fire" (1902, 1908), have been more widely reprinted and celebrated, in a short piece that he wrote for an article entitled "My Best Short Story and Why I Think So," published in *Grand Magazine* in 1906, London stated, "I incline to the opinion that 'The League of the Old Men' is the best short story I have written." Elaborating further, London declared: "The voices of millions are in the voice of Old Imber, the tears and sorrows of millions in his throat as he tells his story; and his story epitomises the whole vast tragedy of the contact of the Indian with the white man." Interestingly enough, he added, "I may say that nobody else agrees with me in the selection which I have made and which has been my selection for years."

Another work that reflects London's consistent desire to speak for the down-trodden of the world is "The Apostate," likely inspired in large part by London's own horrific experiences working in a jute mill in 1893 at the age of sixteen, and what he witnessed while living in the poor East End of London. London's likely intentions for this story are suggested both by where he chose to publish it (*Woman's Home Companion* magazine) and by its subtitle ("A Child Labor Parable").

*Readers should be aware that "The League of the Old Men" includes some language which, while commonly used during this time period, is no longer considered acceptable because of its offensive nature.

THE LEAGUE OF THE OLD MEN (1902)

At the Barracks[1] a man was being tried for his life. He was an old man, a native from the Whitefish River, which empties into the Yukon below Lake Le Barge. All Dawson was wrought up over the affair, and likewise the Yukon-dwellers for a thousand miles up and down.[2] It has been the custom of the land-robbing and sea-robbing Anglo-Saxon to give the law to conquered peoples, and ofttimes this law is harsh. But in the case of Imber the law for once seemed inadequate and weak. In the mathematical nature of things equity did not reside in the punishment to be accorded him. The punishment was a foregone conclusion—there could be no doubt of that; and though it was capital,[3] Imber had but one life, while the tale against him was one of scores.

In fact, the blood of so many was upon his hands that the killings attributed to him did not permit of precise enumeration. Smoking a pipe by the trailside or lounging around the stove, men made rough estimates of the numbers that had perished at his hand. They had been whites, all of them, these poor murdered people; and they had been slain singly, in pairs, and in parties. And so purposeless and wanton had been these killings that they had long been a mystery to the mounted police, even in the time of the captains, and later, when the creeks realized, and a governor came from the Dominion to make the land pay for its prosperity.[4]

But more mysterious still was the coming of Imber to Dawson to give himself up. It was in the late spring, when the Yukon was growling and writhing under its ice, that the old Indian climbed painfully up the bank from the river trail and stood blinking on the main street. Men who had witnessed his advent noted that he was weak and tottery, and that he staggered over to a heap of cabin logs and sat down. He sat there a full day, staring straight before him at the unceasing tide of white men that flooded past. Many a head jerked curiously to the side to meet his stare, and more than one remark was dropped anent the old Siwash[5] with so strange a look upon his face. No end of men remembered afterward that they had been struck by his extraordinary figure, and forever afterward prided themselves upon their swift discernment of the unusual.

But it remained for Dickensen—Little Dickensen—to be the hero of the occasion. Little Dickensen had come into the land with great dreams and a pocketful of cash; but with the cash the dreams vanished, and to earn his passage back to the States he had accepted a clerical position with the brokerage firm of Holbrook and Mason. Across the street from the office of Holbrook & Mason was the heap of cabin logs upon which Imber sat. Dickensen looked out of the window at him before he went to lunch; and when he came back from lunch he looked out of the window, and the old Siwash was still there.

Dickensen was a romantic little chap, and he likened the immobile old heathen to the genius of the Siwash race, gazing calm-eyed upon the hosts of the invading Saxon. The hours swept along, but Imber did not vary his posture, did not move a muscle; and Dickensen remembered a man who once sat upright on a sled in the main street where men passed to and fro. They thought the man was resting, but later they found him stiff and cold, frozen to death in the midst of the busy street. To undouble him, that he might fit into a coffin, they had been forced to lug him to a fire and thaw him out a bit. Dickensen shivered at the recollection.

Later on Dickensen went out on the sidewalk to smoke a cigar and cool off; and a little later Emily Travis happened along. Emily Travis was dainty and delicate and rare, and whether in London or Klondike she gowned herself as befitted the daughter of a millionaire mining engineer. Little Dickensen deposited his cigar on an outside window ledge, where he could find it again, and lifted his hat.

They chatted for ten minutes or so, when Emily Travis, glancing past Dickensen's shoulder, gave a startled little scream. Dickensen turned about to see, and was startled too. Imber had crossed the street and was standing there, a gaunt and hungry-looking shadow, his gaze riveted upon the girl.

"What do you want?" Little Dickensen demanded, tremulously plucky.

Imber grunted and stalked up to Emily Travis. He looked her over, keenly and carefully. Especially did he appear interested in her silky brown hair and in the color of her cheek, faintly sprayed and soft, like the downy bloom of a butterfly wing. He walked around her, surveying her with the calculating eye of a man who studies the lines upon which a horse or a boat is builded. In the course of his circuit the pink shell of her ear came between his eye and the westering sun, and he stopped to contemplate its rosy transparency. Then he returned to her face and looked long and intently into her blue eyes. He grunted and laid a hand on her arm midway between the shoulder and elbow. With his other hand he lifted her forearm and doubled it back. Disgust and wonder showed in his face, and he dropped her arm with a contemptuous grunt. Then he muttered a few guttural syllables, turned his back upon her, and addressed himself to Dickensen.

Dickensen could not understand his speech, and Emily Travis laughed. Imber turned from one to the other, frowning, but both shook their heads. He was about to go away, when she called out:

"Oh Jimmy! Come here!"

Jimmy came from the other side of the street. He was a big, hulking Indian[6] clad in approved white-man style, with an Eldorado king's sombrero[7] on his head. He talked with Imber, haltingly, with throaty spasms.[8] Jimmy was a Sit-kan,[9] possessed of no more than a passing knowledge of the interior dialects.[10]

"Him Whitefish man," he said to Emily Travis. "Me savve um talk no very much. Him want to look see chief white man."

"The governor," suggested Dickensen.

Jimmy talked some more with the Whitefish man, and his face became grave and puzzled.

"I t'ink um want Cap'n Alexander," he explained. "Him say um kill white man, white woman, white boy, plenty kill um white people. Him want to die."

"Insane, I guess," said Dickensen.

"What you call dat?" queried Jimmy.

Dickensen thrust a finger figuratively inside his head and imparted a rotary motion thereto.

"Mebbe so, mebbe so," said Jimmy, returning to Imber, who still demanded the chief man of the white men.

A mounted policeman (unmounted for Klondike service) joined the group and heard Imber's wish repeated. He was a stalwart young fellow, broad-shouldered, deep-chested, legs clean-built and stretched wide apart, and tall though Imber was, he towered above him by half a head. His eyes were cool and gray and steady, and he carried himself with the peculiar confidence of power that is bred of blood and tradition. His splendid masculinity was emphasized by his excessive boyishness,—he was a mere lad,—and his smooth cheek promised a blush as willingly as the cheek of a maid.

Imber was drawn to him at once. The fire leaped into his eyes at sight of a sabre slash that scarred his cheek. He ran a withered hand down the young fellow's leg and caressed the swelling thew.[11] He smote the broad chest with his knuckles, and pressed and prodded the thick muscle-pads that covered the shoulders like a cuirass.[12] The group had been added to by curious passers-by—husky miners, mountaineers, and frontiersmen, sons of the long-legged and broad-shouldered generations. Imber glanced from one to another; then he spoke aloud in the Whitefish tongue.[13]

"What did he say?" asked Dickensen.

"Him say um all the same one man, dat p'liceman," Jimmy interpreted.

Little Dickensen was little, and because of Miss Travis he felt sorry for having asked the question. The policeman was sorry for him, and stepped into the breach.

"I fancy there may be something in his story. I'll take him up to the captain for examination. Tell him to come along with me, Jimmy."

Jimmy indulged in more throaty spasms, and Imber grunted and looked satisfied.

"But ask him what he said, Jimmy, and what he meant when he took hold of my arm?" So spoke Emily Travis, and Jimmy put the question and received the answer.

"Him say you no afraid," said Jimmy.

Emily Travis looked pleased.

"Him say you no *skookum*,[14] no strong, all the same very soft like little baby. Him break you, in um two hands, to little pieces. Him t'ink much funny, very strange, how you can be mother of men so big, so strong, like dat p'liceman."

Emily Travers kept her eyes up and unfaltering, but her cheeks were sprayed with scarlet. Little Dickensen blushed and was quite embarrassed. The police-man's face blazed with his boy's blood.

"Come along, you," he said gruffly, setting his shoulder to the crowd and forcing a way.

Thus it was that Imber found his way to the Barracks, where he made full and voluntary confession, and from the precincts of which he never emerged.

*   *   *   *   *   *   *   *

Imber looked very tired. The fatigue of hopelessness and age was in his face. His shoulders drooped depressingly, and his eyes were lack-lustre. His mop of hair should have been white, but sun and weatherbeat had burned and bitten it so that it hung limp and lifeless and colorless. He took no interest in what went on around him. The courtroom was jammed with the men of the creeks and trails, and there was an ominous note in the rumble and grumble of their low-pitched voices, which came to his ears like the growl of the sea from deep caverns.

He sat close by a window, and his apathetic eyes rested now and again on the dreary scene without. The sky was overcast and a gray drizzle was falling. It was floodtime on the Yukon. The ice was gone and the river was up in the town. Back and forth on the main street, in canoes and poling-boats, passed the people that never rested. Often he saw these boats turn aside from the street and enter the flooded square that marked the Barracks parade-ground. Sometimes they disappeared beneath him, and he heard them jar against the house logs and their occupants scramble in through the window. After that came the slush of water against men's legs as they waded across the lower room and mounted the stairs. Then they appeared in the doorway, with doffed hats and dripping sea boots, and added themselves to the waiting crowd.

And while they centered their looks on him and in grim anticipation enjoyed the penalty he was to pay, Imber looked at them and mused on their ways and on their law that never slept, but went on unceasing, in good times and bad, in flood and famine, through trouble and terror and death, and which would go on unceasing, it seemed to him, to the end of time.

A man rapped sharply on a table, and the conversation droned away into silence. Imber looked at the man. He seemed one in authority, yet Imber divined the square-browed man who sat by a desk farther back to be the one chief over them all and over the man who had rapped. Another man by the same table uprose and began to read aloud from many fine sheets of paper. At the top of each sheet he cleared his throat; at the bottom moistened his fingers. Imber did not understand his speech, but the others did, and he knew that it made them angry. Sometimes it made them very angry, and once a man cursed him, in single syllables, stinging and tense, till a man at the table rapped him to silence.

For an interminable period the man read. His monotonous, sing-song utterance lured Imber to dreaming, and he was dreaming deeply when the man ceased. A voice spoke to him in his own Whitefish tongue, and he roused up, without surprise, to look upon the face of his sister's son, a young man who had wandered away years agone to make his dwelling with the whites.

"Thou dost not remember me," he said, by way of greeting.

"Nay," Imber answered. "Thou art Howkan, who went away. Thy mother be dead."

"She was an old woman," said Howkan.

But Imber did not hear, and Howkan, with hand upon his shoulder, roused him again.

"I shall speak to thee what the man has spoken, which is the tale of the troubles thou hast done and which thou hast told, O fool, to the Captain Alexander. And thou shalt understand and say if it be true talk or talk not true. It is so commanded."

Howkan had fallen among the mission folk[15] and been taught by them to read and write. In his hands he held the many fine sheets from which the man had read aloud, and which had been taken down by a clerk when Imber first made confession, through the mouth of Jimmy, to Captain Alexander. Howkan began to read. Imber listened for a space, when a wonderment rose up in his face and he broke in abruptly:

"That be my talk, Howkan. Yet from thy lips it comes when thy ears have not heard."

Howkan smirked with self-appreciation. His hair was parted in the middle. "Nay, from the paper it comes, O Imber. Never have my ears heard. From the paper it comes, through my eyes, into my head, and out of my mouth to thee. Thus it comes."

"Thus it comes? It be there in the paper?" Imber's voice sank in whisperful awe as he crackled the sheets betwixt thumb and finger and stared at the characters scrawled thereon. "It be a great medicine, Howkan, and thou art a worker of wonders."

"It be nothing; it be nothing," the young man responded, carelessly and pridefully. He read at random from the document: "In that year, before the break of the ice, came an old man, and a boy who was lame of one foot. These also did I kill, and the old man made much noise—"

"It be true," Imber interrupted breathlessly. "He made much noise and would not die for a long time. But how dost thou know, Howkan? The chief man of the white men told thee, mayhap? No one beheld me, and him alone have I told."

Howkan shook his head with impatience. "Have I not told thee it be there in the paper, O fool?"

Imber stared hard at the ink-scrawled surface. "As the hunter looks upon the snow and says, Here but yesterday there passed a rabbit; and here by the willow scrub it stood and listened and heard and was afraid; and here it turned upon its trail; and here it went with great swiftness, leaping wide; and here, with greater swiftness and wider leapings, came a lynx; and here, where the claws cut deep into the snow, the lynx made a very great leap; and here it struck, with the rabbit under and rolling belly up; and here leads off the trail of the lynx alone, and there is no more rabbit,—as the hunter looks upon the markings of the snow and says thus and so and here, dost thou, too, look upon the paper and say thus and so and here be the things old Imber hath done?"

"Even so," said Howkan. "And now do thou listen, and keep thy woman's tongue between thy teeth till thou art called upon for speech."

Thereafter, and for a long time, Howkan read to him the confession, and Imber remained musing and silent. At the end, he said:

"It be my talk, and true talk, but I am grown old, Howkan, and forgotten things come back to me which were well for the head man there to know. First, there was the man who came over the Ice Mountains, with cunning traps made of iron, who sought the beaver of the Whitefish; him I slew. And there were three men seeking gold on the Whitefish long ago; them also I slew, and left them to the wolverines. And at the Five Fingers[16] there was a man with a raft and much meat."

At the moments when Imber paused to remember Howkan translated, and a clerk reduced to writing. The courtroom listened stolidly to each unadorned little tragedy, till Imber told of a red-haired man whose eyes were crossed and whom he had killed with a remarkably long shot.

"Hell!" said a man in the forefront of the onlookers. He said it slowly and soulfully. He was red-haired. "Hell!" he repeated; "that was my brother Bill." And at regular intervals throughout the session his solemn "Hell!" was heard in the courtroom. His comrades did not check him, nor did the man at the table rap him to order.

Imber's head drooped once more, and his eyes grew dull, as though a film rose up and covered them from the world. And he dreamed as only age can dream upon the colossal futility of youth.

Later Howkan roused him again, saying, "Stand up, O Imber. It be commanded that thou tellest why you did these troubles and slew these people and at the end journeyed here seeking the law."

Imber rose feebly to his feet and swayed back and forth. He began to speak in a low and faintly rumbling voice, but Howkan interrupted him.

"This old man, he is crazy," he said in English to the square-browed man. "His talk is foolish and like that of a child."

"We will hear his talk which is like that of a child," said the square-browed man. "And we will hear it word for word, as he speaks it. Do you understand?"

Howkan understood, and Imber's eyes flashed; for he had witnessed the play between his sister's son and the man in authority. And then began the story, the epic of a bronze patriot which itself might well be wrought into bronze for generations unborn. The crowd fell strangely silent, and the square-browed judge leaned head on hand and pondered his soul and the soul of his race. Only were heard the deep tones of Imber, rhythmically alternating with the shrill voice of the interpreter, and now and again, like the bell of the Lord, the wondering and meditative "Hell!" of the red-haired man.

"I am Imber, of the Whitefish people." So ran the interpretation of Howkan, whose inherent barbarism gripped hold of him, and who lost his mission culture and veneered civilization as he caught the savage ring and rhythm of old Imber's tale. "My father was Otsbaok, a strong man. The land was warm with sunshine and gladness when I was a boy. The people did not hunger after strange things nor hearken to new voices, and the ways of their fathers were their ways. The women found favor in the eyes of the young men, and the young men looked upon them with content. Babes hung at the breasts of the women, and they were heavy-hipped with increase of the tribe. Men were men in those days. In peace and plenty, and in war and famine, they were men.

"At that time there was more fish in the waters than now, and more meat in the forest. Our dogs were wolves, warm with thick hides and hard to the frost and storm. And as with our dogs, so with us; for we were likewise hard to the frost and storm. And when the Pellys[17] came into our land we slew them and were slain; for we were men, we Whitefish, and our fathers and our fathers' fathers had fought against the Pellys and determined the bounds of the land.

"As with our dogs, I say, so with us. And one day came the first white man. He dragged himself, so, on hand and knee, in the snow. And his skin was stretched tight, and his bones were sharp beneath. Never was such a man, we thought, and we wondered of what strange tribe he was and of its land. And he was weak, most weak, like a little child, so that we gave him a place by the fire, and warm furs to lie upon, and we gave him food as little children are given food.

"And with him was a dog, large as three of our dogs, and very weak. The hair of this dog was short and not warm, and the tail was frozen so that the end fell off. And this strange dog we fed and bedded by the fire, and fought from it our dogs, which else would have killed him. And what of the moose meat and the sun-dried salmon, the man and dog took strength to themselves; and what of the strength they became big and unafraid. And the man spoke loud words and laughed at the old men and young men and looked boldly upon the maidens. And the dog fought with our dogs, and for all of his short hair and softness slew three of them in one day.

"When we asked the man concerning his people he said, 'I have many brothers,' and laughed in a way that was not good. And when he was in his full strength he went away, and with him went Noda, daughter to the chief. First, after that, was one of our bitches brought to pup. And never was there such a breed of dogs,—big-headed, thick-jawed, and short-haired and helpless. Well do I remember my father, Otsbaok, a strong man. His face was black with anger at such helplessness, and he took a stone, so, and so, and there was no more help-lessness. And two summers after that came Noda back to us with a man-child in the hollow of her arm.[18]

"And that was the beginning. Came a second white man, with short-haired dogs, which he left behind him when he went. And with him went six of our strongest dogs, for which, in trade, he had given Koo-So-Tee, my mother's brother, a wonderful pistol that fired with great swiftness six times. And Koo-So-Tee was very big, what of the pistol, and laughed at our bows and arrows. 'Woman's things,' he called them, and went forth against the bald-face grizzly, with the pistol in his hand. Now it be known that it is not good to hunt the bald-face with a pistol, but how were we to know? And how was Koo-So-Tee to know? So he went against the bald-face, very brave, and fired the pistol with great swiftness six times; and the bald-face but grunted and broke in his head like it were an egg, and like honey from a bee's nest dripped the brains of Koo-So-Tee upon the ground. He was a good hunter, and there was no one to bring meat to his squaw[19] and children. And we were bitter, and we said, 'That which for the white men is well is for us not well.' And this be true. There be many white men and fat, but their ways have made us few and lean.

"Came the third white man, with great wealth of all manner of wonderful foods and things. And twenty of our strongest dogs he took from us in trade. Also, what of presents and great promises, ten of our young hunters did he take with him on a journey which fared no man knew where. It is said they died in the snow of the Ice Mountains, where man has never been, or in the Hills of Silence, which are beyond the edge of the earth. Be that as it may, dogs and young hunters were seen never again by the Whitefish people.

"And more white men came with the years, and ever, with pay and presents, they led the young men away with them. And sometimes the young men came back with strange tales of dangers and toils in the lands beyond the Pellys, and sometimes they did not come back. And we said: 'If they be unafraid of life, these white men, it is because they have many lives; but we be few by the Whitefish, and the young men shall go away no more.' But the young men did go away; and the young women went also; and we were very wroth.

"It be true we ate flour and salt pork and drank tea which was a great delight; only when we could not get tea it was very bad and we became short of speech and quick of anger. So we grew to hunger for the things the white men brought in trade. Trade! trade! all the time was it trade! One winter we sold our meat for clocks that would not go, and watches with broken works, and files worn smooth, and pistols without cartridges and worthless. And then came famine, and we were without meat, and twoscore[20] died ere the break of spring.

"'Now are we grown weak,' we said; 'and the Pellys will fall upon us, and our bounds be overthrown.' But as it fared with us, so had it fared with the Pellys, and they were too weak to come against us.

"My father, Otsbaok, a strong man, was now old and very wise. And he spoke to the chief, saying: 'Behold, our dogs be worthless. No longer are they thick-furred and strong, and they die in the frost and harness. Let us go into the village and kill them, saving only the wolf ones, and these let us tie out in the night that they may mate with the wild wolves of the forest. Thus shall we have dogs warm and strong again.'

"And his word was harkened to, and we Whitefish became known for our dogs, which were the best in the land. But known we were not for ourselves. The best of our young men and women had gone away with the white men to wander on trail and river to far places. And the young women came back old and broken, as Noda had come, or they came back not at all. And the young men came back to sit by our fires for a time, full of ill speech and rough ways, drinking evil drinks and gambling through long nights and days, with a great unrest always in their hearts, till the call of the white men came to them and they went away again to the unknown places. And they were without honor and respect, jeering the old-time customs and laughing in the faces of chief and shamans.

"As I say, we were become a weak breed, we Whitefish. We sold our warm skins and furs for tobacco and whiskey and thin cotton things that left us shivering in the cold. And the coughing sickness[21] came upon us, and men and women coughed and sweated through the long nights, and the hunters on trail spat blood upon the snow. And now one and now another bled swiftly from the mouth and died. And the women bore few children, and those they bore were weak and given to sickness. And other sicknesses came to us from the white men, the like of which we had never known and could not understand. Smallpox, likewise measles, have I heard these sicknesses named, and we died of them as die the salmon in the still eddies when in the fall their eggs are spawned and there is no longer need for them to live.

"And yet—and here be the strangeness of it—the white men come as the breath of death. All their ways lead to death; their nostrils are filled with it, and yet they do not die. Theirs the whisky and tobacco and short-haired dogs; theirs the many sicknesses, the smallpox and measles, the coughing and mouth-bleeding; theirs the white skin and softness to the frost and storm; and theirs the pistols that shoot six times very swift and are worthless. And yet they grow fat on their many ills, and prosper, and lay a heavy hand over all the world and tread mightily upon its peoples. And their women, too, are soft as little babes, most breakable and never broken, the mothers of men. And out of all this softness and sickness and weakness come strength, and power, and authority. They be gods, or devils, as the case may be. I do not know. What do I know, I, old Imber of the Whitefish? Only do I know that they are past understanding, these white men, far-wanderers and fighters over the earth that they be.

"As I say, the meat in the forest became less and less. It be true the white man's gun is most excellent and kills a long way off; but of what worth the gun when there is no meat to kill? When I was a boy on the Whitefish there was moose on every hill, and each year came the caribou uncountable, but now the hunter may take the trail ten days and not one moose gladden his eyes, while the caribou uncountable come no more at all. Small worth the gun, I say, killing a long way off, when there be nothing to kill.

"And I, Imber, pondered upon these things, watching the while the Whitefish and the Pellys and all the tribes of the land perishing as perished the meat of the forest. Long I pondered. I talked with the shamans and the old men who were wise. I went apart that the sounds of the village might not disturb me, and I ate no meat so that my belly should not press upon me and make me slow of eye and ear. I sat long and sleepless in the forest, wide-eyed for the sign, my ears patient and keen for the word that was to come. And I wandered alone in the blackness of night to the river bank, where was wind moaning and sobbing of water, and where I sought wisdom from the ghosts of old shamans in the trees and dead and gone.

"And in the end, as in a vision, came to me the short-haired and detestable dogs, and the way seemed plain. By the wisdom of Otsbaok, my father and a strong man, had the blood of our own wolf-dogs been kept clean, wherefore had they remained warm of hide and strong in the harness. So I returned to my village and made oration to the men. 'This be a tribe, these white men,' I said. 'A very large tribe, and doubtless there is no longer meat in their land and they are come among us to make a new land for themselves. But they weaken us and we die. They are a very hungry folk. Already has our meat gone from us, and it were well, if we would live, that we deal by them as we have dealt by their dogs.'

"And further oration I made, counselling fight. And the men of the Whitefish listened, and some said one thing and some another, and some spoke of other and worthless things, and no man made brave talk of deeds and war. But while the young men were weak as water and afraid, I watched that the old men sat silent and that in their eyes fires came and went. And later, when the village slept and no one knew, I drew the old men away into the forest and made more talk. And now we were agreed, and we remembered the good young days, and the free land, and the times of plenty, and the gladness and sunshine; and we called ourselves brothers, and swore great secrecy, and a mighty oath to cleanse the land of the evil breed that had come upon it. It be plain we were fools, but how were we to know, we old men of the Whitefish?

"And to hearten the others I did the first deed. I kept guard upon the Yukon till the first canoe came down. In it were two white men, and when I stood upright upon the bank and raised my hand they changed their course and drove in to me. And as the man in the bow lifted his head, so, that he might know wherefore I wanted him, my arrow sang through the air straight to his throat, and he knew. The second man, who held paddle in the stern, had his rifle half to his shoulder when my spear smote him.

"'These be the first,' I said, when the old men had gathered to me. 'Later we will bind together all the old men of all the tribes, and after that the young men who remain strong, and the work will become easy.'

"And then the two dead white men we cast into the river. And of the canoe, which was a very good canoe, we made a fire, and a fire also of the things within the canoe. But first we looked at the things, and they were pouches of leather which we cut open with our knives. And inside these pouches were many papers, like that from which thou hast read, O Howkan, with markings on them which we marveled at and could not understand. Now I am become wise and I know them for the speech of men as thou hast told me."

A whisper and buzz went around the courtroom when Howkan finished interpreting the affair of the canoe, and one man's voice spoke up: "That was the lost '91 mail—Peter James and Delaney bringing it in and last spoken at Le Barge by Matthews going out." The clerk scratched steadily away, and another paragraph was added to the history of the North.

"There be little more," Imber went on slowly. "It be there on the paper, the things we did. We were old men, and we did not understand. Even I, Imber, do not now understand. Secretly we slew and continued to slay, for with our years we were crafty and we had learned the swiftness of going without haste. When white men came among us with black looks and rough words and took away six of the young men with irons binding them helpless we knew we must slay wider and farther. And one by one we old men departed up river and down to the unknown lands. It was a brave thing. Old we were and unafraid, but the fear of far places is a terrible fear to men who are old.

"So we slew, without haste and craftily. On the Chilcoot and in the Delta[22] we slew, from the passes to the sea, wherever the white men camped or broke their trails. It be true, they died, but it was without worth. Ever did they come over the mountains, ever did they grow and grow, while we, being old, became less and less. I remember, by the Caribou Crossing, the camp of a white man. He was a very little white man, and three of the old men came upon him in his sleep. And the next day I came upon the four of them. The white man alone still breathed, and there was breath in him to curse me once and well before he died.

"And so it went, now one old man, and now another. Sometimes the word reached us long after of how they died, and sometimes it did not reach us. And the old men of the other tribes were weak and afraid, and would not join with us. As I say, one by one, till I alone was left. I am Imber, of the Whitefish people. My father was Otsbaok, a strong man. There are no Whitefish now. Of the old men I am the last. The young men and young women are gone away, some to live with the Pellys, some with the Salmons,[23] and more with the white men. I am very old and very tired, and it being vain fighting the law, as thou sayest, Howkan, I am come seeking the law."

"O Imber, thou art indeed a fool," said Howkan.

But Imber was dreaming. The square-browed judge likewise dreamed, and all his race rose up before him in a mighty phantasmagoria—his steel-shod, mail-clad race, the lawgiver and world-maker among the families of men. He saw it dawn red-lickering across the dark forests and sullen seas; he saw it blaze, bloody and red, to full and triumphant noon; and down the shaded slope he saw the blood-red sands dropping into night. And through it all he observed the law, pitiless and potent, ever unswerving and ever ordaining, greater than the motes of men who fulfilled it or were crushed by it, even as it was greater than he, his heart speaking for softness.

NOTES

1. Buildings where police or military forces are stationed.
2. These place-names situate the story concretely in an area along the Yukon River, which is almost two thousand miles long and flows from the Canadian province of British Columbia through Yukon Territory, across Alaska, and to the Bering Sea. During the Klondike gold rush (1896–99), tens of thousands of non-Indigenous people—mostly men—came to the region in hopes of finding gold and becoming rich; most landed by boat at Skagway, along the coast of Alaska, traveled overland to the newly formed city of Whitehorse (in Yukon Territory), and then journeyed north on the Yukon River toward Dawson City (also in Yukon Territory).
3. A capital offense that he committed.
4. In 1873, the government of the Dominion of Canada (the country's formal name) created the North-West Mounted Police to serve in its Northwest Territories, which included the Yukon, and a governor was appointed to enforce laws and collect tax revenues. "The creeks realized" refers to the creeks of the area beginning to yield ("realize") gold to prospectors.
5. A derogatory and offensive term derived from the French word *sauvage* used by many non-Indigenous people at the time to refer generally to First Nations peoples of the Yukon area.
6. Here London uses a general term commonly used by non-Indigenous people at the time to refer to Indigenous peoples of North America; in Canada, since the 1980s, they are known chiefly as First Nations peoples.
7. El Dorado was a mythical place of untold gold and riches for early Spanish explorers in the New World. A sombrero is a type of broad-brimmed hat formerly worn by many people in Mexico.
8. Here, as well as many other times later in the story, London engages in a practice common to White writers of the time: representing Indigenous people's English-language as deficient and thus "humorous."
9. London, like almost all non-Indigenous people who came to the Yukon in the late nineteenth century, had no actual direct knowledge of the First Nations peoples of the area. This led London here—and elsewhere in the story—to classify First Nations peoples by the White settlement areas from which they came, rather than by their actual First Nations name. Sitka is a settlement on an island in what is now southeastern Alaska.
10. This area was (and still is) inhabited by many different First Nations peoples speaking a wide variety of languages.
11. Muscular lineaments.
12. A covering intended to protect, here probably made of leather.
13. London here creates a language and name for one of the First Nations peoples from the Whitefish River, located in the southeast area of what is now Yukon Territory; this would be London's term, not Jimmy's, for the latter would almost certainly know which First Nations people Imber came from.
14. A word meaning "strong" or "brave" in Chinook Jargon, a trade language developed from the Chinook people's language in the nineteenth century.
15. Along with White settlers and prospectors, Christian missionaries came to the Yukon area in the late nineteenth century; many in this last group set up schools

whose object was to not only convert First Nations people to their religion but also forcibly assimilate students into settler colonial Canadian culture, thereby eradicating Indigenous customs and languages. In many cases, too, this project of missionaries and the Canadian government was carried out by forcibly taking First Nations children from their families and sending them to boarding schools long distances away.

16. An area of rapids in the Yukon River.

17. Again, this would be London's designation, not Imber's. It is another inaccurate term used by non-Indigenous people to refer to a First Nations people, in this case those who either lived along the Pellys River or in the Pellys Mountains, northeast of Whitehorse; they likely would have come from the Little Salmon / Carmacks First Nation or Kaska Nation.

18. Many First Nations women were raped by non-Indigenous men during this period or promised the security of marriage with them if they left their nation; as seen here, however, many First Nations women were deserted and left to return to their nation without a husband.

19. A derogatory term commonly used by non-Indigenous people at the time to refer to an Indigenous woman. It is considered offensive and no longer used.

20. Forty years (one score is twenty).

21. Tuberculosis. One major way the British, French, and then Americans damaged First Nations communities was by introducing tuberculosis (as well as smallpox) to populations that had no natural immunity.

22. The Chilkoot River is located in what is now southeastern Alaska; numerous river deltas are found in the area.

23. London's own name for another First Nations people. It is possible he was referring to members of the Little Salmon / Carmacks First Nation, but since salmon are important to many First Nations peoples, London's term could apply to any of them.

THE APOSTATE:[1] A CHILD LABOR PARABLE (1906)

> *Now I wake me up to work;*
> *I pray the Lord I may not shirk.*
> *If I should die before the night,*
> *I pray the Lord my work's all right.*
> *Amen.*[2]

"If you don't git up, Johnny, I won't give you a bite to eat!"

The threat had no effect on the boy. He clung stubbornly to sleep, fighting for its oblivion as the dreamer fights for his dream. The boy's hands loosely clenched themselves, and he made feeble, spasmodic blows at the air. These blows were intended for his mother, but she betrayed practised familiarity in avoiding them as she shook him roughly by the shoulder.

"Lemme 'lone!"

It was a cry that began, muffled, in the deeps of sleep, that swiftly rushed upward, like a wail, into passionate belligerence, and that died away and sank down into an inarticulate whine. It was a bestial cry, as of a soul in torment, filled with infinite protest and pain.

But she did not mind. She was a sad-eyed, tired-faced woman, and she had grown used to this task, which she repeated every day of her life. She got a grip on the bed-clothes and tried to strip them down; but the boy, ceasing his punching, clung to them desperately. In a huddle, at the foot of the bed, he still remained covered. Then she tried dragging the bedding to the floor. The boy opposed her. She braced herself. Hers was the superior weight, and the boy and bedding gave, the former instinctively following the latter in order to shelter against the chill of the room that bit into his body.

As he toppled on the edge of the bed it seemed that he must fall head-first to the floor. But consciousness fluttered up in him. He righted himself and for a moment perilously balanced. Then he struck the floor on his feet. On the instant his mother seized him by the shoulders and shook him. Again his fists struck out, this time with more force and directness. At the same time his eyes opened. She released him. He was awake.

"All right," he mumbled.

She caught up the lamp and hurried out, leaving him in darkness.

"You'll be docked,"[3] she warned back to him.

He did not mind the darkness. When he had got into his clothes, he went out into the kitchen. His tread was very heavy for so thin and light a boy. His legs dragged with their own weight, which seemed unreasonable because they were such skinny legs. He drew a broken-bottomed chair to the table.

"Johnny!" his mother called sharply.

He arose as sharply from the chair, and, without a word, went to the sink. It was a greasy, filthy sink. A smell came up from the outlet. He took no notice of it. That a sink should smell was to him part of the natural order, just as it was a part of the natural order that the soap should be grimy with dish-water and hard to lather. Nor did he try very hard to make it lather. Several splashes of the cold water from the running faucet completed the function. He did not wash his teeth. For that matter he had never seen a toothbrush, nor did he know that there existed beings in the world who were guilty of so great a foolishness as tooth washing.

"You might wash yourself wunst a day without bein' told," his mother complained.

She was holding a broken lid on the pot as she poured two cups of coffee. He made no remark, for this was a standing quarrel between them, and the one thing upon which his mother was hard as adamant. "Wunst" a day it was compulsory that he should wash his face. He dried himself on a greasy towel, damp and dirty and ragged, that left his face covered with shreds of lint.

"I wish we didn't live so far away," she said, as he sat down. "I try to do the best I can. You know that. But a dollar on the rent is such a savin', an' we've more room here. You know that."

He scarcely followed her. He had heard it all before, many times. The range of her thought was limited, and she was ever harking back to the hardship worked upon them by living so far from the mills.

"A dollar means more grub," he remarked sententiously. "I'd sooner do the walkin' an' git the grub."

He ate hurriedly, half chewing the bread and washing the unmasticated chunks down with coffee. The hot and muddy liquid went by the name of coffee. Johnny thought it was coffee—and excellent coffee. That was one of the few of life's illusions that remained to him. He had never drunk real coffee in his life.

In addition to the bread, there was a small piece of cold pork. His mother refilled his cup with coffee. As he was finishing the bread, he began to watch if more was forthcoming. She intercepted his questioning glance.

"Now, don't be hoggish, Johnny," was her comment. "You've had your share. Your brothers an' sisters are smaller'n you."

He did not answer the rebuke. He was not much of a talker. Also, he ceased his hungry glancing for more. He was uncomplaining, with a patience that was as terrible as the school in which it had been learned. He finished his coffee, wiped his mouth on the back of his hand, and started to rise.

"Wait a second," she said hastily. "I guess the loaf kin stand you another slice—a thin un."

There was legerdemain[4] in her actions. With all the seeming of cutting a slice from the loaf for him, she put loaf and slice back in the bread box and conveyed to him one of her own two slices. She believed she had deceived him, but he had noted her sleight-of-hand. Nevertheless, he took the bread shamelessly. He had a philosophy that his mother, because of her chronic sickliness, was not much of an eater anyway.

She saw that he was chewing the bread dry, and reached over and emptied her coffee cup into his.

"Don't set good somehow on my stomach this morning," she explained.

A distant whistle, prolonged and shrieking, brought both of them to their feet. She glanced at the tin alarm-clock on the shelf. The hands stood at half-past five. The rest of the factory world was just arousing from sleep. She drew a shawl about her shoulders, and on her head put a dingy hat, shapeless and ancient.

"We've got to run," she said, turning the wick of the lamp and blowing down the chimney.[5]

They groped their way out and down the stairs. It was clear and cold, and Johnny shivered at the first contact with the outside air. The stars had not yet begun to pale in the sky, and the city lay in blackness. Both Johnny and his mother shuffled their feet as they walked. There was no ambition in the leg muscles to swing the feet clear of the ground.

After fifteen silent minutes, his mother turned off to the right.

"Don't be late," was her final warning from out of the dark that was swallowing her up.

He made no response, steadily keeping on his way. In the factory quarter, doors were opening everywhere, and he was soon one of a multitude that pressed onward through the dark. As he entered the factory gate the whistle blew again. He glanced at the east. Across a ragged sky-line of housetops a pale light was beginning to creep. This much he saw of the day as he turned his back upon it and joined his work gang.

He took his place in one of many long rows of machines. Before him, above a bin filled with small bobbins, were large bobbins revolving rapidly. Upon these he wound the jute-twine[6] of the small bobbins. The work was simple. All that was required was celerity. The small bobbins were emptied so rapidly, and there were so many large bobbins that did the emptying, that there were no idle moments.

He worked mechanically. When a small bobbin ran out, he used his left hand for a brake, stopping the large bobbin and at the same time, with thumb and forefinger, catching the flying end of twine. Also, at the same time, with his right hand, he caught up the loose twine-end of a small bobbin. These various acts with both hands were performed simultaneously and swiftly. Then there would come a flash of his hands as he looped the weaver's knot and released the bobbin. There was nothing difficult about weaver's knots. He once boasted he could tie them in his sleep. And for that matter, he sometimes did, toiling centuries long in a single night at tying an endless succession of weaver's knots.

Some of the boys shirked, wasting time and machinery by not replacing the small bobbins when they ran out. And there was an overseer to prevent this. He caught Johnny's neighbour at the trick, and boxed his ears.

"Look at Johnny there—why ain't you like him?" the overseer wrathfully demanded.

Johnny's bobbins were running full blast, but he did not thrill at the indirect praise. There had been a time . . . but that was long ago, very long ago. His apathetic face was expressionless as he listened to himself being held up as a shining example. He was the perfect worker. He knew that. He had been told so, often. It was a commonplace, and besides it didn't seem to mean anything to him any more. From the perfect worker he had evolved into the perfect machine. When his work went wrong, it was with him as with the machine, due to faulty material. It would have been as possible for a perfect nail-die[7] to cut imperfect nails as for him to make a mistake.

And small wonder. There had never been a time when he had not been in intimate relationship with machines. Machinery had almost been bred into him, and at any rate he had been brought up on it. Twelve years before, there had been a small flutter of excitement in the loom room of this very mill. Johnny's mother had fainted. They stretched her out on the floor in the midst of the shrieking machines. A couple of elderly women were called from their looms. The foreman assisted. And in a few minutes there was one more soul in the loom room than had entered by the doors. It was Johnny, born with the pounding, crashing roar of the looms in his ears, drawing with his first breath the warm, moist air that was thick with flying lint. He had coughed that first day in order to rid his lungs of the lint; and for the same reason he had coughed ever since.

The boy alongside of Johnny whimpered and sniffed. The boy's face was convulsed with hatred for the overseer who kept a threatening eye on him from a distance; but every bobbin was running full. The boy yelled terrible oaths into the whirling bobbins before him; but the sound did not carry half a dozen feet, the roaring of the room holding it in and containing it like a wall.

Of all this Johnny took no notice. He had a way of accepting things. Besides, things grow monotonous by repetition, and this particular happening he had witnessed many times. It seemed to him as useless to oppose the overseer as to defy the will of a machine. Machines were made to go in certain ways and to perform certain tasks. It was the same with the overseer.

But at eleven o'clock there was excitement in the room. In an apparently occult way the excitement instantly permeated everywhere. The one-legged boy who worked on the other side of Johnny bobbed swiftly across the floor to a bin truck that stood empty. Into this he dived out of sight, crutch and all. The superintendent of the mill was coming along, accompanied by a young man. He was well dressed and wore a starched shirt—a gentleman, in Johnny's classification of men, and also, "the Inspector."

He looked sharply at the boys as he passed along. Sometimes he stopped and asked questions. When he did so, he was compelled to shout at the top of his lungs, at which moments his face was ludicrously contorted with the strain of making himself heard. His quick eye noted the empty machine alongside of Johnny's, but he said nothing. Johnny also caught his eye, and he stopped abruptly. He caught Johnny by the arm to draw him back a step from the machine; but with an exclamation of surprise he released the arm.

"Pretty skinny," the superintendent laughed anxiously.

"Pipe stems," was the answer. "Look at those legs. The boy's got the rickets[8]—incipient, but he's got them. If epilepsy doesn't get him in the end, it will be because tuberculosis gets him first."

Johnny listened, but did not understand. Furthermore he was not interested in future ills. There was an immediate and more serious ill that threatened him in the form of the inspector.

"Now, my boy, I want you to tell me the truth," the inspector said, or shouted, bending close to the boy's ear to make him hear. "How old are you?"

"Fourteen," Johnny lied, and he lied with the full force of his lungs. So loudly did he lie that it started him off in a dry, hacking cough that lifted the lint which had been settling in his lungs all morning.

"Looks sixteen at least," said the superintendent.

"Or sixty," snapped the inspector.

"He's always looked that way."

"How long?" asked the inspector, quickly.

"For years. Never gets a bit older."

"Or younger, I dare say. I suppose he's worked here all those years?"

"Off and on—but that was before the new law was passed," the superintendent hastened to add.

"Machine idle?" the inspector asked, pointing at the unoccupied machine beside Johnny's, in which the part-filled bobbins were flying like mad.

"Looks that way." The superintendent motioned the overseer to him and shouted in his ear and pointed at the machine. "Machine's idle," he reported back to the inspector.

They passed on, and Johnny returned to his work, relieved in that the ill had been averted. But the one-legged boy was not so fortunate. The sharp-eyed inspector haled[9] him out at arm's length from the bin truck. His lips were quivering, and his face had all the expression of one upon whom was fallen profound and irremediable disaster. The overseer looked astounded, as though for the first time he had laid eyes on the boy, while the superintendent's face expressed shock and displeasure.

"I know him," the inspector said. "He's twelve years old. I've had him discharged from three factories inside the year. This makes the fourth."

He turned to the one-legged boy. "You promised me, word and honour, that you'd go to school."

The one-legged boy burst into tears. "Please, Mr. Inspector, two babies died on us, and we're awful poor."

"What makes you cough that way?" the inspector demanded, as though charging him with crime.

And as in denial of guilt, the one-legged boy replied: "It ain't nothin'. I jes' caught a cold last week, Mr. Inspector, that's all."

In the end the one-legged boy went out of the room with the inspector, the latter accompanied by the anxious and protesting superintendent. After that monotony settled down again. The long morning and the longer afternoon wore away and the whistle blew for quitting time. Darkness had already fallen when Johnny passed out through the factory gate. In the interval the sun had made a golden ladder of the sky, flooded the world with its gracious warmth, and dropped down and disappeared in the west behind a ragged sky-line of housetops.

Supper was the family meal of the day—the one meal at which Johnny encountered his younger brothers and sisters. It partook of the nature of an encounter, to him, for he was very old, while they were distressingly young. He had no patience with their excessive and amazing juvenility. He did not understand it. His own childhood was too far behind him. He was like an old and irritable man, annoyed by the turbulence of their young spirits that was to him arrant silliness. He glowered silently over his food, finding compensation in the thought that they would soon have to go to work. That would take the edge off of them and make them sedate and dignified—like him. Thus it was, after the fashion of the human, that Johnny made of himself a yardstick with which to measure the universe.

During the meal, his mother explained in various ways and with infinite repetition that she was trying to do the best she could; so that it was with relief, the scant meal ended, that Johnny shoved back his chair and arose. He debated for a moment between bed and the front door, and finally went out the latter. He did not go far. He sat down on the stoop, his knees drawn up and his narrow shoulders drooping forward, his elbows on his knees and the palms of his hands supporting his chin.

As he sat there, he did no thinking. He was just resting. So far as his mind was concerned, it was asleep. His brothers and sisters came out, and with other children played noisily about him. An electric globe at the corner lighted their frolics. He was peevish and irritable, that they knew; but the spirit of adventure lured them into teasing him. They joined hands before him, and, keeping time with their bodies, chanted in his face weird and uncomplimentary doggerel.[10] At first he snarled curses at them—curses he had learned from the lips of various foremen. Finding this futile, and remembering his dignity, he relapsed into dogged silence.

His brother Will, next to him in age, having just passed his tenth birthday, was the ringleader. Johnny did not possess particularly kindly feelings toward him. His life had early been embittered by continual giving over and giving way to Will. He had a definite feeling that Will was greatly in his debt and was ungrateful about it. In his own playtime, far back in the dim past, he had been robbed of a large part of that playtime by being compelled to take care of Will. Will was a baby then, and then, as now, their mother had spent her days in the mills. To Johnny had fallen the part of little father and little mother as well.

Will seemed to show the benefit of the giving over and the giving way. He was well-built, fairly rugged, as tall as his elder brother and even heavier. It was as though the life-blood of the one had been diverted into the other's veins. And in spirits it was the same. Johnny was jaded, worn out, without resilience, while his younger brother seemed bursting and spilling over with exuberance.

The mocking chant rose louder and louder. Will leaned closer as he danced, thrusting out his tongue. Johnny's left arm shot out and caught the other around the neck. At the same time he rapped his bony fist to the other's nose. It was a pathetically bony fist, but that it was sharp to hurt was evidenced by the squeal of pain it produced. The other children were uttering frightened cries, while Johnny's sister, Jennie, had dashed into the house.

He thrust Will from him, kicked him savagely on the shins, then reached for him and slammed him face downward in the dirt. Nor did he release him till the face had been rubbed into the dirt several times. Then the mother arrived, an anaemic whirlwind of solicitude and maternal wrath.

"Why can't he leave me alone?" was Johnny's reply to her upbraiding. "Can't he see I'm tired?"

"I'm as big as you," Will raged in her arms, his face a mass of tears, dirt, and blood. "I'm as big as you now, an' I'm goin' to git bigger. Then I'll lick you—see if I don't."

"You ought to be to work, seein' how big you are," Johnny snarled. "That's what's the matter with you. You ought to be to work. An' it's up to your ma to put you to work."

"But he's too young," she protested. "He's only a little boy."

"I was younger'n him when I started to work."

Johnny's mouth was open, further to express the sense of unfairness that he felt, but the mouth closed with a snap. He turned gloomily on his heel and stalked into the house and to bed. The door of his room was open to let in warmth from the kitchen. As he undressed in the semi-darkness he could hear his mother talking with a neighbor woman who had dropped in. His mother was crying, and her speech was punctuated with spiritless sniffles.

"I can't make out what's gittin' into Johnny," he could hear her say. "He didn't used to be this way. He was a patient little angel."

"An' he *is* a good boy," she hastened to defend. "He's worked faithful, an' he did go to work too young. But it wasn't my fault. I do the best I can, I'm sure."

Prolonged sniffling from the kitchen, and Johnny murmured to himself as his eyelids closed down, "You betcher life I've worked faithful."

The next morning he was torn bodily by his mother from the grip of sleep. Then came the meagre breakfast, the tramp through the dark, and the pale glimpse of day across the housetops as he turned his back on it and went in through the factory gate. It was another day, of all the days, and all the days were alike.

And yet there had been variety in his life—at the times he changed from one job to another, or was taken sick. When he was six, he was little mother and father to Will and the other children still younger. At seven he went into the mills—winding bobbins. When he was eight, he got work in another mill. His new job was marvellously easy. All he had to do was to sit down with a little stick in his hand and guide a stream of cloth that flowed past him. This stream of cloth came out of the maw of a machine, passed over a hot roller, and went on its way elsewhere. But he sat always in one place, beyond the reach of daylight, a gas-jet flaring over him, himself part of the mechanism.

He was very happy at that job, in spite of the moist heat, for he was still young and in possession of dreams and illusions. And wonderful dreams he dreamed as he watched the steaming cloth streaming endlessly by. But there was no exercise about the work, no call upon his mind, and he dreamed less and less, while his mind grew torpid and drowsy. Nevertheless, he earned two dollars a week, and two dollars represented the difference between acute starvation and chronic under-feeding.

But when he was nine, he lost his job. Measles was the cause of it. After he recovered, he got work in a glass factory. The pay was better, and the work demanded skill. It was piecework, and the more skilful he was, the bigger wages he earned. Here was incentive. And under this incentive he developed into a remarkable worker.

It was simple work, the tying of glass stoppers into small bottles. At his waist he carried a bundle of twine. He held the bottles between his knees so that he might work with both hands. Thus, in a sitting position and bending over his own knees, his narrow shoulders grew humped and his chest was contracted for ten hours each day. This was not good for the lungs, but he tied three hundred dozen bottles a day.

The superintendent was very proud of him, and brought visitors to look at him. In ten hours three hundred dozen bottles passed through his hands. This meant that he had attained machine-like perfection. All waste movements were eliminated. Every motion of his thin arms, every movement of a muscle in the thin fingers, was swift and accurate. He worked at high tension, and the result was that he grew nervous. At night his muscles twitched in his sleep, and in the daytime he could not relax and rest. He remained keyed up and his muscles continued to twitch. Also he grew sallow and his lint-cough grew worse. Then pneumonia laid hold of the feeble lungs within the contracted chest, and he lost his job in the glass-works.

Now he had returned to the jute mills where he had first begun with winding bobbins. But promotion was waiting for him. He was a good worker. He would next go on the starcher,[11] and later he would go into the loom room. There was nothing after that except increased efficiency.

The machinery ran faster than when he had first gone to work, and his mind ran slower. He no longer dreamed at all, though his earlier years had been full of dreaming. Once he had been in love. It was when he first began guiding the cloth over the hot roller, and it was with the daughter of the superintendent. She was much older than he, a young woman, and he had seen her at a distance only a paltry half-dozen times. But that made no difference. On the surface of the cloth stream that poured past him, he pictured radiant futures wherein he performed prodigies of toil, invented miraculous machines, won to the mastership of the mills, and in the end took her in his arms and kissed her soberly on the brow.

But that was all in the long ago, before he had grown too old and tired to love. Also, she had married and gone away, and his mind had gone to sleep. Yet it had been a wonderful experience, and he used often to look back upon it as other men and women look back upon the time they believed in fairies. He had never believed in fairies nor Santa Claus; but he had believed implicitly in the smiling future his imagination had wrought into the steaming cloth stream.

He had become a man very early in life. At seven, when he drew his first wages, began his adolescence. A certain feeling of independence crept up in him, and the relationship between him and his mother changed. Somehow, as an earner and breadwinner, doing his own work in the world, he was more like an equal with her. Manhood, full-blown manhood, had come when he was eleven, at which time he had gone to work on the night shift for six months. No child works on the night shift and remains a child.

There had been several great events in his life. One of these had been when his mother bought some California prunes. Two others had been the two times when she cooked custard. Those had been events. He remembered them kindly. And at that time his mother had told him of a blissful dish she would sometime make—"floating island," she had called it, "better than custard." For years he had looked forward to the day when he would sit down to the table with floating island before him, until at last he had relegated the idea of it to the limbo of unattainable ideals.

Once he found a silver quarter lying on the sidewalk. That, also, was a great event in his life, withal a tragic one. He knew his duty on the instant the silver flashed on his eyes, before even he had picked it up. At home, as usual, there was not enough to eat, and home he should have taken it as he did his wages every Saturday night. Right conduct in this case was obvious; but he never had any spending of his money, and he was suffering from candy hunger. He was ravenous for the sweets that only on red-letter days he had ever tasted in his life.

He did not attempt to deceive himself. He knew it was sin, and deliberately he sinned when he went on a fifteen-cent candy debauch. Ten cents he saved for a future orgy; but not being accustomed to the carrying of money, he lost the ten cents. This occurred at the time when he was suffering all the torments of conscience, and it was to him an act of divine retribution. He had a frightened sense of the closeness of an awful and wrathful God. God had seen, and God had been swift to punish, denying him even the full wages of sin.

In memory he always looked back upon that as the one great criminal deed of his life, and at the recollection his conscience always awoke and gave him another twinge. It was the one skeleton in his closet. Also, being so made, and circumstanced, he looked back upon the deed with regret. He was dissatisfied with the manner in which he had spent the quarter. He could have invested it better, and, out of his later knowledge of the quickness of God, he would have beaten God out by spending the whole quarter at one fell swoop. In retrospect he spent the quarter a thousand times, and each time to better advantage.

There was one other memory of the past, dim and faded, but stamped into his soul everlasting by the savage feet of his father. It was more like a nightmare than a remembered vision of a concrete thing—more like the race-memory of man that makes him fall in his sleep and that goes back to his arboreal ancestry.

This particular memory never came to Johnny in broad daylight when he was wide awake. It came at night, in bed, at the moment that his consciousness was sinking down and losing itself in sleep. It always aroused him to frightened wakefulness, and for the moment, in the first sickening start, it seemed to him that he lay crosswise on the foot of the bed. In the bed were the vague forms of his father and mother. He never saw what his father looked like. He had but one impression of his father, and that was that he had savage and pitiless feet.

His earlier memories lingered with him, but he had no late memories. All days were alike. Yesterday or last year were the same as a thousand years—or a minute. Nothing ever happened. There were no events to mark the march of time. Time did not march. It stood always still. It was only the whirling machines that moved, and they moved nowhere—in spite of the fact that they moved faster.

* * * * * * * *

When he was fourteen, he went to work on the starcher. It was a colossal event. Something had at last happened that could be remembered beyond a night's sleep or a week's pay-day. It marked an era. It was a machine Olympiad,[12] a thing to date from. "When I went to work on the starcher," or, "after," or "before I went to work on the starcher," were sentences often on his lips.

He celebrated his sixteenth birthday by going into the loom room and taking a loom. Here was an incentive again, for it was piece-work. And he excelled, because the clay of him had been moulded by the mills into the perfect machine. At the end of three months he was running two looms, and, later, three and four.

At the end of his second year at the looms he was turning out more yards than any other weaver, and more than twice as much as some of the less skilful ones. And at home things began to prosper as he approached the full stature of his earning power. Not, however, that his increased earnings were in excess of need. The children were growing up. They ate more. And they were going to school, and school-books cost money. And somehow, the faster he worked, the faster climbed the prices of things. Even the rent went up, though the house had fallen from bad to worse disrepair.

He had grown taller; but with his increased height he seemed leaner than ever. Also, he was more nervous. With the nervousness increased his peevishness and irritability. The children had learned by many bitter lessons to fight shy of him. His mother respected him for his earning power, but somehow her respect was tinctured with fear.

There was no joyousness in life for him. The procession of the days he never saw. The nights he slept away in twitching unconsciousness. The rest of the time he worked, and his consciousness was machine consciousness. Outside this his mind was a blank. He had no ideals, and but one illusion; namely, that he drank excellent coffee. He was a work-beast. He had no mental life whatever; yet deep down in the crypts of his mind, unknown to him, were being weighed and sifted every hour of his toil, every movement of his hands, every twitch of his muscles, and preparations were making for a future course of action that would amaze him and all his little world.

It was in the late spring that he came home from work one night aware of unusual tiredness. There was a keen expectancy in the air as he sat down to the table, but he did not notice. He went through the meal in moody silence, mechanically eating what was before him. The children um'd and ah'd and made smacking noises with their mouths. But he was deaf to them.

"D'ye know what you're eatin'?" his mother demanded at last, desperately.

He looked vacantly at the dish before him, and vacantly at her.

"Floatin' island," she announced triumphantly.

"Oh," he said.

"Floating island!" the children chorussed loudly.

"Oh," he said. And after two or three mouthfuls, he added, "I guess I ain't hungry to-night."

He dropped the spoon, shoved back his chair, and arose wearily from the table.

"An' I guess I'll go to bed."

His feet dragged more heavily than usual as he crossed the kitchen floor. Undressing was a Titan's[13] task, a monstrous futility, and he wept weakly as he crawled into bed, one shoe still on. He was aware of a rising, swelling something inside his head that made his brain thick and fuzzy. His lean fingers felt as big as his wrist, while in the ends of them was a remoteness of sensation vague and fuzzy like his brain. The small of his back ached intolerably. All his bones ached. He ached everywhere. And in his head began the shrieking, pounding, crashing, roaring of a million looms. All space was filled with flying shuttles[14] They darted in and out, intricately, amongst the stars. He worked a thousand looms himself, and ever they speeded up, faster and faster, and his brain unwound, faster and faster, and became the thread that fed the thousand flying shuttles.

He did not go to work next morning. He was too busy weaving colossally on the thousand looms that ran inside his head. His mother went to work, but first she sent for the doctor. It was a severe attack of la grippe,[15] he said. Jennie served as nurse and carried out his instructions.

It was a very severe attack, and it was a week before Johnny dressed and tottered feebly across the floor. Another week, the doctor said, and he would be fit to return to work. The foreman of the loom room visited him on Sunday afternoon, the first day of his convalescence. The best weaver in the room, the foreman told his mother. His job would be held for him. He could come back to work a week from Monday.

"Why don't you thank 'im, Johnny?" his mother asked anxiously.

"He's ben that sick he ain't himself yet," she explained apologetically to the visitor.

Johnny sat hunched up and gazing steadfastly at the floor. He sat in the same position long after the foreman had gone. It was warm outdoors, and he sat on the stoop in the afternoon. Sometimes his lips moved. He seemed lost in endless calculations.

Next morning, after the day grew warm, he took his seat on the stoop. He had pencil and paper this time with which to continue his calculations, and he calculated painfully and amazingly.

"What comes after millions?" he asked at noon, when Will came home from school. "An' how d'ye work 'em?"

That afternoon finished his task. Each day, but without paper and pencil, he returned to the stoop. He was greatly absorbed in the one tree that grew across the street. He studied it for hours at a time, and was unusually interested when the wind swayed its branches and fluttered its leaves. Throughout the week he seemed lost in a great communion with himself. On Sunday, sitting on the stoop, he laughed aloud, several times, to the perturbation of his mother, who had not heard him laugh for years.

Next morning, in the early darkness, she came to his bed to rouse him. He had had his fill of sleep all the week, and awoke easily. He made no struggle, nor did he attempt to hold on to the bedding when she stripped it from him. He lay quietly, and spoke quietly.

"It ain't no use, ma."

"You'll be late," she said, under the impression that he was still stupid with sleep.

"I'm awake, ma, an' I tell you it ain't no use. You might as well lemme alone. I ain't goin' to git up."

"But you'll lose your job!" she cried.

"I ain't goin' to git up," he repeated in a strange, passionless voice.

She did not go to work herself that morning. This was sickness beyond any sickness she had ever known. Fever and delirium she could understand; but this was insanity. She pulled the bedding up over him and sent Jennie for the doctor.

When that person arrived, Johnny was sleeping gently, and gently he awoke and allowed his pulse to be taken.

"Nothing the matter with him," the doctor reported. "Badly debilitated, that's all. Not much meat on his bones."

"He's always been that way," his mother volunteered.

"Now go 'way, ma, an' let me finish my snooze."

Johnny spoke sweetly and placidly, and sweetly and placidly he rolled over on his side and went to sleep.

At ten o'clock he awoke and dressed himself. He walked out into the kitchen, where he found his mother with a frightened expression on her face.

"I'm goin' away, ma," he announced, "an' I jes' want to say good-bye."

She threw her apron over her head and sat down suddenly and wept. He waited patiently.

"I might a-known it," she was sobbing.

"Where?" she finally asked, removing the apron from her head and gazing up at him with a stricken face in which there was little curiosity.

"I don't know—anywhere."

As he spoke, the tree across the street appeared with dazzling brightness on his inner vision. It seemed to lurk just under his eyelids, and he could see it whenever he wished.

"An' your job?" she quavered.

"I ain't never goin' to work again."

"My God, Johnny!" she wailed, "don't say that!"

What he had said was blasphemy to her. As a mother who hears her child deny God, was Johnny's mother shocked by his words.

"What's got into you, anyway?" she demanded, with a lame attempt at imperativeness.

"Figures," he answered. "Jes' figures. I've ben doin' a lot of figurin' this week, an' it's most surprisin'."

"I don't see what that's got to do with it," she sniffled.

Johnny smiled patiently, and his mother was aware of a distinct shock at the persistent absence of his peevishness and irritability.

"I'll show you," he said. "I'm plum' tired out. What makes me tired? Moves. I've ben movin' ever since I was born. I'm tired of movin', an' I ain't goin' to move any more. Remember when I worked in the glass-house? I used to do three hundred dozen a day. Now I reckon I made about ten different moves to each bottle. That's thirty-six thousan' moves a day. Ten days, three hundred an' sixty thousan' moves. One month, one million an' eighty thousan' moves. Chuck out the eighty thousan'"—he spoke with the complacent beneficence of a philanthropist—"chuck out the eighty thousan', that leaves a million moves a month—twelve million moves a year.

"At the looms I'm movin' twic'st as much. That makes twenty-five million moves a year, an' it seems to me I've ben a movin' that way 'most a million years.

"Now this week I ain't moved at all. I ain't made one move in hours an' hours. I tell you it was swell, jes' settin' there, hours an' hours, an' doin' nothin'. I ain't never ben happy before. I never had any time. I've ben movin' all the time. That ain't no way to be happy. An' I ain't going to do it any more. I'm jes' goin' to set, an' set, an' rest, an' rest, and then rest some more."

"But what's goin' to come of Will an' the children?" she asked despairingly.

"That's it, 'Will an' the children,'" he repeated.

But there was no bitterness in his voice. He had long known his mother's ambition for the younger boy, but the thought of it no longer rankled. Nothing mattered any more. Not even that.

"I know, ma, what you've ben plannin' for Will—keepin' him in school to make a book-keeper out of him. But it ain't no use, I've quit. He's got to go to work."

"An' after I have brung you up the way I have," she wept, starting to cover her head with the apron and changing her mind.

"You never brung me up," he answered with sad kindliness. "I brung myself up, ma, an' I brung up Will. He's bigger'n me, an' heavier, an' taller. When I was a kid, I reckon I didn't git enough to eat. When he come along an' was a kid, I was workin' an' earnin' grub for him too. But that's done with. Will can go to work, same as me, or he can go to hell, I don't care which. I'm tired. I'm goin' now. Ain't you goin' to say goodbye?"

She made no reply. The apron had gone over her head again, and she was crying. He paused a moment in the doorway.

"I'm sure I done the best I knew how," she was sobbing.

He passed out of the house and down the street. A wan delight came into his face at the sight of the lone tree. "Jes' ain't goin' to do nothin'," he said to himself, half aloud, in a crooning tone. He glanced wistfully up at the sky, but the bright sun dazzled and blinded him.

It was a long walk he took, and he did not walk fast. It took him past the jute-mill. The muffled roar of the loom room came to his ears, and he smiled. It was a gentle, placid smile. He hated no one, not even the pounding, shrieking machines. There was no bitterness in him, nothing but an inordinate hunger for rest.

The houses and factories thinned out and the open spaces increased as he approached the country. At last the city was behind him, and he was walking down a leafy lane beside the railroad track. He did not walk like a man. He did not look like a man. He was a travesty of the human. It was a twisted and stunted and nameless piece of life that shambled like a sickly ape, arms loose-hanging, stoop-shouldered, narrow-chested, grotesque and terrible.

He passed by a small railroad station and lay down in the grass under a tree. All afternoon he lay there. Sometimes he dozed, with muscles that twitched in his sleep. When awake, he lay without movement, watching the birds or looking up at the sky through the branches of the tree above him. Once or twice he laughed aloud, but without relevance to anything he had seen or felt.

After twilight had gone, in the first darkness of the night, a freight train rumbled into the station. When the engine was switching cars on to the side-track, Johnny crept along the side of the train. He pulled open the side-door of an empty box-car and awkwardly and laboriously climbed in. He closed the door. The engine whistled. Johnny was lying down, and in the darkness he smiled.

NOTES

1. One who renounces their religious faith.
2. A morning variation of the prayer many Christian children once learned to say before going to bed. The evening/bedtime version is: "Now I lay me down to sleep, / I pray the Lord my soul to keep; / If I should die before I wake, / I pray the Lord my soul to take. / Amen." The amended version presented here had appeared in many magazines around the time London composed this story, so it's highly unlikely he wrote it.
3. To have one's pay reduced.
4. Skillful maneuvering, associated with magic tricks.
5. The mother is using a lamp that burns a wick of cotton which draws liquid fuel from a receptacle below it; the "chimney" is the clear part of the lamp, in which the wick burns and emits light.
6. A twine made of jute, a type of rough fiber made from the bark of certain plants; London himself worked in a jute mill as a teenager in 1893 and hated it.
7. A mold into which some type of material—in the case of nails it would be molten steel—is poured to form a product; when the material has cooled and the die is opened, the product is released.
8. A bone disease caused by vitamin D deficiency, other nutritional deficiencies, or lack of exposure to sunlight. It often softens and weakens the bones of infants and young children, and bowed legs are a common visible characteristic.
9. A synonym for "haul."
10. Badly composed writing or speech.
11. Machine for starching fabrics to make them stiffer.
12. A reference to the Olympic games, which tested athletes' endurance and strength every four years during this time period. Here the term "Olympiad" suggests a great physical and mental challenge.
13. The Titans were immense and powerful Greek gods who came before the better-known Olympians.
14. A small yet heavy tool used to move thread between layers of other threads in fabric making.
15. Influenza (French).

LUCY BATES MACOMBER

(Unknown Birth and Death Dates)

Very little is known about Lucy Bates Macomber except that she was born Lucy Virginia Bates and was listed as being from Grand Rapids, Michigan, when she married a twenty-seven-year-old Presbyterian minister named William Wirt Macomber in 1863. A biographical listing for Reverend Macomber in *General Biographical Catalogue of Auburn [NY] Theological Seminary 1818–1918* (1918) indicates that he graduated from Western Reserve College in Cleveland in 1860 and served fourteen different congregations during his career. Among the places the couple lived were Marysville, California, and the Nevada mining towns of Gold Hill, Silver City, and Nevada City. Given the seven years she lived in these Sierra Nevada towns, Macomber undoubtedly came to possess what scholar Julie Meloni terms "true 'insider's knowledge' of the region." Macomber transformed her observations into "The Gossip of Gold Hill," the excellent short story reprinted here, which Meloni, the person responsible for bringing it to light in a scholarly article published in 2010, notes is Macomber's "only documented work of fiction I have been able to locate." It was originally published in the March 1873 issue of the *Overland Monthly,* a San Francisco magazine intended to showcase the talent of western writers to the rest of the country, especially to the many easterners who thought of the West as a cultural desert. After reading the story, which offers a viewpoint on the "Western experience" that is far different from what most male authors depicted, one in which a woman's (and mother's) experience is placed at the forefront, most will agree with Meloni's conclusion: "If it does comprise her complete literary output, this is truly a shame."

 *Readers should be aware that this story includes some language which, while commonly used during this time period, is no longer considered acceptable because of its offensive nature.

THE GOSSIP OF GOLD HILL (1873)

The Pioneer stage-coach that had rumbled its way along from Sacramento, attended by a pillar of cloud—more alkaline, doubtless, but none the less faithful than that of Israelitish renown-—suddenly projected itself upon the Silver City[1] vision, according to its daily wont, one languid July afternoon. Of course, it was a remote July, when stage companies flourished and fattened, and railroad monopolies existed only in the covetous visions of greedy speculators. The passengers, twelve in number—ten, including a little child, inside, and two on the box—had passed through the experience common to travelers on that route. They had sweltered uncomfortably through the day, and had shivered in the coolness of the mountain night-air. From serenest altitudes of ribbon-like smoothness, they had gazed upon the rugged picture of the pine-clad heights beneath them, calmly sleeping in the moonlight, and had instinctively drawn toward the inside of the grade, as the sharp-faced man on the middle seat designated the precise locality of the last stage disaster, when horses, coach, and passengers were precipitated into a heterogeneous compound, two hundred feet below. They had fallen into fitful dozes, and proved, by severe cranial experiences, the equality of action and reaction, until their powers of philosophizing on the subject were quite benumbed; and, with the general exhaustion and the democratic level of beauty to which they had been reduced by alluvial deposits, they had almost lost their individuality, and had quite forgotten the intensity of interest with which they had looked forward to the wonderful new mining towns which had sprung up almost in a night, when, "Passing through Devil's Gate,"[2] pronounced with appropriate solemnity by the sharp-faced man, startled the torpid life into a momentary spasm of rebellion. Then a brutal voice outside was heard, saying, "D—n you, let go, or I'll make a corpse of you," adding a catalogue of expletives impossible of repetition; and the little lady on the back-seat looked out of the window and saw the veritable Devil's Gate, in all its wild beauty, closing behind her, and felt a sudden oppression, as if she had been unexpectedly thrust into Satanic regions, with no hope of reprieve.

Up the long, irregular cañon, bristling with quartz-mills, and lined with queer, little houses, hastily improvised of wood, and cloth, and paper; through the narrow main street, blocked with a tangle of teams and men, the verdureless mountains rising bleakly on either side, covered to a certain height with a medley of buildings, trestles, and dumps of blue earth; bewildered by the thunder of the mills and the jargon of blasphemous tongues, they rattled on into what seemed to be a very pandemonium. They passed a few saloons, a store or two, then suddenly drew up, and the driver shouted, "Vesey House." The coach-door opened from without, there was a stir inside, an uncomfortable compression of dry-goods and humanity, a folding together of the middle-seat, and a gentleman with the child alighted, and handed out the little lady from the back-seat. As they passed into the hotel, a group of loungers on the steps took careful observations, and one exclaimed, "What the devil's Bliss up to now?" "D—d if she don't look like a lady, anyhow," came the quick response. "Not one of his kind, I reckon." As the lady was passing to her room, Bliss, as he had been dubbed at the door, with quick instinct, divined her look of sudden hopelessness, and, with charming courtesy and kindliness spoke a few cheerful words, adding, "So, hasten your toilet, or he'll be here before you are ready."

Twenty years before, this same little lady had made her embryonic appearance in a quiet New England village. She had met her mother on the threshold of eternity, received her first, last kiss, and, passing into time, had unconsciously taken up the broken threads of affection that had once encircled the departed. She crept quietly into her father's vacant heart and warmed it with her soft nestling. She became the Little Amy of the village, whose claim to love was neither questioned nor limited. With a certain royalty of birthright, she had made childish appropriation of the most promising boy of the village, and had grown up in the enjoyment of his tacit proprietorship; so that when, with characteristic precipitation, he had declared his purpose to seek a quick fortune in the new *dorados*[3] of the West, the good old deacon conceded to him the first right to his little Amy, and the village pronounced a quiet amen. The honey-moon passed in a subdued pathos begotten of the impending separation, and then he was gone. At nineteen, little Amy became a mother, and, with the development of maternity, received a full supplement of character—a strength born of weakness—for an all-potent motherhood, in its infinite necessities, laid strong hold of an Almighty arm, and was exalted in the two best possibilities of love—the love of God and that of little children.

Another year passed, redolent of baby bloom, and then the old man died. It was Amy's first grief, and, in her sore extremity, she naturally turned to her distant husband for sympathy and shelter. With an energy born of intense loneliness, she heralded her approach by telegram, then set out in the care of friends to San Francisco, and pushed on to the Washoe mines[4] alone. By accident of conversation, she had heard her fellow-traveler, Mr. Bliss, mention Gold Hill,[5] and then speak in a familiar way of the mine in which she knew her husband to be most interested, and, in response to some proffered courtesy at one of the stations, she had timidly made herself known, and found in him an old comrade of Harry's, and thenceforth her own kind friend and escort.

The dust and stain of travel removed, and baby dressed in dainty white muslin and fresh blue ribbons, she sat in tremulous expectation of she scarce knew what, so strangely had her spirits sunk. She even betrayed no surprise when Mr. Bliss returned alone, and, with forced cheerfulness, told her that Harry was out of town, he did not know exactly where; had gone on a sort of exploring expedition to the Reese River country, and possibly to San Francisco; had missed her telegram, starting the day before it arrived, but would doubtless return soon, and in the meantime no effort should be spared to find and hasten him.

When she went to dinner that afternoon, there was the usual stare at the newcomer, with a reaction of excessive masculine deference, which quite disconcerted poor Amy, and made her feel very much out of place. She had begun to entertain a conscious longing for companionship with her own sex, but a generous specimen of female corpulency at the end of the table, talking incessantly with a most gratuitous prodigality of voice, to a select coterie of admirers, and two elaborately-dressed young ladies, with a dash of bold prettiness and an extravagance of white powder on their faces, bandying jokes and slang phrases with their *vis-a-vis* across the table, robbed isolation of its sense of loss. Her convictions on this point were somewhat confirmed, when, an hour later, Mr. Bliss, at her request, guided her to the little cabin on the side-hill where Harry had been "baching it,"[6] whence she discovered what seemed to her a singular phenomenon in the person of a richly-dressed lady sitting in a remote doorway, smoking a cigar, with all the *nonchalance* of one well accustomed to that innocent diversion.

Harry's cabin was a rude one, like its fellows, which seemed to have perched like so many crows in the most precarious situations on the barren hill-side; but Harry was proverbially nice in his tastes, and so the legendary dishes, cleaned by

turning on the other side, were put away in all the dull neatness of the most orthodox propriety, and the bunk on which Harry had enjoyed his Bohemian slum-
bers, shut off from the main room by the ordinary cloth partition, was cleanly
draped; while, in spite of the thick covering of dust which had sifted through
the inevitable cracks, the floor gave evidence of intimacy with the broom, doing
inverted penance behind the door. On the table lay a scrap of paper full of
penciled figures, and, over all, "Amy" was scribbled in two or three places, as if
the writer's mind had involuntarily wandered from his mathematical computa-
tions to the dearer thoughts of home; and, in one corner, "Harry" was carefully
executed in large hand, then, within the parallels of the H, "Amy" was written
in small characters, and within the A was the tiny word, "Baby." This papery
circumstance, through the subtle kinship of mind and matter, threw Amy into a
lachrymose condition, alike distressing to Mr. Bliss and baby; and, after a little,
the three returned.

Next day, Amy learned the fabulous cost of living at the hotel, counted her
money twice over, calculated just how long it would give her a right to stay there,
looked greatly perplexed for half an hour, then paid her bill, and with baby
made her way to Harry's cabin on the hill. When Mr. Bliss found her there, he
remonstrated, as he would have done to any independent mind, on the ground
of unsafety, with a hint that it was not best, for some other reason wholly unintelligible to Amy; but she, with child-like innocence, trusted all humanity, and
was not afraid. Dependent all her life upon the wisdom of others, she would
have readily obeyed a command, but none came, and so her own judgement
prevailed.

Her appearance at the hotel as the *protégée* of a notoriously "fast man," had
inspired some unhallowed conjectures, in spite of the contradiction in her face
and demeanor, and now, from her sudden disappearance, had sprung up a whole
crop of wicked inferences. Nevada society never has adjusted itself to the stereo-
typed grooves of social teas and neighborly gossip, and it never will. Two unsophisticated ladies from the East once conceived the benevolent device of both
leavening the community and benefiting the poor, by means of a sewing society.
It began well, with the moral support of the best female influence in town; but a
discouraging deficiency of that mild type of gossip which is the natural pabulum
of such institutions, and a series of social shocks which caused everybody to
regard everybody else with that distant deference which one might naturally
accord to an electric eel, caused it soon to degenerate into an uproarious evening
sociable, which few ladies found time to attend, and where gentlemen, to whom
the attractions of the saloons had become monotonous, made free contributions,
ranging from "four bits" to five dollars, until the treasury was overburdened.
Everybody was then living in the enjoyment of prospective opulence, since the
fat washerwoman down the cañon had "struck it rich," and two or three illiterate
miners had suddenly found themselves transformed to wealthy speculators, while
several Irish ladies had risen, by means of wildcat stock, from despised biddies to
a high state of matrimonial eligibility, not to mention those of more pretentious

quality who had taken fortune "at the flood;" so, in sheer lack of more legitimate beneficiaries, the money was donated to the minister's wife, and the society abandoned to a quiet death.

Physical barrenness and moral rankness and excess is the law of life there. The same climatic influences which dry up the springs of a sanitary vegetation, seem to foster a tropical luxuriance of evil in the moral soil. There are a few souls whose unsoiled spotlessness has proved their utter lack of chemical affinity with the surrounding elements, or rather the steadfastness of that mystic anchor within the vail; but the great multitude of men and women are intent on "making their pile"[7] and their escape as speedily as possible, and meanwhile they are willing to free themselves of the hampering amenities of a more decorous life. Timid natures do not seek such fields of enterprise; and so, where hundreds of buildings go up in a day, and fortunes are made and lost in intoxicating succession, slander bursts full-blown into existence, without the ordinary germ and bud of gossip. The women—be it said to their praise—being vastly in the minority, and their services much in demand, generally attended to their own business, and found little time to form original conclusions concerning their neighbors. The rigidly conservative among them seemed inclined to consign new-comers of their own sex, who lacked the flourish of an indorsement, to an eternal quarantine, fearing doubtless some deadly contagion; but, with feminine inconsistency, they welcomed newly-arrived gentlemen as if their manhood was mail-proof against infection.

Amy's lonely life and the unvitalizing air of that great altitude were well calculated to induce an unhealthy state of depression, both physical and mental. For prudential reasons known to that gentleman, Mr. Bliss had not called for two or three days; and so, one stifling afternoon, when baby's feverish state filled her with anxiety, she resolved upon an effort at friendship with the woman whom she had seen in a cabin near. Approaching timidly, she essayed a propitiatory form of speech, but was rudely interrupted with, "I am a dacent woman, mum, and wuddent wish to associate with the likes of you; so ye may as well take yerself off." Amy did not comprehend this rebuff, but she went home and wept bitterly. The next day, when she went down the hill for water, and a miner took the pail, filled, and carried it back for her, then said, awkwardly, "I'm always at your service, miss, if I can do anything for you—errands, or the like o' that; you don't look like you were used to roughing it much," her voice failed her to make answer, and the miner, looking back, saw her weeping just as bitterly as she had wept the day before. This was apparently unreasonable; but she was learning the value of kindness by contrast—a miserable lesson that must come, sooner or later, to all. Two or three more days passed, and baby pined and grew worse, until Amy, who could not leave it, took it in her arms and went down the hill, then up the main street toward the divide, looking wistfully for doctors' signs. Seeing one at length, she turned into the office. The doctor was not there, and, after waiting some time, she left an urgent order, describing as well as she could on the slate, the situation of her cabin, and went home. The day was hot, and the trip did not benefit the child. At evening, it was so much worse that she left it, and ran quickly to a house where she had seen children playing, and so hoped to touch a mother's sympathy. Fearing she should again be repulsed before her errand was told, she precipitately cried out, "O won't you come and stay with me to-night? my baby is sick." A kindly glance overspread the woman's face for an instant, but she was the unwilling mother of a numerous offspring, which had persisted intact through all the minor details of childhood, from colic to scarlet fever, so that she did not regard a sick child as a very appalling circumstance. Moreover, she was a good Methodist sister, who had given the small entirety of her being to her Lord, but had not yet burst the chrysalis-shell of her narrow limitations, and, thinking thus to please her Master, she was always making the gate straiter and the way narrower than did He who built them. To her, falling from grace seemed like an ever-impending calamity, ready to surprise her at any instant, and since her residence at Gold Hill, its Protean[8] form most often assumed the shape of the "world's people," especially those of reputed laxity of virtue. So when she asked Amy where she lived, and what friends she had, an unfortunate memory of something she had overheard "the men folks" saying prompted a frigid excuse. Amy turned away with a chill at her heart. The world that had hitherto been her nursing-mother, had suddenly cast her off. The air was stifling, and the blue concavity of sky above seemed like the cover of an exhausted receiver closing down upon her.

All that night she carried her little one to and fro, and sang tender lullabies, until her own voice frightened her into silence. The whir of the mills[9] never ceased, and a confused sound of bacchanal[10] revelry mingled with it from the saloons below. The night previous, in her wakefulness, Amy had heard vaguely a short altercation, a scuffling sound, and then two quick reports of a pistol near her dwelling, and, while in the doctor's office, she had read an item in the paper which made her blood run cold. The paragraph was quite unique in its way, being couched in an emotionless brevity worthy of a Euclid.[11] It is, however, but justice to the editorial heart of that period and locality to say, that the frequency of such occurrences necessitated either an unobtrusive terseness or an attractive facetiousness of statement, in order to add to the popularity and financial success of the paper. Yet it did not have a good effect upon Amy, who had imbibed certain antiquated notions concerning the sacredness of human life. Still, she was not afraid now. A certain pallor and blueness about the eyes, and a pinched contraction of baby's dimpled chin, lifted her above fear, into the regions of awe. She heard an approaching footstep, and ran out and asked a man, who was passing, to go for a doctor quick. The man consented, and turned back, as if to go at once, but he was drunk, and never reached his destination.

Some hours later, the miner who had compassionated Amy at the spring, passed along on his way to his "morning shift." He had a tin lunch-pail in his hand, and a hard, prosaic expression on his grimy face. He was not apparently a favorable medium through which a subtle spiritual influence might scent out

trouble and send relief. But as he neared the little cabin, he remembered its occupant, and fell to wondering who she was, and how such a little timid creature
came to be there alone. Perhaps it was the peaceful hush of earth, and air, and
sky, that sent a rush of gentle thoughts through his mind; perhaps it was the
sudden uprising of a far-off memory that made him turn when he had passed,
with a look of protection at the cabin. All was quiet, and he wondered to see the
flickering of a lamp within, dimmed by the morning sun. The door was ajar,
and he felt a strange impulse to enter. There was no response to his light knock,
and he pushed the door a trifle further open. There sat Amy—tearless, and rigid
almost as the lifeless baby in her arms. The horror that had rested in the child's
eyes during the last convulsive agony, had transferred itself now to the amazed
mother's, and there was only peace and beauty on the baby face.

O! ye whose tender buds of promise have been plucked from fairest gardens,
which lacked neither dew nor rain, thank God that you were spared the sharper
anguish of those patient mourners who have watched the light of life go out, for
lack of the abundance just beyond their grasp—forever haunted by the memory
of childish eyes full of unreasoning appeals for simplest comforts which they
could not give.

The miner dropped his lunch-pail and his awkwardness together, and gently disengaging the child, laid Amy on her bed, and ran for brandy and female
assistance. Entertaining a vague conviction that a minister would constitute
an appropriate feature of the scene, he afterwards left the Methodist sister,
devoutly hoping that the Lord's dealings might not be in vain, and giving the
hapless mother many pious exhortations, walked to Virginia,[12] in quest of a
recent ecclesiastical importation which that city possessed in the person of a
young Episcopal rector. There was a funeral that afternoon, at the expense
of the miner and his friends, for sympathy in that climate generally takes a
circuitous route through the pocket. Amy was quiet and tearless again; and
the Methodist sister despairingly remarked, as she was enjoying her first drive
in Washoe at the vicarious expense already mentioned, "that it was mighty
strange how hard-hearted some folks were; for if Mollie should die now, in
one of her croupy spells, she should take on awfully, she was sure; but then,
there was no accountin' for the difference in people, and for her part, she could
never be too thankful that the Lord had made her to differ; and she hoped it
would be a lesson to them all." Probably it was a lesson, for they all seemed dis-
inclined to talk, and so she gradually subsided into silence. A decent colored[13]
woman, who dropped in to the service at the house, took Amy's hand as she
went out, and said: "Bress you, honey; I'se sure de Lord hisself is wid you, or
you couldn't be so quiet-like, an' de dear baby gone." A kind lady from Virginia
came down with the rector, and insisted on taking the stricken mother home
with her; but Amy, docile in all else, refused to go.

They did not leave her again; and after a few days of delirium, in which
Harry was painfully absent, while baby seemed ever before her—now a child of

earth, with wants unsatisfied; then an angel child, treading with charmed feet the courts of Paradise; and, again, a happy babe, pressing with soft clasp the mother's aching breast—she gathered herself up, one early twilight, and with the mother-love flashing from her eyes, put out both her arms, saying softly, "Mamma is coming," and was gone.

In a different community, this martyrdom of innocent life might at least have borne a harvest of love and charity for other starving souls to reap; but in that strange land, whose silver-hoards benumb the heart, the sacrifice was lost, like a bubble in the sea. I do not even know that there was any record of it in the *Daily News*, for the next day there was a "development in the mines" which made every one wild with excitement, and editors and readers alike were absorbed in their own sordid possibilities.

NOTES

1. From the late 1850s through the 1860s, Silver City, Nevada, was a productive mining town where Macomber once lived; it is now a near ghost town.
2. Once a prominent Nevada landmark, Devil's Gate is a narrow gorge north of Silver City that now marks the boundary between Storey and Lyon Counties.
3. This term derives from the widespread belief among Spanish explorers during the sixteenth century that somewhere in the New World there was a city or kingdom known as "El Dorado" filled with vast amounts of gold and riches; here it colloquially refers to the belief of many Americans during the nineteenth century that one could discover gold in the West and become rich.
4. During this period, the Washoe mining district, southeast of what is now Reno, Nevada, and east of Lake Tahoe, was the site of many very productive gold and silver mines as well as, consequently, a number of "boomtowns" filled with miners.
5. The small former mining town of Gold Hill, Nevada, which Macomber also once lived in, still exists today.
6. Living as a bachelor, alone.
7. Making a great deal of money.
8. In ancient Greek mythology, Proteus is a sea god who can easily change forms to avoid capture; the adjective "protean" conveys the sense of something constantly changing.
9. Stamping mills were used to crush large amounts of mined rock in order to help extract the gold or silver contained in it.
10. An adjective derived from the proper name "Bacchus," who was the Roman god of agriculture, fertility, and wine. He is often associated with large drunken celebrations.
11. Possibly the most famous mathematician of ancient Greece, Euclid is commonly known as the "Father of Geometry" and thus was renowned for his straightforward reasoning.
12. Short for "Virginia City," a large mining town located near Gold Hill.
13. A term commonly used at this time to refer to African Americans. It is now considered offensive and no longer acceptable.

MARÍA CRISTINA MENA

(1893–1965)

María Cristina Mena is among the large group of writers now considered American but who were not originally from the United States. Born in Mexico to a Mexican father and Spanish mother in 1893, Mena in 1907 was sent to live with relatives in New York City in order to shield her from the violence then gripping her home country. Already fluent in English when she arrived, Mena did well in school and began writing stories about Mexico. She began submitting these stories—which often included Spanish phrases and words—to American magazines for publication. From 1910 to 1913 ten of Mena's short stories and one nonfiction article were published, mostly in the New York–based magazines the *Century* and *Cosmopolitan*, which circulated nationally. Significantly, none of Mena's stories are about Mexicans' experiences in the United States, for she preferred to limit herself to explaining Mexico to Americans. In addition, while these magazines' editors eagerly wished to include Mena's tales in their publications for their "exotic" element, they also frequently shortened or excised the Spanish phrases and words she had used.

After her marriage to Henry Kellers Chambers in 1916, Mena—now María Cristina Chambers—stopped writing almost completely. Between 1916 and 1942 she published only one short story, "A Son of the Tropics," in 1931, but this was likely written much earlier. After her husband's death in 1935, Mena returned to writing, publishing four juvenile novels, all about Mexican subjects, between 1942 and 1946. In part because of her anglicized last name, these and her earlier works were not recovered as early examples of Latinx literature until 1978. Scholars are divided in their opinions about Mena's works, with some applauding the very fact that a Latina was able to successfully negotiate the American publishing world and be paid for her productions, and others disparaging them for their condescending treatment of Mexican characters, which they say Mena did to please American editors and readers.

"The Education of Popo" was one of Mena's first published works, originally having appeared in the March 1914 issue of *Century Magazine;* it was later included in *The Collected Stories of María Cristina Mena* (1997). One can definitely see in this story certain elements of American cultural condescension toward the Mexican characters, but there are also subtle criticisms of particular attitudes among the American characters as well. Overall, the way in which Mena subtly portrays the interplay between these two cultures offers a good example of the type of negotiation and compromise many immigrant authors were forced to engage in if they wanted their works to be published in the United States.

THE EDUCATION OF POPO (1914)

Governor Fernando Arriola and his amiable señora[1] were confronted with a critical problem in hospitality: it was nothing less than the entertaining of American

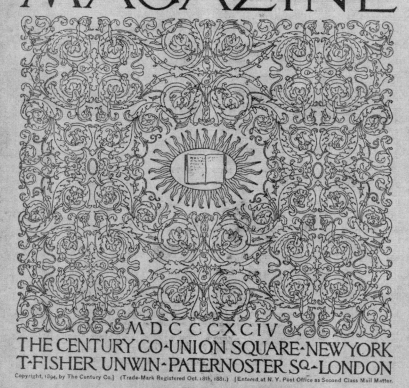

A NOVELETTE IN THREE PARTS "A Cumberland Vendetta" BEGINS IN THIS NUMBER.

VOL. XLVIII.   JUNE, 1894.   No. 2.

THE CENTURY ILLUSTRATED ❋ MONTHLY ❋ MAGAZINE

MDCCCXCIV

THE CENTURY CO · UNION SQUARE · NEW YORK
T · FISHER UNWIN · PATERNOSTER SQ · LONDON

Cover of the *Century Illustrated Monthly Magazine* (June 1894).

ladies, who by all means must be given the most favorable impressions of Mexican civilization.

Hence some unusual preparations. On the backs of men and beasts were arriving magnificent quantities, requisitioned from afar, of American canned soups, fish, meats, sweets, *hors d'oeuvres*, and nondescripts; ready-to-serve cereals, ready-to-drink cocktails, a great variety of pickles, and much other cheer of American manufacture. Even an assortment of can-openers had not been forgotten. Above all, an imperial call had gone out for ice, and precious consignments of that exotic commodity were now being delivered in various stages of dissolution, to be installed with solicitude in cool places, and kept refreshed with a continual agitation of fans in the hands of superfluous servants. By such amiable extremities it was designed to insure the ladies Cherry against all danger of going hungry or thirsty for lack of conformable aliment or sufficiently frigid liquids.

The wife and daughter of that admirable Señor Montague Cherry of the United States, who was manipulating the extension of certain important concessions in the State of which Don Fernando was governor, and with whose operations his Excellency found his own private interests to be pleasantly involved, their visit was well-timed in a social way, for they would be present on the occasion of a great ball to be given by the governor. For other entertainment the Arriola family would provide as God might permit. Leonor, the only unmarried daughter, was practicing several new selections on the harp, her mama sagaciously conceiving that an abundance of music might ease the strain of conversation in the event of the visitors having no Spanish. And now Próspero, the only son, aged fourteen, generally known as Popo, blossomed suddenly as the man of the hour; for, thanks to divine Providence, he had been studying English, and could say prettily, although slowly, "What o'clock it is?" and "Please you this," and "Please you that," and doubtless much more if he were put to it.

Separately and in council the rest of the family impressed upon Popo that the honor of the house of Arriola, not to mention that of his native land, reposed in his hands, and he was conjured to comport himself as a true-born caballero.[2] With a heavy sense of responsibility upon him, he bought some very high collars, burned much midnight oil over his English "method," and became suddenly censorious of his stockinged legs,[3] which, accompanying him everywhere, decoyed his down-sweeping eyes and defied concealment or palliation. After anxious consideration, he put the case to his mama.

"Thou amiable companion of all my anguishes," he said tenderly, "thou knowest my anxiety to comport myself with credit in the view of the honored Meesees Cherry. Much English I have already, with immobile delivery the most authentic and distinguished. So far I feel myself modestly secure. But these legs, Mama—these legs of my nightmares—"

"*Chist, chist!* Thou hadst ever a symmetrical leg, Popo mine," expostulated Doña[4] Elvira, whose soul of a young matron dreaded her boy's final plunge into manhood.

"But consider, little Mama," he cried, "that very soon I shall have fifteen years. Since the last day of my saint I have shaved the face scrupulously on alternate mornings; but that no longer suffices, for my maturing beard now asks for the razor every day, laughing to scorn these legs, which continue to lack the investment of dignity. Mother of my soul, for the honor of our family in the eyes of the foreign ladies, I supplicate thy consent that I should be of long pantaloons!"

Touched on the side of her obligations as an international hostess, Doña Elvira pondered deeply, and at length confessed with a sigh:

"It is unfortunately true, thou repose of my fatigues, that in long pantaloons thou wouldst represent more."

And it followed, as a crowning graciousness toward Mrs. Montague Cherry and her daughter, that Popo was promoted to trousers.

When the visitors arrived, he essayed gallantly to dedicate himself to the service of the elder lady, in accordance with Mexican theories of propriety, but found his well-meaning efforts frustrated by the younger one, who, seeing no other young man thereabout, proceeded methodically to attach the governor's handsome little son to herself.

Popo found it almost impossible to believe that they were mother and daughter. By some magic peculiar to the highly original country of the *Yanquis*,[5] their relation appeared to be that of an indifferent sisterliness, with a balance of authority in favor of the younger. That revolutionary arrangement would have scandalized Popo had he not perceived from the first that Alicia Cherry was entitled to extraordinary consideration. Never before had he seen a living woman with hair like daffodils, eyes like violets, and a complexion of coral and porcelain. It seemed to him that some precious image of the Virgin[6] had been changed into a creature of sweet flesh and capricious impulses, animate with a fearless urbanity far beyond the dreams of the dark-eyed, demure, and now despised damsels of his own race. His delicious bewilderment was completed when Miss Cherry, after staring him in the face with a frank and inviting smile, turned to her mother, and drawled laconically,

"He just simply talks with those eyes!"

There was a moon on the night of the day that the Cherrys arrived. There was also music, the bi-weekly *serenata*[7] in the plaza fronting the governor's residence. The band swept sweetly into its opening number at the moment when Don Fernando, with Mrs. Cherry on his arm, stepped out upon his long balcony, and all the town began to move down there among the palms. Miss Cherry, who followed with Popo, exclaimed at the romantic strangeness of the scene, and you may be sure that a stir and buzzing passed through the crowd as it gazed up at the glittering coiffure and snowy shoulders of that angelic señorita from the United States.

Popo got her seated advantageously, and leaned with somewhat exaggerated gallantry over her chair, answering her vivacious questions, and feeling as one translated to another and far superior planet. He explained as well as he could the social conventions of the *serenata* as unfolded before their eyes in a concerted coil of languid movement—how the ladies, when the music begins, rise and promenade slowly around the kiosk of the band, and how the gentlemen form an outer wheel revolving in the reverse direction, with constant interplay of salutations, compliments, seekings, avoidings, coquetries, intrigues, and a thousand other manifestations of the mysterious forces of attraction and repulsion.

Miss Cherry conceived a strong desire to go down and become merged in that moving coil. No, she would not dream of dragging Doña Elvira or Leonor or mama from the dignified repose of the balcony; but she did beg the privilege, however unprecedented, of promenading with a young gentleman at her side, and showing the inhabitants how such things were managed in America—beg pardon, the United States.

So they walked, together under the palms, Alicia Cherry and Próspero Arriola, and although the youth's hat was in the air most of the time in acknowledgment of salutes, he did not really recognize those familiar and astonished faces, for his head was up somewhere near the moon, while his legs, in the proud shelter of their first trousers, were pleasantly afflicted with pins and needles as he moved on tiptoe beside the blonde Americana, a page beside a princess.

Miss Cherry was captivated by the native courtliness of his manners. She thought of a certain junior brother of her own, to whom the business of "tipping his hat,"[8] as he called it, to a lady occasioned such extreme anguish of mind that he would resort to the most laborious maneuvers to avoid occasions when the performance of that rite would be expected of him. As for Próspero, he had held tips of her fingers lightly as they had descended the marble steps of his father's house, and then with a charming little bow had offered her his arm, which she with laughing independence had declined. And now she perused with sidelong glances the infantile curve of his chin, the April fluctuations of his lips, the occasional quiver of his thick lashes, and decided that he was an amazingly cute little cavalier.

With a deep breath she expelled everything disagreeable from her mind, and gave up her spirit to the enjoyment of finding herself for a little while among a warmer, wilder people, with gallant gestures and languorous smiles. And the aromatic air, the tantalizing music, the watchful fire that glanced from under the sombreros of the peons[9] squatting in colorful lines between the benches—all the ardor and mystery of that unknown life caused a sudden fluttering in her breast, and almost unconsciously she took her escort's arm, pressing it impulsively to her side. His dark eyes flashed to hers, and for the first time failed to flutter and droop at the encounter; this time it was her own that lost courage and hastily veiled themselves.

"That waltz," she stammered, "isn't it delicious?"

He told her the name of the composer, and begged her to promise him the privilege of dancing that waltz with her at the ball, in two weeks' time. As she gave the promise, she perceived with amusement, and not without delight, that he trembled exceedingly.

Mrs. Cherry was a little rebellious when she and Alicia had retired to their rooms that night.

"Yes, I suppose it's all very beautiful and romantic," she responded fretfully to her daughter's panegyrics,[10] "but I'm bound to confess that I could do with a little less moonlight for the sake of a few words of intelligible speech."

"One always feels that way at first in a foreign country," said Alicia, soothingly, "and it certainly is splendid incentive to learn the language. You ought to adopt my plan, which is to study Spanish very hard every moment we're here."

"If you continue studying the language," her mother retorted, "as industriously as you have been doing to-night, my dear, you will soon be speaking it like a native."

Alicia was impervious to irony. Critically inspecting her own pink-and-gold effulgence in the mirror, she went on:

"Of course, this is also a splendid opportunity for Próspero to learn some real English, which will please the family very much, as they've decided to send him to an American college. I do hope it won't spoil him. Isn't he a perfect darling?"

"I don't know, not having been given a chance to exchange three words with—Sh-h! Did you hear a noise?"

It had sounded like a sigh, followed by a stealthy shuffle. Alicia went to the door, which had been left ajar, and looked out upon the moonlit gallery just in time to catch a glimpse of a fleeting figure, as Próspero raced for his English dictionary, to look up the strange word "darling."

"The little rascal!" she murmured to herself. "What a baby, after all!" But to her mother she only said, as she closed the door, "It was nothing, dear; just one of those biblical-looking servants covering a parrot's cage."

"Even the parrots here speak nothing but Spanish," Mrs. Cherry pursued fretfully. "Of course I am glad to sacrifice my own comfort to any extent to help your dear father in his schemes, although I do think the syndicate might make some graceful little acknowledgment of my social services; but I'm sure that papa never dreamed of your monopolizing the only member of this household to whom it is possible to communicate the most primitive idea without screaming one's head off. I am too old to learn to gesticulate, and I refuse to dislodge all my hairpins in the attempt. And as for your studies in Spanish," she continued warmly, as Alicia laughed, "I'd like to know how you reconcile that pretext with the fact that I distinctly heard you and that infant Lord Chesterfield[11] chattering away together in French."

"French does come in handy at times," Alicia purred, "and if you were not so shy about your accent, Mama dear, you could have a really good time with Doña Elvira. I must ask her to encourage you."

"Don't do anything of the kind!" Mrs. Cherry exclaimed. "You know perfectly well that my French is not fit for foreign ears. And I do think, Alicia, that you might try to make things as easy as possible for me, after my giving way to you in everything, even introducing you here under false pretenses, so to speak."

"It isn't a case of false pretenses, Mama. I've decided to resume my maiden name, and there was no necessity to enter into long explanations to these dear people, who, living as they do in a Catholic country, naturally know nothing about the blessings of divorce."

"So much the better for them!" retorted Mrs. Cherry. "However much of a blessing divorce may be, I've noticed that since you got your decree your face has not had one atom of real enjoyment in it until to-night."

"Until to-night!" Alicia echoed with a stoical smile. "And to-night, because you see a spark of reviving interest in my face, you try to extinguish it with reproaches!"

"No, no, my darling. Forgive me, I'm a little tired and nervous. And I can't help being anxious about you. It's a very trying position for a woman to be in at your age. It's trying for your mother, too. I could box that wretched Edward's ears."

"Not very hard, I'm thinking. You wanted me to forgive him."

"No, my dear, only to take him back on probation. We can punish men for their favorite sins much more effectually by not giving them their freedom."

"I couldn't be guilty of that meanness, and I shall never regret having shown some dignity. And I think that closes the subject, doesn't it, dearest?" Alicia yawned.

"Poor Edward!" her mother persisted. "How he would have enjoyed this picturesque atmosphere with you!"

Alicia calmly creamed her face.

Próspero spent a great part of the night over his English dictionary. Again and again he conned[12] the Spanish equivalents listed against that word "darling." A significant word, it seemed, heart-agitating, sky-transporting. He had not dreamed that the harsh, baffling English language could contain in seven letters a treasure so rare. *Predilecto, querido, favorito, amado*[13]—which translation should he accept as defining his relation to Mees Cherry, avowed by her own lips? The patient compiler of that useful book could never have foreseen the ecstasy it would one day bring to a Mexican boy's heart.

He was living in a realm of enchantment. To think that already, on the very day of their meeting, he and his blonde Venus should have arrived at intimacies far transcending any that are possible in Mexico except between the wedded or the wicked! In stark freedom, miraculously unchaperoned, they had talked together, walked together, boldly linked their very arms! In his ribs he still treasured the warmth of her; in his fingers throbbed the memory that for one electric instant their hands had fluttered, dove-like, each to each. Small enough, those tender contacts; yet by such is the life force unchained: Popo found himself looking into a seething volcano, which was his own manhood. That discovery, conflicting as it did with the religious quality of his love, disturbed him greatly. Sublimely he invoked all his spiritual strength to subdue the volcano. And his travail was richly rewarded. The volcano became transformed magically into a fount of pellucid purity in which, bathing his exhausted soul, young Popo became a saint.

In that interesting but arduous capacity he labored for many days, during which Miss Cherry created no further occasion for their being alone together, but seemed to throw him in the way of her mama, a trial which he endured with fiery fortitude. He was living the spiritual life with rigorous intensity, a victim of the eternal mandate that those fountains of purity into which idealism has power to transform the most troublesome of volcanoes should be of a temperature little short of the boiling-point.

His dark eyes kept his divinity faithfully informed of his anguish and his worship, and her blue ones discreetly accepted the offering. Once or twice their hands met lightly, and it seemed that the shock might have given birth to flaming worlds. When alone with her mama, Alicia showed signs of an irritable ardor which Mrs. Cherry, with secret complacency, set down to regrets for the too hastily renounced blessings of matrimony.

"Poor old Ned!" the mother sighed one night. "Your father has seen him, and tells me that he looks dreadful."

On the morning of the night of the ball the entire party, to escape from the majordomo[14] and his gang of hammering decorators, motored into the country on a visit to Popo's grandmother, whose house sheltered three priests and a score of orphan girls, and was noted for its florid magnificence of the Maximilian period.[15]

Popo hoped that some mention might be made in Alicia's hearing of his grandmother's oft-expressed intention to bequeath the place to him, and he was much gratified when the saintly old lady, who wore a mustache _á la española_,[16] brought up the subject, and dilated upon it at some length, telling Popo that he must continue to make the house blessed by the presence of the three padres, but that she would make provision for the orphans to be taken elsewhere, out of his way, a precaution she mentioned to an accompaniment of winks and innuendos which greatly amused all the company, including the padres, only Alicia and Popo showing signs of distress.

After dinner, which occurred early in the afternoon, Popo maneuvered Alicia apart from the others in the garden. His eyes telegraphed a desperate plea, to which hers consented, and he took her by the hand, and they ran through a green archway into a terraced Italian garden peopled with marble nymphs and fauns, from which they escaped by a little side gate into an avenue of orange-blossoms. Presently they were laboring over rougher ground, where their feet crushed the fat stems of lilies, and then they turned and descended a roughly cut path winding down the scarred, dripping face of a cliff into the green depth of a little cañon, at the upper end of which a cascade resembling a scarf flung over a wall sang a song of eternity, and baptized the tall tree-ferns that climbed in disorderly rivalry for its kisses.

Alicia breathed deeply the cool, moss-scented air. The trembling boy, suddenly appalled at the bounty of life in presenting him with his sovereign concatenation of the hour, the place, and the woman, could only stammer irrelevantly, as he switched at the leaves with his cane:

"There is a cave in there behind the waterfall. One looks through the moving water as through a thick window, but one gets wet. Sometimes I come here alone, all alone, without going to the house, and _mamagrande_[17] never knows. The road we came by passes just below, crossing this little stream, where thou didst remark the tall bamboos before we saw the porter's lodge. The mud wall is low, and I tie my horse in the bamboo thicket."

"Why do you come here?" she asked, her eyes tracing the Indian character[18] in the clear line of his profile and the dusky undertone of his cheek.

"It is my caprice to meditate here. From my childhood I have loved the *cañon-cito*[19] in a peculiar way. Thou wilt laugh at me—no? Well, I have always felt a presence here, unseen, a very quiet spirit that seemed to speak to me of—*¿quien sabe?*[20] I never knew—never until now."

His voice thrilled, and his eyes lifted themselves to hers, as if for permission, before he continued in ringing exaltation:

"Now that thou hast come, now that thou appearest here in all thy lovely splendor, now I know that the spirit I once felt and loved in secret was a prophecy of thee. Yes, Alicia mine, for thee this place has waited long—for thee, thou adored image of all beauty, queen of my heart, object of my prayers, whose purity has sanctified my life."

Alicia, a confirmed matinée girl,[21] wished that all her woman friends might have seen her at that moment (she had on a sweet frock and a perfectly darling hat), and that they might have heard the speech that had just been addressed to her by the leading man. He was a thorough juvenile, to be sure, but he had lovely, adoring eyes and delightfully passionate tones in his voice; and anyhow, it was simply delicious to be made love to[22] in a foreign language.

She was extremely pleased, too, to note that her own heart was going pitapat in a fashion quite uncomfortable and sweet and girly. She wouldn't have missed that sensation for a good deal. What a comfort to a bruised heart to be loved like this! He was calling her his saint. If that Edward could only hear him! Perhaps, after all, she *was* a saint. Yes, she felt that she certainly was, or could be if she tried. Now he was repeating some verses that he had made to her in Spanish. Such musical words! One had to come to the hot countries to discover what emotion was; and as for love-making! How the child had suffered!

As he bowed his bared head before her she laid her hands, as in bene-diction, where a bronze light glanced upon the glossy, black waves of his hair; and that touch, so tender, felled Popo to the earth, where he groveled with tears and broken words and kisses for her little shoes, damp from the spongy soil. And she suddenly dropped her posings and her parasol, and forgot her complexion and her whalebones,[23] and huddled down beside him in the bracken, hushing his sobs and wiping his face, with sweet epithets and sweeter assurances, finding a strange, wild comfort in mothering him recklessly, straight from the soul. At the height of which really promising situation she was startled by a familiar falsetto hail from her mama as the rest of the party descended into the *cañoncito*, whither it had been surmised that Popo had conducted Miss Cherry.

After flinging an artless yodel in response to the maternal signal, and while composing Popo and herself into lifelike attitudes suggestive of a mild absorp-tion in the beauties of nature, she whispered in his ear:

"The next time you come here you shall have two horses to tie in the bamboos."

"*Ay Dios!* All blessings on thee! But when?" he pleaded. "Tell me when!"

"Well, to-morrow," she replied after a quick thought; "as you would say, my dear, *mañana*. Yes, I'll manage it. I'm dying for a horseback ride, and I've had such a lovely time to-day."

To be the only blonde at a Mexican ball is to be reconciled for a few hours to the fate of being a woman. Alicia, her full-blown figure habited in the palest of pink, which seemed of the living texture of her skin, with a generous measure of diamonds winking in effective constellations upon her golden head and dazzling bosom, absorbed through every pore the enravished admiration of the beholders, and beneficently poured it forth again in magnetic waves of the happiness with which triumph enhances beauty. Popo almost swooned with rapture at this apotheosis[24] of the being who, a few hours earlier, had actually hugged him in the arms now revealed as those of a goddess. And to-morrow! With swimming brain he repeated over and over, as if to convince himself of the incredible, "*Mañana!*"

Almost as acute as the emotions of Popo, in a different way, were those of a foreign gentleman who had just been presented to the governor by the newly arrived Mr. Montague Cherry. So palpably moved was the stranger at the sight of Alicia that Mrs. Cherry laid a soothing hand on his arm and whispered a conspirator's caution. Presently he and Alicia stood face to face. Had they been Mexican, there would have ensued an emotional and edifying scene. But all that Alicia said, after one sharp inspiration of surprise, was, with an equivocal half-smile:

"Why, Edward! Of all people!"

And the gentleman addressed as Edward, finding his voice with difficulty, blurted out hoarsely:

"How are you, Alicia?"

At which Alicia turned smilingly to compliment Doña Elvira on the decorations.

Mr. Edward P. Winterbottom was one of those fortunate persons who seem to prefigure the ideal toward which their race is striving. A thousand conscientious draftsmen, with that national ideal in their subconsciousness, were always hard at work portraying his particular type in various romantic capacities, as those of foot-ball hero, triumphant engineer, "well-known clubman,"[25] and pleased patron of the latest collar, cigarette, sauce, or mineral water. Hence he would give you the impression of having seen him before somewhere under very admirable auspices. Extremely good-looking, with long legs, a magnificent chin, and an expression of concentrated manhood, he had every claim to be classed as "wholesome," cherishing a set of opinions suitable to his excellent station in life, a proper reverence for the female of the species, and an adequate working assortment of simple emotions easily predicable by a reasonably clever woman. Of the weaknesses common to humanity he had fewer than the majority, and in the prostration of remorse and desire in which he now presented himself to Alicia he seemed to offer timber capable of being made over into a prince of lifelong protectors.

Alicia had come to feel that she needed a protector, chiefly from herself. Presently, without committing herself, however, she favored him with a waltz. As they started off, she saw the agonized face of Popo, who had been trying to reach her. She threw him a smile, which he lamentably failed to return. Not until then did she identify the music as that of the waltz she had promised him on the night of that first *serenata*. After it was over she good-naturedly missed a dance or two in search of him, meaning to make amends; but he was nowhere to be found.

With many apologies, Doña Elvira mentioned to Alicia, when she appeared the following morning, that the household was somewhat perturbed over the disappearance of Próspero. No one could remember having seen him since early in the progress of the ball. He had not slept in his bed, and his favorite horse was missing from the stable. Don Fernando had set the police in motion. Moreover, *la mamagrande*, informed by telephone, was causing masses to be said for the safety of her favorite. God would undoubtedly protect him, and meanwhile the honored señorita and her mama would be so very gracious as to attribute any apparent neglect of the canons of hospitality to the anxieties of an unduly affectionate mother.

Alicia opened her mouth to reply to that tremulous speech, but finding no voice, turned and bolted to her room, trying to shut out a vision of a slender boy lying self-slain among the ferns where he had received caresses and whispers of love from a goddess of light fancy and lighter faith. She had no doubt that he was there in his *cañoncito*. But perhaps he yet lived, waiting for her! She would go at once. Old Ned should escort her as far as the bamboos, to be within call in case of the worst.

Old Ned was so grateful for the privilege of riding into the blossoming country with his Alicia that she rewarded him with a full narration of the Popo episode; and he received the confidence with discreet respect, swallowing any qualms of jealousy, and extolling her for the high-minded sense of responsibility which now possessed her to the point of tears.

"It's all your fault, anyway," she declared as they walked their horses up a long hill.

He accepted the blame with alacrity as a breath of the dear connubial days.

"One thing I've demonstrated," she continued fretfully, "and that is that the summer flirtation of our happy land simply cannot be acclimated south of the Rio Grande. These people lack the necessary imperturbability of mind, which may be one good reason why they're not permitted to hold hands before the marriage ceremony. To complicate matters, it seems that I'm the first blonde with the slightest claim to respectability that ever invaded this part of Mexico, and although the inhabitants have a deluded idea that blue eyes are intensely spiritual, they get exactly the same Adam-and-Eve palpitations from them that we do from the lustrous black orbs of the languishing tropics."

"Did you—ah—did you get as far as—um—kissing?" Mr. Winterbottom inquired, with an admirable air of detachment.

"Not quite, Edward; that was where the rest of the folks came tagging along. But I promise you this: if I find that Popo alive, I'm going to kiss him for all I'm worth. The unfortunate child is entitled to nothing less."

"But wouldn't that—hum—add fuel to the flame?" he asked anxiously.

"It would give him back his self-respect," she declared. "It isn't healthy for a high-spirited boy to feel like a worm."

Mr. Winterbottom, while waiting among the bamboos in company with three sociable horses—Popo's was in possession when they arrived,—smoked one very long cigar and chewed another into pulpy remains. Alicia not having yodeled, he understood that she had found the boy alive, and he tried to derive comfort from that reflection. He had promised to preserve patience and silence, and such was his anxiety to propitiate Alicia that he managed to subjugate his native energy, although the process involved the kicking up of a good deal of soil. She reflected, when she noted on her return his carefully cheerful expression, that a long course of such discipline would go far toward regenerating him as a man and a husband.

"Well, how is our little patient today?" he inquired with gentle jocosity as he held the stirrup for her.

"I believe he'll pull through now," Alicia responded gravely, "I've sent him up to his grandmother's to be fed, and he's going to telephone his mother right away."

"That's bully,"[26] Mr. Winterbottom pronounced heartily; and for some moments, as they gained the road, nothing more was said. Alicia seemed thoughtful. Mr. Winterbottom was the first to speak.

"Poor little beggar must have been hungry," he hazarded.

"He had eaten a few bananas, but as they're not recognized as food here, they only increased his humiliation. You know, banana-trees are just grown to shade the coffee-plants, which are delicate."

Mr. Winterbottom signified a proper interest in that phase of coffee culture, and Alicia took advantage of a level stretch of road to put her horse to the gallop. When he regained her side, half a mile farther on, he was agitated.

"Alicia, would you mind enlightening me on one point?" he asked. "Did you—give him back his self-respect?"

"Perhaps I'd better tell you all that happened, Edward."

"By Jove! I wish you would!" he cried earnestly.

"Well, Popo wasn't a bit surprised to see me. In fact, he was expecting me."

"Indeed? Hadn't lost his assurance, then."

"He had simply worked out my probable actions, just as I had worked out his. Of course he looked like a wild thing, hair on end, eyes like a panther, regular young bandit. Well, I rag-timed up[27] in my best tra-la-la style, but he halted me with a splendid gesture, and started a speech. You know what a command of language foreigners have, even the babies. He never fumbled for a word, and all his nouns had verbs waiting, and the climaxes just rolled over one another like waves. It was beautiful."

"But what was it about?"

"Me, of course: my iniquity, the treacherous falseness residing as ashes in the Dead Sea fruit[28] of my beauty, with a lurid picture of the ruin I had made of his belief in woman, his capacity for happiness, and all that. And he wound up with

Drawn by F. Luis Mora

"'"WELL, I RAG-TIMED UP IN MY BEST TRA-LA-LA STYLE, BUT HE HALTED
ME WITH A SPLENDID GESTURE, AND STARTED A SPEECH"'"

Illustration from María Cristina Mena, "The Education of Popo," *Century Magazine* 87 (March 1914).

a burst of denunciation in which he called me by a name which ought not to be applied to any lady in any language."

"Alicia!"

"Oh, I deserved it, Edward, and I told him so. I didn't care how badly he thought of me if I could only give him back his faith in love. It's such a wonderful thing to get *that* back! So I sang pretty small about myself; and when I revealed my exact status as an ex-wife in process of being courted by her divorced husband, his eyes early dropped out of his head. You see, they don't play 'Tag! You're it!' with marriage down here. That boy actually began to hand me out a line of missionary talk. He thinks I ought to remarry you, Ned."

"He must have splendid instincts, after all. So of course you didn't kiss him?"

"Wait a minute. After mentioning that I was eleven years older than he, and that my hair had been an elegant mouse-drab before I started touching it up—"

"Not at all. I liked its color—a very pretty shade of—"

"After that, I told him that he could thank his stars for the education I had given him, in view of the fact that he's going to be sent to college in the U.S.A., and I gave him a few first-rate pointers on the college widow breed.[29] And finally,

Ned, I put it to him that I was anxious to do the square thing, and if he considered himself entitled to a few kisses while you were waiting, he could help himself."

"And he?" Mr. Winterbottom inquired with a pinched look.

"He looked so cute that I could have hugged him. But he nobly declined."

"That young fellow," said Mr. Winterbottom, taking off his hat, and wiping his brow, "is worthy of being an American."

"Why, that was his Indian revenge,[30] the little monkey! But he was tempted, Ned."

"Of course he was. If you'd only tempt *me!* O Alicia, you're a saint!"

"That's what Popo called me yesterday, and it was neither more nor less true than what he called me today. I suppose we're all mixtures of one kind and another. And I've discovered, Ned, that it's the healthiest kind of fun to be perfectly frank with—with an old pal. Let's try it that way next time, shall we, dear?"

She offered her lips for the second time that day, and—

NOTES

1. A married woman (Spanish).
2. Gentleman (Spanish).
3. At this time, a boy wearing stockings signified that he was not yet considered an adult.
4. Lady (Spanish).
5. "Yankees" is a term used in many Spanish-speaking countries to refer to people from the United States; it usually possesses a negative connotation.
6. The Virgin Mary, mother of Jesus.
7. A performance of vocal or instrumental music in the open air, intended to enchant and please its listeners (Spanish).
8. The act of raising one's hat slightly. At this time men were expected to use this respectful gesture when greeting a woman.
9. A poor, unskilled laborer.
10. A speech praising a person or thing.
11. Philip Stanhope, the fourth Earl of Chesterfield (1694–1773). After his death, a poor relative compiled a book consisting of more than four hundred of the Earl's private letters written over a thirty year span and published them as *Letters to His Son on the Art of Becoming a Man of the World and a Gentleman* (1774); this book, regarded as offering sound advice to young men who aspired to worldly success, was quite popular.
12. To study and learn something by repetition.
13. Spanish synonyms for "darling": "preferred," "loved," "favorite," and "beloved," respectively.
14. The head servant of a household (anglicized version of Spanish and Italian terms).
15. The French emperor Napoleon III named Maximilian, archduke of Austria, to the post of emperor of Mexico in 1863; he served in this position until his execution by Mexican soldiers in 1867.
16. In the Spanish style (Spanish).
17. Grandmother (Spanish).

18. This indicates Popo is of mixed Spanish and Indigenous (here referred to as "Indian") ancestry.
19. Small canyon (Spanish).
20. Who knows? (Spanish).
21. Someone who enjoys going to lots of matinée performances of plays, which during this time period typically involved a heterosexual romance.
22. At this time, "to make love to someone" meant simply to court that person with romantic interest and attention.
23. Whalebones were used to stiffen a woman's corset, which was worn under a dress in order to shrink the woman's waistline.
24. Elevation to the status of a divine being.
25. A member of a socioeconomically elite men's club that included dining rooms, a library, gaming rooms, etc.
26. A British term meaning "Great!"
27. Ragtime music is lively and jaunty.
28. Something that appears beautiful and wonderful but is actually quite insubstantial and disappointing.
29. A young woman who dates successive male college students. After they graduate, she is temporarily a "widow."
30. This is meant to suggest that he is being a little "savage" ("Indian") in withholding his kiss from her; today such a stereotype would be deemed offensive.

HANNAH LLOYD NEALL

(1817–1912)

Hannah Lloyd was a member of a prominent Quaker family from Philadelphia, but in 1852 she gave up the privileged life in which she had been raised to marry fellow Quaker James Neall and move far away with him to the then undeveloped state of California. When Hannah Lloyd Neall first arrived in San Francisco in March 1853, she did not anticipate staying very long, but her husband's various business ventures and the birth of two children served as anchors to keep her there and never return to live in Philadelphia. While James's businesses struggled—at one point he had to relocate his family from San Francisco to the small town of Auburn, California, in the Sierra foothills—Hannah not only became active in the suffrage movement but also started to write and publish her poetry and short stories, in part to supplement the family's income. She was encouraged in her efforts by no less a personage than Thomas Starr King (1824–64), the famous Unitarian minister whose fiery sermons have been credited as one of the major reasons California remained on the Union side during the Civil War.

   Only a few of Lloyd Neall's literary efforts were ever published, and chiefly in the *Overland Monthly* magazine, founded in 1868 by Anton Roman to prove to all Americans—especially those on the East Coast—that California possessed not only material wealth but also a culture worthy of respect. Indeed, Bret Harte, the magazine's first editor, as well as its most famous contributor, published some of his most famous stories and poems in the *Overland Monthly* before he left for the East in late 1871 (as editor, he likely was responsible for accepting "Placer" for publication in the October 1871 issue). Harte and those editors who followed him actively sought submissions from talented West Coast authors; Lloyd Neall would have been attracted not only by the opportunity to earn money from selling her writing to the magazine but also by the possibility of representing her adopted region to people such as the relatives and friends she had left behind years before in Philadelphia. Her stories "Spilled Milk" (1870), "Placer" (1871), and "Patty Dree, Schoolmarm" (1872) all deal with aspects of life in California during this period.

"Placer" very pointedly deals with the clash of values between those raised to cherish the type of civilization practiced among genteel easterners and those who believed the former group's beliefs and practices needed to adapt to the conditions found in California. It likely draws on Lloyd Neall's personal experience living in Auburn, a small mining community in the Sierras, far away from her former abodes in Philadelphia and San Francisco and what she would have regarded as "civilization." Possibly of greatest interest to modern readers is the way it deals with racial issues. Having grown up in a family of Quakers during the early part of the nineteenth century, Lloyd Neall would have been very familiar with that religious group's core belief in the divinity and equality before God of all human beings, no matter their gender or their race. Indeed, Quaker adherence to these tenets formed the foundation for the work of many of the faith's prominent members fighting for gender and racial justice, especially the broad antebellum movement calling on the country to abolish slavery.

"Placer" offers a nuanced narrative that challenges yet also confirms the beliefs of many White Americans about Native Americans. At times it appears to satirize the religious hypocrisy and racism of the main character, Esther Hamilton, but in other places it traffics in racial stereotypes. In doing so, it highlights the limitations of even the most well-intentioned White middle-class writers of the period, as well as the White editors of the country's major magazines and most of their readers.

*Readers should be aware that this story includes some language which, while commonly used during this time period, is no longer considered acceptable because of its offensive nature.

PLACER (1871)

I

"Esther, my dear, here is a present for you," said John Hamilton to his wife, carefully placing on the floor a huge bundle, wrapped in a shaggy, tan-colored blanket, not altogether immaculate in the matter of cleanliness. Esther responded

with, "Oh, thank you, John!"—supposing it to be the long-coveted buff and gold
tea-set—adding, "It is so kind in you to bring it yourself, instead of trusting it to
the tender mercies of that careless carrier."

But a sudden movement of the bundle, and a cry proceeding from somewhere
in the middle of it, caused her to start from rather than toward it, exclaiming,
"Mercy! John Hamilton, is it alive?"

"Certainly, my dear, it is alive; and what is more, it will soon be kicking." And
he proceeded gently to unfold the blanket, revealing to the astonished gaze of
Esther a Digger Indian[1] papoose.

The mop of coarse, black hair, the deep-set eyes, the tawny, grimy skin of
the bare-legged creature, suggested any thing rather than a human being. And
Esther shrank away with disgust and repugnance, culminating in aversion, as she
caught a glimpse of the crawling wonders, defying concealment, which doubtless
had been the cause of its uneasiness.

"Take it away at once; I will not have it in the house. How could you be so
cruel, John?" And the voice of the neat little housewife quivered with anger and
tears.

"It has nowhere to go, my dear," said bland and provoking John. "To take it
away means starvation, cold, and death."

"Where in the world did you get it? You are always picking up trash of some
kind, and have any amount of rusty treasures now that I should be glad to throw
in the fire."

"This among them?" questioned John.

"Nonsense! But I really can not have that thing in the house. Who is to take
care of it? I'd rather have a young cinnamon bear."[2]

"Esther Hamilton, have you no bowels of compassion? Of what avail are
all the humanitarian ideas you have been inculcating by precept, if they fail
you when the time comes for their exercise? I have heard you say repeatedly,
that every human creature was endowed with God-given faculties, which needed
only development and proper training to produce a Christian. Where is the benevolence that constituted you a member of every moral reform society in the
past, from anti-slavery down to the prevention of cruelty to animals? Now, here
is a human soul—"

"Oh, bother, John! Don't preach. I am not going to have that Digger baby,
all over filth, in my house; so you can just take it to some squaw.[3] There is the
spade, you can shovel it up; and do not come near me again till you have had a
drenching shower-bath."

"Esther, my dear—"

"Do not 'Esther, my dear,' me. I never could endure Indians. They have
none of the attributes novelists ascribe to them, and the historian who writes of
them should live among them to ascertain that the 'noble Red Man'[4] is a mean,
thieving, revengeful scoundrel, far below the grade of the most indifferent white
human," and Esther began to pat sleek-haired Fidelle, who barked furiously at
the miserable little specimen of our aborigines on the floor.

John Hamilton had calculated upon the charity and tenderness of his wife, when a wretched squaw, dying by the road-side, had implored him, with the instinct of maternity strong in death, to take her papoose. Dismounting from his horse, he had scarcely lifted the child away from the stiffening arms of its mother, when, with a gasp, she died, and he found himself, perforce, obliged either to abandon it or to take it home.

The Diggers generally collect in the autumn from remote localities, and concentrate near some village, gathering acorns; buying salt fish, whisky, and whatever else their scanty means affords; begging, pilfering, and, in a week or two, closing up their annual meeting by a grand fandango, preparatory to migrating, in small companies, to any spot where timber and water will supply them with fuel and serve their necessities. The burdens are strapped upon the backs of their women, and these toil in weariness, and almost nakedness, up and down steep hills, through ravines, and across swollen streams, seldom resting by the way, till the tents are pitched for the winter; their lords, meanwhile, leisurely riding on the bundle of bones, covered with a hide, they miscall a horse. The very aged or sick are often left behind, to linger out a miserable existence by begging, crawling under shelter of a hay-stack, or rooming in a hollow tree, or burrowing like animals in the earth till the rainy season is over. If they survive till spring, and are able to gather grasshoppers and worms, the healthy diet soon recuperates them, and they travel on to join their tribe, or await its return. Many of them, however, unable to help themselves, drift away unseen and unheard of, to the sunset land, and their skeletons, laid bare by the revealing winds, are all the records left of the poor creatures. The mother of the little Digger, now the subject of contest between John Hamilton and his wife, had probably been unable to travel with the tribe, and, deserted and alone, was kept alive only by the animal instinct of preservation for her child.

The face of John Hamilton was one which even a brute would appeal to, in the certainty of finding commiseration; and he was the owner of more lame dogs, lean cats, and wounded hares than his wife cared to number. She was naturally sympathetic toward all phases of suffering, but the universal benevolence of her easy-going husband had slightly acidulated, if not curdled, the milk of human kindness in her nature; and there is something so uncanny and revolting about the Digger tribes, that it requires a strong amalgam of generosity to concentrate the gold of benevolence toward them.

It was a raw, chill evening, peculiarly Californian; for, notwithstanding the generally halcyon character ascribed to the climate by travelers, who brace themselves during a few weeks of relaxation by the salt breezes by the Bay, or the more exhilarating influences of the rarified mountain air, permanent residents cautiously admit that a few months in the year are far from heavenly; and the shivering oldest-inhabitant, dating from '49,[5] will occasionally indulge in expletives of ungentle force in alluding to certain days preceding the setting in of the rainy season, when the sky is veiled in clouds which never reveal a silver lining, and the bare hills brood moodily under a covering which is unflecked with sunshine and shadow. Dull, raw, and cold, such days have not the snap of frost to redeem their cheerless monotony, nor the whiteness of snow to cover their bleak inhospitality, yet are they ominous of the crystal blessing which makes February unequaled in any climate in the world.

John Hamilton looked from his helpless charge to his wife, not at all defeated by her protest, and having no idea of abandoning the little Digger to the tender mercies of the atmosphere. He knew Esther would relent. He was sure of her goodness and its ultimate exercises, and he was content to wait.

Whistling to amuse the baby and keep up his courage, he leisurely took the spade, and with a "here goes, then," carefully lifted his present upon it, and with a courtly bow, approached Esther, saying, "Now, my dear, you can have it served either like John the Baptist's head,[6] or whole, for we must either kill or keep it. If you decide upon the former alternative, it must be speedily dispatched, for I am too tender-hearted to let the little creature perish with either cold or hunger."

The baby, so far from being disconcerted by its iron seat, smiled in Esther's face, and held out its skinny hands to her, as its mother had done to her husband.

A glance between them, laughter and tears, and the matter was settled.

"Have it washed, then, and I will keep it for the present."

To put it, blanket and all, into a warm bath, was the work of a few moments. To shear its locks fell to the lot of Sandy Crup, a shock-headed[7] biped, whose paramount excellence consisted in being endowed with "faculty"; for nothing was out of the line of his skill; and under his manipulations the papoose began to look almost as human as Fidelle, who condescended to sniff at it with a disdainful air of superiority.

There are many men and women, theoretically benevolent, whose purse-strings are more easily relaxed than the tenacious threads which hold in check their self-abnegation.

Esther Hamilton was one of the women whose theory of benevolence had been so continually exercised so as to have given her the reputation of more than average self-sacrifice. She had the advantage, also, of *not* having the outward appearance of a female iconoclast. She never robed herself in unbecoming drapery, and was unconscious of green spectacles and the abomination of cropped hair. Her manners were genial and pleasant, and she deserved the character she had so long held, of being thoroughly good. But missionary work of all kinds, performed amid the pleasant social combinations, which are often so efficient, is far from calling for that absolute surrender of one's own personality, which attends it when individual effort only is required.

This little one could, in a city, have been turned over to a foundling asylum, and perhaps have become quite a pet and the rage among lady managers, and the recipient of generous bounty from the visitor introduced to it, as a California curiosity. But apart from all such means of educating it into membership with its kindred of higher races, Esther felt that she must grapple alone with her problem, and bring into active exercise her especial theory of development; for the isolation of her mountain home precluded the possibility of a sharer in her responsibility.

She looked upon the unwelcome addition to her family with the same emotions of pity she would have felt for a forlorn dog, forsaken and hungry, and was willing to extend toward it the same comfort of food and shelter. But had she not (as her husband had remind her) asserted that to be human was to be susceptible of recipiency, at least; and that education and culture were alone needed to place the races of humanity on a par with each other?

She thought over these things with vexation of spirit. To be brought to the trial of putting one's theories into instant exercise is rather a severe ordeal; but Esther nerved herself for the task.

"No; I will not cast out this perishing human soul," she said. "I will struggle, at least, to mold it into the beautiful likeness of its divine originator;" and taking the poor, skinny babe in her arms, now wrapped in clean garments of her own, she laid it across her lap. Fidelle sprang furiously at the stranger usurping his place, and with angry leaps tried to displace the baby from the soft warmth of a seat so long his own. Nor would he suffer Esther to lift him beside the child. He slunk away, whining piteously; and thereafter, unless the Digger was entirely out of sight, refused the caresses she had lavished so abundantly upon him. Sandy Crup volunteered to take charge of the foundling at night, and Esther heard the good-natured fellow lulling it with a "rock-a-by, baby," as he sat beside the kitchen-fire. Her trials came with the morning.

"This wretched thing will neither drink milk nor eat spoon-victuals, John; what shall I do with it?"

"Call Sandy," suggested John, which certainly was an inspiration, for Sandy's idea was prompt and to the point.

"Get a goat, marm—"

"What, and let it feed itself?"

"Yes'm. I've know'd young uns raised in that way. This un's a half animal, and I shouldn't wonder ef a goat would prewail, where nothin' else couldn't."

Sandy's advice was acted upon at once, Esther saying, "Now, John, you have brought this baby. You must get it a nurse. I have concluded to take a goat."

"Whew!"

"Yes; and that is not all. It must be vaccinated at once."

"What, the goat?"

"No; the Digger. And I want it baptized, and some red flannel."

John jotted on his fingers. "The minister and some red flannel, vaccine and a goat; anything else?"

The little papoose greedily adopted its nurse, and contentedly slept on the warmth of its shaggy skin—creeping after it on all fours, and uttering a strange bleat in its absence. The gradual growth of the Digger baby from infancy to childhood was unlike that of other children. It disliked the fondling and dandling commonly bestowed upon infants, spurning playthings with fretful impatience. It was happy, surrounded by rabbits, cats, or dogs, and made unceasing efforts at friendliness with Fidelle, who invariably snarled at it. As the spring weather yielded to the summer heats, it would roll out to the low door-step, and thence to the soft earth, with a keen instinct of enjoyment and delight; its great, deep eyes peering curiously and unblinkingly sunward, and sometimes seeking those of Esther with eager, questioning looks, which its tongue refused to interpret.

"That child seems always to be asking for something, John. I am sure I do my duty by it. What *can* it want?"

"Do you love it?"

"I can not say I do; neither do I dislike it. But there is some want in its soul, young as it is, unsatisfied, and I can not fathom it."

"Bear with me, wife," said John, tenderly. "I think I can explain the great need of this poor, little waif. It craves mother-love. You are resolute in your sense of duty toward it, but you do not take it into your heart. You speak of it as an indifferent object—a mere *thing.* The goat and Fidelle are as much to you as the child. You have not even named it, for the baptism did not follow the vaccination. To call out the best and highest that is in it, *you must love it.*"

Esther made no reply. She felt that John was right. And as the little creature crept to his knee, he raised it—as he had often done—and held it quietly against his breast; for the little one had found the avenue to his heart, and clung to him with touching dependence and trust. A week after this conversation, the Rev. Arthur Atwill baptized the Indian child. John claiming it as a surface treasure, it was christened PLACER. This event took place in 1853.

II

Animal tendencies of unusual force, strong will, fierce passions, groveling tastes, were Nature's endowment of Esther Hamilton's charge; and repeatedly did she resolve to give up the "horrid little Digger," and assume only the pecuniary responsibility of its keeping, but as often she felt that this strange being was guarding her from her own besetting sins. For to be impatient or hasty with Placer, was to set at naught her own teachings; and the redeeming trait of unbounded affection in the child appealed powerfully to her heart. She manifested her joy at Esther's return, after a few hours' absence, with leapings and shouts of delight. Toward John the demonstration was more quiet, but not less earnest; and the large, wistful eyes would fix themselves upon his with awakening intelligence, as he taught her the meaning of simple words, or lured her to ask questions. For the first few years, objects perceptible to the senses, only, were explained, their uses revealed, and a clear conception of their meaning conveyed in concise words, which Placer readily repeated, and appeared to understand. But the irksomeness of restraint was apparent in every movement.

To keep shoes and stockings on her feet during the summer season, was an impossibility, and she would yell out her disapprobation, with sundry rebellious kicks to enforce it, and passionate tearings of her hair, pitiful to behold and exhausting to contend with.

"I never shall civilize this miserable thing, John! Do let us turn it out to grass. Such unreasoning rage is impossible to control, and I am ready to adopt the enlightened philosophy which places the lower orders in a descending scale toward the brute creation."

"But Darwin's theory of development, my dear, places them in an ascending scale—from the monkey, through the different grades of ape, baboon, and gorilla, till they touch humanity."[8]

"Oh, dear! I think Placer must be a young gorilla. If you had heard her terrific yells this morning, and seen her tear her hair and beat her hands, you would have believed she was one of Du Chaillu's importations[9] escaped from confinement. She even attempted to bite me."

"And how did your doctrine of moral suasion answer, my love?"

John's irony was the feather that broke the camel's back. Esther's flushed face and compressed lips threatened a civilized explosion of temper; but the finer forces of her nature conquered, though the struggle to maintain composure was severe and protracted. She left the room with decided step, and something of emphasis in her manner of closing the door; but as she passed the kitchen, she heard the nasal voice of Sandy Crup reading to the little Digger, and what he read was this: "He that ruleth his spirit, is better than he that taketh a city."[10]

"Come here, naughty little Placer, till I tell you what this means," said Sandy, laying down the book.

"I won't. I don't want to know. I hate every body," was the indignant response of the child. "I won't wear shoes; I won't go to Sunday-school; I won't be made a Christian of. I'd like to lick little Samuel; and those were good children that the bears ate up."[11]

"My, my! Here's Placer settin' at naught all that me an' Mis' Hamilton's bin teachin' her these years," said Sandy, softly. "What's to be did in the premises, ain't for me to determine. But, I reckon, she got all them buttin' propensities from that 'air goat what fetched her up. But me an' Mis' Hamilton ain't got to give in, that's certain, fur Mr. Hamilton he jest lets her alone."

Wise John Hamilton. How may sweet graces have been the fruits of the letting-alone system. "Don't do this," and "I'm ashamed of you," and "What will people say," and "Oh dear! what will become of you?" have been the sources of manifold wicked tendencies in the naturally perverse and rebellious heart; and a judicious letting-alone is often the most adroit management for an unruly temper.

"Wait a little," was the invariably gentle advice of John Hamilton, and by the time Waiting had had its perfect work, Patience was ready for hers, and the conquest was comparatively easy.

The especial cause of Placer's temper on the morning in question, was her aversion to the Sabbath-school drill for the yearly exhibition. Remarks touching her parentage, her nursing by the goat, and various other comments, had reached her ears and made her somewhat conspicuous. If there was any thing irksome to this child of nature, it was the stiffly-starched white dress which was the usual Sunday wear; and even the light hat that shielded her from the sun, was more frequently held by the strings, when out of sight of Mrs. Hamilton, than worn on her head. So that the robes in question were not, perhaps, the most alluring prospect for the little Indian, whose traditionary spirit-land is personal freedom and unlimited space.

"Oh, John, dear!" said Esther, "what a vixen I am. I actually shook Placer this morning and gave her a box on the ear, and then when you twitted me with my moral suasion doctrine, I felt *so* vexed. Do forgive me: I will try hard, in future, to be patient with our little charge."

"Forgive you, wife! I was just thinking I had imposed too heavy a burden upon you. I am out and about, and you have all the weariness, all the contest, and all the responsibility of poor Placer's training. It seems almost cruel; and yet I do love the little one, and could scarcely bear to give her up."

"Nor I. Nor do I intend to. I suppose you will laugh; but, do you know, despite her stealthy eating of grasshoppers and acorns, now and then—despite her inclination to inactivity, and her uncontrolled temper—I do believe we can win her to gentleness, and transform her into an interesting and noble woman. She has strong affections, as well as strong passions; keen perceptions, and ready intuitions; and with the help of Sandy and yourself, I am going to turn over a new leaf, and give up educating her on any *theory*—only following out the indexes leading to purity and truth in her own character."

"Good for you!" said John.

III

"It ain't no use to ask Mis' Hamilton. I'm sure certain she won't give no consent. She an' I's suffered enough by them Diggers now; and they can't camp down here."

"Wall, Sandy; who'd a thought you was that onfeelin'. Here's these poor critters, jes' wantin' a campin'-ground fur a little spell, an' you're so feeble-minded, you won't go an' ask Mister Hamilton to let 'em have that pastur-lot, down by the creek. You're swayed by petticoat gov'ment[12] altogether too much."

"That ain't so, Israel. Why don't you leave 'em have your own pastur? It's not nigh on to the house, while ourn is; an' ef you've so much charity fur Injuns, why all I've got to say, most likely you know where charity *begins.*"

"Ef they would'nt burn up the timber so, they might get into that piece of woodland t'other side; an' that's the best I kin du fur 'em," returned Israel, not noticing Sandy's proverbial hint.

"An' ef they want to shake our oaks, or gather them big snails alongside where the water's brought in on to the divide, I shouldn't mind. But I don't keer about ther bein' round here, along o' Placer."

"That's so, Sandy. I railly didn't think o' that; they might, meybe, steal her away, tho' she's got too big now."

Israel rode on, stopping, as he went, to tell Captain Tom—the Chief among the Diggers—that the tribe might camp in the woodland, "purviding the tember wa'ant teched"; a promise readily given, as there was plenty of dry, broken wood lying round for the present need of Tom and his tribe.

Placer had always wandered about, at her own will, during the hours not employed in study or household duties. Esther Hamilton had attempted to send her to the village school. But to the rude taunts of the boys, she had opposed such a ready aggressiveness, that she had pommeled more than one youngster into black-and-blue remembrance of her. And she was so continually getting into disgrace, for playing truant, that it was finally concluded to teach her at home. Many an evening did John Hamilton spend in directing her mental energies, at last awakening them to question—that being, perhaps, the best training a child can have, eagerness to learn following as a natural consequence; while Sandy Crup devoted hours to explaining, in his crude, yet original way, natural objects and spiritual philosophy. Esther taught the feminine grace of needlework, for which Placer expressed supreme contempt. She was permitted to roam anywhere within a half-dozen miles of the cottage, and often returned laden with wood-mosses and wild-blooms, fresh as when she started. But bare-footed she must and would go. It was pain enough to be compelled to be shod in the house. But out-doors, the soft turf, or the stony road, the long tunnel through the hills, or the surface diggings, often bore the impress of her broad foot; and if she could ride thus astride of Esther's pony, she was supremely happy.

During one of her rambles, Placer came suddenly upon the camping-ground of the Diggers. She knew she was an Indian, but had never realized the depths of degradation, or the squalid misery, from which she had been rescued. Occasionally she saw one or two of the tribe in the village, Mrs. Hamilton having been careful to keep her from their knowledge, lest they might claim her. But now they stood revealed in all their grimy triumph.

Placer stood at the entrance of the wood, looking upon the encampment. It was a warm, summer day, and the half-naked and dwarfish men and wholly nude children were lying about indolently under the trees or at the doors of the tents. An old and elfish-looking creature, smeared with pitch, and the horrible fatty compound constituting an Indian woman's mourning, was pounding a disgusting mass of grasshoppers and acorns in a circular stone, hollowed out like a bowl. Some younger ones were skinning a hare, and with unwashed hands tearing it apart. An iron pot was suspended between forked sticks over some glowing coals, and from this the men would occasionally dip a portion of its contents, passing the dirty tin-cup from one to the other. Rude and altogether repulsive was the scene; no adjuncts of wood or stream could soften the bare ugliness of these brute-like human creatures. They marred the sweet peace and loveliness of Nature with their harsh guttural sounds, and the discordant howl of their exhilarated moments was even more shocking to the poor child than their unmeaning words. The half-drunken laugh of the men frightened Placer; she shrank away unseen, with loathing of soul, and hastened, horror-stricken, home.

"And *I* am one of these! *I* belong to them!" came again and again from her lips, and out of their hearing she almost shrieked in her agony; for in that

moment the seeds which Esther Hamilton had planted quickened their germi-
nating forces, and closed over, in their sudden growth, the torn soil from whence
the weeds had been uprooted.

NOTES

1. A derogatory and offensive term commonly used by non-Native settlers and
   government officials in the mid to late nineteenth century to categorize Native
   Americans of all the various tribes in northern California as subhuman. Doing
   so was essential to justifying what the thousands of non-Native people flooding
   into the state did during and after the California gold rush of 1849: they stole
   land from many different Native American tribes; enslaved countless Native men,
   women, and children; trafficked thousands of young Native women; and killed a
   great many Native people for bounties.
2. A reddish variety of black bear.
3. A derogatory term commonly used by non-Native people at the time to refer to a
   Native American woman. It is now considered offensive and no longer used.
4. This term refers to the idealized Romantic notion that because Native Americans
   (the "savages") had not been exposed to the corrupting influence of European
   and American civilization, they should be regarded as "noble"; it is now recognized that using this condescending term to describe Native Americans justified
   White settlers' efforts to rob Native Americans of their lands.
5. The year of 1849 marked the high point of California's great gold rush, when
   great numbers of non-Native people came to California.
6. Mentioned in all four Gospels of the New Testament, John the Baptist is usually
   depicted as a martyr who is decapitated on the order of King Herod, and his
   head is brought in upon a platter.
7. Having a thick crop of hair.
8. In *The Descent of Man, and Selection in Relation to Sex,* published in England in March
   1871, only eight months before "Placer" appeared, English naturalist Charles
   Darwin applied the theory of evolution to human beings.
9. Paul Du Chaillu (ca. 1831–1903) was a French-American explorer who spent
   several years traveling in West Africa in the 1850s and was the first non-African
   to describe gorillas in detail, which caused him to become a sensation among the
   scientific elite; he brought numerous gorillas and other animals back to Europe
   from his travels.
10. Proverbs 16:32 (King James Version) reads: "He that is slow to anger is better
    than the mighty; and he that ruleth his spirit than he that taketh a city." This is
    usually taken to mean that to be a good Christian, one must control one's temper.
11. The prophet Samuel is a major figure in the Bible. In 2 Kings 2:23–24, a large
    group of children taunt the prophet Elisha, who in response curses them, and
    subsequently two bears appear and devour forty-two of the children.
12. "Petticoat government" was a colloquial reference to "rule by women" (who at
    the time wore petticoats under their dresses); it would appear, then, that the "Mis-
    ter" in the preceding line is a misprint, since the "Mis'" noted earlier clearly refers
    to "Missus" Hamilton.

FRANK NORRIS

(1870–1902)

Despite being born into a business-oriented, well-to-do family in 1870, Norris did not, as a young man, pursue any traditional type of success; instead, he lived a rather desultory, bohemian life and aspired to a career as an author, wishing to emulate two contemporary reporters turned successful writers, Richard Harding Davis and Stephen Crane. Believing that he needed to experience life in order to write about it, just as they had, Norris spent little time on his studies at the University of California, Berkeley, and at Harvard (he attended both these institutions from 1890 to 1895, but did not receive a degree from either); he subsequently went to South Africa for a short time as a newspaper reporter and after returning to the United States became an editor and staff writer for the *Wave*, a small San Francisco weekly publication with a limited regional audience.

In 1897, while working at the *Wave*, Norris dedicated himself to promoting San Francisco as a locale worthy of treatment by literary artists. To demonstrate the many different ways one could write about the city, Norris wrote and published numerous pieces in that magazine. One of these, "The House with the Blinds," appeared in the issue of August 21; it was later reprinted in the book collection *The Third Circle* (1909).

Shortly after publication of "The House with the Blinds," Norris moved to New York City, where for the next few years he worked for various publishing enterprises and turned his attention to writing novels; from 1898 to 1902 he published no fewer than six novels, as well as a great many important essays in literary criticism. Norris's prominent place in American literary history is due chiefly to his novel *McTeague: A Story of San Francisco* (1899), commonly regarded as one of the most important examples of Naturalistic fiction ever written. In this novel, which shocked many critics, Norris depicts many aspects of life among the city's lower-class residents that were deemed unwholesome by many Americans; indeed, in order to win the approval of his publisher, Norris was forced to excise one passage that was deemed offensive. Unfortunately, Norris's life and promising writing career were cut short when, in October 1902, he ignored his doctor's advice to have an appendectomy; despite emergency surgery a day later, Norris died from peritonitis at the young age of thirty-two.

THE HOUSE WITH THE BLINDS (1897)

It is a thing said and signed and implicitly believed in by the discerning few that this San Francisco of ours is a place wherein Things can happen. There are some cities like this—cities that have come to be picturesque—that offer opportunities in the matter of background and local color, and are full of stories and dramas and novels, written and unwritten. There seems to be no adequate explanation for this state of things, but you can't go about the streets anywhere within a mile radius of Lotta's fountain[1] without realizing the peculiarity, just as you would realize the hopelessness of making anything out of Chicago, fancy a novel about Chicago! or Buffalo, let us say, or Nashville, Tennessee. There are just three big cities in the United States that are "story cities"—New York, of course, New Orleans, and best of the lot, San Francisco.

Here, if you put yourself in the way of it, you shall see life uncloaked and bare of convention—the raw, naked thing, that perplexes and fascinates—life that involves death of the sudden and swift variety, the jar and shock of un-leased passions, the friction of men foregathered from every ocean, and you may touch upon the edge of mysteries for which there is no explanation—little eddies on the surface of unsounded depths, sudden outflashings of the inexplicable—troublesome, disquieting, and a little fearful.

About this "House With the Blinds" now.

If you go far enough afield, with your face towards Telegraph Hill, beyond Chinatown, beyond the Barbary Coast, beyond the Mexican quarter and Luna's restaurant, beyond even the tamale factory and the Red House,[2] you will come at length to a park in a strange, unfamiliar, unfrequented quarter. You will know the place by reason of a granite stone set up there by the Geodetic surveyors, for some longitudinal purposes of their own, and by an enormous flagstaff erected in the center. Stockton street flanks it on one side and Powell on the other. It is an Italian quarter as much as anything else, and the *Società Alleanza* holds dances in a big white hall hard by. The Russian Church, with its minarets (that look for all the world like inverted balloons) overlooks it on one side, and at the end of certain seaward streets you may see the masts and spars of wheat ships and the Asiatic steamers. The park lies in a valley between Russian and Telegraph Hills, and in August and early September the trades come flogging up from the bay, overwhelming one with sudden, bulging gusts that strike downward, blanket-wise and bewildering. There are certain residences here where, I am sure, sea-captains and sailing masters live, and on one corner is an ancient house with windows opening door-fashion upon a deep veranda, that was used as a custom office in Mexican times.[3]

I have a very good friend who is a sailing-master aboard the *Mary Baker*, a full-rigged wheat ship, a Cape Horner,[4] and the most beautiful thing I ever re-member to have seen. Occasionally I am invited to make a voyage with him as supercargo, an invitation which you may be sure I accept. Such an invitation came to me one day some four or five years ago, and I made the trip with him to Calcutta[5] and return.

The day before the *Mary Baker* cast off I had been aboard (she was lying in the stream off Meigg's wharf) attending to the stowing of my baggage and the appointment of my stateroom. The yawl[6] put me ashore at three in the after-noon, and I started home via the park I have been speaking about. On my way across the park I stopped in front of that fool Geodetic stone, wondering what it might be. And while I stood there puzzling about it, a nurse-maid came up and spoke to me.

The story of "The House With the Blinds" begins here.

The nurse-maid was most dreadfully drunk, her bonnet was awry, her face red and swollen, and one eye was blackened. She was not at all pleasant. In the baby carriage, which she dragged behind her, an overgrown infant yelled like a sabbath of witches.

"Look here," says she; "you're a gemmleman, and I wantcher sh'd help me outen a fix. I'm in a fix, s'w'at I am—a damn' bad fix."

I got that fool stone between myself and this object, and listened to it pouring out an incoherent tirade against some man who had done it dirt, b'Gawd, and with whom it was incumbent I should fight, and she was in a fix, 's'what she was, and could I, who was evidently a perfick gemmleman, oblige her with four bits?[7] All this while the baby yelled till my ears sang again. Well, I gave her four bits to get rid of her, but she stuck to me yet the closer, and confided to me that she lived in that house over yonder, she did—the house with the blinds, and was nurse-maid there, so she was, b'Gawd. But at last I got away and fled in the direction of Stockton street. As I was going along, however, I reflected that the shrieking infant was somebody's child, and no doubt popular in the house with the blinds. The parents ought to know that its nurse got drunk and into fixes. It was a duty—a dirty duty—for me to inform upon her.

Much as I loathed to do so, I turned towards the house with the blinds. It stood hard by the Russian Church, a huge white-painted affair, all the windows closely shuttered and a bit of stained glass in the front door—quite the most pretentious house in the row. I had got directly opposite, and was about to cross the street when, lo! around the corner, marching rapidly, and with blue coats flapping, buttons and buckles flashing, came a squad of three, seven, nine—ten policemen. They marched straight upon the house with the blinds.

I am not brilliant nor adventurous, but I have been told that I am good, and I do strive to be respectable, and pay my taxes and pew rent. As a corollary to this, I loathe with a loathing unutterable to be involved in a mess of any kind. The squad of policemen were about to enter the house with the blinds, and not for worlds would I have been found by them upon its steps. The nurse-girl might heave that shrieking infant over the cliff of Telegraph Hill, it were all one with me. So I shrank back upon the sidewalk and watched what followed.

Fifty yards from the house the squad broke into a run, swarmed upon the front steps, and in a moment were thundering upon the front door till the stained glass leaped in its leads and shivered down upon their helmets. And then, just at this point, occurred an incident which, though it had no bearing upon or connection with this yarn, is quite queer enough to be set down. The shutters of one of the top-story windows opened slowly, like the gills of a breathing fish, the sash rose some six inches with a reluctant wail, and a hand groped forth into the open air. On the sill of the window was lying a gilded Indian-club,[8] and while I watched, wondering, the hand closed upon it, drew it under the sash, the window dropped guillotine-fashion, and the shutters clapped to like the shutters of a cuckoo clock. Why was the Indian-club lying on the sill? Why, in Heaven's name, was it gilded? Why did the owner of that mysterious groping hand, seize upon it at the first intimation of danger? I don't know—I never will know. But I do know that the thing was eldritch[9] and uncanny, ghostly even, in the glare of that cheerless afternoon's sun, in that barren park, with the trade winds thrashing up from the seaward streets.

Suddenly the door crashed in. The policemen vanished inside the house. Everything fell silent again. I waited for perhaps fifty seconds—waited, watching and listening, ready for anything that might happen, expecting I knew not what—everything.

Not more than five minutes had elapsed when the policemen began to reappear. They came slowly, and well they might, for they carried with them the inert bodies of six gentlemen. When I say carried I mean it in its most literal sense, for never in all my life have I seen six gentlemen so completely, so thoroughly, so hopelessly and helplessly intoxicated. Well dressed they were, too, one of them even in full dress. Salvos of artillery could not have awakened that drunken half dozen, and I doubt if any one of them could even have been racked into consciousness.

Three hacks[10] appeared (note that the patrol-wagon was conspicuously absent), the six were loaded upon the cushions, the word was given and one by one the hacks rattled down Stockton street and disappeared in the direction of the city. The captain of the squad remained behind for a few moments, locked the outside doors in the deserted shuttered house, descended the steps, and went his way across the park, softly whistling a quickstep. In time he too vanished. The park, the rows of houses, the windflogged streets, resumed their normal quiet. The incident was closed.

Or was it closed? Judge you now. Next day I was down upon the wharves, gripsack in hand, capped and clothed for a long sea voyage. The *Mary Baker's* boat was not yet come ashore, but the beauty lay out there in the stream, flirting with a bustling tug that circled about her, coughing uneasily at intervals. Idle sailormen, 'longshoremen and stevedores sat upon the stringpiece of the wharf, chewing slivers and spitting reflectively into the water. Across the intervening stretch of bay came the noises from the *Mary Baker's* decks—noises that were small and distinct, as if heard through a telephone, the rattle of blocks, the straining of a windlass, the bos'n's whistle, and once the noise of sawing. A white cruiser sat solidly in the waves over by Alcatraz,[11] and while I took note of her the flag was suddenly broken out and I heard the strains of the ship's band. The morning was fine. Tamalpais[12] climbed out of the water like a rousing lion. In a few hours we would be off on a voyage to the underside of the earth. There was a note of gayety in the nimble air, and one felt that the world was young after all, and that it was good to be young with her.

A bum-boat[13] woman came down the wharf, corpulent and round, with a roll in her walk that shook first one fat cheek and then the other. She was peddling trinkets amongst the wharf-loungers—pocket combs, little round mirrors, shoe-strings and collar-buttons. She knew them all, or at least was known to all of them, and in a few moments she was retailing to them the latest news of the town. Soon I caught a name or two, and on the instant was at some pains to listen. The bum-boat woman was telling the story of the house with the blinds:

"Sax of um, an' nobs[14] ivry wan. But that bad wid bug-juice! Whoo! Niver have Oi seen the bate! An' divil a wan as can remimber owt for two days by, bory-eyed they were; struck dumb an' deef an' dead wid whiskey and bubble-wather. Not a manjack av um can tell the tale, but wan av um used his knife cruel bad. Now which wan was it? Howse the coort to find out?"

It appeared that the house with the blinds was, or had been, a gambling house, and what I had seen had been a raid. Then the rest of the story came out, and the mysteries began to thicken. That same evening, after the arrest of the six inebriates, the house had been searched. The police had found evidences of a drunken debauch of a monumental character. But they had found more. In a closet under the stairs the dead body of a man, a well dressed fellow—beyond a doubt one of the party—knifed to death by dreadful slashes in his loins and at the base of his spine in true evil hand-over-back fashion.

Now this is the mystery of the house with the blinds.

Beyond all doubt, one of the six drunken men had done the murder. Which one? How to find out? So completely were they drunk that not a single one of them could recall anything of the previous twelve hours. They had come out there with their friend the day before. They woke from their orgy to learn that one of them had worried him to his death by means of a short palm-broad dagger taken from a trophy of Persian arms that hung over a divan.

Whose hand had done it? Which one of them was the murderer? I could fancy them—I think I can see them now—sitting there in their cells, each man apart, withdrawn from his fellow-reveler, and each looking furtively into his fellow's face, asking himself, "Was it you? Was it you? or was it I? Which of us, in God's name, has done this thing?"

Well, it was never known. When I came back to San Francisco a year or so later I asked about the affair of the house with the blinds, and found that it had been shelved with the other mysterious crimes: The six men had actually been "discharged for the want of evidence."

But for a long time the thing harassed me. More than once since I have gone to that windy park, with its quivering flagstaff and Geodetic monument, and, sitting on a bench opposite the house, asked myself again and again the bootless questions. Why had the drunken nurse-maid mentioned the house to me in the first place? and why at that particular time? Why had she lied to me in telling me that she lived there? Why was that gilded Indian-club on the sill of the upper window? and whose—here's a point—whose was the hand that drew it inside the house? and then, of course, last of all, the ever-recurrent question, which one of those six inebriates should have stood upon the drop and worn the cap[15]—which one of the company had knifed his friend and bundled him into that closet under the stairs? Had he done it during the night of the orgy, or before it? Was his friend drunk at the time, or sober? I never could answer these questions, and I suppose I shall never know the secret of "The House With the Blinds."

A Greek family lives there now, and rent the upper story to a man who blows the organ in the Russian Church, and to two Japanese, who have a photograph gallery on Stockton street. I wonder to what use they have put the little closet under the stairs?

NOTES

1. An ornate iron fountain then—and still—located at the intersection of Market, Geary, and Kearny Streets in San Francisco. It was given to the city in 1875 by vaudeville performer Lotta Crabtree.
2. Specific places in San Francisco.
3. What is now the city of San Francisco began as a military post and mission built by the Spanish in 1776; after Mexico achieved independence from Spain in 1821, Mexico controlled the Bay. As early as 1835 the United States government tried to purchase the San Francisco Bay from Mexico, but its offer was declined. In 1846, after the Mexican-American War began, US military forces claimed the settlement of Yerba Buena (which the Americans renamed San Francisco), and in 1848 the entire state of California was officially ceded to the United States in the Treaty of Guadalupe Hidalgo.
4. A ship that, before the Panama Canal opened in 1914, regularly sailed from San Francisco to the East Coast of the United States by traveling around Cape Horn, located at the southern tip of South America.
5. Former spelling of Kolkata, India. The ship would not have gone around Cape Horn to make this voyage.
6. A small boat, usually with four to six oars, designed to shuttle people and goods between shore and a large ship.
7. Fifty cents.
8. Named by nineteenth-century British colonists who encountered them on the Indian subcontinent, so-called Indian clubs are bowling pin–shaped clubs weighing up to a hundred pounds and usually made of wood that are used as exercise equipment to build strength and dexterity.
9. Weird, or frightful.
10. Short for "hackney," a type of small horse-drawn carriage that, along with its driver, could be hired for short trips.
11. An island in San Francisco Bay. From 1850 to 1933 it served as a United States military installation, and from 1934 to 1963 it was a federal prison.
12. Mount Tamalpais is a peak in Marin County, California, which is located on the north side of San Francisco Bay.
13. A small boat that provides or sells supplies to large ships in port.
14. A "nob" is a person of wealth and high social standing. Nob Hill was and still is an exclusive area of San Francisco.
15. Been executed by hanging. Traditionally, a "cap," or hood, is placed over the condemned person's head before they are "dropped" from a sufficient height.

JOHN OSKISON

(1874–1947)

For a variety of reasons, modern scholars have had a difficult time deciding to what degree John Oskison should be termed a "Native American author." One can argue, though, that it is precisely this inability to categorize him and his writings that makes them so interesting—and important—to study.

Oskison was born in 1874 in Indian Territory, which later became the state of Oklahoma, to an English immigrant father and a mother who was one-quarter Cherokee. His mother died when Oskison was only four years old, leaving him to be raised by his father, who by the 1870s had become a cattle rancher. After graduating from a small Oklahoma college in 1894, Oskison went on to the newly founded Stanford University, from which he graduated in 1898 (the first Native American to do so), and then he began pursuing a graduate degree in English at Harvard University. Yet when one of his short stories ("Only the Master Shall Praise") won a *Century Magazine* prize during his first year there, Oskison left Harvard to pursue a writing career in New York City. There, Oskison blended in easily with White mainstream culture and served as an editor at a number of different publications, most notably *Collier's* magazine. He also married Florence Ballard Day, a niece of financier Jay Gould, in 1903, served as a lieutenant in World War I, and after divorcing his first wife in 1920, married Hildegarde Hawthorne, a granddaughter of Nathaniel Hawthorne. Given this history of Oskison's deep involvement in White mainstream culture, one might be led to believe that he had little to do with his Native American heritage as an adult.

However, Oskison's work both as a nonfiction and fiction writer was almost always infused with Native American elements. Even while living in New York, he published numerous articles and editorials about issues important to Native Americans, both in mainstream periodicals and in newspapers back in Indian Territory. In these pieces he argued, time and again, that Native Americans deserved the opportunity to succeed in modern America. Some critics at the time charged him with being overly assimilationist and not being resistant enough to the encroachments of White American culture, but his overall position was that the only way for Native Americans to preserve their culture was to have a stronger voice in matters that affected them, including governance and schooling.

In his editorials, as in his short stories, Oskison was almost always evenhanded, carefully delineating the difficulties and conflicts facing Native American people in their new circumstances, as well as the options open to them, without descending into polemics on one side or the other. "The Problem of Old Harjo" exemplifies this approach. Significantly, Oskison chose to publish it in the *Southern Workman* (April 1907), a magazine sponsored by the Hampton Normal and Agricultural Institute in Virginia. Founded in 1868 to provide a solid education to African Americans, the institute also opened its doors to Native Americans in

1878; by 1910 it had 1,807 students of the former group and 31 of the latter. This magazine, in which the African American author Charles W. Chesnutt also published a handful of stories, reached exactly the type of audience Oskison would have wanted for "The Problem of Old Harjo": those interested in finding solutions to the dilemmas facing both Native Americans and the White Christian missionaries.

Unfortunately, Oskison wrote only a few short stories after 1915 and none after 1925, when he turned his attention to writing novels. Between 1925 and 1935, he published four novels, all of which focus on White settlers in Indian Territory and draw heavily on Oskison's own experiences; none, though, are of the same high quality as his short stories. Thus, when Oskison died in 1947, he was little known as a fiction writer and mostly forgotten. In the 1980s some of his works were rediscovered by literary scholars eager to better understand the viewpoints of previously marginalized authors. Yet because Oskison did not offer hard-line resistance against the dominant White culture, instead choosing to portray his Native American characters as doing their best to maintain their identities but also adapting to settler colonial culture, his works have not received as much attention as those of other Native American authors of his time, such as Zitkala-Ša and Charles Eastman. It is the editors' belief, however, that not only "The Problem of Old Harjo" but also many of his other short stories deserve to be read and discussed more widely.

THE PROBLEM OF OLD HARJO (1907)

The Spirit of the Lord had descended upon old Harjo. From the new missionary, just out from New York, he had learned that he was a sinner. The fire in the new missionary's eyes and her gracious appeal had convinced old Harjo that this was the time to repent and be saved. He was very much in earnest, and he assured Miss Evans that he wanted to be baptized and received into the church at once. Miss Evans was enthusiastic and went to Mrs. Rowell with the news. It was Mrs. Rowell who had said that it was no use to try to convert the older Indians, and she, after fifteen years of work in Indian Territory missions,[1] should have known. Miss Evans was pardonably proud of her conquest.

"Old Harjo converted!" exclaimed Mrs. Rowell. "Dear Miss Evans, do you know that old Harjo has two wives?" To the older woman it was as if some one had said to her "Madame, the Sultan of Turkey wishes to teach one of your mission Sabbath school classes."

"But," protested the younger woman, "he is really sincere, and—"

"Then ask him," Mrs. Rowell interrupted a bit sternly, "if he will put away one of his wives. Ask him, before he comes into the presence of the Lord, if he is willing to conform to the laws of the country in which he lives, the country that guarantees his idle existence. Miss Evans, your work is not even begun." No one who knew Mrs. Rowell would say that she lacked sincerity and patriotism.

Her own cousin was an earnest crusader against Mormonism, and had gathered a goodly share of that wagonload of protests that the Senate had been asked to read when it was considering whether a certain statesman of Utah should be allowed to represent his state at Washington.[2]

In her practical, tactful way, Mrs. Rowell had kept clear of such embarrassments. At first, she had written letters of indignant protest to the Indian Office against the toleration of bigamy amongst the tribes. A wise inspector had been sent to the mission, and this man had pointed out that it was better to ignore certain things, "deplorable, to be sure," than to attempt to make over the habits of the old men. Of course, the young Indians would not be permitted to take more than one wife each.

So Mrs. Rowell had discreetly limited her missionary efforts to the young, and had exercised toward the old and bigamous only that strict charity which even a hopeless sinner might claim.

Miss Evans, it was to be regretted, had only the vaguest notions about "expediency;" so weak on matters of doctrine was she that the news that Harjo was living with two wives didn't startle her. She was young and possessed of but one enthusiasm—that for saving souls.

"I suppose," she ventured, "that old Harjo *must* put away one wife before he can join the church?"

"There can be no question about it, Miss Evans."

"Then I shall have to ask him to do it." Miss Evans regretted the necessity for forcing this sacrifice, but had no doubt that the Indian would make it in order to accept the gift of salvation which she was commissioned to bear to him.

Harjo lived in a "double" log cabin three miles from the mission. His ten acres of corn had been gathered into its fence-rail crib; four hogs that were to furnish his winter's bacon had been brought in from the woods and penned conveniently near to the crib; out in a corner of the garden, a fat mound of dirt rose where the crop of turnips and potatoes had been buried against the corrupting frost; and in the hayloft of his log stable were stored many pumpkins, dried corn, onions (suspended in bunches from the rafters) and the varied forage that Mrs. Harjo number one and Mrs. Harjo number two had thriftily provided. Three cows, three young heifers, two colts, and two patient, capable mares bore the Harjo brand, a fantastic "H ⊣" that the old man had designed. Materially, Harjo was solvent; and if the Government had ever come to his aid he could not recall the date.

This attempt to rehabilitate old Harjo morally, Miss Evans felt, was not one to be made at the mission; it should be undertaken in the Creek's[3] own home where the evidences of his sin should confront him as she explained.

When Miss Evans rode up to the block in front of Harjo's cabin, the old Indian came out, slowly and with a broadening smile of welcome on his face. A clean gray flannel shirt had taken the place of the white collarless garment, with crackling stiff bosom, that he had worn to the mission meetings. Comfortable, well-patched moccasins had been substituted for creaking boots, and brown corduroys, belted in at the waist, for tight black trousers. His abundant gray hair fell down on his shoulders. In his eyes, clear and large and black, glowed the light of true hospitality. Miss Evans thought of the patriarchs as she saw him lead her horse out to the stable; thus Abraham[4] might have looked and lived.

"Harjo," began Miss Evans before following the old man to the covered passageway between the disconnected cabins, "is it true that you have two wives?" Her tone was neither stern nor accusatory. The Creek had heard that question before, from scandalized missionaries and perplexed registry clerks when he went to Muscogee to enroll himself and his family in one of the many "final" records ordered to be made by the Government preparatory to dividing the Creek lands among the individual citizens.[5]

For answer, Harjo called, first into the cabin that was used as a kitchen and then, in a loud, clear voice, toward the small field, where Miss Evans saw a flock of half-grown turkeys running about in the corn stubble. From the kitchen emerged a tall, thin Indian woman of fifty-five, with a red handkerchief bound severely over her head. She spoke to Miss Evans and sat down in the passageway. Presently, a clear, sweet voice was heard in the field; a stout, handsome woman, about the same age as the other, climbed the rail fence and came up to the house. She, also, greeted Miss Evans briefly. Then she carried a tin basin to the well near by, where she filled it to the brim. Setting it down on the horse block, she rolled back her sleeves, tucked in the collar of her gray blouse, and plunged her face in the water. In a minute she came out of the kitchen freshened and smiling. 'Liza Harjo had been pulling dried bean stalks at one end of the field, and it was dirty work. At last old Harjo turned to Miss Evans and said, "These two my wife—this one 'Liza, this one Jennie."

It was done with simple dignity. Miss Evans bowed and stammered. Three pairs of eyes were turned upon her in patient, courteous inquiry.

It was hard to state the case. The old man was so evidently proud of his women, and so flattered by Miss Evans' interest in them, that he would find it hard to understand. Still, it had to be done, and Miss Evans took the plunge.

"Harjo, you want to come into our church?" The old man's face lighted.

"Oh, yes, I would come to Jesus, please, my friend."

"Do you know, Harjo, that the Lord commanded that one man should mate with but one woman?" The question was stated again in simpler terms, and the Indian replied, "Me know that now, my friend. Long time ago"—Harjo plainly meant the whole period previous to his conversion—"me did not know. The Lord Jesus did not speak to me in that time and so I was blind. I do what blind man do."

"Harjo, you must have only one wife when you come into our church. Can't you give up one of these women?" Miss Evans glanced at the two, sitting by with smiles of polite interest on their faces, understanding nothing. They had not shared Harjo's enthusiasm either for the white man's God or his language.

"Give up my wife?" A sly smile stole over his face. He leaned closer to Miss Evans. "You tell me, my friend, which one I give up." He glanced from 'Liza to Jennie as if to weigh their attractions, and the two rewarded him with their pleasantest smiles. "You tell me which one," he urged.

"Why, Harjo, how can I tell you!" Miss Evans had little sense of humor; she had taken the old man seriously.

"Then," Harjo sighed, continuing the comedy, for surely the missionary was jesting with him, "'Liza and Jennie must say." He talked to the Indian women for a time, and they laughed heartily. 'Liza, pointing to the other, shook her head. At length Harjo explained, "My friend, they cannot say. Jennie, she would run a race to see which one stay, but 'Liza, she say no, she is fat and cannot run."

Miss Evans comprehended at last. She flushed angrily, and protested, "Harjo, you are making a mock of a sacred subject; I cannot allow you to talk like this."

"But did you not speak in fun, my friend?" Harjo queried, sobering. "Surely you have just said what your friend, the white woman at the mission (he meant Mrs. Rowell) would say, and you do not mean what you say."

"Yes, Harjo, I mean it. It is true that Mrs. Rowell raised the point first, but I agree with her. The church cannot be defiled by receiving a bigamist into its membership." Harjo saw that the young woman was serious, distressingly serious. He was silent for a long time, but at last he raised his head and spoke quietly, "It is not good to talk like that if it is not in fun."

He rose and went to the stable. As he led Miss Evans' horse up to the block it was champing a mouthful of corn, the last of a generous portion that Harjo had put before it. The Indian held the bridle and waited for Miss Evans to mount. She was embarrassed, humiliated, angry. It was absurd to be dismissed in this way by—"by an ignorant old bigamist!" Then the humor of it burst upon her, and its human aspect. In her anxiety concerning the spiritual welfare of the sinner Harjo, she had insulted the man Harjo. She began to understand why Mrs. Rowell had said that the old Indians were hopeless.

"Harjo," she begged, coming out of the passageway, "please forgive me. I do not want you to give up one of your wives. Just tell me why you took them."

"I will tell you that, my friend." The old Creek looped the reins over his arm and sat down on the block. "For thirty years Jennie has lived with me as my wife. She is of the Bear people,[6] and she came to me when I was thirty-five and she was twenty-five. She could not come before, for her mother was old, very old, and Jennie, she stay with her and feed her.

"So, when I was thirty years old I took 'Liza for my woman. She is of the Crow people.[7] She help me make this little farm here when there was no farm for many miles around.

"Well, five years 'Liza and me, we live here and work hard. But there was no child. Then the old mother of Jennie she died, and Jennie got no family left in this part of the country. So 'Liza say to me, 'Why don't you take Jennie in here?' I say, 'You don't care?' and she say, 'No, maybe we have children here then.' But we have no children—never have children. We do not like that, but God He would not let it be. So, we have lived here thirty years very happy. Only just now you make me sad."

"Harjo," cried Miss Evans, "forget what I said. Forget that you wanted to join the church." For a young mission worker with a single purpose always before her, Miss Evans was saying a strange thing. Yet she couldn't help saying it; all of her zeal seemed to have been dissipated by a simple statement of the old man.

"I cannot forget to love Jesus, and I want to be saved." Old Harjo spoke with solemn earnestness. The situation was distracting. On one side stood a convert eager for the protection of the church, asking only that he be allowed to fulfill the obligations of humanity and on the other stood the church, represented by Mrs. Rowell, that set an impossible condition on receiving old Harjo to itself. Miss Evans wanted to cry; prayer, she felt, would be entirely inadequate as a means of expression.

"Oh! Harjo," she cried out, "I don't know what to do. I must think it over and talk with Mrs. Rowell again."

But Mrs. Rowell could suggest no way out; Miss Evans' talk with her only gave the older woman another opportunity to preach the folly of wasting time on the old and "unreasonable" Indians. Certainly the church could not listen even to a hint of a compromise in this case. If Harjo wanted to be saved there was one way and only one—unless—

"Is either of the two women old? I mean, so old that she is—an—"

"Not at all," answered Miss Evans. "They're both strong and—yes, happy. I think they will outlive Harjo."

"Can't you appeal to one of the women to go away? I dare say we could provide for her." Miss Evans, incongruously, remembered Jennie's jesting proposal to race for the right to stay with Harjo. What could the mission provide as a substitute for the little home that 'Liza had helped to create there in the edge of the woods? What other home would satisfy Jennie?

"Mrs. Rowell, are you sure that we ought to try to take one of Harjo's women from him? I'm not sure that it would in the least advance morality amongst the tribe, but I'm certain that it would make three gentle people unhappy for the rest of their lives."

"You may be right, Miss Evans." Mrs. Rowell was not seeking to create unhappiness, for enough of it inevitably came to be pictured in the little mission building. "You may be right," she repeated, "but it is a grievous misfortune that old Harjo should wish to unite with the church."

No one was more regular in his attendance at the mission meetings than old Harjo. Sitting well forward, he was always in plain view of Miss Evans at the organ. Before the service began, and after it was over, the old man greeted the young woman. There was never a spoken question, but in the Creek's eyes was always a mute inquiry.

Once Miss Evans ventured to write to her old pastor in New York, and explain her trouble. This was what he wrote in reply: "I am surprised that you are troubled, for I should have expected you to rejoice, as I do, over this new and wonderful evidence of the Lord's reforming power. Though the church cannot receive the old man so long as he is confessedly a bigamist and violator of his country's just laws, you should be greatly strengthened in your work through bringing him to desire salvation."

"Oh! it's easy to talk when you're free from responsibility!" cried out Miss Evans. "But I woke him up to a desire for this water of salvation that he cannot take. I have seen Harjo's home, and I know how cruel and useless it would be to urge him to give up what he loves—for he does love those two women who have spent half their lives and more with him. What, what can be done!"

Month after month, as old Harjo continued to occupy his seat in the mission meetings, with that mute appeal in his eyes and a persistent light of hope on his face, Miss Evans repeated the question, "What can be done?" If she was sometimes tempted to say to the old man, "Stop worrying about your soul; you'll get to Heaven as surely as any of us," there was always Mrs. Rowell to remind her that she was not a Mormon missionary.[8] She could not run away from her perplexity. If she should secure a transfer to another station, she felt that Harjo would give up coming to the meetings, and in his despair become a positive influence for evil amongst his people. Mrs. Rowell would not waste her energy on an obstinate old man. No, Harjo was her creation, her impossible convert, and throughout the years, until death—the great solvent which is not always a solvent—came to one of them, would continue to haunt her.

And meanwhile, what?

NOTES

1. "Indian Territory" refers to a large area of land just west of Arkansas whose borders were set by the Indian Intercourse Act of 1834 and that was originally designed to be reserved for those Native Americans forced by the US government and US Army to leave their ancestral homelands further east; numerous missionaries worked in the area, trying to convert Native Americans to Christianity. Part of Indian Territory became the state of Oklahoma in 1907.
2. In 1903, Reed Smoot (1862–1941) of Utah was elected to the US Senate; however, because many people believed that as a leader of the Church of Jesus Christ of Latter-day Saints (Mormons) he not only condoned polygamy but also had taken an oath against the United States government, extensive Senate hearings were conducted to determine whether he could rightfully serve in the Senate. A 1907 Senate vote confirmed his place there, and he continued as a Utah Senator until 1933.
3. A member of the Muscogee (Creek) Nation, whose members were forced in the 1830s from their homes in what is now the southeastern United States and now live throughout Oklahoma.
4. Originally named Abram. In Genesis 17:5 (King James Version), God says to him, "Neither shall thy name any more be called Abram, but thy name shall be Abraham; for a father of many nations have I made thee." Abraham is one of the most venerated figures in Christianity, as well as in Judaism and Islam.
5. A city in Indian Territory whose spelling was changed by the US Post Office in 1900 to "Muskogee." In 1887 the Dawes Act (also known as the General Allotment Act or the Dawes Severalty Act) authorized the United States government

to survey Native American tribal lands and divide them into allotments for individual registered Native Americans; those who took one of these allotments
and agreed to live apart from other tribal members were granted US citizenship.
Amended in 1891, 1898, and 1906, this legislation's purpose was to separate Native Americans from their communal identities and make them more like the
individualized landowners of European heritage.

6. Most Native American peoples have multiple clans within them; one's clan membership depends on that of one's mother. Members of the Creek people's Bear
Clan come from the older Native ancestral clans of the Muklasalgi and Nokosalgi.

7. There is no known Crow Clan among the Creek, and thus this might be a reference to the Crow people, whose ancestral lands are located in what is now
northwestern Wyoming, western North Dakota, and almost the entire state of
Montana. In marrying her, Harjo thus married outside of his community.

8. The Church of Jesus Christ of Latter-day Saints (Mormons), in 1852, endorsed
"plural marriages" in which men could have multiple wives. In order to make
Utah Territory eligible for statehood, in 1890 church president Wilford Woodruff
called for an end to new plural marriages, but it was only in 1904, eight years after
Utah became a state, that church president Joseph F. Smith disavowed polygamy
before Congress, issued a declaration that all plural marriages should cease, and
publicly stated that anyone who did not comply would be excommunicated.

ELIA WILKINSON PEATTIE

(1862–1935)

Elia Wilkinson was born in Michigan in 1862 but moved with her family to
Chicago in 1871. Shortly thereafter, at the age of thirteen, she had to drop out of
school, first to help at her father's printing business and afterward to stay at home
and help her mother take care of the family's younger children. Elia married
Chicago journalist Robert Peattie in 1883, and even after the birth of two children she was able to work as a columnist for the *Chicago Daily News* and, a little
while later, as a reporter for the *Chicago Tribune;* she also began to write short stories and submit them to prize contests, winning first place in many of them. The
first story she published in a national periodical was "Grizel Cochrane's Ride,"
in the February 1887 issue of *St. Nicholas,* a very popular children's magazine.

In 1888, Elia and her family moved to Omaha, Nebraska, where her husband
had been hired as managing editor of the *Omaha Daily Herald;* Elia also became
a regular columnist. Unfortunately, Robert contracted double pneumonia in
1890 and never recovered fully enough to continue as an editor. In response
to the family's reduced financial fortunes, Elia began to write more fiction and
was very successful at placing her short stories in many prominent, well-paying
national magazines, including *Harper's Bazar, Harper's Weekly, Cosmopolitan, Lippincott's, St. Nicholas,* and *Youth's Companion.* Many of these stories were collected in

book volumes; possibly the strongest of these was *A Mountain Woman* (1896). In addition to the hundreds of short stories and newspaper pieces she published, Peattie wrote a number of novels, plays, and nonfiction books.

Peattie and her family were forced to return to Chicago in 1896 for financial reasons. There, she continued to publish prolifically and serve as literary critic for the *Chicago Tribune* from 1901 to 1917. Yet it is clear that living in Nebraska for eight years had made an enormous impact on her. One result is the present story, "After the Storm: A Story of the Prairie," which originally appeared in the prestigious *Atlantic Monthly* magazine in September 1897. Its subject—the incredibly difficult life for women on the plains—might be similar to that explored by Hamlin Garland, Kate Cleary, and Willa Cather, but Peattie's stark, matter-of-fact, and Naturalistic prose speaks in a voice uniquely hers.

AFTER THE STORM: A STORY OF THE PRAIRIE (1897)

When the men drove up for supper, they found the table unset, the fire out, and the woman tossing on the bed.

There were six of the men, besides Tennant, the Englishman, who, "by the bitter road the younger son must tread,"[1] had come to Nebraska and the sandhill country, ranching, and who was put over the rest of the men because he did not get drunk as often as they did.

Sharpneck, the cattleman, was in town. So was his daughter, whose hungry cats darted about the disorderly room, crying to be fed.

The men were astonished at the condition of affairs. The woman had never failed them before in all the months that she had cooked, and made beds, and washed and scrubbed for them. They swore hungry oaths, for the autumn air gets up a sharp appetite when a man is in saddle all day.

"Poor old prairie dog," said Fitzgerald, who was rather soft-hearted, "she's clean petered out!"

Tennant had been feeling her head.

"Get in your saddles again," he said, "and ride down to Smithers' for something to eat. You, Fitzgerald, go on to town and get the doctor. Get Sharpneck, too—if you can. And you might look up Kitty."

Kitty was the daughter who owned the cats. These animals appeared to be voracious. Their eyes shone with evil phosphorescence as Tennant sent the men off and closed the door. He lit a fire in the stove, and then tried to make the woman more comfortable. Her toil-stained clothes were twisted about her; her wisps of hair straggled about her face.

"Poor old prairie dog!" he murmured, repeating Fitzgerald's words. "Not one of us noticed at noon that she was not as usual—and why should we? What do we care?"

He had his own reasons for being out of love with his kind, and with himself, and he smiled sardonically, as, in making her more comfortable on the bed, he noticed the wretched couch, the poor garments smelling of smoke, the uncared-for body.

"She has borne two sons and a daughter," he went on, "and known the brutal boot of that drunken Dutchman, and, after all, she lies here alone, dies here alone, perhaps—and it doesn't make any difference."

The sick woman was a stranger to him. To be sure, he had known her for three months. He had eaten at her table three times a day. Her little brown parchment-like face looked familiar to him from the first, not because he had seen it before, but because some things have, for certain persons, an indefinable familiarity. Besides doing the housework, she milked three cows, fed the pigs and chickens, and made the butter. Tennant had often seen her working far into the night. When he was on the night shift with the cattle, he had seen her moving about noiselessly, while the others slept.

As for Sharpneck, the proprietor of the land, the cattle, and her, he was a big fellow from Pennsylvania, who got drunk on vile compounds. Tennant never heard him address her except to give an order, and he usually gave it with an oath. Once Tennant had brought her some bell-like yellow flowers that he picked among the tall grasses. She nodded her thanks hurriedly,—she was cooking cakes for the men,—and put the blossoms in a glass. Her husband got up and tossed the flowers out of the window. Tennant did not find it worth his while even to be angry. After that, however, he thought it the part of kindness to leave her alone.

He lit his pipe now, and sat down near her. The hours passed, and the men did not return. Tennant guessed, with a good deal of accuracy, that in the allurements of a rousing game of poker they had forgotten him and his charge. It was not surprising; on the contrary, it seemed perfectly natural. Tennant decided to bend his energies to the getting up of a meal for himself. He found some bacon, which he fried, and some cold prune sauce, and plenty of bread. Then he made tea, and persuaded the sick woman to take a little of it by giving it to her a tea-spoonful at a time. He placated the cats, too, but they would not sleep. He drove them all from the house, but they ran in again through holes they had scratched in the structure, near the floor—for the shack was built of sod. Their eyes, red and green, seemed to light the whole place with a baleful radiance. Once, in anger, Tennant hurled a glowing brand at them, but furious, they rushed up the sides of the room, hissing and spitting, and making themselves much more hideous than before.

Toward morning, he could see that the sick woman was sinking into a state of coma. He grew seriously worried, and wondered if Fitzgerald had forgotten to go for the doctor. When it came time for the men to be at their places, he signaled them, and Fitzgerald came in answer to his summons. He had seen the physician, who had said he would be along in the course of the day. Sharpneck had been fool-drunk, and in no mood to listen to anything. Kitty said she would be home in the morning. But the whole forenoon passed without word from any of them. In the afternoon, however, Dr. Bender came out. He was a young man, with avaricious eyes and a sensual mouth. His long body was lank and ill-constructed. His hair was red, and an untidy mustache gave color to an otherwise colorless face. When he saw the unconscious figure on the bed, so inert, so mortally stricken, a peculiar gleam came to his eye.

"Her chance is small, I'm afraid," said Tennant, "but do what you can. She is here with you and me, and none beside. We mustn't fail her, you know, by Jove!"

The physician leered at him, stupidly. He looked the woman over, put some powders in a glass of water, and arose to go.

"Then you don't know what is the matter with her!" exclaimed Tennant roughly. "You're going to leave her to her fate?"

"I've done all there is to do," said the doctor sullenly. "I ought to have been called sooner."

"You were called sooner, you fool!" almost shouted Tennant. "Get out, will you? I'd take more interest in a dying cow than you do in this woman."

There was a sort of menace in the man's white face as he quitted the place, but Ralph Tennant was not worrying about expressions of countenance. He gave the stuff the doctor had left—merely to satisfy his conscience, and watched the road for Sharpneck. About three o'clock, the woman's breathing became so slight, he could no longer hear it. He tried to arouse her with stimulants, but it was of no avail. The last spark of life presently went out.

He rode four miles for a neighbor woman, who came and performed the last offices for the poor creature. She got supper for Tennant, too, and then left him. He had to sit up all night to keep off the cats, and one of the other fellows sat up with him; the two men played poker gloomily, occasionally varying the monotony by throwing brands at the cats, which, smelling death, were seized with some grim carnivorous atavism.[2] The jungle awoke in them, and they were wild beasts, only more contemptible.

When morning came, Tennant set about making preparations for the funeral. He imagined how dismal the whole thing would be; he never dreamed that events would shape themselves otherwise than monotonously and drearily. But to his astonishment, the men came in their best clothes. They were, in fact, in a state of fine excitement.

"I'll be riding down to Gester's to see if they have a spring seat[3] to give us the loan of," said young Fitzgerald, who was the first to appear in the morning. The other men were close behind him. They had all breakfasted at Smithers'; Smithers' was a place which sometimes served as a road-house, and they were well-fed and in form for some novel entertainment.

"Spring seats?" gasped Tennant. "What is wanting with spring seats?"

"To accommodate the mourners, to be sure! You don't want the mourners to ride on boards, do you, man?"

"Mourners!" Tennant's voice was almost hollow. He felt a terrible kinship with the "poor little prairie dog," who, a small mass of mortality, lay under the cold sheet in her miserable home. "Who in God's name are the mourners?"

"We are the mourners!" cried Fitzgerald, with grandiloquence, sweeping his hand around to indicate his companions.

"And the cattle, and the other work—who, pray, will attend to them?" Tennant put this question more to drown the sardonic guffaw that was ready to leap out, than because of any care for Sharpneck's possessions.

"In times of mourning," said the Irishman, winking to his companions, but drawing a lugubrious face to Tennant, "other matters have to go to the wall."

The men nodded. Tennant wanted to roar—or would, if he had not wanted to weep. So he went back to his watch, and to fighting the cats, and let the humans have their way.

There had not been so much riding in that part of the country since Tennant came into it. Gester sent up two spring seats, which Fitzgerald and Duncan brought home across their horses' backs. Abner Farish dashed to town with the news of the event—no one, it seemed, considered the death a catastrophe—and encountered Sharpneck on the way. Sharpneck made back for town, to interview his brother, Martin Sharpneck, the undertaker, and then turned his face homeward again. With him came his daughter, silent and straight, carrying in her lap a black crape hat she had borrowed for the occasion. There was a keg of something in the rear of the wagon calculated to raise the spirits of the mourners, and the sight of this insured Sharpneck a welcome from his men.

The air was indeed charged with excitement. The horses were combed and brushed, the wagons were washed. A missionary clergyman, who happened to be passing through the next town west, was sent over by the thoughtful neighbors, who had somehow learned of Mrs. Sharpneck's demise, and he was warmly received. The house swarmed with people. There were even a number of women present, though few of or none had come to see the lonely little creature while she still lived. Tennant would have fled from it all and got out with the cattle, only he felt as if he could not desert that pitiful body. He stayed to appease his conscience, which cried out to him that he was on guard.

Kitty Sharpneck showed a bright red spot on each cheek, but her eyes were dry. The Englishman could not make her out at all. He had sometimes seen her about the house, though she spent most of her time in town, where she was serving a sort of apprenticeship with a milliner. She was little and brown, like her mother, with the same restless, nervous glance that she had had. The cats all rubbed up against her as she entered, and leaped to her shoulders and her lap. The women poured questions upon her; the men regarded her fixedly. Every one was alert to see what her deportment would be, and was quite willing that there should be a scene. They were disappointed. The girl, after a few moments' rest, brushed away her pets, and, walking over to the place where the form of her mother was lying in a cold inner room, lifted the sheet and looked at the face. The body had been wrapped in a clean sheet.

"Mother used to have a shawl," she said to Tennant; "I'll see if I can find it."

She searched about in the drawers and finally drew it forth, a great shawl of gray silk, delicately brocaded.

"It was her wedding shawl," said Kitty. "It came from Holland."

The women made a shroud of it. Tennant still kept watch. His presence was a check on the conversation and kept it within bounds. The women baked a great meal, and they all sat down to it—except Kitty, who could not be found. The men were convivial. It was part of the inevitable programme, apparently. Tennant needed sleep, but when night came, every one went away, and he was left there alone again. Kitty could not be found even now. He had been up two nights, and being a young fellow with a fixed habit of sleeping, the strain was telling on him a little. But the red eyes of the cats showed through the holes in the shack, and his aversion to the creatures keyed him to his task.

About midnight he heard some one cautiously approaching the shack from the outside. The door opened softly. Kitty Sharpneck came in. She stole past Tennant and into the room where her mother lay. She closed the door behind her, and there was silence. Presently she came out. There were no tears in her eyes; a look of peculiar hardness marred her young face.

She went up to Tennant and stood before him, looking at him.

"You have been good," she whispered. "Why?"

"Why not?" said Tennant, horribly afraid of sentiment. But he need not have feared it from Kitty.

"No doubt you had your reason," she said sharply. "Now go to sleep. I'll watch."[4]

Tennant demurred.

"Get over there on the settle, I say, and go to sleep. I'll watch."

He obeyed her and lay on the settle. She took his seat before the fire, and from time to time made flourishes at the cats, even as he had done. Periodically she went to the inner room to change the cloths on the dead woman's face. The rest of the time she sat still, looking straight before her, and as she looked, her little brown face hardened ever more and more. Sometimes for a moment bright red spots would burn on her cheeks, and then die away again.

Tennant had passed the point where he was sleepy. He lay awake, watching the girl. Her low brow, her thin, delicately curved lips, her shapely nose, the high cheek bones and dainty chin, the pretty ears and sloping shoulders, all indicated femininity and intelligence. It was difficult to account for the fineness of her quality. And yet, who could tell what the "poor little prairie dog" might have been? Women make strange marriages and travel strange roads. Tennant knew by what devious paths a human creature could tread. He himself—But that had nothing to do with the case, and he banished thoughts of self, for they were not pleasant. Anyhow, what was the use of reminiscence? Here he was, with one good lung and one not quite so good, out in the semi-arid belt, on horseback from twelve to sixteen hours a day, eating like a Zulu,[5] and waiting for events. He reflected that the things which affected him personally he looked upon as events. Those which touched him indirectly, such as the death of Maria Sharpneck, he looked upon as episodes. Such is the involuntary egotism of man.

"I'm not sleeping," Tennant announced to the girl.

"I know it," she said.

"What are you thinking about?" he asked.

Her eye involuntarily went toward the room where the silent Thing was.

"The cats, of course," said she, her lip curling a trifle.

"Don't be angry with me," pleaded Tennant. "I feel very sorry for you."

"You needn't."

"Why not?"

"It's none of your funeral."

She had meant merely to use the slang, not to refer to the actual event.

"Shall I keep still?"

"Yes, I guess you'd better."

The minutes passed. Outside, silence—silence—silence. It reaches so far on the plains, does silence. The sky is higher above the earth than in other places. The night is of velvet. Vast breaths of wind and mystery blow backward and forward.

This night a wolf bayed, and gave the voice of life. Dismal as was the sound, it was not so bleak as the utter stillness it had been.

"You were with mother when she died?" asked the girl suddenly.

She arose and stood near Tennant, looking down into his eyes.

"I was with her."

"Tell me what happened."

He told her.

"I'm glad she's dead. Of course you know I'm glad."

"If you loved her, I know you must be glad."

"I ought to have stayed with her."

"But—well, it was—Oh, you know what it was."

"I can guess."

"You know what I did. I went to town and worked for my board. My father is a rich man. I washed dishes in another woman's kitchen and went to school. Then I went to the milliner. I apprenticed myself to her. But I was sorry. I did not like her, nor the other girls, nor things that happened. I did not like the town. I dared not come home. Father was worse then. We always quarreled. He and mother quarreled about me."

"I never heard your mother say anything."

"No, she didn't say much, except when father pitched on me. But it was different—once."

She turned, went into the inner room, opened a drawer, and took something out. When she came back, she placed it in Tennant's hand. It was an ambrotype[6] of a young girl with a face like that of the girl before him. The hair was parted smoothly from the low, lovely brow. Alert dark eyes looked gently from the picture. Around the bared neck was a coral necklace with a gold clasp, and the miniature-maker had gilded the clasp and tinted the cheeks and lips, and made the coral its natural tint. A dainty low-necked gown and big puffed sleeves confessed to the coquetry of the wearer.

"That was mother," said Kitty.

And then the storm broke at last, and she was on the floor, face downward, in a passion of weeping, and the young man—he who had trod the bitter road—felt his own frame quiver at sight of her woe, at thought of his own, at knowledge of the world's big burden.

By and by, when Kitty lay on the settle and Tennant sat beside her, she grew confidential, and told him in detail the life at which he had guessed.

"He'll expect me to be the drudge now," she said in conclusion, referring to her father.

"Now I'll be the one to get breakfast and dinner and supper, and breakfast and dinner and supper, and stay here at home forever, and wear dirty clothes, and scrub and wash and iron! I know how it will be. That is—if"—

"If what?"

"If I stay."

"What else can you do? Go back to the millinery shop?"

"No. He wouldn't give me a minute's peace there. He never comes to town that he doesn't make me ashamed of him. I suppose you wonder why I didn't come out as soon as you sent word that mother was sick. Well, he would n't let me. He sat himself down there, and swore I ought to stay. Miss Hiner, the milliner, was having her fall opening, and she got round him and said I ought to stay. So I stayed."

She set her teeth hard and looked unutterable protest at the young man.

Tennant was a gentleman, and not given to parading his own troubles, yet now, in the desolation and silence, with the dead within and the wolves without, it seemed natural that he should tell the girl something of his own life. It was a familiar tale. Thousands of young Englishmen, crowded out of their own land and their own families, who come here to wring something from fortune's greedy grasp, could tell a similar one. But given the personal quality, it seemed unique, particularly to the inexperienced girl who listened. The two had a community of suffering and deprivation and loneliness. They looked at each other with eyes of profound sympathy. Each felt so deep a pity for the other that for a time self-pity was submerged.

Morning dawned. Presently the men came from the adjoining buildings for breakfast. Kitty had risen to the emergency,—the emergency of breakfast; she had it ready,—corn bread, salt pork, potatoes, eggs, and black coffee. In her fear lest she should not have enough to satisfy these men of prodigious appetite, she had cooked even more than they could eat. She had set the table just as her mother had been in the habit of doing. Everything was cluttered together. As she worked, imitating in each most trifling particular the ways of the dead woman, a gray look settled about her face. Tennant, who had both sympathy and imagination, knew she was looking down the long, long road of monotonous and degrading toil which lay before her. He saw her soul shuddering at the captivity to which it was doomed. Now and then she cast at him a glance of mute horror.

The men were excited, and eager to do anything to help to the success of the day. Sharpneck himself was restless. His little green eyes rolled around in their fleshy sockets. He shuffled about constantly, and at last said he was going to town to make the final arrangements, but would be back soon. A number of men immediately offered to go for him. In spite of all they knew of the truth, they had created a fiction regarding him now in this supreme hour, and had actually persuaded themselves that he was a sufferer. He insisted on making the journey himself, and some of the simple fellows chose to believe this to be an evidence of devotion.

Kitty did not share this belief. She cast an apprehensive glance at Tennant. He looked as reassuring as he could. They both feared he was going to get drunk and shirk the funeral altogether. But he was back in a wonderfully short time, wearing a new suit of clothes. Kitty had the house cleared up, and the neighbors began to arrive. The coffin came,—a brilliantly varnished coffin, with much nickel plate[7] on it. It was placed in the front room. The men stood around, the big sombreros in their hands, their pretty, high-heeled boots carefully cleaned. Five women were present. Their sobs, oddly enough, were genuine, and at moments became even violent, though none of them had known the dead woman well. But who could know that silent and inscrutable creature?

The minister wore squeaky boots, and had a red beard, which claimed much of his attention. Fitzgerald, who found the whole proceeding tamer than it ought to have been, took him into an inner room and braced him for his melancholy duties. The clergyman had never met Mrs. Sharpneck, but he seemed to be cognizant of all her virtues, and exploited them in tones at once strident and nasal. Poor Kitty, behind her crape veil, grew hard and angry, and Tennant knew that the quivering of her frame did not denote grief so much as inarticulate rage and revolt. The girl's passion was setting her apart from her world in his estimations. Something tragic in her surroundings and her soul put her above the others.

The men did not appear to be at all surprised at the way the women wept. They considered weeping the function of women at a funeral. That they were weeping from self-pity did not once occur to them. The minister neglected none of his duties, and they included an address lasting forty-five minutes and two prayers, one of thirty minutes' duration. The people sang Nearer, my God, to Thee.[8] At this Kitty grew almost rigid, and at last, her misery passing all bounds, she caught Tennant's hand in hers—he was sitting near her—and pressed it in a bitter grasp.

"What is it? What is it?" he whispered.

"The song!" she managed to say. "As if she knew anything about God, or ever thought"—

"Hush! Hush! Perhaps it wasn't as bad as you think. She did her duty well, you know, and may be she will be rewarded."

Kitty looked about the room,—at the stove where she had seen the soiled little figure of her mother standing these years and years, at the pots she had patiently scoured, at the low walls, the deep windows, the unstable sandhills beyond, the wind-stricken pool where the cattle stood,—she looked at it all, and thought of the slave bound to it, loaded with heavy chains, starved in the midst of it, and her eyes turned to meet those of Tennant, big with knowledge which knew no words.

Since Ralph Tennant put the world behind him and came out into the wilderness with the cattle and the men who herd them, he had never seen so comprehensive a glance, or been so conscious of the fact of mind. Though the hour was so hideous, though the poor girl beside him was bowed with shame and tortured with inexpressible grief, yet a joy came to his heart at finding once more the human soul, sane, susceptible, responsive, courageous. He drew his chair a little closer, as if he would protect her from the facts that confronted her.

But the people, watching him and her, while the minister droned on and on in dull explanation to his Creator, saw in his sympathy only what was natural and the outcome of the occasion. They guessed at nothing more.

The getting of the coffin into the wagon was no easy task.

"By the saints, it ought to go in feet first," said Fitzgerald, who was one of the pall-bearers. "You'll not be launchin' the woman head foremost into her own grave!"

"It goes head on, you fool!" replied Watson.

The six men stood still, arguing.

"Oh, what's the difference?" asked a bystander. But Watson, who had been an Englishman some time or other,—or at least the father before him had,—was not one to yield to a man who had once called the British jack[9] a dirty rag, as Fitzgerald had, more than once, in the heat of argument. So the discussion waxed hot, and might have ended in a manner more or less sensational, for the men had had a taste of novelty and their appetites were whetted by it, had it not been for Tennant, who came out, leaving Kitty standing in the door, and pointed a stern finger at the wagon; and poor Maria Sharpneck was laid in, head foremost as it happened. It was thought proper that Sharpneck should ride in this wagon, but he was somewhat loath to do so, as the owner of the team, who insisted on driving his own horses, was not of the same politics as himself, and was, moreover, stone-deaf. He had an offensive way of airing his own opinions, and he was so deaf—or affected to be—that he never could hear anything his opponent might say. There was only one bond of sympathy between them, and that was plug tobacco. Some sympathizing friend, endeavoring to mitigate present woes, loaded Sharpneck up with this succulent commodity, and, thus placated, the enemies sat side by side in a semblance of amicability. Behind came two wagon-loads of mourners, composed of the men of the ranch, and Kitty. After them came five or six loads of neighbors who took this opportunity to enjoy an outing, to which they considered themselves entitled after weeks of monotonous toil. It happened that the horses which drew the wagon containing the coffin were very frisky, and it was not long before this wagon was well in advance of the others, the coffin bumping meantime from side to side.

"Hold on, man!" cried Sharpneck to his deaf driver, "hold on, I say! There's reasons why I don't want that there coffin scratched up. Hold in the horses, I say!"

The driver did not hear, and the horses were really too excitable for Sharp-neck to risk meddling with the reins.

The mourners were soon left well behind, though they did their utmost to urge on their animals. In fact, the Dickeys, who had some freshly broken colts of their own raising, had taken another road to town, boasting confidently to the Abernethys that their colts would get them there before the far-famed black team of the Abernethys saw the first church spire. The Abernethys were behind the mourners, and when it developed that the off horse on the second wagon was winded, and it was proved to be impossible for one team to get ahead of another on the steep grade of the road, indignation ran high. The Abernethys fumed, knowing that their neighbors were amused at their predicament.

The mourners were not very far distant, and, being on a rise of ground, they could see the Sharpneck wagon brought to a halt by a horseman who had dashed out from town.

"It's Martin Sharpneck. He's the undertaker," the men made out. He had apparently brought out a big rubber cloth to protect the coffin, for it was beginning to look like rain, and by the time the others were with the group, the coffin was wrapped from sight.

Tennant began to wonder what this could mean. Not a man living would have ridden out that way to meet the "poor little prairie dog" in her lifetime—not a man!

"You're to come around to my place after it's over," the undertaker said. "You'll need to steady your nerves a bit. Come around as soon as you can, boys. You must be about used up." He looked with solicitude at the strapping bronzed men in the wagons.

Tennant glanced sharply at Kitty. Was she not conscious that there was something in the wind? But she watched the wheels rolling in the sand,—watched them turning and dripping the sallow granules from the wheels, as if she dared look neither behind nor before,—and she did not see his look.

The minister had not accompanied the cortège[10] to the cemetery. (One always refers to a cortège in the West, on even a very slight provocation.) So the coffin, shining and gleaming with its nickel plate, was dropped gently into the grave, and then, presently, the undertaker was urging all the boys to come around to his place and brace up, and they all went—Tennant with the rest. Etiquette in such matters is imperative in that section of the country. Tennant could not have refused without paying the penalty of a quarrel, and it was no time for self-assertion. So he cast a look of appeal and apology at Kitty, and went. Sharpneck followed them. There was no one left save the gravedigger, who insisted that he knew his business and did not need anyone to help him.

The women drove the wagons back to town, and went into the stores to gossip and trade. Kitty accompanied them. She had no place to go except the millinery shop, and it had never seemed more dreadful to her than this day. She felt she could not endure the scrutiny of the girls. She crept out of the big store at the back, and sat on a pair of stairs which made their way to the upper story. The day was growing bleak, and gray shadows trailed along the plain. Kitty was not warmly clothed, and the wind sifted through her black garments and chilled her. She had not an idea of what was to happen next. She did not know whether her father would look for her or not. She did not believe Tennant would remember to seek her. Indeed, why should he? She had known him no better than she had known the other men in her father's employ. She had, of course, always felt him to be different. No one could help noticing that he was not a part of his environment. But, after all, young English gentlemen were not an uncommon sight in the sandhill country, and every one was quite aware that of all fools an Englishman was the worst, and could go to the dogs generally with a rapidity which none could rival. With the reasons for this the natives did not trouble themselves. These poor tragedies merely amused them, or awoke their contempt.

The afternoon grew late. Kitty still sat crouched upon the stairs. She was facing her future. She was looking into the eyes of her destiny—and it was a fearsome thing to do.

The base drudgery of the ranch presented itself to her vision with no compensation. The life at the little millinery shop, with its temptations, its wretched scandal, its petty, never-ending talk, came before her too. On every side there seemed to be only what was unspeakably distasteful and disgustingly common. Romance and youth were fair and fleeting things; they were as the mirage which in August days trembled on the heat-misted horizon.

In the midst of all this she saw Tennant crossing over from the millinery shop, which stood, almost solitary, on the street behind the main one. He was looking for her. Kitty ran to meet him, glad to set aside her terrible scrutiny of the future. Perhaps he represented a change or a possibility.

His face was white. He had been drinking a little, but some sudden knowledge had banished all trace of it, save that in the shock his face had suffered.

"We went with your uncle," he began at once, too full of his theme to use judgement or mercy,—"we all went with him, and he 'braced us up,' though God knows why! I scented something in the wind—else why such generosity? It isn't your uncle's way—no, nor your father's—to give something for nothing. The others drank heavily. I drank some, but not enough to dull my curiosity. I got out unnoticed, Miss Kitty, and went back to—to the grave."

"Well—well?" gasped Kitty.

"Well, it was already empty!"

"What?"

"Yes, the coffin was"—

"Where?"

"Back in Martin Sharpneck's shop, by God!"

"And the—and my"—

"And the red-headed doctor had—had the rest!"

The wind blew the sand into dirty yellow spirals, and these danced in drunken fashion about the two who stood there. Down the street could be heard the voices of the drunken men. Kitty saw her father come out of his brother's shop and reel along the street. The women who had ridden to the funeral were coming out of the stores with their arms full of parcels. Their vociferous husbands were about to join them.

"Shall I go to the doctor," asked Tennant, "and"—

"No. What does it matter! It is of a piece with the rest."

Ralph Tennant felt a sudden revulsion. The girl seemed—but, after all, how could he judge her?

"There's no use in trying to do anything. We couldn't. There's no one to help us. Besides, father can do what he pleases—with his own."

"But if he was exposed?"

"No one would care—it would only give them something to talk about. They would pretend to care—but they wouldn't, really."

"Then you are going back, to-night, of course, with"—

"I'm not going back with anybody. I am never going back."

At the last her resolution was taken quite suddenly.

"What will you do, then?"

"In half an hour the train will be here. I am going to take it."

"I'll take it with you."

They were very young; they were half-mad with horror and disgust. They stood alone, and they were in revolt. This accounted for it.

"Very well," said Kitty.

"It is impossible to stay here longer," said the poor younger son, who might, had things been different, have wooed some sweet and well-bred girl in England, instead of this poor, angry savage of the sand wastes.

"It is impossible," said she. "We will go away."

"I have a little money with me."

"I have a little."

"I know the men on the freight, due here in an hour. If you like"—

"Do you think we could manage it?"

"I feel sure of it."

"Then we can save our money."

"Yes. We will go to Omaha."

"As you please."

The gray sky showed a gleam of pale gold at the horizon. The sun was setting. The wagons were driving out of town. Tennant and Kitty saw her father looking for her, and she and Tennant hid in a coal-shed, till Sharpneck's patience being exhausted he drove furiously out of town, cursing.

"He thinks I have gone home with some of the others," said Kitty.

The passenger train rushed into the town and out again. After a time they heard the freight in the distance, and ran down to the little station. Every one was home at supper. Only the station agent saw them talking with the conductor of the freight.

"Goin' away, Miss Sharpneck?" he asked. He did not blame her, but he wanted to know.

"I'm going away," she replied steadily, but hardly hearing him.

Tennant looked too severe to be questioned. He helped the girl into the caboose. She was famished with cold, hunger, and misery. He and the blowzy Irishman on the train built up a brisk fire, and laid her down on a bench near it, wrapped in their cloaks. The Irishman shared his luncheon with them, and made coffee on the stove.

Kitty felt no anticipation. She looked forward to the morning with no emotion whatever. She did not taste the food she put in her mouth. But little by little the warmth of the friendly fire reached her, and she fell asleep and lay as still as—her mother.

* * * * * * * *

"Better come on to Council Bluffs," said the conductor when they reached Omaha.

"Why not?" said Tennant, and laughed.

"Why not?" echoed Kitty.

Both "why nots" sounded bitter. These young persons were adventurers by force of circumstances.

Council Bluffs is a charming place. Part of it lies on a flat lowland, beyond which are the bottom-lands of the river. The rest of the town is built on serrated bluffs, covered with foliage. Although the yellow Missouri separates it from the great American plain, yet it has the sky of the plain, which is a throbbing and impenetrable blue. Its abrupt bluffs have made precipitous and irregular streets. Some of them are almost in the shape of a scimitar; some run like a creek between high terraces; others look up to heights which drip with vineyards; many of them present yellow clay banks which the graders have cut like gigantic cheeses to make way for practical thoroughfares. In these clay cuts the swallows burrow industriously, and perforate the face of the cut with innumerable Zuñi-like residences.[11] The squirrels chatter in the fine old trees. Charming houses stand in the "dells," that is, in the umbrageous cul-de-sacs where the graded streets terminate in bluffs too bold to be penetrated.

Why nature is more prolific there than across the river it would be hard to say; but it is a fact that flowers and vines, and, no doubt, vegetables and fruit, grow better in that locality than in the great grain State over the way. It often happens in America that natural beauty fails to instruct the people who live in the midst of it. This has not been the case at Council Bluffs. From the time when the Mormons first settled there in their historical hegira[12] and built their odd little huts with the numerous outside doors,—cutting an entrance for each housewife,—there has been something involuntarily quaint about the architecture of the place. Roofs slope off into the bluffs, houses are built on green ledges of earth, and back yards shoot skyward, so that the vineyards grow at an angle of forty-five degrees, and he who goes to look at his garden must needs take an alpenstock in his hands. Hammocks hang under the trees;

cottages riot in porches; old mansions wander with a sort of elegant negligence over ground which has never been held at a fictitious value. An exclusive and self-conscious aristocracy looks down upon the ostentation of the fashionable set of Omaha, and lives its quiet life of sociable exclusion, making much of music and ceramics, and attaching no very great importance to commercial aggression or to literature.

Into this peaceful town the adventurers came one bleak autumn day, when the leaves were stirring about the narrow and tortuous streets and the nuts were rattling to the ground. Coming as they did from the treeless region, the place was enchanting to them. No sooner had they sat down to their breakfast than things began to wear a rosier hue. They ate in a fascinating restaurant, where a steel engraving of the destruction of Johnstown,[13] with innumerable remarques,[14] hung above them. Kitty had never eaten a breakfast just like it, and even Tennant, who had known flesh-pots,[15] found it delicious.

As they sipped their coffee, they talked, scrutinizing each other all the time. Tennant was thinking the situation enchanting. Kitty was waiting—waiting for events—for life! She did not reflect. Her hour was a subjective one.

"What shall we do after breakfast?" asked Kitty.

"We must be married," said Tennant decidedly. The girl paled, then blushed and paled again.

"Oh, no, no!" she gasped.

"There is nothing else to do," went on Tennant decidedly. "You needn't worry about it a bit. You needn't pay any particular attention to me, you know. But we've got to be married, my dear. We have cut loose from every one and everything. We must go into partnership. Perhaps you don't love me now,—how could you?—but we have cast in our lot together, and we're coming out on top, somehow. We're going to succeed. Moreover, I don't mind telling you that I'm happier with you here, this morning, and was happier and more contented all last night, while we were rushing along through the darkness escaping from all manner of hideous things, than I have been since—well, since I was a little boy, and thought my mother was greater than the Queen of England and lovelier than all the angels."

The blush came gently back to the girl's cheeks and stayed there this time. She ventured on her confession, too.

"I never felt—well—safe, I guess you call it, before in all my life. Until that night when I talked with you (and I was so cross at first), there in the shack, with poor mother, I never told any one the whole truth about anything, or cared what they thought, or was glad to have them understand what I was thinking."

"What made you so cross with me?"

"Oh, I don't know. You bothered me. You made me want to be different. I thought you were hating me."

"I guess we were just hating the world."

"Probably that was it. Anyhow, fate has thrown us together. It's a case of united we stand."

They looked about the town after breakfast, and found a tiny cottage with three rooms on the side of a hill. A grassy bluff rose immediately behind it, and the roof of the kitchen ran into the bluff. Grapevines rioted down the side. Catalpas grew on the level ledge of ground, and straggling up the hill, holding on tenaciously by their roots, were great chestnut-trees. The little house was painted green, and in summer, Kitty could imagine, it would seem quite to melt into the hill.

"We can have a hammock up there," cried Tennant, after he had arranged to rent it for a trifle, and forgetful that winter was coming. There was actually a rude brick fireplace in the front room—indeed, the place had been the summer retreat of an artist. This filled the young Englishman with delight, and he was off to order some wood.

"To think that we shall have a wood fire!" he exclaimed over and over again. "I will put my pipe on the shelf, and smoke evenings, eh?"

"Yes," cried Kitty. Then she was silent, and something troubled came into her face.

"Well," said Tennant, seeing it, "what is it, my child?"

"I was thinking."

"Yes?"

"Well, please don't be offended with me. But—well, I don't like drinking."

"Don't you, my dear? Well, neither do I."

"But"—

"Oh, I know. But what else was there to do out there? You don't know how lonely I was. You needn't worry about that now!"

They had a wonderful day. They bought a pine table and three pine chairs, and a little second-hand cook-stove, and some shades for the window. Then Tennant asked every man he met for work. He would have made a nuisance of himself if he had not been so excited and generally filled with anticipation that the people pardoned him for his effervescence.

"I've got to have work," he declared to every one. "Anything—anything—manual, clerical, it makes no difference to me. I'll chop wood, or keep books, or coach for college, or work on the road—but I've got to have work!"

He got it—never mind what it was. It was not the sort that he was destined to do by and by, but it served for bread and butter, and a little more. Incidentally, that day, he and Kitty were married. Tennant would have a clergyman perform the ceremony, though Kitty, poor little heathen, was indifferent about it. So they stood before the altar of a curious church up one of the tortuous streets, and were married by a young Episcopal priest, while the merry wind sang outside and red leaves tumbled down the wild hills beyond. They told a bit of their story to the young priest, and he took them to his home, which was on the very top of one of the hills, and they had dinner there, and met the young man's wife, who was a lovely girl from the East, and who took to Kitty at once. That was the beginning of many things—friendships, and little gayeties, and hours of study,—but it is easy to guess what could happen.

Ah, how bare the little green cottage was! But what of it? What of it?

Frequently Kitty spent an hour of her day up at the little wind-haunted rec-
tory, hemming tablecloths and pillow-cases, and she learned to keep a potted
fern on her table,—the minister's wife taught her that,—and to have the hearth
swept at night, and the big chunks of wood blazing. Then Tennant smoked, and
she read to him in the evening.

It was delightful to watch the new home grow! Neat clothes finally were hung
up in the closets, and the demure little lady who was Kitty's friend taught her
all manner of things that could not be learned in books. She helped her buy her
furniture bit by bit, and Tennant and Kitty would sit a whole evening and look at
a new chair in amazement at the knowledge that it was their own.

Presently they had their hospitalities and their institutions and their beaten
paths. It was quite wonderful how quickly they became an orderly part of the
community—these two from the wilderness. Moreover, they were very happy.
It was all simple and common-place enough; but it was their life, and they lived
it with honesty and with courage. Still, perhaps that is not remarkable either.
Honesty and courage are so common—in the West.

NOTES

1. Lines from the poem "Song of the Banjo" (1894), by British writer Rudyard
   Kipling (1865–1936). The poem refers to how sons with no hope of inheritance
   must leave home to pursue their fortunes.
2. A tendency to recur to how one's ancestors acted or thought.
3. A type of fancy horse-drawn carriage.
4. In ancient times, people watched over a person's body after death to safeguard it,
   or in hopes that the person might come to life; even in modern times, the custom
   of this type of vigil is still practiced.
5. A person from the largest ethnic group in what is now the country of South
   Africa. At the time when this story was written, it would have been understood by
   most readers as suggesting a "savage" warrior.
6. A photographic image reproduced on glass, with a black backing.
7. Not solid metal. Meant to suggest its relative cheapness.
8. A popular Christian hymn written and published in 1841 by British writer Sarah
   Fuller Flower Adams (1805–48). Its career in the United States began with its
   publication in Rev. James Freeman Clarke's *Service Book* (1844).
9. Since the union of Great Britain and Northern Ireland in 1801, the United Kingdom's flag has often been referred to as the "Union Jack" (a "jack flag" is one
   flown at the bow of a ship).
10. A funeral procession (French).
11. The Zuñi are a tribe of Native Americans who live in west-central New Mexico;
    most lived, and still live, in Zuñi Pueblo, a complex of residences and other build-
    ings built out of adobe (baked mud and straw) bricks.
12. A "hegira" is a journey undertaken to flee some type of danger or threat; from
    1846 to 1869, fleeing persecution in the American Midwest, approximately
    seventy thousand members of the Church of Jesus Christ of Latter-day Saints
    (Mormons) made the long journey to what is now the state of Utah.

13. Johnstown, Pennsylvania, was destroyed on May 31, 1889, by a flood caused by the failure of a dam fourteen miles north of the city.
14. A sketch on the margin of a larger print, often portraying greater detail of the central image.
15. Referring to pots in which meat was boiled, this term suggests luxuries or delicacies.

HARRIET PRESCOTT SPOFFORD

(1835–1921)

Harriet Prescott was born in Maine in 1835 but at an early age moved with her family to Newburyport, Massachusetts. As early as her high school years, she showed a good deal of promise as a writer. Her talents were only put to full use, however, when both her father and mother became invalids in the early 1850s and someone in the family needed to start providing income sufficient to support them and their other children. Consequently, Harriet began to submit her work to numerous "story papers"—popular weekly periodicals that looked like newspapers but were filled mostly with fiction and other features—and their frequent acceptances and payments kept the family afloat. Her first recognition as a serious writer came with the publication of three stories in the renowned *Atlantic Monthly* magazine in 1859 and 1860, including her frequently anthologized piece entitled "The Amber Gods." Even after her marriage to lawyer Richard Spofford Jr. in 1865, Harriet continued to bear the burden of familial responsibilities until the 1880s. Out of necessity, she had to produce a great many fictions in a condensed time frame, and thus their quality was quite uneven.

In part because Spofford continued to write in the Romantic vein even after Realism had become the favored genre, literary critics often depicted her as an author whose early promise had gone unfulfilled. It should be noted, though, that Spofford in fact experimented with writing in many different genres, including the romance, the detective story, and supernatural fiction; her work is known to have positively influenced a good number of prominent contemporary women writers. In addition, her fictions remained quite popular among readers all the way to the end of the century, as evidenced by their frequent publication in all the leading magazines of her day, such as the *Atlantic Monthly*, *Harper's Monthly*, *Cosmopolitan*, *Lippincott's*, and *Harper's Bazar*.

"Her Story" was originally published in the December 1872 issue of *Lippincott's*. Although the majority of Spofford's stories that appeared serially, both in well-known and lesser-known periodicals, were not reprinted in her lifetime, "Her Story" was, eventually appearing in *Old Madame and Other Tragedies* (1900). Whether Charlotte Perkins Gilman ever read "Her Story" is unknown, but elements of Spofford's tale are clearly evident in Gilman's famous work "The

THIS NUMBER CONTAINS

QUEEN OF SPADES

AND

"A NATIVE AUTHOR CALLED ROE."

BY

E. P. ROE.

OCTOBER, 1888

LIPPINCOTT'S

MONTHLY MAGAZINE

CONTENTS

PRICE TWENTY-FIVE CENTS

J: B: LIPPINCOTT: CO: PHILADELPHIA:

LONDON: 10 HENRIETTA STREET, COVENT GARDEN.

Cover of *Lippincott's* (October 1888).

Yellow Wall-Paper" (1892), demonstrating that the latter story was not the first fictional exploration of how marriage and motherhood could take a severe toll on women's mental health.

HER STORY (1872)

Wellnigh the worst of it all is the mystery.

If it was true, that accounts for my being here. If it wasn't true, then the best thing they could do with me was to bring me here. Then, too, if it was true, they would save themselves by hurrying me away; and if it wasn't true—You see, just as all roads lead to Rome,[1] all roads led me to this Retreat. If it was true, it was enough to craze me; and if it wasn't true, I was already crazed. And there it is! I can't make out, sometimes, whether I am really beside myself or not; for it seems that whether I was crazed or sane, if it was true, they would naturally put me out of sight and hearing—bury me alive, as they have done, in this Retreat. They? Well, no—he. She stayed at home, I hear. If she had come with us, doubtless I should have found reason enough to say to the physician at once that she was the mad woman, not I—she, who, for the sake of her own brief pleasure, could make a whole after-life of misery for three of us. She—Oh no, don't rise, don't go. I am quite myself, I am perfectly calm. Mad! There was never a drop of crazy blood in the Ridgleys or the Bruces, or any of the generations behind them, and why should it suddenly break out like a smothered fire in me? That is one of the things that puzzle me—why should it come to light all at once in me if it wasn't true?

Now, I am not going to be incoherent. It was too kind in you to be at such trouble to come and see me in this prison, this grave. I will not cry out once: I will just tell you the story of it all exactly as it was, and you shall judge. If I can, that is—oh, if I can! For sometimes, when I think of it, it seems as if Heaven itself would fail to take my part if I did not lift my own voice. And I cry, and I tear my hair and my flesh, till I know my anguish weighs down their joy, and the little scale that holds that joy flies up under the scorching of the sun, and God sees the festering thing for what it is! Ah, it is not injured reason that cries out in that way: it is a breaking heart!

How cool your hand is, how pleasant your face is, how good it is to see you! Don't be afraid of me: I am as much myself, I tell you, as you are. What an absurdity! Certainly any one who heard me make such a speech would think I was insane and without benefit of clergy. To ask you not to be afraid of me because I am myself. Isn't it what they call a vicious circle? And then to cap the climax by adding that I am as much myself as you are myself! But no matter—you know better. Did you say it was ten years? Yes, I knew it was as much as that—oh, it seems a hundred years! But we hardly show it: your hair is still the same as when we were at school; and mine—Look at this lock—I cannot understand why it is only sprinkled here and there: it ought to be white as the driven snow. My babies are almost grown women, Elizabeth. How could he do without me all this time?

Hush now! I am not going to be disturbed at all; only that color of your hair puts me so in mind of his: perhaps there was just one trifle more of gold in his. Do you remember that lock that used to fall over his forehead and which he always tossed back so impatiently. I used to think that the golden Apollo of Rhodes[2] had just such massive, splendid locks of hair as that; but I never told him; I never had the face to praise him; she had. She could exclaim how like ivory the forehead was—that great wide forehead—how that keen aquiline was to be found in the portrait of the Spencer of two hundred years ago.[3] She knew how, by a silent flattery, as she shrank away and looked up at him, to admire his haughty stature, and make him feel the strength and glory of his manhood and the delicacy of her womanhood.

She was a little thing—a little thing, but wondrous fair. Fair, did I say? No: she was as dark as an Egyptian, but such perfect features, such rich and splendid color, such great soft eyes—so soft, so black—so superb a smile; and then such hair! When she let it down, the backward curling ends lay on the ground and she stood on them, or the children lifted them and carried them behind her as pages carry a queen's train. If I had my two hands twisted in that hair! Oh, how I hate that hair! It would make as good a bowstring as ever any Carthaginian woman's made.[4] Ah, that is too wicked! I am sure you think so. But living all these lonesome years as I have done seems to double back one's sinfulness upon one's self. Because one is sane it does not follow that one is a saint. And when I think of my innocent babies playing with the hair that once I saw him lift and pass across his lips! But I will not think of it!

Well, well! I was a pleasant thing to look at myself once on a time, you know, Elizabeth. He used to tell me so: those were his very words. I was tall and slender, and if my skin was pale it was clear with a pearly clearness, and the lashes of my gray eyes were black as shadows; but now those eyes are only the color of tears.

I never told any one anything about it—I never could. It was so deep down in my heart, that love I had for him: it slept there so dark and still and full, for he was all I had in the world. I was alone, and orphan—if not friendless, yet quite dependent. I see you remember it all. I did not even sit in the pew with my cousin's family, that was so full, but down in one beneath the gallery, you know. And altogether life was a thing to me that hardly seemed worth the living. I went to church one Sunday, I recollect, idly and dreamingly as usual. I did not look off my book till a voice filled my ear—a strange new voice, a deep sweet voice, that invited you and yet commanded you—a voice whose sound divided the core of my heart, and sent thrills that were half joy, half pain, coursing through me. And then I looked up and saw him at the desk. He was reading the first lesson: "Fear not, for I have redeemed thee, I have called thee by thy name: thou art mine."[5] And I saw the bright hair, the upturned face, the white surplice, and I said to myself, It is a vision, it is an angel; and I cast down my eyes. But the voice went on, and when I looked again he was still there. Then I bethought me that it must be the one who was coming to take the place of our superannuated rector—the last of a fine line, they had been saying the

day before, who, instead of finding his pleasure otherwise, had taken all his
wealth and prestige into the Church.

Why will a trifle melt you so—a strain of music, a color in the sky, a perfume? Have you never leaned from the window at evening, and had the scent
of a flower float by and fill you with as keen a sorrow as if it had been disaster
touching you? Long ago, I mean—we never lean from any windows here. I don't
know how, but it was in that same invisible way that this voice melted me; and
when I heard it saying, "But thou hast not called upon me, O Jacob, but thou
hast been weary of me, O Israel,"[6] I was fairly crying. Oh, nervous tears, I dare
say. The doctor here would tell you so, at any rate. And that is what I complain
of here: they give a physiological reason for every emotion—they could give you
a chemical formula for your very soul, I have no doubt. Well, perhaps they were
nervous tears, for certainly there was nothing to cry for, and the mood went as
suddenly as it came—changed to a sort of exaltation, I suppose—and when they
sang the psalm, and he had swept in, in his black gown, and had mounted the
pulpit stairs, and was resting that fair head on the big Bible in his silent prayer, I
too was singing—singing like one possessed:

> *Awake, my glory; harp and lute,*
> *No longer let your strains be mute;*
> *And I, my tuneful part to take,*
> *Will with the early dawn awake!*[7]

And as he rose I saw him searching for the voice unconsciously, and our eyes
met. Oh, it was a fresh young voice, let it be mine or whose. I can hear it now
as if it were someone else singing. Ah, ah, it has been silent so many years! Does
it make you smile to hear me pity myself? It is not myself I am pitying: it is that
fresh young girl that loved so. But it used to rejoice me to think that I loved him
before I laid eyes on him.

He came to my cousin's in the week—not to see Sylvia or to see Laura: he
talked of church-music with my cousin, and then crossed the room and sat down
by me. I remember how I grew cold and trembled—how glad, how shy I was;
and then he had me sing; and at first Sylvia sang with us, but by and by we sang
alone—I sang alone. He brought me yellow old church music, written in quaint
characters: he said those characters, those old square breves, were a text guarding secrets of enchantment as much as the text of Merlin's book did; and so we
used to find it. Once he brought a copy of an old Roman hymn, written only in
the Roman letters: he said it was a hymn which the ancients sang to Maia, the
mother-earth, and which the Church fathers adopted, singing it stealthily in the
hidden places of the Catacombs; and together we translated it into tones. A rude
but majestic thing it was.

And once—The sunshine was falling all about us in the bright lonely room,
and the shadows of the rose leaves at the window were dancing over us. I had
been singing a Gloria[8] while he walked up and down the room, and he came up

behind me: he stooped and kissed me on the mouth. And after that there was no singing, for, lovely as the singing was, the love was lovelier yet. Why do I complain of such a hell as this is now? I had my heaven once—oh, I had my heaven once! And as for the other, perhaps I deserve it all, for I saw God only through him: it was he that waked me to worship. I had no faith but Spencer's faith; if he had been a heathen, I should have been the same, and creeds and systems might have perished for me had he only been spared from the wreck. And he had loved me from the first moment that his eyes met mine. "When I looked at you," he said, "singing that simple hymn that first day, I felt as I do when I look at the evening star leaning out of the clear sunset lustre: there is something in your face as pure, as remote, as shining. It will always be there," he said, "though you should live a hundred years." He little knew, he little knew!

But he loved me then—oh yes, I never doubted that. There were no happier lovers trod the earth. We took our pleasure as lovers do: we walked in the fields; we sat on the river's side; together we visited the poor and sick; he read me the passages he liked best in his writing from week to week; he brought me the verse from which he meant to preach, and up in the organ-loft I improvised to him the thoughts that it inspired in me. I did that timidly indeed: I could not think my thoughts were worth his hearing till I forgot myself, and only thought of him and the glory I would have revealed to him, and then the great clustering chords and the full music of the diapason[9] swept out beneath my hands—swept along the aisles and swelled up the raftered roof as if they would find the stars, and sunset and twilight stole around us there as we sat still in the succeeding silence. I was happy: I was humble too. I wondered why I had been chosen for such a blest and sacred lot. It seemed *that* to be allowed to minister one delight to him. I had a little print of the angel of the Lord appearing to Mary with the lily of annunciation in his hand, and I thought—I dare not tell you what I thought. I made an idol of my piece of clay.[10]

When the leaves had turned we were married, and he took me home. Ah, what a happy home it was! Luxury and beauty filled it. When I first went into it and left the chill October night without, fires blazed upon the hearths; flowers bloomed in every room; a marble Eros held a light up, searching for his Psyche.[11] "Our love has found its soul," said he. He led me to the music-room—a temple in itself, for its rounded ceiling towered to the height of the house. There were golden organ-pipes and banks of keys fit for St. Cecilia's hand;[12] there were all the delightful outlines of violin and piccolo and harp and horn for any who knew how to use them; there was a pianoforte near the door for me—one such as I had never touched before; and there were cases on all sides filled with the rarest musical works. The floor was bare and inlaid; the windows were latticed in stained glass, so that no common light of day ever filtered through, but light bluer than the sky, gold as the dawn, purple as the night; and then there were vast embowering chairs, in any of which he could hide himself away while I made my incantation, as he sometimes called it, of the great spirits of song. As I tried the piano that night he tuned the old Amati[13] which he himself now and then played upon himself, and together we improvised our own epithalamium.[14] It was the violin that took the strong assuring part with strains of piercing sweetness, and the music of the piano flowed along in a soft cantabile[15] of undersong. It seemed to me as if his part was like the flight of some white and strong-winged bird above a sunny brook.

But he had hardly created this place for the love of me alone. He adored music as a regenerator; he meant to use it so among his people: here were to be pursued those labors which should work miracles when produced in the open church. For he was building a church with the half of his fortune—a church full of restoration of the old and creation of the new: the walls within were to be a frosty tracery of vines running to break into the gigantic passion-flower that formed the rose-window; the lectern a golden globe upon a tripod, clasped by a silver dove holding on outstretched wings the book.

I have feared, since I have been here, that Spencer's piety was less piety than partisanship: I have doubted if faith were so much alive in him as the love of a great perfect system, and the pride in it I know he always felt. But I never thought about it then: I believed in him as I would have believed in an apostle. So stone by stone the church went up, and stone by stone our lives followed it—lives of such peace, such bliss! Then fresh hopes came into it—sweet trembling hopes; and by and by our first child was born. And if I had been happy before, what was I then? There are some compensations in this world: such happiness could not come twice, such happiness as there was in that moment when I lay, painless and at peace, with the little cheek nestled beside my own, while he bent above us both, proud and glad and tender. It was a dear little baby—so fair, so bright! and when she could walk she could sing. Her sister sang earlier yet; and what music their two shrill sweet voices made as they sat in their little chairs together at twilight before the fire, their curls glistening and their red shoes glistening, while they sang the evening hymn, Spencer on one side of the hearth and I upon the other! Sometimes we let the dear things sit up for a later hour in the music-room—for many a canticle[16] we tried and practiced there that hushed hearts and awed them when the choir gave them on succeeding Sundays—and always afterward I heard them singing in their sleep, just as a bird stirs in his nest and sings his stave in the night. Oh, we were happy then; and it was then she came.

She was the step-child of his uncle, and had a small fortune of her own, and Spencer had been left her guardian; and so she was to live with us—at any rate, for a while. I dreaded her coming. I did not want the intrusion; I did not like the things I heard about her; I knew she would be a discord in our harmony. But Spencer, who had only seen her once in her childhood, had been told by some one who traveled in Europe with her that she was delightful and had a rare intelligence. She was one of those women often delightful to men indeed, but whom other women—by virtue of their own kindred instincts, it may be, perhaps by virtue of temptations overcome—see through and know for what they are. But she had her own way of charming: she was the being of infinite variety—to-day glad, to-morrow sad, freakish, and always exciting you by curiosity as to her next caprice, and so moody that after a season of the lowering weather of one of her dull humors you were ready to sacrifice something for the sake of the sunshine that she knew how to make so vivid and so sweet. Then, too, she brought forward her forces by detachment. At first she was the soul of domestic life, sitting at night beneath the light and embossing on weblike muslin designs of flower and leaf which she had learned in her convent, listening to Spencer as he read, and taking from the little wallet of her work-basket apropos scraps which she had preserved from the sermon of some Italian father of the Church or of some French divine. As for me, the only thing I knew was my poor music; and I used to burn with indignation when she interposed that unknown tongue between my husband and myself. Presently her horses came, and then, graceful in her dark riding-habit, she would spend a morning fearlessly subduing one of the fiery fellows, and dash away at last with plume and veil streaming behind her. In the early evening she would dance with the children—witch-dances they were—with her round arms linked above her head, and her feet weaving the measure in and out as deftly as any flashing-footed Bayadere[17] might do—only when Spencer was there to see: at other times I saw she pushed the little hindering things aside without a glance.

By and by she began to display a strange dramatic sort of power: she would rehearse to Spencer scenes that she had met with from day to day in the place, giving now the old churchwarden's voice and now the sexton's, their gestures and very faces; she could tell the ailments of half the old women in the parish who came to me with them, and in their own tone and manner to the life; she told us once of a street scene, with the crier crying a lost child, the mother following with lamentations, the passing strangers questioning, the boys hooting, and the child's reappearance, followed by a tumult, with kisses and blows and cries, so that I thought I saw it all; and presently she had found the secret and vulnerable spot of every friend we had, and could personate them all as vividly as if she did it by necromancy.

One night she began to sketch our portraits in charcoal: the likenesses were not perfect; she exaggerated the careless elegance of Spencer's attitude; perhaps the primness of my own; but yet he saw there the ungraceful trait for the first time, I think. And so much led to more: she brought out her portfolios, and there were her pencil-sketches from the Rhine and from the Guadalquivir,[18] rich water-colors of Venetian scenes, interiors of old churches, and sheet after sheet covered with details of church architecture. Spencer had been admiring all the others—in spite of something that I saw in them, a something that was not true, a trait of her own identity, for I had come to criticise her sharply—but when his eye rested on those sheets I saw it sparkle, and he caught them up and pored over them one by one.

"I see you have mastered the whole thing," he said: "you must instruct me here." And so she did. And there were hours, while I was busied with servants and accounts or with the children, when she was closeted with Spencer in the study, criticising, comparing, make drawings, hunting up authorities; other hours when they walked away together to the site of the new church that was building, and here an arch was destroyed, and there an aisle was extended, and here a row of cloisters sketched into the plan, and there a row of windows, till the whole design was reversed and made over. And they had the thing between them, for, admire and sympathize as I might, I did not *know*. At first Spencer would repeat the day's achievement to me, but the contempt for my ignorance which she did not deign to hide soon put an end to it when she was present.

It was this interest that now unveiled a new phase of her character: she was devout. She had a little altar in her room; she knew all about albs[19] and chasubles;[20] she would have persuaded Spencer to burn candles in the chancel;[21] she talked of a hundred mysteries and symbols; she wanted to embroider a stole to lay across his shoulders. She was full of small church sentimentalities, and as one after another she uttered them, it seemed to me that her belief was no sound fruit of any system—if it were belief, and not a mere bunch of fancies—but only, as you might say, a rotten windfall of the Romish Church:[22] it had none of the round splendor of that Church's creed, none of the pure simplicity of ours: it would be no stay in trouble, no shield in temptation. I said as much to Spencer.

"You are prejudiced," said he: "her belief is the result of long observation abroad, I think. She has found the need of outward observances: they are, she has told me, a shrine to the body of her faith, like that commanded in the building of the tabernacle, where the ark of the covenant was enclosed in the holy of holies."

"And you didn't think it profane in her to speak so? But I don't believe it, Spencer," I said. "She has no faith: she has some sentimentalisms."

"You are prejudiced," he repeated. "She seems to me a wonderful and gifted being."

"Too gifted," I said. "Her very gifts are unnatural in their abundance. There must be scrofula[23] there to keep such a fire in the blood and sting the brain to such action: she will die in a madhouse, depend upon it." Think of me saying such a thing as that!

"I have never heard you speak so before," he replied coldly. "I hope you do not envy her powers."

"I envy her nothing," I cried. "For she is as false as she is beautiful!" But I did—oh I did!

"Beautiful?" said Spencer. "Is she beautiful? I never thought of that."

"You are very blind, then," I said with a glad smile.

Spencer smiled too. "It is not the kind of beauty I admire," said he.

"Then I must teach you, sir," said she. And we both started to see her in the doorway, and I, for one, did not know, till shortly before I found myself here, how much or how little she had learned of what we said.

"Then I must teach you, sir," said she again. And she came deliberately into the firelight and paused upon the rug, drew out the silver arrows and shook down all her hair about her, till the great snake-like coils unrolled upon the floor.

"Hyacinthine,"[24] said Spencer.

"Indeed it is," said she—"the very color of the jacinth,[25] with that red tint in its darkness that they call black in the shade and gold in the sun. Now look at me."

"Shut your eyes, Spencer," I cried, and laughed.[26]

But he did not shut his eyes. The firelight flashed over her: the color in her cheeks and on her lips sprang ripe and red in it as she held the hair away from them with her rosy finger-tips; her throat curved small and cream-white from the bosom that the lace of her dinner-dress scarcely hid; and the dark eyes glowed with a great light as they lay full on his.

"You mustn't call it vanity," said she. "It is only that it is impossible, looking at the picture in the glass, not to see it as I see any other picture. But for all that, I know it is not every fool's beauty: it is no daub for the vulgar gaze, but a master-piece that it needs the educated eye to find. I could tell you how this nostril is like that in a famous marble, how the curve of this cheek is that of a certain Venus,[27] the line of this forehead like the line in the dreamy Antinous'[28] forehead. Are you taught? Is it beautiful?"

Then she twisted her hair again and fastened the arrows, and laughed and turned away to look over the evening paper. But as for Spencer, as he lay back in his lordly way, surveying the vision from crown to toe, I saw him flush—I saw him flush and start and quiver, and then he closed his eyes and pressed his fingers on them, and lay back again and said not a word.

She began to read aloud something concerning services at the recent dedi-cation of a church. I was called out as she read. When I came back, a half hour afterward, they were talking. I stopped at my work-table in the next room for a skein of floss that she had asked me for, and I heard her saying, "You cannot expect me to treat you with reverence. You are a married priest, and you know what opinion I necessarily must have of married priests." Then I came in and she was silent.

But I knew, I always knew, that if Spencer had not felt himself weak, had not found himself stirred, if he had not recognized that, when he flushed and quivered before her charm, it was the flesh and not the spirit that tempted him, he would not have listened to her subtle invitation to austerity. As it was, he did. He did—partly in shame, partly in punishment; but to my mind the listening was confusion. She had set the wedge that was to sever our union—the little seed in a mere idle cleft that grows and grows and splits the rock asunder.

Well, I had my duties, you know. I never felt my husband's wealth a reason why I should neglect them any more than another wife should neglect her duties. I was wanted in the parish, sent for here and waited for there: the dying liked to see me comfort their living, the living liked to see me touch their dead; some wanted help, and others wanted consolation; and where I felt myself too young and unlearned to give advice, I could at least give sympathy. Perhaps I was the more called upon for such detail of duty because Spencer was busy with the greater things, the church-building and the sermons—sermons that once on a

time lifted you and held you on their strong wings. But of late Spencer had
been preaching old sermons. He had been moody and morose too: sometimes he
seemed oppressed with melancholy. He had spoken to me strangely, had looked
at me as if he pitied me, had kept away from me. But she had not regarded
his moods: she had followed him in his solitary strolls, had sought him in his
study; and she had ever a mystery or symbol to be interpreted, the picture of
a private chapel that she had heard of when abroad, or the ground-plan of an
ancient one, or some new temptation to his ambition, as I divine; and soon he
was himself again.

I was wrong to leave him so to her, but what was there else for me to do? And
as for those duties of mine, as I followed them I grew restive; I abridged them,
I hastened home. I was impatient even with the detentions the children caused.
I could not leave them to their nurses, for all that; but they kept me away from
him, and he was alone with her.

One day at last he told me that his mind was troubled by the suspicion that
his marriage was a mistake; that on his part at least it had been wrong; that he
had been thinking a priest should have the Church only for his bride, and should
wait at the altar mortified in every affection; that it was not for hands that were
full of caresses and lips that were covered with kisses to break sacramental bread
and offer praise. But for answer I brought my children and put them in his arms.
I was white and cold and shaking, but I asked him if they were not justification
enough; and I told him that he did his duty better abroad for the heartening
of a wife at home, and that he knew better how to interpret God's love to men
through his own love for his children; and I laid my head on his breast beside
them, and he clasped us all and we cried together, he and I.

But that was not enough, I found. And when our good bishop came, who had
always been like a father to Spencer, I led the conversation to that point one evening, and he discovered Spencer's trouble, and took him away and reasoned with
him. The bishop was a power with Spencer, and I think that was the end of it.

The end of that, but only the beginning of the rest. For she had accustomed
him to the idea of separation from me—the idea of doing without me. He had
put me away from himself once in his mind: we had been one soul, and now we
were two.

One day, as I stood in my sleeping-room with the door ajar, she came in. She
had never been there before, and I cannot tell you how insolently she looked
about her. There was a bunch of flowers on a stand that Spencer himself placed
there for me every morning. He had always done so, and there had been no reason for breaking off the habit; and I had always worn one of them at my throat.
She advanced a hand to pull out a blossom. "Do not touch them," I cried: "my
husband puts them there."

"Suppose he does?" said she lightly. "What devotion!" Then she overlooked
me with the long sweeping glance of search and contempt, shrugged her shoulders, and with a French sentence that I did not understand turned back and
coolly broke off the blossom she had marked and hung it in her hair. I could

not take her by the shoulders and put her from the room: I could not touch the flowers that she had desecrated. I left the room myself, and left her in it, and went down to dinner for the first time without the flower at my throat. I saw Spencer's eye note the omission: perhaps he took it as a release from me, for he never put the flowers in my room again after that day.

Nor did he ask me any more into his study, as he had been used, or read his sermons to me: there was no need of his talking over the church-building with me—he had her to talk it over with. And as for our music, that had been a rare thing since she arrived, for her conversation had been such as to leave but little time for it, and somehow when she came into the music-room and began to dictate to me the time in which I should take an Inflammatus[29] and the spirit in which I should sing a ballad, I could not bear it. Then, too, to tell you the truth, my voice was hoarse and choked with tears full half the time.

It was some weeks after the flowers ceased that our youngest child fell ill. She was very ill—I don't think Spencer knew how ill. I dared not trust her with any one, and Spencer said no one could take such care of her as her mother could; so, although we had nurses in plenty, I hardly left the room by night or day. I heard their voices down below, I saw them go out for their walks. It was a hard fight, but I saved her.

But I was worn to a shadow when all was done—worn with anxiety for her, with alternate fevers of hope and fear, with the weight of my responsibility as to her life; and with anxiety for Spencer too, with a despairing sense that the end of peace had come, and with the total sleeplessness of many nights. Now, when the child was mending and gaining every day, I could not sleep if I would.

The doctor gave me anodynes,[30] but to no purpose: they only nerved me wide awake. My eyes ached, and my brain ached, and my body ached, but it was of no use: I could not sleep. I counted the spots on the wall, the motes upon my eyes, the notes of all the sheets of music I could recall; I remembered the Eastern punishment of keeping the condemned awake till they die, and I wondered what my crime was; I thought if I could but sleep I might forget my trouble, or take it up freshly and master it. But no, it was always there—a heavy cloud, a horror of foreboding. As I heard that woman's step go by the door I longed to rid the house of it, and I dinted my palms with my nails till she had passed.

I did not know what to do. It seemed to me that I was wicked in letting the thing go on, in suffering Spencer to be any longer exposed to her power; but then I feared to take a step lest I should thereby rivet the chains she was casting on him. And I longed so for one hour of the old dear happiness—the days when I and the children had been all and enough. I did not know what to do; I had no one to counsel with; I was wild within myself, and all distraught. Once I thought if I could not rid the house of her I could rid it of myself; and as I went through a dark passage and chanced to look up where a bright-headed nail glittered, I questioned if it would bear my weight. For days the idea haunted me. I fancied that when I was gone perhaps he would love me again, and at any rate I might be asleep and at rest. But the thought of the children prevented me, and one other thought—I was not certain that even my sorrows would excuse me before God.

I went down to dinner again at last. How she glowed and abounded in her beauty as she sat there! And I—I must have been very thin and ghastly: perhaps I looked a little wild in all my bewilderment and hurt. His heart smote him, it may be, for he came round to where I sat by the fire afterward and smoothed my hair and kissed my forehead. He could not tell all I was suffering then—all I was struggling with; for I thought I had better put him out of the world than let him, who was once so pure and good, stay in it to sin. I could have done it, you know. For though I still lay with the little girl, I could have stolen back into our own room with the chloroform,[31] and he would never have known. I turned the handle of the door one night, but the bolt was slipped. I never thought of killing her, you see: let her live and sin, if she would. She was the thing of slime and sin, a splendid tropical growth of the passionate heat and the slime: it was only her nature. But then we think it no harm to kill reptiles, however splendid.

But it was by that time that the voices had begun to talk with me—all night long, all day. It was they, I found, that had kept me so sleepless. Go where I might, they were ever before me. If I went to the woods, I heard them in the whisper of every pine tree. If I went down to the seashore, I heard them in the plash of every wave; I heard them in the wind, in the singing of my ears, in the children's breath as I hung above them, for I had decided that if I went out of the world I would take the children with me. If I sat down to play, the things would twist the chords into discords: if I sat down to read, they would come between me and the page. Then I could see them: they had wings like bats. I did not dare speak of them, although I fancied she suspected me, for once she said, as I was kissing my little girl, "When you are gone to a madhouse, don't think they'll have many such kisses." I did not answer her, I did not look up: I suppose I should have flown at her throat if I had.

I took the children out with me on my long rambles: we went for miles; sometimes I carried one, sometimes the other. I took such long, long walks to escape those noisome things: they would never leave me till I was quite tired out. Now and then I was gone all day; and all the time that I was gone he was with her, I knew, and she was tricking out her beauty and practicing her arts.

I went to a little festival with them, for Spencer insisted. And she made shadow-pictures on the wall, wonderful things with her perfect profile and her perfect arms and her subtle curves—she out of sight, the shadow only seen. Now it was Isis,[32] I remember, and now it was the head and shoulders and trailing hair of a floating sea-nymph. And then there were charades in which she played; and I can't tell you the glorious thing she looked when she came on as Helen of Troy[33] with all her "beauty shadowed in white veils," you know—that brown and red beauty with its smiles and radiance under the wavering of the flower-wrought veil. I sat by Spencer, and I felt him shiver. He was fighting and struggling too within himself, very likely; only he knew that he was going to yield after all—only he longed to yield while he feared. But as for me, I saw one of those bat-like things perched on her ear as she stood before us, and when she opened her mouth to speak I saw them flying in and out. And I said to Spencer, "She is tormenting me. I cannot stay and see her swallowing the souls of men in this way." And I would have gone, but he held me down fast in my seat. But if I was crazy then—as they say I was, I suppose—it was only with a metaphor, for she was sucking Spencer's soul out of his body.

But I was not crazy. I should admit I might have been if I alone had seen those evil spirits. But Spencer saw them too. He never exactly told me so, but I knew he did; for when I opened the church door late, as I often did at that time after my long walks, they would rush in past me with a whizz, and as I sat in the pew I would see him steadily avoid looking at me; and if he looked by any chance, he would turn so pale that I have thought he would drop where he stood; and then he would redden afterward as though one had struck him. He knew then what I endured with them; but I was not the one to speak of it. Don't tell me that his color changed and he shuddered so because I sat there mumbling and nodding to myself: it was because he saw those things mopping and mowing beside me and whispering in my ear. Oh what loathsomeness the obscene creatures whispered!—foul quips and evil words I had never heard before, ribald songs and oaths; and I would clap my hands over my mouth to keep from crying out at them. Creatures of the imagination, you may say. It is possible, but they were so vivid that they seem real to me even now: I burn and tingle as I recall them. And how could I have imagined such sounds, such shapes, of things I had never heard or seen or dreamed?

And Spencer was very unhappy, I am sure. I was the mother of his children, and if he loved me no more, he had an old kindness for me still, and my distress distressed him. But for all that the glamour was on him, and he could not give up that woman and her beauty and her charm. Once or twice he may have thought about sending her away, but perhaps he could not bring himself to do it—perhaps he reflected it was too late, and now it was no matter. But every day she stayed he was the more like wax in her hands. Oh, he was weaker than water that is poured out. He was abandoning himself, and forgetting earth and heaven and hell itself, before a passion—a passion that soon would cloy, and then would sting.

It was the spring season then: I had been out several hours. The sunset fell while I was in the wood, and the stars came out; and at one time I thought I would lie down there on last year's leaves and never get up again; but I remembered the children, and went home to them. They were both in bed and asleep when I took off my shoes and opened the door of their room—breathing so sweetly and evenly, the little yellow heads close together on one pillow, their hands tossed about the coverlid, their parted lips, their rosy cheeks. I knelt to feel the warm breath on my own cold cheek, and then the voices began whispering again: "If only they never waked! they never waked!"

And all I could do was to spring to my feet and run from the room. I ran shoeless down the great staircase and through the long hall. I thought I would go to Spencer and tell him all—all my sorrows, all the suggestions of the voices, and maybe in the endeavor to save me he would save himself. And I ran down the long dimly-lighted drawing-room, led by the sound I heard, to the music-room, whose doors were open just beyond. It was lighted only by the pale glimmer from the other room and by the moonlight through the painted panes. And I paused to listen to what I had never listened to there—the sound of the harp and a voice with it. Of course they had not heard me coming, and I hesitated and looked, and then I glided within the door and stood just by the open piano there.

She sat at the harp singing—the huge gilded harp. I did not know she sang—she had kept that for her last reserve—but she struck the harp so that it sang itself, like some great prisoned soul, and her voice followed it—oh so rich a voice! My own was white and thin, I felt, beside it. But mine had soared, and hers still clung to earth—a contralto sweet with honeyed sweetness—the sweetness of unstrained honey that has the earth-taste and the heavy blossom-dust yet in it—sweet, though it grew hoarse and trembling with passion. He sat in one of the great arm-chairs just before her: he was white with feeling, with rapture, with forgetfulness; his eyes shone like stars. He moved restlessly, a strange smile kindled all his face: he bent toward her, and the music broke off in the middle as they threw their arms around each other, and hung there lip to lip and heart to heart. And suddenly I crashed down both my hands on the keyboard before me, and stood and glared upon them.

And I never knew anything more till I woke up here. And that is the whole of it. That is the puzzle of it—was it a horrid nightmare, an insane vision, or was it true? Was it true that I saw Spencer, my white, clean lover, my husband, a man of God, the father of our spotless babies,—was it true that I saw him so, or was it only some wild, vile conjuration of disease? Oh, I would be willing to have been crazed a lifetime, a whole lifetime, only to wake one moment before I died and find that that had never been!

Well, well, well! When time passed and I became more quiet, I told the doctor here about the spirits—I never told him of Spencer or of her—and he bade me dismiss care; he said I was ill—excitement and sleeplessness had surcharged my nerves with that strange magnetic fluid that has worked so much mischief in the world. There was no organic disease, you see; only when my nerves were rested and right, my brain would be right. And the doctor gave me medicines and books and work, and when I saw the spirits again I was to go instantly to him. And after a little while I was not sure that I did see them; and in a little while longer they had ceased to come altogether, and I have had no more of them. I was on my parole then in the parlor, at the table, in the grounds. I felt that I was cured of whatever had ailed me: I could escape at any moment that I wished.

And it came Christmas-time. A terrible longing for home overcame me—for my children. I thought of them at this time when I had been used to take such pains for their pleasure. I thought of the little empty stockings, the sad faces; I fancied I could hear them crying for me. I forgot all about my word of honor. It seemed to me that I should die, that I might as well die, if I could not see my little darlings, and hold them on my knees, and sing to them while the chimes were ringing in the Christmas Eve; and winter was here and there was so much to do for them. And I walked down the garden, and looked out at the gate, and opened it and went through. And I slept that night in a barn—so free, so free and glad; and the next day an old farmer and his sons, who thought they did me a service, brought me back, and of course I shrieked and raved; and so would you.

But since then I have been in this ward and a prisoner. I have my work, my amusements. I send such little things as I can make to my girls; I read; sometimes of late I sing in the Sunday service. The place is a sightly place; the grounds, when we are taken out, are fine; the halls are spacious and pleasant. Pleasant—but ah, when you have trodden them ten years! And so, you see, if I were a clod, if I had no memory, no desires, if I had never been happy before, I might be happy now. I am confident the doctor thinks me well, but he has no orders to let me go. Sometimes it is so wearisome; and it might be worse if lately I had not been allowed a new service, and that is to try to make a woman smile who came here a year ago. She is a little woman, swarthy as a Malay,[34] but her hair, that grows as rapidly as a fungus grows in the night, is whiter than leprosy: her eyebrows are so long and white that they veil and blanch her dark dim eyes, and she has no front teeth. A stone from a falling spire struck her from her horse, they say—the blow battered her and beat out reason and beauty. Her mind is dead: she remembers nothing, knows nothing; but she follows me about like a dog: she seems to want to do something for me, to propitiate me. All she ever says is to beg me to do her no harm. She will not go to sleep without my hand in hers. Sometimes, after long effort, I think there is a gleam of intelligence, but the doctor says there was once too much intelligence, and her case is hopeless. Hopeless, poor thing!—that is an awful word: I could not wish it said for my worst enemy. In spite of these ten years I cannot feel that it has yet been said for me. If I am strange just now, it is only the excitement of seeing you, only the habit of the strange sights and sounds here. I should be calm and well enough at home. I sit and picture to myself that some time Spencer will come for me—will take me to my girls, my fireside, my music. I shall hear his voice, I shall rest in his arms, I shall be blest again. For, oh, Elizabeth, I do forgive him all! Or if he will not dare to trust himself at first, I picture to myself how he will send another—some old friend who knew me before my trouble—who will see me and judge, and carry back report that I am all I used to be—some friend who will open the gates of heaven to me, or close the gates of hell upon me—who will hold my life and my fate. If—oh if it should be you, Elizabeth!

NOTES

1. During the Roman Empire, most roads did indeed "lead to Rome," its capital; this expression means that no matter what choice one makes, one will end up in the same place.
2. To celebrate a military victory, the Greeks erected a large statue of the Titan Helios, over one hundred feet tall, on the Greek island of Rhodes in 280 BCE.

Also known as the "Colossus of Rhodes" and one of the Seven Wonders of the Ancient World, it was destroyed during an earthquake in 226 BCE. Here the narrator mistakenly conflates Helios, god of the sun, with Apollo, a later Greek god of sun, light, medicine, and many other things.

3. A likely reference to a painting of one of Spencer's ancestors that hangs in the house.

4. The city of Carthage, located in what is now Tunisia, in northern Africa, was founded in 813 BCE and served as the capital of a powerful empire that rivaled that of Rome. According to legend, during the final battle for Carthage (149–146 BCE) against the Romans, Carthaginian women cut off their hair to make bowstrings for their soldiers. After the city was destroyed by the Romans in 146 BCE, it became the Roman Empire's most important city in Africa; in 698 CE it was destroyed by Arab conquerors.

5. Isaiah 43:1 (King James Version): "But now thus saith the LORD that created thee, O Jacob, and he that formed thee, O Israel, Fear not: for I have redeemed thee, I have called thee by thy name; thou art mine." This passage is typically used to reassure Christian believers that God is always with them.

6. In Isaiah 43:19 (KJV), God tells Jacob and his followers: "Behold, I will do a new thing; now it shall spring forth; shall ye not know it? I will even make a way in the wilderness, and rivers in the desert." God then, in Isaiah 43:22, chastises them for not worshiping him sufficiently, saying: "But thou hast not called upon me, O Jacob; but thou hast been weary of me, O Israel."

7. Part of a Christian hymn originally published in *The Sunday School Liturgy* (1860) and thus regularly taught to young people at this time. It is loosely based on Psalm 57:8–11.

8. The mass performed in many Christian churches includes a hymn entitled "Glory Be to God in the Highest," which begins with the Latin original, *Gloria in excelsis Deo;* singing "a Gloria" demonstrates one's faith in God.

9. The entire range of notes in an organ.

10. She is guiltily confessing that contrary to God's wishes not to idolize earthly things, she did so with this picture, which she describes as "clay"; this latter term is often used in the Bible to represent something that is frail and liable to decay.

11. Eros is the Greek god of love, and Psyche, the goddess of the soul, becomes his wife.

12. St. Cecilia is the patron saint of musicians and has often been depicted as playing a small organ.

13. The Amati family were well-known and highly respected Italian violin makers.

14. A song that praises a bride and groom at their wedding and expresses a desire for their happiness.

15. A very expressive musical tune (Italian).

16. A hymn.

17. An Indian dancing girl (French).

18. The Rhine River flows through Switzerland, Germany, and the Netherlands and was often associated at this time with highly Romantic scenes. The Guadalquivir River is a major river in southwestern Spain.

19. A white robe worn by those conducting church services.

20. A kind of sleeveless vest, usually worn over the alb.

21. The part of a church that is cordoned off from the main area and is used by those conducting the religious services.
22. A Roman Catholic church. Many Protestants at this time felt Roman Catholic beliefs were decadent and heretical.
23. Tuberculosis of the lymph nodes.
24. Resembling the hyacinth flower; a dark shade of purple.
25. A reddish-orange precious stone; also a synonym for "hyacinth."
26. In Greek mythology, Medusa was a female monster who turned to stone all those who looked at her face; here the narrator is warning Spencer not to suffer a similar fate by looking at his enchantress.
27. The Roman goddess of love, reputed to be the most beautiful woman in existence.
28. A servant to the Roman emperor Hadrian, regarded as the epitome of masculine beauty.
29. A certain type of musical composition for both voice and instruments. Musical time (the signature) tells the number of beats per measure.
30. A type of medicine that relieves pain.
31. A toxic liquid that was often used to anesthetize patients undergoing medical procedures. If too much was administered, it could cause death.
32. An Egyptian goddess associated with ideal motherhood and healing the sick.
33. In Greek mythology, Helen of Troy—allegedly the daughter of Zeus and the mortal princess Leda—was the most beautiful woman in the world.
34. A person from Malaysia or Indonesia.

RUTH McENERY STUART

(1849–1917)

Mary Routh McEnery was born in Louisiana in 1849 and spent the first forty-one years of her life in that state, except for a brief period during which she lived in Washington, Arkansas, with her husband, the wealthy cotton planter Alfred Oden Stuart. After his death in 1883, she returned to New Orleans, where the rest of her family resided, and began writing under the name Ruth McEnery Stuart. She soon achieved success as a writer and in 1890 moved to the New York City area, where she lived for the rest of her life. She never left Louisiana or Arkansas behind, however, for they were always present in almost every story or novel she ever wrote. Her books—the novels and short story collections—sold very well, and she was consequently one of the highest-paid women writers of her era.

Modern readers may find it difficult to understand why Stuart was much more popular than her contemporary and fellow Louisianian Kate Chopin, who is now widely celebrated by academic critics. Both writers had as their main subjects various aspects of life in Louisiana at the end of the nineteenth century; however, Stuart's stereotypical, romanticized portrayals of African Americans and Italian immigrants were much preferred by White readers—both in the North and the South—to Chopin's more nuanced and realistic depictions of Creole culture. At a time when magazine and book editors in the North were clamoring for works about the "exotic" South, and when their mostly White readers fervently wished to leave the past behind and reunite the country, Stuart's tales of formerly enslaved Black people, most of them either stereotypically lazy men or kind-hearted women, satisfied those who wished to believe that African Americans in the South were content under the firm control of southern Whites. The latter group was often represented in Stuart's fictions by an educated White (and usually male) framing narrator. Stuart was also widely applauded by critics for what they presumed was a very accurate portrayal of African American dialect. However, given the paternalistic, condescending attitude toward African Americans that Stuart displayed in so many of her works, as well as her frequent use of terms now deemed offensive, it is little wonder that since her death in 1917 she has been almost entirely excised from literary history and her work rarely read.

Despite the shortcomings of many of her fictions, though, a good number of others deserve to be examined more carefully. Chief among these are ones in the Regionalist fiction vein that deal with dialect-speaking Whites in the fictional village of Simpkinsville, a setting modeled on her one-time home of Washington, Arkansas. In many of these stories Stuart, as befits someone who was a lifelong advocate of women's rights, portrays strong women who dare to defy convention. "The Unlived Life of Little Mary Ellen," which originally appeared in *Harper's Monthly* in October 1896, does not include such a figure but is nonetheless an incisive examination of how a small southern community deals with mental illness and treats fellow townspeople who differ from the norm. After its original serial appearance, it was included in the collection *In Simpkinsville: Character Tales* (1897) and then, due to its popularity, was printed as a separate volume in 1910.

*Readers should be aware that this story includes some language which, while commonly used during this time period, is no longer considered acceptable because of its offensive nature.

THE UNLIVED LIFE OF LITTLE MARY ELLEN (1896)

When Simpkinsville sits in shirt sleeves along her store fronts in summer, she does not wish to be considered *en deshabillé.*[1] Indeed, excepting in extreme cases she would—after requiring that you translate it into plain American, perhaps—deny the soft impeachment.

Simpkinsville knows about coats, and she knows about ladies, and she knows that coats and ladies are to be taken together.

But there are hot hours during August when nothing should be required to be taken with anything—unless, indeed, it be ice—with everything excepting more ice.

During the long afternoons in fly-time no woman who has any discretion—or, as the Simpkinsville men would say, any "management"—would leave her comfortable home to go "hangin' roun' sto'e counters to be waited on." And if they will—as they sometimes do—why, let them take the consequences.

Still, there are those who, from the simple prestige which youth and beauty give, are regarded in the Simpkinsville popular mind-masculine as belonging to a royal family before whom all things must give way—even shirt sleeves.

For these, and because any one of them may turn her horse's head into the main road and drive up to any of the stores any hot afternoon, there are coat pegs within easy reach upon the inside door-frames—pegs usually covered with the linen dashers and seersucker cutaways[2] of the younger men without.

Very few of the older ones disturb themselves about these trivial matters. Even the doctors, of whom there are two in town, both "leading physicians," are wont to receive their most important "office patients" in this comfortable fashion as, palmetto fans in hand, they rise from their comfortable chairs, tilted back against the weather-boarded fronts of their respective drug stores, and step forward to the buggies of such ladies as drive up for quinine[3] or capsules, or to present their ailing babies for open-air glances at their throats or gums, without so much as displacing their linen lap-robes.[4]

When any of the village belles drive or walk past, such of the commercial drummers[5] as may be sitting trigly coated,[6] as they sometimes do, among the shirt sleeves, have a way of feeling of their ties and bringing the front legs of their chairs to the floor, while they sit forward in supposed parlor attitudes, and easily doff their hats with a grace that the Simpkinsville boys fiercely denounce while they vainly strive to imitate it.

A country boy's hat will not take on that repose which marks the cast of the metropolitan hatter, let him try to command it as he may.

It was peculiarly hot and sultry to-day in Simpkinsville, and business was abnormally dull—even the apothecary business, this being the mid-season's lull when even drugs are drugs on the market, the annual lull between spring fevers and green chinquapins.[7]

Old Dr. Alexander, after nodding for an hour over his fan beneath his tarnished gilt sign of the pestle and mortar, had strolled diagonally across the street to join his friend and *confrère*,[8] Dr. Jenkins, in a friendly chat.

The doctors were not much given to this sort of sociability, but sometimes when times were unbearably dull and healthy, and neither was called to visit any one else, they would visit one another and talk to keep awake.

"Well, I should say so!" The visitor dropped into the vacant chair beside his host as he spoke. "I should say so. Ain't it hot enough *for you!* Ef it ain't, I'd advise you to renounce yo' religion an' prepare for a climate thet'll suit you."

This pleasantry was in reply to the common summer-day greeting, "Hot enough for you to-day, doc?"

"Yas," continued the guest, as he zigzagged the back legs of his chair forward by quick jerks until he had gained the desired leaning angle—"Yas, it's too hot to live, an' not hot enough to die. I reckon that's why we have so many chronics[9] a-hangin' on."

"Well, don't let's quarrel with sech as the Lord provides, doctor," replied his host, with a chuckle. "Ef it wasn't for the chronics, I reckon you an' I'd have to give up practisin' an' go to makin' soap. Ain't that about the size of it?"

"Yas, chronics an—an' babies. Ef *they* didn't come so punctual, summer an' winter, I wouldn't be able to feed mine thet're a'ready here. But talkin' about the chronics, do you know, doctor, thet sometimes when I don't have much else to think about, why, I think about them. It's a strange providence to me thet keeps people a-hangin' on year in an' year out, neither sick nor well. I don't doubt the Almighty's goodness, of co'se; but we've got Scripture for callin' Him the Great Physician, an' why, when He could ef He would, He don't—"

"I wouldn't dare to ask myself sech questions as that, doctor, ef I was you. *I* wouldn't, I know. Besides"—and now he laughed—"besides, I jest give you a reason for lettin' 'em remain as they are—to feed us poor devils of doctors. An' besides that, I've often seen cases where it seemed to me that they were allowed to live to sanctify them thet had to live *with* 'em. Of co'se in this I'm not speakin' of great sufferers. An' no doubt they all get pretty tired an' wo'e out with them-selves sometimes. I do with myself, even, an' I'm well. Jest listen at them boys a-whistlin' 'After the Ball'[10] to Brother Binney's horse's trot! They haven't got no mo' reverence for a minister o' the gospel than nothin'. I s'pose as long as they ricollect his preachin' against dancin' they'll make him ride into town to that tune. They've made it up among 'em to do it. Jest listen—all the way up the street that same tune. An' Brother Binney trottin' in smilin' to it."

While they were talking the Rev. Mr. Binney rode past, and following, a short distance behind him, came a shabby buggy, in which a shabby woman sat alone. She held her reins a trifle high as she drove, and it was this somewhat awkward position which revealed the fact, even as she approached in the distance, that she carried what seemed an infant lying upon her lap.

"There comes the saddest sight in Simpkinsville, doctor. I notice them boys stop their whistlin' jest as soon as her buggy turned into the road. I'm glad there's some things they respect," said Dr. Alexander.

"Yas, and I see the fellers at Rowton's sto'e are goin' in for their coats. She's drawin' rein there now."

"Yas, but she ain't more'n leavin' an order, I reckon. She's comin' this way."

The shabby buggy was bearing down upon them now, indeed, and when Dr. Jen-kins saw it he too rose and put on his coat. As its occupant drew rein he stepped out to her side, while his companion, having raised his hat, looked the other way.

"Get out an' come in, Mis' Bradley." Dr. Jenkins had taken her hand as he spoke.

"No, thanky, doctor. 'Tain't worth while. I jest want to consult you about little Mary Ellen. She ain't doin' well, some ways."

At this she drew back the green barége[11] veil that lay spread over the bundle upon her lap, exposing, as she did so, the blond head and chubby face of a great wax doll, with eyes closed as if in sleep.

"GET OUT AN' COME IN, MIS' BRADLEY."

Illustration from Ruth McEnery Stuart, "The Unlived Life of Little Mary Ellen,"
Harper's Monthly 93 (October 1896).

The doctor drew the veil back in its place quickly.

"I wouldn't expose her face to the evenin' sun, Mis' Bradley," he said, gently. "I'll call out an' see her to-morrow; an' ef I was you I think I'd keep her indoors for a day or so." Then, as he glanced into the woman's haggard and eager face, he added: "She's gettin' along as well as might be expected, Mis' Bradley. But I'll be out to-morrow, an' fetch you somethin' thet'll put a little color in *yo'* face."

"Oh, don't mind me, doctor," she answered, with a sigh of relief, as she tucked the veil carefully under the little head. "Don't mind me. I ain't sick. Ef I could jest see *her* pick up a little, why, I'd feel all right. When you come to-morrer, better fetch somethin' *she* can take, doctor. Well, good-by."

"Good-by, Mis' Bradley."

It was some moments before either of the doctors spoke after Dr. Jenkins had returned to his place. And then it was he who said:

"Talkin' about the ways o' Providence, doctor, what do you call that?"

"That's one o' the mysteries thet it's hard to unravel, doctor. Ef anything would make me doubt the mercy of God Almighty, it would be some sech thing as that. And yet I don't know. Ef there ever was a sermon preached without words, there's one preached along the open streets of Simpkinsville by that pore little half-demented woman when she drives into town nursin' that wax doll. An' it's preached where it's much needed, too—to our young people. There ain't many preachers thet can reach 'em, but—Did you take notice jest now how, as soon as she turned into the road, all that whistlin' stopped? They even neglected to worry Brother Binney. An' she's the only woman in town thet'll make old Rowton put on a coat. He'll wait on yo' wife or mine in his shirt sleeves, an' it's all right. But there's somethin' in that broken-hearted woman nursin' a wax doll thet even a fellow like Rowton'll feel. Didn't you ever think thet maybe you ought to write her case up, doctor?"

"Yas; an' I've done it—as far as it goes. I've called it 'A Psychological Impossibility.' An' then I've jest told her story. A heap of impossible things have turned out to be facts—facts that had to be argued backwards from. You can do over argiments, but you can't undo facts. Yas, I've got her case all stated as straight as I can state it, an' some day it'll be read. But not while she's livin'. Sir? No, not even with names changed an' everything. It wouldn't do. It couldn't help bein' traced back to her. No: some day, when we've all passed away, likely it'll all come out in a medical journal, signed by me. An' I've been thinkin' thet I'd like to have you go over that paper with me some time, doctor, so thet you could testify to it. An' I thought we'd get Brother Binney to put his name down as the minister thet had been engaged to perform the marriage, an' knew all the ins and outs of it. And then it'll hardly be believed."

Even as they spoke they heard the whistling start up again along the street, and looking up, they saw the Rev. Mr. Binney approaching.

"We've jest been talkin' about you, Brother Binney—even before the boys started you to dancin'," said Dr. Jenkins; as he rose and brought out a third chair.

"No," answered the dominie,[12] as with a good-natured smile he dismounted. "No, they can't make me dance, an' I don't know as it's a thing my mare'll have to answer for. She seems to take naturally to the sinful step, an' so, quick as they start a-whistlin', I try to ride as upright an' godly as I can, to sort o' equalize things. How were you two discussin' me, I'd like to know?"

He put the question playfully as he took his seat.

"Well, we were havin' a pretty serious talk, brother," said Dr. Jenkins—"a pretty serious talk, doc. and me. We were talkin' about pore Miss Mary Ellen. We were sayin' thet we reckoned ef there were any three men in town thet were specially qualified to testify about her case, we must be the three—you an' him an' me. I've got it all written out, an' I thought some day I'd get you both to read it over an' put your names to it, with any additions you might feel disposed to make. After we've all passed away, there ought to be some authorized account. You know about as much as we do, I reckon, Brother Binney."

"Yes, I s'pose I do—in a way. I stood an' watched her face durin' that hour an' a quarter they stood in church waitin' for Clarence Bradley to come. Mary Ellen never was to say what you'd call a purty girl, but she always did have a face thet would hold you ef you ever looked at it. An' when she stood in church that day, with all her bridemaids strung around the chancel, her countenance would 'a' done for any heavenly picture. An' as the time passed, an' he didn't show up—Well, I don't want to compare sinfully, but there's a picture I saw once of Mary at the Cross—Reckon I ought to take that back, lest it might be sinful; but there ain't any wrong in my telling you here thet as I stood out o' sight, waitin' that day in church, behind the pyramid o' flowers the bridemaids had banked up for her, with my book open in my hand at the marriage service, while we waited for him to come, as she stood before the pulpit in her little white frock and wreath, I could see her face. An' there come a time, after it commenced to git late, when I fell on my knees."

The good man stopped speaking for a minute to steady his voice.

"You see," he resumed presently, "we'd all heard things. I *knew* he'd *seemed* completely taken up with this strange girl; an' when at last he came for me to marry him and Mary Ellen, I never was so rejoiced in my life. Thinks I, I've been over-suspicious. Of co'se I knew he an' Mary Ellen had been sweethearts all their lives. I tell you, friends, I've officiated at funerals in my life—buried little children an' mothers of families—an' I've had my heart in my throat so thet I could hardly do my duty; but I tell you I never in all my life had as sad an experience as I did at little Mary Ellen Williams's weddin'—the terrible, terrible weddin' thet never came off."

"An' I've had patients," said Dr. Jenkins, coming into the pause—"I've had patients, Brother Binney, thet I've lost—lost 'em because the time had come for 'em to die—patients thet I've grieved to see go more as if I was a woman than a man, let alone a doctor; but I never in all my life come so near *clair* givin' way an' breakin' down as I did at that weddin' when you stepped out an' called me out o' the congregation to tell me she had fainted. God help us, it was terrible!

I'll never forget that little white face as it lay so limpy and still against the lilies tied to the chancel rail, not ef I live a thousand years. Of co'se we'd all had our fears, same as you. We knew Clarence's failin', an' we saw how the yaller-haired girl had turned his head; but, of co'se, when it come to goin' into the church, why, we thought it was all right, But even after the thing had happened—even knowin' as much as I did—I never to say fully took in the situation till the time come for her to get better. For two weeks she lay 'twixt life an' death, an' the one hope I had was for her to recognize me. She hadn't recognized anybody since she was brought out o' the church. But when at last she looked at me one day, an' says she, 'Doctor what you reckon kep' him—so late?' I tell you I can't tell you how I felt."

"What did you say, doctor?"

It was the minister who ventured the question.

"What can a man say when he 'ain't got nothin' to say? I jest said, 'Better not talk any today, honey.' An' I turned away an' made pertence o' mixin' powders[13]—an' mixed 'em, for that matter—give her sech as would put her into a little sleep. An' then I set by her till she drowsed away. But when she come out o' that sleep an' I see how things was—when she called herself Mis' Bradley an' kep' askin' for him, an' I see she didn't know no better, an' likely never would—God help me! but even while I prescribed physic for her to live, in my heart I prayed to see her die. She thought she had been married, an' from that day to this she 'ain't never doubted it. Of co'se she often wonders why he don't come home; an' sence that doll come she—"

"Didn't it ever strike you as a strange providence about that doll—thet would allow sech a thing, for instance, doctor?"

Dr. Jenkins did not answer at once.

"Well," he said, presently, "yas—yas an' no. Ef a person looks at it *close-t enough*, it ain't so hard to see mercy in God's judgments. I happened to be at her bedside the day that doll come in—Christmas eve fo' years ago. She was mighty weak an' porely. She gen'ally gets down in bed long about the holidays, sort o' reelizin' the passin' o' time, seein' he don't come. She had been so worried and puny thet the old nigger[14] 'Pollo come for me to see her. An', well, while I set there tryin' to think up somethin' to help her, 'Pollo, he fetched in the express package."

"I've always blamed her brother, Brother Binney," Dr. Alexander interposed, "for *allowin'* that package to go to her."

"*Allowin'!* Why, he never allowed it. You might jest as well say you blame him for namin' his one little daughter after her aunt Mary Ellen. That's how the mistake was made. No, for my part I never thought so much of Ned Williams in my life as I did when he said to me the day that baby girl was born, 'Ef it's a girl, doctor, we're a-goin' to name it after sis' Mary Ellen. Maybe it'll be a comfort to her.' An' they did. How many brothers, do you reckon, would name a child after a sister thet had lost her mind over a man thet had jilted her at the church door, an' called herself by his name ever sence? Not many, I reckon. No, don't blame Ned—for anything. He hoped she'd love the little thing, an' maybe it would help her. An' she did notice it consider'ble for a while, but it didn't seem to have the power to bring her mind straight. In fact, the way she'd set an' look at it for hours, an' then go home an' set down an' seem to be thinkin', makes me sometimes suspicion thet that was what started her a-prayin' God to send her a child. She's said to me more than once-t about that time—she'd say, 'You see, doctor, when he's away so much—ef it was God's will—a child would be a heap o' company to me while he's away.' This, mind you, when he hadn't shown up at the weddin'; when we all knew he ran away an' married the yaller-hair that same night. Of co'se it did seem a strange providence to be sent to a God-fearin' woman as she always was; it did seem strange thet she should be allowed to make herself redic'lous carryin' that wax doll around the streets; an' yet, when you come to think—"

"Well, I say what I did befo'," said Dr. Alexander. "Her brother should 'a' *seen* to it thet no sech express package intended for his child should 'a' been sent to the aunt—not in her state o' mind."

"How could he see to it when he didn't send it—didn't know it was comin'? Of co'se we Simpkinsville folks, we all know thet she's called Mary Ellen, an' thet Ned's child has been nicknamed Nellie. But his wife's kin, livin' on the other side o' the continent, they couldn't be expected to know that, an' when they sent her that doll, why, they nachelly sent it to her full name; an' it was sent up to Miss Mary Ellen's. Even then the harm needn't to 've been done exceptin' for her bein' sick abed, an' me, her doctor, hopin' to enliven her up a little with an unexpected present, makes the nigger 'Pollo set it down by her bedside, an' opens it befo' her eyes, right there. Maybe I'm to blame for that—*but I ain't.* We can't do mo' than *try* for the best. I thought likely as not Ned had ordered her some little Christmas things—as he had, in another box."

The old doctor stopped, and taking out his handkerchief, wiped his eyes.

"Of co'se, as soon as I see what it was, I knew somebody had sent it to little Mary Ellen, but—"

"You say, Brother Binney, thet the look in her face at the weddin' made you fall on yo' knees. I wish you could 'a' seen the look thet come into her face when I lifted that doll-baby out o' that box. Heavenly Father! That look is one o' the things thet'll come back to me sometimes when I wake up too early in the mornin's, an' I can't get back to sleep for it. But at the time I didn't fully realize it, somehow. She jest reached an' took the doll from me, an' turnin' over, with her face to the wall, held it tight in her arms without sayin' a word. Then she lay still for so long that-a-way thet by-an'-by I commenced to get uneasy less'n she'd fainted. So I leaned over an' felt of her pulse, an' I see she was layin' there cryin' over it without a sound, an' I come away. I don't know how came I to be so thick-headed, but even then I jest supposed seein' the doll nachelly took her mind back to the time she was a child, an' that in itself was mighty sad an' pitiful to me, knowin' her story, and I confess to you I was glad there wasn't anybody I had to speak to on my way out. I tell you I was about cryin' myself—jest over the pitifulness of even that. But next day when I went back of co'se I see how it was. She never had doubted for a minute thet that doll was the baby she'd been prayin' for—not a minute. An' she don't, *not to this day*—straight as her mind is on some things. That's why I call it a psychological impossibility, she bein' so rational an' so crazy at the same time. Sent for me only last week, an' when I got there I found her settin' down with *it* a-layin' in her lap, an' she lookin' the very picture of despair. 'Doctor,' says she, 'I'm sure they's mo' wrong with Mary Ellen than you let on to me. *She don't grow, doctor.*' An' with that she started a-sobbin' an' a-rockin' back an' fo'th over it.' An' even the few words she could say, doctor, she seems to forget 'em,' says she. 'She 'ain't called my name for a week.' It's a fact; the little talkin'-machine inside it has got out o' fix some way, an' it don't say' mamma 'and' papa' any mo'."

"Have you ever thought about slippin' it away from her, doctor, an' seein' if maybe she wouldn't forget it? If she was my patient I'd try it."

"Yas, but you wouldn't keep it up. I did try it once-t. Told old Milly thet ef she fretted too much not to give her the doll, but to send for me. An' she did—in about six hours. An' I—well, when I see her face I jest give it back to her. An' I'll never be the one to take it from her again. It comes nearer givin' her happiness than anything else could—an' what could be mo' innocent? She's even mo' contented since her mother died an' there ain't anybody to prevent her carryin' it on the street. I know it plegged[15] Ned at first to see her do it, but he's never said a word. He's one in a thousand. He cares mo' for his sister's happiness than for how she looks to other folks. Most brothers don't. There ain't a mornin' but he drives in there to see ef she wants anything, an', of co'se, keepin' up the old place jest for her to live in it costs him consider'ble. He says she wouldn't allow it, but she thinks Clarence pays for everything, an' of co'se he was fully able."

"I don't think it's a good way for her to live, doctor, in that big old place with jest those two old niggers. I never have thought so. Ef she was *my* patient—"

"Well, pardner, that's been talked over between Ned an' his wife, an' they've even consulted me. An' I b'lieve she ought to be let alone. Those two old servants take about as good care of her as anybody could. Milly nursed her when she was a baby, an' she loves the ground she walks on, an' she humors her in everything. Why, I've gone out there an' found that old nigger walkin' that doll up an' down the po'ch, singing to it for all she was worth; an' when I'd drive up, the po' ol' thing would cry so she couldn't go in the house for ten minutes or mo'. No, it ain't for us to take away sech toys as the Lord sends to comfort an' amuse his little ones; an' the weak minded, why, they always seem that-a-way to me. An' sometimes, when I come from out of some of our homes where everything is regular and straight accordin' to our way o' lookin' at things, an' I see how miserable an' unhappy everything *is*, an' I go out to the old Williams place, where the birds are singin' in the trees an' po' Miss Mary Ellen is happy sewin' her little doll-clo'es, an' the old niggers 'ain't got a care on earth but to look after her—Well, I dun'no'. Ef you'd dare say the love o' God wasn't there, *I* wouldn't. Of co'se she has her unhappy moments, an' I can see she's failin' as time passes;

but even so, ain't *this* for the best? They'd be somethin' awful about it, *to me,* ef she kep' a-growin' stronger through it all. One o' the sweetest providences o' sorrow is thet we poor mortals fail under it. There ain't a flower thet blooms but some seed has perished for it."

It was at a meeting of the woman's prayer meeting, about a week after the conversation just related, that Mrs. Blanks, the good sister who led the meeting today, upon opening the services with a short Scripture reading and prayer, rose to her feet, and after a silence that betokened some embarrassment in the subject she essayed, she said:

"My dear sisters, I've had a subjec' on my mind for a long time, a subjec' thet I've hesitated to mention, but the mo' I put it away the mo' it seems to come back to me. I've hesitated because she's got kinfolks in this prayer meetin', but I don't believe thet there's anybody kin to Miss Mary Ellen thet feels any nearer to her than what the rest of us do."

"Amen!" "Amen!" and "Amen!" came in timid women's voices from different parts of the room.

"I know how you all feel befo' you answer me, my dear sisters," she continued, presently. "And now I propose to you thet we, first here as a body of worshippers, an' then separately as Christian women at home in our closets, make her case a subjec' of special prayer. Let us ask the good Lord to relieve her jest so—*unconditionally;* to take this cloud off her life an' this sorrow off our streets, an' I believe He'll do it."

There were many quiet tears shed in the little prayer meeting that morning as, with faltering voice, one woman after another spoke her word of exhortation or petition in behalf of the long-suffering sister.

That this revival of the theme by the wives and mothers of the community should have resulted in renewed attentions to the poor distraught woman was but natural. It is sound orthodoxy to try to help God to answer our prayers. And so the faithful women of the churches—there were a few of every denomination in town in the union prayer-meeting—began to go to her, fully resolved to say some definite word to win her, if possible, from her hallucination, to break the spell that held her; but they would almost invariably come away full of contrition over such false and comforting words as they had been constrained to speak "over a soulless and senseless doll."

Indeed, a certain Mrs. Lynde, one of the most ardent of these good women, but a sensitive soul withal, was moved, after one of her visits, to confess in open meeting both her sin and her chagrin in the following humiliating fashion:

"I declare I never felt so 'umbled in my life ez I did after I come away from there, a week ago come Sunday. Here I goes, full of clear reasonin' an' Scripture texts, to try to bring her to herself, an' I 'ain't no mo'n set down sca'cely, when I looks into her face, as she sets there an' po's out her sorrers over that ridic'lous little doll, befo' I'm consolin' her with false hopes, like a perfec' Ananias an' Sapphira.[16] Ef any woman could set down an' see her look at that old doll's face when she says, 'Honey, do you reckon I'll ever raise her, when she keeps so puny?'—I say ef any woman with a human heart in her bosom could hear her say that, an' not tell her, 'Cert'n'y she'd raise her,' an' that 'punier children than that had growed up to be healthy men an' women'— well, maybe they might be better Christians than I am, but I don't never expec' to be sanctified up to that point. I know I'm an awful sinner, deservin' of eternal punishment for deceit which is the same as a lie, but I not only told her I thought she could raise her, but I felt her pulse, an' said it wasn't quite what a reel hearty child's ought to be. Of co'se I said that jest to save myself from p'int blank lyin'. An' then, when I see how it troubled her to think it wasn't *jest right,* why, God forgive me, but I felt it over again, an' counted it by my watch, an' then I up an' told her it was *all right,* an' thet ef it had a-been any different to the way it was under the circumstances, I'd be awful fearful, which, come to think of it, that last is true ez God's word, for ef I'd a-felt a pulse in that doll's wrist—which, tell the truth, I was so excited while she watched me I half expected to feel it pulsate—I'd 'a' shot out o' that door a ravin' lunatic. I come near enough a-doin' it when she patted its chest an' it said 'mamma' an' 'papa' in reply. I don't know, but I think thet the man thet put words into a doll's breast, to be hugged out by a po' bereft weak-minded woman, has a terrible sin to answer for. Seems to me it's a-breakin' the second commandment, which forbids the makin' of anything in the likeness of anything in the heavens above or the earth beneath, which a baby is if it's anything, bein' the breath o' God fresh-breathed into human clay. I don't know, but I think that commandment is aimed jest as direct at talkin' dolls ez it is at heathen idols, which, when you come to think of it, ain't p'intedly made after the image of anything *in* creation thet we've seen samples of, after all. Them thet I've seen the pictures of ain't no mo'n sech outlandish deformities thet anybody could conceive of ef he imagined a strange-figgured person standin' befo' a cracked merror so ez to have his various an' sundry parts duplicated, hit an' miss. No, I put down the maker of that special an' partic'lar doll ez a greater idolitor than them thet, for the want o' knowin' better, stick a few extry members on a clay statute an' pray to it *in faith.* Ef it hadn't a-called her 'mamma' first time she over-squeezed it, I don't believe *for a minute* thet that doll would ever'a' got the holt upon Mary Ellen thet it has—I don't indeed."

"Still"—it was Mrs. Blanks who spoke up in reply, wiping her eyes as she began—"still, Sister Lynde, you know she frets over it jest ez much sence it's lost its speech."

"Of co'se," said another sister; "an' why shouldn't she? Ef yo' little Katie had a-started talkin' an' then stopped of a sudden, wouldn't you 'a' been worried, I like to know?"

"Yas, I reckon I would," replied Mrs. Blanks; "but it's hard to put her in the place of a mother with a reel child—even in a person's imagination."

There had been in Simpkinsville an occasional doll whose eyes would open and shut as she was put to bed or taken up, and the crying doll was not a thing unknown.

That the one which should play so conspicuous a part in her history should have developed the gift of speech, invested it with a weird and peculiar interest.

It was, indeed, most uncanny and sorrowful to hear its poor piping response to the distraught woman's caresses as she pressed it to her bosom.

To the little doll-loving girls of Simpkinsville it had always been an object of semi-superstitious reverence—a thing half doll, half human, almost alive.

When her little niece Nellie, a tall girl of eight years now, would come over in the mornings and beg Aunt Mary Ellen to let her hold the baby, she never quite knew, as she walked it up and down the yard, under the mulberry-trees, with the green veil laid lovingly over its closed lids, whether to look for a lapse from its human quality into ordinary dollhood, or to expect a sudden progression on the life side.

She would, no doubt, long ago have lost this last hope, in the lack of progression in its mechanical speech, but for the repeated confidences of her aunt Mary Ellen. She really believed the marvellous stories she told the child of the things "little Mary Ellen" did when she was alone with her mother.

"Why, honey, she often laughs out an' turns over in bed, an sometimes she wakes me up cryin' so pitiful." So the good aunt, who had never told a lie in all her pious life, often assured her—assured her with a look in her face that was absolutely invincible in its expression of perfect faith in the thing she said.

There had been several serious conferences between her father and mother in the beginning, before the child had been allowed to go to see Aunt Mary Ellen's dolly—to see and hold it, and inevitably to love it with all her child heart; but even before the situation had developed its full sadness, or they had realized how its contingencies would familiarize every one with the strange sad story, the arguments were in the child's favor. To begin with, the doll was really hers, though it was thought best, in the circumstances, that she should never know it. Indeed, at first her father had declared that she should have one just like it; but when it was found that its price was nearly equal to the value of a bale of cotton, the good man was moved to declare that "the outlandish toy, with its heathenish imitations, had wrought sorrer enough in the family a'ready, without trying to duplicate it."

Still, there couldn't be any harm in letting her see the beautiful toy. And so, as she held it in her arms, the child came vaguely to realize that a great mystery of anxious love hovered about this strange weird doll, a mystery that, to her young perception, as she read it in the serious home faces, was as full of tragic possibilities as that which concerned the real baby sister that lay and slept and waked and grew in the home cradle—the real, warm, heavy baby that she was sometimes allowed to hold "just for a minute" while the nurse-mammy followed close beside her.

If the toy-baby gave her the greater pleasure, may it not have been because she dimly perceived in it a meeting-point between the real and the imaginary? Here was a threshold of the great wonder-world that primitive peoples and children love so well. They are the great mystics, after all. And are they not, perhaps, wise mystics who sit and wonder and worship, satisfied not to understand?

Summer waned and went out, and September came in—September, hot and murky and short of breath, as one ill of heart-failure. Even the prayer-meeting women who had taken up Miss Mary Ellen's case in strong faith, determined not to let it go, were growing faint of heart under the combined pressure of disappointed hope and the summer's weight. The poor object of their prayers, instead of seeming in any wise improved, grew rather more wan and weary as time wore on. Indeed, she sometimes appeared definitely worse, and would often draw rein in the public road to lift the doll from her lap and discuss her anxieties concerning it with any passing acquaintance, or even on occasion to exult in a fancied improvement.

This was a thing she had never done before the women began to pray, and it took a generous dispensation of faith to enable them to continue steadfast in the face of such discouragement. But, as is sometimes the case, greater faith came from the greater need, and the prayer-meeting grew. In the face of its new and painful phases, as the tragedy took on a fresh sadness, even a few churchly women who had stood aloof at the beginning waived their sectarian differences and came into the meeting. And there were strange confessions sometimes at these gatherings, where it was no uncommon thing for a good sister to relate how, on a certain occasion, she had either "burst out cryin' to keep from laughin'," or "laughed like a heathen jest to keep from cryin'."

The situation was now grown so sad and painful that the doctors called a consultation of neighboring physicians, even bringing for the purpose a "specialist" all the way from the Little Rock Asylum, hoping little, but determined to spare no effort for the bettering of things.

After this last effort and its discouraging result, all hope of recovery seemed gone, and so the good women, when they prayed, despairing of human agency, asked simply for a miracle, reading aloud, for the support of their faith, the stories of marvellous healing as related in the gospels.

It was on a sultry morning, after a night of rain, near the end of September. Old Dr. Jenkins stood behind the showcase in his drug-store dealing out quinine pills and earache drops to the poor country folk and negroes,[17] who, with sallow faces or heads bound up, confessed themselves "chillin'" or "painful" while they waited. Patient as cows, they stood in line while the dispensing hand of healing passed over to their tremulous, eager palms the promised "help" for their assorted "miseries."

It was a humble crowd of sufferers, deferring equally, as they waited, to the dignitary who served them and to his environment of mysterious potencies, whose unreadable Latin labels glared at them in every direction as if in challenge to their faith and respect. To the thoughtful observer it seemed an epitome of suffering humanity—patient humanity waiting to be healed by some great and mysterious Unknowable.

It may have been their general attitude of unconscious deference that moved the crowd to fall quickly back at the entrance of the first assertive visitor of the morning, or perhaps old 'Pollo, the negro, as he came rushing into the shop, would have been accorded right of way in a more pretentious gathering. There was certainly that in his appearance which demanded attention.

He had galloped up to the front door, his horse in a lather from the long hot ride from the Williams homestead, four miles away, and throwing his reins across the pommel of his saddle, had burst into the drugstore with an excited appeal:

"Doctor Jinkins, come quick! For Gord's sake! Miss Mary Ellen *need* you, Marse Doctor—she need you—*right off!*"

He did not wait for a response. He had delivered his summons, and turning without another word, he remounted his horse and rode away.

It was not needed that the doctor should offer any apologies to his patients for following him. He did not, indeed, seem to remember that they were there as he seized his coat, and, without even waiting to put it on, quickly unhitched his horse tied at the front door, and followed the negro down the road.

It was a matter of but a few moments to overtake him, and when the two were riding abreast, the doctor saw that the old man was crying.

"De dorg, he must 'a' done it, Marse Doctor," he began, between sobs. "He must 'a' got in las' night. It was so hot we lef' all de do's open same lak we *been* doin'—But it warn't we-alls fault, doctor. But de dorg, he must 'a' snatch de doll out'n de cradle an' run out in de yard wid it, an' it lay asoakin' in de rain all night. When Miss Mary Ellen fust woked up dis mornin', she called out to Milly to fetch de baby in to her. Milly she often tecks it out'n de cradle early in de mornin' 'fo' missy wakes up, an' make pertend lak she feeds it in de kitchen. An' dis mornin', when she call for it, Milly, she 'spon' back, 'I 'ain't got her, missy!' jes dat-a-way. An' wid dat, 'fo' you could bat yo' eye, missy was hop out'n d bed an' stan' in de middle o' de kitchen in her night-gownd, white in de face as my whitewash-bresh. An' when she had look at Milly an' den at me, she sclaim out, '*Whar my child?*' I tell you, Marse Doctor, when I see dat look an' heah inquiry, I trimbled so dat dat kitchen flo' shuck tell de kittle leds on de stove rattled. An' Milly, she see how scarified missy look, an' she commence to tu'n roun' an' seek for words, when we heah pit-a-pat, pit-a-pat, on de po'ch; an', good Gord, Marse Doctor! heah come Rover, draggin' dat po' miser'ble little doll-baby in his mouf, drippin' wid mud an' sopped wid rain-water. Quick as I looked at it I see dat bofe eyes was done soaked out an' de paint gone, an' all its yaller hair it had done eve'y bit soaked off. Sir? Oh, I don't know, sir, how she gwine teck it. Dey ain't no sayin' as to dat. She hadn't *come to* when I come away. She had jes drapped down in a dead faint in de mids' o' de kitchen, an' I holp Milly lif' her on to de bed, an' I come for you. Co'se I had to stop an' ketch de horse; an' de roads, dey was so awful muddy an'—"

It was long ride over the heavy roads, and as the good doctor trotted along, with the old darky[18] steadily talking beside him, he presently ceased to hear.

Having once realized the situation, his professional mind busied itself in speculations as to the probable result of so critical an incident to his patient. Accident, chance, or mayhap a kind providence, had done for her the thing he had long wished to try but had not dared. The mental shock with the irreparable loss of the doll would probably have a definite effect for good or ill—if, indeed, she would consent even now to give it up. Of course there was no telling.

This question was almost immediately answered, however, for when presently the old negro led the way into the lane leading to the Williams gate, preceding the doctor so as to open the gate for him, he leaned suddenly over his horse's neck and peered eagerly forward. Then drawing rein for a moment, he called back:

"Marse Doctor, look hard, please, sir, an' see what dat my ol' 'oman Milly is doin' out at de front gate."

The doctor's eyes were little better than his companion's. Still, he was able in a moment to reply:

"Why, old man, she is tying a piece of white muslin upon the gate post. Something has happened."

"White is for babies, ain't it, Marse Doctor?"

"Yes—or for—"

"Den it mus' be she's give it up for dead."

The old man began sobbing again.

"Yes; thank God!" said the doctor. And he wiped his eyes.

The bit of fluttering white that hung upon the gate it the end of the lane had soon told its absurd and pitiful little tale of woe to the few passers-by on the road—playfully announcing half the story, the comedy side, even suggested the tragedy that was enacting within.

Before many hours all Simpkinsville knew what had happened, and the little community had succumbed to an attack of hysteria.

Simpkinsville was not usually of a particularly nervous or hysterical temper, but a wholesome sense of the ludicrous, colliding with her maternal love for her afflicted child, could not do less than find relief in simultaneous laughter and tears.

And still, be it said to their credit, when the good women separated, after meeting in the various houses to talk it over, it was the mark of tears that remained upon their faces.

But when it was presently known that their emotional poise was to be critically tested by a "funeral" announced for the next day, there was less emotion exhibited, perhaps, and there were more quiet consultations among the serious-minded.

When Miss Mary Ellen, prostrate and wan with the burden of her long-borne sorrow, had from her pillow quietly given instructions for the funeral, the old doctor, who solicitously watched beside her, in the double capacity of friend and physician, had not been able to say her nay.

And when on the next day he had finally invited a conference on the subject with her brother, the minister, his fellow doctor, and several personal friends of the family, there were heavy lines about his eyes, and he confessed that before daring his advice on so sensitive a point he had "walked the flo' the livelong night."

And then he had strongly, unequivocally, advised the funeral.

"We've thought it best to humor her all the way through," he began, "an' now, when the end is clairly in sight, why, there ain't any consistency in changin' the treatment. Maybe when it's buried she'll forget it, an' in time come to herself. Of co'se it'll be a try in' ordeel, but there's enough of us sensible relations an' friends thet'll go through it, if need be." He had walked up and down the room as he spoke, his hands clasped behind him, and now he stopped before the minister. "Of co'se, Brother Binney"—he spoke with painful hesitation—"of co'se she'll look for you to come an' to put up a prayer, an' maybe read a po'tion o' Scripture. An' I've thought *that* over. Seems to me the whole thing is sad enough for religious services—ef anything is. I've seen reel funerals thet wasn't half so mo'nful, ef I'm any judge of earthly sorrers. There wouldn't be any occasion to bring in the doll in the services, I don't think. But there ain't any earthly grief, in my opinion, but's got a Scripture tex' to match it, ef it's properly selected."

A painful stillness followed this appeal. And then, after closing his eyes for a moment as if in prayer, the good minister said:

"Of course, my dear friends, *you* can see thet this thing can't be conducted *as a funeral*. But, as our good brother has jest remarked, for all the vicissitudes of life—and—death—for our safety in joy and our comfort in sorrow, we are given precious words of sweet and blessed consolation."

The saddest funeral gathering in all the annals of Simpkinsville—so it is still always called by those who wept at the obsequies—was that of Miss Mary Ellen's doll, led by the good brother on the following day.

The prayer-meeting women were there, of course, fortified in their faith by the supreme demand laid upon it, and even equipped with fresh self-control for this crucial test of their poise and worthiness. Their love was deep and sincere, and yet, so sensitive were they to the dangers of this most precarious situation that when presently the minister entered, book in hand, a terrible apprehension seized them.

It was as a great wave of indescribable fright, so awful that for a moment their hearts seemed to stop beating, so irresistible in its force that unless it should be quickly stayed it must presently break in some emotion.

No doubt the good brother felt it too, for instead of opening his book, as had been his intention, he laid it down upon the table before him—the small centre table upon which lay what seemed a tiny mound heaped with flowers—and placing both hands upon the bowed head of the little woman who sat beside it, closed his eyes, and raised his face heavenward.

"Dear Lord, Thou knowest," he said, slowly. Then finding no other words, perhaps, and willing to be still, he waited a moment in silence.

When he spoke again the wave had broken. The air seemed to sway with the indescribable vibrations that tell of silent weeping, and every face was buried in a handkerchief.

"Thou knowest, O Lord," he resumed, presently, raising his voice a little as if in an access of courage—"Thou knowest how dear to our hearts is Thy handmaiden, this beloved sister who sits in sorrow among us to-day. Thou knowest how we love her. Thou knowest that her afflictions are ours. And oh, dear Father, if it be possible, grant that when we have reverently put this poor little symbol of our common sorrow out of sight forever, Thy peace may descend and fill her heart and ours with Thy everlasting benediction."

The words, which had come slowly, though without apparent effort, might have been inspired. Surely they sounded to the women who waited as if uttered by a voice from Heaven, and to their spiritually attuned ears it was a voice comforting, composing, quieting.

After this followed a reading of Scripture—a selection taken for its wide application to all God's sorrowing people—and the singing of the beautiful hymn,

> *"God shall charge His angel legions*
> *Watch and ward o'er thee to keep."*[19]

This was sung, without a break, from the beginning clear through to the end, with its sweet promise to the grief-stricken of "life beyond the grave." Then came the benediction—the benediction of the churches since the days of the apostles, used of all Christians the world over, but ever beautiful and new—"The peace of God, which passeth all understanding, keep your hearts and minds," etc.[20]

All the company had risen for this—all excepting Miss Mary Ellen, who during the entire ceremony had not changed her position—and when it was finished, when the moment of silent prayers was over and one by one the women rose from their knees, there came an awkward interval pending the next step in this most difficult and exceptional service.

The little woman in whose behalf it had been conducted, for whom all the prayers had been said, made no sign by which her further will should be made known. It had been expected that she would herself go to the burial, and against this contingency a little grave had been prepared in the family burial-ground, which, happily, was situated upon her own ground, in a grove of trees a short distance from the house.

After waiting for some moments, and seeing that she still did not move, the reverend brother finally approached her and laid his hand as before upon her head. Then quickly reaching around, he drew her hand from beneath her cheek, felt her pulse, and now, turning, he motioned to the doctor to come.

The old man, Dr. Jenkins, lifted her limp arm tenderly and felt her wrist, listened with his ear against her bosom, waited, and listened again. And then, laying back the hand tenderly, he took his handkerchief from his pocket and wiped his eyes.

"Dear friends," he said, huskily, "your prayers have been answered. Sister Mary Ellen has found peace."

NOTES

1. Undressed (French).
2. Types of summer jackets made from lightweight fabrics.

3. A medicine formerly used to reduce fevers or serve as an energy tonic. Its more common use is to treat malaria.
4. A thin blanket. At this time it was common for people riding in horse-drawn wagons during the summer to cover themselves with a lap robe in order to protect their clothing from dust.
5. Traveling salesmen.
6. Well dressed in a stylish coat.
7. A chinquapin is a small type of chestnut tree with a very sweet nut; the immature nuts, coming in early summer, are green on the outside.
8. Colleague (French). Because of Louisiana's historical relationship with France, French was commonly used in the state during the nineteenth century.
9. Those patients with ailments that required ongoing treatment.
10. "After the Ball," composed in waltz time (a time signature of 3/4) by Charles K. Harris (1867–1930) and published in 1891, was an extremely popular dance song of its day.
11. A light, silky fabric.
12. In this context, "dominie" refers to Brother Binney's role as a minister or pastor.
13. At this time, prescription medicines were often made by mixing ground-up solid ingredients together.
14. An extremely derogatory and offensive term sometimes used by non-Black people to refer to Black people. While sometimes used among Black people to refer to other Black people, in both the past and the present this term was and is usually intended to be derogatory and hurtful when used by non-Black people; it is thus deeply offensive and should not be used.
15. Colloquial pronunciation of "plagued," which at this time meant "greatly bothered or disturbed."
16. In Acts 5:1–11, Ananias and Sapphira, a married couple, lie to the apostle Peter about their keeping some of the money from the sale of their property to themselves rather than donating all their money to the service of the Lord; for their punishment, they die on the spot. What the "false hopes" are in this story is unknown.
17. A term commonly used at this time to refer to African Americans. It is now considered offensive and no longer acceptable.
18. A highly derogatory and offensive term that some White people during this era used to refer to African Americans. It is completely unacceptable today.
19. "God Shall Charge His Angel Legions" was a Christian hymn published by English composer and newspaper editor James Montgomery (1771–1854) in *Songs of Zion* (1822).
20. Many Christian church services employ as a benediction (a wish for someone's happiness and prosperity) all or part of the apostle Paul's address in Philippians 4:4–7 (King James Version): "Rejoice in the Lord always: and again I say, Rejoice. Let your moderation be known unto all men. The Lord is at hand. Be careful for nothing; but in every thing by prayer and supplication with thanksgiving let your requests be made known unto God. And the peace of god, which passeth all understanding, shall keep your hearts and minds through Christ Jesus."

OCTAVE THANET (ALICE FRENCH)

(1850–1934)

Alice French was born in 1850 to patrician parents in Massachusetts but moved as a young girl to Davenport, Iowa, where her father became a successful businessman and civic leader. When she was eighteen years old, French, under the pseudonym "Octave Thanet," published her first piece, a nonfiction article entitled "Communists and Capitalists: A Sketch from Life," in the Philadelphia-based *Lippincott's*. Only later did Thanet turn to writing fiction; her first published short story was "The Bishop's Vagabond," which appeared in the January 1884 issue of the *Atlantic Monthly*. From this point until about 1900, Thanet was one of the most prominent authors of her era. Dozens of her short stories appeared in all the leading periodicals, and many of them were afterward collected in volume form and published by major publishers; she also published a handful of novels that were well-received. Thanet was primarily a Regionalist author who wrote about life in the locations she knew best: a midsize midwestern city (Davenport was known in her fiction as "Fairport") and rural Arkansas (beginning in 1885 she and her partner Jane Allen Crawford spent winters at their plantation house in Clover Bend, Arkansas). As the craze for Regionalist fiction waned toward the end of the century, however, Thanet increasingly wrote more about labor conflicts and ethical dilemmas.

Thanet serves as an excellent example of how an author who was incredibly popular and well-respected during her most productive period can later be deemed unworthy of being read or studied. In part this is due to the way that she typically adopted a more Romantic than Realistic view toward her materials, infusing almost all her fiction with an ethos of individualism that highlighted her characters' powers of self-determination; in her view, all "failures" were the result of individuals not seizing their opportunities. This basic outlook led Thanet, in both her life and fiction, to take positions completely at odds with the progressives of her era. For instance, she believed White farmers and members of the laboring classes, as well as African Americans, not only required the guidance of their more educated "betters" but also needed to work harder to succeed instead of blaming external forces for their plight. Furthermore, Thanet made numerous speeches during and after World War I criticizing pacifists and those who advocated for women's suffrage. Thanet also celebrated midwestern culture and the people living there, putting her at odds with the views of writers such as Hamlin Garland in the 1890s and Sinclair Lewis in the 1920s, both of whom depicted the "reality" of the Midwest in highly negative terms. None of these positions have endeared her to modern, generally liberal, cosmopolitan literary scholars, and even as early as 1965 her sole biographer aptly entitled his book *Journey to Obscurity: The Life of Octave Thanet*. Fifty years later her name and her fiction are even less known.

Whatever one makes of Thanet's positions on certain ideological issues, one must acknowledge that her fictions offer an important counterpoint to the idea that all "good" writers about the Midwest during this era disliked the region and that all of the period's women writers worth reading today offered strong critiques of the patriarchy. One sees all of this quite clearly in "The Face of Failure," which originally appeared in the September 1892 issue of *Scribner's Magazine,* one of the more conservative literary monthlies. This piece, along with a number of other Thanet stories appearing in *Scribner's* that year, was subsequently collected and published in *Stories of a Western Town* (1893), which garnered many positive reviews and sold quite well. In all of these stories, the town of Fairport is portrayed as a very livable place inhabited by many different types of industrious, honest people and where kind members of the upper class are always willing to help people lower on the socioeconomic ladder succeed—as long as they are willing to work hard for it. Significantly, a great number of these people are women.

Indeed, despite her stance against women's suffrage, Thanet cannot be classified so easily as completely conservative regarding women's issues; not only did she choose the name "Octave" because she liked how it could be taken as either male or female and enjoy a long-term relationship with Jane Allen Crawford, but she also depicted a great many strong, independent, self-reliant women in her fiction—including Alma Brown, from "The Face of Failure." It is interesting to note in this context that Thanet served as a major inspiration for a younger woman from Davenport, Susan Glaspell, to pursue her own literary career; Glaspell, who took a stronger stance against the patriarchy in her work, is, as a result, much better known today. Reading Thanet's "The Face of Failure," especially if one compares it to her fellow Iowan Hamlin Garland's story "Up the Coulé" (1891), allows one to see that there was far less consensus among writers in the Midwest about certain issues than many modern students have been led to believe.

THE FACE OF FAILURE (1892)

After the week's shower the low Iowa hills looked vividly green. At the base of the first range of hills the Blackhawk road winds from the city to the prairie. From its starting-point, just outside the city limits, the wayfarer may catch bird's-eye glimpses of the city, the vast river that the Iowans love, and the three bridges tying three towns to the island arsenal. But at one's elbow spreads Cavendish's melon farm. Cavendish's melon farm it still is, in current phrase, although Cavendish, whose memory is honored by lovers of the cantaloupe melon, long ago departed to raise melons for larger markets; and still a weather-beaten sign creaks from a post announcing to the world that "the celebrated Cavendish Melons are for Sale here!" To-day the melon-vines were softly shaded by rain-drops. A pleasant sight they made, spreading for acres in front of the green-houses where mushrooms and early vegetables strove to outwit the seasons, and before the brown cottage in which Cavendish had begun a successful career. The black roof-tree of the cottage sagged in the middle, and the weather-boarding was dingy with the streaky dinginess of old paint that has never had enough oil. The fences, too, were unpainted and rudely patched. Nevertheless a second glance told one that there were no gaps in them, that the farm machines kept their bright colors well under cover, and that the garden rows were beautifully straight and clean. An old white horse switched its sleek sides with its long tail and drooped its untrammeled neck in front of the gate. The wagon to which it was harnessed was new and had just been washed. Near the gate stood a girl and boy who seemed to be mutually studying each other's person. Decidedly the girl's slim, light figure in its dainty frock repaid one's eyes for their trouble; and her face, with its brilliant violet eyes, its full, soft chin, its curling auburn hair and delicate tints, was charming; but her brother's look was anything but approving. His lip curled and his small gray eyes grew smaller under his scowling brows.

"Is *that* your best suit?" said the girl.

"Yes, it is; and it's *going* to be for one while," said the boy.

It was a suit of the cotton mixture that looks like wool when it is new, and cuts a figure on the counters of every dealer in cheap ready-made clothing. It had been Tim Powell's best attire for a year; perhaps he had not been careful enough of it, and that was why it no longer cared even to imitate wool; it was faded to the hue of a clay bank, it was threadbare, the trousers bagged at the knees, the jacket bagged at the elbows, the pockets bulged flabbily from sheer force of habit, although there was nothing in them.

"I thought you were to have a new suit," said the girl. "Uncle told me himself he was going to buy you one yesterday when you went to town."

"I wouldn't have asked him to buy me anything yesterday for more'n a suit of clothes."

"Why?" The girl opened her eyes. "Didn't he do anything with the lawyer? Is that why you are both so glum this morning?"

"No, he didn't. The lawyer says the woman that owns the mortgage[1] has got to have the money. And it's due next week."

The girl grew pale all over her pretty rosy cheeks; her eyes filled with tears as she gasped, "Oh, how hateful of her, when she promised——"

"She never promised nothing, Eve; it ain't been hers for more than three months. Sloan, that used to have it, died, and left his property to be divided up between his nieces; and the mortgage is her share. See?"

"I don't care, it's just as mean. Mr. Sloan promised."

"No, he didn't; he jest said if Uncle was behind he wouldn't press him; and he did let Uncle get behind with the interest two times and never kicked. But he died; and now the woman, she wants her money!"

"I think it is mean and cruel of her to turn us out! Uncle says mortgages are wicked anyhow, and I believe him!"

"I guess he couldn't have bought this place if he didn't give a mortgage on it. And he'd have had enough to pay cash, too, if Richards hadn't begged him so to lend it to him."

"When is Richards going to pay him?"

"It come due three months ago; Richards ain't never paid up the interest even, and now he says he's got to have the mortgage extended for three years; anyhow for two."

"But don't he *know* we've got to pay our own mortgage? How can we help *him?* I wish Uncle would sell him out!"

The boy gave her the superior smile of the masculine creature. "I suppose," he remarked with elaborate irony, "that he's like Uncle and you; he thinks mortgages are wicked."

"And just as like as not Uncle won't want to go to the carnival," Eve went on, her eyes filling again.

Tim gazed at her, scowling and sneering; but she was absorbed in dreams and hopes with which as yet his boyish mind had no point of contact.

"All the girls in the A class were going to go to see the fireworks together, and George Dean and some of the boys were going to take us, and we were going to have tea at May Arlington's house, and I was to stay all night;"—this came in a half sob. "I think it is just too mean! I never have any good times!"

"Oh, yes, you do, sis, lots! Uncle always gits you everything you want. And he feels terrible bad when I—when he knows he can't afford to git something you want—"

"I know well enough who tells him we can't afford things!"

"Well, do you want us to git things we can't afford? I ain't never advised him except the best I knew how. I told him Richards was a blow-hard, and I told him those Alliance grocery folks[2] he bought such a lot of truck of would skin him, and they did; those canned things they sold him was all musty, and they said there wasn't any freight[3] on 'em, and he had to pay freight and a fancy price besides; and I don't believe they had any more to do with the Alliance than our cow!"

"Uncle always believes everything. He always is so sure things are going to turn out just splendid; and they don't—only just middling; and then he loses a lot of money."

"But he is an awful good man," said the boy, musingly.

"I don't believe in being so good you can't make money. I don't want always to be poor and despised, and have the other girls have prettier clothes than me!"

"I guess you can be pretty good and yet make money, if you are sharp enough. Of course you got to be sharper to be good and make money than you got to be mean and make money."

"Well, I know one thing, that Uncle ain't *ever* going to make money. He—" The last word shriveled on her lips, which puckered into a confused smile at the warning frown of her brother. The man that they were discussing had come round to them past the henhouse. How much had he overheard?

He didn't seem angry, anyhow. He called: "Well, Evy, ready?" and Eve was glad to run into the house for her hat without looking at him. It was a relief that she must sit on the back seat where she need not face Uncle Nelson. Tim sat in front; but Tim was so stupid he wouldn't mind.

Nor did he; it was Nelson Forrest that stole furtive glances at the lad's profile, the knitted brows, the freckled cheeks, the undecided nose, and firm mouth.

The boyish shoulders slouched forward at the same angle as that of the fifty-year-old shoulders beside him. Nelson, through long following of the plough, had lost the erect carriage painfully acquired in the army. He was a handsome man, whose fresh-colored skin gave him a perpetual appearance of having just washed his face. The features were long and delicate. The brown eyes had a liquid softness like the eyes of a woman. In general the countenance was alertly intelligent; he looked younger than his years; but this afternoon the lines about his mouth and in his brows warranted every gray hair of his pointed short beard. There was a reason. Nelson was having one of those searing flashes of insight that do come occasionally to the most blindly hopeful souls. Nelson had hoped all his life. He hoped for himself, he hoped for the whole human race. He served the abstraction that he called *"Progress"* with unflinching and unquestioning loyalty. Every new scheme of increasing happiness by force found a helper, a fighter, and a giver in him; by turns he had been an Abolitionist, a Fourierist, a Socialist, a Greenbacker, a Farmers' Alliance man.[4] Disappointment always was followed hard on its heels by a brand-new confidence. Progress ruled his farm as well as his politics; he bought the newest implements and subscribed trustfully to four agricultural papers; but being a born lover of the ground, a vein of saving doubt did assert itself sometimes in his work; and, on the whole, as a farmer he was successful. But his success never ventured outside his farm gates. At buying or selling, at a bargain in any form, the fourteen-year-old Tim was better than Nelson with his fifty years' experience of a wicked and bargaining world.

Was that any part of the reason, he wondered to-day, why at the end of thirty years of unflinching toil and honesty, he found himself with a vast budget of experience in the ruinous loaning of money, with a mortgage on the farm of a friend, and a mortgage on his own farm likely to be foreclosed? Perhaps it might have been better to stay in Henry County. He had paid for his farm at last. He had known a good moment, too, that day he drove away from the lawyer's with the cancelled mortgage in his pocket and Tim hopping up and down on the seat for joy. But the next day Richards—just to give him the chance of a good thing—had brought out that Maine man who wanted to buy him out. He was anxious to put the money down for the new farm, to have no whip-lash of debt forever whistling about his ears as he ploughed, ready to sting did he stumble in the furrows; and Tim was more anxious than he; but—there was Richards! Richards was a neighbor who thought as he did about Henry George[5] and Spiritualism,[6] and belonged to the Farmers' Alliance, and had lent Nelson all the works of Henry George that he (Richards) could borrow. Richards was in deep trouble. He had lost his wife; he might lose his farm. He appealed to Nelson, for the sake of old friendship, to save him. And Nelson could not resist; so, two thousand of the thirty-four hundred dollars that the Maine man paid went to Richards, the latter swearing by all that is holy, to pay his friend off in full at the end of the year. There was money coming to him from his dead wife's estate, but it was tied up in the courts. Nelson would not listen to Tim's prophecies of evil. But he was a little dashed when Richards paid neither interest nor principal at the year's end, although he gave reasons of weight; and he experienced veritable consternation when the renewed mortgage ran its course and still Richards could not pay. The money from his wife's estate had been used to improve his farm (Nelson knew how rundown everything was), his new wife was sickly and "didn't seem to take hold," there had been a disastrous hail-storm—but why rehearse the calamities? they focussed on one sentence: it was impossible to pay.

Then Nelson, who had been restfully counting on the money from Richards for his own debt, bestirred himself, only to find his patient creditor gone and a woman in his stead who must have her money. He wrote again—sorely against his will—begging Richards to raise the money somehow. Richards's answer was in his pocket, for he wore the best black broadcloth in which he had done honor to the lawyer, yesterday. Richards plainly was wounded; but he explained in detail to Nelson how he (Nelson) could borrow money of the banks on his farm and pay Miss Brown. There was no bank where Richards could borrow money; and he begged Nelson not to drive his wife and little children from their cherished home. Nelson choked over the pathos when he read the letter to Tim; but Tim only grunted a wish that HE had the handling of that feller. And the lawyer was as little moved as Tim. Miss Brown needed the money, he said. The banks were not disposed to lend just at present; money, it appeared, was "tight;" so, in the end, Nelson drove home with the face of Failure staring at him between his horses' ears.

There was only one way. Should he make Richards suffer or suffer himself? Did a man have to grind other people or be ground himself? Meanwhile they had reached the town. The stir of a festival was in the air. On every side bunting streamed in the breeze or was draped across brick or wood. Arches spanned some of the streets, with inscriptions of welcome on them, and swarms of colored lanterns glittered against the sunlight almost as gayly as they would show when they should be lighted at night. Little children ran about waving flags. Grocery wagons and butchers' wagons trotted by with a flash of flags dangling from the horses' harness. The streets were filled with people in their holiday clothes. Everybody smiled. The shopkeepers answered questions and went out on the sidewalks to direct strangers. From one window hung a banner inviting visitors to enter and get a list of hotels and boarding-houses. The crowd was entirely good-humored and waited outside restaurants, bandying jokes with true Western philosophy. At times the wagons made a temporary blockade in the street, but no one grumbled. Bands of music paraded past them, the escort for visitors of especial consideration. In a window belonging, the sign above declared, to the Business Men's Association, stood a huge doll clad in blue satin, on which was painted a device of Neptune[7] sailing down the Mississippi amid a storm of fireworks. The doll stood in a boat arched about with lantern-decked hoops, and while Nelson halted, unable to proceed, he could hear the voluble explanation of the proud citizen who was interpreting to strangers.

This, Nelson thought, was success. Here were the successful men. The man who had failed looked at them. Eve roused him by a shrill cry, "There they are. There's May and the girls. Let me out quick, Uncle!"

He stopped the horse and jumped out himself to help her. It was the first time since she came under his roof that she had been away from it all night. He cleared his throat for some advice on behavior. "Mind and be respectful to Mrs. Arlington. Say yes, ma'am, and no, ma'am—" He got no further, for Eve gave him a hasty kiss and the crowd brushed her away.

"All she thinks of is wearing fine clothes and going with the fellers!" said her brother, disdainfully. "If I had to be born a girl, I wouldn't be born at all!"

"Maybe if you despise girls so, you'll be born a girl the next time," said Nelson. "Some folks thinks that's how it happens with us."

"Do *you*, Uncle?" asked Tim, running his mind forebodingly over the possible business results of such a belief. "S'posing he shouldn't be willing to sell the pigs to be killed, 'cause they might be some friends of his!" he reflected, with a rising tide of consternation.

Nelson smiled rather sadly. He said, in another tone: "Tim, I've thought so many things, that now I've about given up thinking. All I can do is to live along the best way I know how and help the world move the best I'm able."

"You bet *I* ain't going to help the world move," said the boy; "I'm going to look out for myself!"

"Then my training of you has turned out pretty badly, if that's the way you feel."

A little shiver passed over the lad's sullen face; he flushed until he lost his freckles in the red veil and burst out passionately: "Well, I got eyes, ain't I? I ain't going to be bad, or drink, or steal, or do things to git put in the penitentiary; but I ain't going to let folks walk all over me like you do; no, sir!"

Nelson did not answer; in his heart he thought that he had failed with the children, too; and he relapsed into that dismal study of the face of Failure.

He had come to the city to show Tim the sights, and, therefore, though like a man in a dream, he drove conscientiously about the gay streets, pointing out whatever he thought might interest the boy, and generally discovering that Tim had the new information by heart already. All the while a question pounded itself, like the beat of the heart of an engine, through the noise and the talk: "Shall I give up Richards or be turned out myself?"

When the afternoon sunlight waned he put up the horse at a modest little stable where farmers were allowed to bring their own provender.[8] The charges were of the smallest and the place neat and weather-tight, but it had been a long time before Nelson could be induced to use it, because there was a higher-priced stable kept by an ex-farmer and member of the Farmers' Alliance. Only the fact that the keeper of the low-priced stable was a poor orphan girl, struggling to earn an honest livelihood, had moved him.

They had supper at a restaurant of Tim's discovery, small, specklessly tidy, and as unexacting of the pocket as the stable. It was an excellent supper. But Nelson had no appetite; in spite of an almost childish capacity for being diverted, he could attend to nothing but the question always in his ears: "Richards or me—which?"

Until it should be time for the spectacle they walked down the hill, and watched the crowds gradually blacken every inch of the river-banks. Already the swarms of lanterns were beginning to bloom out in the dusk. Strains of music throbbed through the air, adding a poignant touch to the excitement vibrating in all the faces and voices about them. Even the stolid Tim felt the contagion. He walked with a jaunty step and assaulted a tune himself. "I tell you, Uncle," says Tim, "it's nice of these folks to be getting up all this show, and giving it for nothing!"

"Do you think so?" says Nelson. "You don't love your book as I wish you did; but I guess you remember about the ancient Romans, and how the great, rich Romans used to spend enormous sums in games and shows that they let the people in free to—well, what for? Was it to learn them anything or to make them happy? Oh, no, it was to keep down the spirit of liberty, Son, it was to make them content to be slaves! And so it is here. These merchants and capitalists are only looking out for themselves, trying to keep labor down and not let it know how oppressed it is, trying to get people here from everywhere to show what a fine city they have and get their money."

"Well, 'tis a fine town," Tim burst in, "a boss town! And they ain't gouging folks a little bit. None of the hotels or the restaurants have put up their prices one cent. Look what a dandy supper we got for twenty-five cents! And ain't the boy at Lumley's grocery given me two tickets to set on the steamboat? There's nothing mean about this town!"

Nelson made no remark; but he thought, for the fiftieth time, that his farm was too near the city. Tim was picking up all the city boys' false pride as well as their slang. Unconscious Tim resumed his tune. He knew that it was "Annie Rooney"[9] if no one else did, and he mangled the notes with appropriate exhilaration.

Now, the river was as busy as the land, lights swimming hither and thither; steamboats with ropes of tiny stars bespangling their dark bulk and a white electric glare in the bow, low boats with lights that sent wavering spear-heads into the shadow beneath. The bridge was a blazing barbed fence of fire, and beyond the bridge, at the point of the island, lay a glittering multitude of lights, a fairy fleet with miniature sails outlined in flame as if by jewels.

Nelson followed Tim. The crowds, the ceaseless clatter of tongues and jar of wheels, depressed the man, who hardly knew which way to dodge the multitudinous perils of the thoroughfare; but Tim used his elbows to such good purpose that they were out of the levee, on the steamboat, and settling themselves in two comfortable chairs in a coign[10] of vantage on deck, that commanded the best obtainable view of the pageant, before Nelson had gathered his wits together enough to plan a path out of the crush.

"I sized up this place from the shore," Tim sighed complacently, drawing a long breath of relief; "only jest two chairs, so we won't be crowded."

Obediently, Nelson took his chair. His head sank on his thin chest. Richards or himself, which should he sacrifice? So the weary old question droned through his brain. He felt a tap on his shoulder. The man who roused him was an acquaintance, and he stood smiling in the attitude of a man about to ask a favor, while the expectant half-smile of the lady on his arm hinted at the nature of the favor. Would Mr. Forrest be so kind?—there seemed to be no more seats. Before Mr. Forrest could be kind Tim had yielded his own chair and was off, wriggling among the crowd in search of another place.

"Smart boy, that youngster of yours," said the man; "he'll make his way in the world, he can push. Well, Miss Alma, let me make you acquainted with Mr. Forrest. I know you will be well entertained by him. So, if you'll excuse me, I'll get back and help my wife wrestle with the kids. They have been trying to see which will fall overboard first ever since we came on deck!"

Under the leeway of this pleasantry he bowed and retired. Nelson turned with determined politeness to the lady. He was sorry that she had come, she looking to him a very fine lady indeed, with her black silk gown, her shining black ornaments, and her bright black eyes. She was not young, but handsome in Nelson's judgment, although of a haughty bearing. "Maybe she is the principal of the High School," thought he. "Martin has her for a boarder, and he said she was very particular about her melons being cold!"

But however formidable a personage, the lady must be entertained.

"I expect you are a resident of the city, ma'am?" said Nelson.

"Yes, I was born here." She smiled, a smile that revealed a little break in the curve of her cheek, not exactly a dimple, but like one.

"I don't know when I have seen such a fine appearing lady," thought Nelson. He responded: "Well, I wasn't born here; but I come when I was a little shaver of ten and stayed till I was eighteen, when I went to Kansas to help fight the border ruffians.[11] I went to school here in the Warren Street school-house."

"So did I, as long as I went anywhere to school. I had to go to work when I was twelve."

Nelson's amazement took shape before his courtesy had a chance to control it. "I didn't suppose you ever did any work in your life!" cried he.

"I guess I haven't done much else. Father died when I was twelve and the oldest of five, the next only eight—Polly, that came between Eb and me, died—naturally I had to work. I was a nurse-girl by the day, first; and I never shall forget how kind the woman was to me. She gave me so much dinner I never needed to eat any breakfast, which was a help."

"You poor little thing! I'm afraid you went hungry sometimes." Immediately he marvelled at his familiar speech, but she did not seem to resent it.

"No, not so often," she said, musingly; "but I used often and often to wish I could carry some of the nice things home to mother and the babies. After a while she would give me a cookey or a piece of bread and butter for lunch; that I could take home. I don't suppose I'll often have more pleasure than I used to have then, seeing little Eb waiting for sister; and the baby and mother—" She stopped abruptly, to continue, in an instant, with a kind of laugh; "I am never likely to feel so important again as I did then, either. It was great to have mother consulting me, as if I had been grown up. I felt like I had the weight of the nation on my shoulders, I assure you."

"And have you always worked since? You are not working out now?" with a glance at her shining gown.

"Oh, no, not for a long time. I learned to be a cook. I was a good cook, too, if I say it myself. I worked for the Lossings for four years. I am not a bit ashamed of being a hired girl, for I was as good a one as I knew how. It was Mrs. Lossing that first lent me books; and Harry Lossing, who is head of the firm now, got Ebenezer into the works. Ebenezer is shipping-clerk with a good salary and stock in the concern; and Ralph is there, learning the trade. I went to the business-college and learned book-keeping, and afterward I learned typewriting and shorthand. I have been working for the firm for fourteen years. We have educated the girls. Milly is married, and Kitty goes to the boarding-school, here."

"Then you haven't been married yourself?"

"What time did I have to think of being married? I had the family on my mind, and looking after them."

"That was more fortunate for your family than it was for my sex," said Nelson, gallantly. He accompanied the compliment by a glance of admiration, extinguished in an eye-flash, for the white radiance that had bathed the deck suddenly vanished.

"Now you will see a lovely sight," said the woman, deigning no reply to his tribute; "listen! That is the signal."

The air was shaken with the boom of cannon. Once, twice, thrice. Directly the boat-whistles took up the roar, making a hideous din. The fleet had moved. Spouting rockets and Roman candles, which painted above it a kaleidoscopic archway of fire, welcomed by answering javelins of light and red and orange and blue and green flares from the shore; the fleet bombarded the bridge, escorted Neptune in his car, manoeuvred and massed and charged on the blazing city with a many-hued shower of flame.

After the boats, silently, softly, floated the battalions of lanterns, so close to the water that they seemed flaming water-lilies, while the dusky mirror repeated and inverted their splendor.

"They're shingles, you know," explained Nelson's companion, "with lanterns on them; but aren't they pretty?"

"Yes, they are! I wish you had not told me. It is like a fairy story!"

"Ain't it? But we aren't through; there's more to come. Beautiful fireworks!"

The fireworks, however, were slow of coming. They could see the barge from which they were to be sent; they could watch the movements of the men in white oil-cloth who moved in a ghostly fashion about the barge; they could hear the tap of hammers; but nothing came of it all.

They sat in the darkness, waiting; and there came to Nelson a strange sensation of being alone and apart from all the breathing world with this woman. He did not perceive that Tim had quietly returned with a box which did very well for a seat, and was sitting with his knees against the chair-rungs. He seemed to be somehow outside of all the tumult and the spectacle. It was the vainglorying triumph of this world. He was the soul outside, the soul that had missed its triumph. In his perplexity and loneliness he felt an overwhelming longing for sympathy; neither did it strike Nelson, who believed in all sorts of occult influences, that his confidence in a stranger was unwarranted. He would have told you that his "psychic instincts" never played him false, although really they were traitors from their astral cradles to their astral graves.

He said in a hesitating way: "You must excuse me being kinder dull; I've got some serious business on my mind and I can't help thinking of it."

"Is that so? Well, I know how that is; I have often stayed awake nights worrying about things. Lest I shouldn't suit and all that—especially after mother took sick."

"I s'pose you had to give up and nurse her then?"

"That was what Ebenezer and Ralph were for having me do; but mother—my mother always had so much sense—mother says, 'No, Alma, you've got a good place and a chance in life, you sha'n't give it up. We'll hire a girl. I ain't never lonesome except evenings, and then you will be home. I should jest want to die,' she says, 'if I thought I kept you in a kind of prison like by my being sick—now, just when you are getting on so well.' There never *was* a woman like my mother!" Her voice shook a little, and Nelson asked gently:

"Ain't your mother living now?"

"No, she died last year." She added, after a little silence, "I somehow can't get used to being lonesome."

"It *is* hard," said Nelson. "I lost my wife three years ago."

"That's hard, too."

"My goodness! I guess it is. And it's hardest when trouble comes on a man and he can't go nowhere for advice."

"Yes, that's so, too. But—have you any children?"

"Yes, ma'am; that is, they ain't my own children. Lizzie and I never had any; but these two we took and they are most like my own. The girl is eighteen and the boy rising of fourteen."

"They must be a comfort to you; but they are considerable of a responsibility, too."

"Yes, ma'am," he sighed softly to himself. "Sometimes I feel I haven't done the right way by them, though I've tried. Not that they ain't good children, for they are—no better anywhere. Tim, he will work from morning till night, and never need to urge him; and he never gives me a promise he don't keep it, no ma'am, never did since he was a little mite of a lad. And he is a kind boy, too, always good to the beasts; and while he may speak up a little short to his sister, he saves her many a step. He doesn't take to his studies quite as I would like to have him, but he has a wonderful head for business. There is splendid stuff in Tim if it could only be worked right."

While Nelson spoke, Tim was hunching his shoulders forward in the darkness, listening with the whole of two sharp ears. His face worked in spite of him, and he gave an inarticulate snort.

"Well," the woman said, "I think that speaks well for Tim. Why should you be worried about him?"

"I am afraid he is getting to love money and worldly success too well, and that is what I fear for the girl, too. You see, she is so pretty, and the idols of the tribe and the market, as Bacon calls them,[12] are strong with the young."

"Yes, that's so," the woman assented vaguely, not at all sure what either Bacon or his idols might be. "Are the children relations of yours?"

"No, ma'am; it was like this: When I was up in Henry County there came a photographic artist to the village near us, and pitched his tent and took tintypes in his wagon. He had his wife and his two children with him. The poor woman fell ill and died; so we took the two children. My wife was willing; she was a wonderfully good woman, member of the Methodist church till she died. I—I am not a church member myself, ma'am; I passed through that stage of spiritual development a long while ago." He gave a wistful glance at his companion's dimly outlined profile. "But I never tried to disturb her faith; it made *her* happy."

"Oh, I don't think it is any good fooling with other people's religions," said the woman, easily. "It is just like trying to talk folks out of drinking; nobody knows what is right for anybody else's soul any more than they do what is good for anybody else's stomach!"

"Yes, ma'am. You put things very clearly."

"I guess it is because you understand so quickly. But you were saying——"

"That's all the story. We took the children, and their father was killed by the cars[13] the next year, poor man; and so we have done the best we could ever since by them."

"I should say you had done very well by them."

"No, ma'am; I haven't done very well somehow by anyone, myself included, though God knows I've tried hard enough!"

Then followed the silence natural after such a confession when the listener does not know the speaker well enough to parry abasement by denial.

"I am impressed," said Nelson, simply, "to talk with you frankly. It isn't polite to bother strangers with your troubles, but I am impressed that you won't mind."

"Oh, no, I won't mind."

It was not extravagant sympathy; but Nelson thought how kind her voice sounded, and what a musical voice it was. Most people would have called it rather sharp.

He told her—with surprisingly little egotism, as the keen listener noted—the story of his life; the struggle of his boyhood; his random self-education; his years in the army (he had criticised his superior officers, thereby losing the promotion that was coming for bravery in the field); his marriage (apparently he had married his wife because another man had jilted her); his wrestle with nature (whose pranks included a cyclone) on a frontier farm that he eventually lost, having put all his savings into a "Greenback" newspaper,[14] and being thus swamped with debt; his final slow success in paying for his Iowa farm; and his purchase of the new farm, with its resulting disaster. "I've farmed in Kansas," he said, "in Nebraska, in Dakota, in Iowa. I was willing to go wherever the land promised. It always seemed like I was going to succeed, but somehow I never did. The world ain't fixed right for the workers, I take it. A man who has spent thirty years in hard, honest toil oughtn't to be staring ruin in the face like I am to-day. They won't let it be so when we have the single tax and when we farmers send our own men instead of city lawyers, to the Legislature and halls of Congress.[15] Sometimes I think it's the world that's wrong and sometimes I think it's me!"

The reply came in crisp and assured accents, which were the strongest contrast to Nelson's soft, undecided pipe: "Seems to me in this last case the one most to blame is neither you nor the world at large, but this man Richards, who is asking *you* to pay for *his* farm. And I notice you don't seem to consider your creditor in this business. How do you know she don't need the money? Look at me, for instance; I'm in some financial difficulty myself. I have a mortgage for two thousand dollars, and that mortgage—for which good value was given, mind you—falls due this month. I want the money. I want it bad. I have a chance to put my money into stock at the factory. I know all about the investment; I haven't worked there all these years and not know how the business stands. It is a chance to make a fortune. I ain't likely to ever have another like it; and it won't wait for me to make up my mind forever, either. Isn't it hard on me, too?"

"Lord knows it is, ma'am," said Nelson, despondently; "it is hard on us all! Sometimes I don't see the end of it all. A vast social revolution—"

"Social fiddlesticks! I beg your pardon, Mr. Forrest, but it puts me out of patience to have people expecting to be allowed to make every mortal kind of fools of themselves and then have 'a social revolution' jump in to slew off the consequences. Let us understand each other. Who do you suppose I am?"

"Miss—Miss Almer, ain't it?"

"It's Alma Brown, Mr. Forrest. I saw you coming on the boat and I made Mr. Martin fetch me over to you. I told him not to say my name, because I wanted a good plain talk with you. Well, I've had it. Things are just about where I thought they were, and I told Mr. Lossing so. But I couldn't be sure. You must have thought me a funny kind of woman to be telling you all those things about myself."

Nelson, who had changed color half a dozen times in the darkness, sighed before he said: "No, ma'am; I only thought how good you were to tell me. I hoped maybe you were impressed to trust me as I was to trust you."

Being so dark Nelson could not see the queer expression on her face as she slowly shook her head. She was thinking: "If I ever saw a babe in arms trying to do business! How did *he* ever pay for a farm?" She said: "Well, I did it on purpose; I wanted you to know I wasn't a cruel aristocrat, but a woman that had worked as hard as yourself. Now, why shouldn't you help me and yourself instead of helping Richards? You have confidence in me, you say. Well, show it. I'll give you your mortgage for your mortgage on Richards's farm. Come, can't you trust Richards to me? You think it over."

The hiss of a rocket hurled her words into space. The fireworks had begun. Miss Brown looked at them and watched Nelson at the same time. As a good business woman who was also a good citizen, having subscribed five dollars to the carnival, she did not propose to lose the worth of her money; neither did she intend to lose a chance to do business. Perhaps there was an obscurer and more complex motive lurking in some stray corner of that queer garret, a woman's mind. Such motives—aimless softenings of the heart, unprofitable diversions of the fancy—will seep unconsciously through the toughest business principles of woman.

She was puzzled by the look of exaltation on Nelson's features, illumined as they were by the uncanny light. If the fool man had not forgotten all his troubles just to see a few fireworks! No, he was not that kind of a fool; maybe—and she almost laughed aloud in her pleasure over her own insight—maybe it all made him think of the war, where he had been so brave. "He was a regular hero in the war," Miss Brown concluded, "and he certainly is a perfect gentleman; what a pity he hasn't got any sense!"

She had guessed aright, although she had not guessed deep enough in regard to Nelson. He watched the great wheels of light, he watched the river aflame with Greek fire, then, with a shiver, he watched the bombs bursting into myriads of flowers, into fizzing snakes, into fields of burning gold, into showers of jewels that made the night splendid for a second and faded. They were not fireworks to him; they were a magical phantasmagoria that renewed the incoherent and violent emotions of his youth; again he was in the chaos of the battle, or he was dreaming by his camp-fire, or he was pacing his lonely round on guard. His heart leaped again with the old glow, the wonderful, beautiful worship of Liberty that can do no wrong. He seemed to hear a thousand voices chanting:

> "*In the beauty of the lilies*
> *Christ was born across the sea,*
> *As He died to make men holy,*
> *let us die to make men free!*"[16]

His turbid musings cleared—or they seemed to him to clear—under the strong reaction of his imagination and his memories. It was all over, the dream and the glory thereof. The splendid young soldier was an elderly, ruined man. But one thing was left: he could be true to his flag.

"A poor soldier, but enlisted for the war," says Nelson, squaring his shoulders, with a lump in his throat and his eyes brimming. "I know by the way it hurts me to think of refusing her that it's a temptation to wrong-doing. No, I can't save myself by sacrificing a brother soldier for humanity. She is just as kind as she can be, but women don't understand business; she wouldn't make allowance for Richards."

He felt a hand on his shoulder; it was Martin apologizing for hurrying Miss Brown; but the baby was fretting and—

"I'm sorry—yes—well, I wish you didn't have to go!" Nelson began; but a hoarse treble rose from under his elbows: "Say, Mr. Martin, Uncle and me can take Miss Brown home."

"If you will allow me the pleasure," said Nelson, with the touch of courtliness that showed through his homespun ways.

"Well, I *would* like to see the hundred bombs bursting at once and Vulcan at his forge!"[17] said Miss Brown.

Thus the matter arranged itself. Tim waited with the lady while Nelson went for the horse, nor was it until afterward that Miss Brown wondered why the lad did not go instead of the man. But Tim had his own reasons. No sooner was Nelson out of earshot than he began: "Say, Miss Brown, I can tell you something."

"Yes?"

"That Richards is no good; but you can't get Uncle to see it. At least it will take time. If you'll help me we can get him round in time. Won't you please not sell us out for six months and give me a show? I'll see you get your interest and your money, too."

"You?" Miss Brown involuntarily took a business attitude, with her arms akimbo, and eyed the boy.

"Yes, ma'am, me. I ain't so very old, but I know all about the business. I got all the figures down—how much we raise and what we got last year. I can fetch them to you so you can see. He is a good farmer, and he will catch on to the melons pretty quick. We'll do better next year, and I'll try to keep him from belonging to things and spending money; and if he won't lend to anybody or start in raising a new kind of crop just when we get the melons going, he will make money sure. He is awful good and honest. All the trouble with him is he needs somebody to take care of him. If Aunt Lizzie had been alive he never would have lent that dead-beat Richards that money. He ought to get married."

Miss Brown did not feel called on to say anything. Tim continued in a judicial way: "He is awful good and kind, always gets up in the morning to make the fire if I have got something else to do; and he'd think everything his wife did was the best in the world; and if he had somebody to take care of him he'd make money. I don't suppose *you* would think of it?" This last in an insinuating tone, with evident anxiety.

"Well, I never!" said Miss Brown.

Whether she was more offended or amused she couldn't tell; and she stood staring at him by the electric light. To her amazement the hard little face began

"'Well, I never!' said Miss Brown." Illustration from Octave Thanet [Alice French], "The Face of Failure," *Scribner's Magazine* 12 (September 1892).

to twitch. "I didn't mean to mad you," Tim grunted, with a quiver in his rough voice. "I've been listening to every word you said, and I thought you were so sensible you'd talk over things without nonsense. Of course I know he'd have to come and see you Saturday nights, and take you buggy riding, and take you to the theatre, and all such things—first. But I thought we could sorter fix it up between ourselves. I've taken care of him ever since Aunt Lizzie died, and I did my best he shouldn't lend that money, but I couldn't help it; and I did keep him from marrying a widow woman with eight children, who kept telling him how much her poor fatherless children needed a man; and I never did see anybody I was willing—before—and it's—it's so lonesome without Aunt Lizzie!" He choked and frowned. Poor Tim, who had sold so many melons to women and seen so much of back doors and kitchen humors that he held the sex very cheap, he did not realize how hard he would find it to talk of the one woman who had been kind to him! He turned red with shame over his own weakness.

"You poor little chap!" cried Miss Brown; "you poor little sharp, innocent chap!" The hand she laid on his shoulder patted it as she went on: "Never mind, if I can't marry your uncle, I can help you take care of him. You're a real nice boy, and I'm not mad; don't you think it. There's your uncle now."

Nelson found her so gentle that he began to have qualms lest his carefully prepared speech should hurt her feelings. But there was no help for it now. "I have thought over your kind offer to me, ma'am," said he, humbly, "and I got a proposition to make to you. It is your honest due to have your farm, yes, ma'am. Well, I know a man would like to buy it; I'll sell it to him, and pay you your money."

"But that wasn't my proposal."

"I know it, ma'am. I honor you for your kindness; but I can't risk what—what might be another person's idea of duty about Richards. Our consciences ain't all equally enlightened, you know."

Miss Brown did not answer a word.

They drove along the streets where the lanterns were fading. Tim grew uneasy, she was silent so long. On the brow of the hill she indicated a side street and told them to stop the horse before a little brown house. One of the windows was a dim square of red.

"It isn't quite so lonesome coming home to a light," said Miss Brown.

As Nelson cramped the wheel to jump out to help her from the vehicle, the light from the electric arc fell full on his handsome face and showed her the look of compassion and admiration, there.

"Wait one moment," she said, detaining him with one firm hand. "I've got something to say to you. Let Richards go for the present; all I ask of you about him is that you will do nothing until we can find out if he is so bad off. But, Mr. Forrest, I can do better for you about that mortgage. Mr. Lossing will take it for three years for a relative of his and pay me the money. I told him the story."

"And *you* will get the money all right?"

"Just the same. I was only trying to help you a little by the other way, and I failed. Never mind."

"I can't tell you how you make me feel," said Nelson.

"Please let him bring you some melons to-morrow and make a stagger at it, though," said Tim.

"Can I?" Nelson's eyes shone.

"If you want to," said Miss Brown. She laughed; but in a moment she smiled.

All the way home Nelson saw the same face of Failure between the old mare's white ears; but its grim lineaments were softened by a smile, a smile like Miss Brown's.

NOTES

1. When someone cannot pay the full price of a property (usually land or buildings), they apply to a bank or lender for a loan, usually called a mortgage; if obtained, the mortgage allows the borrower to use the property while paying back the loan, even though the bank or lender still actually owns the property.

2. The Farmers' Alliance was a group of affiliated organizations in the late nineteenth century dedicated to obtaining fairer treatment for farmers; one of its enterprises involved selling groceries and other goods to member farmers at prices supposedly below those charged by other businesses, which many farmers felt were too high. Here Tim is implying that the Alliance is actually making his uncle pay too much (and later insinuates that they might be frauds).

3. Shipping and handling costs.

4. A variety of nineteenth-century political movements, all of which promised to improve the conditions for various groups of people but whose idealist goals were not always achieved. These movements all influenced the Populist Party, founded in 1891, which sought fairer conditions for farmers and workers through government regulation of corporations and large businesses.

5. Henry George (1839–97) was a political economist, journalist, and politician whose best-selling book *Progress and Poverty* (1879) made a case for the "single tax" on land, which he believed would reduce the disparity in America between what he viewed as the hard-working poor and the rich, who he posited had obtained most of their wealth from land ownership and speculation.

6. A religious movement whose followers believed that not only can the living communicate with the dead but the dead can provide important advice about how to deal with the world's problems; extremely popular in the United States during the mid to late nineteenth century, it lost many followers beginning in the 1880s as many practitioners were exposed as frauds.

7. The Roman god of both freshwater and the sea.

8. Dry food for horses or cattle.

9. "Little Annie Rooney" (1889), composed by Michael Nolan (ca. 1868–1910), was a popular song of the day.

10. An excellent viewing position.

11. Pro-slavery activists and militia members from Missouri who at various times from 1854 to 1860 crossed into Kansas Territory to intimidate people there into accepting slavery.

12. Sir Francis Bacon (1561–1626) was an English philosopher and statesman who promoted empirical logic and what would come to be known as the scientific

method. One of his most famous works was written in Latin and entitled *Novum Organum: Sive Indicia Vera de Interpretationes Naturae* (*New Organon; or, True Directions concerning the Interpretation of Nature*); in it he delineated four categories of logical fallacies (idols), including "Idols of the Tribe" and "Idols of the Market," that he believed prevent humans from acting on a more rational basis.

13. Railroad cars.

14. The Greenback movement, which flourished from approximately 1868 to 1888, advocated putting much more paper money into circulation and thus fueling inflation; this was quite popular among farmers who had borrowed large sums of money to purchase their land, for they could pay back their loans with dollars worth less (due to inflation) than when they originally borrowed them.

15. Here Uncle Nelson repeats the typical arguments of Populist Party supporters in the 1890s, contrasting the supposedly hard-working rural people with the educated urbanites they felt controlled the government.

16. These lines are from "The Battle Hymn of the Republic," written in November 1861 by Julia Ward Howe (1819–1910) after the outbreak of the Civil War, and first published in February 1862; the song became the unofficial anthem of the North (Union) during the Civil War, associating God's righteousness with defeating slavery.

17. Vulcan was the Roman god of fire; this likely refers to the fireworks display.

MARK TWAIN
(SAMUEL LANGHORNE CLEMENS)

(1835–1910)

Born in the small town of Florida, Missouri, in 1835, Samuel Langhorne Clemens spent his youth in poverty, tried out a number of different occupations in the East and South as a young man, and then served very briefly as an irregular soldier in a Confederate militia during the early days of the Civil War. Instead of remaining a soldier, Twain left for Nevada in 1861 with his brother. Between then and 1866, he lived both in Nevada and California and made his living writing straight journalistic pieces as well as humorous sketches for many different newspapers; in February 1863 he used the pen name of "Mark Twain" for the first time.

Despite the fact that Twain is one of the most famous and highly regarded American authors, the majority of his literary output remains rarely read and little known, even among scholars. This is quite understandable, for the prodigious number of sketches, tales, short stories, novels, and nonfiction pieces he wrote between the early 1860s and his death in 1910 makes it impossible for even the most devoted readers to be familiar with more than a small portion of his oeuvre. For many readers in the United States and around the world, Twain was—and still is—regarded chiefly as a folksy American humorist (and sometimes children's author) who wrote chiefly about the West and lower Mississippi valley. Yet Twain was, as we know now, much more than that.

One other important facet of Twain's career is here represented by "The Facts concerning the Recent Carnival of Crime in Connecticut." Published in the same year as Twain's extremely popular novel of American small-town boy-hood, *The Adventures of Tom Sawyer* (1876), this story offers a much less Romantic outlook on life and human nature. Twain originally wrote it to be read before members of the Monday Evening Club in Hartford, Connecticut, in January 1876; also in the audience for its first reading was Twain's friend, the writer and editor William Dean Howells, who had come from Boston for the event. Having experienced the club members' exceptional interest in this thought-provoking story, Howells published it a few months later in the June issue of the *Atlantic Monthly* magazine, of which he was the editor. One sees in "The Facts Concern-ing" Twain's desire, at this point in his career, to turn his attention from solely writing humorous stories about those living in the West and lower Mississippi valley to also satirizing members of the genteel middle and upper classes of the East. By 1876, Twain had had numerous opportunities to experience life among such people firsthand; in 1870 he had married Olivia Langdon, from a well-to-do, eastern, cultured, religious family, and since 1871 had lived in Hartford among very prosperous and successful people. Ironically, it must be acknowledged that Twain simultaneously wished to win the approval of such people, including eastern literary critics; because of this desire, the publication of this story in the *Atlantic Monthly*, the premier magazine of the educated eastern elite, undoubtedly pleased him a great deal.

The second Twain story included here, "The Second Advent," is representative of the posthumous phase of his career. When Twain died in 1910, he left behind a great many unfinished, as well as completed yet unpublished, manuscripts; "The Second Advent" is among the latter. Twain made notes for a story such as this in 1867 during a visit to the Christian Holy Land, in the Middle East; however, he did not flesh it out as a full story until 1881, and it did not appear in print until 1972. Twain probably did not try to publish this piece or the many others like it because he did not wish to offend his religious wife or her respectable family. He also likely feared that expressing such views could hurt the sales of his books and the attendance at his many readings and lectures, all of which would have greatly reduced the income he needed to support his family. Indeed, Twain is famously reported by his first biographer, Albert Bigelow Paine, to have told the illustrator Dan Beard in 1905 that he would not try to publish his own hard-hitting piece "The War Prayer," because "only dead men can tell the truth in this world." Twain did, however, recognize that after his death, previously unpublished works from his hand, no matter what their subject matter, would be in demand and bring a high price. As a result, he left a sizable number of these in the hands of his literary executor, Albert Bigelow Paine, with instructions to take some out at regular pe-riods, sell them, and use the proceeds to support Twain's children after his death. Unfortunately, only one of Twain's children, his daughter Clara, survived him.

Indeed, the deaths of two of his daughters (a son died in infancy in 1872) and his wife during the period of 1896 to 1909 made Twain's later years quite unhappy ones. In August 1896, his beloved daughter Susy died of meningitis while Twain, his wife Olivia, and daughter Clara were in England for a reading tour. That same year, his daughter Jean was diagnosed with epilepsy; she subsequently suffered from poor health for many years and died in December 1909 when a seizure caused her to drown in her bathtub. The greatest blow, however, came when his wife became severely ill in August 1902 and never fully recovered, passing away in Florence, Italy, in June 1904. Given these personal losses, as well as the severe financial crises he had suffered in the mid-1890s, it is understandable why Twain's writing from these later years—almost all of it published only after his death in 1910—exhibited his disappointment with life, great bitterness toward his fellow human beings, and a profound sense of religious skepticism.

To understand Twain, one must acknowledge that he wrote about much more than western roughs and small-town youths, and that his humor was not always offered as genial entertainment. Indeed, it is precisely because he was such a multitalented writer who wrote so well about a wide variety of topics, and with a great range of viewpoints, that he is regarded as one of America's greatest authors.

THE FACTS CONCERNING THE RECENT CARNIVAL OF CRIME IN CONNECTICUT (1876)

I was feeling blithe, almost jocund. I put a match to my cigar, and just then the morning's mail was handed in. The first superscription I glanced at was in a handwriting that sent a thrill of pleasure through and through me. It was aunt Mary's; and she was the person I loved and honored most in all the world, outside of my own household. She had been my boyhood's idol; maturity, which is fatal to so many enchantments, had not been able to dislodge her from her pedestal; no, it had only justified her right to be there, and placed her dethronement permanently among the impossibilities. To show how strong her influence over me was, I will observe that long after everybody else's "*do*-stop-smoking" had ceased to affect me in the slightest degree, aunt Mary could still stir my torpid conscience into faint signs of life when she touched upon the matter. But all things have their limit in this world. A happy day came at last, when even aunt Mary's words could no longer move me. I was not merely glad to see that day arrive; I was more than glad—I was grateful; for when its sun had set, the one alloy that was able to mar my enjoyment of my aunt's society was gone. The remainder of her stay with us that winter was in every way a delight. Of course she pleaded with me just as earnestly as ever, after that blessed day, to quit my pernicious habit, but to no purpose whatever; the moment she opened the subject I at once became calmly, peacefully, contentedly indifferent—absolutely, adamantinely[1] indifferent. Consequently the closing weeks of that memorable visit melted away as pleasantly as a dream, they were so freighted for me with tranquil satisfaction. I could not have enjoyed my pet vice more if my gentle tormentor had been a smoker herself, and an advocate of the practice. Well, the sight of her handwriting reminded me that I was getting very hungry to see her again. I easily guessed what I should find in her letter. I opened it. Good! just as I expected; she was coming! Coming this very day, too, and by the morning train; I might expect her any moment.

I said to myself, "I am thoroughly happy and content now. If my most pitiless enemy could appear before me at this moment, I would freely right any wrong I may have done him."

Straightway the door opened, and a shriveled, shabby dwarf entered. He was not more than two feet high. He seemed to be about forty years old. Every feature and every inch of him was a trifle out of shape; and so, while one could not put his finger upon any particular part and say, "This is a conspicuous deformity," the spectator perceived that this little person was a deformity as a whole—a vague, general, evenly blended, nicely adjusted deformity. There was a fox-like cunning in the face and the sharp little eyes, and also alertness and malice. And yet, this vile bit of human rubbish seemed to bear a sort of remote and ill-defined resemblance to me! It was dully perceptible in the mean form, the countenance, and even the clothes, gestures, manner, and attitudes of the creature. He was a far-fetched, dim suggestion of a burlesque upon me, a caricature of me in little. One thing about him struck me forcibly and most unpleasantly: he was covered all over with a fuzzy, greenish mold, such as one sometimes sees upon mildewed bread. The sight of it was nauseating.

He stepped along with a chipper air, and flung himself into a doll's chair in a very free-and-easy way, without waiting to be asked. He tossed his hat into the waste-basket. He picked up my old chalk pipe from the floor, gave the stem a wipe or two on his knee, filled the bowl from the tobacco-box at his side, and said to me in a tone of pert command,—

"Gimme a match!"

I blushed to the roots of my hair; partly with indignation, but mainly because it somehow seemed to me that this whole performance was very like an exaggeration of conduct which I myself had sometimes been guilty of in my intercourse with familiar friends—but never, never with strangers, I observed to myself. I wanted to kick the pygmy into the fire, but some incomprehensible sense of being legally and legitimately under his authority forced me to obey his order. He applied the match to the pipe, took a contemplative whiff or two, and remarked, in an irritatingly familiar way,—

"Seems to me it's devilish odd weather for this time of year."

I flushed again, and in anger and humiliation as before; for the language was hardly an exaggeration of some that I have uttered in my day, and moreover was delivered in a tone of voice and with an exasperating drawl that had the seeming of a deliberate travesty of my style. Now there is nothing I am quite so sensitive about as a mocking imitation of my drawling infirmity of speech. I spoke up sharply and said,—

"Look here, you miserable ash-cat! you will have to give a little more attention to your manners, or I will throw you out of the window!"

The manikin smiled a smile of malicious content and security, puffed a whiff of smoke contemptuously toward me, and said, with a still more elaborate drawl,—

"Come—go gently now; don't put on *too* many airs with your betters."

This cool snub rasped me all over, but it seemed to subjugate me, too, for a moment. The pygmy contemplated me awhile with his weasel eyes, and then said, in a peculiarly sneering way:

"You turned a tramp away from your door this morning."

I said crustily,—

"Perhaps I did, perhaps I didn't. How do *you* know?"

"Well, I know. It isn't any matter *how* I know."

"Very well. Suppose I did turn a tramp away from the door—what of it?"

"Oh, nothing; nothing in particular. Only you lied to him."

"I *didn't!* That is, I"—

"Yes, but you did; you lied to him."

I felt a guilty pang—in truth, I had felt it forty times before that tramp had traveled a block from my door,—but still I resolved to make a show of feeling slandered; so I said,—

"This is a baseless impertinence. I said to the tramp"—

"There—wait. You were about to lie again. *I* know what you said to him. You said the cook was gone down town and there was nothing left from breakfast. Two lies. You knew the cook was behind the door, and plenty of provisions behind *her.*"

This astonishing accuracy silenced me; and it filled me with wondering speculations, too, as to how this cub could have got his information. Of course he could have culled the conversation from the tramp, but by what sort of magic had he contrived to find out about the concealed cook? Now the dwarf spoke again:—

"It was rather pitiful, rather small, in you to refuse to read that poor young woman's manuscript the other day, and give her an opinion as to its literary value; and she had come so far, too, and so hopefully. Now *wasn't* it?"

I felt like a cur! And I had felt so every time the thing had recurred to my mind, I may as well confess. I flushed hotly and said,—

"Look here, have you nothing better to do than prowl around prying into other people's business? Did that girl tell you that?"

"Never mind whether she did or not. The main thing is, you did that contemptible thing. And you felt ashamed of it afterward. Aha! you feel ashamed of it *now!*"

This was a sort of devilish glee. With fiery earnestness I responded,—

"I told that girl, in the kindest, gentlest way, that I could not consent to deliver judgment upon *any* one's manuscript, because an individual's verdict was worthless. It might underrate a work of high merit and lose it to the world, or it might overrate a trashy production and so open the way for its infliction upon the world: I said that the great public was the only tribunal competent to sit in judgment upon a literary effort, and therefore it must be best to lay it before that tribunal in the outset, since in the end it must stand or fall by that mighty court's decision anyway."

"Yes, you said all that. So you did, you juggling, small-souled shuffler! And yet when the happy hopefulness faded out of that poor girl's face, when you saw her furtively slip beneath her shawl the scroll she had so patiently and honestly scribbled at,—so ashamed of her darling now, so proud of it before,—when you saw the gladness go out of her eyes and the tears come there, when she crept away so humbly who had come so"—

"Oh, peace! peace! peace! Blister your merciless tongue, haven't all these thoughts tortured me enough without *your* coming here to fetch them back again?"

Remorse! remorse! It seemed to me that it would eat the very heart out of me! And yet that small fiend only sat there leering at me with joy and contempt, and placidly chuckling. Presently he began to speak again. Every sentence was an accusation, and every accusation a truth. Every clause was freighted with sarcasm and derision, every slow-dropping word burned like vitriol. The dwarf reminded me of times when I had flown at my children in anger and punished them for faults which a little inquiry would have taught me that others, and not they, had committed. He reminded me of how I had disloyally allowed old friends to be traduced in my hearing, and been too craven to utter a word in their defense. He reminded me of many dishonest things which I had done; of many which I had procured to be done by children and other irresponsible persons; of some which I had planned, thought upon, and longed to do, and been kept from the performance by fear of consequences only. With exquisite cruelty he recalled to my mind, item by item, wrongs and unkindnesses I had inflicted and humiliations I had put upon friends since dead, "who died thinking of those injuries, maybe, and grieving over them," he added, by way of poison to the stab.

"For instance," said he, "take the case of your younger brother, when you two were boys together, many a long year ago. He always lovingly trusted in you with a fidelity that your manifold treacheries were not able to shake. He followed you about like a dog, content to suffer wrong and abuse if he might only be with you; patient under these injuries so long as it was your hand that inflicted them. The latest picture you have of him in health and strength must be such a comfort to you! You pledged your honor that if he would let you blindfold him no harm should come to him; and then, giggling and choking over the rare fun of the joke, you led him to a brook thinly glazed with ice, and pushed him in; and how you did laugh! Man, you will never forget the gentle, reproachful look he gave you as he struggled shivering out, if you live a thousand years! Oho! you see it now, you see it *now!*"

"Beast, I have seen it a million times, and shall see it a million more! and may you rot away piecemeal, and suffer till doomsday what I suffer now, for bringing it back to me again!"

The dwarf chuckled contentedly, and went on with his accusing history of my career. I dropped into a moody, vengeful state, and suffered in silence under the merciless lash. At last this remark of his gave me a sudden rouse:—

"Two months ago, on a Tuesday, you woke up, away in the night, and fell to thinking, with shame, about a peculiarly mean and pitiful act of yours toward a poor ignorant Indian in the wilds of the Rocky Mountains in the winter of eighteen hundred and"—

"Stop a moment, devil! Stop! Do you mean to tell me that even my very *thoughts* are not hidden from you?"

"It seems to look like that. Didn't you think the thoughts I have just mentioned?"

"If I didn't, I wish I may never breathe again! Look here, friend—look me in the eye. Who *are* you?"

"Well, who do you think?"

"I think you are Satan himself. I think you are the devil."

"No."

"No? Then who *can* you be?"

"Would you really like to know?"

"*Indeed* I would."

"Well, I am your *Conscience!*"

In an instant I was in a blaze of joy and exultation. I sprang at the creature, roaring,—

"Curse you, I have wished a hundred million times that you were tangible, and that I could get my hands on your throat once! Oh, but I will wreak a deadly vengeance on"—

Folly! Lightning does not move more quickly than my Conscience did! He darted aloft so suddenly that in the moment my fingers clutched the empty air he was already perched on the top of the high book-case, with his thumb at his nose in token of derision. I flung the poker at him, and missed. I fired the boot-jack.[2] In a blind rage I flew from place to place, and snatched and hurled any missile that came handy; the storm of books, inkstands, and chunks of coal gloomed the air and beat about the manikin's perch relentlessly, but all to no purpose; the nimble figure dodged every shot; and not only that, but burst into a cackle of sarcastic and triumphant laughter as I sat down exhausted. While I puffed and gasped with fatigue and excitement, my Conscience talked to this effect:—

"My good slave, you are curiously witless—no, I mean characteristically so. In truth, you are always consistent, always yourself, always an ass. Otherwise it must have occurred to you that if you attempted this murder with a sad heart and a heavy conscience, I would droop under the burdening influence instantly. Fool, I should have weighed a ton, and could not have budged from the floor; but instead, you are so cheerfully anxious to kill me that your conscience is as light as a feather; hence I am away up here out of your reach. I can almost respect a mere ordinary sort of fool; but *you*—pah!"

I would have given anything, then, to be heavy-hearted, so that I could get this person down from there and take his life, but I could no more be heavy-hearted over such a desire than I could have sorrowed over its accomplishment. So I could only look longingly up at my master, and rave at the ill luck that denied me a heavy conscience the one only time that I had ever wanted such a thing in my life. By and by I got to musing over the hour's strange adventure, and of course my human curiosity began to work. I set myself to framing in my mind some questions for this fiend to answer. Just then one of my boys entered, leaving the door open behind him, and exclaimed,—

"My! what *has* been going on here? The book-case is all one riddle of"—

I sprang up in consternation, and shouted,—

"Out of this! Hurry! jump! Fly! Shut the door! Quick, or my Conscience will get away!"

The door slammed to, and I locked it. I glanced up and was grateful, to the bottom of my heart, to see that my owner was still my prisoner. I said,—

"Hang you, I might have lost you! Children are the heedlessest creatures. But look here, friend, the boy did not seem to notice you at all; how is that?"

"For a very good reason. I am invisible to all but you."

I made a mental note of that piece of information with a good deal of satisfaction. I could kill this miscreant now, if I got a chance, and no one would know it. But this very reflection made me so lighthearted that my Conscience could hardly keep his seat, but was like to float aloft toward the ceiling like a toy balloon. I said, presently,—

"Come, my Conscience, let us be friendly. Let us fly a flag of truce for a while. I am suffering to ask you some questions."

"Very well. Begin."

"Well, then, in the first place, why were you never visible to me before?"

"Because you never asked to see me before; that is, you never asked in the right spirit and the proper form before. You were just in the right spirit this time, and when you called for your most pitiless enemy I was that person by a very large majority, though you did not suspect it."

"Well, did that remark of mine turn you into flesh and blood?"

"No. It only made me visible to you. I am unsubstantial, just as other spirits are."

This remark prodded me with a sharp misgiving. If he was unsubstantial, how was I going to kill him? But I dissembled, and said persuasively,—

"Conscience, it isn't sociable of you to keep at such a distance. Come down and take another smoke."

This was answered with a look that was full of derision, and with this observation added:—

"Come where you can get at me and kill me? The invitation is declined with thanks."

"All right," said I to myself; "so it seems a spirit *can* be killed, after all; there will be one spirit lacking in this world, presently, or I lose my guess." Then I said aloud,—

"Friend"—

"There; wait a bit. I am not your friend. I am your enemy; I am not your equal, I am your master. Call me 'my lord,' if you please. You are too familiar."

"I don't like such titles. I am willing to call you *sir.* That is as far as—"

"We will have no argument about this. Just obey, that is all. Go on with your chatter."

"Very well, my lord—since nothing but my lord will suit you—I was going to ask you how long you will be visible to me?"

"Always!"

I broke out with strong indignation: "This is simply an outrage. That is what I think of it! You have dogged, and dogged, and *dogged* me, all the days of my life, invisible. That was misery enough; now to have such a looking thing as you tagging after me like another shadow all the rest of my days is an intolerable prospect. You have my opinion my lord; make the most of it."

"My lad, there was never so pleased a conscience in this world as I was when you made me visible. It gives me an inconceivable advantage. *Now* I can look you straight in the eye, and call you names, and leer at you, jeer at you, sneer at you; and *you* know what eloquence there is in visible gesture and expression, more especially when the effect is heightened by audible speech. I shall always address you henceforth in your o-w-n s-n-i-v-e-l-i-n-g d-r-a-w-l—baby!"

I let fly with the coal-hod.[3] No result. My lord said,—

"Come, come! Remember the flag of truce!"

"Ah, I forgot that. I will try to be civil; and *you* try it, too, for a novelty. The idea of a *civil* conscience! It is a good joke; an excellent joke. All the consciences *I* have ever heard of were nagging, badgering, fault-finding, execrable savages! Yes; and always in a sweat about some poor little insignificant trifle or other—destruction catch the lot of them, *I* say! I would trade mine for the smallpox and seven kinds of consumption,[4] and be glad of the chance. Now tell me, why is it that a conscience can't haul a man over the coals once, for an offense, and then let him alone? Why is it that it wants to keep on pegging at him, day and night and night and day, week in and week out, forever and ever, about the same old thing? There is no sense in that, and no reason in it. I think a conscience that will act like that is meaner than the very dirt itself."

"Well, *we* like it; that suffices."

"Do you do it with the honest intent to improve a man?"

That question produced a sarcastic smile, and this reply:—

"No, sir. Excuse me. We do it simply because it is 'business.' It is our trade. The *purpose* of it *is* to improve the man, but we are merely disinterested agents. We are appointed by authority, and haven't anything to say in the matter. We obey orders and leave the consequences where they belong. But I am willing to admit this much: we *do* crowd the orders a trifle when we get a chance, which is most of the time. We enjoy it. We are instructed to remind a man a few times of an error; and I don't mind acknowledging that we try to give pretty good measure. And when we get hold of a man of a peculiarly sensitive nature, oh, but we do haze him! I have known consciences to come all the way from China and Russia to see a person of that kind put through his paces, on a special occasion. Why, I knew a man of that sort who had accidentally crippled a mulatto baby; the news went abroad, and I wish you may never commit another sin if the consciences didn't flock from all over the earth to enjoy the fun and help his master exercise him. That man walked the floor in torture for forty-eight hours, without eating or sleeping, and then blew his brains out. The child was perfectly well again in three weeks."

"Well, you are a precious crew, not to put it too strong. I think I begin to see now why you have always been a trifle inconsistent with me. In your anxiety to get all the juice you can out of a sin, you make a man repent of it in three or four different ways. For instance, you found fault with me for lying to that tramp, and I suffered over that. But it was only yesterday that I told a tramp the square truth, to wit, that, it being regarded as bad citizenship to encourage vagrancy, I would give him nothing. What did you do *then?* Why, you made me say to myself, 'Ah, it would have been so much kinder and more blameless to ease him off with a little white lie, and send him away feeling that if he could not have bread, the gentle treatment was at least something to be grateful for!' Well, I suffered all day about *that.* Three days before I had fed a tramp, and fed him freely, supposing it a virtuous act. Straight off you said, 'Oh, false citizen, to have fed a tramp!' and I suffered as usual. I gave a tramp work; you objected to it,—*after* the contract was made, of course; you never speak up beforehand. Next, I *refused* a tramp work; you objected to *that.* Next, I proposed to kill a tramp; you kept me awake all night, oozing remorse at every pore. Sure I was going to be right *this* time, I sent the next tramp away with my benediction; and I wish you may live as long as I do, if you didn't make me smart all night again because I didn't kill him. Is there *any* way of satisfying that malignant invention which is called a conscience?"

"Ha, ha! this is luxury! Go on!"

"But come, now, answer me that question. *Is* there any way?"

"Well, none that I propose to tell *you,* my son. Ass! I don't care *what* act you may turn your hand to, I can straightway whisper a word in your ear and make you think you have committed a dreadful meanness. It is my *business*—and my joy—to make you repent of *every*thing you do. If I have fooled away any opportunities it was not intentional; I beg to assure you it was not intentional!"

"Don't worry; you haven't missed a trick that *I* know of. I never did a thing in all my life, virtuous or otherwise, that I didn't repent of in twenty-four hours. In church last Sunday I listened to a charity sermon. My first impulse was to give three hundred and fifty dollars; I repented of that and reduced it a hundred; repented of that and reduced it another hundred; repented of that and reduced it another hundred; repented of that and reduced the remaining fifty to twenty-five; repented of that and came down to fifteen; repented of that and dropped to two dollars and a half; when the plate came around at last, I repented once more and contributed ten cents. Well, when I got home, I did wish to goodness I had that ten cents back again! You never *did* let me get through a charity sermon without having something to sweat about."

"Oh, and I never shall, I never shall. You can always depend on me."

"I think so. Many and many's the restless night I've wanted to take you by the neck. If I could only get hold of you now!"

"Yes, no doubt. But I am not an ass; I am only the saddle of an ass. But go on, go on. You entertain me more than I like to confess."

"I am glad of that. (You will not mind my lying a little, to keep in practice.) Look here; not to be too personal, I think you are about the shabbiest and most contemptible little shriveled-up reptile that can be imagined. I am grateful enough that you are invisible to other people, for I should die with shame to be seen with such a mildewed monkey of a conscience as *you* are. Now if you were five or six feet high, and"—

"Oh, come! who is to blame?"

"*I* don't know."

"Why, you are; nobody else."

"Confound you, I wasn't consulted about your personal appearance."

"I don't care, you had a good deal to do with it, nevertheless. When you were eight or nine years old, I was seven feet high, and as pretty as a picture."

"I wish you had died young! So you have grown the wrong way, have you?"

"Some of us grow one way and some the other. You had a large conscience once; if you've a small conscience now I reckon there are reasons for it. However, both of us are to blame, you and I. You see, you used to be conscientious about a great many things; morbidly so, I may say. It was a great many years ago. You probably do not remember it now. Well, I took a great interest in my work, and I so enjoyed the anguish which certain pet sins of yours afflicted you with that I kept pelting at you until I rather overdid the matter. You began to rebel. Of course I began to lose ground, then, and shrivel a little—diminish in stature, get moldy, and grow deformed. The more I weakened, the more stubbornly you fastened on to those particular sins; till at last the places on my person that represent those vices became as callous as shark-skin. Take smoking, for instance. I played that card a little too long, and I lost. When people plead with you at this late day to quit that vice, that old callous place seems to enlarge and cover me all over like a shirt of mail. It exerts a mysterious, smothering effect; and presently I, your faithful hater, your devoted Conscience, go sound asleep! Sound? It is no name for it. I couldn't hear it thunder at such a time. You have some few other vices—perhaps eighty, or maybe ninety—that affect me in much the same way."

"This is flattering; you must be asleep a good part of your time."

"Yes, of late years. I should be asleep *all* the time, but for the help I get."

"Who helps you?"

"Other consciences. Whenever a person whose conscience I am acquainted with tries to plead with you about the vices you are callous to, I get my friend to give his client a pang concerning some villainy of his own, and that shuts off his meddling and starts him off to hunt personal consolation. My field of usefulness is about trimmed down to tramps, budding authoresses, and that line of goods now; but don't you worry—I'll harry you on *them* while they last! Just you put your trust in me."

"I think I can. But if you had only been good enough to mention these facts some thirty years ago, I should have turned my particular attention to sin, and I think that by this time I should not only have had you pretty permanently asleep on the entire list of human vices, but reduced to the size of a homeopathic pill, at that. That is about the style of conscience *I* am pining for. If I only had you shrunk you down to a homeopathic pill, and could get my hands on you, would I put you in a glass case for a keepsake? No, sir. I would give you to a yellow dog! That is where you ought to be—you and all your tribe. You are not fit to be in society, in my opinion. Now another question. Do you know a good many consciences in this section?"

"Plenty of them."

"I would give anything to see some of them! Could you bring them here? And would they be visible to me?"

"Certainly not."

"I suppose I ought to have known that without asking. But no matter, you can describe them. Tell me about my neighbor Thompson's conscience, please."

"Very well. I know him intimately; have known him many years. I knew him when he was eleven feet high and of a faultless figure. But he is very rusty and tough and misshapen now, and hardly ever interests himself about anything. As to his present size—well, he sleeps in a cigar-box."

"Likely enough. There are few smaller, meaner men in this region than Hugh Thompson. Do you know Robinson's conscience?"

"Yes. He is a shade under four and a half feet high; used to be a blond; is a brunette now, but still shapely and comely."

"Well, Robinson is a good fellow. Do you know Tom Smith's conscience?"

"I have known him from childhood. He was thirteen inches high, and rather sluggish, when he was two years old—as nearly all of us are at that age. He is thirty-seven feet high now, and the stateliest figure in America. His legs are still racked with growing-pains, but he has a good time, nevertheless. Never sleeps. He is the most active and energetic member of the New England Conscience Club; is president of it. Night and day you can find him pegging away at Smith, panting with his labor, sleeves rolled up, countenance all alive with enjoyment. He has got his victim splendidly dragooned now. He can make poor Smith imagine that the most innocent little thing he does is an odious sin; and then he sets to work and almost tortures the soul out of him about it."

"Smith is the noblest man in all this section, and the purest; and yet is always breaking his heart because he cannot be good! Only a conscience *could* find pleasure in heaping agony upon a spirit like that. Do you know my aunt Mary's conscience?"

"I have seen her at a distance, but am not acquainted with her. She lives in the open air altogether, because no door is large enough to admit her."

"I can believe that. Let me see. Do you know the conscience of that publisher who once stole some sketches of mine for a 'series' of his, and then left me to pay the law expenses I had to incur in order to choke him off?"

"Yes. He has a wide fame. He was exhibited, a month ago, with some other antiquities, for the benefit of a recent Member of the Cabinet's conscience that was starving in exile. Tickets and fares were high, but I traveled for nothing by pretending to be the conscience of an editor, and got in for half-price by representing myself to be the conscience of a clergyman. However, the publisher's conscience, which was to have been the main feature of the entertainment, was a failure—as an exhibition. He was there, but what of that? The management had provided a microscope with a magnifying power of only thirty thousand diameters, and so nobody got to see him, after all. There was great and general dissatisfaction, of course, but"—

Just here there was an eager footstep on the stair; I opened the door, and my aunt Mary burst into the room. It was a joyful meeting and a cheery bombardment of questions and answers concerning family matters ensued. By and by my aunt said,—

"But I am going to abuse you a little now. You promised me, the day I saw you last, that you would look after the needs of the poor family around the corner as faithfully as I had done it myself. Well, I found out by accident that you failed of your promise. *Was* that right?"

In simple truth, I never had thought of that family a second time! And now such a splintering pang of guilt shot through me! I glanced up at my Conscience. Plainly, my heavy heart was affecting him. His body was drooping forward; he seemed about to fall from the bookcase. My aunt continued:—

"And think how you have neglected my poor *protégée* at the almshouse, you dear, hard-hearted promise-breaker!" I blushed scarlet, and my tongue was tied. As the sense of my guilty negligence waxed sharper and stronger, my Conscience began to sway heavily back and forth; and when my aunt, after a little pause, said in a grieved tone, "Since you never once went to see her, maybe it will not distress you now to know that that poor child died, months ago, utterly friendless and forsaken!" My Conscience could no longer bear up under the weight of my sufferings, but tumbled headlong from his high perch and struck the floor with a dull, leaden thump. He lay there writhing with pain and quaking with apprehension, but straining every muscle in frantic efforts to get up. In a fever of expectancy I sprang to the door, locked it, placed my back against it, and bent a watchful gaze upon my struggling master. Already my fingers were itching to begin their murderous work.

"Oh, what *can* be the matter!" exclaimed by aunt, shrinking from me, and following with her frightened eyes the direction of mine. My breath was coming in short, quick gasps now, and my excitement was almost uncontrollable. My aunt cried out,—

"Oh, do not look so! You appall me! Oh, what can the matter be? What is it you see? Why do you stare so? Why do you work your fingers like that?"

"Peace, woman!" I said, in a hoarse whisper. "Look elsewhere; pay no attention to me; it is nothing—nothing. I am often this way. It will pass in a moment. It comes from smoking too much."

My injured lord was up, wild-eyed with terror, and trying to hobble toward the door. I could hardly breathe, I was so wrought up. My aunt wrung her hands, and said,—

"Oh, I knew how it would be; I knew it would come to this at last! Oh, I implore you to crush out that fatal habit while it may yet be time! You must not, you shall not be deaf to my supplications longer!" My struggling Conscience showed sudden signs of weariness! "Oh, promise me you will throw off this hateful slavery of tobacco!" My Conscience began to reel drowsily, and grope with his hands—enchanting spectacle! "I beg you, I beseech you, I implore you! Your reason is deserting you! There is madness in your eye! It flames with frenzy! Oh, hear me, hear me, and be saved! See, I plead with you on my very knees!" As she sank before me my Conscience reeled again, and then drooped languidly to the floor, blinking toward me a last supplication for mercy, with heavy eyes. "Oh, promise, or you are lost! Promise, and be redeemed! Promise! Promise and live!" With a long-drawn sigh my conquered Conscience closed his eyes and fell fast asleep!

With an exultant shout I sprang past my aunt, and in an instant I had my life-long foe by the throat. After so many years of waiting and longing, he was mine at last. I tore him to shreds and fragments. I rent the fragments to bits. I cast the bleeding rubbish into the fire, and drew into my nostrils the grateful incense of my burnt-offering. At last, and forever, my Conscience was dead!

I was a free man! I turned upon my poor aunt, who was almost petrified with terror, and shouted:

"Out of this with your paupers, your charities, your reforms, your pestilent morals! You behold before you a man whose life-conflict is done, whose soul is at peace; a man whose heart is dead to sorrow, dead to suffering, dead to remorse; a man WITHOUT A CONSCIENCE! In my joy I spare you, though I could throttle you and never feel a pang! Fly!"

She fled. Since that day my life is all bliss. Bliss, unalloyed bliss. Nothing in all the world could persuade me to have a conscience again. I settled all my old outstanding scores, and began the world anew. I killed thirty-eight persons during the first two weeks—all of them on account of ancient grudges. I burned a dwelling that interrupted my view. I swindled a widow and some orphans out of their last cow, which is a very good one, though not thoroughbred, I believe. I have also committed scores of crimes, of various kinds, and have enjoyed my work exceedingly, whereas it would formerly have broken my heart and turned my hair gray, I have no doubt.

In conclusion, I wish to state, by way of advertisement, that medical colleges desiring assorted tramps for scientific purposes, either by the gross, by cord measurement, or per ton, will do well to examine the lot in my cellar before purchasing elsewhere, as these were all selected and prepared by myself, and can be had at a low rate, because I wish to clear out my stock and get ready for the spring trade.

NOTES

1. Unwaveringly.
2. A device for helping people pull off their boots. Often it was very heavy.
3. A box-like tool used to carry bricks, mortar, or in this case, coal.
4. A disease with many causes, usually associated with the deterioration of one's body.

THE SECOND ADVENT (WRITTEN 1881; FIRST PUBLISHED 1972)

Black Jack is a very small village lying far away back in the western wilds and solitudes of Arkansas. It is made up of a few log cabins; its lanes are deep with mud in wet weather; its fences and gates are rickety and decayed; its cornfields and gardens are weedy, slovenly, and poorly cared for; there are no newspapers, no railways, no factories, no library; ignorance, sloth and drowsiness prevail. There is a small log church, but no school. The hogs are many, and they wallow by the doors, they sun themselves in the public places.

It is a frontier village; the border of the Indian Territory[1] is not a day's walk away, and the loafing savage[2] is a common sight in the town. There are some other sleepy villages thereabouts: Tublinsonville, three or four miles off; Brunner, four or five; Sugarloaf, ten or twelve. In effect, the region is a solitude, and far removed from the busy world and the interests which animate it.

A gentle and comely girl, Nancy Hopkins, lived in Black Jack, with her parents. The Hopkinses were old residents; in fact neither they nor their forerunners for two generations had ever known any other place than Black Jack. When Nancy was just budding into womanhood, she was courted by several of the young men of the village, but she finally gave the preference to Jackson Barnes the blacksmith, and was promised to him in marriage by her parents. This was soon known to everybody, and of course discussed freely, in village fashion. The young couple were chaffed,[3] joked, and congratulated in the frank, rude, frontier way, and the discarded suitors were subjected to abundance of fat-witted raillery.

Then came a season of quiet, the subject being exhausted; a season wherein tongues were still, there being nothing whatever in that small world to talk about. But by and by a change came; suddenly all tongues were busy again. Busier, too, than they had ever been at any time before, within any one's memory; for never before had they been furnished with anything like so prodigious a topic as now offered itself: Nancy Hopkins, the sweet young bride elect, was—

The news flew from lip to lip with almost telegraphic swiftness; wives told it to their husbands; husbands to bachelors; servants took hold of it and told it to the young misses; it was gossiped over in every corner; rude gross pioneers coarsely joked about it over their whisky in the village grocery, accompanying their witticisms with profane and obscene words and mighty explosions of horse laughter. The unsuspecting blacksmith was called into this grocery and the crushing news sprung upon him with a brutal frankness and directness. At first he was bowed with grief and misery; but very soon anger took the place of these feelings, and he went forth saying he would go and break the engagement. After he was gone, the grocery crowd organized itself into a public meeting to consider what ought to be done with the girl. After brief debate it was resolved—

1. That she must name her betrayer.
2. And immediately marry him.
3. Or be tarred and feathered and banished to Indian Territory.

The proceedings were hardly ended when Jackson Barnes was seen returning; and, to the general astonishment, his face was seen to be calm, placid, content—even joyful. Everybody crowded around to hear what he might say in explanation of this strange result. There was a deep and waiting silence for some moments; then Barnes said solemnly, and with awe in his voice and manner:

"She has explained it. She has made everything clear. I am satisfied, and have taken her back to my love and protection. She has told me all, and with perfect frankness, concealing nothing. She is pure and undefiled. She will give birth to a son, but no man has had to do with her. God has honored her, God has overshadowed her, and to Him she will bear this child. A joy inexpressible is ours, for we are blessed beyond all mankind."[4]

His face was radiant with a holy happiness while he spoke. Yet when he had finished a brutal jeer went up from the crowd, and everybody mocked at him, and he was assailed on all sides with insulting remarks and questions. One said—

"How does she know it was God?"

Barnes answered: "An angel told her."[5]

"When did the angel tell her?"

"Several months ago."

"Before, or after the act?"

"Before."

"Told her it was going to happen?"

"Yes."

"But she didn't mention the matter to you at the time?"

"No."

"Why didn't she?"

"I do not know."

"Had she any other evidence as to the facts than the angel?"

"No."

"What did the angel look like?"

"Like a man."

"Naked?"

"No—clothed."

"How?"

"In ancient times the angels came clothed in a robe, the dress of the people of the day. Naturally this one was clothed according to the fashion of our day. He wore a straw hat, a blue jeans roundabout and pants, and cowhide boots."

"How did she know he was an angel?"

"Because he said he was; and angels cannot lie."

"Did he speak English?"

"Of course; else she would not have understood him."

"Did he speak like an American, or with an accent?"

"He had no accent."

"Were there any witnesses?"

"No—she was alone."

"It might have been well to have some witnesses. Have you any evidence to convince you except her word?"

"Yes. While I talked with her, sleep came upon me for a moment, and I dreamed. In my dream I was assured by God that all she had said was true, and He also commanded me to stand by her and marry her."

"How do you know that the dream came from God and not from your dinner? How could you tell?"

"I knew because the voice of the dream distinctly said so."

"You believe, then, that Nancy Hopkins is still pure and undefiled?"

"I know it. She is still a virgin."

"Of course you may know that, and know it beyond doubt or question, if you have applied the right test. Have you done this?"

"I have not applied any test. I do not need to. I know perfectly that she is a virgin, by better evidence than a test."

"By what evidence? How can you know—how do you know—that she is still a virgin?"

"I know it because she told me so herself, with her own lips."

"Yes, and you dreamed it besides."

"I did."

"Absolutely overwhelming proof—isn't it?"

"It seems so to me."

"Isn't it possible that a girl might lie, in such circumstances, to save her good name?"

"To save her good name, yes; but to lie in this case would be to rob herself of the unspeakable honor of being made fruitful by Almighty God. It would be more than human heroism for Nancy Hopkins to lie in this case, and deny the illustrious fatherhood of her child, and throw away the opportunity to make her name revered and renowned forever in the world. She did right to confess her relations with the Deity. Where is there a girl in Black Jack who would not be glad to enjoy a like experience, and proud to proclaim it?"

"You suspect none but God?"

"How should I?"

"You do not suspect the angel in the straw hat?"

"He merely brought the message, that is all."

"And delivered it and left immediately?"

"I suppose so. I do not know."

"Suppose he had staid away and sent it by mail—or per dream, which is cheaper and saves paper and postage—would the result to Nancy have been the same, do you think?"

"Of course; for the angel had nothing to do but convey the prophecy; his functions ceased there."

"Possibly they did. Still, it would be helpful to hear from the angel. What shall you do with this child when it comes?"

"I shall rear it carefully, and provide for it to the best of my means."

"And call it your own?"

"I would not dare to. It is the child of the most high God. It is holy."

"What shall you call it, if it be a girl?"

"It will not be a girl."

"Then if it be a boy?"

"It shall be called Jesus Christ."

"What—is there to be another Jesus Christ?"

"No, it is the same that was born of Mary, ages ago, not another. This is merely the Second Advent; I was so informed by the Most High in my dream."[6]

"You are in error, manifestly. He is to come the second time not humbly, but in clouds and great glory."

"Yes, but that has all been changed. It was a question if the world would believe it was Jesus if he came in that way, so the former method was reinstituted. He is to be again born of an obscure Virgin, because the world cannot help but believe and be convinced by that circumstance, since it has been convinced by it before."

"To be frank with you, we do not believe a word of this flimsy nonsense you are talking. Nancy Hopkins has gone astray; she is a disgraced girl, and she knows it and you know it and we all know it. She must not venture to show her face among our virtuous daughters; we will not allow it. If you wish to marry her and make an honest woman of her, well and good; but take her away from here, at least till the wind of this great scandal has somewhat blown over."

So the Hopkinses and the blacksmith shut themselves up in their house, and were shunned and despised by the whole village.

But the day of their sorrow was to have an end, in time. They felt it, they knew it, in truth, for their dreams said it. So they waited, and were patient. Meantime the marvelous tale spread abroad; village after village heard of the new Virgin and the new Christ, and presently the matter traveled to the regions of newspapers and telegraphs; then instantly it swept the world as upon myriad wings, and was talked of in all lands.

So at last came certain wise men from the far east, to inquire concerning the matter, and to learn for themselves whether the tale was true or false. These were editors from New York and other great cities, and presidents of Yale and Princeton and Andover and other great colleges. They saw a star shining in the east—it was Venus—and this they resolved to follow.[7] Several astronomers said that a star could not be followed—that a person might as well try to follow a spot on the sun's disk, or any other object that was so far away it could not be seen to move. Other astronomers said that if a star should come down low enough to be valuable as a guide, it would roof the whole earth in, and make total darkness and give forth no relieving light itself—and that then it would be just as useful, as a guide, as is the eternal roof of the Mammoth Cave[8] to the explorer of its maze of halls and chambers. And they also said that a star could not descend thus low without disorganizing the universe and hurling all the worlds together in confusion.

But the wise men were not disturbed. They answered that what had happened once could happen again. And they were right. For this talk had hardly ended when Venus did actually leave her place in the sky and come down and hang over the very building in which the sages were assembled. She gave out a good light, too, and appeared to be no larger than a full moon.

The wise men were greatly rejoiced; and they gathered together their baggage, and their editorial passes, and clerical half-rate tickets,[9] and took the night train westward praising God. In the morning they stopped at Pittsburg and laid over till Venus was visible again in the evening. And so they journeyed on, night after night. At Louisville they got news of the child's birth. That night they resumed their journey; and so continued, by rail and horse conveyance, following the star until it came and stood over the house in Black Jack where the young child lay. Then the star retired into the sky, and they saw it go back and resume its glimmering function in the remote east.

It was about dawn, now; and immediately the whole heavens were filled with flocks of descending angels, and these were joined by a choir of drovers who were ranching in the vicinity, and all broke forth into song—the angels using a tune of their own, and the others an Arkansas tune, but all employing the same words. The wise men assisted, as well as they could, until breakfast time; then the angels returned home, the drovers resumed business, and the wise men retired to the village tavern.

After breakfast, the wise men being assembled privately, the President of Princeton made a brief speech and offered this suggestion:

1. That they all go, in a body, to see the child and hear the evidence;
2. That they all question the witnesses and assist in sifting the testimony;
3. But that the verdict be voted and rendered, not by the full body, but by a jury selected out of it by ballot.

Mr. Greeley, Mr. Bennett and Mr. Beach[10] saw no good reason for this. They said the whole body was as good a jury as a part of it could be.

The President of Princeton replied that the proposed method would simplify matters.

A vote was then taken and the measure carried, in spite of the editorial opposition.

The President of Andover then proposed that the jury consist of six persons, and that only members of some orthodox church be eligible.

Against this the editors loudly protested, and remarked that this would make a packed jury and rule out every editor, since none of their faction would be eligible. Mr. Greeley implored the President of Andover to relinquish his proposition; and reminded him that the church had always been accused of packing juries and using other underhand methods wherever its interests seemed to be concerned; and reminded him, further, as an instance, that church trials of accused clergymen nearly always resulted in a barefaced whitewashing of the accused. He begged that the present opportunity to improve the church's reputation would not be thrown away, but that a fair jury, selected without regard to religious opinion or complexion might be chosen.

The plea failed, however, and a jury composed solely of church members was chosen, the church faction being largely in the majority and voting as a unit. The editors were grieved over the advantage which had been taken of their numerical weakness, but they could not help themselves.

Then the wise men arose and went in a body to see the Hopkinses. There they listened to the evidence offered by Nancy and Barnes; and when the testimony was all in, it was examined and discussed. The religious faction maintained that it was clear, coherent, cogent, and without flaw, discrepancy, or doubtful feature; but the editorial faction stoutly maintained the directly opposite view, and implored the jury to consider well, and not allow their judgment to be influenced by prejudice and what might seem to be ecclesiastical interest.

The jury then retired; and after a brief absence brought in a verdict, as follows:

"We can doubt no whit. We find these to be the facts: An angel informed Nancy Hopkins of what was to happen; this is shown by her unqualified declaration. She is still a virgin; we know this is so, because we have her word for it. The child is the actual child of Almighty God—a fact established by overwhelming testimony, to-wit, the testimony of the angel, of Nancy, and of God Himself, as delivered to Jackson Barnes in a dream. Our verdict, then, is that this child is truly the Christ the Son of god, that his birth is miraculous, and that his mother is still a virgin."

Then the jury and their faction fell upon their knees and worshiped the child, and laid at its feet costly presents: namely, a History of the Church's Dominion During the First Fourteen Centuries; a History of the Presbyterian Dominion in Scotland; a History of Catholic Dominion in England; a History of the Salem Witchcraft; a History of the Holy Inquisition;[11] in addition, certain toys for the child to play with—these being tiny models of the Inquisition's instruments of torture; and a little Holy Bible with the decent passages printed in red ink.

But the other wise men, the editors, murmured and were not satisfied. Mr. Horace Greeley delivered their opinion. He said:

"Where an individual's life is at stake, hearsay evidence is not received in courts; how, then, shall we venture to receive hearsay evidence in this case, where the eternal life of whole nations is at stake? We have hearsay evidence that an angel appeared; none has seen that angel but one individual, and she an interested person. We have hearsay evidence that the angel delivered a certain message; whether it has come to us untampered with or not, we can never know, there being none to convey it to us but a party interested in having it take a certain form. We have the evidence of dreams and other hearsay evidence—and still, as before, from interested parties—that God is the father of this child, and that its mother remains a virgin; the first a statement which never has been and never will be possible of verification, and the last a statement which could only have been verified before the child's birth, but not having been done then can never hereafter be done. Silly dreams, and the unverifiable twaddle of a family of nobodies who are interested in covering up a young girl's accident and shielding her from disgrace—such is the 'evidence!' 'Evidence' like this could not affect even a dog's case, in any court in Christendom. It is rubbish, it is foolishness. No court would listen to it; it would be an insult to judge and jury to offer it."

Then a young man of the other party, named Talmage,[12] rose in a fury of generous enthusiasm, and denounced the last speaker as a reprobate and infidel, and said he had earned and would receive his right reward in the fulness of time in that everlasting hell created and appointed for his kind by this holy child, the God of the heavens and the earth and all that in them is. Then he sprang high in the air three times, cracking his heels together and praising God. And when he had finally alighted and become in a measure stationary, he shouted in a loud voice, saying:

"Here is divine evidence, evidence from the lips of very God Himself, and it is scoffed at! Here is evidence from an angel of God, coming fresh from the fields of heaven, from the shadow of the Throne, with the odors of Eternal Land upon his raiment, and it is derided! Here is evidence from God's own chosen handmaid, holy and pure, whom He has fructified without sin, and it is mocked at! here is evidence of one who has spoken face to face with the Most High in a dream, and even his evidence is called lies and foolishness! and on top of all, here is *cumulative* evidence: for the fact that all these things have happened before, in exactly the same way, establishes the genuineness of this second happening beyond shadow or possibility of doubt to all minds not senile, idiotic or given hopelessly over to the possession of hell and the devil! If men cannot believe *these* evidences, taken together, and piled, Pelion on Ossa,[13] mountains high, what *can* they believe!"

Then the speaker flung himself down, with many contortions, and wallowed in the dirt before the child, singing praises and glorifying God.

The Holy Family remained at Black Jack, and in time the world ceased to talk about them, and they were forgotten.

But at the end of thirty years they came again into notice; for news went abroad that Jesus had begun to teach in the churches, and to do miracles. He appointed twelve disciples, and they went about proclaiming Christ's kingdom and doing good.[14] Many of the people believed, and confessed their belief; an time these became a multitude. Indeed there was a likelihood that by and by all the nation would come into the fold, for the miracles wrought were marvelous, and men found themselves unable to resist such evidences. But after a while there came a day when murmurings began to be heard, and dissatisfaction to show its head. And the cause of this was the very same cause which had worked the opposite effect, previously,—namely, the miracles. The first notable instance was on this wise:

One of the twelve disciples—the same being that Talmage heretofore referred to—was tarrying for a time in Tumblinsonville, healing the sick and teaching in the public places of the village. It was summer, and all the land was parched with a drouth which had lasted during three months. The usual petitions had been offered up, daily at the hearth-stone and on Sundays from the pulpit, but without result—the rain did not come. The governor finally issued his proclamation for a season of fasting and united prayer for rain, naming a certain Sunday for the beginning. St. Talmage sat with the congregation in the Tumblinsonville church that Sunday morning. There was not a cloud in the sky; it was blistering hot; everybody was sad; the preacher said, mournfully, that it was now plan that the rain was withheld for a punishment, and it would be wisest to ask for it no more for the present. At that moment the saint rose up and rebuked the minister before the whole wondering assemblage, for his weak and faltering faith; then he put his two hands together, lifted up his face, and began to pray for rain. With his third sentence an instant darkness came, and with it a pouring deluge! Perhaps one may imagine the faces of the people—it is a thing which cannot be described. The blessed rain continued to come down in torrents all day long, and the happy people talked of nothing but the miracle. Indeed, they were so absorbed in it that it was midnight before they woke up to a sense of the fact that this rain, which began as a blessing, had gradually turned into a calamity—the country was flooded, the whole region was well nigh afloat. Everybody turned out and tried to save cattle, hogs, and bridges; at this work they wrought despairingly and uselessly two or three hours before it occurred to anybody that *if* that disciple's prayer had brought the deluge, possibly another prayer from him might stop it. Some hurried away and called up the disciple out of his bed, and begged him to stay the flood if he could. He told them to cease from their terrors and bear witness to what was about to happen. He then knelt and offered up his petition. The answer was instantaneous; the rain stopped immediately and utterly.

There was rejoicing in all religious hearts, because the unbelieving had always scoffed at prayer and said the pulpit had claimed that it could accomplish everything, whereas none could prove that it was able to accomplish anything at all. Unbelievers had scoffed when prayers were offered up for better weather, and for the healing of the sick, and the staying of epidemics, and the averting of war—prayers which no living man had ever seen answered, they said. But the holy disciple had shown, now, that special providences were at the bidding of the prayers of the perfect. The evidence was beyond dispute.

But on the other hand there was a widespread discontent among such of the community as had had their all swept away by the flood. It was a feeling which was destined to find a place, later, in other bosoms.

When but a few days had gone by, certain believers came and touched the hem of the disciple's garment and begged that once more he would exert his miraculous powers in the name of Him whom he and they served and worshiped. They desired him to pray for cold weather, for the benefit of a poor widow who was perishing of a wasting fever. He consented; and although it was midsummer, ice formed, and there was a heavy fall of snow. The woman immediately recovered. The destruction of crops by the cold and snow was complete; in addition, a great many persons who were abroad and out of the way of help had their ears and fingers frostbitten, and six children and two old men fell by the wayside, being benumbed by the cold and confused and blinded by the snow, and were frozen to death. Wherefore, although numbers praised God for the miracle, and marveled at it, the relatives and immediate friends of the injured and the killed were secretly discontented, and some of them even gave voice to murmurs.

Now came divers of the elect, praising God, and asked for further changes of the weather, for one reason or another, and the holy disciple, glad to magnify his Lord, willingly gratified them. The calls became incessant. As a consequence, he changed the weather many times, every day. These changes were very trying to the general public, and caused much sickness and death, since alternate drenchings and freezings and scorchings were common, and none could escape colds, in consequence, neither could any ever know, upon going out, whether to wear muslin or furs. A man who dealt in matters of science and had long had a reputation as a singularly accurate weather prophet, found himself utterly baffled by this extraordinary confusion of weather; and his business being ruined, he presently lost his reason and endeavored to take the life of the holy disciple. Eventually so much complaint was made that the saint was induced, by a general petition, to desist, and leave the weather alone. Yet there were many that protested, and were not able to see why they should not be allowed to have prayers offered up for weather to suit their private interests—a thing, they said, which had been done in all ages, and been encouraged by the pulpit, too, until now, when such prayers were found to be worth something. There was a degree of reasonableness in the argument, but it plainly would not answer to listen to it.

An exceedingly sickly season followed the confused and untimely weather, and every house became a hospital. The holy Talmage was urged to interfere with prayer. He did so. The sickness immediately disappeared, and no one was unwell in the slightest degree, during three months. Then the physicians, undertakers and professional nurses of all the region round about rose in a body and made such an outcry that the saint was forced to modify the state of things. He agreed to pray in behalf of special cases, only. Now a young man presently fell sick, and when he was dying his mother begged hard for his life, and the saint yielded, and by his prayers restored him to immediate health. The next day he killed a comrade in a quarrel, and shortly was hanged for it. His mother never forgave herself for procuring the plans of God to be altered. By request of another mother, another dying son was prayed back to health, but it was not a fortunate thing; for he strangely forsook his blameless ways, and in a few months was in a felon's cell for robbing his employer, and his family were broken hearted and longing for death.

By this time the miracles of the Savior himself were beginning to fall under criticism. He had raised many poor people from the dead; and as long as he had confined himself to the poor these miracles brought large harvests of glory and converts, and nobody found fault, or even thought of finding fault. But a change came at last. A rich bachelor died in a neighboring town, leaving a will giving all his property to the Society for the Encouragement of Missions. Several days after the burial, an absent friend arrived home, and learning of the death, came to Black Jack, and prevailed with the Savior to pray him back to life and health. So the man was alive again, but found himself a beggar; the Society had posses- sion of all his wealth and legal counsel warned the officers of the Society that if they gave it up they would be transcending their powers and the Society could come on them for damages in the full amount, and they would unquestionably be obliged to pay. The officers started to say something about Lazarus,[15] but the lawyer said that if Lazarus left any property behind him he most certainly found himself penniless when he was raised from the dead; that if there was any dis- pute between him and his heirs, the law upheld the latter. Naturally, the Society decided to hold on to the man's property. There was an aggravating lawsuit; the Society proved that the man had been dead and been buried; the court dismissed the case, saying it could not consider the complaints of a corpse. The matter was appealed; the higher courts sustained the lower one. It went further, and said that for a dead man to bring a suit was a thing without precedent, a violation of privilege, and hence was plainly contempt of court—whereupon it laid a heavy fine upon the transgressor. Maddened by these misfortunes, the plaintiff killed the presiding officer of the Society and then blew his own brains out, previously giving warning that if he was disturbed again he would make it a serious matter for the disturber.

The Twelve Disciples were the constant though innocent cause of trouble. Every blessing they brought down upon an individual was sure to fetch curses in its train for other people. Gradually the several communities among whom they labored grew anxious and uneasy; these prayers had unsettled everything; they had so disturbed the order of nature, that nobody could any longer guess, one day, what was likely to happen the next. So the popularity of the Twelve wasted gradually away. The people murmured against them, and said they were a pes- tilent incumbrance and a dangerous power to have in the State. During the time that they meddled with the weather, they made just one friend every time they changed it, and not less than a hundred enemies—a thing which was natural, and to be expected.—When they agreed to let the weather and the public health alone, their popularity seemed regained, for a while, but they soon lost it once more, through indiscretions. To accommodate a procession, they prayed that the river might be divided; this prayer was answered, and the procession passed over dry-shod. The march consumed twenty minutes, only, but twenty minutes was ample time to enable the backed-up waters to overflow all the country for

more than a hundred and fifty miles up the river, on both sides; in consequence
of which a vast number of farms and villages were ruined, many lives were lost,
immense aggregations of live stock destroyed, and thousands of people reduced
to beggary. The disciples had to be spirited away and kept concealed for two
or three months, after that, so bitter was the feeling against them, and so widespread the desire to poison or hang them.

In the course of time so many restrictions came to be placed upon the disciples' prayers, by public demand, that they were at last confined to two things,
raising the dead and restoring the dying to health. Yet at times even these services
produced trouble, and sometimes as great in degree as in the case of the rich
bachelor who was raised by the Savior. A very rich old man, with a host of needy
kin, was snatched from the very jaws of death by the disciples, and given a long
lease of life. The needy kin were not slow to deliver their opinions about what
they termed "this outrage;" neither were they mild or measured in their abuse of
the holy Twelve. Almost every time a particularly disagreeable person died, his
relatives had the annoyance of seeing him walk into their midst again within a
week. Often, when such a person was about to die, half the village would be in
an anxious and uncomfortable state, dreading the interference of the disciples,
each individual hoping they would let nature take its course but none being
willing to assume the exceedingly delicate office of suggesting it.

However, a time came at last when people were forced to speak. The region
had been cursed, for many years, by the presence of a brute named Marvin, who
was a thief, liar, drunkard, blackguard, incendiary, a loathsome and hateful creature in every way. One day the news went about that he was dying. The public
joy was hardly concealed. Everybody thought of the disciples in a moment, (for
they would be sure to raise him up in the hope of reforming him), but it was too
late. A dozen men started in the direction of Marvin's house, meaning to stand
guard there and keep the disciples away; but they were too late; the prayer had
been offered, and they met Marvin himself, striding down the street, hale and
hearty, and good for thirty years more.

An indignation meeting was called, and there was a packed attendance. It was
difficult to maintain order, so excited were the people. Intemperate speeches were
made, and resolutions offered in which the disciples were bitterly denounced.
Among the resolutions finally adopted were these:

Resolved, That the promise "Ask and ye shall receive" shall henceforth be accepted as sound in theory, and true; but it shall stop there; whosoever ventures to
actually follow the admonition shall suffer death.

Resolved, That to pray for the restoration of the sick; for the averting of
war; for the blessing of rain; and for other special providences, were things
righteous and admissible whilst they were mere forms and yielded no effect;
but henceforth, whosoever shall so pray shall be deemed guilty of crime and
shall suffer death.

Resolved, That if the ordinary prayers of a nation were answered during a
single day, the universal misery, misfortune, destruction and desolation which

would ensue, would constitute a cataclysm which would take its place side by side with the deluge and so remain in history to the end of time.

Resolved, That whosoever shall utter his belief in special providences in answer to prayer, shall be adjudged insane and shall be confined.

Resolved, That the Supreme Being is able to conduct the affairs of this world without the assistance of any person in Arkansas; and whosoever shall venture to offer such assistance shall suffer death.

Resolved, That since no one can improve the Creator's plans by procuring their alteration, there shall be but one form of prayer allowed in Arkansas henceforth, and that form shall begin and end with the words, "*Lord, Thy will, not mine, be done;*" and whosoever shall add to or take from this prayer, shall perish at the stake.

During several weeks the holy disciples observed these laws, and things moved along, in nature, in a smooth and orderly way which filled the hearts of the harassed people with the deepest gratitude; but at last the Twelve made the sun and moon stand still ten or twelve hours once, to accommodate a sheriff's posse who were trying to exterminate a troublesome band of tramps. The result was frightful. The tides of the ocean being released from the moon's control, burst in one mighty assault upon the shores of all the continents and islands of the globe and swept millions of human beings to instant death. The Savior and the disciples, being warned by friends, fled to the woods, but they were hunted down, one after the other, by the maddened populace, and crucified. With the exception of St. Talmage. For services rendered the detectives, he was paid thirty pieces of silver and his life spared.[16] Thus ended the Second Advent, AD 1881.

NOTES

1. "Indian Territory" referred to a large area of land just west of Arkansas whose borders were set by the Indian Intercourse Act of 1834 and that was originally designed to be reserved for those Native Americans displaced from their home territories. Part of Indian Territory became the state of Oklahoma in 1907.
2. A demeaning and offensive reference to a "lazy" Native American. Such a stereotype was commonly believed by many White people at this time.
3. Light, good-natured kidding or banter.
4. An allusion to the narrative in the New Testament Gospels of Luke and Matthew of how Mary, the wife of Joseph, was chosen by God to become pregnant with the baby Jesus through the Holy Spirit rather than through sexual intercourse.
5. Luke 1:26–38 tells of when the archangel Gabriel appeared to Mary and told her that God had chosen her to be the virgin mother of Jesus; this is known as the "Annunciation."
6. The First Advent was the period just before Jesus's birth on what is now celebrated as Christmas; today this period is defined as the four Sundays leading up to Christmas. Many Christians regard the Second Advent as the long-awaited Second Coming of Jesus Christ to the world.
7. In the Gospel of Matthew, "wise men from the East" (Magi) are inspired by a bright star to travel to Jerusalem and herald the birth of Christ; similarly, in this story the supposed wise men (the editors, as well as university and theological

seminary presidents) saw the star while "in the east" and travel west to greet the new Jesus.

8. An extensive and massive cave complex in central Kentucky. It was declared a US national park in 1941.

9. In the nineteenth century, newspaper employees and members of the clergy were often given discount railway tickets.

10. Horace Greeley (1811–1872), James Gordon Bennett (1795–1872), and Moses Yale Beach (1800–1868) were all famous New York newspaper editors; because Beach died in 1868, the events in the story must have taken place earlier than that.

11. The Inquisition was a powerful division of the Catholic Church established to identify Christian heretics through extensive interrogations and eliminate them from the church. The historical era known as the Inquisition extended from the twelfth through the nineteenth centuries.

12. Thomas DeWitt Talmage (1832–1902) was one of the most influential religious leaders in the United States during the mid-nineteenth century.

13. Both Mount Pelion and Mount Ossa are located in Greece; the expression "to pile Pelion on Ossa" means to engage in a futile act.

14. Christ's twelve disciples were fervent believers in Christianity who dedicated their lives to spreading their religion throughout the world.

15. Chapter 11 of the Gospel of John tells of how Jesus miraculously raised Lazarus of Bethany from the dead.

16. The Gospel of Matthew 26:15 indicates that Judas Iscariot betrayed Jesus to the chief priests for thirty pieces of silver.

EDITH WHARTON

(1862–1937)

Edith Wharton (née Edith Newbold Jones) was born in 1862 into the privileged circle of a prominent New York family whose social standing and wealth granted her access to the exclusive sphere that provided inspiration for much of her writing. As a child, Wharton rejected the idea, pushed on her by her family and her surrounding social set, that she should focus all her energy on becoming marriageable. Instead, as she traveled Europe with her family, she read extensively and became fluent in French, German, and Italian. Wharton also enjoyed inventing stories for her family, and she attempted to write her first novel at the age of eleven. In her teens, Wharton published translations of poems and original verse, both under a pseudonym and privately (due to the belief among her social class that writing was not an appropriate activity for a young woman). However, after "coming out" into society in 1879, semiofficially marking her as eligible for marriage, Wharton put her writing aside for the next decade.

In 1885, succumbing to familial and social pressure, Wharton married Edward "Teddy" Wharton, a man thirteen years her senior from a notable Boston family. Although perhaps not a perfect match, the Whartons during the early years of their marriage enjoyed traveling together, furnishing their houses, and spending time with their dogs. While residing in the high-society enclave of Newport, Rhode Island, Wharton collaborated with Ogden Codman Jr. and coauthored her first major book, *The Decoration of Houses* (1897), a successful nonfiction work about design and architecture that continues to be cited as an important reference. In 1901 the Whartons bought The Mount, a large house and estate of more than a hundred acres located in Lenox, Massachusetts. The Mount embodied Wharton's architectural ideals, but the Whartons sold it in 1911 as Teddy's mental health deteriorated and Edith became increasingly intolerant of Teddy's extramarital affairs; they divorced two years later. In 1911, Wharton left the United States and moved to Paris. She remained a US citizen and returned occasionally, but France was her primary residence until her death in 1937.

Over the course of Wharton's career she published more than forty books, including many novels, short story collections, and works of nonfiction. Some of her best-known novels are *The House of Mirth* (1905), *Ethan Frome* (1911), and *The Age of Innocence* (1920). Wharton's depictions of the American upper class during the late nineteenth and early twentieth centuries especially captivated readers desperate for a peek at its exclusive elegance. She rarely portrayed the elite in a positive light, however; they are usually depicted as cruel, decadent, corrupt, and hypocritical. Wharton also frequently explored issues concerning women's place in society. A true trailblazer, she was the first woman awarded the Pulitzer Prize for Fiction (1921) and also the first to be granted an honorary doctorate of letters from Yale University (1923); furthermore, she was honored as a member of the American Academy of Arts and Letters. More than eighty years after her death, Wharton's vivid renderings of New York's rarified high society continue to capture the imagination of popular culture, as evidenced by many of her works being made into movies.

Wharton's story "Xingu" was first published in December 1911 in *Scribner's Magazine*, a publication with a quite stodgy, conservative reputation. In this story, Wharton humorously satirizes a group of upper-class women readers; in doing so, it echoes Wharton's plaintive essay "The Vice of Reading," which she had previously published in the *North American Review* in October 1903.

XINGU (1911)

I

Mrs. Ballinger is one of the ladies who pursue Culture in bands, as though it were dangerous to meet alone. To this end she had founded the Lunch Club, an association composed of herself and several other indomitable huntresses of erudition. The Lunch Club, after three or four winters of lunching and debate, had acquired such local distinction that the entertainment of distinguished strangers became one of its accepted functions; in recognition of which it duly extended to the celebrated "Osric Dane," on the day of her arrival in Hillbridge, an invitation to be present at the next meeting.

The Club was to meet at Mrs. Ballinger's. The other members, behind her back, were of one voice in deploring her unwillingness to cede her rights in favor of Mrs. Plinth, whose house made a more impressive setting for the entertainment of celebrities; while, as Mrs. Leveret observed, there was always the picture-gallery to fall back on.

Mrs. Plinth made no secret of sharing this view. She had always regarded it as one of her obligations to entertain the Lunch Club's distinguished guests. Mrs. Plinth was almost as proud of her obligations as she was of her picture-gallery; she was in fact fond of implying that the one possession implied the other, and that only a woman of her wealth could afford to live up to a standard as high as that which she had set herself. An all-round sense of duty, roughly adaptable to various ends, was, in her opinion, all that Providence exacted of the more humbly stationed; but the power which had predestined Mrs. Plinth to keep footmen clearly intended her to maintain an equally specialized staff of responsibilities. It was the more to be regretted that Mrs. Ballinger, whose obligations to society were bounded by the narrow scope of two parlour-maids, should have been so tenacious of the right to entertain Osric Dane.

The question of that lady's reception had for a month past profoundly moved the members of the Lunch Club. It was not that they felt themselves unequal to the task, but that their sense of the opportunity plunged them into the agreeable uncertainty of the lady who weighs the alternatives of a well-stocked wardrobe. If such subsidiary members as Mrs. Leveret were fluttered by the thought of exchanging ideas with the author of "The Wings of Death," no forebodings of the kind disturbed the conscious adequacy of Mrs. Plinth, Mrs. Ballinger and Miss Van Vluyck. "The Wings of Death" had, in fact, at Miss Van Vluyck's suggestion, been chosen as the subject of discussion at the last club meeting, and each member had thus been enabled to express her own opinion or to appropriate whatever seemed most likely to be of use in the comments of the others. Mrs. Roby alone had abstained from profiting by the opportunity thus offered; but it was now openly recognised that, as a member of the Lunch Club, Mrs. Roby was a failure. "It all comes," as Miss Van Vluyck put it, "of accepting a woman on a man's estimation." Mrs. Roby, returning to Hillbridge from a prolonged sojourn in exotic regions—the other ladies no longer took the trouble to remember where—had been emphatically commended by the distinguished biologist, Professor Foreland, as the most agreeable woman he had ever met; and the members of the Lunch Club, awed by an encomium that carried the weight of a diploma, and rashly assuming that the Professor's social sympathies would follow the line of his scientific bent, had seized the chance of annexing a biological member. Their disillusionment was complete. At Miss Van Vluyck's first off-hand mention of the pterodactyl Mrs. Roby had confusedly murmured: "I know so little about metres—" and after that painful betrayal of incompetence she had prudently withdrawn from farther participation in the mental gymnastics of the club.[1]

"I suppose she flattered him," Miss Van Vluyck summed up—"or else it's the way she does her hair."

The dimensions of Miss Van Vluyck's dining-room having restricted the membership of the club to six, the non-conductiveness of one member was a serious obstacle to the exchange of ideas, and some wonder had already been expressed that Mrs. Roby should care to live, as it were, on the intellectual bounty of the others. This feeling was augmented by the discovery that she had not yet read "The Wings of Death." She owned to having heard the name of Osric Dane; but that—incredible as it appeared—was the extent of her acquaintance with the celebrated novelist. The ladies could not conceal their surprise, but Mrs. Ballinger, whose pride in the club made her wish to put even Mrs. Roby in the best possible light, gently insinuated that, though she had not had time to acquaint herself with "The Wings of Death," she must at least be familiar with its equally remarkable predecessor, "The Supreme Instant."

Mrs. Roby wrinkled her sunny brows in a conscientious effort of memory, as a result of which she recalled that, oh, yes, she *had* seen the book at her brother's, when she was staying with him in Brazil, and had even carried it off to read one day on a boating party; but they had all got to shying things at each other in the boat, and the book had gone overboard, so she had never had the chance—

The picture evoked by this anecdote did not advance Mrs. Roby's credit with the club, and there was a painful pause, which was broken by Mrs. Plinth's remarking: "I can understand that, with all your other pursuits, you should not find much time for reading; but I should have thought you might at least have *got up* 'The Wings of Death' before Osric Dane's arrival."

Mrs. Roby took this rebuke good-humouredly. She had meant, she owned to glance through the book; but she had been so absorbed in a novel of Trollope's that—[2]

"No one reads Trollope now," Mrs. Ballinger interrupted impatiently.

Mrs. Roby looked pained. "I'm only just beginning," she confessed.

"And does he interest you?" Mrs. Plinth inquired.

"He amuses me."

"Amusement," said Mrs. Plinth sententiously, "is hardly what I look for in my choice of books."

"Oh, certainly, 'The Wings of Death' is not amusing," ventured Mrs. Leveret, whose manner of putting forth an opinion was like that of an obliging salesman with a variety of other styles to submit if his first selection does not suit.

"Was it *meant* to be?" enquired Mrs. Plinth, who was fond of asking questions that she permitted no one but herself to answer. "Assuredly not."

"Assuredly not—that is what I was going to say," assented Mrs. Leveret, hastily rolling up her opinion and reaching for another. "It was meant to—to elevate."

Miss Van Vluyck adjusted her spectacles as though they were the black cap of condemnation. "I hardly see," she interposed, "how a book steeped in the bitterest pessimism can be said to elevate, however much it may instruct."

"I meant, of course, to instruct," said Mrs. Leveret, flurried by the unexpected distinction between two terms which she had supposed to be synonymous. Mrs. Leveret's enjoyment of the Lunch Club was frequently marred by such surprises;

and not knowing her own value to the other ladies as a mirror for their mental complacency she was sometimes troubled by a doubt of her worthiness to join in their debates. It was only the fact of having a dull sister who thought her clever that saved her from a sense of hopeless inferiority.

"Do they get married in the end?" Mrs. Roby interposed.

"They—who?" the Lunch Club collectively exclaimed.

"Why, the girl and man. It's a novel, isn't it? I always think that's the one thing that matters. If they're parted it spoils my dinner."

Mrs. Plinth and Mrs. Ballinger exchanged scandalised glances, and the latter said: "I should hardly advise you to read 'The Wings of Death,' in that spirit. For my part, when there are so many books that one *has* to read, I wonder how any one can find time for those that are merely amusing."

"The beautiful part of it," Laura Glyde murmured, "is surely just this—that no one can tell *how* 'The Wings of Death' ends. Osric Dane, overcome by the dread significance of her own meaning, has mercifully veiled it—perhaps even from herself—as Apelles, in representing the sacrifice of Iphigenia, veiled the face of Agamemnon."[3]

"What's that? Is it poetry?" whispered Mrs. Leveret nervously to Mrs. Plinth, who, disdaining a definite reply, said coldly: "You should look it up. I always make it a point to look things up." Her tone added—"though I might easily have it done for me by the footman."

"I was about to say," Miss Van Vluyck resumed, "that it must always be a question whether a book *can* instruct unless it elevates."

"Oh—" murmured Mrs. Leveret, now feeling herself hopelessly astray.

"I don't know," said Mrs. Ballinger, scenting in Miss Van Vluyck's tone a tendency to depreciate the coveted distinction of entertaining Osric Dane; "I don't know that such a question can seriously be raised as to a book which has attracted more attention among thoughtful people than any novel since 'Robert Elsmere.'"[4]

"Oh, but don't you see," exclaimed Laura Glyde, "that it's just the dark hopelessness of it all—the wonderful tone-scheme of black on black—that makes it such an artistic achievement? It reminded me so when I read it of Prince Rupert's *manière noire*[5] . . . the book is etched, not painted, yet one feels the colour values so intensely . . ."[6]

"Who is *he?*" Mrs. Leveret whispered to her neighbour. "Some one she's met abroad?"

"The wonderful part of the book," Mrs. Ballinger conceded, "is that it may be looked at from so many points of view. I hear that as a study of determinism Professor Lupton ranks it with 'The Data of Ethics.'"

"I'm told that Osric Dane spent ten years in preparatory studies before beginning to write it," said Mrs. Plinth. "She looks up everything—verifies everything. It has always been my principle, as you know. Nothing would induce me, now, to put aside a book before I'd finished it, just because I can buy as many more as I want."

"And what do _you_ think of 'The Wings of Death'?" Mrs. Roby abruptly asked her.

It was the kind of question that might be termed out of order, and the ladies glanced at each other as though disclaiming any share in such a breach of discipline. They all knew that there was nothing Mrs. Plinth so much disliked as being asked her opinion of a book. Books were written to read; if one read them what more could be expected? To be questioned in detail regarding the contents of a volume seemed to her as great an outrage as being searched for smuggled laces at the Custom House. The club had always respected this idiosyncrasy of Mrs. Plinth's. Such opinions as she had were imposing and substantial: her mind, like her house, was furnished with monumental "pieces" that were not meant to be suddenly disarranged; and it was one of the unwritten rules of the Lunch Club that, within her own province, each member's habits of thought should be respected. The meeting therefore closed with an increased sense, on the part of the other ladies, of Mrs. Roby's hopeless unfitness to be one of them.

I I

Mrs. Leveret, on the eventful day, had arrived early at Mrs. Ballinger's, her volume of Appropriate Allusions in her pocket.

It always flustered Mrs. Leveret to be late at the Lunch Club: she liked to collect her thoughts and gather a hint, as the others assembled, of the turn the conversation was likely to take. To-day, however, she felt herself completely at a loss; and even the familiar contact of Appropriate Allusions, which stuck into her as she sat down, failed to give her any reassurance. It was an admirable little volume, compiled to meet all the social emergencies; so that, whether on the occasion of Anniversaries, joyful or melancholy (as the classification ran), of Banquets, social or municipal, or of Baptisms, Church of England or sectarian, its student need never be at a loss for a pertinent reference. Mrs. Leveret, though she had for years devoutly conned[7] its pages, valued it, however, rather for its moral support than for its practical services; for though in the privacy of her own room she commanded an army of quotations, these invariably deserted her at the critical moment, and the only line she retained—_Canst thou draw out leviathan with a hook?_—was one she had never yet found the occasion to apply.

To-day she felt that even the complete mastery of the volume would hardly have insured her self-possession; for she thought it probable, even if she _did_, in some miraculous way, remember an Allusion, it would be only to find that Osric Dane used a different volume (Mrs. Leveret was convinced that literary people always carried them), and would consequently not recognise her quotations.

Mrs. Leveret's sense of being adrift was intensified by the appearance of Mrs. Ballinger's drawing-room. To a careless eye its aspect was unchanged; but those acquainted with Mrs. Ballinger's way of arranging her books would instantly have detected the marks of recent perturbation. Mrs. Ballinger's province, as a member of the Lunch Club, was the Book of the Day. On that, whatever it was, from a novel to a treatise on experimental psychology, she was confidently, authoritatively "up." What became of last year's books, or last week's even; what she did with the "subjects" she had previously professed with equal authority; no one had ever yet discovered. Her mind was an hotel where facts came and went like transient lodgers, without leaving their address behind, and frequently without paying for their board. It was Mrs. Ballinger's boast that she was "abreast with the Thought of the Day," and her pride that this advanced position should be expressed by the books on her drawing-room table. These volumes, frequently renewed, and almost always damp from the press, bore names generally unfamiliar to Mrs. Leveret, and giving her, as she furtively scanned them, a disheartening glimpse of new fields of knowledge to be breathlessly traversed in Mrs. Ballinger's wake. But today a number of maturer-looking volumes were adroitly mingled with the primeurs[8] of the press—Karl Marx jostled Professor Bergson, and the "Confessions of St. Augustine" lay beside the last work on "Mendelism"; so that even to Mrs. Leveret's fluttered perceptions it was clear that Mrs. Ballinger didn't in the least know what Osric Dane was likely to talk about, and had taken measures to be prepared for anything.[9] Mrs. Leveret felt like a passenger on an ocean steamer who is told that there is no immediate danger, but that she had better put on her life-belt.

It was a relief to be roused from these forebodings by Miss Van Vluyck's arrival.

"Well, my dear," the new-comer briskly asked her hostess, "what subjects are we to discuss to-day?"

Mrs. Ballinger was furtively replacing a volume of Wordsworth by a copy of Verlaine.[10] "I hardly know," she said somewhat nervously. "Perhaps we had better leave that to circumstances."

"Circumstances?" said Miss Van Vluyck drily. "That means, I suppose, that Laura Glyde will take the floor as usual, and we shall be deluged with literature."

Philanthropy and statistics were Miss Van Vluyck's province, and she naturally resented any tendency to divert their guest's attention from these topics.

Mrs. Plinth at this moment appeared.

"Literature?" she protested in a tone of remonstrance. "But this is perfectly unexpected. I understood we were to talk of Osric Dane's novel."

Mrs. Ballinger winced at the discrimination, but let it pass. "We can hardly make that our chief subject—at least not *too* intentionally," she suggested. "Of course we can let our talk *drift* in that direction; but we ought to have some other topic as an introduction, and that is what I wanted to consult you about. The fact is, we know so little of Osric Dane's tastes and interests that it is difficult to make any special preparation."

"It may be difficult," said Mrs. Plinth with decision, "but it is absolutely necessary. I know what that happy-go-lucky principle leads to. As I told one of my nieces the other day, there are certain emergencies for which a lady should always be prepared. It's in shocking taste to wear colours when one pays a visit of condolence, or a last year's dress when there are reports that one's husband is on the wrong side of the market;[11] and so it is with conversation. All I ask is that I should know beforehand what is to be talked about; then I feel sure of being able to say the proper thing."

"I quite agree with you," Mrs. Ballinger anxiously assented; "but—"

And at that instant, heralded by the fluttered parlour-maid, Osric Dane appeared upon the threshold.

Mrs. Leveret told her sister afterward that she had known at a glance what was coming. She saw that Osric Dane was not going to meet them half way. That distinguished personage had indeed entered with an air of compulsion not calculated to promote the easy exercise of hospitality. She looked as though she were about to be photographed for a new edition of her books.

The desire to propitiate a divinity is generally in inverse ratio to its responsiveness, and the sense of discouragement produced by Osric Dane's entrance visibly increased the Lunch Club's eagerness to please her. Any lingering idea that she might consider herself under an obligation to her entertainers was at once dispelled by her manner: as Mrs. Leveret said afterward to her sister, she had a way of looking at you that made you feel as if there was something wrong with your hat. This evidence of greatness produced such an immediate impression on the ladies that a shudder of awe ran through them when Mrs. Roby, as their hostess led the great personage into the dining-room, turned back to whisper to the others: "What a brute she is!"

The hour about the table did not tend to correct this verdict. It was passed by Osric Dane in the silent deglutition[12] of Mrs. Ballinger's menu, and by the members of the Club in the emission of tentative platitudes which their guest seemed to swallow as perfunctorily as the successive courses of the luncheon.

Mrs. Ballinger's deplorable delay in fixing a topic had thrown the Club into a mental disarray which increased with the return to the drawing-room, where the actual business of discussion was to open. Each lady waited for the other to speak; and there was a general shock of disappointment when their hostess opened the conversation by the painfully commonplace inquiry: "Is this your first visit to Hillbridge?"

Even Mrs. Leveret was conscious that this was a bad beginning; and a vague impulse of deprecation made Miss Glyde interject: "It is a very small place indeed."

Mrs. Plinth bristled. "We have a great many representative people," she said, in the tone of one who speaks for her order.

Osric Dane turned to her thoughtfully. "What do they represent?" she asked.

Mrs. Plinth's constitutional dislike to being questioned was intensified by her sense of unpreparedness; and her reproachful glance passed the question on to Mrs. Ballinger.

"Why," said that lady, glancing in turn at the other members, "as a community I hope it is not too much to say that we stand for culture."

"For art—" Miss Glyde eagerly interjected.

"For art and literature," Mrs. Ballinger emended.

"And for sociology, I trust," snapped Miss Van Vluyck.

"We have a standard," said Mrs. Plinth, feeling herself suddenly secure on the vast expanse of a generalisation: and Mrs. Leveret, thinking there must be room for more than one on so broad a statement, took courage to murmur: "Oh, certainly; we have a standard."

"The object of our little club," Mrs. Ballinger continued, "is to concentrate the highest tendencies of Hillbridge—to centralise and focus its complex intellectual effort."

This was felt to be so happy that the ladies drew an almost audible breath of relief.

"We aspire," the President went on, "to stand for what is highest in art, literature and ethics."

Osric Dane again turned to her. "What ethics?" she asked.

A tremor of apprehension encircled the room. None of the ladies required any preparation to pronounce on a question of morals; but when they were called ethics it was different. The club, when fresh from the "Encyclopaedia Britannica," the "Reader's Handbook" or Smith's "Classical Dictionary," could deal confidently with any subject; but when taken unawares it had been known to define agnosticism as a heresy of the Early Church and Professor Froude as a distinguished histologist; and such minor members as Mrs. Leveret still secretly regarded ethics as something vaguely pagan.[13]

Even to Mrs. Ballinger, Osric Dane's question was unsettling, and there was a general sense of gratitude when Laura Glyde leaned forward to say, with her most sympathetic accent: "You must excuse us, Mrs. Dane, for not being able, just at present, to talk of anything but 'The Wings of Death.'"

"Yes," said Miss Van Vluyck, with a sudden resolve to carry the war into the enemy's camp. "We are so anxious to know the exact purpose you had in mind in writing your wonderful book."

"You will find," Mrs. Plinth interposed, "that we are not superficial readers."

"We are eager to hear from you," Miss Van Vluyck continued, "if the pessimistic tendency of the book is an expression of your own convictions or—"

"Or merely," Miss Glyde hastily thrust in, "a sombre background brushed in to throw your figures into more vivid relief. *Are* you not primarily plastic?"

"*I* have always maintained," Mrs. Ballinger interposed, "that you represent the purely objective method—"

Osric Dane helped herself critically to coffee. "How do you define objective?" she then inquired.

There was a flurried pause before Laura Glyde intensely murmured: "In reading *you* we don't define, we feel."

Osric Dane smiled. "The cerebellum," she remarked, "is not infrequently the seat of the literary emotions."[14] And she took a second lump of sugar.

The sting that this remark was vaguely felt to conceal was almost neutralised by the satisfaction of being addressed in such technical language.

"Ah, the cerebellum," said Miss Van Vluyck complacently. "The Club took a course in psychology last winter."

"Which psychology?" asked Osric Dane.

There was an agonising pause, during which each member of the Club secretly deplored the distressing inefficiency of the others. Only Mrs. Roby went on placidly sipping her chartreuse.[15] At last Mrs. Ballinger said, with an attempt at a high tone: "Well, really, you know, it was last year that we took psychology, and this winter we have been so absorbed in——"

She broke off, nervously trying to recall some of the Club's discussions; but her faculties seemed to be paralysed by the petrifying stare of Osric Dane. What *had* the club been absorbed in lately? Mrs. Ballinger, with a vague purpose of gaining time, repeated slowly: "We've been so intensely absorbed in——"

Mrs. Roby put down her liqueur glass and drew near the group with a smile.

"In Xingu?" she gently prompted.

A thrill ran through the other members. They exchanged confused glances, and then, with one accord, turned a gaze of mingled relief and interrogation on their unexpected rescuer. The expression of each denoted a different phase of the same emotion. Mrs. Plinth was the first to compose her features to an air of reassurance: after a moment's hasty adjustment her look almost implied that it was she who had given the word to Mrs. Ballinger.

"Xingu, of course!" exclaimed the latter with her accustomed promptness, while Miss Van Vluyck and Laura Glyde seemed to be plumbing the depths of memory, and Mrs. Leveret, feeling apprehensively for Appropriate Allusions, was somehow reassured by the uncomfortable pressure of its bulk against her person.

Osric Dane's change of countenance was no less striking than that of her entertainers. She too put down her coffee-cup, but with a look of distinct annoyance: she too wore, for a brief moment, what Mrs. Roby afterward described as the look of feeling for something in the back of her head; and before she could dissemble these momentary signs of weakness, Mrs. Roby, turning to her with a deferential smile, had said: "And we've been so hoping that to-day you would tell us just what you think of it."

Osric Dane received the homage of the smile as a matter of course; but the accompanying question obviously embarrassed her, and it became clear to her observers that she was not quick at shifting her facial scenery. It was as though her countenance had so long been set in an expression of unchallenged superiority that the muscles had stiffened, and refused to obey her orders.

"Xingu——" she murmured, as if seeking in her turn to gain time.

Mrs. Roby continued to press her. "Knowing how engrossing the subject is, you will understand how it happens that the Club has let everything else go to the wall for the moment. Since we took up Xingu I might almost say—were it not for your books—that nothing else seems to us worth remembering."

Osric Dane's stern features were darkened rather than lit up by an uneasy smile. "I am glad to hear there is one exception," she gave out between narrowed lips.

"Oh, of course," Mrs. Roby said prettily; "but as you have shown us that—so very naturally!—you don't care to talk about your own things, we really can't let you off from telling us exactly what you think about Xingu; especially," she added, with a persuasive smile, "as some people say that one of your last books was simply saturated with it."

It was an *it*, then—the assurance sped like fire through the parched minds of the other members. In their eagerness to gain the least little clue to Xingu they almost forgot the joy of assisting at the discomfiture of Mrs. Dane.

The latter reddened nervously under her antagonist's direct assault. "May I ask," she faltered out in an embarrassed tone, "to which of my books you refer?"

Mrs. Roby did not falter. "That's just what I want you to tell us; because, though I was present, I didn't actually take part."

"Present at what?" Mrs. Dane took her up; and for an instant the trembling members of the Lunch Club thought that the champion Providence had raised up for them had lost a point. But Mrs. Roby explained herself gaily: "At the discussion, of course. And so we're dreadfully anxious to know just how it was that you went into the Xingu."

There was a portentous pause, a silence so big with incalculable dangers that the members with one accord checked the words on their lips, like soldiers dropping their arms to watch a single combat between their leaders. Then Mrs. Dane gave expression to their inmost dread by saying sharply: "Ah—you say *the* Xingu, do you?"

Mrs. Roby smiled undauntedly. "It *is* a shade pedantic, isn't it? Personally, I always drop the article; but I don't know how the other members feel about it."

The other members looked as though they would willingly have dispensed with this deferential appeal to their opinion, and Mrs. Roby, after a bright glance about the group, went on: "They probably think, as I do, that nothing really matters except the thing itself—except Xingu."

No immediate reply seemed to occur to Mrs. Dane, and Mrs. Ballinger gathered courage to say: "Surely every one must feel that about Xingu."

Mrs. Plinth came to her support with a heavy murmur of assent, and Laura Glyde breathed emotionally: "I have known cases where it has changed a whole life."

"It has done me worlds of good," Mrs. Leveret interjected, seeming to herself to remember that she had either taken it or read it in the winter before.

"Of course," Mrs. Roby admitted, "the difficulty is that one must give up so much time to it. It's very long."

"I can't imagine," said Miss Van Vluyck tartly, "grudging the time given to such a subject."

"And deep in places," Mrs. Roby pursued; (so then it was a book!) "And it isn't easy to skip."

"I never skip," said Mrs. Plinth dogmatically.

"Ah, it's dangerous to, in Xingu. Even at the start there are places where one can't. One must just wade through."

"I should hardly call it *wading*," said Mrs. Ballinger sarcastically.

Mrs. Roby sent her a look of interest. "Ah—you always found it went swimmingly?" Mrs. Ballinger hesitated. "Of course there are difficult passages," she conceded modestly.

"Yes; some are not at all clear—even," Mrs. Roby added, "if one is familiar with the original."

"As I suppose you are?" Osric Dane interposed, suddenly fixing her with a look of challenge.

Mrs. Roby met it by a deprecating smile. "Oh, it's really not difficult up to a certain point; though some of the branches are very little known, and it's almost impossible to get at the source."

"Have you ever tried?" Mrs. Plinth enquired, still distrustful of Mrs. Roby's thoroughness.

Mrs. Roby was silent for a moment; then she replied with lowered lids: "No—but a friend of mine did; a very brilliant man; and he told me it was best for women—not to . . ."

A shudder ran around the room. Mrs. Leveret coughed so that the parlourmaid, who was handing the cigarettes, should not hear; Miss Van Vluyck's face took on a nauseated expression, and Mrs. Plinth looked as if she were passing some one she did not care to bow to. But the most remarkable result of Mrs. Roby's words was the effect they produced on the Lunch Club's distinguished guest. Osric Dane's impassive features suddenly melted to an expression of the warmest human sympathy, and edging her chair toward Mrs. Roby's she asked: "Did he really? And—did you find he was right?"

Mrs. Ballinger, in whom annoyance at Mrs. Roby's unwonted assumption of prominence was beginning to displace gratitude for the aid she had rendered, could not consent to her being allowed, by such dubious means, to monopolise the attention of their guest. If Osric Dane had not enough self-respect to resent Mrs. Roby's flippancy, at least the Lunch Club would do so in the person of its President.

Mrs. Ballinger laid her hand on Mrs. Roby's arm. "We must not forget," she said with a frigid amiability, "that absorbing as Xingu is to *us*, it may be less interesting to—"

"Oh, no, on the contrary, I assure you," Osric Dane energetically intervened.

"—to others," Mrs. Ballinger finished firmly; "and we must not allow our little meeting to end without persuading Mrs. Dane to say a few words to us on a subject which, to-day, is much more present in all our thoughts. I refer, of course, to 'The Wings of Death.'"

The other members, animated by various degrees of the same sentiment, and encouraged by the humanised mien of their redoubtable guest, repeated after Mrs. Ballinger: "Oh, yes, you really *must* talk to us a little about your book."

Osric Dane's expression became as bored, though not as haughty, as when her work had been previously mentioned. But before she could respond to Mrs. Ballinger's request, Mrs. Roby had risen from her seat, and was pulling her veil down over her frivolous nose.

"I'm so sorry," she said, advancing toward her hostess with outstretched hand, "but before Mrs. Dane begins I think I'd better run away. Unluckily, as you know, I haven't read her books, so I should be at a terrible disadvantage among you all; and besides, I've an engagement to play bridge."

If Mrs. Roby had simply pleaded her ignorance of Osric Dane's works as a reason for withdrawing, the Lunch Club, in view of her recent prowess, might have approved such evidence of discretion; but to couple this excuse with the brazen announcement that she was foregoing the privilege for the purpose of joining a bridge party, was only one more instance of her deplorable lack of discrimination.

The ladies were disposed, however, to feel that her departure—now that she had performed the sole service she was ever likely to render them—would probably make for greater order and dignity in the impending discussion, besides relieving them of the sense of self-distrust which her presence always mysteriously produced. Mrs. Ballinger therefore restricted herself to a formal murmur of regret, and the other members were just grouping themselves comfortably about Osric Dane when the latter, to their dismay, started up from the sofa on which she had been deferentially enthroned.

"Oh wait—do wait, and I'll go with you!" she called out to Mrs. Roby; and, seizing the hands of the disconcerted members, she administered a series of farewell pressures with the mechanical haste of a railway-conductor punching tickets.

"I'm so sorry—I'd quite forgotten—" she flung back at them from the threshold; and as she joined Mrs. Roby, who had turned in surprise at her appeal, the other ladies had the mortification of hearing her say, in a voice which she did not take the pains to lower: "If you'll let me walk a little way with you, I should so like to ask you a few more questions about Xingu . . ."

III

The incident had been so rapid that the door closed on the departing pair before the other members had had time to understand what was happening. Then a sense of the indignity put upon them by Osric Dane's unceremonious desertion began to contend with the confused feeling that they had been cheated out of their due without exactly knowing how or why.

There was an awkward silence, during which Mrs. Ballinger, with a perfunctory hand, rearranged the skillfully grouped literature at which her distinguished guest had not so much as glanced; then Miss Van Vluyck tartly pronounced: "Well, I can't say that I consider Osric Dane's departure a great loss."

This confession crystallised the fluid resentment of the other members, and Mrs. Leveret exclaimed: "I do believe she came on purpose to be nasty!"

It was Mrs. Plinth's private opinion that Osric Dane's attitude toward the Lunch Club might have been very different had it welcomed her in the majestic setting of the Plinth drawing-rooms; but not liking to reflect on the inadequacy of Mrs. Ballinger's establishment she sought a round-about satisfaction in depreciating her savoir faire.[16]

"I said from the first that we ought to have had a subject ready. It's what always happens when you're unprepared. Now if we'd only got up Xingu—"

The slowness of Mrs. Plinth's mental processes was always allowed for by the Club; but this instance of it was too much for Mrs. Ballinger's equanimity.

"Xingu!" she scoffed. "Why, it was the fact of our knowing so much more about it than she did—unprepared though we were—that made Osric Dane so furious. I should have thought that was plain enough to everybody!"

This retort impressed even Mrs. Plinth, and Laura Glyde, moved by an impulse of generosity, said: "Yes, we really ought to be grateful to Mrs. Roby for introducing the topic. It may have made Osric Dane furious, but at least it made her civil."

"I am glad we were able to show her," added Miss Van Vluyck, "that a broad and up-to-date culture is not confined to the great intellectual centres."

This increased the satisfaction of the other members, and they began to forget their wrath against Osric Dane in the pleasure of having contributed to her defeat.

Miss Van Vluyck thoughtfully rubbed her spectacles. "What surprised me most," she continued, "was that Fanny Roby should be so up on Xingu."

This frank admission threw a slight chill on the company, but Mrs. Ballinger said with an air of indulgent irony: "Mrs. Roby always has the knack of making a little go a long way; still, we certainly owe her a debt for happening to remember that she'd heard of Xingu." And this was felt by the other members to be a graceful way of cancelling once for all the Club's obligation to Mrs. Roby.

Even Mrs. Leveret took courage to speed a timid shaft of irony: "I fancy Osric Dane hardly expected to take a lesson in Xingu at Hillbridge!"

Mrs. Ballinger smiled. "When she asked me what we represented—do you remember?—I wish I'd simply said we represented Xingu!"

All the ladies laughed appreciatively at this sally, except Mrs. Plinth, who said, after a moment's deliberation: "I'm not sure it would have been wise to do so."

Mrs. Ballinger, who was already beginning to feel as if she had launched at Osric Dane the retort which had just occurred to her, looked ironically at Mrs. Plinth. "May I ask why?" she enquired.

Mrs. Plinth looked grave. "Surely," she said, "I understood from Mrs. Roby herself that the subject was one it was as well not to go into too deeply?"

Miss Van Vluyck rejoined with precision: "I think that applied only to an investigation of the origin of the—of the—"; and suddenly she found that her usually accurate memory had failed her. "It's a part of the subject I never studied myself," she concluded lamely.

"Nor I," said Mrs. Ballinger.

Laura Glyde bent toward them with widened eyes. "And yet it seems—doesn't it?—the part that is fullest of an esoteric fascination?"

"I don't know on what you base that," said Miss Van Vluyck argumentatively.

"Well, didn't you notice how intensely interested Osric Dane became as soon as she heard what the brilliant foreigner—he *was* a foreigner, wasn't he?—had told Mrs. Roby about the origin—the origin of the rite—or whatever you call it?"

Mrs. Plinth looked disapproving, and Mrs. Ballinger visibly wavered. Then she said in a decisive tone: "It may not be desirable to touch on the—on that part of the subject in general conversation; but, from the importance it evidently has to a woman of Osric Dane's distinction, I feel as if we ought not to be afraid to discuss it among ourselves—without gloves—though with closed doors, if necessary."

"I'm quite of your opinion," Miss Van Vluyck came briskly to her support; "on condition, that is, that all grossness of language is avoided."

"Oh, I'm sure we shall understand without that," Mrs. Leveret tittered; and Laura Glyde added significantly: "I fancy we can read between the lines," while Mrs. Ballinger rose to assure herself that the doors were really closed.

Mrs. Plinth had not yet given her adhesion. "I hardly see," she began, "what benefit is to be derived from investigating such peculiar customs—"

But Mrs. Ballinger's patience had reached the extreme limit of tension. "This at least," she returned; "that we shall not be placed again in the humiliating position of finding ourselves less up on our own subjects than Fanny Roby!"

Even to Mrs. Plinth this argument was conclusive. She peered furtively about the room and lowered her commanding tones to ask: "Have you got a copy?"

"A—a copy?" stammered Mrs. Ballinger. She was aware that the other members were looking at her expectantly, and that this answer was inadequate, so she supported it by asking another question. "A copy of what?"

Her companions bent their expectant gaze on Mrs. Plinth, who, in turn, appeared less sure of herself than usual. "Why, of—of-the book," she explained.

"What book?" snapped Miss Van Vluyck, almost as sharply as Osric Dane.

Mrs. Ballinger looked at Laura Glyde, whose eyes were interrogatively fixed on Mrs. Leveret. The fact of being deferred to was so new to the latter that it filled her with an insane temerity. "Why, Xingu, of course!" she exclaimed.

A profound silence followed this direct challenge to the resources of Mrs. Ballinger's library, and the latter, after glancing nervously toward the Books of the Day, returned in a deprecating voice: "It's not a thing one cares to leave about."

"I should think *not!*" exclaimed Mrs. Plinth.

"It *is* a book, then?" said Miss Van Vluyck.

This again threw the company into disarray, and Mrs. Ballinger, with an impatient sigh, rejoined: "Why—there *is* a book—naturally . . ."

"Then why did Miss Glyde call it a religion?"

Laura Glyde started up. "A religion? I never—"

"Yes, you did," Miss Van Vluyck insisted; "you spoke of rites; and Mrs. Plinth said it was a custom."

Miss Glyde was evidently making a desperate effort to reinforce her statement; but accuracy of detail was not her strongest point. At length she began in a deep murmur: "Surely they used to do something of the kind at the Eleusinian mysteries—"[17]

"Oh—" said Miss Van Vluyck, on the verge of disapproval; and Mrs. Plinth protested: "I understood there was to be no indelicacy!"

Mrs. Ballinger could not control her irritation. "Really, it is too bad that we should not be able to talk the matter over quietly among ourselves. Personally, I think that if one goes into Xingu at all—"

"Oh, so do I!" cried Miss Glyde.

"And I don't see how one can avoid doing so, if one wishes to keep up with the Thought of the Day—"

Mrs. Leveret uttered an exclamation of relief. "There—that's it!" she interposed.

"What's it?" the President curtly took her up.

"Why—it's a—a Thought: I mean a philosophy."

This seemed to bring a certain relief to Mrs. Ballinger and Laura Glyde, but Miss Van Vluyck said dogmatically: "Excuse me if I tell you that you're all mistaken. Xingu happens to be a language."

"A language!" the Lunch Club cried.

"Certainly. Don't you remember Fanny Roby's saying that there were several branches, and that some were hard to trace? What could that apply to but dialects?"

Mrs. Ballinger could no longer restrain a contemptuous laugh. "Really, if the Lunch Club has reached such a pass that it has to go to Fanny Roby for instruction on a subject like Xingu, it had almost better cease to exist!"

"It's really her fault for not being clearer," Laura Glyde put in.

"Oh, clearness and Fanny Roby!" Mrs. Ballinger shrugged. "I daresay we shall find she was mistaken on almost every point."

"Why not look it up?" said Mrs. Plinth.

As a rule this recurrent suggestion of Mrs. Plinth's was ignored in the heat of discussion, and only resorted to afterward in the privacy of each member's home. But on the present occasion the desire to ascribe their own confusion of thought to the vague and contradictory nature of Mrs. Roby's statements caused the members of the Lunch Club to utter a collective demand for a book of reference.

At this point the production of her treasured volume gave Mrs. Leveret, for a moment, the unusual experience of occupying the centre front; but she was not able to hold it long, for Appropriate Allusions contained no mention of Xingu.

"Oh, that's not the kind of thing we want!" exclaimed Miss Van Vluyck. She cast a disparaging glance over Mrs. Ballinger's assortment of literature, and added impatiently: "Haven't you any useful books?"

"Of course I have," replied Mrs. Ballinger indignantly; "but I keep them in my husband's dressing-room."

From this region, after some difficulty and delay, the parlourmaid produced the W-Z volume of an Encyclopaedia and, in deference to the fact that the demand for it had come from Miss Van Vluyck, laid the ponderous tome before her.

There was a moment of painful suspense while Miss Van Vluyck rubbed her spectacles, adjusted them, and turned to Z; and a murmur of surprise when she said: "It isn't here."

"I suppose," said Mrs. Plinth, "it's not fit to be put in a book of reference."

"Oh, nonsense!" exclaimed Mrs. Ballinger. "Try X."

Miss Van Vluyck turned back through the volume, peering shortsightedly up and down the pages, till she came to a stop and remained motionless, like a dog on a point.

"Well, have you found it?" Mrs. Ballinger enquired, after a considerable delay.

"Yes. I've found it," said Miss Van Vluyck in a queer voice.

Mrs. Plinth hastily interposed: "I beg you won't read it aloud if there's anything offensive."

Miss Van Vluyck, without answering, continued her silent scrutiny.

"Well, what *is* it?" exclaimed Laura Glyde excitedly.

"*Do* tell us!" urged Mrs. Leveret, feeling that she would have something awful to tell her sister.

Miss Van Vluyck pushed the volume aside and turned slowly toward the expectant group.

"It's a river."

"A *river?*"

"Yes: in Brazil. Isn't that where she's been living?"

"Who? Fanny Roby? Oh, but you must be mistaken. You've been reading the wrong thing," Mrs. Ballinger exclaimed, leaning over her to seize the volume.

"It's the only *Xingu* in the Encyclopaedia; and she *has* been living in Brazil," Miss Van Vluyck persisted.

"Yes: her brother has a consulship there," Mrs. Leveret eagerly interposed.

"But it's too ridiculous! I—we—why we *all* remember studying Xingu last year—or the year before last," Mrs. Ballinger stammered.

"I thought I did when *you* said so," Laura Glyde avowed.

"I said so?" cried Mrs. Ballinger.

"Yes. You said it had crowded everything else out of your mind."

"Well, *you* said it had changed your whole life!"

"For that matter, Miss Van Vluyck said she had never grudged the time she'd given it."

Mrs. Plinth interposed: "I made it clear that I knew nothing whatever of the original."

Mrs. Ballinger broke off the dispute with a groan. "Oh, what does it all matter if she's been making fools of us? I believe Miss Van Vluyck's right—she was talking of the river all the while!"

"How could she? It's too preposterous," Miss Glyde exclaimed.

"Listen." Miss Van Vluyck had repossessed herself of the Encyclopaedia, and restored her spectacles to a nose reddened by excitement. "'The Xingu, one of the principal rivers of Brazil, rises on the plateau of Mato Grosso, and flows in a northerly direction for a length of no less than one thousand one hundred and eighteen miles, entering the Amazon near the mouth of the latter river. The upper course of the Xingu is auriferous and fed by numerous branches. Its source was first discovered in 1884 by the German explorer von den Steinen, after a difficult and dangerous expedition through a region inhabited by tribes still in the Stone Age of culture.'"

The ladies received this communication in a state of stupefied silence from which Mrs. Leveret was the first to rally. "She certainly *did* speak of its having branches."

The word seemed to snap the last thread of their incredulity. "And of its great length," gasped Mrs. Ballinger.

"She said it was awfully deep, and you couldn't skip—you just had to wade through," Miss Glyde subjoined.

The idea worked its way more slowly through Mrs. Plinth's compact resistances. "How could there be anything improper about a river?" she inquired.

"Improper?"

"Why, what she said about the source—that it was corrupt?"

"Not corrupt, but hard to get at," Laura Glyde corrected. "Some one who'd been there had told her so. I daresay it was the explorer himself—doesn't it say the expedition was dangerous?"

"'Difficult and dangerous,'" read Miss Van Vluyck.

Mrs. Ballinger pressed her hands to her throbbing temples. "There's nothing she said that wouldn't apply to a river—to this river!" She swung about excitedly to the other members. "Why, do you remember her telling us that she hadn't read 'The Supreme Instant' because she'd taken it on a boating party while she was staying with her brother, and some one had 'shied' it overboard—'shied' of course was her own expression?"

The ladies breathlessly signified that the expression had not escaped them.

"Well—and then didn't she tell Osric Dane that one of her books was simply saturated with Xingu? Of course it was, if some of Mrs. Roby's rowdy friends had thrown it into the river!"

This surprising reconstruction of the scene in which they had just participated left the members of the Lunch Club inarticulate. At length Mrs. Plinth, after visibly labouring with the problem, said in a heavy tone: "Osric Dane was taken in too."

Mrs. Leveret took courage at this. "Perhaps that's what Mrs. Roby did it for. She said Osric Dane was a brute, and she may have wanted to give her a lesson."

Miss Van Vluyck frowned. "It was hardly worth while to do it at our expense."

"At least," said Miss Glyde with a touch of bitterness, "she succeeded in interesting her, which was more than we did."

"What chance had we?" rejoined Mrs. Ballinger. "Mrs. Roby monopolised her from the first. And *that*, I've no doubt, was her purpose—to give Osric Dane a false impression of her own standing in the Club. She would hesitate at nothing to attract attention: we all know how she took in poor Professor Foreland."

"She actually makes him give bridge-teas every Thursday," Mrs. Leveret piped up.

Laura Glyde struck her hands together. "Why, this is Thursday, and it's *there* she's gone, of course; and taken Osric with her!"

"And they're shrieking over us at this moment," said Mrs. Ballinger between her teeth.

This possibility seemed too preposterous to be admitted. "She would hardly dare," said Miss Van Vluyck, "confess the imposture to Osric Dane."

"I'm not so sure: I thought I saw her make a sign as she left. If she hadn't made a sign, why should Osric Dane have rushed out after her?"

"Well, you know, we'd all been telling her how wonderful Xingu was, and she said she wanted to find out more about it," Mrs. Leveret said, with a tardy impulse of justice to the absent.

This reminder, far from mitigating the wrath of the other members, gave it a stronger impetus.

"Yes—and that's exactly what they're both laughing over now," said Laura Glyde ironically.

Mrs. Plinth stood up and gathered her expensive furs about her monumental form. "I have no wish to criticise," she said; "but unless the Lunch Club can protect its members against the recurrence of such—such unbecoming scenes, I for one—"

"Oh, so do I!" agreed Miss Glyde, rising also.

Miss Van Vluyck closed the Encyclopaedia and proceeded to button herself into her jacket. "My time is really too valuable—" she began.

"I fancy we are all of one mind," said Mrs. Ballinger, looking searchingly at Mrs. Leveret, who looked at the others.

"I always deprecate anything like a scandal—" Mrs. Plinth continued.

"She has been the cause of one to-day!" exclaimed Miss Glyde.

Mrs. Leveret moaned: "I don't see how she *could!*" and Miss Van Vluyck said, picking up her note-book: "Some women stop at nothing."

"—but if," Mrs. Plinth took up her argument impressively, "anything of the kind had happened in *my* house" (it never would have, her tone implied), "I should have felt that I owed it to myself either to ask for Mrs. Roby's resignation—or to offer mine."

"Oh, Mrs. Plinth—" gasped the Lunch Club.

"Fortunately for me," Mrs. Plinth continued with an awful magnanimity, "the matter was taken out of my hands by our President's decision that the right to entertain distinguished guests was a privilege vested in her office; and I think the other members will agree that, as she was alone in this opinion, she ought to be alone in deciding on the best way of effacing its—its really deplorable consequences."

A deep silence followed this unexpected outbreak of Mrs. Plinth's long-stored resentment.

"I don't see why *I* should be expected to ask her to resign—" Mrs. Ballinger at length began; but Laura Glyde turned back to remind her: "You know she made you say that you'd got on swimmingly in Xingu."

An ill-timed giggle escaped from Mrs. Leveret, and Mrs. Ballinger energetically continued "—but you needn't think for a moment that I'm afraid to!"

The door of the drawing-room closed on the retreating backs of the Lunch Club, and the President of that distinguished association, seating herself at her writing-table, and pushing away a copy of "The Wings of Death" to make room for her elbow, drew forth a sheet of the club's note-paper, on which she began to write: "My dear Mrs. Roby—"

NOTES

1. Mrs. Roby here confuses the "pterodactyl," a winged, flying dinosaur, with a "dactyl," a metrical pattern in poetry, in which the first of three syllables is stressed and the next two are unstressed.
2. Anthony Trollope (1815–82) was a very popular British novelist of the period.
3. In "The Sacrifice of Iphigenia," Apelles of Kos (fourth century BCE, Greece) depicted the father, King Agamemnon, with a cloth over his face as he witnessed the sacrifice of his daughter, Iphigenia; his face is hidden to suggest that his pain is too great to reveal.
4. *Robert Elsmere* (1888), by Mary Augusta Ward (1851–1920), is a novel about a British clergyman who begins to doubt the doctrine of the Anglican Church.
5. Dark ways (French).
6. Prince Rupert of the Rhine, Duke of Cumberland (1619–82), was known for producing etched prints tinted only with black ink.
7. To read over numerous times in order to memorize something.
8. A scoop (French), here referring to a news story exclusive to a particular newspaper.
9. Karl Marx (1818–83) was a German philosopher, scholar, and socialist revolutionary and is best known for *The Communist Manifesto* (1848), which he coauthored with the German philosopher Friedrich Engels (1820–95). Henri-Louis Bergson (1859–1941) was a French-Jewish philosopher known for works such as *Time and Free Will* (1889) and *Matter and Memory* (1896). *The Confessions of Saint Augustine* is an autobiographical work by Saint Augustine of Hippo (354–430 CE) written in Latin between 397 and 400 CE. "Mendelism" is the theory of genetic heredity posited by scientist Gregor Mendel (1822–84).
10. William Wordsworth (1770–1850), British Romantic poet, and Paul Verlaine (1844–96), French Decadent poet.
11. An expression used chiefly among those involved in the stock market. It means to have made a wrong decision resulting in a loss of money.
12. The act of swallowing.
13. These are common reference books for general knowledge and literature, as well as works of Greek and Roman mythology, biography, and history. "Agnosticism" is the belief that God or the divine is unknowable. James Anthony Froude

(1818–94) was an English historian and author. A "histologist" is a medical professional who studies the microscopic structure of tissue.

14. The cerebellum is actually the part of the brain that controls motor movement, not emotions.

15. A fine French liqueur produced in southeastern France since the early eighteenth century.

16. Knowledge of how to speak and act properly in various social situations (French).

17. Secret initiation rituals to the cult of Demeter and Persephone, in ancient Greece.

OWEN WISTER

(1860–1938)

Owen Wister, best known as the author of what is regarded as the prototypical Western novel, *The Virginian: A Horseman of the Plains* (1902), never actually spent any extended period of time living in the West. Born near Philadelphia in 1860 to wealthy parents, he attended a handful of European and American boarding schools and graduated from Harvard in 1882. To improve his physical and mental health, a doctor advised him in June 1885 to spend the summer in Wyoming. Wister fell in love with what he perceived as the simpler life there, one more in contact with nature and supposedly unspoiled by eastern civilization and its constraints. To satisfy his parents and family, however, upon his return to the East he began Harvard Law School; after graduation in 1888 he became a member of a prominent Philadelphia law firm.

Despite enjoying a good measure of success as a lawyer, Wister was unhappy and increasingly thought of becoming a writer. He recalled in his 1930 memoir that he wrote his first Western story, "Hank's Woman," in the library of a Philadelphia men's club sometime during the fall of 1891. He did not, however, immediately submit it to a magazine for publication, because he believed that Westerns were not serious literature. Fortunately, Wister's physician, S. Weir Mitchell (who also treated Charlotte Perkins Gilman), encouraged him to send his story to Henry Mills Alden, the editor of *Harper's Monthly.* The story was not published in that periodical but instead in *Harper's Weekly* (August 27, 1892), a publication that appeared in more of a newspaper format and blended news and features with its fictions. "Hank's Woman" did not attract wide notice, but it did catch the attention of a rising young politician named Theodore Roosevelt, Wister's former Harvard classmate, who liked it very much and encouraged Wister to write more about the West, an area Roosevelt also loved. Wister and Roosevelt—who served as president of the United States from 1901 to 1909—became lifelong friends.

Between 1892 and when *The Virginian* came out, in 1902, Wister not only visited the West (particularly Wyoming) numerous times but also published a great many Western stories in various periodicals, along with a number of story collections in volume form. It was *The Virginian*, however, that made Wister famous. Unlike "Hank's Woman," it gave readers an extremely Romanticized view of the West, including an idealized rugged cowboy, a love story with a schoolmarm from the East, and a stereotypical black-hatted evil villain. Such a vision of the West greatly appealed to urban readers; it sold fifty thousand copies in two months and was reprinted dozens of times. Later it was made into a Broadway play, four movies, and even a popular television series that ran from 1962 to 1971.

"Hank's Woman," in its original 1892 text, offers a very different view of the West than *The Virginian* does. Although "Hank's Woman" did contain humorous incidents and vernacular dialogue, its violence was so stark and brutal that Wister's own mother voiced her displeasure with it. Possibly in reaction not only to her response but also to that of other readers, Wister greatly revised this story for inclusion in his collection *The Jimmyjohn Boss and Other Stories* (1900), transforming it into only a weak shadow of its former self. Those who wish to gain insight into more of the realities of Western life at this time will strongly prefer the *Harper's Weekly* version presented here.

HANK'S WOMAN (1892)

"He decided second thoughts were best, too," I said. This was because a very large trout, who had been flirting with my brown hackle[1] for some five minutes, suddenly saw through the whole thing, and whipped into the deep water that wedged its calm into the riffle from below.

"Try a grasshopper on him." And Lin McLean, whom among all cow-punchers I love most, handed me one from the seat pocket of his overalls.

An antelope earlier that day had given us his attention, as, huddled down in some sage-brush under the burning cloudless sun, I waved a red handkerchief, while Lin lay on his back and shook his boots in the air. But the antelope, after considering these things from a point of view some hundred yards away, had irrelevantly taken off to the foot-hills. We fired the six-shooter, and watched his exasperating white tailless rear twinkle out of sight across the flats.

"If you hadn't gone on so with your crazy boots," I said, "he'd have come up close."

"And if yu'd brought yer rifle along, as I said yu'd ought to," responded Lin, "we'd have had some fresh meat to pack into camp."

Of fish, however, we certainly had enough for lunch now, and enough to take back for supper and breakfast. We had ridden down Snake River from camp on Pacific Creek to where Buffalo Fork comes sweeping in;[2] and there on the shingle point and on a log half sunk in the swimming stream, we had persuaded out of the depths some dozen of that silver-sided, many-speckled sort that does fight. None was shorter than twelve inches; one measured twenty. Therefore, in satisfaction, Lin and I hauled our boots off, tore open shirts and breeches so they dropped where we stood, and regardless of how many trout we might now disturb, splashed into the cool slow breadth of back water the bend makes just there. Then I set about cleaning a couple of fish, and Lin made the fire, and got the lunch from our saddles, setting the teapot to boil, and slicing bacon into the pan.

"As fer second thoughts," said Lin, "animals in this country has 'em more'n men do."

I thought so too, and said nothing.

"Yu' take the way they run the Bar-Circle-Zee.[3] Do yu' figure Judge Henny knows his foreman's standin' in with rustlers like Ed Rogers is? If he'd taken time to inquire why that foreman left Montana, he'd not be gettin' stole from right along, you bet! And Ed Rogers'll be dealt with one of these days. He's a-growin' bold, the way he takes calves this year. He's forgettin' about second thoughts, I expect."

We were silent, and ate some fish and drank some tea—you cannot make good coffee out-of-doors. But Mr. McLean's mind was for the moment running in a channel of prudence.

You would have supposed he had never acted hastily in the whole of his twenty-eight years.

"Folks is poor in Wyoming through bein' too quick," he resumed. "Look at the way them fellers in Douglas got cinched."[4]

"Who, and how?" I inquired.

"Bankers and stockmen. They figured on Douglas bein' a big town, and all because the railroad come there on its way somewheres else that ain't nowheres its own self. I've been in this country since '77, and that's eleven years, and I say yu' can't never make a good town out o' sage-brush."

Lin paused, looking southward across the great yellow-gray plain of the Teton Basin. The Continental Divide rose to the left of us; to the right were the Tetons, shutting us in from Idaho, with their huge magical peaks of blue cutting sharp and sudden into the sky.[5]

"Take marriage," continued the cow-puncher, stretching himself till he sank flat backward on the ground, with his long legs spread wide. "Sometimes there ain't so much as first thoughts before a man's been and done it."

"Wyoming is not peculiar in that respect," I said.

"We come over this trail," said Lin, not listening to me, "the year after the President and Sheridan did. Me and Hank and Honey Wiggin. I'd quit workin' fer the old '76 outfit, and come to Lander after a while and met up with them two fellers, and we figured we'd take a trip through the Park.[6] Now, there was Hank. Yu' never knowed Hank?"

I never had.

"Well, yu' didn't lose much." Lin now rolled comfortably over on his stomach. "Hank, he married a woman. He was small, and she was big—awful big; and neither him nor her was any account—him 'specially."

"Probably they would not agree with you," I said.

"She would now, you bet!" said Lin, sitting up and laying his hand on my knee. "They got married on one week's acquaintance, which ain't enough."

"That's true, I think."

"Folks try it in this Western country," Lin pursued, "where a woman's a scarce thing anyhow, and men unparticular and hasty, but it ain't sufficient in nine times out o' ten. Hank, yu' see, he staid sober that one week, provin' she'd ought to seen him fer two any ways; and if I was a woman, knowin' what I know about men, it wouldn't be two weeks nor two months neither." The cow-puncher paused and regarded me with his wide-open jocular eyes. "When are you goin' to tie up with a woman?" he inquired. "I'm comin' that day."

"Was Hank married when you went to the Park?" said I.

"Of course he weren't. Ain't I tryin' to tell yu'? Him and me and Honey joined a prospectin' outfit when we was through seein' the Park, and Hank and me come into the Springs[7] after grub from Galena Creek, where camp was. We lay around the Springs and Gardner[8] fer three days, playin' cards with friends; and one noon he was settin' in the hotel at the Mammoth Springs waitin' fer to see the stage come in, though that wasn't nuthin' he hadn't seen, nor nuthin' was on it fer him. But that was Hank. He'd set around waitin' fer nuthin' like that till somebody said whiskey, and he'd drink and wait some more. Well, the hotel kid he yells out, 'Stage!' after a while, soon as he seen the dust comin' up the hill. Ever notice that hotel at the Hot Springs before and after that kid says, 'Stage'?"

I shook my head.

"Well, sir," said Lin, "yu' wouldn't never suppose the place was any relation to itself. Yu' see, all them guests and Raymonds clears out for the Norris Basin[9] right after breakfast, and none comes in new from anywheres till round noon, and you bet the hotel folks has a vacation! Yes, sir, a regular good lay-off. Yu'd ought to see the Syndicate manager[10] a sleepin behind the hotel counter, and nobody makin' no noise high nor low, but all plumb quiet and empty-like—maybe a porter foolin' around the ice-cooler, and the flies buzzin'. Then that kid—he's been on the watch-out; he likes it, you bet!—he sings out, 'Stage!' suddenlike, and shoo! the entire outfit stampedes, startin' with them electric bells ring-jinglin' all over. The Syndicate manager flops his hair down quick front of a lookin'-glass he keeps handy fer his private satisfaction, and he organizes himself behind the hotel register-book; and the young photograph chap comes out of his door and puts his views out for sale right acrosst from where the cigar-seller's a clawin' his goods into shape. Them girls quits leanin' over the rail upstairs and skips, and the porters they line up on the front steps, and the piano man he digs his fingers into the keys, and him and the fiddlers starts raisin' railroad accidents. Yes, sir. That hotel gets that joyous I expect them arrivin' Raymonds judge they've struck ice-cream and balance partners right on the surface.

"Well, Hank, now, he watched 'em that day same as every day, and the guests they clumb down off the stage like they always do—young ladies hoppin' spry and squealin' onced in a while, and dusty old girls in goggles clutchin' the porters, and snuffin', and sayin', 'Oh dear!'

"Then out gets a big wide-faced woman, thick all through, any side yu' looked at her, and she was kind o' dumb-eyed, but fine appearin', with lots of yaller hair.

Yu' could tell she were raised in one of them German countries like Sweden, for she acted slow, and started at the folks hustlin', and things noisy, and waltzes playin' inside. Hank seen her, and I expect he got interested on sight, for he was a small man, and she was big, and twiced as big as him. Did yu' ever notice that about small fellers? She was a lady's maid, like they have in the States."

Lin stopped and laughed.

"If any woman in this country was to have to hire another one to help her clothes off her, I guess she'd be told she'd ought to go to bed soberer," he remarked. "But this one was sure a lady's maid, and out comes her lady right there. And my! 'Where have you put the keys, Willomene?'"

Lin gave a scornful imitation of the lady's voice.

"Well, Willomene fussed around her pockets, and them keys wasn't there, so she started explainin' in tanglefoot English to her lady how her lady must have took them from her in the 'drain,' as she said, meaning the cars. But the lady was gettin' madder, tappin' her shoe on the floor, like Emma Yoosh does in the opera—Carmen, or somethin' I see onced in Cheyenne."[11]

"Them ladies," said Lin, after a silence, during which I deplored his commentative propensity, "seems to enjoy hustlin' themselves into a rage. This one she got a-goin', and she rounded up Willlomene with words yu' seldom see outside a book. 'Such carelessness,' says she, 'is too exasperatin';' and a lot more she said, and it were all up to that standard, you bet! Then she says, 'You are discharged,' and off she struts. A man come out soon (her husband, most likely), and he paid the lady's maid some cash (a good sum it was, I expect), and she stood right there for a spell; then all of a sudden she says, 'Ok yayzoo!' and sits down and starts cryin'.

"When yu' see that, yu' feel sorry, but yu' can't say nuthin': so we was all standin' round on the piazza, kind o' shiftless. Then the baggage-wagon come in, and they picked the keys up on the road from Gardner; so the lady was all right, but that didn't do no good to Willomene. They stood her trunk down along with the rest—a brass-nailed concern it was, I remember, same as an Oswego starch-box[12] in size—and there was Willomene out of a job and afoot a long ways from anywheres, settin' in the chair, and onced in a while she'd cry some more. We got her a room in the cheap hotel where the Park drivers sleeps when they're in at the Springs, and she acted grateful like, thankin' everybody in her tanglefoot English. And she was a very nice-speakin' woman. Her folks druv off to the Fountain[13] next mornin', and she seemed dazed like; fer I questioned her where she'd like to go, and she was told about how to get to the railroad, and she couldn't say if she wanted to travel east or west. There's where she weren't no account, yu' see.

"Over acrosst at the post-office I told the postmistress about Willomene, and she had a spare bed, an' bein' a big-hearted woman, she had her to stay and help wait on the store. That store's popular with the soldiers. The postmistress is a little beauty, and they come settin' round there, privates and sergeants, too, expectin' some day she'll look at 'em twiced. But she just stays good-natured to all, and minds her business, you bet! So Hank come round, settin' like the soldiers, and he'd buy a pair of gloves, maybe, or cigars, and Willomene she'd wait on him. I says to Hank we'd ought to pull out for camp, but he wanted to wait. So I played cards, and had a pretty fair time with the boys, layin' round the Springs and over to Gardner.

"One night I come on 'em—Hank and Willomene—walkin' among the pines where the road goes down. Yu'd ought to have seen that pair! Her big shape was plain and kind of steadfast in the moon, and alongside of her little black Hank. And there it was. He'd got stuck on her all out of her standin' up so tall and round above his head. I passed close, and nobody said nuthin', only next day, when I remarked to Hank he appeared to be catchin' on. And he says, 'That's my business, I guess'; and I says, 'Why, Hanky, I'm sure pleased to notice your earnest way.' It wasn't my business if he wanted to be a fool, and take a slow-understandin' woman like she was up to the mines.

"Well, that night I caught 'em again, near the formation, and she says to me 'how beautifool was de wasser steamin' and tricklin' over them white rocks!' And I laffed.

"'Hank,' says I (not then, but in the mornin'), 'before you've made yer mind up right changeless, if I was you, I'd take Miss Willomene over to the Syndicate store and get her weighed.'

"And he says, 'What do yu' mean?'

"So I gave my opinion that if the day was to come when him and her didn't want to travel the same road, why, he'd travel hern, and not his'n. 'Fer she could pack yu' on her back and lift yu' down nice anywheres she pleased,' says I to Hank.

"And I tell yu' it's a queer thing I come to say that."

Lin stopped, and jerked his overalls into a more comfortable fit. "They was married the Toosdy after, at Livingston,"[14] he went on; "and Hank was that pleased with himself he gave Willomene a weddin'-present with the balance of his cash, spendin' his last nickel on buyin' her a red-tailed parrot they had for sale at the First National Bank. The feller hollered so at the bank, the president told the cashier he must get rid of it.

"Hank and Willomene staid a week up in Livingston on her money, and then he brought her back to Gardner, and bought their grub and come up to the camp we had on Galena Creek.[15] She'd never slep' out before, and she'd never been on a horse, neither, and near rolled off down into Little Death Cañon[16] comin' up by the cut-off trail. Now just see that foolishness—to fetch that woman and pack-horses heavy loaded along such a turruble bad place like that cut-off trial is, where a man wants to lead his own horse 'fear of goin' down. You know them big tall grass-topped mountains over in the Hoodoo country, and how they comes slam down through the cross timber yu' can't go through hardly on foot, till they pitches over into lots and lots of little Cañons, with maybe two inches of water runnin' in the bottom? All that's East Fork water, and over the divide's Clark's Fork, or Stinkin' Water if yu' take the country further southeast. But anywheres yu' go is them turrble steep slopes, and the cut-off trail takes along about the worst in the business.

"Well, Hank he got his bride over it somehow, and yu'd ought to have seen them two pull into our camp. Yu'd sure never figured it were a weddin' trip. He was leadin', but skewed around in his saddle to jaw back at Willomene fer ridin' so poorly. And what kind of a man's that, I'd like to know, jawin' at her in the hearin' of the whole outfit of us fellers, and them not married two weeks? She was settin' straddeways like a mountain, and between him and her went the three pack animals, plumb played out, and the flour—they had two hundred pounds—tilted over down-wards, with the red-tailed parrot a-hollerin' landslides in his cage tied on top.

"Hank, he'd had a scare over Willomene comin' so near fallin', and it turned him sour, so he'd hardly speak, but just said, 'How!' kind of gruff, when we come up to congratulate him. But Willomene, she says when she seen me, 'Oh, I am so glad to see you!' and we shook hands right friendly; fer I'd talked to her down at the Springs, yu' know. And she told me how near she come to gettin' killed. Yu' 'ain't been over that there trail?" inquired Lin of me. "Yu'd ought to see that Cañon."

"No," said I; "I've seen enough of the Park, and the Grand Cañon satisfies me."

"'Tain't the same thing. That Grand Cañon's pretty, but Little Death Cañon ain't; it's one of them queer places, somethin' the same style as a geyser is, surprisin' a feller. If Willomene had went down there that afternoon—well, I'll tell yu', so yu' can judge. She seen the trail gettin' nearer and nearer the edge, between the timber and the jumpin'-off place, and she seen how them little loose stones and the crumble stuff kep' a-slidin' away under the horse's feet, and rattlin' down out of sight she didn't know where to, so she tried to git off and walk without sayin' nuthin to Hank. He kep' a-goin', and Willomene's horse she had pulled up, started to follow as she was half off, and that gave her a tumble, but she got her arm hitched around a rock just as the stones started to slide her over. But that's only the beginning of what fallin' into that hole is. A man sometimes falls down a place all right and crawls out after a while. There ain't no crawlin' out in Little Death Cañon, you bet! Down in there, where yu' can't see, is sulphur caves. Yu' can smell 'em a mile away. That Cañon's so narrer where they open out and puff steam that there's no breathin' to be done, for no wind gets in to clean out the smell. If yu' lean pretty far over yu' can see the bottom, and a little green water tricklin' over cream-colored stuff like pie. Bears and elk climbin' round the sides onced in a while gets choked by the risin' air, and tumbles and stays fer good. Why, us fellers looked in one time and seen two big silver-tip carcasses, and didn't dare go in after the hides, though I don't say yu' couldn't never make the trip. Somedays the steam comes out scantier; but how's a man to know if them caves ain't a-goin' to start up again sudden like a cough? I have seen it come in two seconds. And when it comes that way after sundown, risin' out of the Cañon with a fluffy kind of a sigh—yes, sir, I tell yu' that's sick noise it makes! Why, I don't like to be passin' that way myself, though knowin' so well it's only them sulphur caves down in there. Willomene was in luck when she come out safe.

"Anyway, there they was, come to camp without any accident. She looked surprised when she seen Hank's tent him and her was to sleep in. And Hank he looked surprised at the bread she cooked.

"'What kind of a Dutch woman are yu',' says he, half jokin', 'if yu' can't use a dutch-oven?'

"'You said to me you have a house to live in,' says Willomene. 'Where is that house?'

"'I didn't figure on gettin' a woman when I left camp,' says Hank, grinnin', but not pleasant, 'or I'd have hurried up with the shack I'm a-buildin'.'"

"He was buildin' one. Well, that's the way they started into matrimony, and in three weeks they quit havin' much to say to each other. The only steady talkin' done in that home was done by the parrot, and he was a rattlin' talker. Willomene she used to talk with me at first, but she gave it up soon; I don't know why. I liked her mighty well, and so we all did. She done her best, but I guess she hadn't never seen this style of life, and kindness such as we could show her, I suppose, didn't show up fer as well as it was intended.

"There was six of us workin' claims. Some days the gold washed out good in the pan, but mostly it was that fine it floated off without ever settlin' at all. But we had a good crowd, and things was pleasant, and not too lively nor yet too slow. Willomene used to come round the ditch silent like and watch us workin', and then she'd be apt to move off into the woods, singin' German songs, not very loud. I knowed well enough she felt lonesome, but what can yu' do? As fer her, she done her best; only it ain't the sensible way fer a wife to cry at her husband gettin' full,[17] as of course Hank done, same as always since I'd knowed him, bar one week at the Mammoth. A native American woman[18] could have managed Hank so he'd treated her good and been sorry instead of glad every time he'd been drunk. But we liked Willomene, because she'd do anything she could for us, cookin' up an extra meal if we come back from a hunt, and patchin' our clothes. Nor she wouldn't take pay. She was a good woman, but no account in a country like Galena Creek was. Honey Wiggin and me helped her finish the shack, so she and Hank could move in there, and then she fixed up one of them crucifixes she had in the little trunk, and used to squat down at it night and morning, makin' Hank crazy.

"There it was again! Yu' see he couldn't make no allowances fer her bein' Dutch and different. Not because he was bad—there weren't enough of Hank to be bad—but because he had no thoughts. I kind of laffed myself first time I seen Willomene at it. Hank says to me, soft, 'Come here, Lin,' and I peeped in where she was a-prayin' to that crucifix. She seen us, too, but she didn't quit. Them are things yu' don't know about. I figured it this way—that she couldn't make no friends with Hank, and couldn't with us neither, and bein' far away from all she was used to, why, that crucifix was somethin' that staid by her, remindin' her of home, I expect, and anyway keepin' her a sort of company when she felt lonesome. And of course, over in Europe, I guess, she'd been accustomed to believin' in God and a hereafter, and hearin' a lot of singin' in them Catholic churches. So yu' see what she must have thought about Galena Creek.

"One day Hank told her he was goin' to take his dust to town, and when he come back if he found that thing in the house he'd do it up fer her. 'So yu'd better pack off yer wooden dummy somewheres,' says he.

"I tell you," said Lin, fixing his eyes on mine, "a man don't always know how what he speaks is a-goin' to act on others. She said nuthin', and I guess Hank forgot all about it. But I can see the way she looked right now—kind o' stone like and solemn. And I happened to go into the shack around noon to get some matches, and there she was prayin', and that time she jumped.

"The night before Hank was to start fer town, a young chap they called Chalkeye come into camp. He'd been drivin' a bunch of horses to sell round Helena and Bozeman,[19] and he'd lost the trail over to Stinkin' Water where he was goin' back to Meeteetsee. Chalkeye had cigars and good whiskey, and he set up royal fer the gang. That night was the first time I ever knowed him, but him and me has knowed each other pretty well since. He was a surprisin' hand at gettin' on the right side of women without doin' nuthin' special. I've been there some myself first and last, but there's no use tryin' if Chalkeye happens to be on the same trail. Willomene she h'arkened to his talk, and I noticed her, and I concluded she was comparin' him with Hank. After a while we started a game of stud-poker, and Chalkeye cleaned Hank out, who couldn't play cards good.

"He played horses against Hank's gold dust, and by midnight he'd got away with the dust.[20] And Willomene took to his eye, which was jovial like, and I guess she may have been figurin' that if she was a-goin' to marry over again she'd 'a' liked to have been acquainted with Chalkeye before the ceremony with Hank. I think she had them thoughts goin' through her mind in a mixed sort of a way.

"There was one occurrence as to the crucifix which Hank's eye lit on during the game, and he said something nasty. And Chalkeye claimed such things must be a godsend to them as took stock in 'em. He spoke serious all the while he was dealin' the cards; nor it wasn't through desirin' to get in his work with Willomene, but because of feelin's on his part that ain't common in this country, and do a man credit, no matter what his acts may sometimes be. Next day he pulled out for Stinkin' Water, havin' treated Willomene with respect, and Hank not havin' any dust left, went to town all the same, leavin' Willomene at the camp. She come down after a while, and watched us as usual, walkin' around slow, and singin' her German songs that hadn't no tune to 'em. And so it was fer about a week. She'd have us all in to supper up at the shack, and look at us eatin' while she'd walk around puttin' grub on your plate. Mighty pleasant she acted always, but she'd not say nuthin' hardly at all.

"Hank come back, and he was used up, you bet! His little winkin' eyes was sweatin' from drink, and Willomene she took no notice of him, nor she didn't cry, neither, for she didn't care no more.

"Hank seen the crucifix same as always, and he says, 'Didn't I tell yu' to take that down?'

"'You did,' says Willomene, very quiet; and she looked at him, and he quit talkin'.

"We was out of meat, and figured we'd go on a hunt before snow came. Yu' see, October was gettin' along, and though we was havin' good weather, all the same, when yu' find them quakin'-asps all turned yaller, and the leaves keeps a-fallin' without no wind to blow 'em down, you're liable to get snowed in on short notice. Hank staid in camp, and before we started up the mountain, I says to him: 'Hank, yu'd ought to leave Willomene do what she wants about prayin'. It don't hurt neither of yu'.'

"And Hank, bein' all trembly from spreein' in town, he says, 'You're all agin me,' like as if he was a baby.

"We was away three days, and awful cold it got to be, with the wind never stoppin' all night roarin' through the timber down the big mountain below where we was camped. We come back to Galena Creek one noon with a good load of elk meat, and looked around. It was plain nobody was there, fer always Willomene come to the door when we'd been out fer a hunt, and, anyway, it was dinner-time, but no smoke was comin' from their chimney.

"'They've quit,' says Honey to me.

"'Well,' I says, 'then they've left word somewheres.'

"'Why, the door's wide open,' says Honey, as we come round that corner of the shack. So we all hollered. Well, it was beginnin' to be strange, and I stepped in inside, after waitin' to hear if anybody'd answer. The first thing I seen was that crucifix and a big hole plumb through the middle of it. I don't know why we took the concern down, but we did, and there was the bullet in the log. Things was kind of tossed around in that shack, and Honey says, 'He's shot her too.'

"While we was a-wonderin', something made a noise, and us fellows jumped. It was that parrot, and he was a-crouchin' flat on the floor of the cage, a-swingin' his head sideways, and when we come up he commenced talkin' and croakin' fast, but awful low, and never screechin' oncet, but lookin' at us with his cussed eye. And would yu' believe it, us fellers come and stood around that cage like fools, watchin' the bird, and Honey whispers to me, 'You bet he knows!' And then his foot trod on somethin', and he gets down and pulls out an axe a raw bear-hide was half folded around; and we knowed well enough it weren't no bear's blood we seen dried on the axe. I was along that time, and Hank skinned that bear with his knife, and didn't use no axe. We found nuthin' further till I stepped outside the shack and seen Willomene's trail heavylike in the gravel.

"That set me on trails, and I seen Hank's leadin' into the shack, but not out. So we hunted some more, but gave up, and then I says. 'We must follow up Willomene.' And them big marks took us right by the ditch, where they sunk deep in the soil that was kind of soggy, and then down the cut-off trail. Mighty clear them marks were, and like as they had been made by a person moving slow. We come along to Little Death Cañon, and just gettin' out of the timber to where the trail takes on to that ledge of little slidin' stones, Honey Wiggin says, 'Look a-there!'

"We stopped, and all seen a black thing ahead. 'Can yu' make it out?' says Honey, and we starts runnin'.

"'It's a man,' somebody says.

"'What's he pointin' that way for?' says Honey, and we kep' a-runnin', and come closer, and, my God! it was Hank. He was kind of leanin' queer over the edge of the Cañon, and we run up to him. He was stiff and stark, and caught in the roots of a dead tree, and the one arm wheeled around like a scarecrow, pointin', and a big cut in his skull. The slide was awful steep where he was, and we crawled and looked over the edge of them brown rock walls. Well, sir, it's a wonder Honey didn't go over that place; and he would, but I seen him stagger and I gripped his arm. Down there in the bottom, tumbled all in a heap, was Willomene, and Hank's finger was a-pointin' straight at her. She was just a humped-up brown bundle, and one leg twisted up like it was stuffed with bran. If fallin' didn't kill her, she must have got choked soon. And we figured out what them two had done, and how she come to fall. Yu' see, Hank must have shot the crucifix when they was havin' hot words, and likely he said she'd be the next thing he'd pump his lead into, and she just settled him right there, and I guess more on account of what he done to the crucifix than out of bein' scared for herself. So she packed him on her back when she got cool, figurin' she'd tip him over into the Cañon where nobody would suspicion he hadn't fell through accident or bein' drunk. But heftin' him all that ways on her back, she got played out, and when she was on that crumble stuff there she'd slipped. Hank got hooked in the tree root, and she'd gone down 'stead of him, with him stuck on top pointin' at her exactly like if he'd been sayin',

'I have yu' beat after all.'

"While we was a-starin', puff! up comes the steam from them sulphur caves, makin that fluffy sigh. And Honey says, 'Let's get out of here.'

"So we took Hank and buried him on top of a little hill near camp, but Willomene had to stay where she'd fell down in there. We felt kind of bad at havin' to leave her that way, but there was no goin' into that place, and wouldn't be to rescue the livin', let alone to get the dead." Lin paused.

"I think," said I, "you'd have made a try for Willomene if she had been alive, Lin."

The cow-puncher laughed indifferently, as his way is if you discuss his character. "I guess not," he said. "Anyway, what's a life? Why, when yu' remember we're all no better than coyotes, yu' don't seem to set much store by it."

But though Lin occasionally will moralize in this strain, and justify vice and a number of things, I don't think he means it.

NOTES

1. A fishing lure made out of brown feathers.
2. The Snake River has its origins in northwest Wyoming and flows through Idaho, Oregon, and Washington. Pacific Creek and Buffalo Fork both are in Teton County, Wyoming, and empty into the Snake River.
3. The name of a cattle ranch, taken from the lettering on its brand.

4. Douglas, Wyoming. "Cinched" here means to have gotten into a tight or difficult financial position.

5. This location is in northwest Wyoming; much of this area—what is known as Jackson Hole—is now part of Grand Teton National Park.

6. North of the Teton Basin is Yellowstone National Park, established in 1872. In August 1883, Lieutenant General Philip Sheridan, an avid supporter of preserving the park's natural wonders, led President Chester Arthur's fishing expedition to the area; it included an escort of seventy-five US cavalry members and almost two hundred pack animals. They crossed the Continental Divide at Lincoln Pass, which is now known as Sheridan Pass.

7. Mammoth Springs is an extensive cascade of hot water springs just inside Yellowstone's northern boundary.

8. Gardiner (with an *i*), Montana, is located just outside the northern boundary of Yellowstone, a few miles north of Mammoth Springs.

9. A "Raymond" here appears to be local slang for a tour guide. The Norris Basin is located in Yellowstone National Park and contains many geysers and hot springs.

10. Today a syndicate manager is one who puts together financing for a particular business proposition; here, though, the "Syndicate" likely refers to the company that owns the hotel (and the store), and the "Syndicate manager" is the local person in charge.

11. A very popular opera soprano of the 1880s and 1890s, Emma Juch (1861–1939) was born in Austria but raised in the United States. The narrator here refers to an operatic performance in Wyoming's capital city by the Emma Juch Grand English Opera Company, which toured the United States in 1889–90.

12. Oswego, New York, was known across the country for its production of starch, which at this time was frequently used for both washing laundry and cooking; two of the most prominent products, which came in large boxes, were Kingsford's Corn Starch and Silver Gloss Starch.

13. Fountain Geyser, less well known than Old Faithful, is an impressive site in Yellowstone National Park.

14. Livingston, Montana, is located fifty-five miles north of Gardiner, Montana.

15. Galena Creek is located east of the Teton Basin in what is now the Shoshone National Forest.

16. An unidentified location.

17. Drunk.

18. A woman born in the United States, not necessarily a Native American.

19. Cities in Montana.

20. In other words, he bet his horses against gold dust of equal value.

CONSTANCE FENIMORE WOOLSON

(1840–94)

Constance Fenimore Woolson, born in New Hampshire in 1840, is best known for her writings about the Great Lakes region and southern United States, as well as stories about American expatriates in Europe. The grandniece of James Fenimore Cooper, a renowned author of Romantic American novels, including *The Last of the Mohicans* (1826), Woolson made many significant contributions herself to nineteenth-century American literature.

Because her papers were largely scattered or destroyed upon her death, biographers and scholars have had difficulty piecing together the details of Woolson's life, especially the later years. Woolson was her parents' sixth daughter, but three of her young sisters died of scarlet fever within a month of her birth. The family soon thereafter left New Hampshire for Cleveland, Ohio, where she attended the Cleveland Female Seminary and received a science-rich education that complemented her love of nature and the outdoors. She and her family also took many trips throughout the Great Lakes region, including the northern reaches of Michigan. In 1858, Woolson graduated first in her class from Madame Chegaray's School, a finishing school in New York City. Unfortunately, Woolson's family continued to be beset by tragedy; by 1869 two more of her sisters, two brothers-in-law, and her father had passed away. To help support her remaining female family members—her mother and two sisters—Woolson turned to writing.

Woolson succeeded in publishing her fictions and travel essays in a range of notable periodicals, including *Harper's Monthly* and the *Atlantic Monthly*. Woolson's first book—*The Old Stone House* (1873), published under the pseudonym Anne March—was for children, and this was followed by *Castle Nowhere: Lake-Country Sketches* (1875), a short story collection that drew upon her experiences in the Great Lakes region. In the 1870s, Woolson also lived for an extended period of time in Florida and the Carolinas, chiefly to attend to her mother, whose health required a warmer climate. Woolson's experiences in this region produced some of her best fictions, including the well-regarded short story collection *Rodman the Keeper: Southern Sketches* (1880).

After her mother's death in 1879, Woolson left the United States for Europe, living at different times in England, France, Germany, Italy, and Switzerland. *Anne,* her first novel, was published in 1882, and it would be followed by four others, plus two short story collections, many individual poems, and numerous essays. While in Europe, Woolson used her connections to secure an introduction to the novelist Henry James. Interpretations of Woolson's relationship with James vary; some biographers have suggested she was romantically interested in James, while others believe she only admired him as a literary peer. Woolson never returned to the United States, and sadly, her later years in Europe were plagued by deafness, pain, and anxiety. The circumstances leading to her 1894 death in Venice are not entirely clear; what is known is that Woolson either fell or jumped from her fourth-floor apartment.

Woolson is especially well-known for her contributions to American Local Color writing, which attempted to faithfully render a region or its people by accurately depicting the landscape and lifestyle that made an area distinct. "Miss Grief," which originally appeared in the pages of *Lippincott's* in May 1880, may not be an overt example of Woolson's Local Color writing—perhaps in part because Woolson had not yet been to Rome when it was written—but it does bring up issues regarding female authorship and the tensions between raw literary talent and a refined approach to literature. Some critics have suggested the story reflects or draws upon Woolson's own relationship to Henry James, which is particularly interesting since the reader's sympathies may shift throughout the engaging story.

MISS GRIEF (1880)

"A conceited fool" is a not uncommon expression. Now, I know that I am not a fool, but I also know that I am conceited. But, candidly, can it be helped if one happens to be young, well and strong, passably good-looking, with some money that one has inherited and more that one has earned—in all, enough to make life comfortable—and if upon this foundation rests also the pleasant superstructure of a literary success? The success is deserved, I think: certainly it was not lightly gained. Yet even with this I fully appreciate its rarity. Thus, I find myself very well entertained in life: I have all I wish in the way of society, and a deep, though of course carefully concealed, satisfaction in my own little fame; which fame I foster by a gentle system of non-interference. I know that I am spoken of as "that quiet young fellow who writes those delightful little studies of society, you know"; and I live up to that definition.

A year ago I was in Rome, and enjoying life particularly. I had a large number of my acquaintances there, both American and English, and no day passed without its invitation. Of course I understood it: it is seldom that you find a literary man who is good-tempered, well-dressed, sufficiently provided with money, and amiably obedient to all the rules and requirements of "society." "When found, make a note of it"; and the note was generally an invitation.

One evening, upon returning to my lodgings, my man[1] Simpson informed me that a person had called in the afternoon, and upon learning that I was absent had left not a card, but her name—"Miss Grief." The title lingered—Miss Grief! "Grief has not so far visited me here," I said to myself, dismissing Simpson and seeking my little balcony for a final smoke, "and she shall not now. I shall take care to be 'not at home' to her if she continues to call." And then I fell to thinking of Ethelind Abercrombie,[2] in whose society I had spent that and many evenings: they were golden thoughts.

The next day there was an excursion; it was late when I reached my rooms, and again Simpson informed me that Miss Grief had called.

"Is she coming continuously?" I said, half to myself.

"Yes, sir: she mentioned that she should call again."

"How does she look?"

"Well, sir, a lady, but not so prosperous as she was, I should say," answered Simpson, discreetly.

"Young?"

"No, sir."

"Alone?"

"A maid with her, sir."

But once outside in my little high-up balcony with my cigar, I again forgot Miss Grief and whatever she might represent. Who would not forget in that moonlight, with Ethelind Abercrombie's face to remember?

The stranger came a third time, and I was absent; then she let two days pass, and began again. It grew to be a regular dialogue between Simpson and myself when I came in at night: "Grief to-day?"

"Yes, sir."

"What time?"

"Four, sir."

"Happy the man," I thought, "who can keep her confined to a particular hour!"

But I should not have treated my visitor so cavalierly if I had not felt sure that she was eccentric and unconventional—qualities extremely tiresome in a woman no longer young or attractive. If she were not eccentric she would not have persisted in coming to my door day after day in this silent way, without stating her errand, leaving a note, or presenting her credentials in any shape. I made up my mind that she had something to sell—a bit of carving or some intaglio[3] supposed to be antique. It was known that I had a fancy for oddities. I said to myself, "She has read or heard of my 'Old Gold' story, or else 'The Buried God,' and she thinks me an idealizing ignoramus upon whom she can impose. Her sepulchral[4] name is at least not Italian; probably she is a sharp country-woman of mine, turning, by means of the present æsthetic craze,[5] an honest penny when she can."

She had called seven times during a period of two weeks without seeing me, when one day I happened to be at home in the afternoon, owing to a pouring rain and a fit of doubt concerning Miss Abercrombie. For I had constructed a careful theory of that young lady's characteristics in my own mind, and she had lived up to it delightfully until the previous evening, when with one word she had blown it to atoms and taken flight, leaving me standing, as it were, on a desolate shore, with nothing but a handful of mistaken inductions wherewith to console myself. I do not know a more exasperating frame of mind, at least for a constructor of theories. I could not write, and so I took up a French novel (I model myself a little on Balzac).[6] I had been turning over its pages but a few moments when Simpson knocked, and, entering softly, said, with just a shadow of a smile on his well-trained face, "Miss Grief." I briefly consigned Miss Grief to all the Furies,[7] and then, as he still lingered—perhaps not knowing where they resided—I asked where the visitor was.

"Outside, sir—in the hall. I told her I would see if you were at home."

"She must be unpleasantly wet if she had no carriage."

"No carriage, sir: they always come on foot. I think she is a little damp, sir."

"Well, let her in; but I don't want the maid. I may as well see her now, I suppose, and end the affair."

"Yes, sir."

I did not put down my book. My visitor should have a hearing, but not much more: she had sacrificed her womanly claims by her persistent attacks upon my door. Presently Simpson ushered her in. "Miss Grief," he said, and then went out, closing the curtain behind him.

A woman—yes, a lady—but shabby, unattractive, and more than middle-aged.

I rose, bowed slightly, and then dropped into my chair again, still keeping the book in my hand. "Miss Grief?" I said interrogatively as I indicated a seat with my eyebrows.

"Not Grief," she answered—"Crief: my name is Crief."

She sat down, and I saw that she held a small flat box.

"Not carving, then," I thought—"probably old lace, something that belonged to Tullia or Lucrezia Borgia."[8] But as she did not speak I found myself obliged to begin: "You have been here, I think, once or twice before?"

"Seven times; this is the eighth."

A silence.

"I am often out; indeed, I may say that I am never in," I remarked carelessly.

"Yes; you have many friends."

"—Who will perhaps buy old lace," I mentally added. But this time I too remained silent; why should I trouble myself to draw her out? She had sought me; let her advance her idea, whatever it was, now that entrance was gained.

But Miss Grief (I preferred to call her so) did not look as though she could advance anything; her black gown, damp with rain, seemed to retreat fearfully to her thin self, while her thin self retreated as far as possible from me, from the chair, from everything. Her eyes were cast down; an old-fashioned lace veil with a heavy border shaded her face. She looked at the floor, and I looked at her.

I grew a little impatient, but I made up my mind that I would continue silent and see how long a time she would consider necessary to give due effect to her little pantomime. Comedy? Or was it tragedy? I suppose full five minutes passed thus in our double silence; and that is a long time when two persons are sitting opposite each other alone in a small still room.

At last my visitor, without raising her eyes, said slowly, "You are very happy, are you not, with youth, health, friends, riches, fame?"

It was a singular beginning. Her voice was clear, low, and very sweet as she thus enumerated my advantages one by one in a list. I was attracted by it, but repelled by her words, which seemed to me flattery both dull and bold.

"Thanks," I said, "for your kindness, but I fear it is undeserved. I seldom discuss myself even when with my friends."

"I am your friend," replied Miss Grief. Then, after a moment, she added slowly, "I have read every word you have written."

I curled the edges of my book indifferently; I am not a fop, I hope, but—others have said the same.

"What is more, I know much of it by heart," continued my visitor. "Wait: I will show you"; and then, without pause, she began to repeat something of mine word for word, just as I had written it. On she went, and I—listened. I intended interrupting her after a moment, but I did not, because she was reciting so well, and also because I felt a desire gaining upon me to see what she would make of a certain conversation which I knew was coming—a conversation between two of my characters which was, to say the least, sphinx-like,[9] and somewhat incandescent as well. What won me a little, too, was the fact that the scene she was reciting (it was hardly more than that, though called a story) was secretly my favorite among all the sketches from my pen which a gracious public has received with favor. I never said so, but it was; and I had always felt a wondering annoyance that the aforesaid public, while kindly praising beyond their worth other attempts of mine, had never noticed the higher purpose of this little shaft, aimed not at the balconies and lighted windows of society, but straight up toward the distant stars. So she went on, and presently reached the conversation: my two people began to talk. She had raised her eyes now, and was looking at me soberly as she gave the words of the woman, quiet, gentle, cold, and the replies of the man, bitter, hot, and scathing. Her very voice changed, and took, though always sweetly, the different tones required, while no point of meaning, however small, no breath of delicate emphasis which I had meant, but which the dull types could not give, escaped an appreciative and full, almost overfull, recognition which startled me. For she had understood me—understood me almost better than I had understood myself. It seemed to me that while I had labored to interpret, partially, a psychological riddle, she, coming after, had comprehended its bearings better than I had, though confining herself strictly to my own words and emphasis. The scene ended (and it ended rather suddenly), she dropped her eyes, and moved her hand nervously to and fro over the box she held; her gloves were old and shabby, her hands small.

I was secretly much surprised by what I had heard, but my ill-humor was deep-seated that day, and I still felt sure, besides, that the box contained something which I was expected to buy.

"You recite remarkably well," I said carelessly, "and I am much flattered also by your appreciation of my attempt. But it is not, I presume, to that alone that I owe the pleasure of this visit?"

"Yes," she answered, still looking down, "it is, for if you had not written that scene I should not have sought you. Your other sketches are interiors—exquisitely painted and delicately finished, but of small scope. *This* is a sketch in a few bold, masterly lines—work of entirely different spirit and purpose."

I was nettled by her insight. "You have bestowed so much of your kind attention upon me that I feel your debtor," I said, conventionally. "It may be that there is something I can do for you—connected, possibly, with that little box?"

It was impertinent, but it was true; for she answered, "Yes."

I smiled, but her eyes were cast down and she did not see the smile.

"What I have to show you is a manuscript," she said after a pause which I did not break; "it is a drama. I thought that perhaps you would read it."

"An authoress! This is worse than old lace," I said to myself in dismay.— Then, aloud, "My opinion would be worth nothing, Miss Crief."

"Not in a business way, I know. But it might be—an assistance personally." Her voice had sunk to a whisper; outside, the rain was pouring steadily down. She was a very depressing object to me as she sat there with her box.

"I hardly think I have the time at present—" I began.

She had raised her eyes and was looking at me; then, when I paused, she rose and came suddenly toward my chair. "Yes, you will read it," she said with her hand on my arm—"you will read it. Look at this room; look at yourself; look at all you have. Then look at me, and have pity."

I had risen, for she held my arm, and her damp skirt was brushing my knees.

Her large dark eyes looked intently into mine as she went on; "I have no shame in asking. Why should I have? It is my last endeavor; but a calm and well-considered one. If you refuse I shall go away, knowing that Fate has willed it so. And I shall be content."

"She is mad," I thought. But she did not look so, and she had spoken quietly, even gently.—"Sit down," I said, moving away from her. I felt as if I had been magnetized; but it was only the nearness of her eyes to mine, and their intensity. I drew forward a chair, but she remained standing.

"I cannot," she said in the same sweet, gentle tone, "unless you promise."

"Very well, I promise; only sit down."

As I took her arm to lead her to the chair I perceived that she was trembling, but her face continued unmoved.

"You do not, of course, wish me to look at your manuscript now?" I said, temporizing; "it would be much better to leave it. Give me your address, and I will return it to you with my written opinion; though, I repeat, the latter will be of no use to you. It is the opinion of an editor or publisher that you want."

"It shall be as you please. And I will go in a moment," said Miss Grief, pressing her palms together, as if trying to control the tremor that had seized her slight frame.

She looked so pallid that I thought of offering her a glass of wine; then I remembered that if I did it might be a bait to bring her there again, and this I was desirous to prevent. She rose while the thought was passing through my mind. Her pasteboard box lay on the chair she had first occupied; she took it, wrote an address on the cover, laid it down, and then, bowing with a little air of formality, drew her black shawl round her shoulders and turned toward the door.

I followed, after touching the bell. "You will hear from me by letter," I said.

Simpson opened the door, and I caught a glimpse of the maid, who was waiting in the anteroom. She was an old woman, shorter than her mistress, equally thin, and dressed like her in rusty black. As the door opened she turned toward it a pair of small, dim blue eyes with a look of furtive suspense. Simpson dropped the curtain, shutting me into the inner room; he had no intention of allowing me to accompany my visitor further. But I had the curiosity to go to a bay-window in an angle from whence I could command the street-door, and presently I saw them issue forth in the rain and walk away side by side, the mistress, being the taller, holding the umbrella: probably there was not much difference in rank between persons so poor and forlorn as these.

It grew dark. I was invited out for the evening, and I knew that if I should go I should meet Miss Abercrombie. I said to myself that I would not go. I got out my paper for writing, I made my preparations for a quiet evening at home with myself; but it was of no use. It all ended slavishly in my going. At the last allowable moment I presented myself, and—as a punishment for my vacillation, I suppose—I never passed a more disagreeable evening. I drove homeward in a murky temper; it was foggy without, and very foggy within. What Ethelind really was, now that she had broken through my elaborately-built theories, I was not able to decide. There was, to tell the truth, a certain young Englishman—But that is apart from this story.

I reached home, went up to my rooms, and had a supper. It was to console myself; I am obliged to console myself scientifically once in a while. I was walking up and down afterward, smoking and feeling somewhat better, when my eye fell upon the pasteboard box. I took it up; on the cover was written an address which showed that my visitor must have walked a long distance in order to see me: "A. Crief."—"A Grief," I thought; "and so she is. I positively believe she has brought all this trouble upon me: she has the evil eye." I took out the manuscript and looked at it. It was in the form of a little volume, and clearly written; on the cover was the word "Armor" in German text, and, underneath, a pen-and-ink sketch of a helmet, breastplate, and shield.

"Grief certainly needs armor," I said to myself, sitting down by the table and turning over the pages. "I may as well look over the thing now; I could not be in a worse mood." And then I began to read.

Early the next morning Simpson took a note from me to the given address, returning with the following reply: "No; I prefer to come to you; at four; A. Crief." These words, with their three semicolons, were written in pencil upon a piece of coarse printing-paper, but the handwriting was as clear and delicate as that of the manuscript in ink.

"What sort of a place was it, Simpson?"

"Very poor, sir, but I did not go all the way up. The elder person came down, sir, took the note, and requested me to wait where I was."

"You had no chance, then, to make inquiries?" I said, knowing full well that he had emptied the entire neighborhood of any information it might possess concerning these two lodgers.

"Well, sir, you know how these foreigners will talk, whether one wants to hear or not. But it seems that these two persons have been there but a few weeks; they live alone, and are uncommonly silent and reserved. The people round there call them something that signifies 'the Madames American, thin and dumb.'"

At four the "Madames American" arrived; it was raining again, and they came on foot under their old umbrella. The maid waited in the anteroom, and Miss Grief was ushered into my bachelor's parlor. I had thought that I should meet her with great deference; but she looked so forlorn that my deference changed to pity. It was the woman that impressed me then, more than the writer—the fragile, nerveless body more than the inspired mind. For it was inspired: I had sat up half the night over her drama, and had felt thrilled through and through more than once by its earnestness, passion, and power.

No one could have been more surprised than I was to find myself thus enthusiastic. I thought I had outgrown that sort of thing. And one would have supposed, too (I myself should have supposed so the day before), that the faults of the drama, which were many and prominent, would have chilled any liking I might have felt, I being a writer myself, and therefore critical; for writers are as apt to make much of the "how," rather than the "what," as painters, who, it is well known, prefer an exquisitely rendered representation of a commonplace theme to an imperfectly executed picture of even the most striking subject. But in this case, on the contrary, the scattered rays of splendor in Miss Grief's drama had made me forget the dark spots, which were numerous and disfiguring; or, rather, the splendor had made me anxious to have the spots removed. And this also was a philanthropic state very unusual with me. Regarding unsuccessful writers, my motto had been "Væ victis!"[10]

My visitor took a seat and folded her hands; I could see, in spite of her quiet manner, that she was in breathless suspense. It seemed so pitiful that she should be trembling there before me—a woman so much older than I was, a woman who possessed the divine spark of genius, which I was by no means sure (in spite of my success) had been granted to me—that I felt as if I ought to go down on my knees before her, and entreat her to take her proper place of supremacy at once. But there! one does not go down on one's knees, combustively, as it were, before a woman over fifty, plain in feature, thin, dejected, and ill-dressed. I contented myself with taking her hands (in their miserable old gloves) in mine, while I said cordially, "Miss Crief, your drama seems to me full of original power. It has roused my enthusiasm: I sat up half the night reading it."

The hands I held shook, but something (perhaps a shame for having evaded the knees business) made me tighten my hold and bestow upon her also a reassuring smile. She looked at me for a moment, and then, suddenly and noiselessly, tears rose and rolled down her cheeks. I dropped her hands and retreated. I had not thought her tearful: on the contrary, her voice and face had seemed rigidly controlled. But now here she was bending herself over the side of the chair with her head resting on her arms, not sobbing aloud, but her whole frame shaken by the strength of her emotion. I rushed for a glass of wine; I pressed her to take it. I did not quite know what to do, but, putting myself in her place, I decided to praise the drama; and praise it I did. I do not know when I have used so many adjectives. She raised her head and began to wipe her eyes.

"Do take the wine," I said, interrupting myself in my cataract of language.

"I dare not," she answered; then added humbly, "that is, unless you have a biscuit here or a bit of bread."

I found some biscuit; she ate two, and then slowly drank the wine, while I resumed my verbal Niagara.[11] Under its influence—and that of the wine too, perhaps—she began to show new life. It was not that she looked radiant—she could not—but simply that she looked warm. I now perceived what had been the principal discomfort of her appearance heretofore: it was that she had looked all the time as if suffering from cold.

At last I could think of nothing more to say, and stopped. I really admired the drama, but I thought I had exerted myself sufficiently as an anti-hysteric, and that adjectives enough, for the present at least, had been administered. She had put down her empty wine-glass, and was resting her hands on the broad cushioned arms of her chair with, for a thin person, a sort of expanded content.

"You must pardon my tears," she said, smiling; "it was the revulsion of feeling. My life was at a low ebb: if your sentence had been against me it would have been my end."

"Your end?"

"Yes, the end of my life; I should have destroyed myself."

"Then you would have been a weak as well as wicked woman," I said in a tone of disgust. I do hate sensationalism.

"Oh no, you know nothing about it. I should have destroyed only this poor worn tenement of clay. But I can well understand how *you* would look upon it. Regarding the desirableness of life the prince and the beggar may have different opinions.—We will say no more of it, but talk of the drama instead." As she spoke the word "drama" a triumphant brightness came into her eyes.

I took the manuscript from a drawer and sat down beside her. "I suppose you know that there are faults," I said, expecting ready acquiescence.

"I was not aware that there were any," was her gentle reply.

Here was a beginning! After all my interest in her—and, I may say under the circumstances, my kindness—she received me in this way! However, my belief in her genius was too sincere to be altered by her whimsies; so I persevered. "Let us go over it together," I said. "Shall I read it to you, or will you read it to me?"

"I will not read it, but recite it."

"That will never do; you will recite it so well that we shall see only the good points, and what we have to concern ourselves with now is the bad ones."

"I will recite it," she repeated.

"Now, Miss Crief," I said bluntly, "for what purpose did you come to me? Certainly not merely to recite: I am no stage-manager. In plain English, was it not your idea that I might help you in obtaining a publisher?"

"Yes, yes," she answered, looking at me apprehensively, all her old manner returning.

I followed up my advantage, opened the little paper volume and began. I first took the drama line by line, and spoke of the faults of expression and structure; then I turned back and touched upon two or three glaring impossibilities in the plot. "Your absorbed interest in the motive of the whole no doubt made you forget these blemishes," I said apologetically.

But, to my surprise, I found that she did not see the blemishes—that she appreciated nothing I had said, comprehended nothing. Such unaccountable obtuseness puzzled me. I began again, going over the whole with even greater minuteness and care. I worked hard: the perspiration stood in beads upon my forehead as I struggled with her—what shall I call it—obstinacy? But it was not exactly obstinacy. She simply could not see the faults of her own work, any more than a blind man can see the smoke that dims a patch of blue sky. When I had finished my task the second time she still remained as gently impassive as before. I leaned back in my chair exhausted, and looked at her.

Even then she did not seem to comprehend (whether she agreed with it or not) what I must be thinking. "It is such a heaven to me that you like it!" she murmured dreamily, breaking the silence. Then, with more animation, "And *now* you will let me recite it?"

I was too weary to oppose her; she threw aside her shawl and bonnet, and, standing in the centre of the room, began.

And she carried me along with her: all the strong passages were doubly strong when spoken, and the faults, which seemed nothing to her, were made by her earnestness to seem nothing to me, at least for that moment. When it was ended she stood looking at me with a triumphant smile.

"Yes," I said, "I like it, and you see that I do. But I like it because my taste is peculiar. To me originality and force are everything—perhaps because I have them not to any marked degree myself—but the world at large will not overlook as I do your absolutely barbarous shortcomings on account of them. Will you trust me to go over the drama and correct it at my pleasure?" This was a vast deal for me to offer; I was surprised at myself.

"No," she answered softly, still smiling. "There shall not be so much as a comma altered." Then she sat down and fell into a reverie as though she were alone.

"Have you written anything else?" I said after a while, when I had become tired of the silence.

"Yes."

"Can I see it? Or is it *them?*"

"It is *them*. Yes, you can see all."

"I will call upon you for the purpose."

"No, you must not," she said, coming back to the present nervously. "I prefer to come to you."

At this moment Simpson entered to light the room, and busied himself rather longer than was necessary over the task. When he finally went out I saw that my visitor's manner had sunk into its former depression: the presence of the servant seemed to have chilled her.

"When did you say I might come?" I repeated, ignoring her refusal.

"I did not say it. It would be impossible."

"Well, then, when will you come here?" There was, I fear, a trace of fatigue in my tone.

"At your good pleasure, sir," she answered humbly.

My chivalry was touched by this: after all, she was a woman. "Come to-morrow," I said.

"By the way, come and dine with me then; why not?" I was curious to see what she would reply.

"Why not, indeed? Yes, I will come. I am forty-three: I might have been your mother."

This was not quite true, as I am over thirty: but I look young, while she—Well, I had thought her over fifty. "I can hardly call you 'mother,' but we might compromise upon 'aunt,'" I said, laughing. "Aunt what?"

"My name is Aaronna," she gravely answered. "My father was much disappointed that I was not a boy, and gave me as nearly as possible the name he had prepared—Aaron."

"Then come and dine with me to-morrow, and bring with you the other manuscripts, Aaronna," I said, amused at the quaint sound of the name. On the whole, I did not like "aunt."

"I will come," she answered.

It was twilight and still raining, but she refused all offers of escort or carriage, departing with her maid, as she had come, under the brown umbrella. The next day we had the dinner. Simpson was astonished—and more than astonished, grieved—when I told him that he was to dine with the maid; but he could not complain in words, since my own guest, the mistress, was hardly more attractive. When our preparations were complete I could not help laughing: the two prim little tables, one in the parlor and one in the anteroom, and Simpson disapprovingly going back and forth between them, were irresistible.

I greeted my guest hilariously when she arrived, and, fortunately, her manner was not quite so depressed as usual: I could never have accorded myself with a tearful mood. I had thought that perhaps she would make, for the occasion, some change in her attire; I have never known a woman who had not some scrap of finery, however small, in reserve for that unexpected occasion of which she is ever dreaming. But no: Miss Grief wore the same black gown, unadorned and unaltered. I was glad that there was no rain that day, so that the skirt did not at least look so damp and rheumatic.

She ate quietly, almost furtively, yet with a good appetite, and she did not refuse the wine. Then, when the meal was over and Simpson had removed the dishes, I asked for the new manuscripts. She gave me an old green copybook filled with short poems, and a prose sketch by itself; I lit a cigar and sat down at my desk to look them over.

"Perhaps you will try a cigarette?" I suggested, more for amusement than anything else, for there was not a shade of Bohemianism about her; her whole appearance was puritanical.

"I have not yet succeeded in learning to smoke."

"You have tried?" I said, turning round.

"Yes: Serena and I tried, but we did not succeed."

"Serena is your maid?"

"She lives with me."

I was seized with inward laughter, and began hastily to look over her manuscripts with my back toward her, so that she might not see it. A vision had risen before me of those two forlorn women, alone in their room with locked doors, patiently trying to acquire the smoker's art.

But my attention was soon absorbed by the papers before me. Such a fantastic collection of words, lines, and epithets I had never before seen, or even in dreams imagined. In truth, they were like the work of dreams: they were *Kubla Khan*,[12] only more so. Here and there was radiance like the flash of a diamond, but each poem, almost each verse and line, was marred by some fault or lack which seemed wilful perversity, like the work of an evil sprite. It was like a case of jeweler's wares set before you, with each ring unfinished, each bracelet too large or too small for its purpose, each breastpin without its fastening, each necklace purposely broken. I turned the pages, marveling. When about half an hour had passed, and I was leaning back for a moment to light another cigar, I glanced toward my visitor. She was behind me, in an easy-chair before my small fire, and she was—fast asleep! In the relaxation of her unconsciousness I was struck anew by the poverty her appearance expressed; her feet were visible, and I saw the miserable worn old shoes which hitherto she had kept concealed.

After looking at her for a moment I returned to my task and took up the prose story; in prose she must be more reasonable. She was less fantastic perhaps, but hardly more reasonable. The story was that of a profligate and commonplace man forced by two of his friends, in order not to break the heart of a dying girl who loves him, to live up to a high imaginary ideal of himself which her pure but mistaken mind has formed. He has a handsome face and sweet voice, and repeats what they tell him. Her long, slow decline and happy death, and his own inward ennui and profound weariness of the role he has to play, made the vivid points of the story. So far, well enough, but here was the trouble: through the whole narrative moved another character, a physician of tender heart and exquisite mercy, who practised murder as a fine art, and was regarded (by the author) as a second Messiah! This was monstrous. I read it through twice, and threw it down; then, fatigued, I turned round and leaned back, waiting for her to wake. I could see her profile against the dark hue of the easy-chair.

Presently she seemed to feel my gaze, for she stirred, then opened her eyes. "I have been asleep," she said, rising hurriedly.

"No harm in that, Aaronna."

But she was deeply embarrassed and troubled, much more so than the occasion required; so much so, indeed, that I turned the conversation back upon the manuscripts as a diversion. "I cannot stand that doctor of yours," I said, indicating the prose story; "no one would. You must cut him out."

Her self-possession returned as if by magic. "Certainly not," she answered haughtily.

"Oh, if you do not care—I had labored under the impression that you were anxious these things should find a purchaser."

"I am, I am," she said, her manner changing to deep humility with wonderful rapidity. With such alternations of feeling as this sweeping over her like great waves, no wonder she was old before her time.

"Then you must take out that doctor."

"I am willing, but do not know how," she answered, pressing her hands together helplessly. "In my mind he belongs to the story so closely that he cannot be separated from it."

Here Simpson entered, bringing a note for me: it was a line from Mrs. Abercrombie inviting me for that evening—an unexpected gathering, and therefore likely to be all the more agreeable. My heart bounded in spite of me; I forgot Miss Grief and her manuscripts for the moment as completely as though they had never existed. But, bodily, being still in the same room with her, her speech brought me back to the present.

"You have had good news?" she said.

"Oh no, nothing especial—merely an invitation."

"But good news also," she repeated. "And now, as for me, I must go."

Not supposing that she would stay much later in any case, I had that morning ordered a carriage to come for her at about that hour. I told her this. She made no reply beyond putting on her bonnet and shawl.

"You will hear from me soon," I said; "I shall do all I can for you."

She had reached the door, but before opening it she stopped, turned and extended her hand. "You are good," she said: "I give you thanks. Do not think me ungrateful or envious. It is only that you are young, and I am so—so old." Then she opened the door and passed through the anteroom without pause, her maid accompanying her and Simpson with gladness lighting the way. They were gone. I dressed hastily and went out—to continue my studies in psychology.

Time passed; I was busy, amused and perhaps a little excited (sometimes psychology is exciting). But, though much occupied with my own affairs, I did not altogether neglect my self-imposed task regarding Miss Grief. I began by sending her prose story to a friend, the editor of a monthly magazine, with a letter making a strong plea for its admittance. It should have a chance first on its own merits. Then I forwarded the drama to a publisher, also an acquaintance, a man with a taste for phantasms and a soul above mere common popularity, as his own coffers knew to their cost. This done, I waited with conscience clear.

Four weeks passed. During this waiting period I heard nothing from Miss Grief. At last one morning came a letter from my editor. "The story has force, but I cannot stand that doctor," he wrote. "Let her cut him out, and I might print it." Just what I myself had said. The package lay there on my table, travel-worn and grimed; a returned manuscript is, I think, the most melancholy object on earth. I decided to wait, before writing to Aaronna, until the second letter was received. A week later it came. "Armor" was declined. The publisher had been "impressed" by the power displayed in certain passages, but the "impossibilities of the plot" rendered it "unavailable for publication"—in fact, would "bury it in ridicule" if brought before the public, a public "lamentably" fond of amusement, "seeking it, undaunted, even in the cannon's mouth." I doubt if he knew himself what he meant. But one thing, at any rate, was clear: "Armor" was declined.

Now, I am, as I have remarked before, a little obstinate. I was determined that Miss Grief's work should be received. I would alter and improve it myself, without letting her know: the end justified the means. Surely the sieve of my own good taste, whose mesh had been pronounced so fine and delicate, would serve for two. I began; and utterly failed.

I set to work first upon "Armor." I amended, altered, left out, put in, pieced, condensed, lengthened; I did my best, and all to no avail. I could not succeed in completing anything that satisfied me, or that approached, in truth, Miss Grief's own work just as it stood. I suppose I went over that manuscript twenty times: I covered sheets of paper with my copies. But the obstinate drama refused to be corrected; as it was it must stand or fall.

Wearied and annoyed, I threw it aside and took up the prose story: that would be easier. But, to my surprise, I found that that apparently gentle "doctor" would not out: he was so closely interwoven with every part of the tale that to take him out was like taking out one especial figure in a carpet: that is, impossible, unless you unravel the whole. At last I did unravel the whole, and then the story was no longer good, or Aaronna's: it was weak, and mine. All this took time, for of course I had much to do in connection with my own life and tasks. But, though slowly and at my leisure, I really did try my best as regarded Miss Grief, and without success. I was forced at last to make up my mind that either my own powers were not equal to the task, or else that her perversities were as essential a part of her work as her inspirations, and not to be separated from it. Once during this period I showed two of the short poems to Isabel, withholding of course the writer's name. "They were written by a woman," I explained.

"Her mind must have been disordered, poor thing!" Isabel said in her gentle way when she returned them—"at least, judging by these. They are hopelessly mixed and vague."

Now, they were not vague so much as vast. But I knew that I could not make Isabel comprehend it, and (so complex a creature is man) I do not know that I wanted her to comprehend it. These were the only ones in the whole collection that I would have shown her, and I was rather glad that she did not like even these. Not that poor Aaronna's poems were evil: they were simply unrestrained, large, vast, like the skies or the wind. Isabel was bounded on all sides, like a violet in a garden-bed. And I liked her so.

One afternoon, about the time when I was beginning to see that I could not "improve" Miss Grief, I came upon the maid. I was driving, and she had stopped on the crossing to let the carriage pass. I recognized her at a glance (by her general forlornness), and called to the driver to stop: "How is Miss Grief?" I said. "I have been intending to write to her for some time."

"And your note, when it comes," answered the old woman on the crosswalk fiercely, "she shall not see."

"What?"

"I say she shall not see it. Your patronizing face shows that you have no good news, and you shall not rack and stab her any more on *this* earth, please God, while I have authority."

"Who has racked or stabbed her, Serena?"

"Serena, indeed! Rubbish! I'm no Serena: I'm her aunt. And as to who has racked and stabbed her, I say you, *you*—YOU literary men!" She had put her old head inside my carriage, and flung out these words at me in a shrill, menacing tone. "But she shall die in peace in spite of you," she continued. "Vampires! you take her ideas and fatten on them, and leave her to starve. You know you do—*you* who have had her poor manuscripts these months and months!"

"Is she ill?" I asked in real concern, gathering that much at least from the incoherent tirade.

"She is dying," answered the desolate old creature, her voice softening and her dim eyes filling with tears.

"Oh, I trust not. Perhaps something can be done. Can I help you in any way?"

"In all ways if you would," she said, breaking down and beginning to sob weakly, with her head resting on the sill of the carriage-window. "Oh, what have we not been through together, we two! Piece by piece I have sold all."

I am good-hearted enough, but I do not like to have old women weeping across my carriage-door. I suggested, therefore, that she should come inside and let me take her home. Her shabby old skirt was soon beside me, and, following her directions, the driver turned toward one of the most wretched quarters of the city, the abode of poverty, crowded and unclean. Here, in a large bare chamber up many flights of stairs, I found Miss Grief.

As I entered I was startled: I thought she was dead. There seemed no life present until she opened her eyes, and even then they rested upon us vaguely, as though she did not know who we were. But as I approached a light came into them: she recognized me, and this sudden revivification, this return of the soul to the almost deserted body, was the most wonderful thing I ever saw. "You have good news of the drama?" she whispered as I bent over her: "tell me. I *know* you have good news."

What was I to answer? Pray, what would you have answered, puritan?

"Yes, I have good news, Aaronna," I said. "The drama will appear." (And who knows? Perhaps it will in some other world.)

She smiled, and her now brilliant eyes did not leave my face.

"He knows I'm your aunt: I told him," said the old woman, coming to the bedside.

"Did you?" whispered Miss Grief, still gazing at me with a smile. "Then please, dear Aunt Martha, give me something to eat."

Aunt Martha hurried across the room, and I followed her. "It's the first time she's asked for food in weeks," she said in a husky tone.

She opened a cupboard-door vaguely, but I could see nothing within. "What have you for her?" I asked with some impatience, though in a low voice.

"Please God, nothing!" answered the poor old woman, hiding her reply and her tears behind the broad cupboard-door. "I was going out to get a little something when I met you."

"Good Heavens! is it money you need? Here, take this and send; or go yourself in the carriage waiting below."

She hurried out breathless, and I went back to the bedside, much disturbed by what I had seen and heard. But Miss Grief's eyes were full of life, and as I sat down beside her she whispered earnestly, "Tell me."

And I did tell her—a romance invented for the occasion. I venture to say that none of my published sketches could compare with it. As for the lie involved, it will stand among my few good deeds, I know, at the judgment-bar.

And she was satisfied. "I have never known what it was," she whispered, "to be fully happy until now." She closed her eyes, and when the lids fell I again thought that she had passed away. But no, there was still pulsation in her small, thin wrist. As she perceived my touch she smiled. "Yes, I am happy," she said again, though without audible sound.

The old aunt returned; food was prepared, and she took some. I myself went out after wine that should be rich and pure. She rallied a little, but I did not leave her: her eyes dwelt upon me and compelled me to stay, or rather my conscience compelled me. It was a damp night, and I had a little fire made. The wine, fruit, flowers, and candles I had ordered made the bare place for the time being bright and fragrant. Aunt Martha dozed in her chair from sheer fatigue—she had watched many nights—but Miss Grief was awake, and I sat beside her.

"I make you my executor," she murmured, "as to the drama. But my other manuscripts place, when I am gone, under my head, and let them be buried with me. They are not many—those you have and these. See!"

I followed her gesture, and saw under her pillows the edges of two more copybooks like the one I had. "Do not look at them—my poor dead children!" she said tenderly. "Let them depart with me—unread, as I have been."

Later she whispered, "Did you wonder why I came to you? It was the contrast. You were young—strong—rich—praised—loved—successful: all that I was not. I wanted to look at you—and imagine how it would feel. You had success—but I had the greater power. Tell me, did I not have it?"

"Yes, Aaronna."

"It is all in the past now. But I am satisfied."

After another pause she said with a faint smile, "Do you remember when I fell asleep in your parlor? It was the good and rich food. It was so long since I had had food like that!"

I took her hand and held it, conscience-stricken, but now she hardly seemed to perceive my touch. "And the smoking?" she whispered. "Do you remember how you laughed? I saw it. But I had heard that smoking soothed—that one was no longer tired and hungry—with a cigar."

In little whispers of this sort, separated by long rests and pauses, the night passed. Once she asked if her aunt was asleep, and when I answered in the affirmative she said, "Help her to return home—to America: the drama will pay for it. I ought never to have brought her away."

I promised, and she resumed her bright-eyed silence.

I think she did not speak again. Toward morning the change came, and soon after sunrise, with her old aunt kneeling by her side, she passed away.

All was arranged as she had wished. Her manuscripts, covered with violets, formed her pillow. No one followed her to the grave save her aunt and myself; I thought she would prefer it so. Her name was not "Crief," after all, but "Moncrief;" I saw it written out by Aunt Martha for the coffin-plate, as follows: "Aaronna Moncrief, aged forty-three years, two months, and eight days."

I never knew more of her history than is written here. If there was more that I might have learned, it remained unlearned, for I did not ask.

And the drama? I keep it here in this locked case. I could have had it published at my own expense; but I think that now she knows its faults herself, perhaps, and would not like it.

I keep it; and, once in a while, I read it over—not as a *memento mori*[13] exactly, but rather as a memento of my own good fortune, for which I should continually give thanks. The want of one grain made all her work void, and that one grain was given to me. She, with the greater power, failed—I, with the less, succeeded. But no praise is due to me for that. When I die "Armor" is to be destroyed unread: not even Isabel is to see it. For women will misunderstand each other; and, dear and precious to me as my sweet wife is, I could not bear that she or any one should cast so much as a thought of scorn upon the memory of the writer, upon my poor dead, "unavailable,"[14] unaccepted "Miss Grief."

NOTES

1. His servant, or possibly butler.
2. In the story's original appearance in *Lippincott's* (May 1880), this character is named "Ethelind Abercrombie," but when it was reprinted in 1884 in volume 4 of *Stories by American Authors* (New York: Charles Scribner's Sons), the name was changed to "Isabel Abercrombie"; the reason for this emendation is unknown.
3. An "intaglio" is a drawing, sketch, or engraving created by first etching into some type of surface, most commonly a metal plate or wood, then pushing ink into the etching, and then impressing paper onto the surface, thereby taking up the ink from the recessed etched lines.
4. Gloomy, or dismal.
5. A period of intense interest in objects (especially art works) that were valued chiefly for the way they pleased the senses, not because of their utility.
6. French novelist and playwright Honoré de Balzac (1799–1850) was known for pioneering French Realism in literature and creating complex, multifaceted characters.
7. In Greco-Roman mythology, the three Furies were goddesses of vengeance.

8. Tullia (79–45 BCE), daughter of Cicero, a Roman politician. Lucretia Borgia (1480–1519), a Spanish-Italian noblewoman, daughter of Pope Alexander VI (1431–1503), who ruled as governor of Spoleto, an area now part of central Italy.

9. According to Greek legend, the Sphinx was a creature with the head of a human and the body of a lion; it guarded the gate to the city of Thebes, and one could enter the city only by correctly answering the riddle that the Sphinx asked. Here the term "sphinx-like" is meant to convey an air of mystery and perplexity.

10. Woe to the conquered (Latin).

11. Niagara Falls is a group of three large waterfalls on the border of Ontario, Canada, and New York State.

12. "Kubla Khan," or "A Vision in a Dream: A Fragment" (1797), is a poem by British Romantic poet Samuel Taylor Coleridge (1772–1834) that he claimed was inspired by an opium-induced dream.

13. Remember you must die (Latin). A work of art that focuses on the inevitability of death.

14. Reference to a phrase that magazine editors of the time commonly used when returning rejected manuscript submissions to their authors—that is, "We must inform you that we do not find this piece available."

ZITKALA-ŠA
(GERTRUDE SIMMONS BONNIN)

(1876–1938)

Gertrude Simmons was born on the Yankton Sioux Reservation in South Dakota in 1876; she adopted the pen name Zitkala-Ša ("Red Bird") much later, around 1900. Her mother was Native American, but her biological father was a White man who left before she was born; the name "Simmons" is that of another White man her mother had married previously but who had died in 1874. From age six until twenty-four she attended a number of schools run by White Christians who wished to educate Native Americans so they could fit into modern American society, albeit in an ancillary position. Such "education," whether well intended or not, unfortunately always involved an attempt to make students leave their own tribal heritages and ways behind. Zitkala-Ša first attended a Presbyterian school on the Yankton reservation; in 1884 she left for White's Indiana Manual Labor Institute, a school run by Quakers. She stayed there for three years, then returned to the reservation for three years, and subsequently went back, eventually graduating in December 1894. After graduation she attended Earlham College, a Quaker-affiliated college in Indiana, from 1895 to 1897, leaving due to poor health and the need to obtain employment to support herself and her mother. For just two years she taught at the Carlisle Indian Industrial School in Pennsylvania, which was under the direction of former general Richard Henry

Pratt. Although by the end of her involvement with these schools she had become highly literate in English, an accomplished violinist, and an acute thinker, she had also become highly critical of the goals and methods of these schools, and expressed her views in three autobiographical essays published in the January, February, and March 1900 issues of *Atlantic Monthly* magazine: "Impressions of an Indian Childhood," "The School Days of an Indian Girl," and "An Indian Teacher among Indians." These pieces are highly critical of White Christian efforts at the turn of the twentieth century to forcefully assimilate Native Americans into White mainstream American society through education, and they well represent the feelings of many Native Americans at the time of being betrayed by White people's promises and left in between cultures.

Feeling this betrayal, Zitkala-Ša spent the rest of her life putting her talents—especially her excellent writing and editorial skills—to work on behalf of all Native Americans, consistently promoting the idea that they deserved a greater say in their futures. After marrying fellow Yankton Sioux Raymond Bonnin in May 1902, she moved with him to the Uintah and Ouray Reservation in Utah and remained there for the next fourteen years. One of the original founders of the Society of American Indians in 1916, she moved to Washington, DC, to serve as its secretary, remaining there even after it disbanded in 1920; later, in 1936, she and her husband would found a pan-tribal advocacy organization, the National Council of American Indians, which she served until her death in 1938. She also worked diligently at preserving tribal legends—in English—so they would not be lost to future generations; many of these were collected in her first book, *Old Indian Legends* (1901). Most of her writings from 1902 on were nonfiction articles and editorials published in Native American periodicals such as the *American Indian Magazine;* one especially notable publication during her later years was a short volume entitled *Oklahoma's Poor Rich Indians: An Orgy of Graft and Exploitation of the Five Civilized Tribes—Legalized Robbery* (1924).

Just thirty years ago, few scholars or students had heard of Zitkala-Ša. Due to the rediscovery of her and her works in the 1990s, though, instructors at the college level now regularly assign some of her writing, and there is a large body of scholarship devoted to her work. Unfortunately, most scholars have limited the scope of their investigations to the three aforementioned autobiographical essays published in the *Atlantic Monthly* in 1900 and have overlooked a number of other things that deserve to be more widely known, including "The Soft-Hearted Sioux," a short story that originally appeared in the March 1901 issue of *Harper's Monthly.* Perceiving the story as an attack on Whites' attempts to assimilate Native Americans, Richard Henry Pratt, Zitkala-Ša's former boss at the Carlisle Indian Industrial School, bitterly denounced her both in private letters and in public articles, trying to cast her as an ungrateful Native American who was (according to Zitkala-Ša's account of these attacks in a letter she wrote to her friend Carlos Montezuma) "worse than Pagan." Zitkala-Ša had the last word, though, countering Pratt's slander with an essay sarcastically entitled "Why I Am a Pagan" (*Atlantic Monthly,* December 1902).

THE SOFT-HEARTED SIOUX (1901)

I

Beside the open fire I sat within our tepee. With my red blanket wrapped tightly about my crossed legs, I was thinking of the coming season, my sixteenth winter. On either side of the wigwam were my parents. My father was whistling a tune between his teeth while polishing with his bare hand a red stone pipe he had recently carved. Almost in front of me, beyond the centre fire, my old grandmother sat near the entranceway.

She turned her face toward her right and addressed most of her words to my mother. Now and then she spoke to me, but never did she allow her eyes to rest upon her daughter's husband, my father. It was only upon rare occasions that my grandmother said anything to him. Thus his ears were open and ready to catch the smallest wish she might express. Sometimes when my grandmother had been saying things which pleased him, my father used to comment upon them. At other times, when he could not approve of what was spoken, he used to work or smoke silently.

On this night my old grandmother began her talk about me. Filling the bowl of her red stone pipe with dry willow bark, she looked across at me.

"My grandchild, you are tall and are no longer a little boy." Narrowing her old eyes, she asked, "My grandchild, when are you going to bring here a handsome young woman?" I stared into the fire rather than meet her gaze. Waiting for my answer, she stooped forward and through the long stem drew a flame into the red stone pipe.

I smiled while my eyes were still fixed upon the bright fire, but I said nothing in reply. Turning to my mother, she offered her the pipe. I glanced at my grandmother. The loose buckskin sleeve fell off at her elbow and showed a wrist covered with silver bracelets. Holding up the fingers of her left hand, she named off the desirable young women of our village.

"Which one, my grandchild, which one?" she questioned.

"Hoh!" I said, pulling at my blanket in confusion. "Not yet!" Here my mother passed the pipe over the fire to my father. Then she too began speaking of what I should do.

"My son, be always active. Do not dislike a long hunt. Learn to provide much buffalo meat and many buckskins before you bring home a wife." Presently my father gave the pipe to my grandmother, and he took his turn in the exhortations.

"Ho, my son, I have been counting in my heart the bravest warriors of our people. There is not one of them who won his title in his sixteenth winter. My son, it is a great thing for some brave of sixteen winters to do."

Not a word had I to give in answer. I knew well the fame of my warrior father. He had earned the right of speaking such words, though even he himself was a brave only at my age. Refusing to smoke my grandmother's pipe because my heart was too much stirred by their words, and sorely troubled with a fear lest I should disappoint them, I arose to go. Drawing my blanket over my shoulders,

I said, as I stepped toward the entranceway: "I go to hobble my pony. It is now late in the night."

II

Nine winters' snows had buried deep that night when my old grandmother, together with my father and mother, designed my future with the glow of a camp fire upon it.

Yet I did not grow up the warrior, huntsman, and husband I was to have been. At the mission school I learned it was wrong to kill. Nine winters I hunted for the soft heart of Christ,[1] and prayed for the huntsmen who chased the buffalo on the plains.

In the autumn of the tenth year I was sent back to my tribe to preach Christianity to them. With the white man's Bible in my hand, and the white man's tender heart in my breast, I returned to my own people.

Wearing a foreigner's dress, I walked, a stranger, into my father's village.

Asking my way, for I had not forgotten my native tongue, an old man led me toward the tepee where my father lay. From my old companion I learned that my father had been sick many moons. As we drew near the tepee, I heard the chanting of a medicine-man within it. At once I wished to enter in and drive from my home the sorcerer of the plains, but the old warrior checked me. "Ho, wait outside until the medicine-man leaves your father," he said. While talking he scanned me from head to feet. Then he retraced his steps toward the heart of the camping-ground.

My father's dwelling was on the outer limits of the round-faced village. With every heart-throb I grew more impatient to enter the wigwam.

While I turned the leaves of my Bible with nervous fingers, the medicine-man came forth from the dwelling and walked hurriedly away. His head and face were closely covered with the loose robe which draped his entire figure.

He was tall and large. His long strides I have never forgot. They seemed to me then the uncanny gait of eternal death. Quickly pocketing my Bible, I went into the tepee.

Upon a mat lay my father, with furrowed face and gray hair. His eyes and cheeks were sunken far into his head. His sallow skin lay thin upon his pinched nose and high cheek-bones. Stooping over him, I took his fevered hand. "How, Ate?"[2] I greeted him. A light flashed from his listless eyes and his dried lips parted. "My son!" he murmured, in a feeble voice. Then again the wave of joy and recognition receded. He closed his eyes, and his hand dropped from my open palm to the ground.

Looking about, I saw an old woman sitting with bowed head. Shaking hands with her, I recognized my mother. I sat down between my father and mother as I used to do, but I did not feel at home. The place where my old grandmother used to sit was now unoccupied. With my mother I bowed my head. Alike our throats were choked and tears were streaming from our eyes; but far apart in spirit our ideas and faiths separated us. My grief was for the soul unsaved; and I thought my mother wept to see a brave man's body broken by sickness.

Useless was my attempt to change the faith in the medicine-man to that abstract power named God. Then one day I became righteously mad with anger that the medicine-man should thus ensnare my father's soul. And when he came to chant his sacred songs I pointed toward the door and bade him go! The man's eyes glared upon me for an instant. Slowly gathering his robe about him, he turned his back upon the sick man and stepped out of our wigwam. "Hā, hā, hā! my son, I cannot live without the medicine-man!" I heard my father cry when the sacred man was gone.

III

On a bright day, when the winged seeds of the prairie-grass were flying hither and thither, I walked solemnly toward the centre of the camping-ground. My heart beat hard and irregularly at my side. Tighter I grasped the sacred book I carried under my arm. Now was the beginning of life's work.

Though I knew it would be hard, I did not once feel that failure was to be my reward. As I stepped unevenly on the rolling ground, I thought of the warriors soon to wash off their war-paints and follow me.[3]

At length I reached the place where the people had assembled to hear me preach. In a large circle men and women sat upon the dry red grass. Within the ring I stood, with the white man's Bible in my hand. I tried to tell them of the soft heart of Christ.

In silence the vast circle of bareheaded warriors sat under an afternoon sun. At last, wiping the wet from my brow, I took my place in the ring. The hush of the assembly filled me with great hope.

I was turning my thoughts upward to the sky in gratitude, when a stir called me to earth again.

A tall, strong man arose. His loose robe hung in folds over his right shoulder. A pair of snapping black eyes fastened themselves like the poisonous fangs of a serpent upon me. He was the medicine-man. A tremor played about my heart and a chill cooled the fire in my veins.

Scornfully he pointed a long forefinger in my direction and asked:

"What loyal son is he who, returning to his father's people, wears a foreigner's dress?" He paused a moment, and then continued: "The dress of that foreigner of whom a story says he bound a native of our land, and heaping dry sticks around him, kindled a fire at his feet!" Waving his hand toward me, he exclaimed, "Here is the traitor to his people!"

I was helpless. Before the eyes of the crowd the cunning magician turned my honest heart into a vile nest of treachery. Alas! the people frowned as they looked upon me.

"Listen!" he went on. "Which one of you who have eyed the young man can see through his bosom and warn the people of the nest of young snakes hatching there? Whose ear was so acute that he caught the hissing of snakes whenever the young man opened his mouth? This one has not only proven false to you, but even to the Great Spirit who made him. He is a fool! Why do you sit here giving ear to a foolish man who could not defend his people because he fears to kill, who could not bring venison to renew the life of his sick father? With his prayers, let him drive away the enemy! With his soft heart, let him keep off starvation! We shall go elsewhere to dwell upon an untainted ground."

With this he disbanded the people. When the sun lowered in the west and the winds were quiet, the village of cone-shaped tepees was gone. The medicine-man had won the hearts of the people.

Only my father's dwelling was left to mark the fighting-ground.

I V

From a long night at my father's bedside I came out to look upon the morning. The yellow sun hung equally between the snow-covered land and the cloudless blue sky. The light of the new day was cold. The strong breath of winter crusted the snow and fitted crystal shells over the rivers and lakes. As I stood in front of the tepee, thinking of the vast prairies which separated us from our tribe, and wondering if the high sky likewise separated the soft-hearted Son of God from us, the icy blast from the North blew through my hair and skull. My neglected hair had grown long and fell upon my neck.

My father had not risen from his bed since the day the medicine-man led the people away. Though I read from the Bible and prayed beside him upon my knees, my father would not listen. Yet I believed my prayers were not unheeded in heaven.

"Hā, hā, hā! my son," my father groaned upon the first snowfall. "My son, our food is gone. There is no one to bring me meat! My son, your soft heart has unfitted you for everything!" Then covering his face with the buffalo-robe, he said no more. Now while I stood out in that cold winter morning, I was starving. For two days I had not seen any food. But my own cold and hunger did not harass my soul as did the whining cry of the sick old man.

Stepping again into the tepee, I untied my snow-shoes, which were fastened to the tent-poles.

My poor mother, watching by the sick one, and faithfully heaping wood upon the centre fire, spoke to me:

"My son, do not fail again to bring your father meat, or he will starve to death."

"How, Ina,"[4] I answered, sorrowfully. From the tepee I started forth again to hunt food for my aged parents. All day I tracked the white level lands in vain. Nowhere, nowhere were there any other footprints but my own! In the evening of this third fast-day I came back without meat. Only a bundle of sticks for the fire I brought on my back. Dropping the wood outside, I lifted the door-flap and set one foot within the tepee.

There I grew dizzy and numb. My eyes swam in tears. Before me lay my old gray-haired father sobbing like a child. In his horny hands he clutched the buffalo-robe, and with his teeth he was gnawing off the edges. Chewing the dry stiff hair and buffalo-skin, my father's eyes sought my hands. Upon seeing them empty, he cried out:

"My son, your soft heart will let me starve before you bring me meat! Two hills eastward stand a herd of cattle. Yet you will see me die before you bring me food!"

Leaving my mother lying with covered head upon her mat, I rushed out into the night.

With a strange warmth in my heart and swiftness in my feet, I climbed over the first hill, and soon the second one. The moonlight upon the white country showed me a clear path to the white man's cattle. With my hand upon the knife in my belt, I leaned heavily against the fence while counting the herd.

Twenty in all I numbered. From among them I chose the best-fattened creature. Leaping over the fence, I plunged my knife into it.

My long knife was sharp, and my hands, no more fearful and slow, slashed off choice chunks of warm flesh. Bending under the meat I had taken for my starving father, I hurried across the prairie.

Toward home I fairly ran with the life-giving food I carried upon my back. Hardly had I climbed the second hill when I heard sounds coming after me. Faster and faster I ran with my load for my father, but the sounds were gaining upon me. I heard the clicking of snowshoes and the squeaking of the leather straps at my heels; yet I did not turn to see what pursued me, for I was intent upon reaching my father. Suddenly like thunder an angry voice shouted curses and threats into my ear! A rough hand wrenched my shoulder and took the meat from me! I stopped struggling to run. A deafening whir filled my head. The moon and stars began to move. Now the white prairie was sky, and the stars lay under my feet. Now again they were turning. At last the starry blue rose up into place. The noise in my ears was still. A great quiet filled the air. In my hand I found my long knife dripping with blood. At my feet a man's figure lay prone in blood-red snow. The horrible scene about me seemed a trick of my senses, for I could not understand it was real. Looking long upon the blood-stained snow, the load of meat for my starving father reached my recognition at last. Quickly I tossed it over my shoulder and started again homeward.

Tired and haunted I reached the door of the wigwam. Carrying the food before me, I entered with it into the tepee.

"Father, here is food!" I cried, as I dropped the meat near my mother. No answer came. Turning about, I beheld my gray-haired father dead! I saw by the unsteady firelight an old gray-haired skeleton lying rigid and stiff.

Out into the open I started, but the snow at my feet became bloody.

V

On the day after my father's death, having led my mother to the camp of the medicine-man, I gave myself up to those who were searching for the murderer of the paleface.

"At my feet a man's figure lay." Illustration from Zitkala-Ša [Gertrude Simmons Bonnin], "The Soft-Hearted Sioux," *Harper's Monthly* 102 (March 1901).

They bound me hand and foot. Here in this cell I was placed four days ago.

The shrieking winter winds have followed me hither. Rattling the bars, they howl unceasingly: "Your soft heart! your soft heart will see me die before you bring me food!" Hark! something is clanking the chain on the door. It is being opened. From the dark night without a black figure crosses the threshold. . . . It is the guard. He comes to warn me of my fate. He tells me that tomorrow I must die. In his stern face I laugh aloud. I do not fear death.

Yet I wonder who shall come to welcome me in the realm of strange sight. Will the loving Jesus grant me pardon and give my soul a soothing sleep? or will my warrior father greet me and receive me as his son? Will my spirit fly upward to a happy heaven? or shall I sink into the bottomless pit, an outcast from a God of infinite love?

Soon, soon I shall know, for now I see the east is growing red. My heart is strong. My face is calm. My eyes are dry and eager for new scenes. My hands hang quietly at my side. Serene and brave, my soul awaits the men to perch me on the gallows for another flight. I go.

NOTES

1. As part of their efforts to convert Native Americans to Christianity, many churches established "mission schools" on reservations; here the narrator indicates he had studied for nine years at such a school. The object of these schools was not only to convert Native Americans but also to forcibly assimilate the Native students into White-dominated mainstream American culture, thereby eradicating Native customs and languages.
2. Hello, Father (Lakota). "How" is an Americanized representation of the Lakota greeting of *hau*, and was subsequently used inaccurately in many motion pictures as a greeting made by members of many other different tribes.
3. To stop fighting the White people and instead become peaceful Christians.
4. Yes, Mother (Lakota).

PRINCIPLES OF TEXT SELECTION

According to traditional textual studies theory and practice, propounded most prominently by W. W. Greg and Fredson Bowers, the version of any fiction text that most deserves to be read and studied (the "copy-text") is that which best reflects the final intentions of its author. This "rule" reflects—and derives from—the Romantic notion that the meaning of any text is inextricably connected to its individual author, and that the critical reader's goal is to understand and assess what that artist intended. Based on these assumptions, the version of most any nineteenth- and early twentieth-century American fiction found in most anthologies—and thus the one most widely read and studied—has rarely been the one published in the pages of a newspaper or magazine. After all, it is argued, these texts represent at best early drafts of what authors intended and were often altered by periodical editors to suit limitations of space or to not offend readers; such adulterated texts, it is argued, thus do not represent the authors' final intentions and are not the versions their authors would have wished readers to be exposed to. Instead, in most cases, the version of American fictions used as copy-text has been its first publication in book form, based on the reasoning that this was the version the author usually had more input in composing and reviewing before publication.

With the advent of New Historicism in the 1980s, however, the decision about which version or versions of a text to study became more complicated. Because one of the main goals of New Historicism is understanding how literary texts influenced readers and society in general, it became imperative to study those textual versions read by the most people, no matter how different they were from what the author intended. Since, in the late nineteenth and early twentieth centuries, these texts were usually those that appeared in various periodicals, more attention began to be paid to those versions.

For this anthology, we, the editors, have chosen, with few exceptions, to use the serialized, first appearances of the short fictions we have included. One reason for this is that, as New Historicists, we believe an important part of literary study involves understanding how authors interacted with other agents of the literary market, such as editors, readers, and publishers, in order to negotiate the terms and conditions under which their texts would be produced. In the case of periodicals, each one had its own editorial preferences and target audiences, both of which greatly affected whether a particular submitted fiction would be welcomed there and how many people (and what kind of people) would read it if published. Having a work appear in the *Atlantic Monthly*, a Boston magazine known for its conservative values and genteel readership, meant something very different than if it were published, say, in the Los Angeles magazine *Land of Sunshine*, whose chief goal was to promote Southern California to prospective residents and business owners. It is for this reason that we often highlight, in the material prefatory to each story presented here, the particular periodical in which it first appeared.

In addition, we feel that in many cases the first, serialized versions of these texts are more interesting for readers and raise issues often obscured by the author's own later emendations. This is certainly the case with Stephen Crane's "An Experiment in Misery" and Owen Wister's "Hank's Woman." The former first appeared in the *New York Press* newspaper on April 22, 1894, surrounded by a fascinating frame in which two presumably middle-class men contemplate a tramp on the street and speculate about how he feels; this leads one of them to embark on an experiment that involves his posing as a tramp and then later writing about his experiences. Crane himself eliminated this frame when he revised the story for inclusion in *The Open Boat and Other Tales of Adventure* (1898). However, we have chosen to disregard his intentions because we feel that the millions of *New York Press* readers got to read a text that more directly engaged issues of how the middle class was forming its opinions of the urban poor and of how those same poor could be turned into entertainment and profit. We feel our readers should have the opportunity to read this version too.

In the instance of Wister's "Hank's Woman," which first appeared in 1892 in the pages of *Harper's Weekly*, published in a newspaper-like format, its original text contains instances of stark and brutal violence that Wister would soon learn not to include in his fiction if he wanted it to be popular among eastern readers seeking a Romanticized West—and the periodical editors who wanted to satisfy that desire. When Wister greatly altered this story a few years later for publication in his book collection *The Jimmyjohn Boss and Other Stories* (1900), he transformed it into only a weak shadow of its former self. We believe that greater insights into the realities of western life at this time can be gained from the version presented here.

In a few cases, however, we have chosen to present the versions that represent a text's first appearance in book form. It is important for readers to remember that many authors during this time period found it impossible to have certain stories accepted by periodical editors because of their controversial subject matter, as was the case with both of the Paul Laurence Dunbar stories presented here, "The Lynching of Jube Benson" and "One Man's Fortunes." Some texts, too, did not appear in periodical or in book form during the author's lifetime, only being republished much later. For instance, Mark Twain wrote "The Second Advent" in 1881, but it did not appear in print until 1972, chiefly because Twain believed its subject matter would damage his reputation among readers and thus purposely did not submit it to any editor or publisher for publication.

One thing we hope readers will appreciate, too, is that although some of the fictions included here were published in the era's premier monthly magazines—*Atlantic Monthly, Harper's Monthly, Century,* and *Scribner's*—not all come from these sources. Just because a well-known author's story first appeared in a relatively obscure periodical, such as a local or regional newspaper or a non–East Coast–based magazine, or has rarely, if ever, been reprinted, this should not automatically be taken as evidence of its insignificance or low quality and thus used as grounds for noninclusion in an anthology. A number of high-quality literary gems by such authors can still be discovered if only one is willing to comb through less-prominent publications. Recovering and studying these stories provides insight into the authors' intentions and artistry, as well as a better understanding of the types of texts various audiences encountered during this period.

There are numerous examples in this anthology of excellent works that appeared in lesser-known publications. Sarah Orne Jewett's "Stolen Pleasures," for instance, was syndicated to multiple newspapers across the country by S. S. McClure's Associated Literary Press in 1885 but was not included in any of her major collections. Louisa May Alcott's "Hospital Sketches: A Day" was originally serialized in the *Commonwealth,* a Massachusetts-based miscellany. Readers first encountered Ambrose Bierce's "The Affair at Coulter's Notch" in the pages of the *San Francisco Examiner.* Sui Sin Far's trenchant "Sweet Sin" appeared only in *Land of Sunshine,* described above, and her "The Success of a Mistake" was printed solely in the *Westerner,* a short-lived magazine published in the Seattle area that similarly sought to attract new residents and businesses. Significantly, Jack London chose to publish "The Apostate: A Child Labor Parable" in the *Woman's Home Companion* magazine. And Charlotte Perkins Gilman's wonderful satire "Mrs. Beazley's Deeds" was published first in *Woman's World* magazine before it appeared years later in Gilman's own *Forerunner.* Most notably, too, those early Western writers who are sometimes labeled as belonging to the "Sagebrush school," all highly regarded in their own time, had most of their works appear first in small-circulation newspapers such as the *Territorial Enterprise* (Virginia City, Nevada), the *Virginia Chronicle* (Nevada), and the *Salt Lake Tribune* (Utah). Few, though, had their works collected during their lifetimes, and as a result these fictions, unlike those of their friend and compatriot Mark Twain, sank into obscurity. To rectify this situation, we have included not only C. C. Goodwin's iconoclastic "Sister Celeste" but also Samuel Post Davis's skillful "A Christmas Carol."

Finally, we have prioritized periodical publication because we wish to emphasize the point that in the late nineteenth and early twentieth centuries, Realist fiction was not regarded as something apart from "real life" but was instead firmly situated in it. These stories grapple with many of the same social, political, and economic issues that the nonfiction material surrounding them in newspapers and magazines did. Their readers almost certainly made connections between all of these fiction texts and current events, and this is why readers need to familiarize themselves as much as possible with the historical contexts of this era. To assist anyone wishing to investigate in greater detail the original appearances of these works, a complete bibliography of these publications appears at the end of this volume.

Bibliography of Textual Versions Used in This Anthology

Alcott, L[ouisa]. M[ay]. "Hospital Sketches: A Day." *Commonwealth* 1 (May 22, 1863): 1.

Bierce, Ambrose. "The Affair at Coulter's Notch." *San Francisco Examiner* (October 20, 1889): 13.

Cable, George Washington. "Belles Demoiselles Plantation." In *Old Creole Days,* 60–87. New York: Charles Scribner's Sons, 1879. Originally appeared in *Scribner's Monthly* 7 (April 1874): 739–47.

Cahan, Abraham. "The Daughter of Reb Avrom Leib." *Cosmopolitan* 29 (May 1900): 53–64.

Cather, Willa. "On the Divide." *Overland Monthly* 27 (January 1896): 65–75.

Chesnutt, Charles W. "The March of Progress." *Century Magazine* 61 (January 1901): 422–27.

Chopin, Kate. "A Gentleman of Bayou Têche." In *Bayou Folk,* 291–303. Boston: Houghton, Mifflin, 1894.

Cleary, Kate. "Feet of Clay." *Belford's Monthly Magazine* 10 (April 1893): 720–31.

Crane, Stephen. "An Experiment in Misery." *New York Press,* April 22, 1894, iii, 2.

Davis, Rebecca Harding. "A Day with Doctor Sarah." *Harper's Monthly* 57 (June 1878): 430–51.

Davis, Sam[uel] P. "A Christmas Carol." Originally appeared in the *Virginia Chronicle* (Virginia City, Nevada) sometime in the late 1870s. This text is taken from Sam P. Davis, *Short Stories* (San Francisco: Golden Era, 1886), 1–9.

Dreiser, Theodore. "Free." *Saturday Evening Post* 190 (March 16, 1918): 13–15, 81–89.

Dunbar, Paul Laurence. "The Lynching of Jube Benson." In *The Heart of Happy Hollow,* 223–40. New York: Dodd, Mead, 1904.

———. "One Man's Fortunes." In *The Strength of Gideon and Other Stories,* 131–61. New York: Dodd, Mead, 1900.

Dunbar Nelson, Alice. "Titee." In *Violets and Other Tales,* 44–55. Boston: Monthly Review, 1895.

———. "When the Bayou Overflows." In *The Goodness of St. Rocque and Other Stories,* 99–107. New York: Dodd, Mead, 1899.

Far, Sui Sin [Edith Maude Eaton]. "The Success of a Mistake." *Westerner* 8 (February 1908): 18–21.

———. "Sweet Sin. A Chinese-American Story." *Land of Sunshine* 8 (April 1, 1898): 223–26.

Freeman, Mary E. Wilkins. "Old Woman Magoun." *Harper's Monthly* 111 (October 1, 1905): 727–37.

————. "One Good Time." *Harper's Monthly* 94 (January 1897): 309–19.

Garland, Hamlin. "Up the Coulé. A Story of Wisconsin." In *Main-Travelled Roads: Six Mississippi Valley Stories,* 75–146. Boston: Arena, 1891.

Gilman, Charlotte Perkins. "Mrs. Beazley's Deeds." Originally appeared in *Woman's World* 27 (March 1911): 12–13, 58. Because this text is unavailable, the version used here is from the *Forerunner* 7 (September 1916): 225–32.

Goodwin, C[harles]. C[arroll]. "Sister Celeste." *Salt Lake Tribune,* April 5, 1885, 6.

Harte, Bret. "The Luck of Roaring Camp." *Overland Monthly* 1 (August 1868): 183–89.

————. "Wan Lee, the Pagan." *Scribner's Monthly* 8 (September 1874): 552–58.

Hearn, Lafcadio. "In the Twilight of the Gods." *Atlantic Monthly* 75 (June 1895): 791–94.

Henry, O. [William Sydney Porter]. "A Municipal Report." First published in *The Complete Edition of O. Henry: Strictly Business* (Garden City, NY: Doubleday, Doran, 1910), 141–60.

Howells, William Dean. "A Romance of Real Life." *Atlantic Monthly* 25 (March 1870): 305–12.

James, Henry. "The Jolly Corner." *English Review* 1 (December 1908): 5–35.

Jewett, Sarah Orne. "Stolen Pleasures." *Buffalo Express,* October 18, 1885, 7. Also syndicated in multiple newspapers across the United States, with slight textual variations.

————. "Tom's Husband." *Atlantic Monthly* 49 (February 1882): 205–13.

King, Grace. "Making Progress." *Harper's Monthly* 102 (February 1901): 423–30.

London, Jack. "The Apostate: A Child Labor Parable." *Woman's Home Companion* 33 (September 1906): 5–7, 49.

————. "The League of the Old Men." *Brandur Magazine* 1, no. 3 (October 4, 1902): 7–11.

Macomber, Lucy Bates. "The Gossip of Gold Hill." *Overland Monthly* 10, no. 3 (March 1873): 209–14.

Mena, María Cristina. "The Education of Popo." *Century Magazine* 87 (March 1914): 653–62.

Neall, Hannah Lloyd. "Placer." *Overland Monthly* 7 (October 1871): 317–24.

Norris, Frank. "The House with the Blinds." *Wave* 16 (August 21, 1897): 5.

Oskison, John. "The Problem of Old Harjo." *Southern Workman* 36 (April 1907): 235–41.

Peattie, Elia. "After the Storm: A Story of the Prairie." *Atlantic Monthly* 80 (September 1897): 393–405.

Spofford, Harriet Prescott. "Her Story." *Lippincott's* 10 (December 1872): 678–89.

Stuart, Ruth McEnery. "The Unlived Life of Little Mary Ellen." *Harper's Monthly* 93 (October 1896): 697–709.

Thanet, Octave [Alice French]. "The Face of Failure." *Scribner's Magazine* 12 (September 1892): 346–60.

Twain, Mark [Samuel Langhorne Clemens]. "The Facts concerning the Recent Carnival of Crime in Connecticut." *Atlantic Monthly* 37 (June 1876): 641–50.

————. "The Second Advent." Written in 1881 but not published during Twain's lifetime. First appeared in *Mark Twain's Fables of Man,* edited and with intro. by John S. Tuckey (Berkeley: University of California Press, 1972), 53–68.

Wharton, Edith. "Xingu." *Scribner's Magazine* 50 (December 1911): 684–96.
Wister, Owen. "Hank's Woman." *Harper's Weekly* 36 (August 27, 1892): 821–23.
Woolson, Constance Fenimore. "Miss Grief." *Lippincott's* 25 (May 1880): 574–85.
Zitkala-Ša [Gertrude Simmons Bonnin]. "The Soft-Hearted Sioux." *Harper's Monthly* 102 (March 1901): 505–9.

Index of Authors and Texts